Drawn
by Raw, Hungry Emotions,
They Were Lured by the Land
and a Radiant Dream . . .

Sam Brannan—To some he was a visionary, a Latter-Day Saint leading his flock to the new Zion; to others, a sinner fleecing his people to line his own pockets.

Fiona McKay—An emerald-eyed temptress, her passionate heart led her into the arms of a handsome adventurer to seek her fortune on the harsh frontier.

Robin Gentry—He'd caught the fever, but did he dare risk his family's security and the rich bounty of the land for an elusive harvest of gold?

Susannah Morrison—An outcast among her own people, she found refuge as mistress of a daring aristocrat and hope in his bold vision.

Fairy Radburn—An unholy choice made her an outlaw, forcing her across the desert with her children to beg mercy of Brigham Young's Destroying Angels.

Landry Morrison—Driven by a vengeful fury, he would stop at nothing, determined to see his wife and father pay for his disgrace.

THEY SEIZED A DESTINY OF UNPARALLELED SPLENDOR FROM . . .

Sands
of Gold

Also by Day Taylor

THE BLACK SWAN

MOSS ROSE

THE MAGNIFICENT DREAM

Sands of Gold

Day Taylor

A DELL BOOK

Published by
Dell Publishing Co., Inc.
1 Dag Hammarskjold Plaza
New York, New York 10017

*With love and gratitude
this book is dedicated to
Day's five sons and
Taylor's three daughters.*

Dell ® TM 681510, Dell Publishing Co., Inc.

ISBN: 0-440-17585-2

Printed in the United States of America
First printing—December 1985

One

The sleepy little village of Yerba Buena, dusty and rutted in dry weather, awash with mud in the rainy season, had been awakened and rechristened San Francisco by one of the most vibrant and energetic men ever to seek his destiny on the shores of the Pacific Ocean. Unlike other adventurers who had come seeking their dream only to find it tarnished and unattainable, Samuel Brannan merely adjusted his sights after each blow fate dealt him and kept on striving. He kept San Francisco always at the heart of his dream. The force of his determination swept away the sleepy little tent town forever. Sam and his chosen city were now on a headlong flight into the future, seeking the treasures that lay hidden there.

Sam kept himself at the heart of most of the business and activity in San Francisco. Few inhabitants did not know him, for he had his hand in almost every aspect of northern California life. He was a noted merchant in the city, and also had a store at Captain John Sutter's settlement of New Helvetia. Sam was owner-publisher of *The California Star,* as well as a landowner, husband, and father. Most notably of all, he was First Elder of the Church of Latter-Day Saints in California.

Sam Brannan was everywhere, concerned with everything,

traveling the countryside constantly, coming into and out of San Francisco with every tide, or so it seemed. So there was nothing to mark this May 11, 1848, as unusual when he docked his little launch, *Dice Mi Nada,* at the wharf at the foot of Montgomery Street. Cameron Gentry saw the launch as he left the shipping office and gave Sam a friendly wave.

Sam leapt from the launch and started toward his friend, rival, and occasional partner. Tall, handsome, and notable for the vivacity with which he attacked life, Sam half-ran out to Cameron.

Smiling, his brown eyes alight, Cameron shook his head in mock disapproval. "You look like you just swallowed the whole birdcage. What new venture are you going to try to sell me today?"

Sam threw his arms around the taller man's broad shoulders, giving him a secretive pleasure-filled smile. "My birdcage was full of the most amazing, incredible news you can imagine— come with me, and I'll let you in on it."

"Along with the rest of the town. I know that look you have."

Sam pulled a face. "You wound me! But this time you are right. This news is too great to keep secret. Anyway, if I don't tell it, someone else will, and I want to be the one!"

Cameron laughed. "I'll talk to you later. I'm due at Ezra Morrison's house in fifteen minutes."

"Don't go!" Sam said quickly, holding onto Cameron's arm. "Send a messenger for him. I tell you as a friend, what I have to say is of the utmost importance to all of us who love this city. Once my news is out, nothing will ever be the same!"

Sam's urgency gave Cameron pause. He studied the other man's face. Suddenly his eyes lit. "Congress hasn't finally granted us territorial rights, has it?"

Sam waved a hand impatiently. "Haven't heard a word about that," he said, then began to chuckle. "I must run—today I am the eager town crier. What news I have!"

Cameron stood dumbfounded in the middle of Montgomery Street as Sam Brannan, frock coattails flying, ran full tilt up the street toward the Square, calling to friends to follow him as he had news—great news! Usually unexcitable, Cameron found himself unable to resist. He began to run too, following Sam and the others into the Plaza.

Sam pulled from his pocket a small blue tricornered quinine bottle, holding it up high above his head. He stood for a moment, shaking the contents, a broad smile on his face. Then, with laughter in his voice, he cried out, "Gold! Gold! Gold from the American River!"

For a moment puzzlement passed over the faces of the men gathered in the Plaza. Gold? Everyone knew there was gold in California—but not enough for a man to shout about in the streets. Then, as though an electric current ran through the Plaza, the truth dawned on them. Sam Brannan was not shouting about gold, he meant *"Gold!"* The cry resounded throughout the village as one man after another realized that Sam Brannan meant mother lodes, fabulous, glittering wealth in the hills, just waiting for a man to come by and pick it up.

The Plaza became a mass of confused, excited men questioning Brannan. As new people came hurrying in to see what all the excitement was about, those already privy to the information went racing for their homes and shops to collect gear and be off to the gold hills. The Gold Rush of California had begun.

Sam stood for a moment, watching the results of his handiwork, a look of satisfaction on his face. Then he sprang into action again and went off at a run for his newspaper office.

"Ed!" he called as soon as he had passed through the door.

His young editor, Edward Kemble, poked his head out from behind a mound of papers stacked on a massive rolltop desk.

"Late night tonight, Ed!" Sam said excitely. "Tell the boys to be ready to set type for a special flyer!" He reached across the desk, grabbed pencil and paper and scribbled BUY FROM BRANNAN, then thrust the note into Kemble's hand. "Print a thousand of 'em—no, several thousand—as many as you can."

Ed looked at the paper, then at Sam. He tapped the paper. "What is this?"

Sam laughed deeply. "That, my dear fellow, is gold! Print 'em!"

Kemble was not particularly amused by his employer's unexplained exuberance. He stood unmoving, the paper in his hand.

"You've been out in the sun without a hat for too long," he said with a good deal of exasperation. "Is this a joke?"

As Kemble spoke, Cameron Gentry burst through the office door. "Sam, how rich a strike are you talking about?" the big man asked, his attention so riveted on Sam that he did not even greet Kemble.

For the first time Ed Kemble understood that something very unusual and very important was afoot. If Sam was noted for his volatility, Cameron Gentry was noted for his self-contained stability.

Sam put the blue bottle on the desk. "A man can pick up that much in the time it takes him to squeeze his thumb and forefinger together, and he can keep on doing that through the day and into the night without even thinking of a shovel, or leaving a sign that he's been there."

Cameron took a deep breath, then sat down. He looked up at Sam. "You're sure about this—you've seen it for yourself?"

Ed Kemble's eyes sparkled with interest and with the beginnings of visions of himself as a very wealthy man, his pockets lined with gold. He moved around the side of his desk, taking Sam's flyer to the typesetters. The flyers would be out on the streets that very afternoon, and in months to come would be handed to every man, woman, and child in San Francisco, and to those who would be arriving as soon as the word was out.

Cameron's thoughts were racing ahead. Now that Sam had made his announcement, creating excitement and the anticipation of great wealth in the men of the town, word would spread. Men in Monterey, Mexico, Oregon, Peru . . . men from all over the world would hear about the hills of gold in California, and come. "This will change everything," he said in bemusement, still unable to comprehend just how much change it would create.

The undercurrent of excitement that rode beneath the surface of Cameron's voice wasn't lost on Sam, who laughed exultantly again. "You can bet your ass on that. Once the word spreads, people will throng to San Francisco. This is the beginning of the city I've always dreamed of. A city of gold!" he said with a flourish. Then he tried to regain rational, calm control. He picked a cigar from his humidor, rolled it between his fingers, bit off the tip, lit it and puffed with deliberate slowness. The pretense didn't last long. With a halo of blue cigar smoke wafting above his head, Sam was grinning like a young boy again, and talking with rapid-fire enthusiasm. "You're in at the beginning, Cam. Now, a smart man will stock his store with prospecting equipment, open new stores, and let other men bring the gold right out of the hills and into the till for him. Those of us with a true eye for the future will become millionaires."

He offered a cigar to Cameron, then began to move quickly about the office, his restless mind already on new, finer and grander plans. But Sam wasn't a selfish man, and he stopped his motion long enough to ask, "You sent a messenger for Ezra?"

"I did," Cameron answered distractedly.

"Good," Sam breathed with satisfaction. "He should be in at the start too—good man, Ezra Morrison. He deserves some luck." He fished through his desk for papers, then stuffed them into a carpetbag. "Work to do, Cameron," he said cheerfully. "I'd advise the same for you. It won't be more than a day or two before there isn't a pick or shovel or pan to be had in the city. Those that are around will belong to one Samuel Brannan before the sun sets on this day—that is, if they don't belong to Cameron Gentry."

Sam had just picked up his carpetbag when the door flew open and two men pushed through. "Is it true, Sam?" asked the first man. Dressed all in butter-soft tan suede, he was tall, big, broad-shouldered. His eyes gleamed with the look of the hunter, his straight black hair shining in the sun that streamed through the window.

Before Sam could reply, Cameron Gentry said to his twin, "It's true, Robin."

Ezra Morrison stood in the doorway, confusion written in his expression. He brushed nervously at his hat brim. "The streets are filled with crazy men," he said. "Folks are running out of town on foot, on mule, or in any contraption they can lay hands on—why, they're leaving their shops wide open, with signs on the door saying they've gone to the gold fields. What's to come?"

A look of compassionate understanding flitted across Sam's expressive eyes. He was the only man in the room who could fully understand why Ezra Morrison might have misgivings about this day of excitement. He put his hand on Ezra's shoulder. "Nothing to worry about, brother. This is not a day the Saints need fear. This time the good Lord is with us, and the good fortune is to be shared by all. We need not fear."

Ezra maintained his doubt for a moment. He had never known a time in the past when Gentile excitement did not bode ill for the Mormons who happened to be in their path. But if Sam Brannan believed it . . . "What of the city? What will happen?"

Sam smiled again. Shrugging happily, he said, "Can't say right now, Ezra, but if the exodus to the hills is already upon us, I've got to be on my way, or lose my chance."

"Wait, I'm coming with you," Robin said. He moved with quick agility, one hand reaching for his brother. "Come on, Cam, move along! We've no time to waste in ponderance now."

"Agreed!" Sam said heartily. With that said, he disappeared into the street.

Impatient, Robin gave his brother a shove.

Cameron turned angrily. "We're not in some damned race! Where do you think you're running?"

"I'm going to buy a pick and some other tools while I still can, and you are going to hire wagons and load them with anything useful you can find. Then we'll go stock Susannah's store."

"My God, Robin, you're as crazy as Sam. Susannah runs a ladies' dress shop!"

In no mood for talk, Robin grabbed Cameron's arm. "This is your chance—take it!"

Ezra moved past the arguing brothers and ran after Sam. He felt a little like a faithful, confused hound trying to keep up with its master on some puzzling journey. Sam raced from one of his competitors' stores to another, offering to buy out their entire stock of kitchen pans as well as ropes and picks, shovels, spades, any sort of digging implement. Already he found many stores emptied of their clerks. In these, Sam wrote his own order and left his I.O.U. on the proprietor's desk. By the time he had followed this procedure three times in twenty minutes, the goods from the first store were being loaded on the *Dice Mi*

Nada by the men he had hired for the job. With a satisfied smile, he realized that yet today he would be able to take his goods to Sutter's Fort and stock his store there.

As Ezra trotted along beside him, Sam explained over his shoulder, "Sutter's man, Jim Marshall, found the damnedest gold strike you ever want to see up by the mill, Ezra. Sutter is trying to keep it secret, but that's impossible. The only thing a man can do is take advantage of the opportunity. I'll be opening a store near the mill—going to call the town Coloma after the Indian tribe there. If you want to make a handsome fortune yourself, you'll open a—a bakery there. There will be folks from miles around, and every man-jack of them will eat."

"Everything is happening so fast," Ezra marveled.

"Things always happen fast, Ezra—it's just that most of the time we mortals are slow to take advantage of it. That won't be so this time. I'll see to that."

"Smacks a little of playing God, Elder Brannan," Ezra commented with a smile.

"Not at all," Sam shot back. "I'm just playing with the bounty the Lord has provided. There's the fun in life, man."

Robin and Cameron Gentry had split up soon after they had left Sam's office, with Cameron convinced of the need, if not the wisdom, of such rash action. Robin went to hire two heavy freight wagons to supplement the one Cameron had driven. He quickly discovered just what an effect gold fever could have on a town.

Robin found a distracted John Trent at the rear of one of the shipping offices with which he and Cameron did business. "How much you asking to rent two of these wagons, John?" he asked. He got no response. "Hey, John! You going to give me these wagons for nothing?"

The man glanced up, gave a quick nod of recognition, then returned to his rummaging through an old, beaten trunk.

Robin strode over to Trent and stood near, towering over him. He grabbed hold of his shirt collar, and slowly raised him to his feet. "I'm here to do a little business, John. You are in business? I want to hire two freight wagons. How much?"

"Fifty dollars each—in advance," Trent snapped.

Robin's eyebrows went up. "I could buy them for that! That's a bit steep, isn't it?"

"Not if you want the wagons. When you bring 'em back, I'd appreciate it if you'd put the animals in the stable."

After a moment's hesitation Robin asked softly, "You don't want to check the condition of your animals when they're returned?"

"Won't be here," Trent said curtly, then looked up into the eyes of his former customer. "You want the wagons or not, Gentry? If you do, here's my palm—cross it with a hunnert dollars."

Robin pulled gold pieces from his money pouch, and with a grin put them into Trent's hand. "Here, John, this'll get you started, so you'll know what gold looks like before you bring back a bag of pretty colored stones."

The man spat on the earthen floor. "Don't worry yourself none about me, Gentry. I'll be bathin' in gold on Satiddy night while you're still geein' an' hawin' those damned ornery mules."

Robin laughed, and moved quickly outside. There was no one around to hitch the mules or ready the wagons, so he set to doing it himself. Next time Ezra asked what was to come of San Francisco, Robin would tell him.

Cameron set for himself the same task that had occupied Sam Brannan, and was astonished to find the number of stores that stood open and abandoned by their owners. In the space of a few hours men had thrown over the work of a lifetime to seek elusive gold in uncharted hills. Baffled at such behavior, yet impressed by the power held in the promise of gold, Cameron gathered up what goods he thought would be useful and left his own I.O.U.'s for the absent owners. At two places he found that he had arrived too late. Sam Brannan's note was already there, and the shelves were bare. On another occasion he took great satisfaction in finding a cache of tent canvas and a storeroom filled with woolen blankets that Sam had overlooked in his haste.

Cameron had done better in contracting for supplies than he had expected, being in direct competition with the whirlwind Sam. But there were those who did not like Sam. He might elicit respect from all, but some men welcomed the opportunity to thwart him by selling to someone else.

When Robin brought round the bulky three-wagon train, Cameron was at the docks with a huge pile of equipment and supplies, waiting for more to be delivered. "I got the goods, Robin, but I'll be damned if there is a man willing to do the loading. Men are leaving as fast as they can—most of them don't even know where they're going. Ask them! All you'll get is 'to the gold hills.'" Cameron shook his head, and because he began hoisting boxes onto the bed of the first wagon, he didn't notice the pensive silence of his brother.

Robin's mind was filled with a thousand thoughts. He was going to be one of those fools who would head for the gold fields, not knowing where he was going or if he would find anything of value. Almost as soon as he had heard the news, he had known he was going to take part in this new venture. Sam Brannan's assessment of the way a man could best become a millionaire, he agreed with; but that means was not for him. He wanted to walk the hills, searching for the glittering rock that could send a searing thrill down a man's spine; but only now was he beginning to realize how drastically the gold rush would alter his life. For the first time he questioned the effect his decision would have on Fiona McKay. The last time he had felt a driving need to challenge himself and Nature, he had found her. Would he now lose her, chasing after one more dream? Would she or anyone else understand that it was not the gold itself that lured him? Not wanting to pursue that line of thought, he began to work with furious intensity.

Their task completed, the two men covered the loaded wagons with canvas and then went to Sam's tavern to eat. There, as in so many other places, much of the hired help had left the city that afternoon, and those who remained did nothing but talk of leaving and of making their fortunes. The food was not as good as the men had come to expect. Cameron tossed a dried yesterday's biscuit onto the table and watched it bounce, leaving hard, dark crumbs. He laughed. "I think this is but a foreshadowing of what is yet to come."

Robin chuckled with him. "This may be the *best* of what is yet to come. But then again—maybe not. I pity the poor cook if

Sam gets food like this. If he does, we all may benefit—all but the cook."

The men ate slowly and drank two ales each. Then Robin stretched contentedly, saying, "I'm ready to be on our way—what about you?"

Cameron nodded. "Those wagons will be slow, loaded as they are, but with a straight ride through, we should be there in a couple of days." With a smile, he rubbed his hand across his chin. "I'm getting as bad as you and Sam. I was thinking how much I hate to lose two days' selling to travel. Gold may be a fever, but I have a feeling it spawns automatically the greater disease of greed."

For the past several days Susannah Morrison had been experiencing a peculiar and not altogether pleasant phenomenon at her dress shop in Sutter's town of New Helvetia. Now she was standing on the plank sidewalk in front of the shop, her hands on her hips, her small pointed chin jutting out slightly as she gazed at the colorful display of multicolored, befeathered hats in her window. She stamped a small foot and turned to the large woman with her. "All right, Jane, you tell me what there is about this shop that would bring a bunch of straggly, scraggly men in to ask if I sell picks and shovels!"

Jane Pardee was staring at the dusty street, watching the unusual number of men, donkeys, carts, and horses moving about. "Something is afoot. I've never seen so much activity here, and nobody's telling. Last time I talked to John Sutter he was as close-mouthed as a clam. Now, the day that man doesn't want to exaggerate and brag about every bit of gossip that comes along the road here is the day something big is happening. Well, by all that's holy, John Sutter is going to tell me what's afoot, or my name ain't Jane Pardee."

"What makes you think Captain Sutter will know?" Susannah asked, not willing to trust anything in a world that had suddenly turned itself to nonsense.

"Sutter always knows," Jane said simply, and shrugged. "And why shouldn't he?—it *is* his land. I keep hearing rumors that all this fuss is about gold, but I'll be darned if I can figure why one more rumor about gold would cause all this fuss.

Nearly everybody's found a stray nugget now and then, but . . ."

A man let out a whoop, shouting, "Gold!" Susannah whirled, saying, "Is that possible, Jane?"

"There's been talk off and on since last February that Jim Marshall found a goodly amount up near the mill, but if it was true, or worth shoutin' about, why'd the news take so long to get around?" She was silent for a minute, then said pensively, "But then, we're dealing with John Sutter. Could be the old coot has been trying to keep a real gold find all to himself. Be just like that wily old Swiss rascal."

After Jane went home to harness her horse for the short ride to Sutter's Fort, Susannah went to her small office at the rear of her shop. She sat down dispiritedly. During the past two days she hadn't sold a single dress, piece of yard goods, or hat. The women seemed to have vanished, and the streets were clogged with strange men romping around like crazed animals, barging into her shop, knocking over displays, and asking her for merchandise that no dress shop would ever stock. As she had so many times during the last day and a half, she went to her window to stare down the road. She couldn't imagine why Cameron was taking so long in returning from San Francisco. She wanted him by her side. If he were here, he would help her make sense of what was happening.

The bell on her outside door jangled. She could hear the heavy tread of a booted man. With a sigh of exasperation, she moved quickly to the front, hoping to stop him before he pawed through all her fabrics hunting for equipment she did not carry, and even if she did, would not be kept on tables with her fine silks and linens.

She came face to face with a strapping, curly-red-haired giant of a man.

He said gruffly, "This all you got? All this frippery?"

"You are in a *ladies'* dress shop," Susannah said acidly. "What did you expect to find?"

"Something sensible," he said, and pushed past her, stomping into the back room.

"You can't go back there! That is my office, sir! Stay *out!*"

With a triumphant *"Aha!"* he grabbed a pie pan she had set beneath a potted plant.

"What are you doing? Leave that alone!" Susannah cried, running to grab for the pie pan.

"Three dollars!" the man said, holding the pan high over his head out of her reach. His eyes twinkled with amusement as he watched her struggle with her anger and frustration at not being able to retrieve her property.

Susannah strove for control of herself and the situation. "That isn't for sale—it—it is my private property. What's wrong with you? Get out of my store!" She added waspishly, "And give me my pie pan!" She made another quick grab for it, but he kept it out of her reach.

He laughed, a deep melodious chuckle that rumbled from deep within his broad chest. "Last offer . . . three dollars," he said.

"I don't sell pie pans!" Susannah all but shrieked. "Get out of my shop!"

The big red-haired man looked down at her, then winked. "All right, little lady," he said, "but don't say I didn't try to pay you fair and square." Boldly he reached out with one enormous hand and caressed the side of her face, then he marched through the store with his heavy boots and out the front door with her pie pan in his hand.

Susannah stared after him open-mouthed and said aloud, "Everyone has gone stark, staring mad!"

About noon the following day, Cameron and Robin arrived, dusty and tired, in New Helvetia. Susannah had a "closed" sign placed prominently in her shop window, and another on her door, but she had come to the store that morning as usual, not at all sure that the two signs were enough to keep these maniac men outside. As soon as she saw the handsome identical brothers drive up in the freight wagons, she ran outside. She hesitated for a moment on the sidewalk, her gaze locked with Cameron's, then as he moved to dismount, she ran forward into his arms.

"Oh, Cameron, I have missed you so!" she declared, burying her nose in the warm pleasant smell of his neck. Feeling his muscular bulk enwrapping her, Susannah knew that sense had returned to her world. Cameron was her oak, the tree of her life.

At the sight of her, Cameron realized with a hard pang how much he had missed her. He closed his arms around her as she pressed her head against his chest. The fresh sweet scents of her hair and skin filled his nostrils, and he stood in the road with a foolish, pleased grin on his face, holding her until his brother began to laugh.

Robin jumped down from the wagon he had driven and began to pull back the canvases that covered their loads of merchandise.

Susannah stirred, and lifted her face to be kissed. From the corner of her eye she caught sight of the goods on the wagons. With small hands she pushed away from the safe haven of Cameron's embrace. "Oh, no! Not you too! What is happening, Cameron? Why have you brought a load of picks and shovels and—Cameron, I run a *dress* shop!" She peered in dismay at the heavily loaded drays. "I don't understand. I think the entire world has gone mad. Why have you done this?"

With a small chuckle, Cameron stood by her side and began to soothe her. "It'll be all right, Susannah"—he laughed again —"but no saner. Gold has been found on the American River. A lot of gold. Sam made the announcement in San Francisco three days ago, and the city was nearly deserted by the time we left."

Susannah looked up at him, her blue eyes brilliant with apprehension. "Jane said that might be what had happened. She went to the fort yesterday to talk with John Sutter. I am expecting her to return any time now. What will this mean to us, Cameron? Jane didn't seem to think it would be too good. She had heard that Sutter is already having financial problems, and she thought he might be trying to keep the gold a secret if it had been found."

"We have heard the same rumors," Cameron said.

From the other side of the wagon Robin said, "If the strike is as big as is being claimed, it means that nothing will ever be the same—for Sutter, or for us. I think we ought to send messengers to Mother and Dad at Agua Clara, and to the Campbells and

17

the McKays today, and all of us meet at the ranch to make our plans as soon as we can."

Susannah's eyes widened. If Robin and Cameron were thinking of calling a complete family meeting at their parents' ranch, this was indeed a grave situation. The Gentrys were a close, loving family, but most of their all-family gatherings were celebrations such as a fandango or the christening of a child. A chill ran down her spine. Then, with a sense of delighted surprise, she realized it was not a chill of fear, but one of excitement. Quickly she turned to Cameron again, and saw affirmation in his eyes. She glanced over to Robin. He had an amused look on his face. His eyes twinkled in recognition of what she was realizing. All three of them began to laugh with pleasurable anticipation of what was to come.

At Agua Clara, Carl and Rowena Gentry were not unduly surprised by the message from their sons. They too had heard rumors and had observed an unusual amount of traffic on the road from San Francisco. Carl had kept a close watch, for without the status of territory, California had no official government or law enforcement agency. There were no taxes or public funding for such luxuries as roads, so the road being used by these travelers was Carl's own, built by his men and maintained at his own expense and with his own labor. He had also had to instruct his men—those who were still around—to place heavier guard on their most outlying grazing lands to keep squatters away. Carl Gentry had paid the Mexican government cash for his lands years before, but the United States owned California now. In the absence of legal status conferred by Congress, ownership rights and land claims were precarious in these times.

The Gentrys were always glad to have an excuse to bring all the members of their family together. Carl and Rowena threw themselves into the task of preparing the guest rooms at Agua Clara and planning a festive dinner. They expected their sons, the Morrison family, Jane Pardee and her stepson Brian Campbell and his young wife Coleen, and Coleen's family, the McKays.

Robin left Susannah and Cameron to deal with the complexities of finding space in her small store to accommodate the unusual merchandise the twins had brought. With a jaunty wave and an impish grin, Robin left the two squabbling over the placement of the shovels. He was still chuckling at the sight as he rode out of New Helvetia. Susannah had been harried, and tempted to both laugh and cry, for she and Cameron accomplished nothing. The door to the shop was repeatedly opening to admit one more grubby, rushed, would-be miner who wanted any piece of equipment he could buy—right now!

Robin rode to the McKay ranch, a spread of seven hundred acres Sean McKay had purchased from Sutter the year before. His arrival occasioned no surprise. Sean complained regularly that it had done him little good to forbid Robin to marry his younger daughter Fiona until her eighteenth birthday, for Robin was nearly a resident now.

Sean, standing in front of his partially built new stables, grinned up at his son-in-law-to-be. "You're back? I hardly had time to get used to the idea you were gone."

Robin laughed. "You must have missed having an extra hand with this barn, or you wouldn't be so fiesty."

Sean whistled for a young Mexican boy, directing him to take care of Robin's mare. "Come on inside. Mary will want to feed you. She thinks you're too thin," he said, and smacked the flat of his hand against Robin's hard-muscled stomach.

The two men entered the cool house that still smelled of new wood and fresh stucco. As usual Mary McKay, full of smiles, was standing in her kitchen. Fiona, for whom Robin's heart yearned, was nowhere in sight. Unless he wanted to spend the rest of the afternoon enduring Sean's teasing, Robin dared not ask about her.

"So, what brings you back so soon?" Sean asked, as Mary set a steaming bowl of soup in front of Robin. His blue eyes twinkled. "I suspect that this visit is something just a little bit special."

More than a little piqued, for he knew that Sean was deliberately avoiding mention of Fiona, Robin took his time in answering. He carefully selected cheese, fresh bread, and fruit from the platter Mary had set on the table, then slowly turned his attention to Sean. There was a mischievous glint in his golden-brown eyes. "Have you noticed any unusual activity in the last few days, Sean?"

Robin barely managed to suppress the smile that tugged at his lips. He had gotten Sean's complete attention and interest. There was no more teasing laughter in Sean's blue eyes. "I lost two good cattlemen," he said gruffly. "I called them in for supper and"—he gestured broadly—"gone!"

Robin chuckled. "You wouldn't happen to be missing a couple of shovels, and maybe a pick or two, would you?"

Sean crossed his arms over his chest. "Are you going to get to the point, or am I going to get paid back in full for having a little fun with you?"

"Where's Fiona?" Robin asked.

"She's got her paints out in the field. Now, what's going on that I don't know about?"

Robin was now enjoying himself. Sean was bristling with curiosity, and Robin remained silent until that curiosity threatened to turn into ill humor. "Do you remember meeting Sutter's man, Jim Marshall? Some time ago he found a pretty big gold desposit up by the mill. Sutter apparently tried to keep it a secret, but a few days ago Sam Brannan heard and began to spread the news. Cameron and I were in San Francisco the day Sam made his announcement. Within hours, San Francisco was emptying out. Men left their shops open and unattended. Every vehicle for rent was gone—on its way to the hills. Any kind of digging implement can be sold at a premium."

"Gold?" Sean tried the word out, then he looked hard at Robin. "Is this strike big enough to be looking at?"

Robin shrugged. "There's no way to tell for certain, but my gut instinct says it is. At least it is enough for me to want to try my hand at panning for some of it."

"Oh, Robin," Mary said. "You don't mean that you are really going to the mountains in search of gold? Why, men have done such things since time began, and so seldom do they return with anything to show."

"I know that, Mary. I've told myself that a thousand times already, and I agree with you, but I am going. I think that if I didn't, I'd spend the rest of my life wishing I had."

Mary said nothing for a time, then she gave a deep sigh. "Then you must go. If you were a woman I'd try to talk some sense to you, but being that you are a man, you'll never rest unless you have dug in the earth until your fingers bleed and your back breaks from toil, and your spirit is satisfied." She took another deep breath and let it out slowly. "I think you had better go find Fiona. You should tell her of this decision, and I want to talk to Sean. Pray God, he is old enough that sense may have an effect on him."

Mary, much quicker than the men to peer into the future and assess what this news might mean to all of them, was shaken. Neither man said anything. Sean stared studiously at his hands, and Robin pushed his chair back from the table and quietly left the house to find Fiona. Mary's reaction to his news bothered him. She was not a faint-hearted woman, but she was the only person thus far who did not seem to be excited by the lure of great wealth, or the change this would make in their world, or even the adventure of searching for gold. Robin was more intro-spective than customary, and not as sure of himself as he strode across the field, his eyes scanning the horizon for a sight of Fiona.

He found her in a small valley, her easel set up to face the mountains to the east. The broad-brimmed bonnet that Mary insisted her daughter wear to protect her skin lay on the ground. Fiona's creamy fair skin was flushed and pink, although the sun was not terribly hot. Robin slowed his pace, content to watch her. A lusty man by nature, Robin was often surprised at the pleasure he derived from simple things with Fiona—the sight of her, the sound of her voice, even the gentlest touches of her hands. He moved quietly, almost stealthily through the grass, as if fearing the sight of her would be taken from him if he made a sound.

It was some time before Fiona, deeply engrossed in her paint-ing, noticed him. When she turned, her face lit up with a smile. Her auburn hair, piled loosely atop her head, curled in warm, moist ringlets at her cheeks. She tossed her paintbrush to lie beside her discarded bonnet, and ran to Robin, merry laughter bubbling from her throat. "You came back!" She threw her arms around his neck, her face tilted back to be kissed. He bent his head, his lips touching hers, a soft sensual movement, tast-ing, filling her with an excited contentment.

Together they walked back to her painting. She retrieved her discarded paintbrush, and moved to make a sweeping stroke at the painting. Robin grasped her hand, staying it. "Don't! I didn't know you could paint."

"I can't." Fiona giggled. "But I like to try, and with the mountains right out my back door, and the colorful clothing the men wear, how could I resist trying?"

Robin nodded and looked at her painting again, perhaps more critically, trying to see the faults that she thought so apparent and that he, thus far, had not seen at all. "Perhaps if you worked on a larger paper," he suggested. "This is quite small."

"You have got me cornered, and I suppose nothing short of a full confession will do. I am making a book, and this is to be one of the paintings in it. So much has happened to us in the last year or so, I was thinking that when you and I are very old, and our grandchildren don't know what it was that we knew when we were young, I would have this book for them. So I am keeping a journal, and every now and then I do a painting so that there is a picture of the place or people I write about."

Robin, struggling with a strange tightness in his throat, found it difficult to know what to say. Fiona was only seventeen, and yet he thought that no matter how long he knew her or how old she got, he would never have truly plumbed the depths of this strange and beautiful woman he loved.

His silence lasted too long, for Fiona's vivid green eyes clouded, and she asked, "You don't like the idea of having a journal to give to our grandchildren?"

"I love the idea," he said huskily, and gathered her to him. "I love you." They stood together in each other's arms for a long time. Then he said, "I must talk to you about something, Fiona. When I first came down here, I knew just what I wanted to *tell* you, but as usual, my imaginings of you and the effect you have on me were pale. Now I need to talk with you . . . I need to know your opinion, have your help in deciding what I must do."

Though there were questions in her eyes, she asked none aloud, but said, "In the trees are my horse and cart. You'll find a blanket in the cart—we can spread it and talk for as long as you like."

Robin spread the blanket on the ground deep in the shade of

the trees, near enough to the stream that ran through that part of the ranch that they could hear the sweet music of its movement. All seriousness, Fiona sat down and waited for him to tell her his news.

That evening at supper, Robin told the McKays of the meeting to be held at the Gentry ranch, Agua Clara, in two days. "Do you think I should ride over to tell Brian and Coleen of it myself, or will a message do?" Robin asked, his eyes seeking answers in the faces of each of the McKays.

Mary considered her older daughter, Coleen, and tried to guess how she would react to the invitation. Coleen was pregnant with her first child and was no longer eager to travel unless it was necessary.

Sean said, "It is likely that Brian has at least heard rumors of a gold strike. You said that Jane Pardee knew of it, and if she does, she has probably informed Brian."

"Coleen won't want to travel," Mary reminded him.

"If Brian says it is important, she will," Fiona said with complete confidence. "And anyway, Coleen hasn't seen us for nearly two weeks. I think she will be glad of the excuse."

Mary suddenly smiled. "I agree. A message will probably do just fine." Her eyes took on a dreamy, faraway, maternal look as she began to plan all the things she could load into the wagon to take to Coleen. She had been knitting and crocheting baby blankets and small items of clothing nightly, and even though it had been only two weeks since she had given her daughter all that she made, she already had managed a sizeable number of new things.

Sean knew that look, and he groaned. "Mary, we are going to Agua Clara to discuss business!"

She smiled, knowing he would give in without argument. "Just a few things, Sean dear."

On departure day the McKay wagon was nearly full of furniture for Brian and Coleen Campbell's new and nearly barren house. Also included were Mary's handmade items and some preserves for the Gentry household and for the Campbells. Sean, trying as usual to be gruff and stern, was shaking his head and inwardly thanking the gracious God who had given him Mary to attend to the simple, comforting things of life that made him a happy man.

By the time the McKays and Robin arrived at Agua Clara on the appointed day, the ranch was a hive of activity. Long tables were already set up in the courtyard, and the Spanish servants raced frantically back and forth from the house to arrange all as Senora Gentry wished. Susannah and Cameron had arrived from New Helvetia the evening before, and Ezra and Prudence Morrison had come from San Francisco early that morning. The Campbells had sent a messenger ahead and were expected that evening, so the McKays were the latest arrivals.

Sean pointed at Mary. "She has that wagon loaded to the brim—held us up for hours."

Mary just smiled and embraced Rowena Gentry. "What ever would we do, Rowena, if all this growling from our men was meant?"

"Until that day comes, we'll give it no more thought," said Rowena pleasantly. "Let's all go inside where it is cool and we can be comfortable. If Fiona will consent to play for us, perhaps we could have a good sing while we are waiting for the others?"

All of them gathered around the big square piano and sang, Prudence as always slightly off-key, until the sun was a great red ball coloring everything with a rosy haze as it slid below the horizon. Just a few minutes before they would be called to supper, all of them turned at the sound of a wagon, and the unmistakable "Whooo-ee! Anybody home?" of Jane Pardee.

Six feet tall and muscular as any man, Jane clambered down from her stepson's wagon as the Gentrys, Morrisons, and McKays came out the front door. Her eyes snapping with mischief, she engulfed Sean in a bear hug. "The man of my heart!" she crowed.

Sean blushed mightily. He and Mary had known Jane Pardee for two years, and their daughter had married her stepson, but Sean still wasn't sure how to take her. "Heart!" He snorted. "All you were thinking about was getting here in time for supper."

"Yes, darlin', I was, but there was no danger, for I knew you would be here first in the serving line."

After brief greetings all around, the women's attention turned to Coleen. She glowed with health and with pleasure at the coming of her and Brian's child. The women disappeared into the house and up the stairs to settle their families into the guest rooms, and mostly to talk. Notes were compared on pregnancies, and much laughter could be heard throughout the tiled and stuccoed rooms as the stories unfolded. Fiona and Susannah listened closely, each aware that soon they would be married and it would be one or both of them on whom all this attention would be bestowed.

Prudence Morrison was delighted to be at Agua Clara, even though it was only recently that she had felt herself a part of this open, friendly family. Occasionally it bothered her that she had found a freedom and acceptance within this group that she had not found among the Mormons, who were her own people. The Gentrys, the McKays, the Campbells called themselves a family with only the most distant of blood connections, and now they were including the Morrisons even before Susannah and Cameron were wed. Prudence wasn't at all sure what really brought these people into such a cohesive, cooperative unit, but with or without blood ties, they were indeed a family, and with some puzzlement, she found herself blossoming within it. And since Tolerance Morrison had declined to attend this gathering, Prudence hoped she herself might once again be recognized as Ezra's true and only wife.

It wasn't until after supper that the group got down to the serious talk of what the gold rush would mean to them. All of these men were property owners, and as such each of them recognized his own vulnerability. "I have a deed of purchase from John Sutter," Sean said, "but as his land was granted to him by the Mexican government, I don't suppose his claim is valid any more. Mine probably isn't either."

"I have somewhat the same problem," said Carl Gentry, thinking of the three thousand acres of good farm and cattle land that made up Agua Clara. "But the hitch is, to whom do we make our application for true claim? I paid for my land thirty years ago. Yet we have no way of knowing whether the Mexican deeds will be honored by the United States government, and we can't even apply to the U.S. government yet, for we haven't been granted territorial rights."

"There is the crux of it all," said Ezra. "Why can't they seem to make up their minds—are we part of the United States or not? Why did they fight Mexico just to leave us in limbo with no status at all?"

"It's all a part of the damned dispute over making California a slave state," said Carl in disgust. "The radicals and conservatives in Congress are more interested in their personal political schemes than they are in the whole state of California."

"It has been suggested—rather strongly by some—that we form our own government and declare ourselves an independent nation," Cameron said. "It might not be a bad idea, if we are to have the influx of people we expect. At the least we could protect our lands."

"I think we should all file our claims in the United States," said Robin. "That way, when and if Congress decides to grant us territorial status, the applications will already be on hand."

"And if they never do?" asked his father.

Robin shrugged. "Apply to every bit of officialdom you can find. Whatever we choose to do, I think we had all better resign ourselves to the fact that our land will have to be guarded and protected from prospectors who decide they can stake a claim wherever they want."

"Captain Sutter is already having a problem with that," Jane Pardee said. "He says these people coming in have no regard for a man's property. They're crazed with the notion of gold, and no law is going to keep them from getting what they consider their share."

"Law?!" Robin laughed. "What law? So long as Congress withholds status, we have no law!"

Ezra shook his head gloomily. "What are we going to do about that? How long will it be before some of the people coming to California are going to realize they have a free hand and decide to take the law—the lack of law—into their own hands and advantage?"

"And us with no courts, no judges, no legal mechanism at all," Sean added.

All of them sat silent for some time, sorting through the potential dangers that faced them. Then Sean said, "Well, we have each other. If we band together, we can probably protect our own spreads."

"And what will we do for hired help? I've lost eight men this week—all going to hunt for gold," Carl said.

For the first time Brian spoke. "I wouldn't worry about that too much. Mother Nature should take care of that problem. Hunting for gold is a tedious operation, cold and wet and hard. Many of these men who are going to the hills with no more than a back pack and a shovel will be coming back happy to get a regular wage and good meal every night."

Carl laughed. "Spoken like a true Scotsman, Brian, and undoubtedly correct. Thank heaven none of us has been bitten by the gold bug."

Robin had said little about his own feelings concerning gold, and now he sought Fiona's eyes, then glanced at Sean, hoping he would say nothing. Both Sean and Mary were looking down. They would not speak until Robin was ready to tell his family that he had indeed been bitten.

Fiona looked out the window, her eyes sparkling with excitement and determination. On her lips lingered the memory of a smile. She had plans of her own, but no one knew of them, not even Robin.

Two

Sam Brannan's newspaper rival Benjamin R. Buckelew was just as awed by the gold rush as anyone else, but perhaps not so favorably impressed. On May 29 Buckelew's newspaper, *The Californian,* was little more than a single sheet of paper that Buckelew had to put out nearly alone. He used a bold black print that cried out his dismay for him:

> The Majority of our advertisers have closed their doors and places of business and left town. . . . The whole country, from San Francisco to Los Angeles, and from the seashore to the Sierra Nevada, resounds with the sordid cry of Gold! Gold! Gold! while the field is left half planted, the house half built, and everything neglected but the manufacture of shovels and pickaxes.

Benjamin Buckelew, among others, claimed that Sam Brannan had spread the word about gold in the Sacramento Valley just so that he and his partner C. C. Smith could increase their business in New Helvetia, conveniently located in the path of all the miners heading for the American and Feather rivers. Ben simply couldn't accept that Sam's wild street announcement was coincidental. There had been talk of gold for weeks before. Some said drink had already softened the brain of the twenty-nine-year-old Brannan, but as far as Buckelew was concerned, Sam was as sly as a fox, and about the business of selling his wares in his own opportunistic, flamboyant way.

Occasionally the thought that Sam Brannan simply liked excitement and had the dramatic flair to create it niggled at the back of Buckelew's mind. Whatever the answer, Buckelew admitted that Sam had set in motion a series of events that would leave the city of San Francisco and the lives of all her inhabitants changed for all time. He just hoped the change would be better than it appeared now.

At the first opportunity, Robin Gentry, Fiona McKay, and Brian and Coleen Campbell visited San Francisco. Each saw the rush for gold in a different light, and liked what they saw. The two sisters and their men walked cautiously on the radically changed streets. The sleepy little village of Yerba Buena was gone for good. These streets, as primitive as they were, were definitely the streets of a city—San Francisco. Strangers walked there, and on the face of each of them was an expression that announced that San Francisco was his. Fiona McKay felt the same way. This city was hers, and she liked the feeling of possession.

As Robin helped Fiona across a patch of watery mud that was the road, he laughed, his eyes meeting Brian's. "Some things never change," he said, indicating a sign someone had posted at the crossing of Clay and Kearney Streets: THIS STREET IS IMPASSABLE; NOT EVEN JACKASSABLE.

All of them laughed, but the mud in San Francisco was no laughing matter. It was so watery and deep that horses and mules had become mired up to their bellies in it, and it wasn't unusual to hear an unfortunate man or woman shouting for help to get out of the mud. Any newcomer to the city was instantly recognized by seasoned San Franciscans by the lack of mud stains and spatters on his clothing.

Robin walked backwards across the loose planks that served as sidewalks and bridges over the worst spots. He glanced frequently over his shoulder, fearing the results of a misstep to both himself and Fiona. He grasped her hands tightly and slowly guided her along their precarious way to safety.

Brian had a more difficult task, for Coleen was ungainly, late in her seventh month of pregnancy. Coleen took a deep breath of relief when her feet finally touched firm earth. With a shaky laugh, she released her grip on Brian's arm. "I should never have come to town with you," she said apologetically. "I am holding everyone up, when you are all so anxious to talk to Mr. Foster."

"It's all right, darling one," Brian said. "I am happy you are with me."

Coleen couldn't keep a pleased, proud smile off her face, but she looked at her sister and rolled her eyes.

Fiona laughed happily. "It's better that we're all together. What difference will a few minutes make to us? We're adventurers."

Robin laughed too, saying, "In this town a few minutes can mean a shop has closed its doors and the owner is on his way to the Feather River."

"See, I knew I was holding you back!" Coleen said.

"I'm just joking," Robin said quickly.

"No, you're not! What you say is true," she cried, as they passed a partially constructed building. "Look what happened to the Parker House. How is Robert Parker supposed to finish his hotel? Look!" she cried, pointing now to the hammers, saws, and other tools lying on the ground where their owners had abandoned them. "Those workmen just walked off."

Brian said with certainty, "Mr. Foster will be at his carpentry shop. I promise you that, my love. His gold field is right there. All these miners need his services. He's becoming very rich, very fast."

Fiona listened a dreamy, pleased smile on her face. She would remember this day always. All of them were together moving along an unseen road into their future. Ever since Robin had announced he would be seeking gold, her own view of the world had grown, changed, expanded. There was a wonder-filled excitement that threaded through her days. She turned to Coleen, that excitement lighting up her face. "I am going to write about this trip to San Francisco in my book," she said. Then with a quickening in her voice she added, "Maybe I can do a painting of the four of us walking along the street! Oh, won't it be wonderful to be able to look at my memory book when we're old, and see this day and read about it the way it was? It's like being able to carry today with you always—at least a part of it."

Robin felt his heart swell and threaten to fill his whole chest, as it so often did when he saw the world through Fiona's eyes. With a choke in his voice he said, "No matter how much we forget, my Fiona guards and saves a part for us."

The four of them felt a rush of love and warmth that bound them together. There was great strength in that binding, and great joy in the knowledge of its presence, when some moments later they turned into William Foster's wood shop at the corner of Montgomery and Sacramento Streets. Then they were all business, the feeling quiet now, but locked inside each of them.

Robin and Brian wanted Foster to build a "gold rocker" in the manner Isaac Humphries had described to them. Humphries was one of the few men in San Francisco who had any real knowledge of gold mining. He had come from Georgia, where he had done a bit of prospecting. He was considered an authority by those early gold seekers, who knew nothing at all about hunting for the precious metal.

What Humphries had ordered built for himself, and had described to Robin and Brian, was a box three to four feet long, twenty inches wide and eighteen inches deep, mounted on curved rockers. One end of the box was closed, the other open. Its effectiveness was based on the fact that gold is heavy. When dirt was placed in the rocker and flushed with water, the dirt would be loosened and washed away with the motion of the rocker, leaving gold dust and nuggets in the rocker box. Though it was a simple device, anything having to do with gold mining was new and mysterious to Robin and Brian. Both men had tried their hand at searching for gold before, but had done little more than pan for gold in creeks and rivers in the mountains. A real mining venture was different, and both men were hungry for knowledge.

So engrossed where they that they didn't notice Fiona absorbing every word, every piece of information, with a peculiar intensity. She knew that tonight after they had ridden home,

Robin was going to talk to her about his leaving for the gold fields. Desperately he wanted her approval and her assurance that she would wait faithfully and dutifully in her father's house for his return. She also realized that if he did not get those assurances, or if she protested his going, Robin Gentry loved her so much that he would give up his quest for gold. It both pleased and frightened her to know she had such power over this man she loved.

In some ways Fiona's ordeal in the mountains with the Donner Party two years before had left her with an age-old wisdom that consistently surpassed her mere seventeen years. One of these strange bits of wisdom told her that she never dared exercise the power of Robin's love for her. Another told her that unless she closely aligned her interests to his so that they always worked together, she would not be able to resist the temptation. Tonight when he asked her blessing on his venture, and for her fidelity to him while he was gone, she was going to tell him she was going with him. Those were her terms; there would be no others. She would not risk losing him to chance, or to her own willful ways and the temptations of power.

On the ride back to Brian's and Coleen's small ranch, Robin took the task of driving the team, allowing Brian to concentrate on his very tired wife. Robin was unusually quiet. Still wrapped in the protective warmth of the closeness that existed among the four of them, Robin felt a tiny chink in his armor that was permitting the cold wind of fear to touch him. He knew he was almost obsessive about his desire to go to the gold fields, and in the balance he believed his and Fiona's future hung precariously. Until now his life had been a carefree whirlwind of adventure, his decisions carrying little responsibility and presenting little danger to his future. This time it was different. The choice he was about to make was monumental in its consequences. What would he do if Fiona didn't want to wait? He couldn't give her up. He loved her too much. So long as he lived Fiona would be a part of him, a necessary part. She had invaded his spirit and had become his heart. But could he give up his search for gold? The adventure was also a part of his spirit and of his heart.

Fiona sat at his side, not interrupting his thoughts or disrupting the silence, even though she had a good idea what was consuming his attention. She studied the countryside, confident in her own ability to convince him that she had to join him in this venture, that she had to go with him, be with him to the end of their days. Free in that confidence, she committed to memory all the sights of the passing terrain and the feelings she now felt being with her sister, Brian, and Robin. All of this would go into her book of writing and paintings, and would be designated as one of the most important days of her life—perhaps of all their lives.

After the four of them had had supper, a gay first meal for Coleen's new dining-room table, Fiona and Robin washed and put away the dishes. With the chore finished, Fiona removed her apron, folded it, and laid it on the counter. Her green eyes sparkling, she spun round to look at Robin. She put both her hands out for him to take, an enticing smile on her lips. "Shall we go for a walk? There is a beautiful golden moon tonight, and the sky is crowded with stars."

Robin took the several steps to her in easy strides, his big hard hands engulfing her small soft ones. The lamplight seemed to make his light-brown eyes glow deep and dark, but mostly, Fiona knew, it was the influence of the sultry invitation she had let come through her voice.

Brian sat on the sofa watching them, his arm around Coleen. He chuckled softly, then said, "I don't suppose you two want company?"

Coleen laughed, playfully slapping Brian's chest. "Stop it, you tease. It isn't often they get out from under Papa's eagle eye. He's worse than a nun. And anyway," she added, kissing Brian's hand, "you have more than enough to take care of right here."

His attention instantly and completely caught, Brian turned his head just as Coleen moved hers. His lips met the tip of her upturned nose. "You need attention?"

"Always from you, my love," Coleen breathed contentedly. She took his free hand and placed it on her belly for him to feel the child move as she was feeling it.

Fiona and Robin stepped out of the house unnoticed, closing the door quietly behind them. It was a perfect night. The air was clear and dry. The heavens were a deep midnight blue, brightened by myriad clusters of gleaming stars. A slight breeze whispered soft music to the trees. The golden globe of a moon hung low in the sky, casting a warm light on Robin and Fiona.

Robin took Fiona's hand, and slowly they walked together away from the house, of one accord heading for the line of pines that grew near the pasture. Fiona with her artist's eye and imagination knew exactly how they looked together. Robin tall and dark, his broad shoulders swaying just a bit with each step, his narrow hips a sharply masculine contrast to her own trim well-rounded ones. They were beautiful together, she knew that, just as she knew they belonged together. Happily she shook her head, making her curling mane of auburn hair fly around her face, the long tendrils leaping up to catch on the sleeve of his shirt. Just as he laughed and looked down to see what she was doing, she tossed her head back, uncovering her face, and smiled wickedly at him, her eyes like green fire taunting, teasing, inviting him.

Robin caught his breath and automatically put his hand out to touch the creamy velvet of her cheek. Fiona moved her face into his hand, her lips soft and warm as she kissed his palm. He looked away from her, for he dared not keep tantalizing himself with the sight of her. Tonight especially she was so beautiful he could barely stand it, and she seemed so small and in need of protection—particularly from himself.

He had not realized how difficult it was going to be when he had promised Sean McKay he would not marry Fiona until she had passed her eighteenth birthday. Mary had tried to warn him that Fiona was a sensual creature given to teasing, but he had not realized just how tempting Fiona would become once she was completely recovered. And Fiona had aroused other feelings in him he had not even known a man could have. Though he had been intimate with many women, he had never been in love before this. He had discovered quickly and to his regret that the longing agonies of love were greater and more difficult to deal with even than those caused by a celibacy he was unaccustomed to. And Fiona did nothing to help him on either score.

She stood before him, her head coming only to the height of

his shoulder, her eyes searing up at him, bathing him in a green light of love, her hands moving gently, unbearably across the muscles of his chest. Robin tried desperately to continue to think of Sean and his fatherly wrath, but he couldn't hold any thought. The muscles in his broad back and shoulders ached with the need to crush Fiona against him until he had swallowed her up with his own being. Trembling, he took a deep breath. It was a good thing he would be leaving for the gold fields soon. He would not be able to keep his hands off her much longer.

"What . . . no kisses?" she asked, an impish smile on her lips.

He took both her hands in his, and pushed her away from him a bit, then leaned over and chastely kissed her forehead. "I want to talk with you first," he said in the coolest tone of voice he could muster.

She giggled with wicked glee. "But it isn't talking that I want to do."

He laughed in self-protection. "Fiona, be serious for a moment. I want to tell you—"

"That you and Brian will be going to the gold fields and you want me to be a chaste, faithful woman and be here when you decide to return—that is, if you do not find someone who will turn your head while you are away, and in that case, I should pine away the rest of my life wishing for my true love to return —someday? Isn't that what you wanted to say?"

Shocked, he exclaimed, "Not at all!"

"What part would be different?"

"I will never see anyone to compare to you. I will always come back."

The look she gave him was a hard one with no nonsense or mirth in it. For once Fiona McKay was not teasing, nor was she being impish. "You don't know that. All you can tell me is your intention, and intentions change. I shall not spend my life living for intentions, Robin."

A cold feeling of fear had crept into the region of his heart and stomach. "Are you saying that you would not wait for me?" he asked.

"I am indeed. You will never get a promise of the future from me, Robin. All I can give you is what I am now, and what I have now."

He was shaken to his bones. He wandered away from her, to hide his turmoil. He didn't know what to say to her, or what to do. He'd known she wouldn't be happy at being left behind and asked to wait, but he hadn't expected such firmness; nor had he thought her capable of delivering such an ultimatum with cold deliberation. In one quick lesson he had learned that his young, tender, sweet girl could be a hard woman.

"Take me with you," he heard her say.

Without turning around he answered, "You know that is impossible. Your father would never permit it, and the gold fields are not places you'd want to be."

For the first time Fiona felt a twinge of doubt, and a greater twinge of fear. She ran to him, put her arms around him from behind, her head tight against his back. "Don't you love me after all, Robin?"

He said only, "I can't take you with me. I gave your father my word that we would not marry until you are eighteen." He did not answer her question, or turn around in response to her embrace.

With the suddenness of a streak of lightning flashing from the clear heavens, Fiona's dreams crumbled, and she was overcome with an unbearable sorrow. With a stifled sob, she thrust herself away from him and began to run to the darkness of the deepest part of the pines.

Caught unawares, Robin hesitated, then pursued her. Fiona moved swiftly, driven by an awful need to heal a part of herself she had never thought might be damaged. She ran like a doe in and out of the trees, ducking through passages of bush where he could never follow. Then suddenly she disappeared from his sight. He stopped running and stood in the darkness of the woods trying to catch sight of her dress, or to hear some sound that would give her position away. It was as if he were now alone in the woods. "Fiona!" he called softly. "Fiona, come back to me."

He heard nothing but the normal rustling sounds of a nighttime woods and was assailed by a loneliness that seemed to echo in the words he had called to her.

Fiona was curled up at the base of a large single pine that stood in a clearing. Its broad, deep swinging boughs formed a shelter for her. It was almost like being in a house; she felt comforted and protected. She knew she was being childish. Such dreams of love were for books, and faery stories of her parents' native land, but she didn't care. If Robin did not love her as the gods of old had loved their mates, then she wanted none of love, for that belief in true love was as deep in her as her life's blood. Childish or not, she and Robin had to want each other more than anything else in the world, or it mattered not to her if they one day married. That occasion would make her no more than an ordinary woman marrying an ordinary man, and she was certain God had guided Robin to rescue her from a mountain pass for a greater love than that.

When Robin had not found her for over half an hour, he was both frightened and angry. His call to her now was sharper. So often he had passed right by the tree where she hid, and had not thought to look carefully, for it stood alone, and he expected her to be hiding in the depths of the woods. He had finally decided he would have to go back to the house and enlist the aid of Brian and perhaps Coleen to bring Fiona out of the woods. Feeling disconsolate and empty, he sank to his knees, his eyes fixed on the darker part of the woods. For a moment he knelt there unmoving, without thought, alone with the sense of loss that he now couldn't shake. Though he didn't have the romantic bent that Fiona had in abundance, his feelings were not far different from hers. "Fiona," he said softly and sorrowfully, "why wouldn't you wait for me? Is it you who does not love me?"

"I will always love you," she answered in an equally soft voice.

He jerked in her direction, but still saw nothing. "Fiona?" Silence answered him, and then he wasn't certain if he had heard her or just wished her voice into his mind. "Fiona? Please, Fiona, if you are near . . . come to me."

When she spoke again, he heard the slight tremble of frightened, excited expectancy in her voice. She said, "I am beneath the single pine, Robin. You come here to me."

Robin got to his feet and approached the tree. It was thick

with heavy-scented branches. He parted two boughs, then moved inside the great open space near the trunk. His breath caught. His heart raced so hard it threatened to burst through his chest.

Fiona McKay stood before him in her house of boughs, naked. Her arms were stretched out to him, her head was lifted, and her eyes glowed with an ancient invitation. "This is the only promise I have to give, Robin, and it is for now," she said, her voice husky.

Robin couldn't speak. The sounds that came from him were as deeply primitive and ancient as was her invitation.

Then she lowered her head, her dark eyelashes hiding her eyes. "I don't want to be left behind. Take me with you."

Robin touched her shoulder. Her skin felt like silk, soft and smooth. With a small cry she moved into his embrace, her head cushioned against his chest. She listened to the strong beat of his heart, felt the warmth of his arms enfolding her.

He thought only to protect her, but with his arms around her, the touch of her flesh under his hands, his eyes filled with the sight of her, his thoughts were disjointed and without power. He murmured, "I would do anything to keep you with me always, my darling, but I can't . . . I promised. . . ."

She turned a tear-streaked face up to him. The warmth of her breath touched his lips before he kissed her. Gently their lips met, then his tongue entered her mouth and tasted the sweetness within. He pressed her closer to him, his hands sliding down her back to her buttocks, pulling her closer against him. Then, almost frantically, he freed one hand, pulling his shirt from his trousers, working at his trouser placket. A murmur of joyful passion came from Fiona, as her fingers undid the buttons of his shirt.

With infinite care Fiona pushed his shirt off his shoulders. Her green gaze, like the deepest, hottest flames in a fire, moved across the broad, muscled expanse of his chest. Her hands, tracing the path of that heated gaze, seared right to the core of him. Unable to stand the tension any longer, he drew her close against him. Both trembled at flesh touching flesh, their bodies tempered and heated to fit together perfectly. With a quick motion he picked her up, then knelt, placing her on the mat of pine needles beneath the protective shield of the tree.

Fiona's hands raced across his beloved face and down the column of his throat. Gently, almost reverently, he touched her breast, and then like a starveling his lips greedily followed, kissing, sucking, nibbling at her until she arched her back in a cry of abandon. Waves of impassioned pleasure flowed through Fiona, unleashing a lusty wantonness that only she had known existed until tonight. Robin's lips kept teasing her, his hands roved over her body until she couldn't bear it, and she pulled him against her, comfortably taking his full weight. She opened her legs and enclosed his narrow hips within the grasp of her thighs. The sharp pain that came as he entered her served only to release the wildness she had always known lived within her.

With a cry she began to move against him, then with him in a quick heated rhythm. Caught by the sounds of their own inner music, Fiona and Robin moved gracefully in a delirious dance of mating until a great shudder caught both of them. They clung to each other, their breath mingling, their hearts beating against each other's chest. Robin moved his head to kiss Fiona at the side of her neck. She pulled him back to her, not wanting any of the warmth between them to escape into the night air.

"You are my soul," she murmured on a contented sigh.

Another deep shudder ran through him. "And you are mine."

Robin moved, lying beside her then, his face nuzzled against her neck, her auburn hair caught in his. With a smile Fiona felt for her skirt and pulled it over them. She basked in a contented lethargy, her senses still filled with the sight, sound, smell of him, the memory of him within her. When she spoke, her voice had a sleepy, smug tone to it. "And now we have made our own promise, haven't we, Robin, and it is this promise that will be kept before all others."

Fleetingly Robin thought of Sean McKay and what he would do when he found out, but he got up on one elbow to gaze down on Fiona. With a smile he leaned over and kissed her softly on the lips. "The promise we made to each other tonight will always be kept, Fiona. Always." He lay back down.

But she sensed a withdrawal in him. "What are you thinking, dear one?"

"That I wish you knew what life with me in the gold fields will be like. You are afraid that if I leave you behind something will happen to keep us apart, but Fiona, coming with me may be more than you think, and not pleasant. We will have no home—no house—and there will be times—"

"I have thought of all that. There will be times when it rains and we are soaked to the skin, and can do nothing about it but shiver and be miserable. I imagine supplies will be unreliable at best, and the work will be hard, and we will be tired and short-tempered, but we will get over those things, Robin. Those things we will manage—if we truly love."

Again he propped himself on his elbow to see her better. "And how can you be so certain that we truly love?"

There was mischief in her eyes again, but also a seriousness. "I can't be, not until you have the courage to take me with you."

He laughed softly. "And that will make you sure? There are some people who would say that after tonight, I might have other less noble reasons for wanting you with me."

"I meant as your wife."

He was quiet, pensive as his eyes studied her.

All seriousness now, Fiona said, "My mother and I have talked about men and women. I believe that women are afraid to lust . . . for fear of the consequences they may have to bear alone, but men are afraid to love . . . again for fear of the consequences they may have to bear alone." She looked up at him. "If you do not marry me after what I have done tonight, and I should have your child, then I alone must bear those consequences. But if you do marry me out of love, then it is you who take on the burdens of our life together. That is an awesome task for a man—to—to always provide and take what Providence hands him through a woman."

Robin shook his head. "How can one so young be so old?"

She laughed. "I am not so old! I'm Irish, silly!"

"Oh." He chuckled. "That explains it all!"

"You might be surprised to find out that it does." Shivering, she moved closer to him, then wished she hadn't, for instantly he got up and collected the rest of her clothes. "I don't want to leave here," she said.

"It's getting late, and Brian and Coleen are going to begin to wonder."

She sat up, but looked at him impishly. "What do you suppose they will wonder about?"

"Listen, my lovely tease, if you want to be Mrs. Robin Gentry without the whole countryside knowing it before the fact, we will have to be cautious until the deed is accomplished."

Fiona looked at him wide-eyed for a moment, then her face broke into a delight-filled smile. "You have decided!"

He helped her to her feet. "As you said, a promise was made between us tonight that must never be violated, nor must any other come before it."

She threw her arms around his neck, her breasts against him, her small body stretched out, once more moulding to his longer, lean frame. He kissed her quickly, then gave an uncertain laugh as he removed her arms. "You mustn't do that, or we'll never go inside. Put your clothes on, Fiona."

Feeling much safer and in command once they were dressed, Robin took Fiona's hand, and on the way back to the Campbells' new house, they planned how they would manage their marriage in secret.

Three

Brian Campbell had listened patiently to Robin explain to him why it would be better if Brian went to claim their place in the gold fields alone, with Robin to follow shortly. He hadn't believed any of it, but neither had he argued or asked any questions. He and the Gentry twins had been friends for a long time, and within reason Brian was willing to grant Robin anything he asked for. Not only did he have Robin and Cameron to thank for saving his life in the mountain pass along with the lives of all the McKay family, but Brian Campbell knew the value of a friend in a land where one's nearest neighbor might be as far as fifty miles distant. Friendship was a precious gift, and Brian was a man who always recognized true value.

The week following their supper with Robin and Fiona, Brian loaded up his family wagon and took Coleen to her parents' house to stay there until he returned from the gold fields a richer man—he hoped. Mary and Sean both came out of the house as soon as they heard the wagon drive up. Though he wouldn't admit it, Sean missed having his elder daughter at home. He still had not gotten entirely comfortable with the idea that another man, even a man he liked as much as Brian, was now in charge of the comfort, happiness and well-being of his daughter. With exaggerated gentleness, he helped her out of the wagon, then crushed her to him in a bear-hug of an embrace.

"Papa!" Coleen cried as the breath went out of her. "The baby!"

Flustered, Sean backed away from her, patting at her shoulder as if that would make her all right.

Mary laughed, hugging Coleen. "I hope you have better luck teaching your father that he need not treat a pregnant woman with alternating gentleness and ferocity. I have never succeeded in eliminating his extremes."

"Well, my goodness, Papa, please learn now," Coleen said with mock severity. "I think I might be safer in the gold fields."

Blushing, Sean shrugged helplessly. "I just missed my girl."

Coleen threw her arms around him and kissed him on the cheek. "And I've missed you, Papa. It's good to be home with you and Mama for a while—even if it is sad to be without Brian."

Her father patted her comfortingly. "Now, now, Coleen. He hasn't gone away yet, and he won't be away for long, sweet."

Mary took Brian's arm and started back into the house. "Come along, all you McKays and Campbells. I won't have the neighbors seeing us sniffling in our front yard."

Sean looked around. "Neighbors! What neighbors would you be talking about? Perhaps the man ten miles down the north road is farsighted?"

"Hush, you old reprobate, and bring your daughter into the house."

"Where is Fiona?" Coleen asked, noticing for the first time that her sister was nowhere in sight.

"Fiona is where Fiona always is when Robin is in the vicinity. She claims to be painting," Sean grumbled.

"Why, you are in terrible sorts, Sean McKay," Mary scolded. "You know perfectly well that paint she does. Doesn't she always show you her work?"

Brian breathed a sigh of relief hearing that the McKays knew of Fiona's whereabouts. He had been holding his breath, not even telling Coleen he was certain that Fiona and Robin were going to elope, but hoping against hope that they would wait until he was safely on his way to the Feather River. His greatest worry was that, being as much in love as they were, neither of them would think of such eventualities as Brian's having to stay there to search for Fiona if her father took umbrage. With that heavy weight off his back, he cheerfully set to bringing in the baby cradle and other supplies that Coleen had insisted on bringing with her. He had tried arguing with her that there would be no need to bring these things to Mary's house, but Coleen would have none of it.

"You won't be here when the baby is born," she had said with certainty.

"I will be here!" he had insisted. "Jane has promised to keep an eye on you, and at the smallest sign that the time is near, I'll be home."

Coleen had merely shaken her head and had continued to insist that all her baby things be taken to her parents' house. Brian still didn't like the idea that their first child would not be born in their own home, but on the other hand he was glad that the McKays would be looking after Coleen while he was away. And while he knew Coleen would miss him, he also recognized that she would enjoy the stability of living once again with her family.

Later that evening, under the steady barrage of questions that Sean posed to Brian and Robin, Brian said, "I am going ahead of Robin by a few days. I want to stop at Sutter's and see Jane. She will be our best source of information about where the richest diggings have been found. She not only is the nosiest woman who ever lived, but she also has the ear of Sam Brannan, and there is precious little that Brannan doesn't know."

"I imagine Cameron could give you some good advice too," Sean commented. "Is he going too, Robin?"

Robin laughed. "No, not Cameron. He's too level-headed to be out scratching in the dirt hunting for little yellow rocks. He leaves all that sort of thing to me. All I know is that Cameron will never allow the opportunities afforded by this gold rush to pass him by."

It was close to midnight before the family settled down to sleep. All of them slept in the house except for Robin, who was relegated to the quarters above the stables, for he was the only bachelor, and Sean had a beady eye on him. As he kissed Fiona good night, Robin grumbled that if she weren't such a damnable tease her father would not be banishing him from the house.

"He thinks you are lecherous." She giggled, not in the least sympathetic.

"I am," Robin breathed. He leaned forward and kissed her quickly, then ran the tip of his tongue over her lips.

A small cry came from Fiona as she threw her arms around him and held him tight. "I don't want to be without you tonight," she breathed softly into his ear.

Gently, but with authority, Robin disengaged himself from her. "I love you," he mouthed, then said aloud, "Until tomorrow, Fiona," and hurried off into the darkness before he gave in and wrapped her in his arms as he wanted to do.

The entire family was awake and active early the following morning to see Brian off to the gold fields.

"As soon as you have staked your claim, you'll let us know where to contact you," Sean said for the third time in the last half hour.

"I will, Sean," said Brian with infinite patience. "I want to know what is happening here as much as you want to know how I fare. And don't forget to be cautious about strangers near the ranch."

"We'll be fine, lad. You needn't worry on that score."

Brian looked at Robin. "Robin, make sure he understands how it is out here." He said to Sean, "Until the federal government does something about territorial status, Sean, we are all at the mercy of fate. There is no law to help you here—it's not like it was back East."

"I understand, Brian, I do indeed. You're talkin' my ear to the bone about this."

"But you don't seem to understand how—"

"I do, Brian! I will guard the women well, and not let a stranger near the house without my gun sights on him, and a mouthful of questions for him before he gets so much as a sip of water for himself or his animal. I give you my word!"

When Brian started to speak again, Mary stepped forward and hugged her son-in-law. "May the good Lord be with you, Brian." Then she turned to the others. "Be saying your goodbyes and give him a moment to bid his wife farewell without all of you staring, arguing and gawking."

Standing beside the newly loaded wagon, Brian took Coleen's hands in his. Brian's storm-gray eyes held Coleen's blue ones in a gaze that carried them beyond time to a private place that belonged only to them. During the few seconds while they remained still, held in each other's gaze, Coleen and Brian caressed and loved each other with a passion only the mind can achieve. With a deep sigh of contentment, Coleen broke the moment and moved close to her husband, her unborn child pressed between them. She laughed as she felt movement. "Your son is bidding you good luck, Brian Campbell."

"Perhaps it is my daughter who wishes me well," he said, smiling at her. "I am not a man who needs his firstborn to be a son, my love. Nothing would make me happier than to have a little girl who was the image of her mother."

Tears stood at the edge of Coleen's eyes. "What will I do when you are not beside me in the morning, Brian? How shall I ever know the sun has risen in the sky when the darkness of being without you shrouds my heart?"

"I'll always be with you, my darling. All you need do is to look inside that heart you imagine to be shrouded, and you will find me there, just as I shall find you within mine."

Coleen nodded, her head firmly pressed against his chest. "I know—and now you had better leave, or I won't have the strength to let you go."

He kissed her again, then climbed up to the seat of the wagon. Again he held her in his gaze for a long moment, then called to the horses. With a jolt the wagon sprang forward. Coleen stood in the yard watching until Brian turned onto the main road and was lost from sight.

Brian let the horses slow once he had reached the rutted path that served for a road. As surely as if he had looked behind him, he had known Coleen was watching his departure. He could feel her gaze upon him, making that short drive out of the McKay ranch the most difficult bit of terrain he had ever traveled. He hadn't dared look back at her, or wave to her, and even now as the distance grew between them, he wondered if the search for gold was worth being separated from her. With difficulty he rid himself of such thoughts and began to look to the task at hand. He was going to see his stepmother, Jane Pardee, and then travel up the river to find a good claim for himself and Robin. These were the only thoughts he could permit himself right now.

Brian had plenty of company on his way to New Helvetia and Sutter's Fort. From every direction, even up out of the ground it seemed, men were traveling toward the American River. Some, like Brian, had a horse and wagon and supplies. Others rode horseback with only a bedroll behind, and the inevitable shovel and pick sticking out of the pack. Many men were walking. Their garments were as varied as their nationalities and former occupations. Sailors who had jumped ship still wore their seagoing garb: the broad-brimmed black varnished hats made of tarpaulin, the loose checked shirts and the trousers, tight at the hips but flowing long and loose over their boots. Dandies were dressed in velvet jackets, dark trousers, and ruffled shirts as though they had just gotten up from the gaming table. Reserved mountain men unavoidably traveling the public road wore what seemed the most appropriate clothing; stained and long-worn buckskin shirts and trousers, with broad-brimmed hats pulled low over faces bushy with whiskers. Over their shoulders they carried long rifles, a pick and a shovel. Practically all the men were armed with pistols and hunting knives carried in convenient holsters.

Under other circumstances Brian would have given a ride to the first man he saw. But his wagon was heavily loaded; no sense in straining the horse further. Then, as he neared the *Embarcadero,* the Port of New Helvetia, and the number of men increased, he felt less guilt for not having helped his fellow man. Quite the opposite, he began getting a sense of urgency to reach the gold fields before the rest beat him to it.

When Brian arrived, Jane Pardee echoed his sentiment. She came out of her comfortable sprawling house, her face broadened with a smile of greeting. "I been wonderin' if you wasn't never gonna catch the gold fever. Been lookin' for you for weeks now. Supper'll be over an' the dishes washed in them mines by the time you get there."

Brian laughed and threw his long arms around his hefty six-foot stepmother. "I had to stop and see my best girl."

"Good thing you did too. Well, don't just stand there, let's go put up the horse and you come on in and tell me about everybody. How's Coleen? How's my darlin' little Sean?"

Jane's overwhelming affection for Sean had long been a joke to everyone but Sean. Grinning, Brian said, "He's as feisty as—"

"And you didn't bring him with you. Here I was hopin' I'd get him away from that pretty Mary for once an' show him what a good time's all about."

"Jane, you'd only frighten the poor man. You know he's shy and bashful."

Jane guffawed, and the horse glanced at her, startled. "Then he'd be my first shy Irishman." They gave the horse feed and water, and Brian rubbed him down with handfuls of straw. "Now come on in and let me put some meat on those bones, Brian. How is Coleen holdin' up since the weather's gotten so hot?"

"She's well, and in the best of hands. I left her with Mary and Sean and Fiona. I tried to tell her I'd be back before the baby comes, but she still insisted on taking all the baby things to her parents' house."

"Pshaw, Brian, she was right. Once you get up there you won't come straight back. Nobody else has. Tell me, where do you think you'll be goin'?" As she talked, Jane's hands worked deftly, heaping a plate with cold meats and fruit for Brian.

"That's one reason I stopped here. I thought you might know that best."

Jane grinned. "Well, sure, I know, but everybody an' his uncle thinks the best place is someplace else. But Sam Brannan's just back from the mines—"

Brian yelped in astonishment, "Sam?! Digging for gold?"

"Not any more. Now he's diggin' in the Mormons' pockets," Jane answered wryly. "He goes up around the gold fields and collects tithes from the Mormons. For the Church, or so he tells them. And they think they got to pay it. But he'll be comin' for supper tonight; you can talk to him then."

Something further seemed to be on Jane's mind, so Brian asked, "How is Sam? Getting along all right?"

Jane shook her head sorrowfully. "Now there's a fine man goin' to drink. Pity about him."

"Drink? You mean he can't do his work any longer?"

"No, no, nothin' like that, at least not yet. He's still full o' ideas, still carryin' 'em out, an' rakin' in the money. It's just that when that man bends his knees to sit down, he's got to bend his elbow too, and too often."

"That's sad. He's got so many possibilities here. I don't know any other man who's accomplished half what Sam has in the two years he's been in California."

"John Sutter, maybe—but then John got here first. My saints, but John's a busy man these days. Hundreds of men passin' through every week, an' they all have t' stop at John's fort to provision up."

"So John's got his own private gold mine," Brian observed.

"That's what he says. But all the same, he formed a company with Jim Marshall, Isaac Humphries, and Peter Wimmer to mine for gold at Coloma. They began the first of April, over two months ago."

"Is anything good coming out of their mine?"

"Some, I hear. But I don't think they're talkin' about it. Once you find gold, then you get a lot o' competition for it. Too many others up around Coloma as it is."

"Isn't that where Marshall built the mill for Captain Sutter?"

"That's the place. They sawed lumber with it for a while, but since gold's been discovered, the mill's idle. Can't get anybody to run it. They've all got bit by the gold bug. Sutter put ten thousand in it, but he sold out his interest for six thousand."

Brian had eaten everything but the plate. Now he rubbed his belly and grinned at her. "That was good, Jane. Thanks. Where is Sutter now?"

"Right now? Don't know. But he'll be here for supper too. You came at a good time, Brian." She smiled placidly.

"How are your romances going, Jane?"

Jane guffawed. "Romances—hell, honey, Sam's too young for me, and Sutter's too short. And the rest o' the men who come through New Helvetia are hellbent for the gold fields and

49

couldn't see the most beautiful woman God ever built, which I'm not."

Brian looked at this tall big woman, the only mother he could remember, with her uncompromising yet kind blue eyes and her reddish blonde hair streaked with white, and he grinned. "Next thing to it, though," he declared.

"Bein' next best, maybe I try too hard," said Jane uncomplainingly. "Say, I better get that ham in the oven if I want it done by the time comp'ny comes. You're stayin' a few days, aren't you? Then why don't you go on up to Sutter's Fort and talk to some fellows there. They've all got big stories about gold luck t' tell."

Brian walked up the gentle two-mile hill from the *Embarcadero* to Sutter's Fort. The large adobe enclosure stood on a hill, bordered by a creek which emptied into the American River. Around it were grazing lands and fields enclosed in the European manner by ditches. Everywhere were groves of liveoaks, sycamores, elm and ash. Though summer was here, there were still fields to be planted. Strange, there seemed to be few Indians around. John Sutter always had lots of Indian workers. Maybe they too were digging for gold. Brian walked around and looked inside the fort. It was certainly busy enough —shops everywhere, people buying, people hurrying. But he was struck by how few industries were operating now. There seemed to be no manufacturing as before. He saw at work only a wagon-maker and a blacksmith. Had something happened to Sutter's industrial empire?

During the rest of that afternoon Brian heard about finds of gold that made his eyes bulge: the nugget that weighed seventeen pounds; the cluster of pumpkin-seed–sized nuggets in the hollow stump; the man who owed another one money and, becoming exasperated with his creditor's constantly nagging for payment, asked for ten minutes' time, went out and dug up enough gold to pay off the creditor and buy every man in camp a drink. And best of all, the one about the miner who made his pile and went to Sonoma to get a shave and a haircut. When his mining-camp whiskers lay all around him on the floor, the miner asked the barber if he wanted them. The barber said no, so the miner put them in the wash basin and panned out another ounce of gold dust.

Brian was not so gullible that he took all the stories literally, but there was enough truth in them to rouse his excitement. Maybe, if he played it smart, he could make his lucky strike and get back to Coleen before the baby came. Wouldn't she be surprised! A rich husband and a new baby, all at once!

Jane was right about Sam, except that Sam got himself a drink before he sat down. He was looking a little thin and nervous these days; the pleasant lines around his mouth were grooved deeper than they had used to be. But then Sam had always driven himself like a demon. He might be just plain tired out. Brian and Sam talked desultorily for a few moments before John Sutter came bouncing into the room. "Vell, vell, vell," he said, wringing Brian's hand. "So Jane's son is off to the gold fields. You vant to be careful there, young feller, those men vill thief your shirt off the branch vhere you hang it."

"What're you missin' now, John?" Jane boomed.

"It is nothing, my friend, only a dozen cattle and some sheep. I vouldn't mind giffing them, but I feel resentful vhen they steal from an honest man. Especially vhen that honest man is myself!" He looked around, beaming genially. "So. Did you and Charley Smith have any luck in the mountains, Sam? You came back so soon, hardly a month."

Sam had been slumping a little in his chair. Now he sat up, animation on his face. "No luck, John—but as it turns out, that was the best kind of luck for me. I know now I don't want to pan for gold. I got that all out of my system in a few days. Now I can go back to my merchandising with a free mind. Charley and I want to expand."

"How so? You vant to rent more room in the Fort?"

"Not now, John. We're covered there." Sam revealed nothing of his observation that the Fort was dying, or that he and his partner would soon be moving out to a more lucrative location. He seldom told of big plans before he had carried them out, but he had a way of talking as if he were seeking opinion. "We're thinking of buying up a ship that's lying abandoned in San Francisco Bay, provisioning it and sailing it up here. We might dock it at the *Embarcadero* and sell from it. Any objections to that, John?"

Sutter's face fell a little, for he too worried about the Fort. Nearly all his rentable spaces were occupied and bringing him in a substantial monthly sum; but the goods being sold there were no longer manufactured by any of Sutter's employees. With only rents for income, he was not getting rich from this Gold Rush, as men were calling it. He said, "I haff no objections. I can rent you vharf space as vell as varehousing. But tell me vhy don't you vant to expand at the fort. Certainly plenty of customers are coming there."

Sam said carefully, "The Fort is two miles from the river. When a man is in a great hurry to get rich, he'll buy from the merchant who has goods to sell where he is. I propose to serve these earnest gold seekers right at the river's edge."

Brian said, "I think I'd feel the same way, Sam. You're probably right."

Sam gave him a wryly amused little smile. He was betting quite a lot of money on being right. In a day or two, when the ships arrived, it would be time enough to tell John Sutter that he'd bought three ships and would be anchoring them in the Sacramento River right off Sutter's wharf. He leaned forward, the superb salesman with a fresh idea. "John," he said, "when are you going to sell me enough land right here to start another city? This is where it will be, you know, not two miles away."

Sutter looked mutinous; he and Sam had tangled over this issue before. "I haff tell you, Sam, this is not the place for a city. This is bad land, too low. Effery year since I come here, the river rises up and inundates some land. The place to build a city in Sutterville. It is three miles below here, also close to the river, but on high ground vhere houses vould be safe."

"I don't think a city will grow there," Sam said flatly.

Sutter grew pink. "Of course it vill. Early in May I had John Bidwell survey it for me. Lots are for sale already."

Sam said calmly, "Oh, yes, the location has more advantages, but it hasn't got the sparkle that Sacramento has already. No matter what you might do, Sutterville will remain a pokey little place while Sacramento booms."

"Vell, vell, I von't argue any more. In a year ve shall know."

Jane had been sitting uncharacteristically quiet, simply watching the men as they talked, enjoying having Brian here for a little while. Sam had had two drinks already, but so had Sutter. She said, "Supper'll be on the table in five minutes, gents. John, do you want to tell Brian that story about trying to lease the Indian land?"

"Ah, Jane, I haff tell that story so often. But for you, vunce again."

"You tried to lease some more land?" Brian asked. "I'd have thought you already had enough."

"Yes, vell, there vas gold on it. And I vas selfish, I vas thinking maybe if I could get a big amount of gold out, then I could pay off effery debt and New Helvetia and Fort Ross and Bodega vould be all mine. There is an old Mexican law stating that any man who finds a new mine, or wishes to lay claim to an old abandoned mine, has only to notify the authorities, and he can own all the mineral rights there. So I kept quiet about finding it. I call all these Indians together and I talk vith them. All I asked of them vas the right to dig for minerals for three years, and they vould be protected during that time. The Indians know how I treat them fair, so they agreed. They signed the lease."

"When did this happen?" Brian asked.

"In February. It vas then I put my trust in the wrong feller. I giff this paper to Charles Bennett in greatest secrecy. He carries it to our military governor, Colonel Mason, for approval. But along the vay Bennett brags about gold, he spills the beans as you say. Efferybody who talks with Bennett knows about the gold, so it is no use trying to be quiet any more. Then in early March comes a message from Governor Mason. He says that America does not own this land here, it is simply held under conquest. He says that the old Mexican law vhich vould have protected my mineral rights no longer applies. And United States laws do not apply to this land because America does not own it. So." He waved his hand. "Ve haff no law. That is how ve got back to the beginning again. Of course my lease meant nothing. All those fellers Bennett talked to are mining my gold now."

Sam had poured himself another whiskey, and when Jane

called the men to the meal he topped off his glass and carried it along.

Jane said, "John, have you been able to get anyone to run that gristmill at Coloma for you?"

Sutter shook his head, and forked a generous piece of ham onto his plate. "Efferybody vith half sense is digging for gold. Nobody vants to make flour, Jane. Thirty thousand dollars I sink into that mill. If only I had known, I might haff paid off the rest of my debt on Fort Ross, and haff money left over besides."

"The secret of financial success," Sam said hesitantly, for he was starting to feel his drinks, "is never use your own money for anything. Always borrow from the other man. So if you fail, you haven't lost anything but your reputation."

"I am proud of my reputation," said Sutter stiffly.

"I'm proud of mine," Sam said. "But you can win it back if you lose it honestly."

Brian said, "You men have both been to the gold fields, haven't you? Then could you tell me where the richest diggings are to be found?"

"My boy," Sam said, highly amused, "if I could tell you that, I'd first go there myself, and haul it out by the wagonload."

Sutter smiled too. "You do not belief in vasting time, do you, Brian? There are so many liddle places vhere is gold. Murderer's Bar, Murderer's Gulch, Diamond Springs, Milkpunch, Grizzly Flat, Shirt-tail Canyon, Lousey Level, Coyote Diggings —they all haff names and there is gold, or vas. But my young friend, it has been here for a hundred years, so men vill not dig it all out in a few months."

"The boy's anxious, John, just like you were," said Jane defensively.

"And look how I didn't get anyvhere being anxious," Sutter replied cheerfully. "Besides, this Fourth of July will be our first under the American flag. I am having a big party, and I vant you all to come. Ve vill shoot off the cannons, and haff a grand dinner, and ve vill all get a liddle bit tipsy, and dance and sing."

"To John's party," said Sam, raising his glass. Jane, glancing at his plate, saw that he had managed to eat a normal amount, in spite of the whiskey he had poured down his throat. She wondered if he would be sick later on.

Governor Mason and his entourage arrived at the Fort on July 2, bringing with them a party atmosphere. Sutter had declared a holiday for the Fourth. The day itself dawned sultry with a red flaring sunrise, which all who were awake declared was highly patriotic. The flag was hoisted to the roll of Mexican drums, and several cannon were fired, one after the other. The celebration breakfast, prepared by four cooks, was lavish: cornbread, eggs, ham, venison, fruit, and coffee. At midmorning Sutter's army put on a display of military maneuvers. Unfortunately the effect was dimmed by the scarcity of soldiers; however, those present made up for their absent compatriots by their preciseness and fine bearing. Sutter, who had trained them himself and who truly had served as a captain in the Swiss military service, was proud. As he dismissed them, there were tears in many eyes.

There was no lunch, but there were various entertainments during the day: foot races, horse races, wrestling, feats of strength and endurance. Afterward all those who wished to went down to the pond behind the fort to swim. A festive dinner was served in the afternoon, as the sun was starting down the western sky. John Sutter still had many of his trained Indian servants with him and, dressed in their spotless uniforms, they served the enormous meal faultlessly. Sutter had been able to buy provisions from a French vessel, so the delicacies included Sauterne and brandy, cheeses and other imported foods. In addition there was beef, game and fowl, and sugar for the coffee and tea.

Many toasts were proposed, especially to the few ladies present. Jane was resplendent in the deep-blue satin dress Susannah had made for her to wear to Coleen's wedding. She even managed to blush a time or two. Then later she was in her glory when "Philosopher" Pickett, a tall, fine-looking gentleman and the primary speaker of the evening, sought her out and insisted on her complete attention. After some time had passed, Brian felt he ought to rescue his stepmother, but for some reason he couldn't see either Jane or Pickett. Brian hid his grin in his drink glass. Jane could take care of herself . . . if she needed to.

The party went on, getting noisier, the room stifling with cigar smoke, but the guests remained. At dawn there was the clatter of hoofbeats, and suddenly a messenger appeared at the door. "Gold!" he yelled. "Gold! John Bidwell's found gold at Bidwell's Bar!"

A cheer went up, but nobody left the room to hurry off to the gold fields. They were having a fine time where they were.

With his head full of new information, most of it decidedly disturbing, Brian left his stepmother's home nearly three weeks after his journey had begun. He had decided to drive up along the American River, even though it was likely the best claims were already taken, and then make his way toward the Feather, where he had a hunch the pickings would be better. But, in truth his head was now so filled with stories of fabulous strikes and rich diggings, he hardly knew where to go first. So, without realizing he was like almost every other man who had set out for gold, Brian Campbell searched for his claim by being a wanderer, always moving on to what he thought would be the biggest strike of all.

Brian began his search at the mill where James Marshall had first discovered gold. Even with the plethora of tales about great wealth being taken from this area, Brian was amazed to find miners as thick as ants on a hill thirty miles in either direction from Sutter's mill. He stopped at the camps only long enough to hear stories of success. "Are you bringing out light gold or heavy stuff?" he asked, rapidly becoming more particular about the type of digging he wanted.

The scruffy but delighted miner dug deep into his saddlebags and raised a fistful of brilliant, sparkling grains, some no bigger than grains of sand. "Light as the air, it is!" he said triumphantly. "I figger I'm pannin' near to thirty dollars a day."

Brian smiled and congratulated the miner—but he knew he wanted more. He clapped the man on the back and bade him farewell.

Keeping to a northerly direction, he moved up the Middle Fork of the American River. He had heard many tales of a big find at a place everyone was calling Spanish Bar. With the first miner who went to the city for supplies, Brian sent word back to Robin Gentry that he had staked their first claim, a mere four foot square patch of earth, at Spanish Bar.

Four

Robin Gentry was one of the most nervous prospective bridegrooms who had ever lived. Though Robin's family worshiped regularly, the Gentrys were of no particular denomination, and Robin had never before tangled with the unbending regulations of the Catholic Church. So far as he was concerned, the only function such regulations as the posting of banns could achieve was to allow Sean to discover their plans and stop them. "Isn't that what the posting of banns is for?" he asked Fiona frantically. "Aren't they to allow time for anyone who can give cause that the marriage should not take place to come forth? You told me that."

"It's true," Fiona said calmly.

"I knew it! And Sean will hear, and believe me, Fiona, he'll give that priest of yours a list as long as his black robes, and we won't get married now—or ever!"

"Nothing has happened so far," said Fiona. She looked up from the watercolor she had been working on and turned her attention to Robin. He lay in the hot, dry long grass of deep summer. Instantly she forgot the painting she had been doing, her artist's eye captivated by him. His skin was darkened by long hours in the sun, his thick black hair gleamed with healthy highlights. The long sinewy curves of his body were accentuated by the cushion of long grass. He was the essence of maleness, the lion at rest, the panther overlooking his domain. "I want to paint you just as you are right now, Robin," she said softly, her own voice a feline purr.

He turned his glance upon her, his light-brown eyes golden in the light. "And I want you to go to a minister—any minister, the *alcalde,* anyone who can marry us, and let us be on our way to the gold diggings and be on with our life, Fiona."

"Papa would not recognize such a marriage, Robin. We would be better not to marry at all if that is all you want. My marriage must be the joining of ourselves with each other and with God by a priest, and none other will have meaning." Her hands moved quickly as she placed a new sheet of paper on her easel. "Don't move, Robin, the light won't stay as it is for long, and I want to get the richness of the shadows on your face. You have a beautiful face."

"Women have beautiful faces," he said perfunctorily, though he held still.

"Yours is beautiful—all planes and angles and marks of strength."

He shook his head. "Fi-ona! You've got me arguing with you over whether men are beautiful or if it is women who are. I want to talk about our marrying and leaving here—either we do that or we go to your father and talk to him. Maybe Sean will change his mind and give his permission for us to marry sooner."

She stopped and considered for a moment. "He might. If Mama were on our side, and supported us, then Papa would at least listen."

Robin chuckled softly. "Mary would sympathize with me. Did I tell you that she once warned me that I had better be completely certain of my own mind before I got involved with you, for you were capable of driving a man to drink—actually, she said you could drive the saints to drink." With an impish look at her, he pulled a flask from the jacket he had been using as a pillow, and took a long swallow from it.

Fiona's green eyes glittered. With a quick motion she tossed her wet and well-colored paint rag, hitting him squarely on the forehead.

Robin rolled to the side, his arm reaching out to whip across the legs of the three-legged stool upon which Fiona sat. In seconds she was skirts over head in the long grass with Robin Gentry on top of her. She squealed with laughter, staving off his kisses until he had her pinned to the ground and helpless. "Will you talk with your mother? Get her to help us? Have a little pity on me, Fiona!" Robin wailed in mock despair. "Sean is going to shoot me if I give him a chance!—And I pine for you in my arms at night!" He nuzzled against her, tickling, nipping at her ear, until she once more dissolved into laughter.

"I will! I will!" she cried, tears of laughter streaking down her face. "Robin, stop! We'll go to Mama and Papa."

"And if they won't help us, then will you be married by the *alcalde?*"

"Papa won't accept that."

"But I will, Fiona, and I am the man who wants to be your husband." This time Robin kissed her tenderly, at the corners of her mouth and on her eyelids, his love for her clear to be seen on his face.

"I will," she answered breathlessly, her arms going around his neck as she drew him closer to her. "I want to be your wife. I want to be the mother of your children, dozens and dozens of little boys all looking exactly like you running through golden fields—oh, yes, Robin, I will do whatever you say."

Robin kissed her deeply, his tongue exploring her mouth until they nearly dissolved with their hunger for each other. Then he raised up, his gaze devouring her as his mouth had just moments before. He smoothed her riotously curling auburn hair from her face, his fingers tracing across her eyebrows, down the side of her cheek to her lips. She kissed the tips of his fingers, smiling dreamily at him. "I feel as though we will always love as we do now. Is that possible, Robin? Can love last forever?"

"If it can last for one moment, one hour, one day—then it can last forever." He sat up straight, then got to his feet. He put his hands out for her to take. "Let's go back. Talk to your mother now. I don't want to lose another moment, Fiona. We have so much to do together . . ."

"You are very eager to join Brian, aren't you, Robin? Sometimes I forget because you don't say a lot about it, but it is always there. The gold is always in the back of your mind, isn't it?"

"It's always there," he agreed.

Fiona began to pack up her painting tools. She stopped for a moment to look at the sketch she had begun of Robin. As unfinished as it was, it was special to her. Perhaps one day she would finish it. Even if she didn't, this sketch would go into her book, and someday she would show Robin's sons and daughters and grandchildren this sketch of him. The longer Fiona stared at the drawing the larger her Gentry family became, and in her mind's eye it stretched out through the years, generation upon generation, and always Robin loomed large as the patriarch, the source. She shivered with the force of her feeling for him. Robin.

Robin Gentry, staring off into the distance, was unaware of his love's contemplation of him. With the suddenness of a mountain storm his mood had changed. He had lived all his life in the west, and was accustomed to reacting to the slightest, subtlest change in his environment. Now he squinted as he scanned the horizon, searching the darker depths of the woods and the brush that grew along the banks of the stream. He knew someone was about, though he saw nothing, and he could hear no sound that gave anyone away. In a quiet, even voice he urged Fiona to hurry and put her belongings aboard the small cart. As if trying to facilitate her packing, he removed his guns and holster from the cart, and fastened them around his hips.

Still tied up in her own dreams, Fiona smiled. "I think Mama has been expecting me to come to her about us for a long time. I think she will help us. Even if Papa has to behave like a protective bear, Mama knows what is to want to . . . to be married."

Without seeming to, he hurried her. He helped her onto the cart and took the reins himself, setting the horse to a brisk trot across the field. It was an uncomfortable pace, for the little cart bobbled and hopped over every bump on the field.

Fiona frowned, clutching at her hat with one hand and trying to keep her easel and paints from popping out the back with her other. "Robin, please slow down—there is no hurry!"

Robin gave her a quick smile, but his eyes remained hard and observant on the terrain around them. "You have no spirit of adventure. Just hang onto your hat, love, and enjoy the ride."

With Fiona complaining the whole way, Robin jolted into the stableyard, pulled the horse to a stop, and jumped from the cart. "You go talk to Mary," he called, already halfway across the stableyard.

"*Robin!*" Fiona called out, and started after him.

Mary came out onto the porch. "Fiona, what has happened? Have you and Robin argued? Is something wrong?"

With an exasperated stamp of her foot, Fiona turned to face her mother. "I wasn't aware of anything being wrong until moments ago. I don't know what has gotten into him. Everything was fine until we started home, and then he insisted on making the horse fly over the fields and nearly bounced me out of the cart. And you saw what happened just now."

A worried frown marred Mary's face. "Then he has seen something he did not want you aware of, and has gone for Sean."

As if to prove her worries sound, Robin, Sean, and three of the ranch hands rounded the side of the barn at a run. Moments later the men on horseback thundered out of the yard in the direction Robin and Fiona had just come from. Mary fished her rosary beads from her apron pocket and made a quick sign of the Cross. She loved her new California home, but it was a rough and unpredictable land. "Come inside, Fiona," she said in a thin voice. "We'll find out what this is about soon enough, and in the meantime we should prepare ourselves for the worst."

Coleen, just inside the house, heard the last. "What worst? What has happened, Mama?"

"I don't know, dear. Robin, your father, and three of the men just rode out of here, and they are all armed. May the blessed saints ride with them, but . . . we should be ready with bandages if necessary. Come along, both of you."

Sean and Robin rode in the general direction Robin gave them. Robin had never actually seen the people he thought were squatting on Sean's land, and all he had been able to give Sean's men was a sighting of movement along the stream near the place where Fiona had been painting. Despite the vagueness of

Robin's description, they found the four squatters in less than half an hour. They had pitched a tent near the stream and had taken out gold-panning equipment.

Sean McKay, his Celtic blue eyes blazing, rode up to the man who looked to be in charge. "What are you men doing here? You're on private property."

Robin shook his head, and said under his breath to the man next to him, "They've come from outside. No Californian would pan for gold here."

The man to whom Sean spoke verified that they were looking for gold, then asked, "How'm I supposed to know this is your land? By what authority?"

This was a dangerous question. Sean sat a little straighter. Whoever the stranger was, he had been educated, and probably knew as well as Sean that there was no legal structure by which he could claim ownership of the ranch.

Sean said gruffly, "By authority of my purchasing this land, working it and living on it with my family. Now, just who am I talking to, and by what authority are you here?"

The man smiled smoothly, thrust out his hand and said, "Name's Aaron Wheelwright. Me and my friends are panning for gold—and we're here by the authority that there is no authority."

Robin laughed softly, his hand firmly on his gun. "Well, Wheelwright, there's no authority here, but neither is there any gold. You're looking for gold on a ranch that isn't going to give you much but a panful of dung. You want gold, you go to the hills. Where are you from?"

Wheelwright shook his head. "I guess it's obvious that we're not from around here."

"Couldn't be more so," Sean agreed dryly, feeling a sudden pride in being a man who would know better than to pan for gold in a livestock stream.

"We're from back east," Wheelwright said vaguely, then he looked at Sean. "I don't suppose you could see clear to letting us camp here for the night?"

Sean glanced over at Robin and saw the same look of uncertainty that he himself felt. "I guess I could—if you're willing to pay for the privilege."

"Pay?" Wheelwright shook his head morosely. "Sorry, Mister, it took every cent we had to buy this equipment. I couldn't pay you anything. I was counting on Western hospitality, I guess."

Robin said, "Since gold's been found, Western hospitality has had a considerable strain on it. So far you haven't given very good cause for being here, you don't say where you're from—and I get the feeling you'd just as soon not—and I haven't heard you say when you're moving on, or where you're headed."

"That's quite a speech," Wheelwright drawled. "What if I was to say I don't believe you folks either? What if I was to say I'm thinking of staying right where I am?"

Robin slid his gun from its holster, and leveled it at the man's chest. "I'd say we'd done enough talking."

Wheelwright's dark, hard eyes fixed on Robin. It was difficult to see the man's features for the black unruly beard he had allowed to grow untrimmed all over his face. He was just a dark-visaged man staring with cold eyes at the tall sun-browned man in the saddle, assessing whether Robin would use the pistol.

Robin spoke to the ranch hands with him. "Help Mr. Wheelwright pack up the tents and equipment. He and his friends will be leaving the ranch now."

Wheelwright smiled, and nodded. Taking several steps back, he raised his hands in defeat, then turned away from Robin so his right side was hidden. With a quick move Wheelwright turned, and Robin shot at his feet. Dust and rock spurted up the man's pants legs. Wheelwright jumped back, his own gun in his hand. Robin's eyes were grim and steady on Wheelwright, his gun pointed at the man's chest. He said with deadly calm, "I won't hit dirt and rock with my next shot."

Wheelwright's eyes locked with Robin's. The two men glared at each other in a struggle of wills, then Wheelwright lowered his pistol. "You win this time, Mister, but you won't ever turn your back again without having to wonder where Aaron Wheelwright is."

"Start packing up," Robin ordered.

Wheelwright took a couple of steps forward. "You've got the gunhand now, and I'll do as you say, but mark what I said,

Mister. Aaron Wheelwright doesn't forget a face or a score, and you and me have a score to settle." That said, he turned on his heel, stalking off to pick up his belongings. He kept up a non-stop monologue of curses and threats, but not once did he stop working.

Robin and Sean waited until they were certain the three ranch hands could handle Wheelwright and his men, then they began a leisurely ride home. As they rode, Sean turned to Robin. "You're pretty quick with that gun of yours. Wheelwright believed you'd use it on him. Would you have?"

Robin turned his head just enough for Sean to see the easy curve to his lips and the hard glint to his eyes, but he said nothing.

"Humph," Sean said, and nodded. "That's what I thought . . . just wanted to check. One sure way to take the measure of a man is to see him stretched out against an enemy."

"And did I meet your standard, Sean?"

"You did," Sean said gruffly.

"Enough for you to free me of the promise to wait for Fiona's eighteenth birthday before we marry?"

Sean's eyes darted to Robin's face, but he said nothing.

"Sean, I want Fiona with me when I go to the diggings. I don't want to go without her, and I don't want to marry her without your permission and blessing. Will you give them?"

Sean, as Robin had done before, turned his head just enough for Robin to see the curve of his lips and the glint in his eyes, but he was still silent. He snapped his crop over his horse's flank, and the animal shot ahead of Robin's mount.

When Robin caught up with him, Sean slowed his animal to an unhurried trot and said, "If you prove to be less of a man than I judge you to be, or less of a man than she believes you to be, you'd better be prepared to use that gun of yours, because I'll come after you, and that's the only thing that will stop me. Think about that."

Robin gave him a curt not. "I've always known that, Sean. I wouldn't respect you if it were any other way." Then he broke into a broad grin. "Thanks for your blessings."

As they rode into the yard of the ranch, their attentions were distracted by the worried look on Mary's face. She stood on the porch, her face pale with fright.

Sean waved to her, calling, "All's well." As soon as the stable boy appeared, Sean dismounted and turned his horse over to the youngster. He ran to his wife, putting his arm around her and holding her close and protected against him. He kissed the top of her head, then he said in a low voice, "He kept the wind at our backs, Mary my love. We are safe. We are all safe."

Sean explained to Mary's satisfaction what had happened that afternoon, then he sat in his favorite chair and waited like the king of the manor for his lady to serve him something cool to drink. He took a deep and satisfying draught from the glass of tea Mary had cooled in the springhouse. With a mild twinkle in his eye he said gruffly, "And now I'd like to talk alone with my daughter."

"Which daughter?" Fiona said in a small voice.

"The daughter who has been scurrying about the countryside hunting for a priest to marry her behind her father's back. Which daughter might that be?"

"You know?!" Fiona gasped.

"Of course I know. To whom do you think those black-robed crows come when they want a tithe? To your papa, and in exchange for the Lord's share, they give me a blessing and news of my daughter's doings!"

Mary and Coleen quietly disappeared from the room, Mary tugging fiercely on Robin's sleeve until he went with them, leaving Fiona bright-eyed and frightened with her father. "I didn't mean to deceive you, Papa," she began.

"All your chasing around was an accident? Is that what I'm to believe, girl?"

"No! That isn't what I meant—I mean—oh, Papa, I love Robin and I was afraid you would refuse to give permission because I am not yet eighteen."

"So you decided to ignore your father's wisdom, not to mention the Fourth Commandment—or do the Commandments of the Lord Himself have no more meaning to you?"

Tears formed in Fiona's eyes. "He was going to leave me behind and join Brian, Papa. I—"

"He was coming back, was he not? You *are* betrothed, aren't you? Have you no trust, girl, not in God, not in me, and not in the man you say you love?"

Fiona began to cry harder. She sat alone, her small body becoming even more compact and tiny as she closed into herself with sorrow. Sean watched his younger daughter for a time, then got up from his seat and went to her. He took her hands from over her eyes, and lifted her chin so that she looked at him.

"We are McKays, Fiona, given to each other by God Himself. We keep His rule, and for the keeping He has given us all the gift of love. That gift will be lost through deception. Its foundation is love. Its mechanism is trust, and its preservation is understanding. Never try to find love by turning your back on others who love you, Fiona, for what you find at the end of that journey is disappointment and loneliness, not love."

He pulled her to her feet. "Come with me now," he said not ungently. They went into the kitchen, where Sean knew Mary and Robin waited. Without saying anything he walked over to Robin and placed Fiona's hand in his, then he covered both their hands with his own. "You have my blessings. May the good Lord and His angels guard you always."

Fiona burst into fresh sobs. She looked at Robin, tears flooding down her cheeks, then she turned and threw her arms around her father's neck. "Papa, I love you! I'll never forget again. Thank you, Papa, oh, thank you!"

Fiona and Robin were married in the front room of the McKay house on July 21, 1848. With her usual wizardry, Mary managed to make a lovely wedding dress for Fiona. When they had left Illinois for their journey west, Mary had been carrying with her her mother's wedding gown made in 1800, the same that Mary had worn when she married Sean and had expected her daughters to wear at their weddings. But like everything else the McKays had owned, the gown had been lost when they were trapped in the mountains. Mary and her daughters tried to remember every detail of it, and Fiona drew a sketch from which Mary worked.

The original had been a very simple gown in the Grecian style of Mary's mother's time, a chemise of lightweight silk fabric, cut quite wide and shaped to its wearer by the use of draw-strings at the low neck and just under the bosom. For the short puffed sleeves and the bodice, Fiona selected a fine creamy lace which formed delicate ruffles at the edges and fell into delightful gathers over her breasts. The full-cut thin silk hung in beautiful folds on her slender body. As there was no time to do the elaborate embroidery which had been on her mother's dress, Mary trimmed the skirt and the train with a foot-wide band of the lace. Over her head Fiona wore a long veil of the same delicate lace, from behind which her green eyes sparkled bewitchingly.

On the day that he brought Fiona down the stairs to Robin's side, Sean's eyes shone with love and pride and tears, for she was the image of her mother on the day they had married.

Robin's hand trembled as Sean placed Fiona's in his. There had been many important days in his young life, and most of them had passed by unrealized until much later. However this, his wedding day, was not one of these unmarked days. Ever since Sean had talked to Fiona and later to Robin about what it was to love a McKay and to be a member of that family, he knew fully that his life would be altered for all time once he was married. His heart was beating so hard, he had to concentrate with all his might to hear what the priest was saying to him.

Finally he placed the gold band on Fiona's finger, and was permitted to lift the veil and announce to all the world that they belonged to each other in the eyes of man and God for all time. Breathlessly he kissed his bride, holding her close against him. Then, in an uncontrollable burst of emotion, he lifted her off her feet and swung her around, dancing with her to the accompaniment of the laughter and well-wishes of his lusty new family.

Five

Susannah Morrison was not happy in her dress shop near Sutter's Fort. She was making a great deal of money, and looked upon that development favorably, but she did not like the sudden and seemingly permanent change in her clientele. The stock which she carried in her shop in no way resembled what she had dreamed of. Mixed in among the pretty silk dresses, satin robes, and beautifully designed hand-made hats now gathering dust were the items she loathed and which brought her so much money. Pans and picks, red flannel shirts, gray and blue wool shirts, shovels—things of little beauty, worn and used by men of little culture. She could see herself merely as a shopkeeper, not as someone special who designed and sold special things to the women of a thriving city.

All of Sutter's holdings seemed to be dissolving into chaos. Money, or rather gold, was everywhere, and the rough men who clambered up into the hills seeking the mineral by the cartload had the idea they could buy anything. As more and more men streamed into California, the idea that a man was a law unto himself seemed to gain strength. It was difficult to find a man who had not been drinking, and it was no longer a good idea for a woman to walk the streets unescorted. Susannah hated the *laissez-faire* attitudes of the miners, and mourned the loss of freedom their ill behavior meant to her.

She didn't complain to Cameron, but it wasn't difficult for him to figure out that her sudden reluctance to open her shop, and her willingness to close early at any provocation, were due to the changes in the town. The spirit of sprightly, infinitely ambitious, infinitely curious and adventurous Susannah was slowly being crushed under the weight of the crudity of the miners. As impossible as it was to imagine, Susannah was becoming quiet, reserved, almost withdrawn. Cameron hated that as much as Susannah hated dealing with the miners.

She had so little interest in her shop that it was a simple matter for Cameron to begin clearing the inventory without her noticing. On several occasions he had dropped the word that he and Susannah might be willing to sell the lucrative business. When he was fairly certain he had a buyer for the business, he came into the shop mid-afternoon and gave Susannah a rakish grin. He strode over to her desk, tipping his hat far back on his head. "Could I persuade the lovely lady entrepreneur to take the afternoon off for a jaunt in the country, the best meal available, and later a pleasant evening at home with a cooled bottle of champagne?"

Instantly the sparkle came into Susannah's bright blue eyes. She smiled at him, but then that look of cynical resignation crossed her face, a look he had come to know but hated seeing in her. She said, "I would close shop for no more than a walk in mud and a supper of beef jerky. Put the sign in the window, Cameron, while I lock the back door. These miners will steal what they can't buy." She hurried round her desk, talking as she slipped the bolt on the door. "Do you remember, we never used to lock anything. Now you have to watch every door and window as if we're under seige. They even leave I.O.U. notes promising payment when they strike it rich! Can you imagine?"

"They're used to getting easy credit from Sutter."

"Well, I'm not Sutter, and I don't think even these clods are going to mistake me for him."

Cameron walked back across the room and took her shoulders in his hands. "Susannah, Susannah, are you going to take everything I say and twist it to feed the hostility you feel towards the miners?"

Susannah felt instant remorse. She shook her head, making her black curls bob. "I'm sorry," she said, then leaned against him, feeling relief in his gentle embrace. "Oh, Cameron, what is wrong with me? Every time I open my mouth it is to complain or criticize. I didn't used to be like that, did I?"

"No, my love, and you should not be like that now. Come, let's close this place and get on with our picnic. I would like to talk to you about something."

"What?"

Cameron kissed the tip of her nose. "Patience, good dame. I will tell you later after I have plied you with wine and soothed you into a good mood."

"Cameron! Please tell me now! You know how I hate to wait. Tell me, what are we going to talk about?" She hurried along beside him, trying to keep up as he tossed dust covers over the counters of goods, pulled the shades on the windows, and placed the cases of valuable jewelry into her safe.

"Cameron, say something! You are a terrible tease! Stop smiling!" she cried in frustration. "I'll never be in a good mood if you won't tell me!"

Cameron took her elbow and escorted her out of the shop into his waiting carriage. He drove straight for Sutter's Fort and the hotel there. Leaving Susannah waiting in the carriage, he ran inside, returning with the picnic basket and the chilled wine he had ordered.

His light-brown eyes twinkled with amusement as he noticed Susannah sniffing at the delicious odors emanating from the basket. She kept the expression on her face bland, and refused to look at him, or admit she was interested in the food. He drove out away from the town and away from the direction the miners took. After fifteen minutes of unrelenting silence from Susannah, he said, "Pouting will do you no good. I am going to tell you what I have in mind in my own good time. Meantime, I am going to eat—alone, or with a pleasant companion."

"You wouldn't dare . . ."

He reached over, cupped her chin in his hand, and turned her to face him. "I would," he declared softly. "And that is not all I would dare."

Susannah tried to muster up anger, but failed. She was captured by the merry gleam in his eyes, and began to laugh. She always seemed to be putty in his hands. Every time she set out to have her own way about something, somehow it was always Cameron who had his way.

Cameron found a green valley not too far from town for their picnic. He unpacked the basket, handing the cloth to Susannah to place on the ground. He took out silverware, crystal, china, linen and a succulent meal of chicken breast, fresh tomatoes, *pommes frittes,* and *mousse.* Susannah's blue eyes grew large as he brought out one container after another. He left her to gawk over these treats while he went back to the carriage to fetch the wine. "Any complaints now, my pretty one?" he asked.

She stood up and put her arms around his neck. "You make me feel so privileged, I am ashamed for ever having complained about anything to you. Why do you put up with me, Cameron? I am so much trouble."

Smiling, he kissed the lids of her eyes. "You are a very great trouble, but I love you, and I love the trouble you are. Now, sit down and eat, my lady. I want to get on with plying you with wine and food and soothing you so that you will be completely receptive when I suggest to you that we have had enough of New Helvetia. It is time for us to go to our house in San Francisco as man and wife."

Susannah, open-mouthed, blinked in surprise at him. "That is what you wanted to talk with me about? San F . . . you want us to go to San Francisco . . . to be married . . . now?"

"We agreed that one day we would do so. I think it is time."

Susannah's eyes were shining. "I—I don't know what to say first—there are so many things flying around in my mind. My shop—I'd be your wife— When would we be married? Where? Will I have time to order a gown? I can't just abandon the shop, can I? What will I do with all the stock?" She flung her arms around him and kissed him repeatedly. "Cameron, I love you! Help me decide!"

Laughing, Cameron kissed her, then took her arms from his neck and made her sit down. "First we eat," he said. He fixed a plate of food for her, put it into her hands, handed her fork and napkin, then poured wine, his lips twitching in a pleased, amused smile at her delighted perplexity. "Let's put some order into your thoughts, and rid ourselves of practical worries first. You haven't noticed, but I have already reduced your inventory. I think I can find a buyer for the shop. Unless you want to stay here, the shop can be disposed of."

"You've been planning this for some time."

"Yes, I've been thinking about it for a while. You're not happy here, Susannah, and I am here only because of you. My preference has always been for us to live in San Francisco—"

"The only reason I didn't want to go back there was because of—of what happened when I took Papa's tithe money, Cameron. It was a long time ago, but the Saints will never accept me, and I don't think I could stand always being treated like a pariah. It would be awful to walk into shops and have people refuse to wait on me, or cut me dead in the streets. We'd have no friends, no place to go—I am afraid to go there. I'd have only you, my father and Mama, and even then it isn't like it used to be. Papa and I are reunited, but you know there is—there is a reserve between us, and probably always will be because I sent the money to my brother Landry."

"I know all of that, but I know more than that, things you do not know. San Francisco is no longer the little village overrun with Mormons that you left. Many of the Saints are moving to Salt Lake City. Even Sam Brannan is now only one of many important men. The town is changing, Susannah. Hundreds of people live there now. Streets have been blocked out, hotels and business buildings are being built, houses are under construction. It is a thriving place—no longer the settlement of mud and tents that you left. It has been a long time since you have been there."

"The Saints are not so all-powerful there as they were?" she asked tentatively.

"No. You would have many people to befriend you, and many shops to frequent where you might never have to see a Mormon."

Susannah sighed deeply. "Oh, how I would love it to be so." She looked at Cameron, then down at her hands. "I am a city girl, I guess. I thought it didn't really matter where I lived, but when all these men came looking for gold, I—I am ashamed to say it, but I don't like the way they are. I don't like what is going on in New Helvetia. I've begun to long for the theater, and concerts, and people who talk about the latest novels, and have new ideas. I think maybe—maybe I am a terrible snob."

Cameron laughed. "Oh, my darling, you aren't a snob. These men are suffering from a malady that seems to have gotten the name gold fever. If you were to meet some of them in different circumstances, I am sure you would like them very much. I've met lawyers, doctors, teachers, men from all walks of life heading up into the hills, and it is true they seem to have lost their senses, and most of their manners, but they'll recover, I'm sure."

"Perhaps. I have seen no evidence of it."

"Well, all that will become apparent in time, but for now, let's get on with plans. The shop can be managed. San Francisco is no longer a threat to you. So to the most important matter. Will you marry me, Susannah?"

Susannah scooted over closer to him and nestled her head on his shoulder. "You know that is the one thing you needn't have questioned. I want to spend the rest of my life with you. But now there is nothing I want more than for you to see me walking down an aisle, dressed like a queen with flowers all around, and music from an organ, and everyone we know seeing us as we become man and wife. Of course I want to marry you, Cameron. I want to plan the wedding and revel in every tiny bit of it."

"That sounds like a very big shindig you're planning," he commented.

"The biggest New Helvetia has ever seen—or maybe San Francisco, if it has changed as you say it has. Yes! Oh, let's be married in San Francisco—maybe even in one of the old abandoned missions! Wouldn't that be a wonderful place for our wedding?"

He said hopefully, "We could always get married right here, quietly, and go to San Francisco with the deed already accomplished."

"We could, but it wouldn't be nearly as much fun. I want

everyone who ever snubbed me to see me now. I want all the newspapers to write stories about the prominent citizen Mister Cameron Gentry and his new bride, and to see the most gorgeous wedding gown San Francisco has ever seen—or ever will. The Brannans won't hold a candle to us—or even the Gillespies with their three Chinese servants. We'll outdo them all."

Cameron's eyes became a deeper brown as he watched Susannah. "I never realized other people's opinions meant so much to you."

"They don't," she said airily. "I'm being practical, that's all. If we are going to take our place in society, then it is sensible to give the important people in the city information about who we are, so they know from the outset that we are people to be reckoned with. Never hide your light under a bushel, Cameron, that's always good advice."

He chuckled. "Once you've arrived, I am certain the right people will know it, but if we don't close your shop and sell it, none of this can happen. I suggest we go home and get events in motion."

Susannah began to gather up the picnic remains, then stopped in the midst of folding the tablecloth. "Cameron! Will everything change when I am your wife? Will I be able to open another shop, a very exclusive ladies' shop, when we go to San Francisco?"

"You will always be Susannah, darling, wherever you are," he assured her, "so I suppose if you want another shop, you will have one. Let's not worry about the future, shall we? We have more than enough to keep us busy right now."

Susannah cocked her head to one side, an impish look in her eyes. "Just in case you might turn into a stuffy old husband, I want us to have a completely decadent night tonight. I am going to treasure all these last days when I am your mistress. I want to undress you, and rub your body with oils—scented oils—and drink wine, and fill the tub with warm water and bubbles and bathe in it with you and make love all night long."

"If you can carry that attitude over into marriage, I doubt that I would ever turn into a stuffy old husband. But I might put you in a house with no windows so it would always be night, and I might never get out of bed."

Susannah giggled. As they rode back to New Helvetia, both of them remained in the grasp of initial giddiness over the bright and promising turn their lives would take. But then Susannah began remembering all that had happened to her in San Francisco, and again her doubts and misgivings came to the fore. "Maybe San Francisco isn't as different as you think, Cameron. Maybe when the great rush for gold is over, and all these strangers leave again, it will be just as it was before."

"It isn't likely that it will ever be as it was before, Susannah. But even if that should happen, this is not the time to worry about it. You are borrowing trouble. If San Francisco doesn't suit us in a few years, there is nothing to prevent us from moving on—is there?"

She looked dubious. Her trust in the future wasn't as strong as his, but then Cameron had never been a Saint, had never experienced the hate of Gentiles, or been driven from his home just when he thought all was well. He had never experienced any of the terrors of prejudice that her family had. Susannah feared living in San Francisco with the Saints since she had fallen from favor with them; but she also feared the Gentiles, for she had no idea of what they might do to the Mormons—even one fallen from grace like herself. She sighed deeply, then finally said, "Could we just think about it for a little while—not make any definite decision right now?"

Cameron's voice was still quiet and kind, but an edge had crept into it. "You are being foolish. Nothing is going to happen to you in San Francisco—at least nothing bad."

"I know, I know—you are probably right, but it is such a big move and I'm—"

"If we don't make preparations now for the move—such as packing up the stock you want to take with you from your shop, and selling the rest—we won't be able to do anything properly when the time comes. You have to consider what is happening here too. Sutter's properties are not doing as well as they once were. If we don't sell out at the right time, we may find ourselves in possession of a shop in a ghost town, the proud owners of a property that no one wants, including us."

Susannah groaned and put her hands over her face. "Why does everything always happen at once?"

Cameron put his arm around her. "Don't worry so, my darling. It won't really happen that fast. You've allowed your imagination to run away with you. You will be opening your shop as usual tomorrow, and we have a great deal to do before we actually leave. There will be plenty of time for you to get used to the idea of leaving here and going to San Francisco."

"I don't mind leaving here a bit. I'm just not sure about going to San Francisco. Maybe Monterey would be better, or—"

He squeezed her tight. "Stop it, Susannah, you are making mountains from molehills. Everything will be good for us in San Francisco. You'll see."

"You sound so positive."

"I am, so stop worrying."

Susannah continued to operate her store. Every time one of the mud-spattered, bewhiskered miners came in with their dirty hands, asking to buy items Susannah hated handling, she tried to think of a pretty little shop exclusively for ladies in San Francisco.

Cameron had always encouraged her; now he began coming to the shop with her every morning, and worked with her until she closed it at night. He still refused to wait on customers, but he took over cleaning the shop, taking inventory, and marking stock to be taken with them or left behind for the next owners. He was a cheerful, tireless worker, and his energetic attack on the task at hand made Susannah's spirits rise. She even managed a pleasant smile to some of the miners. Now, whenever she had the mad urge to close the shop and run back to her house next door, she had only to go to the back room and hurl herself into Cameron's strong arms to be refreshed.

"I used to think I wanted to get away from the shop, but what I really wanted was to be with you," she murmured as he stroked her cheek and kissed her hair.

They had been working together and selling without replenishing supplies for a fortnight when a dark-haired man entered the shop. His eyes shaded by his slouch hat, and the rest of his face concealed by a wild growth of black whiskers, the man moved slowly around the shop fingering everything Susannah had laid out on her tables. Not liking the look of him, Susannah did not move forward to wait on him, but remained behind the counter watchful.

The man stopped his seemingly endless wandering, and returned to several of the display tables. He picked out half a dozen gray wool shirts, three red flannel ones, two pairs of denim trousers, several neckerchiefs, a hat, and some digging equipment. He placed all the items in a stack near the front door, then approached Susannah. "I'll give you my chit for that stuff," he said.

Susannah blinked in amazement at the man's presumption. "I'm sorry, sir, but I don't accept chits in this store, and we don't have accounts for any but our oldest and most trusted customers. If you want those goods, you will have to pay cash for them—or gold." She came briskly around the side of the counter, walking toward the sizeable pile of merchandise he had taken.

"I can't pay you cash, and I'm just now on my way to get gold, lady. I'll give you my chit. It's as good as money. There ain't a store around that don't offer credit."

"Then I suggest you go to one of those other stores, because I do not!" Susannah said curtly.

"What's so special about this shop? Or is it that you took a dislike to me?" He was moving slowly toward her.

Susannah backed away, thinking to seek the safety of her counter, but the man had blocked her way. "I don't even know you—and that is reason enough not to extend credit, sir."

"Name's Aaron Wheelwright, and I said I'd give you a chit. What the hell do you want, lady—a formal invitation to tea so's we can shake hands and talk while we're sippin'?"

Cameron, hearing the shrillness in Susannah's voice, came out from the back room. "What's the trouble out here? Susannah?"

"This man is insisting I give him credit, and I've tried to explain, but he—he won't listen."

Wheelwright was staring at Cameron. Under his breath he muttered, "I'll be damned!" Aloud he said, "Now I'm beginning to understand why there's no credit for me here."

Cameron said courteously, "I don't know what you're referring to, sir, but this shop does not extend credit to the miners unless they have been customers before. Once you have established yourself as a reliable customer, then we can discuss credit."

Wheelwright shook his head. "You aren't even going to acknowledge me, are you?" He shook his head again, then grinned. "I'll give you this, you're a cool customer—or mighty stupid."

"I think you'd better leave." Cameron moved out into the shop.

Wheelwright laughed. "Oh, I'll go. That seems to be your way, talk a bit and when you don't like what you hear, just chase the fellow off. But don't you forget that warning I gave you last time, mister. I might let one time go, but by my soul, I'll get you this time."

Cameron took the last few steps to reach Wheelwright, grasped the man by the arm and propelled him out into the street. "Don't come back in here—not even with cash." He closed the door firmly before Wheelwright had a chance to reply. Through the window Cameron glimpsed the fury on Wheelwright's face as he turned and marched down the street.

"He acted as if he knew you, Cameron," Susannah said, her heart still pounding furiously. "Who is he?"

"I don't know. I've never seen him before. He's probably just been up in the hills too long without proper food. A lot of those men who go up there and don't find gold get some funny ideas."

Susannah's eyes were still fixed on the door. "I don't know. He was so menacing. It's as if he hated us."

"I don't think he hated you, darling, no one ever does. It was only me, so let's get back to work and forget him. He'll wander from store to store until he gets his credit somewhere and then he'll forget all about us."

Susannah shuddered. "I hope so! I don't like that man. Cameron, let's close the shop. I really don't want to stay here any more today."

Cameron chuckled and put his arms around her. "A hug won't do it for you this time?"

She smiled weakly at him. "Oh, a hug will make me feel better, but not in here. He might come back. Oh, please, we've been working in the shop every day, can't we just take a ride or go visit Sean and Mary, or Sutter? Let's just go somewhere. Maybe Coleen's had her baby. We could go see."

Cameron watched the play of fear and hope in her eyes. Susannah always seemed so headstrong and independent, it was only at times like this that he could see how much she needed to be protected—how much she needed him. Tenderly he held her, reveling in her soft femininity, aware of his own role in her life. He kissed her, saying, "We'll go back to the house and while away the rest of the afternoon, and then—well, we'll decide what we will do after that. Would that suit you, my love?"

Aaron Wheelwright had not gone far from Susannah's shop. He had gone down the street a short way to Smith and Brannan's Store, joining his two friends at the bar.

"Did you get our stuff, Aaron?"

Wheelwright shook his head, then grinned. "But I got something else. You remember that big bastard that ran us off his land a couple weeks back? Well, I found the son of a bitch. He acted like he never saw me before in his life, and damn if he didn't run me off again. Only this time we got him. He must own that store, and soon's it gets dark we're gonna make him a poorer man by half."

Wheelwright kept talking to his friends and drinking. The little cash the trio possessed was quickly going down their gullets fortifying their courage for Aaron Wheelwright's planned revenge.

It was midnight when the three men left Smith and Brannan's. Wheelwright left the other two for a while, heading for one of the stores that was no more than a tent with its flaps tied to stakes in the ground. With little effort the slim, wiry Wheelwright had wriggled under the flap and helped himself to several tins of lamp oil.

Burdened with the tins, he rejoined his friends. "They in there?" he asked, his eyes steady on the light that dimly shone through one of the shop's shuttered windows.

"I'm not sure," one said. "I think so, but you can't see a damn thing for the shades on the windows."

"Even if he ain't in there," said the other, "he ain't gonna like havin' his store go up in flames."

"I want the son of a bitch!" Wheelwright growled. He put down the lamp oil and crept to the window trying to peer in under the shade. With an angry gesture, he admitted it was difficult to tell. "I think I saw the woman—but it might ha' been one o' thse damn dresses she has perched all over that store. But if it was her, you can be sure he's in there too."

Each of the men took up one of the heavy tins of lamp oil, punching a hole in the tops with their hunting knives. "Make sure there isn't a spot you don't douse. I don't want them left with a way out," Wheelwright said.

Each man took a side of the shop, dousing the wooden foundation with oil, then more cautiously and quietly saturating each of the window frames. The three met at the front of the shop and repeated their action there. The little oil that was left in each container was thrown onto the roof of the shop. With a grin Wheelwright pulled three cigars out of his pocket, giving one to each of his friends. "This looks like a good place to have a nice smoke. Good way to top off a pleasant evening." The others laughed.

He slowly lit the cigar, taking his time to nip off the end, smell the tobacco, making certain it was well lit and drawing well before he tossed the used match at the edge of the foundation. The match almost went out, then flickered and turned blue. The flame began to creep along the trail of oil. Wheelwright then took out his box of matches and began to walk around the perimeter of the shop, dropping flaming matchsticks along the foundation. Any scrap of paper he found, or piece of dry brush, he used as a torch. His compatriots gathered brush and pieces of wood, piling them up on the fireline, so that each stack lit and added fuel. As soon as the fire had a good start the three men hurriedly walked away, but not so far that they couldn't see what was happening.

Susannah and Cameron were in bed drowsily talking about their plans. Their house and Jane Pardee's stood beside the shop in a cluster of three frame buildings. The shop was already an inferno before the wind shifted and they smelled smoke. Fire was such a common and constant threat in towns made mostly of canvas and wood that Cameron was out of bed and reaching for his trousers before Susannah had a moment to react.

"Hurry, get dressed, Susannah," he called, already buttoning clothes and running barefoot down the stairs. Without even bothering to identify the location of the fire or how bad it was, Cameron ran to the back stoop and began frantically ringing the large bell he had put there for instances of alarm.

From the stoop he had a clear view. "Susannah, it's the shop! Hurry, the wind is carrying the fire to Jane's house. Ours will go next."

"We have to save Jane!" she cried, then realized that Jane was still visiting the McKays.

The sky was a fiery pink by the time the first townsmen came running from their dwellings and from the saloons. Cameron was already at the well, shouting for Susannah to bring every receptacle that could hold water. With confidence he filled up one after the other, certain the water brigade would form as soon as the townspeople responded to the bell. One by one nightgowned men took up buckets, pots, and pans, passing them on to the next, the last man throwing water on the fire. Up at Sutter's Fort and all along the way, bells began to ring, and more and more people showed up in the street. Others took positions at nearby establishments wetting down roofs to prevent the fire from sweeping through the whole section of New Helvetia.

With a huge pop, and a spray of fire and sparks, Susannah's own supply of lamp oil burst into a huge flame that shot through the roof of the shop, taking with it slabs of burning wood. With deadly accuracy the flaming materials landed on the roof of Susannah's house as well as Jane's.

Gunpowder, oil, all the materials Susannah did not like to sell in her shop, exploded in vicious bursts of noise and flame. The men in the street backed up, unable to stand the intense heat of the burning building. Soon they were too far from the buildings to be able to quench the fire. One man took Cameron's arm sympathetically. "I'm sorry, Gentry. There's nothing we can do. All I can offer you is my regret, and a promise that I'll be the first one there to help you and Susannah rebuild. This is a dirty shame."

Another said, "This was a set fire, you can bet on that. This thing went up too fast. Someone knew what he was doing."

Susannah, who was clinging to Cameron's other arm, whispered, "It was that man, Cameron, I know it was. He said he'd get you and he—we might have been killed—he wanted to kill us!" Her voice had risen dangerously, and she was trembling all over, her teeth chattering, her eyes crazed with fear.

With the cruel suddenness of hidden memory unleashed, Susannah was thrust back to her childhood flight from the burning Mormon section of Independence, Missouri. She was four years old again, clutching her doll, with her brother Landry jerking her by the hand as they ran screaming toward the stables after Papa, terrified that in his desperate hurry he would drive away in the carriage without them or leave them behind all limp and cold like their mother. Behind them flames licked into the sky as the only home little Susannah had ever known was incinerated. The whole section had been set afire by the Gentiles in retaliation because the Mormons had declared themselves more favored of God. All around them people were running and yelling. One man was a fleeing ball of flame. Hoarsely he was shrieking, "I'm on fire! I'm on fire!" The Gentiles had tarred and feathered him and lit matches to him.

Susannah tried not to look, tried to keep up with nine-year-old Landry—but she could not help seeing mothers and children running in their nightclothes, and saw the Gentiles on their horses laughing as they herded the terrified people like cattle. One woman who stumbled was immediately trampled by her neighbors. The Gentiles had long whips out, and did not hesitate to use them on any victim who appealed to them—like her mother.

Then came the horrifying carriage ride out of town, seeing frightened people's eyes all around them pleading with her father, and hearing their screams, "Take me with you! Take me!" It was then by chance that Ezra Morrison had seen Prudence and her son Asa, hurrying like the rest, and Ezra had stopped and picked them up. The group had fled throughout that night, leaving the awesome orange sky and the stench of burning far behind, but it clung like smoke to the memory, always there waiting for an ill wind to revive it.

Cameron, alarmed, hugged Susannah against him. He had never known her to panic like this. He tried all he could to calm her, but it was as if she didn't know him and didn't see him. "Susannah!" he cried, shaking her, trying to get her to tear her gaze from the flames and look at him. "Susannah!"

Mrs. Wentworth, who lived down the street and had been watching them, came over to Cameron. "She is in shock, Mr. Gentry. You will do no good by shaking her. Come with me— my house seems to be safe. We will go there and give her laudanum to put her to sleep. She will be all right when she awakens."

"Thank you, but—"

"Don't argue, Mr. Gentry. You must go somewhere. You have no house. You have to sleep somewhere."

Cameron tore his attention from Susannah for a moment, finally allowing the sense of the woman's words to register on him. Dazedly he said, "I don't suppose we can stop this fire, can we. Thank you—we'll be grateful for your help."

Mrs. Wentworth took Susannah's hand from Cameron, speaking to Susannah in a kind but firm voice. "Come, dear, we are going to take you where you will be safe."

"Papa!" she cried wildly, looking around with unseeing eyes. "Where is Papa? I can't find Landry!" She tried to throw off Cameron's protective arm, and he held her tighter. "Papa!" she screamed. "Landry! Landry!"

Cameron's eyes met Mrs. Wentworth's. He said helplessly, "I'm not sure what—she must be remembering something else. Her father is in San Francisco, and her brother Landry is still in New York. Perhaps when she was younger there was a fire at her home."

"All the more reason for us to get her calmed and asleep. The sooner she forgets this, the better."

Cameron scooped Susannah up in his arms and carried her the several blocks down the street, with Mrs. Wentworth breathlessly trotting beside him in an effort to keep up.

Wheelwright, standing at a distance, smiled in satisfaction. He and his men had melted into the heated night. Unwilling to aid in putting out the fire, they were afraid their refusal might be noticed.

By dawn the fire was finally beginning to wane. Susannah's shop was nothing but scorched rubble, and all but the rear wall of her pretty new house had burned. Jane's house fared little better. The original part of the house had been constructed of log, and still stood, though it smouldered and was so hot that no one could go near it. The newer frame section was a blackened ruin on the ground.

As soon as the danger to other houses and businesses was over, soot-begrimed men and women wearily made their way back to their own homes, thankful that the fire had been contained and their houses were untouched this time.

Cameron kept watch over Susannah all night long. Mrs. Wentworth soon fell sound asleep in her chair, but Cameron watched Susannah with worry and concern. No matter how well he knew her, it always seemed that there was more to his Susannah than he ever dreamed. He was certain now that they were leaving for San Francisco as soon as she was able to travel, and from now on in he would be more careful with her.

Six

Suddenly the move to San Francisco became a simple matter for Susannah and Cameron. Susannah's fears of events that might await her in San Francisco seemed nothing in comparison to the terror she had experienced in New Helvetia; and as a result of the fire there were no possessions to be moved, no house to vacate, no inventory to be disposed of, no shop to sell. Susannah Morrison owned only what she had on her back. So the move was made simple, but it was also devastatingly clear once again how swiftly and cruelly her life could change. She clung to Cameron with a desperate passion, knowing that she could never trust what fate might bring her and that every moment she had was a precious one, not to be squandered away.

Together Susannah and Cameron made the rounds of the homes in New Helvetia, thanking the many people who had helped them the night of the fire and on many other occasions. With some particular friends whom they would be sad to be leaving behind, they shared a meal and a whole night's conversation filled with pleasant memories. Both Cameron and Susannah issued many heartfelt invitations for their friends to visit them in San Francisco. Sniffing on the day of departure, tears rolling down her cheeks, Susannah let Cameron help her into the carriage that would take them away from New Helvetia and toward their new home. With a final wave, Cameron called to the horses and headed south and west to the coast and the city by the bay.

The day was beautiful, the ride was pleasant, and it took little time for Susannah's spirits to rise. As soon as he noticed that she was once again her natural curious self, Cameron grinned broadly and began telling her who owned which piece of land they traveled through. The closer they came to the city, the more contagious his excitement became, and Susannah was all eyes when he halted the horses at the top of a hill.

Below them was the verdant slope, and beyond that, in the cove of the mountain, the new city. In the streets they could see masses of people moving, and horses, mules, and wagons, most of them headed out toward the gold fields. A little farther out was San Francisco Bay, with numerous ships anchored and others playing in and out among them. White sails billowed in the breeze; at mastheads flew the flags of all the world. For twenty miles beyond that the waters of the bay glittered rose-orange in the evening sun. All around the bay, as far as they could see, were long continuous ranges of mountains, some high, some mere green hills. Looking westward, they saw the outlet of the bay and the foaming billows of the Pacific Ocean. Even this far away they could hear the hushed roar of the sea.

As they began the descent, Susannah was full of questions. The village she had left nearly a year before was no longer there. In its place were the beginnings of a cosmopolitan city that bore little resemblance to the muddy lines of tents and shanties she had left. Hotels were being built; stacks of fresh-milled lumber waited at the sides of roads, some of which were not yet named. Carts and drays hurried up and down the dusty streets. There was a bustle about everyone here. The men on the streets had unfamiliar foreign faces, and spoke to each other in many languages. Spanish dons dressed in beautiful suits mixed and mingled with men attired as miners, sailors and workmen. The only thing these people had in common was that every man she saw wore a pistol on his hip.

When Cameron turned the horses onto Montgomery Street, driving toward the house they had built the year before, Susannah's awe was uncontainable. "The houses! Cameron, ours was almost the only house on the street! Where have all these people come from?" Though she was glad for neighbors, she was also glad that Cameron had bought enough land that they would be at a little distance from the nearest houses. She swiveled around on her seat, trying to see in all directions at once. At the corner of Sacramento and Montgomery there was a cabinet-maker's shop, which she noticed immediately.

Cameron smiled. "I have a feeling Orris Parrish will be an important man to you. There is nothing he can't build—fine furniture, cabinets, anything you could want."

"It really has changed, hasn't it? I must have seen hundreds of people as we drove through, and not one face was familiar to me. I could go for weeks and not even meet one of the Saints I knew before, couldn't I?"

"You could indeed," Cameron agreed, then added, "Even if you should meet some of the Saints with whom you came over on the *Brooklyn*, I think you may find that their attitudes are quite different now."

"In what way?" Susannah asked, her attention now solely on him.

"I haven't said much, because I didn't want to worry you, and I know your fondness for Sam Brannan. But Sam and Brigham Young have been in a struggle for control of the church for some time, and Sam is not winning. A good number of the Mormons have already left San Francisco and have joined Young in Salt Lake, and those who have stayed behind are not what you would call true Mormons."

"What about Papa? Surely he hasn't left the Church—has he?"

Cameron shrugged. "I suppose it depends on what you mean by leaving the church. I think he had better talk for himself."

Susannah nodded. "I want to see him as soon as we are settled. I must talk to him. He has never mentioned this problem. I just can't imagine his thoughts if he is now leaving the Church after all that has taken place in its name. Oh, Cameron, what a terrible toll it will take if everything he did to our family will have been done for nothing." Involuntarily she shuddered, thinking about what Ezra's rigid adherence to the dictates of the church had cost her family. Wanting to be a devout Mormon, Ezra had first cast out Susannah's mother, then her brother, and finally Susannah herself. He had even taken a second wife, Tolerance, yet still there was trouble.

"It will be a comfort to him that you are here and so close to him. Prudence will be glad for a friend too, I'll bet."

"Oh, yes! Poor Mama." Susannah was quiet for several minutes, her eyes holding a faraway look. "I haven't been much of a daughter to them lately, Cameron. I have a great deal to make up for."

"Well, let's not brood about that now. Here is your house. This, I think, will be just as you remember it. Does it feel like home?"

Susannah's blue eyes shone with pleasure as Cameron helped her from the carriage, and they went together up the brick walk to their house. Flourishing a sturdy-looking key, Cameron opened the door and they entered the spacious front hall. To their right was the handsome staircase that led up to the bedrooms and bathroom. On their left was a parlor with a big bay window. Susannah sighed happily, thinking how beautiful the house would look once she got the plaster walls covered and furniture in place. "Do you remember, Cameron, you said I could watch from this bay window for you to come home."

He smiled at her. "It seems like a long time ago, last year at least."

They toured the dining room and the kitchen, telling each other how they wanted things arranged. "Oh, it is a beautiful house!" Susannah exclaimed. "I thought perhaps I had made it lovelier in my imagination, but I hadn't. It is just as I remembered. I can hardly wait until we're married! Let's have a garden, with hundreds and hundreds of flowers all around the house—and children, several children."

"Anything you say," he replied grandly.

In the washhouse Susannah, giggling, threw her arms around him and detained him for several minutes. "If you're going to be like this," he said at last, smiling fondly at her shining loveliness, "shouldn't we wait until we get up to the bedrooms?"

"One floor is no harder than another," she said practically. "And besides, I've never made love in a washhouse before."

"Neither have I. Well, if Sir Walter Ralegh can throw down his cloak, the least I can do is throw down my body." With that, he lay supine on the floor and held up his arms to Susannah.

Laughing, she knelt beside him and began kissing him again. Then he heaved her over on top of him and lay smiling up at her, his expression amused and pleased.

"Cameron!" she wailed. "What do I do next?"

"I am an innocent pioneer here in the washhouse," he replied. "Just be gentle with me."

"Oh, you—" She was still giggling as she inched backwards down his legs and unbuttoned his trousers and released him from confinement.

"What a relief," he said.

"That is nothing compared to coming events," she said saucily, and bent over and kissed him on the head of his penis. It was a thing she had never done before, but it seemed all right. His eyes, watching her, were startled; but his face was alight with pleasure. Holding the shaft, gently she ran her tongue over his penis, feeling the little ridge on the underside, reveling in the silky smoothness and warmth of him. She felt an urge to take him into her mouth, and she did, once or twice running her tongue up and down his length. Then, feeling him throb and realizing that her own satisfaction came from holding him within her another way, she pulled up her skirts and eased herself down onto him. It was very strange, being on top and seeing the dazed sensuality on his face. And it felt good—more exciting than ever—becoming one with him in an entirely new way. Perched comfortably on her knees, she rocked a little to and fro, intensifying their enjoyment.

Cameron lay with his hands on her bare legs, her full skirts covering them both. As she made her movements longer and slower, his hands tightened on her thighs, synchronizing with her motion as he urged her on. With magnificent control she kept up the same pace, so that when they both climaxed at the same time, it went on and on, long and intensely pleasing. Then she collapsed onto his chest, her face rosy with delight, still panting and shuddering as she felt his diminishing spasms within her.

Cameron held her comfortably tight, his lips against her forehead. After a while she eased off him and they stood up stiffly and refastened their clothes. Catching each other's eyes, they grinned, and he embraced her again. He said, "Susannah, my darling, you are a constant surprise to me."

She sighed against his vest. "I can hardly wait until we're married," she said, and they laughed.

"I'd better start making arrangements this afternoon," he said. "It sounds as though we have many things to do instantly."

Susannah playfully slapped him on the arm. "You always make fun of me! But this time you'll be sorry. I am already planning our wedding, the biggest and best San Francisco has ever seen. Everyone is going to know that the Gentrys have arrived!"

"Whoa! How about something a little less flamboyant? Perhaps a nice little affair in the *alcalde*'s office, no fuss or bother?"

Susannah, eyes sparkling, shook her head. "Uh-uh! You told me yourself the rule in this town is glitter and gold, and that's what we're going to have—a wedding fit for a king and queen."

Cameron didn't say anything more, but a slight frown creased his brow. He couldn't tell how much of Susannah's talk was the result of excitement and an immediate acceptance of San Francisco as *her* town, and how much of it was serious.

During the next two weeks, while Cameron and Susannah set up housekeeping, they lived at Brown's Hotel. Though it was only a one-story adobe, it was the best hotel in San Francisco, outdoing the Portsmouth.

Susannah wanted her house to have her marks of good taste, so she declared that the walls needed imported wallpapers and fresh-colored paints. She kept Cameron hopping trying to secure laborers to do the tasks she set forth. The rest of her time and his was spent shopping in the few stores that remained open in San Francisco. Whenever they could not find what Susannah wanted, they ordered from the great shipping houses that seemed to be springing up everywhere.

Susannah remained impressed by all she saw of the city. One day, risking Cameron's jealousy of Sam Brannan, she said, "I just can't help remembering Sam telling all of us what a magnificent city this would be. He said that even before we had sailed from New York. It hasn't happened exactly as he envisioned—I mean, this isn't going to be New Zion for the Saints, but he certainly foresaw the great city, didn't he? He really is a man of vision—a builder of dreams."

"You sound as if you think he put up this place brick by brick with his own hands," Cameron grumbled. "You know there were a few other people who had a hand in this."

"Oh, I know that, please don't twist what I'm saying. All I meant was that Sam put a dream in our minds when we were still in New York. Imagine, more than two hundred saints being asked to give up all they had worked for in New York to come out here to build a new and safe place for our Church. We were all very frightened, and then Sam gave us a dream of this magnificent city that only he could really envision. And now here I am, living in it. Don't you think that is wonderful? Something miraculous?"

"I suppose if you look at it from that standpoint it could be, but there are a few people around here who could give you a very different view. To them your Sam Brannan is little more than a shrewd opportunist willing to use whatever means, and whatever money he can lay hands on, to butter his own bread."

"Well, I don't think that's fair. You tell me which of these other men you refer to have *not* tried to butter their own bread, as you put it. I don't see anything wrong with that. Anyway, no matter what you say, Sam has done a lot for this city."

Cameron sighed. "I suppose he has."

Susannah suddenly giggled. "That's better. You're not really jealous of him any longer, are you?"

Cameron wouldn't answer, but she was right. He didn't know when it had happened, or when he knew it to be true, but Susannah's former relationship with Samuel Brannan no longer bothered him.

She leaned over and gave him a quick kiss on the cheek. "I'm glad. It's about time you got smart and realized I love only you —and always will."

Cameron laughed. "I don't know whether to grin like a fool, because I'm such a lucky man, or to cry in my beer, because you are such a handful and I'm the fellow who gets to try to keep up with you."

And Susannah was a handful. She kept right on with her plans for a huge wedding at the same time her fertile imagination fired her ambitions for the two of them. She did indeed want a new shop in San Francisco, and of course that too had to be the very best and most impressive. She also decided that Cameron had to have his own offices in town just as several other prominent men did, including Sam Brannan. Ezra and Tolerance did not visit—perhaps awaiting an invitation—and Susannah said very little about going to see them until two events happened. The first was entirely coincidental: One day while shopping Susannah saw from a distance Tolerance Morrison, her father's plural wife, and her concern for her father came once more to the fore of her mind. The meeting also occasioned another shopping spree, for Tolerance was perfectly groomed and very fashionably dressed, rivaling Susannah's own spectacular appearance. Susannah purchased four new gowns, the latest fashion fresh off the ship from Paris, before she felt entirely secure again.

The other event was a vehement argument with Cameron over the size and scope of their wedding. "I do not like showy displays!" he had said heatedly.

"And I don't like secret little rituals performed in some back closet of an office as though we had something to be ashamed of!" she had shot back at him.

By the time they had argued for nearly an hour with neither giving ground, Susannah felt badly bruised and in need of an ally. Trying to appear superior, and now above such petty arguments, she said, "I've said all I'm going to on the matter, Cameron. I will not be married by some petty official in an office!"

"Then I guess there will be no wedding. I'm not going to be put on display like some oddity in a carnival!"

"What a ridiculous thing to say! I think we'd better change the subject. I would like to see what Papa and Mama have to say about this. Maybe they can talk some sense into you."

"More than likely your father will talk some sense into you. I can't imagine Ezra Morrison countenancing a public spectacle such as you evidently have in mind."

Susannah, hands on hips, stuck out her small pointed chin. "Well, we'll just see about that! I'll send a calling card to Mama this very afternoon, telling her we'll be over tomorrow."

Cameron and Susannah set out for Ezra Morrison's house mid-morning of the tenth of August. It was a glorious day of bright sunshine and mild breezes. Susannah was in high spirits, eager to see her parents, and certain that Ezra and Prudence would support her in her desire for a big wedding. The only cloud on her horizon was Tolerance. As she adjusted her hat to the perfect angle to compliment her face, Susannah said, "I do hope Tollie has the good sense to go shopping or something. I don't want to sit through a whole afternoon of listening to her inane chatter."

Cameron suppressed a grin. He knew very well it was not Tollie's inane chatter that Susannah wanted to avoid, but the likelihood that Tollie would side against her in whatever she would suggest. And perhaps most important, Susannah, a rare beauty anywhere, but certainly in woman-starved San Francisco, did not like competition from Tollie whom she had previously considered plain.

Susannah had taken great pains in dressing this morning, choosing an outfit that would enhance her high coloring, her brilliant blue eyes and her shining black hair. She had chosen a tailored white wool walking suit trimmed at the lapels and the hem in black velvet piping. The suit fitted her bust perfectly, tapering in sharply at her small waist. Her soft silk blouse was a gentle aqua, heightening the color of her eyes. Her hat was a small pillbox encumbered artistically with a spray of ostrich plumes. She wore white gloves and black kid boots, and carried a parasol of aqua silk that matched her blouse. She made quite a picture, and felt reasonably confident that nothing in Tolerance Morrison's wardrobe could touch this for fashion or sophistication.

With a satisfied smile she glanced over at Cameron. "But if she does have the good sense to find something else to do, I hope she leaves little Elisha with Mama. I really would like to see him. It's been over a year since I've seen my—what do I call Elisha, Cameron? He is really my nephew, but after Papa married Tollie he—"

"He's not your stepbrother, Susannah. He is still your nephew."

"But I don't think Papa will like Elisha calling me Aunt Susannah. Not many people here know what happened between my father and my brother."

"Yes, I know. I have heard unkind talk about the fact that your father has two wives. Even with so many Mormons out here, the idea of plural wives is not looked upon favorably."

"It would be even less favorable if people knew that my father's second wife actually had been my brother's wife. Oh, that Tollie! She has never been anything but trouble. I wish none of my family had ever laid eyes on her! Ever! Not even Landry."

Cameron took her hand in his. "There is no point in getting yourself all upset about that. You can do nothing. It happened, and all we can do is go on with our lives from here."

"Well, it isn't that simple. If what you heard is true, that Brigham is calling the Saints to Salt Lake to be with him, then Papa will be in a very small minority here. You never know what people will do to someone who lives differently from the rest. I know, because I've seen what they can do. Tollie is going to cause us a lot more trouble. Why can't she go to Salt Lake City? If she had any decency she'd leave us alone."

Cameron said, in a way he sometimes had when he seemed at a loss for other words, "Ohh . . . Susannah. You're getting all worked up for nothing. Anyway, from what you've told me, what happened wasn't Tollie's fault, it was Landry's."

Susannah wouldn't answer. If Landry had a fault, it was in seeing both sides of an issue. He had been excommunicated because he had questioned the teachings of the church and then had expressed his questions as doubts in a confrontation with a powerful bishop of the Church. It was true that Landry had been terribly stupid and irresponsible, but in Susannah's eyes, Tollie was still the villain. Tollie hadn't stood by her husband when he most needed her. She had even taken his unborn son away from him—and then, as if to assure that there would be trouble for years to come, she had married Landry's own father. There was no member of Susannah's family who had not suffered because of Tolerance Weber Morrison. And not once had

Tollie ever shown any indication that she felt remorse or guilt for her part in the whole rotten mess.

Cameron and Susannah completed the ride to Ezra's house in pensive silence. But all of Susannah's worries seemed to evaporate when the front door of the Morrison house was flung open and a joyous Prudence stood there, her arms outstretched to receive her stepdaughter.

All thoughts of fashion and sophistication vanished from Susannah as well. As soon as Cameron helped her down from the carriage she flew into Prudence's arms. "Mama! Oh, Mama, I've missed you so much."

Tears stood in Prudence's eyes, but her homely face was a garland of smiles. With Susannah still in her arms she greeted Cameron, and slowly the three of them managed to enter the house with all three voices vying to be heard first.

With a laugh Ezra came out of his study, his reading glasses in his hand. "I just knew that had to be my Susannah," he said. "No one else can make a house come alive the way you can." At first he kissed her shyly, gingerly on the cheek, then on impulse engulfed her in a fatherly bear hug.

"Come along into the parlor," Prudence urged. "I just made some fresh lemonade. We can have a nice chat until our supper is ready."

As casually as she could manage, Susannah asked, "Where is Tollie? Will she be joining us?"

Prudence's eyes twinkled as she glanced over at Ezra. "No, Tolerance remembered she had promised to visit friends this afternoon. Flora and her family will be leaving any day now to join President Young in Salt Lake."

"And Elisha?"

"Elisha is with Tollie, but there will be other times for you to visit with him now that you are living so near to us again. Oh, this is wonderful to have you here, Susannah. San Francisco is getting to be a lonely place for Papa and me. So many of our old friends are leaving, and the newcomers are so strange, I'm afraid I haven't made many new friends."

"I am surprised that Flora is leaving. She has always been one of Sam's strongest supporters, and she certainly liked San Francisco. What made her change her mind?" Susannah asked.

Prudence looked to Ezra. Susannah's father cleared his throat, then said, "To begin with, President Young and Elder Brannan have not been seeing eye to eye."

"Yes, Cameron mentioned that, but I still don't see—"

"It has to do with gold. Of all gold taken out of the hills by the Mormons, Brother Brigham has ordered Sam to take thirty percent for the Church. Of course, he anticipated that Sam would send that gold right to him and Salt Lake. Brother Brigham has in mind to build a magnificent temple in the desert there, and he wants every cent he can lay hands on. However, Sam has not sent whatever he has collected. He has kept it for the Church here—or so he says. Others say his intentions are not so Godly, but that is something else altogether. In any case, a clash between Sam and Brigham is in the offing. Brigham has ordered the Saints living here to move to Salt Lake City, and he has sent his Destroying Angels to deal with Sam."

"The Danites? That's barbaric!" Susannah fumed.

"Oh, don't worry about Sam," Cameron said with a smile. "From what I hear, he has quite a force of his own. He calls them the Exterminators, which I am certain aggravates Brigham sorely."

Susannah's eyes were wide with surprise. "Are you saying that President Young and Sam have—have *armies* they are sending against each other?"

"That's putting it a bit strong," Ezra said, "but essentially that is so. The Church of Latter-Day Saints is a big plum, Susannah, and these are two powerful and power-hungry men."

"Sam?" Susannah asked breathily. She remembered the times when Sam had used to talk with her of his ambitions. *I mean to rise in the Church,* he had said.

Ezra's eyes sought the comfort of the window and a clear blue sky. "The names of President Brigham Young and Elder Samuel Brannan will probably both go down in the history books. Men who make a notable mark on history do not lead peaceable, quiet lives, Susannah. It takes a titanic force to leave an imprint on time." Ezra's gaze returned to his daughter. "Let us just be thankful that as close as our family has been to these two men, we have not suffered as bystanders to their battles."

Prudence let out a gust of air as though she had been holding her breath. "Let us not talk of this any more. It makes me very uneasy. Surely our lunch must be ready by now." She rang a small bell and spoke low to the Mexican woman who appeared almost instantly. Then Prudence turned back to her family. "Rosita says she is ready for us—and just at the proper time, in my opinion!"

The four of them sat down at Prudence's dining table, a new acquisition of which she was very proud. Susannah commented on the lushness of the table setting, remarking on the presence of Prudence's good Bavarian china, her silver and crystal.

Pleased, Prudence said with a huge smile, "But this is a special occasion. Papa and I have our daughter back at last." Then with a coy glance at Cameron, she added, "And we are about to welcome a new son to the family."

Susannah sat up straighter, and said without preamble, "That is something I wanted to talk with you and Papa about. Cameron and I are having a terrible disagreement over our wedding, and—"

"Oh, dear!" Prudence interrupted. "We *are* going to have a wedding, aren't we?"

"Oh, yes!" Susannah said quickly. "It's just that Cameron wants a little hole-in-the-wall ceremony in some petty official's office, and I—"

Laughing, Cameron put up his hand. "Wait a minute! If you are going to present this, do it fairly. Ezra, Prudence, I do not want a little hole-in-the-wall ceremony in some petty official's office, as Susannah so imaginatively put it. All I suggested is that we get married quietly, perhaps having the ceremony performed by the *alcalde.* There is some confusion here as to who should marry us. Susannah is no longer a Saint, so I doubt your First Elder would feel comfortable performing the ceremony. And I am not a member of any particular church. There have been mostly itinerant preachers out here, so my family and I worshiped wherever we could."

Susannah's eyes sparkled. "I don't see that as being important at all! Sam would probably be glad to perform the ceremony, but even if he wasn't, and the *alcalde* does it, we don't have to hide ourselves away in some office! I want a nice wedding."

"I think you should have one," said Prudence.

"She doesn't want a nice wedding," Cameron said. "She wants a spectacle!"

"Oh, Susannah, surely not," said Prudence with a puzzled frown.

"Mama, you know he is exaggerating, but I do think we should have a large wedding and invite the important people in San Francisco. And yes, it should be something people are going to remember and talk about favorably. After all, Cameron is going to be a *very* important man in San Francisco if he ever learns not to hide his light under a bushel. I think we ought to start out on the right foot. Papa—you haven't said anything. Don't you agree that I am right?"

"I am not sure, Susannah. Knowing you, you are telling me only a small portion of what you have in mind. But I do have a suggestion, if you two are willing to listen."

Cameron said, "If it tones down her grandiose ideas at all, I am certainly willing to listen. I am going to feel like a circus elephant on parade if Susannah has her way."

"Cameron! You make me so angry!" Susannah fumed, her small fists doubled up in her lap. "Why do you say such awful things?"

"Because they're true!" he shot back.

"Children!" said Ezra in his best patriarchal voice. "Susannah is my only daughter, and customarily it is proper for the parents of the bride to give her a suitable wedding. Would both of you entrust your wedding plans to Mama and me?"

Cameron looked warily at Ezra.

Ezra laughed. "I promise you there will be no circus parade, Cameron, and you, Susannah, have my promise that you will have no office wedding performed by a petty official. Can we leave it at that?"

Neither Cameron nor Susannah answered immediately. Their eyes locked, each waiting for the other to give agreement. Finally Susannah said, "I will agree. Mama will give us a beautiful wedding—but I don't think Cameron will."

Cameron still didn't answer. All eyes were focused on him. Finally, thoroughly uncomfortable, he gave a curt nod.

"Good! Then it's all settled, and none of us need wrangle over this any more." Ezra rubbed his hands together. "Prudence, my dear, what have you planned for dessert? Suddenly I have a taste for something sweet—and a cup of coffee wouldn't be amiss."

Prudence squeezed his hand affectionately. "He is such an old reprobate. Never could do without his cup of coffee, even if it did mean risking the wrath of the church elders."

After a second helping of Prudence's apple cobbler with its rich heavy cream sauce, Cameron felt stuffed and lethargic. "If I don't take a walk, I am going to fall asleep at the table," he said on a muffled yawn. "Prudence, your cookery could lead a man to a happy death."

"I think I'm complimented," Prudence said wryly, "but it is difficult to tell. Susannah, why don't you take this man out for a walk, while I help Rosita in the kitchen?"

"I think I'll join you, if you don't mind," said Ezra.

The three of them had barely walked three blocks before Susannah declared she wanted to do some shopping. "I would like to get a little something for Mama. She is so proud of her new furniture, I'd like to bring her back a knickknack for the table—and flowers! Yes, fresh flowers for her table. They will set it off perfectly."

Ezra and Cameron exchanged glances. Ezra chuckled. "She isn't happy unless she's spending money."

"I've noticed," said Cameron with mock severity.

"Well, it's been a long time since I've been in a real city," Susannah said gaily. "San Francisco still can't hold a candle to New York, but at least it has some interesting stores and some pretty things to buy."

Susannah purchased flowers and a porcelain vase for Prudence. Many of the shops were still closed, their owners at the gold diggings, but Susannah dragged Cameron and Ezra into and out of any that remained open, or had opened recently. She was having a marvelous time. As they neared the plaza they heard an uproarious commotion.

"What do you suppose caused that?" Ezra asked of no one in particular.

"Let's go see!" Susannah said excitedly, already turning in that direction.

They had just rounded the corner when a man, smiling and

waving his arms in the air, shouted the good news. "California is a possession of the United States! Treaty ratified!"

Cameron quickly gave chase to the man already running on down the street, catching hold of him. "When did this happen? How do you know?"

"A courier rode into San Francisco this very afternoon, just minutes ago. Mexico signed the treaty! We're on American soil again! Pass the word—there's goin' to be good times in the old city tonight!" The man wrenched free, continuing his mad dash down the street shouting his news to everyone he passed.

Cameron raced back to Susannah and Ezra, relaying the news.

"We must go home at once and tell Prudence," Ezra said. "She will be so pleased, and will not want to miss out on the festivities." Even as the threesome hurried home, dozens of people crowded the streets, all of them talking animatedly, and cheering spontaneously. Shutters that had been closed opened up, and houses and tents that had looked innocuous only moments before had suddenly sprouted SALOON signs.

Susannah looked around with a mixture of awe and disapproval. "I was going to ask you how you thought we might celebrate, Cameron, but I guess I don't need to. What this city needs is a few hundred more decent women. All you men know how to do is shoot off guns and drink."

Cameron said for only her ears, "And maybe another thing or two." Susannah had the grace to blush rosily.

Prudence was as excited as the others by the news. No sooner had she heard than her doorbell began to ring. One neighbor after another, and a good number of strangers, came to tell the family of the great event. Finally Prudence kept the door open, and Cameron and Ezra put a sign outside announcing that they already knew. Susannah and Prudence made several big pitchers of lemonade and placed them inside the front door, offering a cool drink to all who passed by.

By nightfall there wasn't a man, woman or child who had not heard and was not celebrating. It was decided that Susannah and Cameron would remain at Ezra's that night so that the family would all be together on this momentous occasion. Little thought was given to sleeping arrangements. At first Prudence had begun to fuss that Susannah and Cameron should not share the same room, but it became quickly apparent that sleep was a moot question. Guns were being shot off; firecrackers snapped and barked everywhere. Revelers could be heard on the streets shouting and singing. An occasional playful brawl noisily broke out, once right outside of Ezra's parlor window. Cameron and Ezra ran out onto the street, laughingly offering themselves as mediators between two men and one bottle. However, Prudence was the heroine of the day when she came to the rescue with two jam jars into which the remaining applejack was poured in even amounts. The two, once again friends, weaved off down the street now offering cheers to Prudence as well as to California, the new United States possession.

At nearly ten o'clock Tollie rushed into the house, barely taking time to say hello as she rushed to her bedroom to change clothes. "There is a big party at Flora's. Elisha has already been put to bed with Flora's children!" She waved goodbye hastily as she once more headed out of the house to join her friends.

Susannah looked at Ezra. "Papa, do you just let her go like that—wherever she wants? She doesn't act like a married woman at all! What will people think?"

Ezra's eyes sought Prudence. Prudence said, "Susannah, in many ways Tolerance isn't a wife. After your visit here last year, your papa and I decided that *I* am his wife—his true wife—and that left Tolerance in a rather peculiar position, don't you see. So she does as she wishes, certainly not what we'd like, but we can hardly keep her prisoner here being Ezra's wife in name but not really his wife, can we?"

Susannah turned her attention to Cameron as though it were all his fault. "See! I told you Tolerance was nothing but trouble —for all of us!"

Ezra sighed. "Yes. I am afraid this whole affair did not turn out too well. Perhaps it is the only part of my life that if I were given it to do over, I would do it differently."

"Oh, Papa!" Susannah cried. "I am so happy to hear you say that!"

"Susannah, this does not mean I would do things to your satisfaction, even if I did have the opportunity to change the past. My own admission of a lack of wisdom does not mean I forgive or condone what your brother Landry did."

Prudence said briskly, "This is nothing for us to be talking about on a day of celebration. Why don't we go out and celebrate too? We could even go to Flora's party. We'd be welcome there."

"I'm not so sure I'm ready for a party at Flora's," Susannah said doubtfully, remembering what good friends they had become on the *Brooklyn*. "I would love to see her, but I don't know how she or the other Saints would feel about me. Above all, Mama, I don't want to have to answer questions about what happened when I left San Francisco." She shuddered. "That would be awful!"

"I don't think we need worry about finding a place to celebrate," Cameron said. "From the sound of things, there is a party on every street corner."

It was nearly one o'clock in the morning before they returned home, hoarse with laughter and cheering, and very hungry. Prudence fixed a plate of cold chicken and fresh salad for them.

It seemed that they had barely closed their eyes to sleep when dawn broke, and with it every ship in the harbor hoisted flags and fired salutes. Barely taking time to wash their faces and dress, the Morrison family and Cameron were back on the streets hurrying toward the bay. Men on the shore fired their pistols to return the boom of the ships' guns. Children had purchased firecrackers from the supply Charles Gillespie had brought with him from China, and were firing them at every opportunity, causing havoc when the noisy, fiery things came too close to a lady's skirt.

Not to be outdone, Lieutenant Edward Gillespie led the New York Volunteers in full dress through the streets of the town in lordly fashion. Throngs of people lined the docks and the streets, all of them waving handkerchiefs, scarves, or flags, and cheering wildly.

That afternoon Robert Semple, a giant Kentuckian who stood close to seven feet tall, and ran the all-important ferry over the Carquinez Strait, gave a speech to a thoroughly appreciative audience. Semple, an ambitious man with an eye to selling lots and developing the community of Benicia, faced his slightly intoxicated, very gleeful audience with a twinkling eye; but his message was deeply heartfelt. To thunderous cheers he declared, "I thank Providence, yeah, I thank Providence that once again that he has so blessed me as to place my feet once more on American soil! Yeah, man! American soil!" he shouted, even then barely to be heard above the roar of applause, whistles and shouts. More guns went off, and firecrackers burst in all directions.

By the time the sun was setting, there was a barrel of tar on every street corner, lit and smoking and flaming brightly to mark the day. San Francisco was a blaze of light. Happy but very tired celebrants tried valiantly to keep up the festivities, certain now that California would become the thirty-first state to enter the Union.

The next day the Californians, not being a people to put things off, began preparations to apply to Congress for entry into the Union. Men jovially and confidently assured each other that it would be only a short time before the next celebration would take place. Sam Brannan was already trying to think what should be done in San Francisco to mark that momentous day when California was granted statehood.

"You may be jumping the gun a bit, Sam." Cameron laughed. "We just got declared a possession of the United States. We aren't going to be a state overnight."

"That's the difference between you and me, Cam," Sam said, his cigar bobbing up and down as he spoke. "It's going to seem like tomorrow to the man who isn't prepared."

Cameron shrugged. "At the least, it will be a couple of months."

"No time at all," declared Sam.

The two men parted, each going their separate ways as they came to the intersection. Sam clapped Cameron on the back. "Give my best to Susannah and her family! And mark my words—it'll feel like tomorrow when we celebrate statehood. Don't let it sneak up on you, Cam, be prepared to cash in on it!"

Cameron thanked Sam and walked on, a smile lingering on his lips. Sam would never let an opportunity pass him by. And maybe he was right. There was nothing to prevent California from gaining entry to the Union after the government had been

set up, and that had been in the works for a year. All California
had been waiting for was ratification of the treaty with Mexico.
Now that the treaty had been signed, what was to stop statehood? Certainly everyone agreed that it was necessary. As it
was now, California was without formal law, and with more
people coming in daily, self-rule was not going to suffice. California was going to be an asset the United States Congress
couldn't fail to recognize. With the wealth and the gold out
there, not to mention the growing commerce and shipping, Congress was going to want its share in taxes as soon as possible.

Slowly Cameron was beginning to look at the probability of
statehood differently. Perhaps he and Susannah *should* be better
prepared. Perhaps she should have her shop as soon as possible.
He had been urging her to take her time, but maybe he had been
wrong. He glanced over at the dock and watched as men were
filing aboard the *Sacramento* for the trip to Sutter's wharf. Every day it seemed there were more and more people. In Sam's
vernacular, there were more and more customers, more and
more opportunities. Cameron Gentry began to walk a little
faster, suddenly eager to get home to Susannah. Perhaps it was
time for him to learn to speak the same commercial language
that Sam Brannan did. Cameron was a very successful land and
commodities speculator, but he needed to become more gregari-
ous to keep apace with the flamboyant exuberance of San Francisco. The one thing he could not bear was being passed by!

Seven

Several dozen eager male passengers poured off the schooner *Sacramento* at the *embarcadero*, Sutter's wharf two miles below his fort. Among them was a slender young man of medium height, blue-eyed, brown-haired. He watched the others crowding each other, shoving to be earliest in line. They had been like that in San Francisco too. To his European eyes this behavior was repulsive. If these were the people his father had associated with for so many years, he was less than certain what would come of his reunion with his father. These rough, crude people had no manners! *Pigs,* he thought resignedly.

He started up the long hill toward Sutter's Fort. The afternoon was sultry; the warm damp wind carried dust on it from the huge freight wagons and the horsemen who passed him. Frequently on the gentle climb he stopped to look around him. His father's fields had a look of neglect, and there were few cattle or horses. The prospect of prosperity was there in the rich red land, but there was little evidence of it. He shook his head in sadness. Even as a child of seven, just before his father had left Switzerland for America, he remembered his mother saying that for Papa it was never the present which was important; all the good in life was always ahead. Here in California, Papa was still neglecting the possessions he had for those he might have. So he had not changed.

He passed through the gates of the fort, weary yet buoyed up. After nearly a year's travel, after fifteen years' separation, he would surprise his father with his arrival. Straightening his posture and setting upon his face an expression suitable to a man of his station, he entered the open door of Sutter's quarters.

Two miners, muddy from head to foot, got up to leave. He stepped aside, giving the men plenty of berth, and unconsciously brushed his coat after they had passed. Only then did he turn his attention to a heavyset man seated at a rude table, who asked, "Help you, sir?"

"Where is Captain Sutter, if you please?"

"He just left, be gone a week." The man added cheerfully, "What can I do for you today? Want to buy hip boots? Panning equipment? We give credit if you need it."

He was completely alert now, and fully the guardian of his family interests. He said, "How much credit?"

"Whatever amount of credit you need."

"Could I still have that if Captain Sutter were here?"

The man at the desk looked surprised. "Sutter'd be the first to say yes. Why, what's wrong? Who are you?"

"I am Johann Augustus Sutter, eldest son of Captain Sutter."

Augustus reached into his coat pocket and withdrew letters. "This is from Peter Shenibuk, my father's agent in San Francisco. It will introduce me."

The man stood up. "Of course. I'm Bert Lang, Mr. Sutter."

"I will need a place to sleep."

"Sam Kyburz has a hotel just across the way. You could try that. Just tell him who you are, and he'll get you in."

At the hotel he was assigned a bunk in a room with three others. He glanced at the rude accommodations, pronounced them satisfactory, and inquired about supper. While he was eating, a gentleman came in whom he recognized from a slight acquaintance in Washington City: Major Samuel J. Hensley. The men greeted each other, and Hensley introduced his companion, George McKinstry. They sat together, talking casually.

Augustus liked these men. Both had been in his father's service, and were well acquainted with his affairs. They seemed honest and open, without personal axes to grind. They were soon all on a first-name basis.

McKinstry said, "What will you be doing, Augustus, now that you're here? Digging for gold, like everyone else?"

"I might come to that." Augustus smiled. Then his face grew somber. He felt he could trust these two, so he said, "From the moment I landed in San Francisco, as soon as men found out I am Captain Sutter's son, they began bombarding me with contradictory reports on his affluence, on his debts. . . ." The young man paused for a moment, gravely in need of a friend and some good advice, but it went against the grain to discuss family matters with strangers. With a sigh he decided the information was more important to him than pride—at least right now. So he continued in a hushed voice, "It has even been intimated that my father drinks too much." He sighed again, deeper and more ragged than before. "It may be that he mishandles his affairs. Everything I hear is a contradiction. I do not know what to think—or do."

"What were you expecting?" McKinstry asked.

Suddenly like a ray of sunshine, Augustus's youthful sincerity shone through. His large blue eyes moved from one man to the other as he said, "When I was waiting to come to this country, I was so afraid that my father would have no need of me as a man. But you see I was wrong. I spoke to Peter Shenibuk, his agent in San Francisco. Mr. Shenibuk advised me specifically to get control of Father's holdings, to discharge all the rogues in his employ, to collect all debts owed him, and pay off all he owes."

Hensley and McKinstry exchanged glances. Hensley said, "Augustus, are you aware that your father owes the Russian American Fur Company thirty thousand dollars with interest?"

"No!"

"So—it seems you have made up your mind to take a hand in John's affairs," said McKinstry.

Hensley said, "I assume you also do not know that the Russian American Fur Company is suing your father, and that the sheriff of San Francisco has levied an attachment on all his properties in order to force payment?"

Augustus looked from one man to the other. "The news is at

least a year old when my father's letters arrive in Switzerland. Gentlemen, I do not even know enough about my father's business to guess if he is capable of payment. But I am worried. I must think of the welfare of my mother, my sister and my two brothers. For the past fifteen years my father's brother has seen to their support—but I resolved that once I came of age, I would try to reunite the family over here."

In the next few days, while waiting for his father, Augustus talked with Emil Hahn, who kept his father's records. Hahn readily turned over the books. Augustus examined them minutely, his dismay growing. Finally he said, "See here, Hahn. Is this all you have? There are no records for the last six months."

"We have been busy," replied Hahn with dignity.

Across the room Augustus could smell the liquor on Hahn's breath. He resolved to get rid of the man as soon as possible. He began walking around the little office, looking with critical eyes at papers on the desk. In a half-open drawer he found a survey map signed by Captain Jean Jacques Vioget. His instincts told him that it was too important, too much at issue, simply to be lying about. He looked Hahn steadily in the eyes as he put it under his arm. Further searching turned up the contracts his father had signed with the Russian-American Fur Company, as well as the accounts adding up to a large debt owed him by Captain John C. Fremont. If that existed, there must be others about.

In the following days Augustus observed that the traders in the fort—Smith and Brannan, men named Ellis, Pettit, Pickett and others—furnished everybody with anything they desired and billed it to Captain Sutter. He had heard his father's generosity was legendary—but had he authorized this profligacy?

Augustus met with Hensley and McKinstry at least once each day. Finally he exploded. "The more I hear, the worse it gets. How could a sane man let his affairs get into such a tangle?"

Hensley said, "You must remember, Augustus, your father is a very kind man. He was poor for so many years that he cannot refuse the entreaties of any fellow with a good story."

"Be that as it may!" said Augustus angrily. "He keeps no account of it. And the men who owe him make no attempt to settle! What is wrong with this country?"

"Men trusted other men, that is all," replied McKinstry. "Nowadays men are changing. The wolves are coming in to prey on the lambs."

"Captain Sutter being one of the lambs," said Augustus bitterly.

"It is bad, but perhaps not so bad as that," said McKinstry. "Patience, and we shall be able to take steps."

John Sutter arrived at the end of the week. By this time Augustus was installed in a bedroom in his father's house. He had been sleeping poorly and was taking a fitful nap when he heard Sutter's voice booming, "My little Augustus! My boy, vhere are you?"

Augustus clattered down the stairs and into his father's embrace. "Oh, Papa!" he said, tears springing to his eyes.

" 'Gustus! My boy, my boy, my boy!" Sutter too was crying, rocking his son in his arms, laughing, pounding him on the shoulders. "You are bigger," said Sutter wonderingly, and Augustus, tears still streaming, began to laugh. It was good to be in his father's arms.

Through all the years there was a part of Johann Sutter who had remained a hero to his son, and today Augustus was not disappointed by this man who stood no more than of medium height, but had an aura that fascinated. Augustus's own eyes seemed to look lovingly back at him. From his father's gaze emanated a strength that gave Augustus the first comfort he had had since he had first arrived in California. Sutter's sideburns were still dark, and came round his powerful jaw to meet under his rounded chin. His nose was long and bony, the kind of nose one might see often in Switzerland, but Augustus had seldom seen since he had been in this country. Sutter's eyebrows were dark and forceful slashes that accentuated the command in his blue eyes. His mustaches were neatly trimmed, and again accentuated another of his features, his fleshy, sensual mouth.

"You have not aged," Augustus declared. "You are still that strong, robust captain of the artillery in the Swiss Guard."

"And you know something?" Sutter laughed. "It is still the greatest delight of my life to hear the cannon roar. Here at Sutter's Fort ve fire the cannon for every occasion, but mainly for my enjoyment. But come, sit, tell me of your mother, of my daughter and my two other sons. And your uncles Heinrich and Friedrich. Haff they let you want for anything?"

"We were adequately provided for, Papa. Mama is well, and sends her love and says she wishes to join you as soon as possible."

"A good voman," said Sutter, fresh tears welling. "Fifteen years—it seems more like a century." Sutter laughed shakily. "My Anna. She sometimes used to hold up the example of myself for myself, when I had fallen short of her hopes."

"She's still using that trick on us all"—Augustus chuckled— "and it works."

Sutter leaned forward eagerly. "Augustus, let me tell you of my splendid plans for the future. These are exciting days now, with new mines of gold being found effery day. Now what I haff in mind is this." Sutter went on speaking, his hands shaping the air in front of him while he told of his grand ideas for becoming even richer. He finally wound down by saying, "And in maybe three years, ve can bring ofer your mama and the other children." He looked at his eldest son, pleased with his own visions and inviting Augustus to be complimentary.

Augustus chose not to be. He was thinking of his father's certainty that the future was always going to be better. He said hesitantly, "About how much would it cost to bring them over now, Papa?"

Sutter looked startled. "Now? Vhy, that is impossible now. Quite impossible."

"Is the sum so great? Or do you have debts?"

"Vell"—his father sputtered—"vell, maybe a little debt. Not a big vun, but—" He suddenly seemed to catch hold of himself. "But ve do not need to vorry ourselves vith such things at present. Come, I show you my fort." He rose, very busy and important.

Augustus sat looking up at him from his chair. "Papa, let us talk now. There is trouble, and we must discuss what to do about it immediately."

Sutter sat back down abruptly. "Trouble? You are in trouble, my 'Gustus? Vot trouble? Tell Papa."

"I am not in trouble. It is Captain Sutter."

Slowly, moving into the subject by degrees, Augustus brought up the matter of the debt on Fort Ross and Bodega, and the threat that one creditor, by attaching Sutter's property, would hold the power to sacrifice the entire estate, to the injury of other creditors and the useless ruin of the Sutter family. He commented on the hopeless state of the record books, at which Sutter protested, "Now, now, I haff that all in my head. Let me see now, McDougall owes me—" Augustus interrupted politely, managing to outline the entire financial problem.

Sutter said uncomfortably, "Vell, it takes a little time to collect from friends—"

"There is no little time. The sheriff could come at any moment with his writ, and no one could save your lands for you then."

"But you think you could?" Sutter's eyes held an angry fire.

"I could try. Papa, George McKinstry is an honest man, is he not?"

Sutter nodded solemnly. "I am proud to call him friend."

"I've been spending my evenings with George and Major Hensley. They have come up with a possible solution for your difficulties."

"Vell, at least I vill listen."

That evening McKinstry and Hensley talked earnestly. After consideration, Sutter agreed to transfer his real estate and personal property to his son. "But," said Sutter, "my son's name on my property is there temporarily, a matter of months only. And Augustus is to pay all my debts off."

"That is my solemn promise to you, Papa," said Augustus. "Furthermore, I will collect all of your debts which I can prove."

Word got around quickly that Augustus Sutter was in charge of John Sutter's finances. Not surprisingly, his debtors kept a safe distance. But his creditors came with their hands out. Augustus dealt with them all, consulting with his father, whose most frequent remark was, "Pay this man vot he says I owe. I trust him. I let him keep track." Augustus asked for signed bills, but soon found out that even the most scrupulous creditors still depended on a man's word. He said one day, "Papa, I do not understand why you did not pay these bills yourself. Some of them are years old."

"I had no money, Augustus. Ve used barter. Ve agreed to pay so many bushels of vheat on such and such a day. If the vheat did not come in, ve did not pay. It is only now that the gold is recognized as a crop that there is anything comparable to money available."

The process was agonizingly slow, but Augustus was also managing to collect some of his father's outstanding debts. Little by little Augustus was setting his father's affairs to rights. This was a considerable feat, for Sutter possessed seventy-six square miles of land which had been granted to him by the Mexican government.

Sutter was in the mountains when Sam Brannan came to see Augustus. The captain owed him $15,000, Sam said. Augustus checked on this, and it was true. He said to Brannan, "I admit the debt, and we will pay you as soon as possible."

"I don't need the money," Sam said.

Augustus was surprised. He replied, "Perhaps then you would be content to wait until all the others have received theirs?"

"No, I wouldn't," Sam said in that same agreeable tone.

"Then what do you want instead?"

"I'll settle for land."

"We have none to barter just now."

"I have a suggestion. Why don't we have a drink and talk about it?"

"Very well."

Sam poured two hefty slugs of brandy from his own flask into Sutter's glasses, and the men sat back to chat.

"Quite some time ago, perhaps a year," Sam began, "I tried to convince Captain Sutter he should build a city."

"He's starting one, at Sutterville."

"But it isn't doing very well yet, is it?"

"It has only just begun," Augustus replied loyally.

Sam chuckled. "As I told John, it's the wrong direction from the *Embarcadero*. Look, young John, I've heard good things about the way you're taking over your father's business and straightening out a five-year mess. I'll be perfectly straightforward with you. Sutter doesn't want a city here, near the fort and the landing, but it could benefit his finances immensely. It's ideal in location. It will grow into an enormous place in no time. Too bad you never saw Sutter's Fort in its heyday, when most of these shops and stores were your dad's. He had hundreds of workmen doing his bidding. This is a natural crossroads. We ought to take advantage of that and build another city on this spot. Hell, man, enough men pass through every day to populate Sutterville and Sacramento too."

Augustus took an appreciative sip of his brandy. Brannan's taste in liquor was superb. "What are you proposing, Mr. Brannan?"

"Subdivide this land right here. I'll hire a surveyor, adding his fee to my bill. When he gets the job done, I'll take two hundred lots of my own choice and call your father's debt paid. I'll also recommend an honest, ambitious man to sell the lots for you."

"Two hundred lots in a developing city? Isn't that a high barter for a debt of only fifteen thousand dollars?"

Sam grinned at him and took another swallow of brandy. *"Only* fifteen thousand dollars? Young John, you are beginning to think like a Californian. Yes, perhaps two hundred lots are too many, but consider this. You don't have to hire the surveyor. You don't have to pay out gold. You don't have to sell any lots yourself. Your father's debt to me is paid in full. And you'll be able to throw off those squatters who've set up in business on the captain's valuable land down by the *embarcadero.*"

Augustus had not known that. "What about his objection to having a city situated here?"

"You'll have to wrestle with that devil alone. But perhaps you secretly agree with me that Captain Sutter's ability to plan sometimes overwhelms his good business sense."

Augustus said, before he thought, "For him, the future is always best."

Sam poured himself some more brandy and waved the flask at Augustus. He said, sighing, "Yes, and he may be right." Absently he sipped. "Well, what do you think? Shall we build a city around the fort and the *Embarcadero?*"

Augustus said, smiling, "You are not trying to hurry me, are you, Mr. Brannan?"

Sam smiled back, full of confidence. "Certainly I'm trying to hurry you. The sooner we start this city, the sooner it will start getting Captain Sutter out of debt."

"I'll think it over for a few days."

Sam rose, tucking his flask into his frock coat pocket and smiling. "Oh, I'll see you at supper. You'll have your mind made up by then. Meantime, I hope you'll be asking around about me and my credentials. I am the largest landholder in the city of San Francisco . . . *my* city, which I built and am continuing to build. In it I own various successful business enterprises. Those three ships tied up at the *Embarcadero,* doing business as warehouses, belong to me. Ask anyone. Everybody knows Sam Brannan."

"Possibly so," said Augustus stiffly. He was not sure he liked this tall man with his wavy brown hair and his vibrant energy. Almost, he had the feeling that Sam was poking fun at him. But possibly, just possibly, the man had a valid idea.

Augustus sought out George McKinstry and told him of his talk with Brannan. "George, what do you think?"

"Do it, Augustus. Sutter's Fort is going to pieces. It's practically deserted now compared to old times. If you can get the land surveyed and give Sam two hundred lots for your father's debt, grab it and run."

Augustus voiced his most perplexing concern. "What will Papa say? He doesn't want a city here."

McKinstry put his hand on the young man's shoulder. "A city has already begun on his land, a scruffy assemblage of tents and brush arbors. Given a choice—which you have at present—it is better to plan this city and be in control of it than to have it grow up around you willy-nilly and receive nothing for it. These squatters could overrun your father's land. They are becoming a powerful and dangerous nuisance."

"Brannan said he would see me at supper."

McKinstry laughed. "Be prepared to answer him, then."

Augustus shook his head, his blue eyes betraying a mixture of disbelief and merriment. "Such a place this California is. A gentleman walks up to me and says my father owes him fifteen thousand dollars, but he does not want money, he wants to build a city. I should give him my reply by dinnertime, and most likely with the rising of the sun we will have a city!" He shook his head again, pondering the insanity of it. "It is no wonder my father has such a muddle in his affairs. California is no place for mere human beings, it is a land of Titans!"

At the Morrison household, Prudence was in a flurry of activity. Her house was turned upside down and inside out as she and her servants cleaned every wall and floor and cranny. She made inventories of china and crystal, and sent out orders for new items with Ezra. It was a mere month until Susannah's September wedding, and Prudence wanted everything to be exactly right. She was honored and thrilled that it had been herself Susannah had entrusted with the plans of this most important event. There was a part of Prudence which sided with Susannah in thinking that this must be the most impressive wedding of the year. Only Prudence's more conservative nature and tastes saved Cameron Gentry from the public spectacle—or circus— he dreaded.

About her most pressing concern, Prudence could talk to no one. Weddings were family ceremonies, Prudence always had felt, and she would so love to have her family around her at this important time. There was only one of her blood—her son Asa Radburn, who was serving as one of Brigham Young's Danites in Salt Lake City. She heard little from Asa, except a message early last year that he had married one of the Saints. Late that night, with Ezra snoring beside her, Prudence gave in to tears. Asa was her only child, born when she was fifteen; they had come through so much together, and she could not attend his wedding. She supposed he had a baby by now, a grandchild she loved without ever having seen or held it.

But even if she could get a message to him now, it would be entirely unsuitable to invite him to Susannah's wedding. Asa had left San Francisco under a cloud, having been accused of trying to rape Susannah, and having fought with Cameron Gentry, who had saved Susannah—if the story was true at all—and having had a violent disagreement with his spiritual leader, Sam Brannan. And all these people would be at the wedding. All the troubles they had had, which were now quieted down, would begin again if Asa were present. No, she could not be responsible for bringing him here. Yet he was her son, greatly beloved, and she yearned to visit with him, to see how he looked, to see what kind of man he had become.

Before he had left Asa had said, "Mama, I'm going to join the Danites."

Prudence had looked at his face, no longer chubby but lean and hard, with the bruises from the fight with Cameron on his jaw and around his eye, and she could hardly speak. Her heart felt as if it had stopped. She whispered, "But . . . they're— they have a bad reputation." Killers, that was what she had heard, the word she couldn't say.

"They're only policemen, Mama. In New York you taught me not to be afraid of policemen."

Looking down, she rubbed a fold of her dress between her thumb and fingers. "But this is different, Asa."

"Don't try to talk me out of it. It's the only thing I want to be. It's the only way I can get back at the people who have hurt me so."

"And I? Have I hurt you too?" Her mouth trembled; she feared his answer.

He reached out and put his arms around her. "No, Mama, you have always loved me, and I you." He kissed her broad shiny forehead. "I have to leave, before they come to arrest me. Goodbye, dear Mama, God bless you."

Then he was out the door, and Prudence's hand was reaching out to the empty air where he had been.

So many times in her mind she had gone over that last meeting and Asa's assurances of the love between them. So many nights she had prayed to God that Asa would never have to take the life of a human being. So often she thought of him and missed him. She wondered if she would ever see her son again. But she never spoke his name anymore, for Ezra hated being reminded of that episode. The book of Asa had been closed forever.

"Honestly, Mama, I think you're working too hard," Susannah said.

Prudence looked up startled from her thoughts of Asa. "Why do you say that? We have plenty of help."

"You're sighing so much. Can't I take over something, and you sit and rest for a while?"

"Perhaps it would be a good idea," Prudence admitted. "I'll just sit here and count napkins—"

"—and then fingers, and toes." Susannah giggled. She whirled around suddenly, her skirt swirling like a lily around her. "Oh, Mama, I am so happy! Cameron is the most wonderful man in the world—we are such good *friends,* and we are so jolly together!"

"He is a fine man," Prudence agreed. "You do have this tendency to run over him sometimes—"

"I know, I know," Susannah said, spreading her fingers before her face in mock shame. "But he's learning to defend himself—when he wants to. Just think, it's only a few days until we'll be married. And Mama, my shop is nearly ready to open too. Oh, I'm so excited I don't know how I'm going to hold it all!"

Ezra came in, laying his hat on the kitchen table, and Susannah greeted him with an enthusiastic hug. "Papa, Papa," she teased, "how can a man of forty-four continue to look so youthful?"

"Your eyes are so full of stars you can't see me well," he said, grinning. "Well, Cameron should be relieved that he won't have to feel like—what was it he said, a gorilla on parade?" Cameron's lament had been turned into a joke now, with a different animal mentioned every time. "I've kept the guest list to a minimum—well, almost—to please him, and asked the most important people in town to please you. And I've been assured that the news will be given full coverage in the paper."

"My gown is nearly finished," Susannah put in. "Mrs. Goodrich is doing such a beautiful job."

Prudence, thinking of her dear stepdaughter as a bride, said, "Is your house going to be ready?"

"Oh, no," said Susannah airily, "but we'll live there anyway. We'll have enough furniture, and the curtains and draperies are up, and we have a couple of servants, so we'll manage. In another week we can probably begin receiving guests. We'll just be on our honeymoon until then." She turned away to hide her blushes, thinking of Cameron, thinking of making love in the empty washhouse, thinking of them sharing meals and a bed as man and wife. Cameron had changed so much since they had met—become more forceful with her, taking his own part more, and yet that core of kindness and tenderness, that inner strength which made him so dear, had not diminished. She was one lucky woman.

Thank God she had not married Sam Brannan. She would always love Sam from her chosen distance, would remember the love they had shared on the *Brooklyn*, but she had been wiser than her years when she had decided not to marry him. His ambitions were too great—and besides, she would have become a plural wife. Ann Eliza would have made life a hell for them both. There was one perfect man for Susannah Morrison, and it was Cameron Gentry.

Their wedding day dawned with fog. For the past two nights Cameron and Susannah had been separated, Susannah staying at her parents' house in a last-minute bow to propriety and practicality, and Cameron sleeping at the hotel. His parents had arrived with Jane Pardee, and were staying there too. The Mc-Kays had not come, as Coleen was so near her time; and Robin, Fiona and Brian were somewhere out in the gold fields. So of dear friends there would be very few. Sam would be there, and Jane, and one or two Saints, close friends of Susannah's parents who, like Ezra and Prudence, were beginning to question the dictates of the church.

The wedding ceremony itself would be in the late afternoon, with a wedding feast to follow, and music and dancing afterwards. Tolerance, who spent most of her days away from Ezra's house, had suggested that two-year-old Elisha be the ring bearer. They had tried him at a rehearsal, but he was totally undisciplined, and Susannah did not want her wedding turned into a circus after all. She thought she was being generous enough in asking Tollie to be her attendant. She was tempted to ask Tollie to wear a dress of gold color, which would completely wash out her pale complexion, but then she was ashamed of such a petty thought, and let her choose a cloud-soft pink tulle trimmed with lace. As it turned out, the girls complemented each other. Both had black hair, Tollie's straight, Susannah's curly; both were well formed and wore their garments with flair.

A quick hard rain two hours before the wedding cleared the air. It was cool and pleasant when the ceremony began. Tollie went into Ezra's parlor first, portrait-pretty in her long full gown. Next Susannah entered, beautiful and queenly on her father's arm. Seated there, on chairs borrowed from the entire neighborhood, were most of the famous and influential men in San Francisco. Sam Brannan and Ann Eliza were in the front, beside Ezra and Prudence. Susannah saw the governor, newly promoted General Richard Mason; Charles Gillespie and William Clark, successful local merchants; newspaper publisher Benjamin Buckelew; John Sutter and his handsome son Augustus; the former Consul Thomas O. Larkin; Lieutenant William "Cump" Sherman; Robert Parker, the hotelman; Reverend Walter Colton, former *alcalde* of Monterey. Some of the men's wives and families had come also. Though not a lavish showing, there were enough men and women of power in Ezra's parlor to satisfy Susannah's social desires while still abiding by Cameron's.

When Susannah first saw Cameron waiting for her, she drew in a quick breath. She was struck as always by his magnificent height and breadth. He was an exceptionally handsome man even without his clothing, as she well knew; today he wore a stark black frock coat and trousers with a white frilled shirt, an outfit which accentuated his lovely coloring, his thick black hair, brown eyes and handsome mouth. There was an eager glow about him she had been seeing a lot lately. It occurred to her how much he loved her and how much this day meant to him. She had been so busy preparing for the ceremony that she had had little time to reflect on its deeper meaning. But there was Cameron, the man she would love throughout eternity— and her heart swelled and tears of joy sprang out of her eyes. The smile she tried to give him trembled at the corners.

Cameron felt his own eyes mist over as he looked at Susannah. Her blue eyes were bright with happiness; her complexion bloomed. Even her dimples seemed deeper today. She was wearing a gown of thin white silk sarcenet, made with a dropped shoulder and a modestly low V neckline that revealed the swell of her full breasts. The sleeves were elaborately puffed above her elbows. The dress was severely nipped in at her slender waistline, coming to a point in front and back. The skirt was three graduated tiers pleated at the waist, and several yards around at the floor. The beautifully cut dress was without lace or other ornamentation save for a large white silk rose and its leaves, pinned at the center of Susannah's bodice. Over her hair she wore a short transparent veil of silk illusion. The sheer lace wrap she draped like a shawl across her arms was the newest fashion, called a Cornelia. The unornamented simplicity of her gown and accessories was the ultimate in sophisticated taste.

The *alcalde* of San Francisco officiated at the ceremony. Susannah looked into Cameron's eyes and gave him her hand. The hardness of his hand was very reassuring. Strange how her knees seemed to want to tremble. She had thought of her gown, her guests, even of her bridegroom—but she had not thought about being so scared on her wedding day!

Automatically, scarcely hearing the words or knowing her own replies, she went through the ceremony. "Do you take this woman, Susannah Naomi Morrison . . . this man Cameron Bruce Gentry . . . love him . . . honor him . . . so long as you both shall live . . ." It was like being in a dream, for later she remembered nothing, only the warmth of Cameron's hand and body beside her, only the love in his shining eyes. Then the ceremony was over, and Cameron had wrapped his arms around her and was placing his lips on hers, and she came to life. Joyous, once more in control of herself, she returned his kiss with an unvirginal fervor that made him suddenly aware of their guests, even though she was oblivious to them.

In the receiving line she was greeted by James King, who called himself James King of William, for William was his father's name. He was an odd little man, with round, dark-brown eyes and a mustache and short beard, whose leathery complexion made him look older than he was. He was some sort of businessman, she knew. He said, "That's a handsome dress. Gives you authority."

Flustered, for she had never thought in those terms at all, she said, "Why, thank you."

He leaned over to speak confidentially in her ear, jerking his thumb briefly toward Tollie. "Makes that other girl look like a box of candies."

She glanced at Tollie. The man was right; but she said loyally, "I thought she looked very pretty."

"Can't hold a candle to you," he said bluntly. He turned to Cameron. "Now Gentry, you've got a clever girl here, hope you'll have the good sense to hang onto her. I'd like to see you in the next week or two. I've just learned about a deal you might want to get in on. Has to do with building a warehouse down by the Bay."

Cameron smiled. There was something compelling about James King of William, a refreshing honesty. "Thanks, Jim, I'll be talking with you."

Next in line came A. J. Ellis, who had a boardinghouse and grog shop on Montgomery Street. He kissed Susannah, who scarcely knew him, and complimented her, and said jovially to Cameron, "I stayed away from the gold fields for an extra week just to come to your wedding, Cameron."

"We appreciate that," Cameron assured him. "When are you leaving?"

"Right after we eat."

"Good luck, Ellis."

When Sam came up to Susannah she was hardly prepared for it. He reached for her in the old way, and pulled her up to him leisurely, and kissed her hard. He whispered, "Tell me I haven't really lost you, Susannah." But he smiled at her teasingly, and she smiled too but did not reply. Next to her Ann Eliza had stood on tiptoe to place a kiss on Cameron's cheek, just to get even with her husband.

Jane Pardee, her bulk and natural dignity accentuated by a deep purple silk paduasoy afternoon suit, and a broad-brimmed flat-crowned hat, hugged Susannah and Cameron with bone-crushing affection. "So you did it at last." She beamed. "Can't think of two I'd rather see tie the knot. Now you stay happy, and God bless you both."

There were others: Lieutenant Edward Gillespie in full military dress; William A. Liedesdorff, agent for the Russian American Fur Company; Joshuah Abraham Norton, a wealthy entrepreneur. Then came the wedding feast, cooked by Prudence and a team of Mexican women, every dish a treat for eyes and palate. Susannah and Cameron, sitting side by side with their thighs touching, tasted each dish but ate sparingly. Frequently their eyes would meet, with that promise in them; and Susannah blushed a great deal.

When all was cleared away and the dancing began, Ezra led his daughter out onto the parlor floor to open the festivities. Soon Cameron claimed her; and for the next hour neither Susannah nor Cameron was ever without a partner, as they danced with all of the guests. Then suddenly Susannah found herself in Sam's arms, being held decorously close, while he chatted inconsequentially. Then as Cameron approached, Sam said to her, "You have married well, my little one. I am glad for your sake."

"That's very generous of you, Sam," she said, and smiled back at him as she waltzed into her husband's embrace. She looked up at Cameron. "Are you ready to go?"

"God, yes. If one more fat matron puts her foot under my boot, I think I'll pretend to faint just to get out of the room."

Susannah giggled. "Lead me away, then."

They danced toward the door, where Cameron had a driver waiting with his horse and carriage, and made their escape. There were objects tied to the carriage—tin cans and old boots and ribbons of various kinds—and several of the wedding guests pursued them, but at the hotel they managed to get into their room and lock the door.

"Whew," said Cameron, with his back to the door, and his eyes large on Susannah. "What a relief." He stood there looking at her, with a little smile on his face. He said softly, "It was a nice wedding, darling."

"Yes, it was, wasn't it? Thanks to Mama and Papa." And Sam, she added silently. It had been his famous friends who had filled the Morrison parlor to wish them well. But in time those people would be her friends and Cameron's too. She looked at Cameron, suddenly amused. "You forgot to carry me over the threshold."

"Tomorrow," he said, coming to her and enfolding her in his embrace. His mouth met hers softly; his tongue traced the outline of her upper lip. He whispered, "Tomorrow."

Eight

Robin and Fiona Gentry had set off for the gold
fields with a titillating sense of adventure. Their emotions were
heightened by their total absorption in each other, and the deli-
ciously roguish feeling they both got from the knowledge that
theirs was not a conventional marriage. They were far more
than mere husband and wife, they were friends, partners in business, partners in fun, partners in life—and they were going to be
rich in every way a man and a woman could be rich.

The last word they had received from Brian Campbell had
come from Spanish Bar. Brian, always terse in his letters, had
been almost non-communicative in this one. Robin and Fiona
didn't know if Brian had staked a claim for them at Spanish
Bar, or if he had merely stopped there on his way to some other
location.

Fiona, her green eyes filled with questions, asked, "If he isn't
there . . . what will we do? How will we find him?"

With a chuckle, Robin shrugged. After a time he said, "Don't
worry about it, darlin', the gold fields have limits like anything
else. Brian will be somewhere within about five hundred miles
along the Sierra Nevada. We won't go any farther north than
the farthest point on the Feather River, or any farther south

than the River Rey. If we don't find him somewhere in there, we'll assume he got tired of waiting for us and went home."

Fiona burst out laughing. "I don't think you care if we find him or not. You'd think it was just a dandy trick if we left him, wouldn't you?" When Robin didn't answer, she grew serious, wondering if what she had said flippantly could be true. "We are going to find him, aren't we?"

Again Robin gave forth a deep chuckle of amusement. "Of course we'll find him. He'll have left a trail for us to follow—wait and see."

"But how do we know where to start?" Fiona cried. "You said five hundred miles, Robin—that's impossible!"

He put his hand over hers where it rested on the wagon seat between them. "We'll go to Coloma. Spanish Bar isn't far from there, and most likely that is where he goes to get supplies. Someone will have heard of him, or he will have left another message with someone."

Fiona shook her head. "I don't know how you ever accomplish anything. You make this all sound so easy, but—you're looking for a message you don't know exists, left with someone you don't know!"

He raised her hand to his lips to kiss her fingers. "Hardly anything is easy, but hardly anything is impossible either. I told you not to worry about it. Brian and I know what we're doing."

"Ha!" Fiona said smartly. But she gave up the conversation and concentrated on the terrain.

Once they had left Sutter's Fort the scenery became wilder. Its untamed beauty sparked Fiona's imagination, and teased her artist's eye. Futilely she attempted to sketch as Robin drove the wagon. After several disastrous bumps which caused her charcoal to streak across her drawing, she gave up, and thereafter confined her artistic impulses to those times when they stopped to eat, to water the horses, or to camp for the night.

Fiona learned to adjust to other hardships as well. The farther they traveled, the rougher the hills became. Instead of going over the fairly easy grades of the foothills, the wagon jolted and bucked over rocks and boulders that shook Fiona's teeth and rattled her bones. Soon she was walking beside the wagon most of every day as Robin coaxed, prodded, and shouted the mules up the steep inclines. It was an awe-inspiring, sometimes frightening terrain with deep gorges yawning, and huge conical rocks jutting high into the air. There was nothing that could properly be called a road.

Robin followed the scars left on the rocks by other wagons that had passed before them. Fiona knew he was moving as slowly and gently as he could, trying to give her a chance to adjust to the rigorous demands of this kind of travel. And she was thankful to be given the extra hours—perhaps days—to learn to properly conserve her energy and to toughen up, but she also worried about just how much she was delaying their progress. There was little she could do about it, however, for most days it took all her concentration and strength to get through the day before she gratefully fell into exhausted slumber after Robin had fixed dinner.

Sometimes at night, after they had eaten and Fiona had managed the day's strenuous travel without exhaustion, she and Robin would lie close together, wrapped in blankets, and listen to the cold night wind whistle down from the Sierra Nevadas, causing the towering pines to bend and sough in song. They looked at the night sky, identifying constellations and always hoping to see a shooting star or perhaps a comet.

When they reached Coloma on the South Fork of the American River they found a strange combination of activity and idleness. Miners could be seen everywhere, hurrying into town or out, calling to each other, rapidly passing news of gold strikes and places that had proved barren. Saloons and makeshift buildings they called hotels did a booming business, but Sutter's mill was ominously quiet. Robin felt a strange pinch of regret as he thought of Captain Sutter. He had always liked John and admired the spirit and generosity of the man. It was not a good thing for anyone, what was happening to Sutter and his dreams for his seventy-five-square-mile empire. Sutter's loss would eventually be everyone's loss, for he was a good man.

Shaking free of these unhappy thoughts, Robin pulled the wagon to a hitching post, alighted, and helped Fiona down. Covered with the red dust of the hills, they entered the hotel looking like all the other dust-laden people who bustled through the town. Robin walked over to the bar at the far end of the room, holding fast to Fiona's hand. The barkeeper glanced at him and lifted a glass in question.

Robin shook his head, then said, "I'm looking for Brian Campbell. You heard of him?"

The man's face was blank as he mentally sorted through names he had heard of late, then suddenly he smiled. "Tall, lanky man?" Before Robin could reply, he asked, "Your name wouldn't be Gender, would it?"

"Gentry."

"Close enough. I got a letter for you. That Campbell fellow left it here—said you'd be through here sooner or later." The man pulled a box out from under the bar, and began to thumb through a disheveled pile of letters and scraps of paper. Finally he came up with a crumpled, dirty folded sheet of paper with Robin's name on it.

Robin read: "Left Spanish Bar. Headed for Middle Fork. B." With a smile Robin handed the paper to Fiona, then asked the barman, "You heard of any good strikes on the Middle Fork?"

The man grinned. "I hear about 'em every day. I hear there's plenty of good digs there. Nobody comes back unhappy from Middle Fork."

"Is there any special place, though?" Robin persisted.

He shook his head. "No-o—maybe Big Bar. It's about eighteen miles up from Spanish Bar. Lots of folks have been talking about taking gold outta there."

Robin nodded. It wasn't much to go on, but at least there'd be miners camped there, and if Brian were anywhere in the vicinity, or if he had left another message, they would know about it.

Before they left Coloma, Robin made an all-important stop to outfit Fiona with her mining clothes. He had left that until now, because he knew Sean would be outraged to think his "little girl" would be in men's britches and boots. But if Fiona was going to work in this rough country, heavy clothes were necessary. Already her calico skirt looked ragged. Soon she would be in tatters, resembling the half-naked Indian squaws they had seen from time to time.

Robin also added to their supply of food, for one piece of information they had been given over and over was that food was very scarce in the camps, and many miners had begun to suffer from a peculiar malady that gave great pain to the legs. It was being called land scurvy, and was thought to come from a lack of vegetables. Ignoring the exorbitant prices, Robin purchased all the fresh or jarred vegetables he was able to lay hands on. Then with a thought for the cold nights when the winds roared down the mountains, he purchased two quarts of New England rum, the only liquor he could get. Its only virtue was that it was better than nothing.

It was mid-afternoon before they set out for Middle Fork. The country between Sutter's mill at Coloma and Middle Fork was a study in contrasts. There were huge hills of red gravelly soil that were dotted with groves of oak trees. Then suddenly at the crest of a hill they would be gazing down into rich, green, well-watered valleys with loam so black it seemed to glow like polished ebony. Merry little streams dashed and curled among the rocks, tumbling downward into the verdant growth of the valley proper. They camped for the night in the second valley they came to.

Fiona awakened before Robin the next morning. The valley looked gray-green in the hazy light of dawn, and Fiona watched it come into glowing color as the sun rose over the eastern range of hills. Sated with its beauty, she went to the stream and, shivering, washed herself in the clean water. Then she dressed in her new clothing.

When Robin opened his eyes to the morning, he was greeted by the sight of Fiona sporting an outfit that was the acme of the latest style in gold camp apparel: black felt slouch hat, red flannel shirt sizes too large for her, and tough denim pants over high leather boots. The expression on Robin's face declared he had just awakened to a nightmare, which sent Fiona into peals of laughter. She posed, sticking her hip out at him, her hands behind her hat so that her bosom stuck out. Then she twirled, striking another provocative pose made ridiculous by the voluminous shirt. Robin propped himself up on his elbows watching her, then he groaned and flopped back onto his bedroll. "I'm taking you home to skirts and perfume and—ooofff!" he half bellowed, half gasped as Fiona leapt onto his chest.

"Don't you love me no matter what I look like, Mr. Gentry? What happened to 'worse'?"

"It's a matter of degree," he panted, then reared up and toppled her to the ground. Her thick auburn hair escaped from the hat and tumbled in riotous rich tresses covering his arm. He lay atop her, losing himself in the depths of her green-witch eyes. "My God, but I do love you. Ugly as a toothless old squaw, and still I love you."

Fiona's eyes flashed a deeper green, and she grabbed the hat and beat him mercilessly. As he tried to protect himself she scrambled out from under him, getting quickly to her feet. "It's no breakfast for you if you think I'll prepare it for you."

He was laughing so hard it was difficult to parry her sharp tongue. "And it's none for you if you think I'll share what I cook!"

Faced with a standoff, Fiona smiled angelically. "I'll make coffee and biscuits if you'll do something to soften that awful beef jerky." She made a terrible face, suitable to complement her terrible outfit, and then set to work. She had learned quickly that Robin was a master at making the most repellent of foods palatable. Beef jerky was made of long strings of bullock flesh that had been hung to dry and harden until it tasted like tree bark. She hated it unless Robin softened it, seasoned it, and made it taste better.

Three days later they found Brian, several miles upriver from Big Bar.

"I thought you'd never get here!" he cried, throwing one arm around Fiona, and pumping Robin's hand with his. Laughing, he added, "I didn't know if you'd eloped and kept on going, or if Sean had caught you and shot holes in the seat of Robin's pants."

After telling him that they had managed to get married properly at home with Sean's blessing, neither Fiona nor Robin got another word in. Usually reticent Brian Campbell told them the diggings were good and asked how everyone at home was faring. "How is Coleen?" he finally asked, and gave them a chance to answer.

"Coleen is grouchy, as big as a house, and impatient for the baby to come," Fiona said quickly and all on one breath, fearing

Brian would start talking and asking questions again before she could finish.

"And she misses you," Robin added.

"She misses me?"

Robin's mouth twitched with the temptation to say something to Brian he daren't in front of Fiona. He rolled his eyes skyward, then said mildly as he separated Brian from an enthusiastic embrace of Fiona, "Almost as much as you miss her."

Brian blushed to the roots of his sandy hair.

"Pay no attention to him, Brian. We McKays are an affectionate clan," Fiona said, and threw herself back into the arms of her brother-in-law. She gave him a quick kiss on the cheek. "That's from Coleen."

Robin didn't ask, and Brian said little of his success or lack of it in finding gold until they had made camp that night and were away from the other miners. Then Brian said, "This Middle Fork is a gold mine from source to mouth. Nobody leaves here poor! And I've heard the North Fork is a close second to this. We ought to go there next."

Robin's eyes sparkled with interest, then he tempered his enthusiasm, saying, "This is the roughest terrain we've seen so far. It isn't a good place to break Fiona in."

The Middle Fork of the American River was a swiftly flowing river of about thirty feet in width, having a current that ran five to six miles per hour. Its banks and bed were rugged, made up of huge granite boulders tumbled into the stream. Some of the mountains that pressed against its sides soared two miles into the sky. It was an eerie and mysterious stream that raced through the protected heart of the gold country.

Brian said, "I admit it's hard, but it's worth the hardship. We can work this area for a month or so, then move on to better ground and make a permanent camp for the rainy season. We have time! Listen, Robin, I'm sure we can take fifteen or twenty thousand dollars' worth out of here with the three of us working —maybe more. This bar alone will yield thousands."

Fiona had been listening intently. She shook her head as if to clear it. "What is all this talk of bars? I keep hearing men say that, but I don't know what a bar is."

Brian rubbed his hands together. "Well, my dear, let the old master unfold for you the mysteries of hunting for gold." Patiently, and with many interruptions from Fiona and an occasional comment from Robin, Brian said, "The richest deposits on the rivers are called bars, because at these spots there is an extension of the bank into the river. The stream has to go around this projection of land, and when it does, it leaves the gold caught in the bank and the rocks. Some folks say the bars were formed when the river changed course for some reason, probably a big thaw or a natural dam. And others say the bars form from annual run-offs, depositing soil and minerals there. Whatever the cause, it's good for us. All we have to do is wash the soil and take the gold."

"I'm ready!" Fiona said happily. "I'll be all right here, Robin. Just tell me when to begin, and where I dig."

Brian exchanged glances with Robin. "Eager, isn't she?"

For the next two weeks the three of them panned and used the rocker at the bar, and rapidly they began to fill chamois bags with cleaned gold dust and nuggets. News of the rich diggings along that stretch of the river spread, and by the end of two weeks the area was so thick with miners that it was difficult to take a full swing with a pick without worrying about hitting your neighbor.

One hot, sunny afternoon, Fiona left the digging, wanting to get away from the constant clang of pick and shovel against rock, and the continuous hum of human voice. She climbed up the rocky bank, moving carefully and noting her route so she wouldn't become lost. Her head was swimming with all the information Robin, Brian and others tried to teach her about finding likely spots for gold. She scrambled up a steep incline, then came to a fairly level spot that suddenly dropped off into a deep and narrow ravine. Staring down into that yawning narrow mouth in the earth, she felt strangely drawn, then shaking free from the mildly morbid fascination, she started back. Then, on an impulse, or a hunch, she stopped, and casually swung her pick at a cluster of rocks.

The rocks split open like an over-ripe squash, and then, with a funny little scurrying sound, gold rolled out with the fragments. She had struck a pocket of nuggets the size of pumpkin seeds. Fiona didn't move for a moment, her eyes fixed and huge on the nuggets. She wanted to shout with joy! Jump! Cry! Laugh! But she had learned well how fast hundreds of men could be drawn to a new strike. So as calmly as she could, she made her way back to Robin and Brian. Clutched in her hand she had three of the nuggets. She tugged on Robin's sleeve and silently bade him look in her hand.

Instantly Robin began to rub his back and complain about not finding anything today. "Let's pack it in today and get an early start in the morning."

Brian looked up with alarm, then Fiona opened her hand in front of his nose, and he agreed.

As fast as they could gather their equipment, they followed after Fiona. When they reached the ravine and were out of earshot, Fiona began to laugh. With her voice trembling, she pointed to her find. "Th-there!" she cried. "Look! Isn't it beautiful?"

The men fell to their knees and Fiona did too, all three scraping in the earth with their fingers, pocketknives and spoons, taking out the small yellow pellets and tossing them in a bucket nearby, laughing like loons. "We'll all be rich as Croesus!" said Robin. They had agreed to share all finds three ways so long as Brian was working with them.

"It's the luck of the Irish!" said Brian. "*And* the Scots!" In an excess of exuberance he threw several nuggets into the air, catching most of them but having to scrabble in the dust for the rest. In half an hour they had cleaned out the pocket and had at least twenty pounds of nuggets to show for it. They sat back on the dry ground, looking at each other, sifting the nuggets through their fingers, and laughing.

"Do you realize that there's four or five thousand dollars right here?" Brian marveled. "We're rich!"

"Not bad for a woman," said Robin generously, and cowered from Fiona's pretended anger. Then he said, "Tell us, where do we search next?"

"You're sitting on it," said Fiona, so seriously that Robin leapt up and he and Brian began digging with their picks. This time they found only a handful of nuggets, but they were all grinning and highly pleased with themselves. They tried digging again where Fiona lightheartedly told them, but came up dry this time. They decided to work this area thoroughly. There were no more pockets of large nuggets, but plenty of little ones, enough that they labored all the daylight hours.

They used two or three methods of mining for the flakes and nuggets that slowly mounted up at an average of several ounces per person per day. Where the gold flakes occurred in a stream, they used the simple but tediously back-breaking method of panning. Standing in the stream from dawn to dark, they would put mud or sand into the pan along with some water, then skillfully swirl the water around so that the waste materials flowed over the sides and the heavier gold and sand settled to the bottom. When that had been sufficiently cleaned, they picked out the gold flakes by hand. More often they poured out the gold and sand onto a cloth to dry, and later blew off the sand, leaving the heavier gold flakes. It was a long, strenuous day's work for one of them to wash fifty pans of earth.

The cradle or rocker they had had built in San Francisco was useful in a "dry diggings" where a source of water was available somewhere nearby. At the top of the rocker was a sieve, and at the bottom a series of cleats. Dirt was poured into the top, followed by a bucketful of water. The cradle was rocked to agitate the mixture and send it flowing through the box. The big rocks were sieved out, most of the mud ran out the lower end, and the heavy gold flakes were caught on the cleats at the bottom.

Robin and Fiona preferred the rocker, because with it they could wash nearly a cubic yard of earth in a day. And their results were good because of a trick Robin had thought of. Out of curiosity he had once visited the mercury mines and refinery a short distance south of San Jose. There he was told that mercury amalgamates with other metals. Remembering that, Robin dipped the copper cleats of the cradle in the heavy liquid metal. The tiny gold flakes that would otherwise have washed out clung to the mercury. After a while he scraped the mercury and gold off the cleats. Then, using great precaution against the deadly vapors, he heated the compound. The mercury distilled, leaving the gold. For little more effort and some risk, they got a greater yield.

This hot day in early fall, Fiona sat still, dreamy and exhausted. She watched Robin climb the hill with two buckets full of water. It would be her turn next. She insisted on doing as much physical work as Robin, though he protested and tried to stop her. Usually while one went for water, the other one was digging with a pick, or rocking the cradle with the slurry of mud, water and gold in it. One kind of work was as hard as another.

She started to rise as he neared, but he put the buckets down and came to sit by her. "Let's just be idle for a while," he suggested. "I'm dead on my feet today."

Fiona put her hand companionably in his. "So am I. It couldn't be because we wore ourselves out in the night, could it?"

He grinned, and rubbed her thigh with the flat of one hand. "Couldn't be," he declared. "Ah, Fiona, what mischief you do in me."

"It's the other way round, Robin," she said, and they laughed. She took off her hat and laid her head on Robin's hard-muscled arm. "What a man," she sighed reminiscently. "But we'll get some rest—I'll be letting you alone for a few days."

"No baby this month?" he said sympathetically.

She shook her head, and tears gathered on her lower eyelashes. "I can't understand it. We've given ourselves every opportunity."

He chuckled in spite of himself, and quickly hugged her. "Don't fret, Fiona. Everything in its own time. We have years ahead of us."

"But I thought I'd have a baby right away."

"Lovely Fiona, if you had, your father would have shot me. Now what good would a baby do you then? Quit being anxious, and the first thing you know we'll be Daddy and Mama."

"I hope so." Taking a deep breath, Fiona stood up and stretched. A little breeze sprang up and blew her hair out behind her, and fluttered her shirt tails. In the time since they had come to the gold fields she had become tanned, her body as muscular as an athlete's, with a strength that even Robin found surprising. In spite of the calluses on her hands, she was more womanly and attractive than ever. Smiling, she reached out a hand to encourage Robin to get up; but he pulled her back down, so that she fell on top of him and was held laughing in his strong arms. "Robin Gentry, you are the baddest," she said, giggling. "Can't you think of anything else?"

"Not very well, with you wiggling right there where you are."

"But we can't now."

"Then let's just lie here and talk." He moved her so that she was lying in the dirt beside him. They looked into each other's eyes smiling, and kissing longingly. "What do you suppose Brian is doing now?" he asked.

"He must be getting very hungry and wondering why he doesn't hear the sounds of us working," she said with a laugh. "While we idle away the day, he's making us rich."

"We've had phenomenal luck, but our luck is bound to change," Robin mused.

"I don't know why," she said seriously. "*I* think we're going to be hideously, embarrassingly, mortifyingly wealthy."

He chuckled. "You don't use very attractive words to describe it. Would you rather not strike the mother lode?"

"Of course I would rather! I *want* us to be *loaded,* Robin! After all, if we're going to have a dozen children—"

"*What!*" he shrieked.

She had the good sense to blush. "Just a figure of speech," she said hastily. "Anyway, if we have several children, we'll need the money."

He was still shaken. "Money, hell. I could use a drink after hearing what you've got in mind."

"There's the bucket," she said cheerfully, giggling.

His fingers on her ribs suddenly dug in to tickle her, and she yelped with surprise and tried to roll away. At the same time she tried to tickle him, and soon they were rolling and scrambling in the dry dusty wash, laughing and poking at each other. Suddenly she cried out, "I give, Robin!" and he captured her and planted a kiss on her dusty mouth. They lay panting, eyeing each other, not sure the game was really over. Finally she said, "Look at us. Covered from head to foot with sand and burrs. Won't we ever grow up?"

"No," he said. "I was grown up once, but I forwent it for you."

"Thanks," she whispered, and rubbed her finger in the dust on his cheek.

Suddenly Robin stood up, and held out his hand. "Time to get back to work," he said. "Why don't you quit for the day, get your bath and start an early supper? Let me finish these last two cradles."

She smiled at him. "I'll do that. And I'll fix us something special." Humming, she swung off down the hill. Robin, working the cradle on the slope, watched her as she stood by the river, stripped off all her clothes, and dived in. He shook his head in wonder. Just when he thought the world had a finite number of dimensions, Fiona showed him a few more.

After she had built the fire and started their supper, Fiona sat down, letting the strain of her day's labors slough away. In the distance she could hear the steady, never-ending sound of pick and shovel against mountain, and the echoes of those same sounds as the rocks bounced them around like a diminishing ball.

Soon, she knew, the sounds would end for the day, and in their place she would hear the cheerful "halloes" that one man shouted across the rocky expanses to another as each returned to his camp for the night. They would pass her camp, a pile of brush carried atop their heads to make tonight's campfire. Even here there were little rituals observed, little habits all the men followed and seemed to take comfort from. Liking that observation, she pulled out her notebook and wrote the thought beside the sketch she had made days ago of the men returning to camp with the fire brush on their heads. Finished, she allowed the notebook to slide from her lap, and she sat there in the dry dirt with her chin resting on her folded arms.

Her eyes roamed the wide fertile valley. They had chosen their campsite well, even though it did mean quite a walk and a climb to get to their digging site each morning. But as Robin had pointed out, this was a suitable place for a winter shelter, and that was something they needed to give special thought and time to. It meant their survival. At the moment, however, it was difficult to think of winter, for everything was green and beautiful.

Supper was cooked and steaming by the time Robin and Brian had washed in the stream and returned to the camp. Robin put a couple more pieces of wood on the fire, for already the cold night winds were beginning to sweep down the mountainside.

Tired, but content with the underlying satisfaction that this had been another good day and their store of gold had grown, the three gold miners ate heartily and in near silence. Toward the end of their meal they could hear soft voices coming from distant camps. Occasionally the wind carried the faint strum of a guitar. With cups of coffee Fiona, Robin and Brian sat near to their own campfire enjoying the pleasant human sounds, and the eerier sounds of the mountain creatures that they could hear but rarely see.

It was nearly dark, and they were thinking of going to bed, when suddenly there were unfamiliar noises. There were creaks and jingles and the sound of plodding hooves. Robin, the hair on the back of his neck rising at the possibility of its being Aaron Wheelwright, grabbed for his rifle. Fiona, seeing his action, quickly got the Colt revolver which she had learned to fire accurately at game. Robin thrust her behind him into the shadows. They waited while the caravan slowly came nearer. Suddenly in the rustling night there came a hearty baritone voice:

"Whiskey gave me a broken nose, Whiskey Johnny;
Whiskey made me pawn my clothes, Whiskey Johnny—

Whiskey drove me 'round Cape Horn, Whiskey Johnny;
'Twas many a month when I was gone, Whiskey Johnny!"

Robin, though he grinned sympathetically, did not relax his hold on his weapon until their visitors were fully revealed in the light from the campfire. Their leader was a big broad-shouldered handsome man of about thirty. His curling hair was a darker red than Fiona's; his smile was as broad and genuine as a man's could be. He dismounted, saying pleasantly, "Good evening! My name is Zane Tyler. We saw your fire two or three miles off. My party and I are passing through on our way upriver."

Robin stood up, extending his hand. Fiona, watching from her hiding place, saw that Zane Tyler was even larger in all directions than her tall muscular husband, who said, "I'm Robin Gentry." In seconds the two men had assessed each other and felt it was safe to be friendly. "Would you drink a cup of coffee? There's half a potful left from supper."

"Thanks, we would. I'd like you to meet Josie."

A tall, long-legged figure which proved to be a woman swung down from a horse and clasped Robin's hand with a manlike grip. "Howdy, Robin. That coffee smells right good. I'da been sorry if you hadn't offered us any."

Fiona, seeing another woman for the first time in two months, could not remain hidden any longer. She came out of the tent to stand by Robin. His eyes widened with momentary apprehension but he introduced her, and the two women smiled at each other. Traveling with the Tylers were three others, with the faces and manners of decent men. One thing learned quickly was not to judge a miner solely by appearance. Under long hair, beards, and dust-laden jeans were doctors, lawyers, clergymen, men of all walks of life in other times.

"If you'll bring your own cups I'll pour the coffee," said Fiona.

They sat talking around the campfire, their weariness forgotten in the cheerful occasion of having company. Robin, so recently a bridegroom, asked, "Have you two been married long?"

Josie laughed. "Matter o' fact, no. Zane an' me just met a couple o' weeks ago in Sacramento. He asked me along, so here I am." She smiled at Zane in evident contentment. "You folks tied the knot?"

Quickly, so as not to embarrass Josie, Fiona said, "Well, we think about it all the time."

Robin, going along with the joke, said, "Before all the kids grow up and start asking questions, I reckon we might."

One young man said, "My wife's back in Monterey. If I knew there'd be women in the gold fields, I'd have brought her along. I sure do miss her."

"I know that feeling," Brian said, with heartfelt sincerity.

"Been having any luck?" asked Tyler.

"Not bad," said Robin, and shrugged. "Where-all have you been?"

"I've been up the American and back, and now I'm going to work the Feather. I heard tell there might be something on the Trinity too, so we're headed in that general direction."

"The Trinity's way up north," Brian said.

Tyler replied, smiling, "I don't mind leading the pack, if I get a good enough headstart."

"How was it on the American when you were there?"

"Crowded. Hardly room to swing a pick. Men standing in the stream all day and half the night. I was talking to John Sinclair. His rancho's three miles above Sutter's. He was employing about fifty Indians on the North Fork close to the main river. In one five-week period he hauled in about sixteen thousand dollars. He was bragging that in one week he got fourteen *pounds* of clean-washed gold."

"Fourteen pounds!" exclaimed Robin and Fiona together.

"But of course that's with fifty men working."

"Still a fine haul," said Tyler. "Wouldn't mind running across a lode that rich."

One of the young men stood up, saying, "I better see about them horses before it gets pitch dark."

"Off that way is good grazing," said Robin, pointing.

The three young men took off the horses' packs and led them toward water and pasture. Tyler looked long at Robin. "Why don't you come along with our party? There's plenty of gold for us all."

"Thanks, but I guess not," Robin replied, forgetting Fiona's story. "We're still on our honeymoon."

Josie laughed, thinking he was joking. "That's a great line, Zane. Why don't you say that next time? 'This is Josie, we're on our honeymoon.'"

Zane grinned at her, chucking her under the chin affectionately. "Maybe I will. It'd sure help me out. Keep men's hands off my woman, and give me a few days' headstart digging in a fresh spot." Then he gave Robin and Brian a sympathetic look and added, "I guess that's what you folks were lookin' for here.

Sorry I spoiled it for you. Once one man beats a path to your door, others won't be far behind."

Brian shrugged. "Someone was bound to come—there's lots of men near here. If it hadn't been you tonight, it would have been one of them." Then Brian rubbed his hands together and his face took on an impish look. "Robin, where'd you stash those two bottles you brought up here with you? Seems like this might be the right night for a bit of fun and merrymaking."

Robin didn't comment, but dived into a carpetbag of supplies he had brought, and came up triumphantly with a bottle of New England rum in each hand.

Zane Tyler's bearded grin was just as broad, and he too was fishing in a satchel of supplies. "Just happens that I have some real corn whiskey left from my last visit to civilization."

The seven new friends dumped their coffee out on the ground and put their cups forward. Even Fiona, after a moment's hesitation, dumped her coffee and asked for the liquor she had never had before.

It wasn't often the miners took a night off from their customary sobriety to celebrate in camp. That entertainment was saved for their trips into towns, but on those rare occasions when they did drink, the result was usually hilarity. Zane's three companions were introduced as Bill, Ted, and Max, who had left his young wife back in Monterey. Max pulled a harmonica from his pocket and, settling comfortably against a rock, began to play beautiful, haunting music.

By the time the bottles had made their third round, Robin and Fiona were dancing, as were Josie and Zane. Soon Josie was clapping and stomping her feet, trying to get Max to play something cheerier, and—more important—faster. "C'mon, Maxie! Give us somethin' with a little life—somethin' I kin move my bones to!" she cried, and gave a quick, impressive demonstration of the wild, frenetic mountain jig she had in mind. "How about 'The Pesky Sarpent' or 'Darlin' Corey'?"

Max gave her a glum look. "Those are hell to play on a mouth organ. Can't dance to 'em either." Then he brightened. "Give me that bottle. I'll see what I can do." He drank, and sat moodily for a while. Then he began a moderately fast rendition of "The Oxen Song," while Bill and Ted sang the one dozen verses. They began with:

> *"Come all you bold ox teamsters, wherever you may be,*
> *I hope you'll pay attention and listen here to me."*

As soon as the lively beat steadied and Max began to enjoy what he was doing, Josie, a tall, rangy, freckle-faced mountain girl from Tennessee, began dancing, then reached for Zane's hands. The big man groaned. "Josie, I can't jump around like that, girl. I'll shake the mountain."

Josie's grin was impish. "That's it, lover man, you jus' shake this big ol' mountain, and make it spill all its treasures right into our pockets!"

Zane began to follow Josie's quick steps with heavy-booted grace that made light of his size.

Faster with every verse, Max played and Bill and Ted went on singing of Johnny Carpenter, who was hauling spruce logs and always trying to keep ahead of his fellow workers. Soon Fiona was on her feet. She took Brian by one hand and Robin with the other, and pulled them into motion with her. With eyes fastened on Josie's flying feet they moved to her rhythm, copying what she did until they were all breathless and laughing. On the last verse they were all singing lustily:

> *"He tried to keep his oxen fat, but found it was no use;*
> *For all that's left is skin and bones, and all their horns are*
> *loose."*

Panting, they all collapsed to the ground, and reached for the cooling liquid in their cups, still laughing and feeling very close to one another. In no more than three minutes Zane was on his feet again, pacing back and forth in front of the waning campfire, his face radiant with drink and excitement. He expanded his great chest, and boomed forth in his deep baritone, "By God! I feel powerful tonight!" Quickly warming up to the feeling and the sound of his own voice bouncing back to him from the rocks, he bellowed again, "I am powerful tonight! I am a tiger of the land! I am a lion of the mountains!" Agilely he leapt up the rocks until he stood about eight feet above his friends. "Hear me out there?" he shouted into the rocky darkness. "Hear me, all you grizzlies? Come on, if you dare challenge me! I'll battle you all with my bare hands! I'll beat you one by one! Hear me, bears?"

Off to the side of the fire a little away from the others Ted, bleary-eyed and slurry of speech, was talking with Celtic eloquence to the stars, preaching a grand sermon on the universe. Bill snored, smiling, and Max had gone back to playing "Juanita" and "Pretty Saro," soft and sad songs that reminded him of his wife in Monterey. Brian Campbell lay in his bedroll and dreamed that its soft folds were Coleen's arms wrapped around him. Fiona and Robin, locked in each other's arms, fell asleep listening to Ted's sermon and the rich, vivid challenges that Zane Tyler kept issuing to the grizzly bears.

When they all awakened in the morning, the camp was in disarray. Zane was sprawled out across the outcropping of rocks that had served as his platform. Ted was still sitting up, and awakened with a very stiff back. It took quite a long time for all of them to shake off their grogginess and start coffee and food. Most of that day was lost for Brian and Robin in working their claim, and Zane and his friends couldn't abide the thought of traveling over the rough terrain on mules until late in the afternoon. It was decided that they might as well give up the day and enjoy the company, getting a fresh start the following morning. The seven of them spent the day dozing, talking, and fastening their new friendships.

Fiona, Robin and Brian were sad to see Zane and Josie and the others leave the next day, knowing it was possible they'd never see each other again.

With the rainy season not far off, Brian and Robin spent a good portion of their time building a log cabin to live in when the cold winds of the Sierras no longer returned to their heights. Already the sun's rays were weaker, and they could feel the chill of winter lingering in the morning air. One day when the cabin was nearly complete, Fiona said to Robin, "Brian is getting very anxious. He still hasn't heard from home about the baby."

Robin nodded. "More and more often he's been mentioning

that he is going home. One of these mornings he's just going to pack and leave." He walked a little away from Fiona and came back. "I hate to lose him, but if he doesn't go soon, he's going to be stuck here until spring."

Fiona nodded in quiet agreement. She knew as well as the men that Brian would be leaving any day, but until now, when the last days were upon her, she hadn't realized how fond she had become of her brother-in-law, or how much she would miss him.

Fiona wrote letters to Mary, Sean, Coleen, and Carl and Rowena Gentry, then added to the packet the notes Robin had scribbled, and gave them to Brian. "When you go home, Brian, would you deliver these, please?" It was her way of saying she had accepted his leavetaking, for she had also realized in the last few days that Brian was as torn between home and these mountains as she and Robin were about wanting him to stay while knowing he should go. Brian packed to leave the following morning.

None of them knew what to say. They had become so much a part of one another, they didn't know how to separate. Finally Brian said, "Well, I'll be back with supplies." He mounted the wagon and drove away. No one said goodbye.

Nine

It was close to noon on a bright day early in October. Brian Campbell was home at last—jumping down from his wagon in Sean McKay's stableyard, with Coleen running to greet him, her hair and her dress flying, arms outstretched, and Mary and Sean following with scarcely less enthusiasm. He and Coleen collided happily, and his long arms wrapped her up. "Oh, *Brian,* I'm so glad you're home!" she crowed.

"So am I," he said, unable to understand why his throat was so choked. He kissed her, to find that everything that had been between them before was still alive, still urgent. "Coleen . . ."

"Brian, Brian," she murmured. Then remembering the presence of her parents, she pulled away from him slightly. Sean and Mary arrived, and everyone hugged everyone else.

"How about that baby? Where is he? Or she? How come he's not out here too?"

"Comin', Brian!" said Jane's deep voice. She came out the back door holding a thoroughly swaddled small bundle carefully in both arms. She thrust the bundle at Brian, saying, "Here's your little bullwhacker."

With Coleen's suddenly nervous help, Brian got a secure hold on the boneless bundle, and Mary reached forward and lifted the blanket from over his face. The baby squirmed at the light, but before he turned his face away, Brian got a first startling glimpse of himself in miniature.

"He's Patrick Brian Campbell, just as we agreed," said Coleen happily. "Brian Og."

Brian looked at his son, tears in his eyes and a smile trembling on his lips. Then he said, surprised, "Brian *Og?*"

"It's Irish for Brian Junior or young Brian," explained Sean. "I'm mighty pleased you wanted to name him after my father and your father, but somehow he wouldn't answer to Paddy, so he's Brian Og."

"Brian Og. Well, you're certainly something, Patrick Brian."

"The worst spoiled kid I ever raised," said Jane cheerfully.

"Here, I'll take the baby," Coleen said. "You haven't greeted your mother yet."

Brian and Jane hugged bone-crushingly, laughing and patting each other. "Jane, is everything all right? I'd have thought you'd be back home a long time ago."

"I went home once. Some son of a bitch had burnt my house down, all but the log part. Not a thing left in it. Burnt up my blue satin dress and them purty underthings and all. I was so mad I'da killed him if I'da known who it was."

Brian was shocked. "Why would anyone burn your house down?" He put his arm around Coleen and the baby and they started toward the back porch.

"If I ever catch him, his name'll be R.I.P. What happened was he took Cameron for Robin, and said he was gonna get even, and so he burnt down Susannah's shop, and my house, and a couple other buildings too."

"What had Robin done to him?" Brian asked in surprise.

"Nothing a real man wouldn't do to protect his own property," said Sean defensively. "He threw the man and his party off my land. At least it's our best guess. When the man saw Cameron in Susannah's shop he made some remarks about getting even with him, and about property rights. So we think it was Aaron Wheelwright."

"Robin never mentioned anything about him to me."

"No reason to," said Sean. "It was an unimportant incident at the time."

"He hasn't come back to threaten you?" Brian asked anxiously, looking at Coleen and the covered-up Brian Og.

"No, we're perfectly safe here," Mary assured him. "The man was out for revenge. He should be satisfied now."

Sean said, "Tell us about Fiona and Robin. Are they well?"

"Well, happy, and prospering. I left them on the Middle Fork of the American, snug in a winter cabin. I expect by now they're rained in. They won't get much mining done now."

"My Fiona mining? You mean using a pick or shovel?" asked Mary in surprise. "I remember in Illinois I had to threaten her to get her to dig up the parsnips."

"She didn't like the earthworms, Mama." Coleen laughed.

"She doesn't even notice them now," Brian replied. Turning to his stepmother, he asked, "So, Jane, what are you going to do next?"

"Mary and Sean've asked me to stay as long as I want. When I get tired o' visiting, or holdin' the baby, I might build a house in Sacramento. Sam Brannan thinks that'll be a big city someday."

Brian looked at her curiously. "Why can't I see you living in a city? What does a city have to attract you?"

"Men, you dumb bunny," said Jane. "I'm still on the lookout for number five, or is it four? Can't seem to keep it straight."

Coleen had been quiet as long as she could, with Brian close to her and warming her with his arm. She looked up and said shyly, "Are you home for good, Brian?"

"I'm afraid not, honey," he said and squeezed her. "But I'll be home for a few days." *And nights,* his eyes added.

Coleen blushed, and had to fix the baby's blanket again. Once they were in the house and seated, Brian said, "What does he look like? I mean, really look like? His little hands and his fingers and his toes? And his eyes? Does he have all the right numbers of everything?"

"You bet he does," Sean assured him. "It was the first thing I noticed."

Coleen unwrapped Brian Og, a little at a time, so he would not become chilled even in the pleasantly warm kitchen, and his proud father counted his toes and marveled at their tininess, and saw the little dimples forming on the backs of his son's hands. It was astonishing, it was uncanny, to see this miniature of himself, the same broad feet, the same ear shape. "And look, Brian," Coleen said, gently turning the baby's head. "He's got your cowlick."

"Son of a gun, he has. And his mother's lovely eyes," said Brian. To make sure he wasn't wrong, he looked into them, and Coleen blushed again, feeling like a new bride. With a newly gained expertise, she put the baby up against her shoulder and, glowing with happiness, patted his little back.

"Why do you have to go back?" she asked anxiously.

"You don't want your sister and her husband to starve, do you?" he teased. "I promised them I'd bring back supplies. They'll be out of everything by the time I get back."

"Tell us about the gold fields," said Sean impatiently. "Was it worth your while, going?"

Brian concealed his feeling of elation at the amount of gold dust and nuggets he had brought home for himself, Fiona, and Robin. "I guess so."

"Did you bring any home? Can we see it?" boomed Jane.

Brian got up. "I'll fetch it in."

"Need any help?" asked Sean.

"Sure, you can carry a box or two."

Sean went outside with him, and Coleen walked as far as the window so as not to let Brian out of her sight. Brian threw back the tarpaulin on the wagon, and revealed about a dozen well-made boxes nailed tightly shut. "That's what we got, Sean."

Sean's eyes bulged. "This is gold? All gold?"

Brian grinned in wicked glee. "All gold. Nearly three hundred pounds. One third mine and Coleen's, one third Fiona's, one third Robin's."

"Blessed Lord," Sean whispered. "And what will that be worth?"

"The ounce price varies a lot, but it's somewhere between ten and fifteen dollars per ounce. At ten dollars, a pound is worth one hundred sixty dollars."

Sean was pale. He said, "In San Francisco only a week ago, Sam Brannan and some other men set the price of gold at sixteen dollars per ounce. You're richer than you knew, Brian."

"Yes, but everything is relative," Brian replied. "Flour at Sutter's Fort is thirty-six dollars a barrel and scarce, so the Sutters are going to raise it to fifty dollars. I'll go to San Francisco for supplies on the way back to the gold fields, and that may cost me a box of gold."

Sean lifted out a box. "They're heavy. About twenty-five–thirty pounds each?"

"About so."

Sean said impishly, "Let's take them in one at a time, for effect."

Silently the men carried in the boxes until the wagon was emptied. Everyone in the kitchen was exclaiming over their number, and asking questions. Then Mary, watching her husband's face and the ostentatious way Brian and Sean set the boxes on the kitchen floor, said, "You're not going, Sean."

"Not going?!" he echoed. "Not going where?"

"To the gold fields. We're rich enough right now. And we need you here."

"Aww, Mary—" he began to protest, then seeing the firmness on her mouth and determination in her green eyes, shrugged and sat down in his rocker.

Carefully with a crowbar Brian pried the boards off the top of one box. "There," he said, and they all crowded around to see.

Coleen knelt down and let some sift through her hands, awed at its glitter. "Is this really gold? All of it?"

"All of it," Brian assured her. "A third of it is ours, Coleen. And I'm going back for more."

"Altogether, what's it worth?" asked Jane in a hushed voice.

"About seventy-six thousand dollars."

The amount was so astronomical that at first nobody spoke, only looked with wide eyes at the others. Then they started chattering and exclaiming, and everybody wanted to feel the gold and see it sparkle in the light.

Sean said at last, "We'll have to have a safe place to keep this. What is to be done with Robin's and Fiona's share? Will they be coming home soon—to haul it in to San Francisco?"

Brian shook his head. "No, Sean, they're going to stay in the mountains. I've got letters from both Robin and Fiona for you. Robin is hoping you'll take care of getting his gold assayed, and handling the money until he comes home."

Sean didn't say anything for a moment, then said, "I was hoping they'd come at least for a visit."

"I can assure you they are both well—and they are happy together, Sean. Robin is a good husband to Fiona."

Sean took a deep breath, forcing himself to accept life as it came, then he said cheerfully, "Robin's a good man, and I'll take care of the gold—damned good care of it."

While Mary and Jane started preparing lunch, and Coleen nursed the baby with Brian raptly watching, Sean creaked his rocker, lost in thought. "Under the cookstove," he said at last.

"What's under the cookstove?" asked Mary in a panic, backing away from it and eyeing it suspiciously.

"That's where we'll hide the gold until we take it to the assayer's office. Take up some floorboards and hide the boxes down there."

"We'll never be able to get at it, Papa," said Coleen, laughing.

"I'll make a trapdoor."

"Sean, I hardly think you'll want to move the stove every time Coleen needs a penny for a spool of thread."

"Make the trapdoor in the middle of the room, under the table," Brian suggested. "Stagger the ends of the boards and it won't be obvious at all. The table legs and the chair legs will usually be over it."

"That's what I'll do," said Sean decisively. "I'll start right now." He hurried out to the barn for his tools.

Brian kissed Coleen lightly and followed him. "Do you really think it's over with Wheelwright, Sean?"

"Yes. But we've taken precautions. After Jane came back I started a regular routine of having a couple of the men ride over the whole rancho every day, at a different time. Now the only trouble with that is that I'm losing men all the time, and when I take on a new one I'm not sure I can trust him."

"Are you checking things yourself occasionally?"

"Oh, yes. And we've discovered two or three other parties of squatters and turned them out. Now tell me—" Guiltily Sean looked around in case his Mary was nearby eavesdropping. "Tell me about the gold fields. Is everybody getting rich this quick?"

"Not at all. In fact, I wasn't having any outstanding luck

until Fiona and Robin caught up with me. I'd go two or three days at a time and not find anything and move on. The minute they came, we started hauling it out by the ton. That Fiona's a gold sniffer."

Sean's eyes moistened fondly. "That's my girl! You're sure she's well?"

"She is not merely well, she can work rings around me. And she is the happiest person I ever knew, Sean."

Sean's eyes twinkled. "Am I going to be a grandfather yet?"

Brian put his hand on his father-in-law's shoulder. "Not yet, but Fiona is determined it will happen soon, and if Fiona puts her mind to something, she usually gets it."

Sean laughed. News of Fiona made him feel good, closer to her. Before he got too sentimental, he shifted back to safer ground. "How much gold do men usually get in a day?"

"An ounce is considered a decent haul."

"Sixteen dollars a day. It's certainly more than I can make farming."

"Coleen is expecting me to farm our land," Brian mused.

"I take it you're not quite ready for that, Brian. What are you going to do?"

"I'm not certain. There's something about those mountains . . . I'm not ready to give it up yet, Sean, but—well, Coleen is already starting in on me about not going back. Somehow I'm going to have to think of something."

Sean gave him a curt nod. "That you do, boy. We'll give it some thought, and talk it out when we can get some time to ourselves. Right now, how about you carrying the hammer and saw and nails? I'll gather some boards."

They worked all afternoon building a secure storage place. After supper the work was finished and the gold was safely cached. By lamplight they sat and talked about the gold camps, but soon Sean started snoring where he sat, and they all went off to bed.

Coleen was changing the baby's diaper on the bed, bent over talking to him matter-of-factly, telling him just what she was doing and that he was to go to sleep right away and be a good baby that night. Brian watched her for a moment. Then he walked up behind her, just touching her body with his. She turned around and smiled at him, her face flushed and happy in the lamplight. He put his big hands on her hips, and slowly ran his palms up her waist—slim once again—to cup her breasts gently. She said, "I'll be done here in just a minute, Brian."

He drew away, disappointed. Before he could stop himself he said acidly, "I didn't know I'd be bothering you." He sat on the edge of their bed and began pulling his boots off.

"I didn't mean it that way!" she protested. "I only have to put him in his cradle and cover him up. Come and help me," she pleaded softly.

He knew she hadn't meant it the way he had taken it, but for some reason he couldn't help himself. He had expected the same mellow closeness with Coleen that he had enjoyed with Robin and Fiona, only with the added delight of lovemaking, and now he seemed out of sorts and unable to control himself. He let one boot drop loudly, and again rash words flowed out of his mouth. "You seemed to manage while I was gone."

She straightened up. "Brian, don't be mean! He's *your* son too!"

"All right," he said ungraciously. "What do you want me to do?"

"Here," she said, and handed Brian Og to his father. "Pull down his little nightgown and then lay him on his blanket with his head in the corner."

"Why? That looks silly," he said, still feeling put off.

"Just do it and I'll show you. See, we pull the bottom up, and the sides over each other, and he's all snug and warm."

"Huh," said Brian, chagrined that he hadn't noticed the way the blankets were folded before. "Now in the cradle?"

"Yes. Oh, hold his head, his neck is still weak. Are you all right, Brian Og?"

Brian said, exasperated and jealous, "I'm not going to break him, you know." Carefully he put his son in the cradle, and together they covered him with more blankets. "Won't he be too hot?"

"He'll be fine," Coleen said, and giggled. "There—aren't you a proud father?" She smiled at him.

He said, just looking into her eyes, "I'd rather be a proud husband."

"We're getting to that too," she promised him softly, and pulled his arms around her. "Oh, my darling Brian, how I have missed you! The long long nights and the empty days—"

"You can live in the house with Sean and Mary and Jane, and call the days empty?" he asked in astonishment.

"Without you, they are," she assured him.

"Mine weren't too wonderful either," he said, and kissed her deeply.

Slowly they moved toward the bed, kissing and caressing each other. "Let me undress you," she said eagerly.

He smiled. "My pleasure." He still had one boot on, so she tugged it off, then in between kisses she unbuttoned his shirt and pulled it out of his trousers. She buried her face in the abundant sandy hair on his chest, twining her fingers in it, caressing his muscular breast. He was working on the buttons down the back of her dress, his hands shaking, scarcely able to concentrate on his task for thinking of the joys that lay ahead. She let the dress drop to the floor and stepped out of it. Then she unbuttoned his trousers, having a slight difficulty because of a certain natural eminence which seemed to be in the way. Then rapidly his trousers and her petticoats were cast aside, and they stood naked in each other's arms.

Any shyness they could have felt because of their long separation was forgotten. Brian ran his hands down from her breasts along her waist and cupped her bottom, then brought his hands back up over her smooth flesh to do it again. He wanted to know the whole of her as he had known her before. Coleen was licking the corners of his lips with tender little motions. They were both chuckling breathlessly. Suddenly Coleen got away from him and dived under the covers. With a short cry quickly stifled, Brian scrambled after her. They held each other, giggling, and then they stopped giggling and began to kiss again.

The tip of Brian's tongue worked its way into Coleen's mouth, and she responded by very gently nipping it with her teeth. He thrust in farther, and her tongue slid along his until they filled each other's mouths. With the palm of his hand he touched her breast, then he kissed it. She moved his head so that he took her nipple into his mouth and was rewarded with the sweet taste of her milk. His desire leapt, and so did hers, for she urged him on top of her. He felt the warm welcoming moistness between her thighs, and he entered her.

Coleen's legs went up around his back, and he knew in reality the comforting snugness that had been so much a factor in his dreams while he had been apart from her. Without haste now, for there was no longer need of it, he thrust and withdrew, thrust and withdrew, at first gently for fear of hurting her, and she moved with him. But feeling the urgency of her response, he moved faster, and still she moved with him. Then like twigs on the breast of a mighty river, they were swept along with the current faster and faster until they knew the highest bliss that earth affords. He continued to thrust, prolonging their delight, and then slowed down and they both lay still, panting and making little murmurs of satisfaction. He kissed her fondly, then without another motion they both fell sound asleep.

The baby cried twice in the night, and Coleen staggered out of bed to nurse him and change his diaper, and each time she and Brian made love, and each time went to sleep still lovingly linked.

At breakfast they were both glowing, and Mary and Sean looked at them and each other smiling, thinking of their own night before. Jane, whose early-morning spirits were unfailingly cheerful, looked at the two pairs of lovers and said enviously, "It sure must be nice to get it regular. I better hurry up an' get to Sacramento an' find number five."

Sean blushed, and said, "He'll be quite a man, Jane, you'll see."

"But first I got to locate him. Pass that honey, will you, Brian? Might as well enjoy what's available."

During the day Brian rode the rancho with Sean, looking for campfire smoke, checking down the gullies for tents or other equipment. That took them two hours, moving as quickly as they could. The rest of the day they worked threshing and cleaning wheat. Because there was a fine crop, and the hired hands were short this year, this was a job that would go on for nearly two more months.

Sean, for all his burning curiosity, did not ask Brian what he intended to do about the gold fields. He waited until Brian worked around to the subject himself. It took nearly three days before Brian was ready to talk. Sweaty and tired from working in the fields, Brian and Sean sat down to eat the lunch Mary had prepared and they had brought into the fields with them.

Brian said, "I've been trying to sort out how I'm going to keep Coleen happy and satisfy myself, ever since we talked a few days back, Sean. Here's what I've come up with—tell me what you think. The folks in the hills are desperate for supplies. No matter how much you cart along with you, you always seem to need something. And then there's the gold. Just like this wagonload of Robin's and mine I brought home—other men have gold that needs to be carried too. What do you think about me starting a freight wagon making regular runs to the camps? I could take supplies up there, and haul the gold back."

Sean weighed what Brian was saying, then said, "To my ears it sound good. You'd make as much as if you were panning for gold, and you'd be home a fair amount too."

Brian brightened immediately. "You think Coleen would be content with that? It isn't exactly the same as if I were farming our land, but . . ."

"Try it out on her," Sean advised, then after a moment put his hand on Brian's arm. "There are times in a man's life he's got to satisfy his own cravings as well as those of his wife, son. As long as what you're craving can stand out in the light of God's eye, you are doing right."

That night at the supper table Brian told the family what he was planning. "So instead of digging, or panning, I'll be doing something else, but just as lucrative—"

"It'd be hard to beat the amount of gold you brought out this time," Jane said.

"It was the changing conditions in the gold field that gave me the idea," Brian began. "Right now I'd say you can automatically trust seventy-five percent of the men you'll meet out there. But as this gold fever goes on—and certainly everything that's happening indicates it will—then we're going to get more people like your squatters. These men will find somebody's land and just sit there on it and won't be moved. They'll claim possession."

"Yes," said Sean angrily, "and with the present lack of law, the men who've paid out good money for their land are help-less."

"I'm not only talking about ranch land, Sean. I'm talking about claim jumping too—waiting until some man who has a good claim leaves it long enough to cook supper, or sleep, and pouncing on it and taking it over. That's already happened twice that I've heard of. More of that will go on as we get men in California who scoff at any sort of law or even regulation, men who are out to grab it all, no matter whose it is."

Coleen looked worried. "Brian, you're not thinking of becoming a law officer, are you?"

He flashed her a tender look. "Not me, Coleen. Although what I'm thinking of goes along with protecting what's yours. The next thing we'll have to contend with in the camps is stealing. At present, miners can leave their stash of gold in their tents and come back in a week and every grain is still there. But there's enough dishonesty in the men who are coming in now that pretty soon we'll hear of thefts of gold that miners have worked for months to get."

"But is there some way to prevent that stealing?" Mary asked.

"Yes, if there's nothing to steal. You see, when I came home to see Coleen and the baby—" He smiled at her. "Robin suggested I might bring home the gold. In the first place, it's getting heavy to carry in the wagon from one camp to the next, and in the second place, once it's known there's a man who's making a good strike, others come as soon as word spreads. So that's why I brought it all home with me."

"You're gonna haul the stuff!" Jane exclaimed.

Brian nodded. "Yes. For a percentage of the miners' gold, I'll take it to a bank for them. On the way back from the bank, so as not to run empty, I'll bring supplies and sell them at the camps. There's plenty of profit in supplies too."

"By hickory, I'd like to do that myself," Jane said lustily. "D'you need a partner, Brian?"

Brian grinned broadly. "I was hoping you'd say that. Between us we could have a regular schedule going. The time between supply wagons would not be long at all."

"We could take the mail for the miners, too."

"Great idea. At present, if you want to contact someone, you have to send a messenger. That's been getting more expensive too. But that's to our advantage, of course. Every time the price of anything goes up, we could profit by it."

"And would it mean you could be home more often?" Coleen asked.

"That's what made me think of it to begin with," he assured her.

"Brian—how long do you think you might be doing this?"

"Why, I don't know, honey. As long as the gold camps hold out, I guess."

Coleen looked down at Brian Og, asleep in her lap. "I'd rather have you at home. What is going to happen to our ranch —our plans? I—I'm a little bit afraid to be all alone on our ranch with only the hired men to protect me and the baby."

"You can always stay here, Coleen," her mother said, though she knew well what her daughter was thinking.

Coleen said stubbornly, "Then I might as well not have married. I might as well be an old maid with a baby and living with my parents."

Jane said, her voice booming cheerfully, "If that's all that's worryin' you, girl, we'll work that out somehow. Surely you're strong enough to be on your own once in a while. A man's got to do a man's job even when it don't agree with a woman's wants." Jane, tall and large-boned, was never afraid of anything or anyone.

"But I'd be l-lonesome!" Coleen said, trying not to cry.

Sean, usually so defensive and protective where his daughters were concerned, said, surprisingly, "Listen to Jane, Coleen. She's right. A man has to do what he thinks best for the both of them, Coleen. And his wife learns how to get along."

"The wife is a partner too," Mary reminded him sharply, and did not smile.

Sean's eyes flashed dangerously. "Partner is the correct word, Mary, and someone has to make the decisions for that partnership. That's the man of the house! The head of the house!"

"Well, well, we won't get this settled right now," said Jane. "Let's talk about what kind of money we might make, Brian. It might turn out that farming'll be better after all. How much freight you figure to carry?"

"With a six-horse team and a Conestoga type wagon, I could haul eight to ten tons at once. Take a reasonable percentage of, say, six tons of gold for our profit on our trip, one way. Does that answer your question roughly?"

Jane smiled, pleased. "Sure does. The hell with farming, let's tote that load."

Coleen stood up abruptly, slinging little Brian up onto her shoulder. "I think you're just horrible! So selfish and money-hungry!" she cried, and with the baby wailing as accompaniment, she ran back to her bedroom and slammed the door.

Brian and Jane looked at each other, stricken. Mary got up to go comfort her daughter, but Sean said sternly, "Mary, let the girl alone. She's got to grow up and take responsibility sometime." Then as Mary still seemed determined to go, he said again, "She's my daughter too. I care for her safety and welfare just as much as you do. But let her work it out with Brian. And let us, for once in our lives, mind our own business."

Mary sat back down, too astonished to argue with him.

Brian, his pleasant attractive face scarlet down to his collar, stood up and went outside, where he walked out and stood looking into the horse corral for a long time. Of all the things he had imagined, Brian had never expected that his first visit home would come to this. He and Coleen could not seem to settle comfortably with each other. Why couldn't she be a little more like Fiona? Where was her spirit? He was unprepared for the critical feelings he was having toward his wife. Had he, at some point, imagined her as having characteristics belonging to Fiona? Or had she changed? Or had he? How could he love her so much, and yet feel so unable to touch or understand her? Then his attention was caught by his son. It hurt him to hear Brian Og's short little screams. Restless, he wandered out beyond the barns where he couldn't hear anything.

Jane, feeling distinctly third party, went out to sit alone on the front porch. Mary, able now to speak her mind freely to her husband, sat silently grim-lipped, her gaze fixed on a picture off to the left of Sean. He waited, his hands folded peaceably in his lap, creaking his rocking chair. When Mary had thought of a good reply, she would speak to him.

Each driving a wagon, Brian and Jane left for San Francisco three days later. Coleen, taking out on her family her hurt and frustration that no one—no one—had come back soon to comfort her and assure her that she was loved, was not among those bidding Brian and Jane goodbye in the stableyard. Brian had been in tears when he had left Coleen in the bedroom, for he honestly did not know if his wife and child would ever belong to him again. Yet talking briefly in private with Sean, he made excuses for her, saying that she was too broken up to come outside now.

"I know, I know." Sean sighed heavily. He felt he was right in this, but Mary still had a little edge to her voice when she said anything to him, which had been seldom these past three days. "If matters don't clear up in a day or two, I'll have to talk with the both of them. That is a thing I'm not looking forward to, two against one and the one being meself."

"Tell Coleen I'll be back in a month," Brian said. "Tell her I—" But his voice broke.

"I'll tell her you love her," said Sean roughly. "Good luck, son."

"Thanks." The men gripped hands, and Brian went to hug Mary good-bye. She clung to him, weeping, but said only, "God go with you, Brian."

As he left, he looked back at the room he and Coleen had shared. For an instant he glimpsed her holding the baby at the window, but then they disappeared.

He was glad Jane was driving her own wagon, for it gave him time to think. He moved the team along steadily, knowing that in two hours he'd stop to water and rest them, and that would be soon enough to talk with his stepmother.

"Hell to pay," said Jane, as soon as they stopped.

"I tried to talk to her, Jane. I tried to get her to see that it's for *our* benefit, not just mine. But she wouldn't listen."

"Women are like that," Jane observed, as detached as though

she were not one herself. "But she certainly loves you. She certainly was lonesome for you while you were gone."

He said angrily, "She picked a poor way to show it when I was there."

"Maybe so. But in a month she'll get herself together. By the time you go back home again, I expect she'll be a different woman."

"I'd settle for the one I married, if she's not mad at me."

Jane laughed a little. "Brian, you've got to understand. Most of the time it's a man's world. Women get sick and tired of always coming second. Once in a while we want to be first. But our weapons are blunt, so we have to use sharp words and tears and silences when we want to be heard. And at those times we don't always want to listen, like Coleen. She wants to be with you, boy, that's all. Pure romance, it's what a woman wants, to be with the man of her choice and have him admirin' an' sweet-talkin' her. But she'll come around. She'll go along with what you want. You'll see."

"You'd have thought she'd at least said goodbye to me with her folks—"

"She was makin' a point. By the time you get back, she'll realize that it was herself she was cheatin' too. Besides, Sean's a sensible man; he'll make her see right."

Brian pulled a harness strap a notch tighter. "I should have been able to do that while I was home."

"Brian, I'm gonna say this to you now, so you'll have the whole month t' think on it before you do anything. When you go back the next time, it's my belief you'd ought to move her out of there and put her back in your own home. I'm not sayin' Sean an' Mary spoil her, but they been lettin' her spoil herself. Her father was right, she has to learn responsibility."

Brian's jaw had a stubborn set to it, but he said, "I'll think it over."

"Fine."

"By the way, I'll be stopping to look at our house. I'd better see if there's anything left of it, and if I've still got any hired hands."

"While we're in San Francisco, I want to get me a couple

pairs o' men's pants. If I'm gonna drive a freight wagon, I don't want to have to mess with no long skirts."

Brian laughed. "Jane, you'll never catch number five that way."

She said imperturbably, "Sean told me I would, an' I will."

In San Francisco Brian and Jane were able to order two freight wagons made, to be ready upon their return in early November. Then they bought two more horses apiece and all the supplies their wagons would carry. They had flour, meal, crackers, sides of bacon, dried apples, sugar, coffee and tea, rice, salt and pepper, medicines and cordials. In among the loads were all the cooking utensils they could find, a large supply of blankets and ammunition, and several new rifles. Brian and Jane were each armed with two pistols. Two loaded rifles rested in secure racks mounted directly in front of them.

Jane was dressed in her new pants, a blue work shirt and the worn leather jacket she had had ever since Brian had known her. She looked doubtfully at the two heavily loaded wagons. "Brian, are you *positive* this stuff'll sell at the gold fields? We sure got a lot to dump out if it don't."

"Jane, we won't get halfway around our intended route before it'll be all gone. Just wait and see."

"All right. I'm ready t' start any time you are, Brian."

For answer Brian cracked his whip over the horses' backs and yelled, "Giddap!"

Ten

Mormon First Elder Sam Brannan had met only once with Brigham Young, President of the Church of Jesus Christ of Latter-Day Saints, since he had brought his group of Saints from New York around Cape Horn to California. The meeting had taken place on June 30, 1847, nearly eighteen months before. At that time, completely out of patience with waiting for Young to bring his party to California as planned, Sam had gone to meet him at the Green River in Wyoming. From there Sam agreed to travel to Great Salt Lake City. In the remarkable city that Young had founded, the two Mormon leaders had a number of conferences, each one calculated to diminish Sam's rightful feeling of self-worth. It was made abundantly clear that Young had no intention of leaving Salt Lake City. Sam's community of New Hope, which he had founded in a fertile spot north of San Francisco, with Young's large party in mind, was not destined to become the New Zion. Furthermore, Young demanded that Sam send to Utah all the moneys that the California Mormons had contributed to the Church. Volubly, Sam refused. Just before they parted Young, white with rage at Sam's reckless audacity, threatened to have Sam "used up" for an apostate.

Sam had discovered early in life that his own anger was pointless unless put to work. So on his way home to San Francisco in a considerable fury, he used its impetus to goad his mind into making plans. It was common knowledge that Young used his Danite bodyguards—his Destroying Angels—to rid himself of annoying opposition. In view of Young's threat, Sam decided to hire bodyguards of his own. Whimsically he dubbed them the Exterminators. It was not his inclination to hound apostates, having been so accused—but having guards for his person rather amused him. And later he discovered the convenience of having a big burly servant who could see him to bed when he was too drunk to go home and risk Ann Eliza's tongue.

Now it was a gloomy November morning, bone-chilling, murky with fog. Sam sat in his office, his desk piled with accounts he must attend to, trying to think of some excuse why he couldn't do them now. He did not need to go to the *Star* office, for that had folded in the summer. He missed having it as an outlet for his vast curiosity. If he had the *Star* now, he might use a story on the three Chinese servants of Mr. Charles Gillespie, late of Hong Kong, telling what their lives had been like in that other country, and what had made them run away from his employ to dig for gold in America. Or he might write an editorial on the need for public protection in his city. He might even say something about the shipping that was coming in at William Clark's new wharf. But he had no one to get the stories for him, or run the presses.

Clark's Point. Sam thought on that a while. Already the wharf was so crowded at times that ships had to anchor in the bay waiting for dock space. Now if he built a wharf, he'd make it a long one, a thousand feet—no, make it two thousand feet long. Stretch it out into the bay half a mile and dock ships on both sides of it. Let's see now, he had about $15,000 he could put into it. It would cost about a hundred dollars a foot, so that would give him 150 or maybe 200 feet. Of course he'd have to get other men in on such a grand project—

His planning was interrupted by a thunderous banging on his door. He called irritably, "Come in! Now what's all the—well, hello, Dick."

Sam's visitor was small, scrawny, filthy with road dust, red and sweating. He panted, "I got here as soon as I could, Mr. Brannan."

"I appreciate that. What's going on?"

"President Young's sent three of his boys to waste you. I started ridin' the minute I got wind of it. I ruined two horses gettin' here."

"Where are Young's men now?"

"Figgerin' them slower'n me, they ought to have a couple days' ride yet."

Sam raised his eyes to the tall, massive man who stood in the doorway waiting for his orders. "You heard that, Luke?"

Luke nodded. "Which way was they comin' from?"

Dick explained. Luke nodded. "Want us to head 'em off?"

"You know what to do," Sam replied. "We sure don't need them in San Francisco."

"I'll take Dick here, an' four o' the boys."

"Keep your head down, Luke."

Luke smiled grimly. "I ain't about t' give 'em no big target."

The men left, and Sam looked after them. He sighed. San Francisco, for all it was his town and he loved it, was pretty dull sometimes. With so many men gone to the mines, it was hard to find a good fight to get into. He drew another breath and was about to let it out when his eyes widened. A good fight! And he would miss it!

He sprang up from his desk, toppling over the chair, and jerked open the door. Shubel, the guard on duty outside, glanced at his employer in surprise, and quickly followed Sam as he ran down the stairs, the men's boots making an echoing tattoo in the narrow stairway. "Luke!" Sam yelled. He cupped his hands and yelled again after the two men who were riding away in the mud of Montgomery Street.

Luke looked around, then came sloshing back. "Somethin' wrong?"

"I'm going with you," Sam announced.

Luke looked distinctly disappointed, though his words were solicitous enough. "Aww, boss, we don't want you gettin' in no danger."

"Well, I want to. I'm going along."

Luke wasted no time in argument. "Now? Or later?"

"Right now. While you're rounding up the boys, I'll go home and get my extra guns and a heavy coat." Sam swung onto his own horse. "I'll see you all here in twenty minutes."

Ann Eliza was at home, wearing a gray muslin housedress she had embroidered with pink roses and green leaves and standing on a chair washing cupboard shelves. Sam burst into the house, and they regarded each other with equal surprise. For a moment he stood irresolute, which gave her the advantage.

"Who did you suppose cleaned out cupboards?" she asked, amused.

"I never thought about it. In fact, I never think about cleaning cupboards at all," he replied. "Coming down, my dear?"

She held out her arms and he swung her down. They stood in light embrace, Ann Eliza's arms around his neck. He smiled at her, and kissed her on the end of her nose. He said admiringly, "No matter what you are doing, you somehow stay immaculate, the very height of fashion and grooming."

She smiled back at him. "How nice to have you home in the middle of a dismal foggy morning. Will you stay for lunch, or—"

"I'm off, I'm afraid." He said genuinely regretful. Ann Eliza in this mood of complaisance could be a pleasure indeed. Just thinking about it began to rouse him, and fleetingly he calculated how long it would take to persuade her into bed, satisfy them both, and be back at his office. Too long, he realized, though it would be well worth being late under other circumstances. To remind himself, he said, "I just came home to kiss you goodbye and pick up my coat."

She snuggled against him, which was something he both enjoyed and dreaded, for not to make love to her in her present frame of mind was to invite bitter recriminations. She murmured, rubbing her palm sensuously on his breast, "Why don't we make the goodbye worthwhile, then?"

Without seeming rude, he took her hand and placed it on his cheek. "I must go now, Ann Eliza. People are waiting for me." Gently he kissed her palm, looking lovingly into her blue eyes. Without warning a vision sprang into his mind of Ann Eliza lying next to him, with her glorious thick blond hair undone and trailing over his arm and his chest. Against the vision he said harshly, "I must go." Hastily he kissed her again, and disengaged himself from her arms.

She followed him to the bedroom, making it difficult to get his extra guns without her knowing. "Will you be home for dinner?" she asked.

He reached up to the back of a high shelf, where the guns were kept away from Sammy and the younger children. "No, as a matter of fact. I—I'll be gone for several days."

"Several days!" she said, stricken. "Don't you want me to pack for you? Won't you need clean shirts and extra trousers—"

He got the guns and buckled them on, and filled a pouch with ammunition under her suddenly alert gaze. He tried to be nonchalant. "I don't think so, but thank you just the same. I'll be in the saddle most of the time."

"Riding for several days?" Her voice rose in alarm. "Sam, tell me where you are going!"

"I don't know exactly. Toward the mountains." To reassure her he added, "I'll have six of my men with me, so I'll be well protected."

She slammed the bedroom door and stood with her back against it. "I insist on knowing about this trip. Where are you going? What are you going for? Why do you need six men to protect you? Sam Brannan, what are you up to now?"

Strangely he felt comforted by her switch in disposition. This Ann Eliza, this shrill-voiced one, he could deal with better than the seductive one whose passion once unbridled could exhaust them both. Although . . . Mentally he shook himself. He straightened up and faced her. "It's only Church business, nothing to be upset about."

"*Only!*" she echoed. "You say *only?* What is it, that you need all your guns for? Sam, *what are you hiding from me?*"

"My dear Liza, there is nothing to hide. I always take my guns when I am outside San Francisco, in case of wild beasts." He smiled at her. "This is nothing special. It's merely a meeting with some men of President Young's."

". . . who has said he'll have you used up for an apostate!" She flew to him, putting her hands on his shoulders, her blue eyes pleading with him. "You are not going! I forbid you to go! Every time you have business on behalf of the church, you endanger yourself. You don't need the church! You can be successful without it! Sam, I won't let you go!"

He would not look at her, but stared at a painting on the wall. Because her own Episcopalian Church did not seem to need Ann Eliza, she could not understand why Sam's Church needed him. "I must do what I must do."

"Send someone else to do it!"

"Let me be the judge of my own business, Ann Eliza."

She raged at his cool superiority. "For God's sake, can't you once think of your wife and family? You are putting yourself at risk, and for what? Pride! That's all it is, Sam, pride—sinful pride! You want to best Brigham Young. You don't care about me or the children, or even the Church, it's only you and your infernal pride!"

"I'd *better* care about that. Left in your hands I'd have no pride at all. You'd tie me to your apron strings as you do my children."

Hurt, angry, and helpless, Eliza muttered cynically, "You never think of anyone but yourself. What Sam wants, what Sam is going to do." Then with a sudden shift she changed directions to something he occasionally responded to, her position in society. It was shallow, but when it came to her, Sam only saw the shallow things, so she said, "What about what *I* want? What about what I want to do?"

"I'm not preventing you from anything," he pointed out.

"We *were* going to a party tonight. Now I can't go, because I won't have an escort!"

"That's a silly argument, when you've gone alone before."

"Precisely what I mean," she said. "You think only of yourself."

"My dear wife, you have all the fine material things you have ever expressed a desire for—and all obtained through *my* efforts. I get a little weary of being criticized because I haven't done something especial for you today."

She said sarcastically, "Oh, but you *are* doing something especial today—you are leaving San Francisco and riding God knows where so you can get into a brawl with Brigham's killers. Well, tell your 'boys' to bury you where you fall!"

He looked at her and then away, his mouth set. "Sometimes I wonder why I come home to you at all."

Her eyes burned at him, and her mouth was ugly from the acidity of her words. "Why, Sam, how easy to answer that. You come home so that I may entertain your *ever-so-important* friends, and maintain your esteem in their eyes. You come home so that I may bear you children to carry on your *ever-so-important* name, why else?"

He blinked at her, then, because he knew it would hurt her as she had hurt him, he added, "An infrequent roll in the hay with you is hardly worth the monumental effort to keep you in the mood for it."

Her eyes widened; she grew scarlet. He did not dream—could not dream—how often she longed to do exactly that. To make love with him in utter abandon was the closest to heaven she would ever come. And yet when she did, the shame afterwards was more than she could bear. She retorted hotly, "Thinking only of yourself again! What Sam wants! Maybe just once I would like to feel loved, instead of used! Maybe just once I would like to be your only woman!"

"Maybe. But this is no time to get into that."

"Pity you can't stay sober while you're among the wild beasts."

This wounded him again, for he knew as well as anyone that he drank too much. But he seemed unable to stop it, or to substitute anything else for it. He made no answer, rummaging in the wardrobe for his heavy coat. He heard the slight splash of a half-full flask in the pocket. With Ann Eliza's stony gaze focused on him, he moved to the decanter that stood on his chest of drawers and deliberately filled the flask. Defiantly, he poured himself a jigger and made three swallows of it.

"You never think of anyone but yourself! You're killing yourself! Who's to take care of me and the children?" she asked shrilly. "It's not even noon yet and you've had two drinks that I know of! From now on that decanter stays in the parlor!"

"Don't touch it," he said coldly.

In the act of reaching, she stopped to stare him down. "I ought to throw out *all* the liquor in this house!"

He said again, "Don't touch it. I warn you, Ann Eliza."

"You warn me?" She sneered. "What would you do?"

His eyes glittered. "Don't push me, or we'll both find out. Now move out of my way. I'm late already." He tried to go to her right, then her left, but each time she blocked him. He stood perfectly still, waiting. "You're not going to stop me, Liza."

She screamed, "Then go! And take this with you!" Lightning-fast, she raked her nails down his cheek.

For an instant only, Sam stood rooted with astonishment. He felt the searing pain of the scratches, felt the blood rush to his head with dizzying force. Then he knew only rage, the urge to kill her.

But Ann Eliza had run out of the bedroom, slamming the door behind her. He heard her footsteps dwindle away into some other part of the house. He half started after her, but instead made himself go out the front door and get on his horse. As he was riding down the muddy street, he wiped the blood off his face again and again.

Luke and Dick, Mike, Bill, Shubel and Ozro were waiting for him. Seeing his wounds, they started grinning, and Luke opened his mouth to make a jovial remark.

Sam quelled them all with one black look. He said tightly, "Let's ride."

Moving quickly through the foggy day, he could not help going over and over their quarrel. All the elements were in this one, the elements of every quarrel they had: his need for autonomy and her dispute of that need; his unfinished business with the Church; his selfishness; his drinking. She accusing, he denying or defending, both sublimating their passion with angry words. He thought it might be more sensible in the long run if they could simply play out their ardor in bed.

The problem was that Ann Eliza wanted an ordinary man to love and cherish her in an ordinary way. That petrified Sam Brannan. Ordinariness and failure were the same word to him, and he could not bear that. Shuddering, he took another long pull from his flask.

They were in the foothills, much farther from San Francisco than Dick had expected to find Young's men. For the past two hours Dick had been muttering that they ought to turn back, somehow they had missed the party. Finally Sam said, "We'll go on today. Tomorrow we'll head for home."

In the late afternoon Dick saw them. "There they are," he whispered. "I reckanize that yella neckerchief."

Sam knew two of the three: Bart Dixon and Percy Hubbard. They were militant Danites, troublemakers from Illinois days with the Prophet Joseph Smith. He said, "Do they know you?"

"Not sure. Dixon might. He knows you, so stay low."

"How close d'you want to get, boss?" Luke asked.

"Within good firing range." Sam looked around. In the vicinity were several other travelers, going to the gold fields or returning home from them. His mind churned with the knowledge that these three men had been sent to kill him—in the name of the Lord. Well, his death or life was in the hands of the Lord now. And if he was going to die at age twenty-nine, he wanted to take his murderers with him. He said, "No matter what happens to me, kill them all—in the name of Sam Bra—"

As he spoke, one of the men raised his pistol and fired. The first bullet zinged past Sam, painfully nicking his ear, which spurted blood all over his coat. The second bullet missed him widely. Then his men were shooting, and Sam saw the middle one of Young's Destroying Angels fall off his horse. He glimpsed the other travelers, caught in this inexplicable crossfire, scurrying for shelter in the underbrush and behind small trees.

Bullets seemed to be whining all around him, but Sam was too angry to care. He spurred his horse and hid behind a twisted tree, and aimed his pistol at Bart Dixon's chest. With a steady hand he pulled the trigger. He was astonished when a red hole seemed to blossom on his target and Dixon's face contorted with agony. Dixon clutched his chest with both hands. His frantic breathing could be heard even at a distance. Two more shots rang out. Hubbard's horse screamed, and his legs buckled under him. Percy leapt off. Another bullet hit Dixon, this time in the head. He spiraled downward from his horse and crumpled to the ground.

But Percy Hubbard was not idle. While attention was on Dixon, he too got behind a tree. He raised a rifle and took expert aim. Dick screamed, dropping his pistol and grabbing his throat to stop the blood that spurted through his fingers. Several shots sounded from Sam's bodyguards. Dick slid sideways off his horse, one foot caught in the stirrup. The horse, feeling no restraints, reared and neighed and began to gallop madly, dragging Dick's lifeless body over the ground.

It was quiet for a moment, while the men who were left sought shelter for reloading. Luke fired into the tree where Hubbard had been, but there was no response. Sam and his men were alert, every hair on end as they crept through the underbrush, hoping to locate Hubbard before he pulled the trigger on one of them.

A shot rang out, and Luke grimaced, but automatically fired in the direction of the shot. A man's high scream was suddenly cut off. An eerie silence followed. Separated from his men, Sam could not see anything. Five breath-held minutes went by. Then Shubel called out, "It's all right. All those sons a bitches are dead. And Luke's been shot."

Sam moved in the direction of Shubel's voice, and found Ozro kneeling beside Luke. With his penknife he was probing Luke's arm, which had been penetrated by a bullet. Luke, green-faced and pop-eyed, was staring into some ghastly distance. Then Ozro said triumphantly, "Got the bastard!" and held up a bullet in bloodied fingers. Mike and Bill were looking in the other direction. Ozro took off his sweaty and dusty neckerchief and bound Luke's arm tightly. "There, Luke, you'll be fine in a day or two."

Luke sat up, looking somewhat relieved—and fainted. They let him lie where he had fallen, with Ozro chafing his wrists to bring him to.

The other travelers had gathered around by now, asking what had happened. Mike, who had been perfectly silent until now, said, "You can get the word to Brigham Young that this is what happens to his Destroying Angels when he sends them to destroy Sam Brannan. All the Angels are dead. Sam and his Exterminators are still alive." He did not point out Sam, whose ear was still dripping blood.

"You boys ought to be more careful," scolded a clerkish-looking foot traveler. "Some innocent person might have been killed."

They camped a few miles back on the trail, beside a clear stream. Luke, though pale, was able to ride. In the morning they began the trip home. It seemed to Sam, whose life four men had died for, that there was meaning in the gray lowering clouds that dogged them the entire way. Without real thought he had killed a man who had intended to kill him. Yet he was alive. Evidently he still had work to do. He thanked God for that.

Moodily, he sipped from his almost empty flask.

Back again in San Francisco, Sam did not feel like going home to Ann Eliza yet. He couldn't bring himself to face her. Instead of heading down the street to his house, he went to his apartment. Their last fight had touched him in a way he wasn't accustomed to. She had screamed at him that he would not put his life at risk if he loved her or his children. But he had put his life at risk, and until it was over, he hadn't given one thought to Ann Eliza or his daughters or his sons. Did that mean she was right? Did he use her to further his own interests? Did he love her at all? Was he capable of loving anyone?

He sat and brooded. For a long time he was unable to break free of the vicious circle of doubt, guilt, self-hate—and pride. Just as Ann Eliza had accused, there was always his pride. Thoughts of her and Susannah, and Harriet, and so many other women tumbled around in his mind, stirring up uncomfortable memories of pleasurable nights, and days of recrimination.

Annoyed, but aching with the awful need to have someone love him uncritically, he got up and had a hot bath drawn for him. For nearly an hour he soaked in the tub, trying to ease the empty ache. He gave it up as a bad job, turning his attention to carefully shaving himself. He took a closer look at the deep scratches Ann Eliza had given him, to remind himself of her fury.

He couldn't seem to make himself feel any better at all until, dressed in fresh, stylish clothing, he went out and ordered himself the best meal in town, found some admirers, and had a few drinks. Finally he began to feel himself again. With clean clothes on, a meal and a drink under his belt, he felt able to face anything that came.

He was in his office looking at the same paperwork of ten days before, when he heard a woman's high heels clack across the floor of his reception area. His interest aroused, he straightened his cravat. Then Shubel opened the door. "Miz Tol'rance Morrison wants to see you."

Sam stood up, and smiled at her. He had unnerved himself for nothing. Ann Eliza was a bitch. She had always been a complainer, she would never be anything else. She simply didn't understand him, or know what a man really needed.

Tollie's bold eyes looked Sam over from head to toe. Her slow smile told him that she knew how to appreciate him.

Eleven

The Fourth and Sixth Wards of New York City encompassed the Bowery and the section called Five Points, the stomping grounds for three kinds of people: life's losers, who would always be at the bottom of the heap; immigrants, fresh off ships and vulnerable to anyone who claimed to know the ways of this country; and those who preyed on the other kinds. Landry Morrison fitted into the latter class. Whistling, hands thrust deep into his trouser pockets, Landry jingled his pocketful of coins as he walked jauntily through the crowded, steamy streets of the district. Tenements shot up from the sidewalk's edge like crumbling cliffs. Hot gusts of steamy cabbage-bloated air burst from nearly every window and mingled with the stale odor of beer that always lingered on the stagnant air of Five Points.

When he had first been forced by penury to live here, these smelly, teeming streets had terrified him. Along with the other smells that were always present, there was another that assaulted a man's survival instinct—pent-up violence. Landry had never before known that violence had an odor, but it did, and he had also learned to live with it, and to give off that same scent from his own body when it served him.

Today he had money in his pocket, a lot of money, and the

prospect of getting a lot more by the end of the week. On days such as this one he could look back with a manageable detachment on the sequence of events that had brought him to this squalid section of the city. Until February 1846 Landry Morrison had been the pampered, beloved, only son of Mormon Elder Ezra Morrison, pillar of the Church. He had been completing the last weeks of his two-year mission for the Church in Canada, and enjoying the first lush passions of a new marriage. Tolerance, his young wife, had been expecting their first child in the spring of that year. He shouldn't have had a complaint in the world, but he had been dissatisfied in spite of the bounty of his life.

Then too, he hadn't yet learned the value of a well-placed lie, for he was still struggling to win salvation, which seemed of the utmost importance to him. The Church of Latter-Day Saints had permeated his life; its influence, its credo affected all he said, thought, and did. His discontent and malaise of spirit rested in the fact that he had not been able to accept certain beliefs of the church. For example, how was it possible for a serious man to believe that the Prophet Joseph Smith saw visions through spectacles made of wire and stone? Most claimed belief, but Landry had not been able to do so, and for that he had been condemned an apostate, driven from the Church, damned, driven from his family, disowned, and had had his wife Tolerance and their unborn child taken from him.

Even on a pleasant afternoon such as this, Landry could not gain a reasonable detachment when he thought of his father taking Tolerance as his wife, then justifying it to Landry as his duty under God! Ezra and Tolerance! He sickened at the thought of it. He removed his hands from his pockets, clenching his fists convulsively. The scent of violence drifted off the fabric of his frock coat and mingled with the other human scents of labor, dissipation, fear and illness. Nothing eased him. Not even the reassuring sounds of jingling money could soothe the rage that came when he thought of Ezra and Tolerance as man and wife. And what of his child? Neither Ezra nor Tolerance had had the decency to tell him if he was the father of a son or of a daughter. He knew no name by which to bring the child to life in his imagination.

As always when he reached this point in his thinking, he remembered the packet of money his sister Susannah had sent to him, urging him to use it for a passage to California. That money had kept a roof over his head and food on his table. There had been no question of going to California at that time, but now he had many times over replaced that money, and he was free to do what he pleased and to go where he wished.

He roughly shouldered his way through a clot of men and women gathered on the sidewalk in front of one of the innumerable groggeries. He wondered what his sweet sister Susannah would think of him now. Would she still urge him to come to California if she knew him now? He was certainly not the green youth he had been when he had allowed himself to be cheated of everything he held dear. She might not find him the loving, playful brother she remembered. He laughed bitterly, the sound blending naturally with the street talk. She might not like him at all. And what about Tolerance? If he were to go to California, what would his peaches and cream wife do? He had once thought her so innocent and fragile, a delicate budding woman he expected to be his wife and helpmeet for all eternity. He still could not stifle the occasional dream that tantalizingly presented visions of Tollie's milky white flesh, the rosy tips of her breasts, the soft fragrance that was hers.

Coming to the door of his tenement, he shoved a youngster out of the doorway, then raced up the stairs taking them two or three at a time until, winded, he reached the corridor outside his room on the fourth floor. Fumbling for his key, he glanced to either side, making certain no one was lurking in the darkened corners of the hallway. One could not be careless in Five Points and live. There was always someone willing to take a man's life for the shoes on his feet or the shirt on his back. Landry had to be doubly careful, for he liked to flaunt the fact that he had money.

Finally getting his key to work in the wobbly, nearly useless lock, he pushed the door open. A wall of stale air that reeked of rat dung, human urine, and cheap soured wine fell into the room with him. He peered cautiously into the dingy room, assuring himself of its emptiness before going in. Immediately upon entering, he closed the door behind him and locked it again, jamming a chair under the knob for added security.

He took three steps across the narrow room and opened the only window, but it offered little relief. He cleared the small table near the window of last night's meal, and pulled the change from his pockets. Then he reached into his breast pocket and carefully removed a substantial envelope of crisp, unfolded bills. With a pleased smile he sat down, opened the envelope, and removed the bills, laying them in three neat stacks. One thousand dollars—twenties, fifties, and hundred-dollar bills. He sat motionless staring at them until his eyes dried and began to smart.

Then with a satisfied sigh, he picked up the money. Almost regretful of having to ruin the flat perfection of new bills, he rolled them tightly, then bound the roll with string. He was well practiced, and when he removed one of the rungs from the footboard of his iron single bed, the roll of bills slid easily into the chamber. He replaced the rung, then picked up the coins from the table, dropped them into a pouch, and stuck them under his mattress. They made a bulge. If someone broke into his room, they would happily rob him of the coins and look no further.

Satisfied with his cleverness, he turned slowly to the scrap of mirror glued to his wall and meticulously began to remove the disguise he had worn that day. Carefully he took off his dark frock coat, his eyes fixed on his image in the glass. He liked his looks—the brown waving hair, the foxy handsome face with its clear coloring. Smiling faintly, he removed his white shirt and the dark trousers. He folded each garment carefully, making certain it would rest neatly in his trunk so that everything he wore the next time would look well cared for and pressed. Once more in front of the looking glass, he carefully removed his false mustache and the wire-rimmed spectacles that sat ridiculously on the bridge of his nose.

The spectacles were always the last thing he removed, for they were the part of his disguise that amused him the most. Joseph Smith had seen visions of angels and gold tablets and Gardens of Eden through stone spectacles, while Landry Morrison saw greed, lust, avarice, and the other dissipating human weaknesses through his spectacles of clear, clear glass. Gently he placed them in the trunk on top of his folded coat. With a last smile of bitter amusement, he looked at the spectacles innocently lying there. Then he shut the trunk and locked it. After that he donned the tattered, dirty clothing of a Five Points runner.

To the people of the streets and the people who patrolled those streets, he was Lanny Morris, a cheap little man who eked out his existence by running to the docks whenever a shipload of immigrants came into New York. Down on South Street, Maiden Lane, and several other streets near the wharves, Landry and hundreds of others like him met the ships, and loudly vied for the attention of the newly arrived. Landry's method was simple. He would hurry up to a new arrival and grab his luggage, talking rapidly. "Need a good cheap place to stay? A job? Money? I know the perfect place—good food—clean and cheap. Yeah, not much money, and he knows about comin' here for the first time. How much money you got? Lemme see it. I can help you—tell you how to keep from gettin' cheated."

It was pathetically easy to get these men and women to turn over all they possessed. Many immigrants didn't speak English, and all of them were bewildered by the dizzying bustle of New York City. The lucky ones who managed to elude the runners were those who had family here, or friends already in this country to guide them. The others were too baffled and lost to refuse to trust anyone who claimed to know what to do and where to go to start a new life in a strange new land.

Landry didn't even need to be subtle. He simply grabbed, talked, and led his victim to the tenement of the man he worked for. Landry got paid his pittance for bringing the lambs to the shearing shed, and the lambs remained trapped until they had been fleeced and had learned the hard ways of the city.

With the business of being a runner, Landry gained a certain notoriety and a readily recognized face, which left him free to don his disguise, slip uptown to spy and collect secrets from snippets of gossip and sly observation regarding the loves and sometimes peculiar preferences of wealthy, respectable men and women who would pay well to keep their indiscretions hidden from the public eye. Uptown, Landry identified himself as Ezra

Morrison, and was always boastful and a little loud in making certain his victims knew the name. Even those few who had tried to find him and put an end to his blackmail had ended in a dead-end in Five Points. No one could ever confuse grubby, foul-mouthed Lanny Morris with the immaculate, well-groomed, well-spoken Ezra Morrison.

The deceit gave Landry great joy, and helped him ease out of those terrible days he had spent brooding about the injustices his father had done to him. Before he had thought of this clever ruse, those had been days of immobility in which he was able to feel only the hurt of the injury and the pain of deeply needed vengeance. By now Landry had honed his desire for vengeance to a fine philosophy that governed his life.

All he lived for now was the one final payment that would be made to him this Friday, and then he would take steps to answer the questions he had asked of himself earlier. What would Susannah think of her brother now? What would Tollie do when confronted with him in the flesh in San Francisco, California? What would Ezra do? Most entertaining of all, what would he, Landry, do to even the score?

Landry checked his room to be certain there was an acceptable disorder to it, then removed the chair from under the doorknob, unlocked it, and went down to the streets to find a decent meal. Five Points had little to offer, so he walked along the narrow lanes toward the Bowery. Though most of the respectable citizens had already left their once-fine houses, the Bowery still had more to offer than Five Points; and for at least a short time he could get the Irish smell of cabbage and turnips out of his nostrils. He entered an eatery and sat at a corner table.

He ate alone. He did almost everything alone. He had not even made an attempt to befriend anyone since he had been excommunicated. He trusted no one, and preferred his own thoughts to the lies he might be told by a friendly stranger. His isolation had not only made him a suspicious, cynical man, it had made him wary and cautious. Even though his ship would not sail for a full week, Landry had already booked passage on the *Falcon,* as well as having bought a through ticket on the steamship *California.* The *Falcon* would carry him by the quickest route, Panama, where he would board the *California,* which had sailed in December making her way through the Straits of Magellan. The *California* would then take him right into San Francisco harbor. It couldn't be simpler—when a man looked ahead.

And it had the added advantage of the possibility of gaining attention upon the ship's arrival in San Francisco. The *California* was making the longest nonstop voyage ever made by a steamship. He just might arrive in San Francisco amid cheers, and maybe even a brass band. Wouldn't he like to see his father standing near the docks with eyes popping out of his head when he, Ezra's well-dressed and obviously prosperous son, disembarked.

In the few days before the *Falcon* was to sail, Landry left his rat-infested flat in Five Points and moved himself into the Astor House. It was a pleasure to use on himself some of the money he had been hoarding for the past two years. He felt very strongly that he deserved pampering. He wore his good uptown suit, having discarded all his Five Points garb. In order to look respectable upon entering the Astor House, he purchased a good carpetbag and stuffed it with paper until he could purchase a wardrobe. He spent his last three days in New York City shopping. Most of his time and money were spent at Stewart's new and modern store. There he purchased every conceivable item of apparel a gentleman of fashion could want.

On a December morning in 1848 when he boarded the *Falcon,* he was wearing a fine pearl gray tailored suit under a darker gray woolen great coat, a gray hat and white gloves, and carrying a gentleman's cane. His carpetbag and a newly purchased trunk were brought aboard by a hired porter. With an air of disdain, Landry stood to one side watching as the man brought his belongings aboard and took them to his cabin. He leaned lightly on the new cane, relishing the secret power of the instrument. The latest rage in crime-ridden New York City, the cane was equipped with a spring device that, when pressed, released a long, lethal knife blade from the tip, should he ever need to defend himself.

Satisfied that his belongings were secure, he flipped a coin to the porter, and grandly turned his back as he strolled back onto the main deck. It occurred to Landry that he might do well to cultivate some shipboard acquaintances who could be of use to him in California. His restless, well-practiced eyes sorted through the passengers who were on deck taking a final look at the bustling city they would probably never see again. He was looking for those who appeared most prosperous, or who gave the air of being important.

Not immediately seeing anyone who caused his instinct for power and money to come alive, he looked appreciatively at the ship. He had never sailed anywhere, and he was ready to be impressed. The *Falcon* was a ship of 700 tons burthen, and most important of all, so far as Landry was concerned, she was bound for Panama, the shortest route to California. The fact that his arrival at Chagres on the Atlantic side of the isthmus would require an overland journey to Panama City on the Pacific side did not trouble him. The clerk who had sold him his ticket had assured him that the trip was uneventful. Landry shrugged. He knew as little about geography as he did about ships.

Once again taking up his search for a suitable traveling companion, he spotted the perfect family. Using all the charm he possessed, he walked over to them and stood near them at the rail. After commenting, "This must be the busiest port in the world," he introduced himself, and waited patiently until the other man said, "I am Jonas Walker. This is my wife Sarah, and these are my children."

With the introductions over, Landry sighed. "I shall miss New York, I fear. It is so alive with noise and bustling humanity, and I have heard that San Francisco is little more than a village. That will make quite a contrast, won't it? Are you also from the city?"

Sarah Walker smiled sweetly at him. "No, we are from Troy, New York. We shall not find so great a contrast as you will, Mr. Morrison."

"That's to my liking," Walker said. "I come to New York City on business occasionally, but I can't say I care much for what you call bustling humanity. I don't believe I have ever been in a dirtier place in my life, and not all that dirt is on the streets, either."

"Jonas," his wife warned gently, then smiled again at Landry. "Mr. Walker does go on a bit about the evils of the city."

Landry nodded solemnly. "And well he should. It teems with every kind of vice."

"Well, but let's not talk about such sordid things now. We are at the start of a voyage, and I for one expect it to be a wonderful time." Mrs. Walker smiled again, and effectively silenced both men.

Landry did not seek the Walkers out any more that day, and had about decided to seek other companions. If Jonas Walker was so aware of vice in other men, Landry Morrison wanted nothing to do with him. However, Landry seemed to have made a favorable impression upon the couple, for the next day Walker joined him on deck.

"Sarah is a bit queasy this morning," Walker said expansively, "but not me. I feel fit! Wonderful air at sea . . . makes a man feel . . . fit."

"Umm," Landry murmured, then found he had nothing more he wished to say.

Walker stretched, doing morning exercises. "What takes you to California, Morrison? Gold, I suppose?"

"Gold?" Landry asked, surprised. "Is that why you are going?"

"My company is sending me out there. I'm a mining engineer. Of course, until I see the lode for myself, I'm not willing to promise a thing. A man has actually got to see for himself before he knows what kind of strike he's talking about."

Landry settled more comfortably, leaning on the rail, his eyes glistening with interest. Perhaps he had chosen the right companion after all. "You and the men who hired you must be fairly certain it's a big strike. After all, a mining company doesn't start hiring men and sending them to the other side of the continent on a whim."

Walker laughed and admitted, "No, they don't. All the reports we've gotten have been encouraging." He paused for a moment, then added, "Most encouraging."

"What reports might those be?" Landry asked.

Walker gave him a sharp, assessing look. "Surely you read the letter James Gordon Bennett published in the *Herald* last August? He even mentioned that Kit Carson delivered the soldier's letter himself."

"What soldier? What letter?" Landry asked, a little curtly. He didn't like being taken lightly, and he suspected Walker was playing with him.

"A man in the New York Volunteers, who saw the gold first-hand, claimed that men are taking it out by the bagful. He exhorted his fellow New Yorkers to come West to wealth."

"And this letter is what your company is basing its hopes on?" Landry asked, with a trace of sarcasm.

"Oh, my, no!" Walker laughed. "We have verification far more substantial than that. Thomas Larkin, once our Consul for California, has verified it, as have Colonel Richard Mason and some others."

"Then it's true," Landry breathed. "And California is now a possession of the United States."

Walker did laugh now, and there was more than a trace of superiority in the sound. "True. You can stake your claim as well as the next fellow. No Mexican government to deal with, just the good old U.S.A. It doesn't take much to give a man gold fever, does it."

"No," said Landry acidly. "No, it doesn't, and it took you less time than it did me."

Walker seemed to enjoy that, and he laughed harder.

After watching the man continue with his calisthenics for a time, Landry bade him good day, and wandered to the other side of the deck to think—and plan. This lent a whole new aspect to his venture. A bright aspect, filled with golden promise.

The next day when he dined with the Walker family, he made no mention of gold. Neither did Jonas Walker, but Landry had the uncomfortable feeling that the man was laughing at him. The feeling was particularly acute, for the previous afternoon he had discovered in a conversation with Mrs. Walker that her husband was an elder of the Second Presbyterian Church of Troy. That alone was enough to make Landry suspicious and wary of anything the man might say, think, or do. He would remain friendly, but alert. Never again would he be done in by some church man spouting moralistic mumbo-jumbo.

Had Landry remained in New York only a few more days, he would have heard that President Polk, now privy to the exciting news of California gold, had added his own weight to the rumors being reported in newspapers around the country. In his annual message to Congress on December 5, 1848, he included a news item. The day would be called a "June day in December." Outside the two houses of Congress men were waiting for the signal that they should take the packets they had been given and distribute them to the names on their lists.

Each packet contained copies of the letters sent by Colonel Richard B. Mason, military governor of California, the other reports of gold, and a copy of the President's message to Congress. These packets were to be given to the newspapers, the telegraph offices, and all the important people in Washington, and in other cities in the country. President Polk on this day in December gave official impetus to the Gold Rush to California, a possession of the United States which had no protection of law. The booming of a cannon signaled the horsemen on their way to inform the whole country of the news.

Gold fever struck the country instantly, and hard. The New York newspapers reported the full story on December 6, and by nightfall of that same day hundreds of men were asking how one dug for gold, and how one could get to San Francisco in the winter. The answer, of course, was by steamship! Steamship offices were immediately swamped, having to put extra ships on the line. Still there were lines of people waiting passage. New businesses started in New York. Gold rockers could be purchased. Official gold hunters' kits were for sale. Instruction books and all manner of equipment, some useful and some not, could soon be purchased on any street corner and in hundreds of shops.

But Landry had left New York three days too soon. The first stop made by the *Falcon* was Charleston, South Carolina, where she took on more passengers. A few days later the ship docked at Havana. Many of the passengers were fascinated with this beautiful island, and Landry was one of them. He and Jonas Walker went ashore, and were enchanted by the busy, quaint streets. They took a ride in an omnibus, and went to see the fortifications of the island at Moora Castle. It provided a pleasant afternoon, and Landry knew that someday when he was a very rich man and in the company of important people, he would tell the tale of his visit to Havana with major embellishments of his "stay" there.

The *Falcon* continued on its pleasant voyage, stopping at New Orleans to take on more coal and more passengers. As the voyage progressed, there was more and more talk about the California gold strike. Two days outside of Chagres, Landry wondered if it would be possible to find a mere half dozen men aboard the *Falcon* who had not been smitten with the idea of easy California wealth.

Near the end of December 1848, the *Falcon* came into the small port of Chagres. The passengers could not have had a better day, nor could the town ever have looked more inviting. A gently warming sun blessed them with a dry warmth and lent a romantic cast to the old Spanish fort that dominated Chagres. Haphazard streets were formed by the positioning of the native huts. The population had the easy, ambling gait of those accustomed to living with heat and of being in no hurry, for whatever was here to be done today would be there tomorrow as well. The population was a mix of Spanish, Indian and Negro, a combination which brought about some exotically handsome faces.

The passengers filled the narrow streets, and swarmed over the sun-baked fort as they waited for a select group of men to make arrangements for the second leg of their journey.

Landry, Jonas Walker and several other men from the *Falcon* bargained successfully for the riverboat *Orus* to take them up the River Chagres.

With a good-natured laugh, Landry put his hand on Walker's shoulder. "We'll be in Panama awaiting the *California* before you know it. When we first set eyes on this village, I anticipated a long wait for a vessel worthy to carry us upriver, but this is marvelous." He laughed happily. "California gold, here come the New Yorkers!"

Walker laughed with him, his own excitement mounting. Now that they had found no cause for delay in this little village,

Chagres seemed to wink at him with sunny promises of bright days to come.

The *Orus* was ready to transport its passengers in short order. The sun was still high in the sky when the company boarded the riverboat and began their journey up the river. Neither Landry nor Jonas Walker nor any of the other passengers had any idea of what the Isthmus of Panama was like, so at first they were enchanted by the lush vegetation along the river banks. All of them relaxed, dozing in the warm sun, enjoying the gentle motion of the boat. Before the journey had well begun, however, both men and women were uncomfortable. The deeper they went into the Isthmus, the more humid it became; and swarms of mosquitoes seemed to appear out of nowhere to hum around one's face and neck.

Seventeen miles up the river, the *Orus* pulled to the bank. With a knowing and unkind smile, the captain told the passengers they would have to make arrangements with native boatmen for the remainder of the journey, as from that point on, the river was too shallow for the *Orus*.

Landry felt a hollow pit where his stomach had been moments before. So far as he knew, no one of their company could speak the native tongue well enough to bargain for boats to take them upriver. He glanced uneasily at the assortment of scantily clothed boatmen who lounged in the shade. There was an assortment to choose from—tall, short, lanky, stocky—but none of them appeared to be at all interested in the arrival of the *Orus*. He reached out to touch Walker's arm. "What are we to do now?"

Walker cleared his throat, then said to the captain, "As we were not told of this need, sir, I ask that you bargain with these natives for the native craft we will need to complete our journey."

The captain's smile grew larger, showing yellowed teeth. He had been through this many times before, and was well aware of the travelers' plight and the profits it meant to him. He agreed to aid in the bargaining.

Landry watched the expression flit through the man's eyes, watched the muscles of his mouth work as he spoke and smiled, and recognized what was happening. There was a profit being made here, and instead of being on the gaining end, he was now on the giving end of it. There was little difference between this captain and Landry himself when he had been a runner in Five Points. Now he had as little choice as the immigrants had when he took advantage of them. He started to say something to Walker about not paying the price asked, for he was certain the captain was taking a large cut. But he said nothing after all. They needed those native boats, whatever the cost.

Shortly, for ten dollars a head for boatmen, the company had the use of five *bungas*, flat-bottomed native boats, and the men to pole them. The captain bade them farewell and good luck, then boarded the *Orus* to return to Chagres and collect another boatload of passengers. For a moment the company stood dumbly watching the riverboat chug easily down the muddy water, stunned at how alone and vulnerable they felt with that last vestige of civilization disappearing around a bend in the river.

Shaking themselves free of the uncomfortable feeling, they turned their attentions to the *bungas*, which all of the Americans pronounced *bongos*. The natives made no move to leave, seeming content to rest upon their poles forever if necessary. The men put the luggage aboard, and then began the rather difficult task of trying to keep families together and fit everyone onto the boats.

Landry jumped into one of the crafts immediately, not having anyone but himself to worry about, and he wanted a seat on the side. Oblivious to the talk and arranging that the others were making, Landry sat complacently waiting for the journey to begin.

Finally with everyone in place, and the babble of talk and jostling quieting, the boatmen began to pole their way upriver. Landry stared at the boatmen open-mouthed, then turned to the man seated next to him. "Surely we will move faster than this!" There was barely any movement, and a small child could have walked along the banks at a faster pace than they were moving. Without seeming to move a muscle or exert any effort, the boatmen put their weight on the pole, and as the weight against the angle of the pole became great enough, the boat inched along.

But they did not move any faster, and the natives calmly

ignored anything they said to urge speed. It was as though no one had spoken. As they traveled, the vegetation became heavier and heavier. Strange vines and fronds reached far over the river bank, dipping low toward the boats. There were strange odors, and an even stranger atmosphere in which everything seemed to have stopped. The air was thick with moisture. Even their breathing became slower.

Landry looked around at his fellow passengers. All of them sat listlessly, their faces frozen in a peculiar configuration of fascinated repulsion and fear. He felt the same way. And he wasn't at all certain that fear would not grow into panic. He had the awful sensation that this boat ride would never end, and one day he would be steaming in the humid air, and simply go mad, jumping from the boat and racing through the sweet rot of the jungle.

He turned his attention to the water, letting his hand into the only slightly cooler river. He tried to think of other things, of the gold he would find in California. However, that did not soothe him, for it also brought to mind that he might never arrive in California. This river, this muddy, insect-ridden river, might be the place where he died. He turned his head and happened to look at the boatman, who was watching him. The man shook his head in a negative, then rolled his eyes toward the river bank. Landry followed the direction of the gesture, and watched as a piece of rotted, gnarled wood slid off a mud embankment, landing without a splash in the river. Then in horror, he watched as yet another log seemed to move from farther up on the bank and make its way to the water.

He snatched his hand into the boat, rubbing it furiously as he stared sickly at the alligators making their lazy way toward the middle of the shallow river, nearer to the boat. He couldn't take his eyes from the murky water now. He began to notice things he hadn't before. It didn't seem like water at all, but thick, and unnatural. Strange bubbles rose to the surface and burst, expelling repulsive odors. Feeling fear rise higher in him, Landry looked beyond the bow of the boat, hoping to see blue sky, some break in the hideously lush vegetation of the river. This journey had to end soon! But there was no break. If anything, the foliage got thicker and the river became shallower.

The flat-bottomed craft began to scrape along the rocky river bottom, the noise and the sensation grating fearfully on the nerves of the passengers, all of them aware that most would not survive if they were stranded. While in the village for even a short time, they had all heard tales of men walking into the jungle never to be seen again. Of course, safe in Chagres, and fresh off a ship that had brought them from New York City, none of them had thought of themselves in those terms. Now, deep in the jungle with the monkeys chattering wildly in the trees overhead, to their sides and all around, and brilliantly colored parrots shrieking as they dived from those same trees, they could think of nothing but themselves.

Frantically Landry motioned to the boatman to hurry. With a broad-toothed smile and a congenial nod of his head, the man slowly pressed his weight into the pole, waiting patiently, effortlessly, for the boat to move over the next shallow stretch of water. "He doesn't listen," Landry said to no one in particular and to anyone who would listen and sympathize. "Can't he understand?" He slapped hard at a mosquito that landed on his cheek. Already he looked like a man suffering from hives, with welted marks all over his face, neck, and hands. One woman sitting ahead of him turned, and he saw that her eyes were nearly swollen shut in reaction to the insect onslaught. Another man put his head in his hands, already feeling ill.

From somewhere behind him he heard Sarah Walker's voice, soft yet clear. "What will we do when night falls, Jonas? Are we near a village?"

Landry cast wary eyes skyward, to notice for the first time that the sun was setting behind them. Another wave of panic overcame him. They were supposed to be traveling to the Pacific Coast! Why was the boat headed east? Trying to keep himself calm enough to think, he tried to envision the map, and what the isthmus looked like, and then to think of the curves the river had taken. Was it possible that they had corkscrewed so much that they were traveling east to go west? Giving up, and not being able to think it through, he turned around seeking Walker, who had had more travel experience than he.

"It is the curve of the Isthmus," Walker said gruffly, his voice seeming hoarse. "The east coast is actually farther west than the west coast is."

Unaccountable rage bubbled out of Landry's mouth, before he could control it. "What kind of place is that! It's the Devil's work! We should be heading west! West!"

There were murmurs of agreement from the others. They must be in the Devil's domain. None of them was certain they would emerge whole from it.

That night they camped along the shore, lying in total discomfort under the trees with a blanket of mosquitoes feeding on them. One of the men kept watch at all times, changing guard every four hours. There was no question of any of the sentries falling asleep on the job. No one slept well that night, most of them only dozing to awaken to the ear-piercing, heart-stopping howls of prowling jungle animals.

Having fallen asleep just before dawn, Landry could barely force his matter-sealed eyes open when the brilliant tropical sun blazed full strength in the morning. Moving nearly as slowly as the boatmen, he rolled over, escaping the hot nails of sun being driven into his eyelids. His mouth was dry, and his saliva thick. He reached for his canteen and slowly let the water clean the hot film from his mouth. Everything felt thick, his body was thick, and even though he was hungry, he could not make himself eat. His mind was slow and sluggish, allowing him to think only as far ahead as the next step his foot would take.

They set out again, at the same slow, monotonous pace that somehow bred a frantic fear. That afternoon they again traveled with the western sun at their backs. No matter how often they told themselves that this was as it should be, it continued to feel wrong and add to the burden of apprehension.

Today Jonas Walker sat on the seat next to Landry, but neither man had spoken a dozen words. It was too much effort, and there was little to say that anyone wanted to hear. Both of them had made the effort that morning to shave, and wash, but here, by midafternoon, the beards of the two men had grown far faster than usual and both looked tired and scruffy. Walker chuckled. "We are a fine-looking company, aren't we—stubble beards and wrinkled gowns. There's not a one of us who could gain entrance to a respectable restaurant in New York."

"What I wouldn't give for some good food," Landry sighed. "What do you know of Panama City—is it civilized?"

"I imagine it is. A great many ships put into port there, and the trade coming across the Isthmus increases each year. I am hoping it is a pleasant place with a good inn and decent food." Walker had a faraway look in his eyes. Then the focus tightened, and he looked down. "One of the men is ill," he said in a low voice.

"I can't say I'm surprised. It's this heat—damnable heat," Landry said, mopping at his face and neck. "It's a wonder we're not all dead from fever."

Walker looked sharply at him. "That's exactly what I fear, Morrison. The fellow may have been sick when he was aboard the *Falcon,* but if he has contracted something from this confounded jungle, we may all be in for a bout. There are several children—it could be very bad for them."

Landry nodded in agreement, then shrugged. "There is no sense in worrying about it. We cannot escape. There is no place to go but through the festering morass, and hope we get out."

Walker said shyly, "We could pray . . . you were once a man of God."

Landry laughed bitterly. "Yes, I was once a man of God, and I prayed. That is why I am no longer a man of God."

"Your prayers were not answered?" asked Walker.

"I have no way of knowing. Perhaps they were, and it is that I do not like the God who grants such boons as He granted me. Or perhaps they were not. Perhaps there was no one there at all to hear my pleas."

"I understand," said Walker.

Landry turned to him, a fire of anger burning in his eyes. "No, you don't. You understand nothing of it at all."

Walker said nothing, and neither man spoke again until toward evening they reached the native village of Gorgona. In their usual steady pace, the half-caste boatmen poled the boats to the river bank and stopped. Grateful for any sign of civilization, no matter how primitive or remote, the passengers got out of the *bungas,* smiling at all new faces. Landry had been one of the first ashore, and now he was giving the village a quick assessment for means of comfort, when behind him there was a commotion: loud American voices in argument with the softer, slower native ones. He took several steps back toward the river. One of four young carpenters, bent on making their fortunes in the West, was gesticulating wildly and screaming at the natives, "Unload the luggage!"

With mouths clamped shut, the natives steadfastly refused. They had been hired to pole the boats, not to unload boxes and luggage.

Jonas Walker then surprised Landry and the rest of the company by pulling a pistol out from his coat. He waved the weapon in front of the natives, then fired one shot into the soft earth, causing mud to spray and a clod of earth to leap high into the air. With the promise of additional money and the threat of the gun, the natives sullenly brought the boxes and luggage from the boats, scattering them on the river bank. Within seconds of the placement of the last box, the natives were back in their boats, speedily disappearing down the River Chagres.

The company from the *Falcon* was left to make arrangements for the overland journey to Panama City, some twenty-four miles through the heavy jungle growth. With the handicap of language, unfamiliarity with the terrain, and not knowing which of many guides was trustworthy, arrangements for the overland trip were time-consuming. The company settled in, resigned to remain in Gorgona for at least two days and perhaps longer, until a bargain could be struck.

From the first steps it promised to be a difficult trip. No one was feeling his best, and several were complaining of severe headaches and a general malaise. The days were steaming hot, but during the night the temperatures dropped drastically, and they huddled together, covering themselves with whatever they could to keep warm. Landry kept reminding himself that Panama City was only twenty-four miles away, and this God-awful trip could not last forever. He studiously avoided anyone who had any health complaint, afraid that he would contract cholera or some unknown jungle fever.

They came to the village of Cruces, and there some of the men were able to hire mules. Though Landry thought he had secured one entirely for his own use, it was commandeered for one of those who were too ill to continue on foot. Grumbling under his breath, but not daring to make his displeasure known, Landry continued walking.

Not far outside of Cruces, the swampy ground became rocky, and the plagued travelers saw before them a range of mountains. Men and mules edged their way along the precarious paths; the cliffs were sheer and steep. Each ledge they managed to negotiate successfully led them to another more dangerous than the last. Finally at the top, they rested, enjoying the momentary sensation of safety. Landry looked out and saw nothing but mountain, and in the distance the rich tangle of green out of which they had come.

Had there been any way of doing so, it was certain that all of them would have refused to continue the journey, for now they had to go down the other side of the mountains, negotiating the same steep cliffs, tiptoeing along similarly narrow ledges. Years before, the Spanish had cut niches in the rock on the steepest declines to give the mules footing, but these were of little comfort when it seemed that at any moment man and animal would hurtle out into space, tumbling down hundreds of feet into a void.

To add to their misgivings, the man who had fallen ill at the outset of the journey died. Several others were now ill, and the spirits of the rest of the travelers were very low. Several had taken to calling the strange malaise "Chagres fever" for lack of a better name. Every man and woman felt a surge of hope and relief when they finally came down the last set of mule steps, and the mountains were behind them. For the first time since they had left Chagres, they had a sense that the journey was nearly over; but many of them wondered at what cost they had taken the shortest route to California.

Walker asked Landry, "Would you have done it if you had been told of this trek through the Isthmus?"

Landry thought for a moment. "I probably would have, because I wouldn't have realized how bad this is—even if told. I would have heard fifty or so miles and thought of two days' hard traveling. Who would ever expect the boatmen to move slower than a man can walk?"

"Well, it's behind us now, and Panama is just ahead. We'll be all right now."

All of them had their eyes to the front, searching for the first sign of Panama City. When it finally came into view, it seemed like Mecca. It was far more civilized than Chagres. The people wore ordinary clothing, and lived in houses made of adobe bricks. It was a pleasant, pretty little village with homes covered with picturesque vines. A few of the families were of Spanish descent. The rest were a mixture, as were the people of Chagres; but to the weary, ill travelers, it was a small piece of heaven, and the last stop before they boarded ship to go to California.

The closer they came to Panama, the more they began to realize their Mecca had a blemish. The travelers from the *Falcon* were not the only ones who were seeking passage to California. The village was clogged with people, all two thousand of them awaiting a ship, any ship that would take them on. Even more disturbing was the discovery that many of the two thousand people waiting were sick. Some of them had cholera, brought with them from the ships that had carried them to Chagres; others had what was now commonly known as Chagres fever. Even the easy-going inhabitants of Panama City, who were accustomed to travelers staying for a time in their village, were alarmed and upset by the presence of so many.

The United States had a Consul here, Mr. William Nelson, and the Pacific Mail Line had set up an office. Mr. Nelson and the company agents had been expecting certain army and government personnel, who had come across the Isthmus, but not the others. Provisions had been made for the army and government people, but the gold seekers, and those who were going to California for the work and high wages, were left on their own to find housing wherever they could.

Many things had become apparent to both Landry and Jonas Walker as soon as they had arrived in Panama City. One was that nearly all of these people waiting were trying to buy tickets on the *California,* the first ship likely to continue the journey to California. Second, with the army and government personnel also waiting, some of these people were going to be unable to book passage. So Landry and Walker quickly struck an agreement. Jonas and Sarah Walker sought housing, which was not easy, for Panama City had no hotel. And Landry went to try to purchase tickets for the Walkers on the Pacific Mail Line, hoping that his already purchased through-ticket might add a little weight to the request.

Late that afternoon Landry and Jonas met in the little market in town to report on their respective successes. Walker had managed to let two rooms above the stables of one of the Spanish families. "It isn't much, but to get that, I had to pay double the going rate, and then beg for it. It was only Sarah's presence that gained us the rooms."

"Manure may be a pleasant odor after some of those we smelled on the crossing," Landry said with a wry grin. "At this point I will be happy to sleep anywhere that is indoors, and away from the mosquitoes and the howling animals." As they talked, the two men filled a small basket with rice, yams, tomatoes and a few other vegetables from the market.

"My own news," Landry said, after Jonas had tried unsuccessfully to purchase a small piece of beef, "also has its drawbacks. I have purchased passage for you and Sarah and the children, but after overhearing two of the clerks in the Pacific Line office, I am convinced that they are overbooking that ship. Not all of these tickets are going to be good. I am not even certain my own is."

"Why, they will have riots!" Walker exclaimed. Then he hurried off to another stall to again try to buy beef.

Catching up with him, Landry said, "I agree with you, and if they continue the practice, it could get quite nasty. I don't know when exactly, but more people are due to arrive here. The *Crescent City* and the *Isthmus* have let off passengers who are in the jungle right now. They should arrive any day now."

"And all of them will be seeking passage to California," said Jonas.

"And if they are sold tickets on the *California?*" Landry asked with raised eyebrows. "Who knows what is likely to happen?"

Walker was silent. He paid the man for the beef, tucked the purchases under his arm, returning the basket to the lady from whom he had borrowed it, then led Landry away from the market toward their lodgings. Finally he said, "We must board that ship."

"I agree, but first we must find a way of achieving that,"

Landry answered. He already had an idea, but he didn't share it with Jonas Walker.

The following day he returned to the Pacific Mail Line offices and purchased as many tickets as he had cash to pay for. With a pleased smile, and certain of what would happen in the following days, he returned to his stable room and carefully hid the tickets. That accomplished, he returned to the main section of town. There he found an old board and several adobe bricks, and set up his shell game near the picturesque walls the Spanish had built around the city many years before to protect it from sea marauders. The walls had fallen into disrepair, but some of the great Spanish guns remained. Every day the Americans stranded in Panama City climbed upon the walls, straddled the big guns, and looked longingly out to sea in hopes of spotting a ship. In the long hours of boredom, Landry Morrison intended to provide them with a pleasant diversion and replenish his wealth at the same time.

Several days after the passengers off the *Falcon* had arrived in Panama City, those from the *John Benson,* the *Crescent City,* and the *Isthmus* poured into the city, making it even more crowded and lively than ever. Several New Orleans gamblers set up shop and gave Landry competition for his money-making scheme, but there seemed to be enough boredom to keep the money rolling into any diversion anyone could provide. As soon as he accumulated enough money, and for as long as the Pacific Mail Line continued to sell tickets, Landry Morrison bought them and hoarded them, waiting for the right day.

The number of men who went to the shore or who sat astride the Spanish guns increased daily, and as soon as Landry heard rumors that the *California* was due in port at any time, he began to work his tickets. At his makeshift table, he held a raffle. One lucky ticket to one lucky winner, all for the price of one dollar a chance! His pockets and fists were soon filled with dollar bills, and a small bag clinked heavily with gold coins. As soon as one ticket was won, Landry would wait long enough for the losers to wish they had one more chance, then he would bring out another of his hoarded passage tickets and begin the raffle over again. His only worry now was that the *California* would reach port before he had raffled off the last ticket. Of course he could always sell it to the highest bidder, but he was sure he would lose money that way.

Twelve

Captain Cleveland Forbes had taken the *California* south out of New York harbor with no inkling of the gold fever that was about to strike and cause him untold troubles. He headed his ship out to sea, planning to make no stop before reaching Rio de Janeiro, thus making this voyage of the *California* the longest non-stop voyage ever made by a steamship. His journey had barely begun before Captain Forbes began to feel ill. However, the Captain was one of life's deft players and an experienced, able seaman. Despite his illness, he accomplished the longest non-stop voyage made by a steamship in record time. Through a hazy blur of headache, fever and general malaise he smiled, feeling a bit better for the noted run between New York and Rio. He still had not heard so much as a whisper about the gold excitement that would obliterate his navigational feat.

While the *California* took on coal and supplies in Rio, and his crew partook of whatever pleasures the city had to offer, Cleveland Forbes rested and coddled himself, expecting the peculiar and persistent illness to release its hold on him. It did not, and the *California* began the second leg of her journey on November 25, 1848, with her captain still ailing.

Forbes had been ill before, but he was a healthy man most often, and he was sure this fever would pass as had other minor illnesses. He was also mightily pleased with his accomplishments thus far on the voyage, and wouldn't be a bit dismayed if the *California* managed another record or two before reaching her destination at San Francisco Bay. He headed his ship for the tip of South America, his mind churning almost as hard as the great steam engines that drove the vessel. Nearing the tip of the continent, Forbes decided that rather than doubling Cape Horn, he would thread the treacherous, narrow 350-mile passage of the Straits of Magellan. On December 7, the *California* entered this dangerous run between the southern tip of Chile and the islands of Tierra del Fuego.

About this same time, in several other parts of the world, men first learned that gold was to be had for the taking in California. These first reports were relatively mild, but nevertheless men began the exodus to California. So, five days later when Captain Cleveland Forbes, aware only that this voyage would be notable for its speed and the expertise of his seamanship, brought the *California* into the Pacific Ocean, hundreds of other men were hastening to Peru and to Panama City expecting to gain passage on his ship. Even if he had heard the tales of instant wealth to be taken from the California ground, Forbes might not have paid much attention. His illness had become much worse. He was no longer confident of his ability to carry the burden of authority for his ship. His challenge of the Straits seemed to have taken the last bit of stamina from him.

Forbes put in at Valparaiso, where two things happened. So far as Forbes was concerned, the agreement between himself and John Marshall, another captain with Pacific experience, was paramount. Captain Marshall agreed to take over much of Forbes's duty, while an officer of the *California* would take command of Marshall's ship. This arrangement allowed Forbes to remain aboard the *California*, but relieved him of the heavy burden of full responsibility.

The second occurrence was, to Forbes, a nuisance, of some interest but little importance. Several South Americans and some other foreigners from a variety of countries clamored for tickets of passage aboard the *California*. In their numerous native tongues, and some peculiar English, these men chattered excitedly about gold in California. Forbes was completely unmoved by such arguments. He was a company man, and his company carried American passengers. He was also patriotic, and preferred his passengers to be American. He refused the men passage from Valparaiso, citing those American passengers awaiting him in Panama City as reason.

The *California,* with John Marshall in command, steamed up the coast of Peru with all her passenger berths empty. Marshall put in at the port of Callao for supplies. At the sight that greeted him there, Marshall immediately called for Forbes to join him. Both captains were stunned as hundreds of wild, manic, gold-hungry Peruvians stormed the ship, not asking but demanding passage to San Francisco.

At a loss, Marshall looked to Forbes. There were some decisions regarding this vessel that Marshall thought it better not to make. But Forbes was as reluctant to deal with this peculiarity as was Marshall. He turned the decision over to his company. Forbes reported to the Pacific Mail Office in Lima, asking for instruction. He returned not entirely pleased. "We're to take on passengers," he told Marshall curtly. Then checking his log, he saw that he was anticipating about fifty Americans to be waiting passage in Panama City. Some of these were company men, some army men, and others were government men on their way to the new United States possession of California. "Take on no more than a hundred men—no women, no families," he instructed Marshall.

When the *California* steamed out of Callao, she had seventeen men in her more expensive cabin berths and about eighty others in steerage. Marshall made one more supply stop in Paita, and again there was a clamor for passage tickets. "No!" roared Forbes, annoyed with all these irregularities in his trip, and a bit confused and grumpy about all the fuss these men gone mad were making about gold in California. "Chattering monkeys!" he yelled. "That's all they are. We'll take on Americans! *Only* Americans in Panama!"

Marshall shrugged, and followed Forbes's orders. He headed the ship for the Isthmus of Panama to pick up the army personnel, the few government men and the company men.

On the morning of January 17, 1849, Landry Morrison, as usual, was near the old Spanish walls offering a variety of games of chance and raffling off one of his seemingly endless supply of steamship tickets. The money was flowing freely when several of the men straddling the Spanish guns and keeping watch on the sea began to shout. In moments the cry was taken up by the crowd that roamed the beaches, then word flew through the town of Panama with lightning speed, "The *California* is coming!"

As was the custom, the vessel anchored offshore, and acting Captain Marshall and several of the other ship's officers rowed toward shore. As soon as they had neared Panama, Marshall had noticed the unusual number of people milling about the beach and sitting atop the Spanish walls, but being busy with final details, he hadn't thought much about it. No matter how many were waiting in Panama, it was unlikely to have any effect on the *California,* or so he reasoned. She was already carrying one hundred people, but she boasted one hundred fifty berths. The fifty remaining empty ones were more than enough to carry her anticipated number of American passengers.

Marshall became uneasy only when the horde of beach roamers plunged into the surf yelling unintelligibly and reaching for the boat. With uncomfortable suddenness, Marshall recalled Captain Forbes's warning against selling passage to any but Americans. But Forbes couldn't have foreseen this—nobody could have foreseen this mob! Marshall turned a little desperately to his first mate, but never got the chance to speak as several hands reached out of the frothy surf to grab the jolly boat. The clawing hands of wild-looking men demanding attention grabbed at his uniform sleeves, and tried to wrestle him and the boat, nearly throwing all aboard into the water. With horrifying rapidity it was dawning on Marshall that every one of these men, and most likely the others ashore, all expected to be given passage on the *California.*

Marshall quickly recovered from his initial surprise. Squaring his shoulders, he mustered a full air of command, and in his most authoritarian voice ordered the men away. He then ungraciously kicked off the remaining grasping hands on the jolly boat, and safely brought his boat and his small crew of officers to dry land. His back ramrod straight, and a stern look plastered on his face, John Marshall stepped lively across the sand with a horde of waving, shouting men following him. Marshall's eyes stared straight ahead, his lips were clamped shut in a hard, firm line. He neither looked at nor spoke to any of the mob, which was growing in number and ferocity as he and his men made their way to the steamship office.

"What in the hell is going on out there?" he barked at the clerk as soon as the office door was closed behind him. Even now faces were pressed to the glass of every window in the building. Men rapped on the doors, windows, and walls.

The harried clerk shook his head. "They're coming in on every native boat. We didn't know what to do with them."

The muscles in Marshall's jaw jumped. "You didn't know what to do with them, so you sold them tickets for passage on the *California?*"

The clerk's eyes slid away from him and fixed on his desk. "Well, not all of them."

"Not all of them!" Marshall shouted. "My God, man, at the best of times—with an empty ship—we could only take a hundred fifty—maybe two hundred if we jammed them in. We're carrying a hundred passengers right now."

"But you can't be!"

"The hell we can't. Your office in Lima ordered us to take on passengers in Callao."

"Oh, my God . . ." The harried clerk moaned. "What'll we do with all these—"

"Goddamned mad, dangerous maniacs," Marshall finished for him. "I don't know what you're going to do, but you'd better make a decision soon or you're going to have a riot on your hands." Marshall turned away, taking several steps toward the door.

"Where are you going? You can't leave—"

Marshall smiled. "I am going to get a good stiff drink, find safe quarters, keep out of sight of this mob, and wait for you and this office to solve your problem." He opened the door, smiled again, and walked out, pushing his way through the crowd. He managed to go about fifteen yards when the crowd became so dense he couldn't move. Once more the hundreds of inquiries were shouted at him, hundreds of hands plucked at his uniform. He raised his arms asking for silence. When the roar had subsided sufficiently for his voice to carry over it he said, "The Pacific Mail Office is working out the schedule of passengers. When their decisions have been made, you will get word from this office—not from me. I can tell you nothing. Talk to the right man to get the right answer. Don't waste any more of your time or mine by asking me."

Jonas Walker and Landry stood on the periphery of the crowd that closed in around John Marshall, and had heard what he said. The two men exchanged glances. Each man had his ticket, Landry's purchased in New York, and Walker's one of the first purchased in Panama City, but neither man was certain how this dilemma would be solved. Fairness and justice were not always practicable in a panic situation.

In fact, as Landry saw it, no matter what the shipping office decided, there would be no equitable means to handle this situation. Most of the people standing in front of the office were ticket holders, and if the captain strung them up on the spars and the rigging, he still could not get all these people aboard. The Peruvians who had purchased tickets in Callao and were now aboard were not helping matters. At least a dozen men were hanging over the side of the ship, waving their arms and shouting derisive remarks across the expanse of water. The furious, stranded Americans responded with their own taunts and hurled rocks.

The man next to Landry shook an angry fist in the air and shouted, "Put the Peruvians off!"

At the same moment others took up this cry, the door to the Pacific Mail Office opened, and an older portly gentleman with thick bushy muttonchops stepped out.

Before the man spoke a word, Landry said in a loud but calm voice, "You are an American steamship line. You're supposed to carry American passengers."

The Pacific Mail officer took note of Landry, then scanned the rest of the crowd. The man next to Landry again shouted, "Put the Peruvians off!"

The Pacific Mail officer raised his hands for silence as the crowd roared its agreement. He didn't get silence, but there was a modest quietening. He said, "Those people bought tickets in good faith. We had no way of anticipating—"

"Those ships are for Americans!"

"We had no way of anticipating so many of you would arri—"

"You gonna put 'em off or are we?" asked a belligerent voice from the rear.

"The tickets already honored were bought in good faith!" the officer shouted.

"What the hell were ours bought in? You sold us tickets," a man yelled, waving his tickets frantically over the heads of the others.

"We're Americans, goddammit! We go first!"

"Get the others off the ship—or we get 'em off for you!"

"Quiet!" the Pacific man shouted. "We will solve nothing by screaming threats. You'll all get passage to California . . ." he said, and backed into the building a few steps, muttering, ". . . somehow."

The terrified clerk appeared at the door. With a shaking voice he said, "We will let you know tomorrow what has been decided." As soon as the words were out of his mouth he scuttled back into the office and slammed the door shut.

The following day when no decision was made, the crowd again thronged around the steamship offices. They were angrier than ever, but the night had given them time to let some of the emotion subside, and cooler, more logical thoughts to come forth. They sent a delegation of men into the office. Landry made certain he was among them. It had cost him one of his remaining tickets to a man who had not been able to get enough tickets for his entire family and had expected to have to leave his eldest son in Panama City until another ship came in.

After several more minutes of talk and useless argument, the Pacific Mail officer sent a man out to the *California* to see if he could persuade the Peruvians to give up their berths. The Peruvians would not budge and boasted that the Americans would have to throw them overboard. With tempers what they were, it was not a particularly wise thing to say.

The refusal was reported by the Pacific Mail officer to the Americans. All of them left the office angry and determined to see their tickets honored one way or another. The men at the steamship office were nearly as frantic as those trying to gain passage. No one was quite certain how such a mess had occurred. Looking to any solution, the Pacific Mail chartered the *Philadelphia* to carry some of the people to San Francisco. This idea caused as much bad temper, and as many threats, as the idea of no ship at all. The *Philadelphia* was an American sailing vessel unloading a cargo of coal at Panama City.

"That ship will take at least two times as long as the *California* to get there!"

"We bought passage on the *California!*"

"Our tickets are paid for! Honor them! On the *California!*"

No one was able to pacify the clamoring crowd this time. Finally in disgust and desperation, Captain John Marshall ordered all the Peruvians out of their berths. "You want to remain on this ship, you'll do it on deck!" he growled. Still in foul humor, he returned to the shipping offices and confronted the crowd himself. "There are as many berths aboard the *California* for you now as there would have been if I came in here with an empty ship. I've got a hundred fifty berths, I'll carry one hundred fifty passengers, and not a damned body more!" He clamped his mouth shut on the final word, and shoved his way through the crowd into the town heading for his favorite tavern and his favorite barmaid.

Marshall's speech quieted people down, or perhaps it is better said that he stunned them into silence. There would not be enough space for anywhere near the number of people in Panama City holding tickets. However, Captain John Marshall's voice carried authority, and every man in the street believed that he would not take more than 150 passengers.

The Pacific Mail Steamship Line wrestled with the problem for several more chaotic days. Finally it was announced in which order the tickets would be honored:

"First, Army officers and government envoys.
Second, All tickets purchased in New York.
Third, Those who hold tickets purchased in Panama City. These tickets will be honored in the order in which they were purchased and registered."

There was great celebrating and jubilation among the passengers who had arrived at Chagres aboard the *Falcon* and the *John Benson,* for they had also been among the first to purchase tickets upon arrival in Panama City. Sarah, Jonas and Landry joined hands, dancing in the street. "California on the *California!*" they chanted, dissolving into delighted, breathless laughter.

Those who would not be granted passage were as angry as ever, and the argument between stranded passengers and the steamship lines continued unabated.

Aboard the *California,* Captain John Marshall rued the day he had ever made the agreement to run Captain Cleveland Forbes's ship for him. This voyage had been a headache from stem to stern, and it wasn't over yet. Steamships, like almost all passenger ships, had a peculiar way of counting. They said one hundred passengers, but a child was counted only as a half; therefore one hundred could actually be considerably more than one would expect. Captain Marshall began preparations for his "funny" one hundred passengers immediately. The *California* had a crew of thirty-six, and all hands were put to work putting up bunks in the hold, where the baggage was normally carried.

Captain Forbes stayed hidden in his cabin as much as possible. Order was a thing of the past on his vessel, and the very sight of his crew threading their way through the hundred Peruvians spread out all over the deck, and hauling lumber to remake his hold, made him feel even worse than his fever did. When the ship was finally ready, there was not a single sanguine temper left on board or in the city of Panama. No one was happy.

As was expected, on January 30, 1849, a great scrambling rush took place among the passengers when it was time to board. A stampede of cattle might have looked like a regimental march in comparison. Men, women and squalling children pushed, shoved and trampled each other, bruising those before and behind with swaying, ungainly luggage. The Pacific Mail agents hurried down to the shore, hoping to restore some kind of order. They succeeded only in rousing the wrath of everyone once again.

An announcement was made. "The *California* will carry no baggage!"

A uniform howl of rage rang out. "The price of a ticket includes the transportation of luggage!"

"Every damn man who gets squeezed aboard means revenue for you! You're bleedin' us for your own profit!"

"Right! Luggage don't mean money!"

"The *California* will not carry baggage!" the angry agent rasped. "You don't want to leave it behind, then give up your ticket to a man who will!"

The passengers boarded the vessel with confusion rampant. Because no one was willing to accept the idea of being left behind, many people whose tickets should not have been honored crowded in among those who were scheduled to board, and Landry Morrison bribed a seaman to stow his baggage. The passengers moved, a great teeming mass of humanity, overwhelming in vehemence and size. None of the ship's officers or agents had time to count those boarding, or to pay much attention to the tickets hastily thrust under their noses. Even if a man had wished to take his time in boarding it was impossible, for the surge of those behind him thrust him along.

By the time the *California* steamed out of Panama harbor heading north toward California, estimates of passengers aboard ranged from 300 to 500 people. The fact that a man had a berth was more joke than fact. There was barely enough room to turn around on the deck without maiming a fellow passenger, let alone room enough to make true use of a berth. But even these evil-tempered passengers who steamed away from Panama on that morning registered a kind of triumphant joy. At least they were not the ones who had to take the slower *Philadelphia*, or to have been left behind entirely to await the second steamer of the Pacific Mail Line. They were on their crowded way to California and *gold!*

In all ways it was a disagreeable voyage. Those who had the quickly constructed bunks slept in an airless hold. Others, like the Peruvians, found any place they could to sleep. Some slept in the open on coils of rope. Landry and the Walker family slept on the dining table in the galley. Hammocks hung from the rigging. Makeshift sleeping contraptions were likely to be found anywhere a man had been able to claim a few inches in which to tie a rope and a piece of sheeting. Food was in short supply, but in spite of all the hardships most of the people's health actually improved once they had left the steamy tropics. Impatience and shortness of temper were the worst dangers they faced. Every man, woman and child aboard was over-anxious to reach San Francisco, and daily their eyes scanned the ocean as if they expected California to simply appear. Actually the voyage was a distance of 3,245 nautical miles. It was not only going to be an unpleasant voyage, it was also a long one.

After what seemed like an unendurably long time, the *California* put into Monterey on February 22, 1849. From the moment the big ship steamed into the harbor, spirits of the passengers began to rise until they had reached a fever pitch. The army personnel were to go ashore there, and the *California* remained in harbor for four days. The docks were jammed with people who had come to greet the vessel. As the passengers disembarked for their first real experience of California life, they were greeted with a population that spent most of its time bored with governmental paper work. What was left of the population of Monterey consisted mostly of army men who could not leave their posts for richer grounds, and government personnel who were responsible to higher authorities back east. The inhabitants of Monterey were ecstatic to have new people in their midst.

The other thing the passengers of the *California* quickly learned was that nothing was cheap in California. As soon as the gold rush had started, prices skyrocketed. The third thing they learned was that impulse was the order of the day. Landry and the Walkers were present when Mrs. Persifor Smith blustered that her maid had eloped to the gold fields. "She only met him day before yesterday!" cried the stunned woman. "Whatever will happen to her?"

"She'll probably become wealthy," Landry said with a chuckle.

Mrs. Smith began to protest, then burst out giggling. Life was going to be unpredictable in California.

Thirteen

Susannah Morrison Gentry awakened quickly the morning of February 28, 1849, as she did most mornings. But as was also her habit, she didn't arise. She took these first few minutes of the morning to luxuriate in contemplation of the pleasures of her present life. In her earlier, more religious days, she would have said she was counting her blessings. To her right her husband of almost seven months rested, still in the embrace of the last minutes of morning sleep. His hand was resting on the gentle but growing mound of their first child. She put her left hand over his, sensing the life of the child under Cameron's hand, and her own and Cameron's life under her own hand. It was a deeply thrilling sensation.

With a long sigh of satisfaction she recognized that there was no part of her life that wasn't deeply thrilling right now. She had a home she loved, was married to the man she loved, was about to have her first child, and was the proprietor of her own very successful shop. And every day she was delighted, stimulated, thoroughly engaged in the energetic, changeable pace of San Francisco. Never did boredom enter a day, for something was always happening, something was always being built. And today was no different.

San Franciscans had been watching the bay and the Pacific for days, awaiting the arrival of the steamship *California*, the first steamship to travel at such speeds from New York around the Cape to California. It would mark a great day. From now on the travel time from New York to California would be negligible. How well Susannah understood the meaning of that! How well she remembered the endless months she and the other Saints had spent at sea, wondering if they would ever land in California. But that appallingly slow means of travel would no longer be necessary with the arrival of the *California*. Mail, goods, people would be carried back and forth from one shore of this vast country to the other with speed and convenience. Like all other San Franciscans, she and Cameron planned to be there when the ship dropped anchor in the bay.

Now, realizing she had used all the luxurious moments of appreciation she could afford, she leaned over and kissed Cameron to wakefulness. "We'll have to hurry," she said softly, "if we're to be there when the *California* comes in. Already I can hear people in the streets."

Cameron's hand moved from the mound of her belly up to her breast. He smiled with proprietory smugness. "We could stay here," he murmured, his mind already far away from steamships and days of celebration. What was one more event in a city that lived in a constant state of celebration?

Playfully Susannah smacked his hand and pushed his head away from her bosom. "Don't you dare make me miss this! Everyone is going to be there, and I am not going to be left out! We'd be missed."

Cameron gave in without an undue amount of urging, but he insisted upon using the carriage in deference to Susannah's delicate condition. She protested, "But we won't be able to get close enough to see anything!" Her words fell on deaf ears.

Cameron pulled the carriage into the crowd of milling people, getting as near to the activity as he dared. They arrived just in time. Most of the townspeople were already crowded on the road and all the way down to where the water lapped at the shore. Flags were being waved frantically as though their owners were trying to be the first recognized. Those who didn't have flags waved newspapers, scarves, neckerchiefs, or anything else handy. In the bay the commodore's flagship and five other ships had taken position. Then in the misty distance Susannah could just make out the indistinct shape of the *California* entering the Golden Gate. As she passed through fully entering the bay, the six ships fired salutes in her honor. The hazy morning cracked with the noise of the big guns, and their smoke hung heavy in the fog-thick air.

Proudly the *California* steamed into San Francisco Bay, her rails cluttered with her passengers as eager for their first look at San Francisco as the San Franciscans were eager for the arrival of the great ship bringing them new blood. Lighters dotted the surface of the water, and one by one the small ships brought passengers and their scanty luggage from the steamer to the shore. The passengers, much the worse for their difficult time in Panama City, straggled ashore to the accompaniment of horns tooting, people cheering, hooting and laughing. San Francisco was in a greater state of excitement than Monterey had been, and it was not bogged down by the boredom of bureaucracy. San Francisco was alive and vital. Every man, woman, and child it seemed came down to the dock or the beach. The *California* was the very first steamship ever to enter San Francisco Bay, and she was bringing with her the very first men from the United States to come to California to hunt for gold.

Both Captain Marshall and Captain Forbes were on the bridge as the *California* steamed through the Golden Gate into the bay. The commodore's flagship and five other ships in the bay fired salutes as the *California* steamed past. It was a glorious day, and even Captain Forbes couldn't help smiling. He turned to John Marshall and the two men shook hands, then as their eyes locked, they embraced like two strange bears bumping chests, and quickly parted to stare hard and seriously at the cheering crowd on the docks.

The passengers, or as many as were able, were on deck, rapidly becoming infected with the sheer joy of the San Franciscans. As a whole the passengers were a haggard, poorly looking bunch, battered, some bruised, tattered, tired and mostly hungry, but on every face there was a glow of triumph and victory. Gamblers, clergymen, opportunists, laborers, courtesans, mothers holding children, businessmen and revenge-seeking sons straggled off the *California* to be welcomed to the wildest, wooliest, richest place in the world—San Francisco, California!

This was California, and these were the Forty-Niners.

"Oh, I'm glad we came," Susannah said, clapping her hands in applause for a bedraggled bunch of strangers.

Cameron smiled as he put his arm around her and gave her an affectionate squeeze. There was a part of Susannah that would always be a child prepared to enter fully into the simpler delights of life. This knowledge gave comfort to his too-adult soul.

Just as he was sitting back, getting fully into this musing, philosophical mood, Susannah sat up straight, gave out a strangled exclamation of surprise, then fell back against the seat shaking.

"What is it? What happened? Are you all right? Is it the baby?" he asked in rapid succession, his hands anxiously checking her well-being.

Susannah waved him away with a dainty white-gloved hand. "I don't know what happened—I guess pregnant women are subject to strange thoughts—and illusions," she said, and laughed self-consciously. Cameron was still looking at her with worry and more than a little curiosity, so she added, "It was nothing. One of the men walking up from the lighter . . . he looked like . . . I thought for a moment he was my brother. . . ." She shrugged, blushing prettily. "I told you it was silly . . . nothing. It couldn't have been Landry."

But it had been he. Landry Morrison, disheveled and irritated at all the delays and illnesses and worries of this trip, put his foot on California soil to the cacophony of hundreds of excited voices. His first thought was that these were a strange and very excessive people. Then he smiled. He was in Susannah's city. He seldom thought of this place as San Francisco. It was mostly Susannah's city. He wondered how difficult it would be to find his sister. He could always ask his father, but he wouldn't. There was only one thing he wanted to do to his father, and that certainly wasn't to ask a favor, however small.

He glanced around the mob, searching for someone he could hire to carry his luggage and lead him to a decent hotel. His attention was momentarily caught by the expensive, shiny black, English-made carriage near the rear of the crowd. Fleetingly he wondered to whom it belonged, and who, in this outpost of civilization, would have the wherewithal or the taste to own such a vehicle. Then he forgot all about it, and called to a young Mexican boy to carry his luggage.

"Hurry up, Chico! I want a good room, and from the looks of this place there aren't many to be had," he snapped, anxiously watching all those who were getting ahead of him on their way to the town proper. Giving the young man a swat on his rear, Landry set off at a rapid pace, expecting the overloaded youngster to keep up with him. Quickly he gained on and passed his fellow passengers, who perhaps did not realize as he did that San Francisco was not likely to have an overabundance of living accommodations. He had learned little in Panama City, but the one thing it had taught him was to be certain he had decent lodgings in a western town.

The boy led Landry first to the Parker House on Portsmouth Square, an imposing structure for San Francisco standards, boasting sixty feet of road frontage. Finding that filled, the boy hurried Landry across the Square to the City Hotel, where he secured a room for twenty-five dollars per week. He then agreed to pay an additional twenty dollars per week for board. Quickly absorbing the shock of the high prices he was going to encounter in Susannah's city, he turned to the boy. "I suppose you think your time is worth a ridiculous amount of money as well," he said brusquely. He added, hoping to cow the boy, "I'll give you what *I* think you're worth."

"Two dollars," the boy said firmly, his small grimy hand out.

Ungraciously Landry slapped coins into the boy's palm, then turned to the hotel clerk. "There damned well better be gold in your hills, otherwise a man can't survive here."

"Oh, it's there," the clerk said genially. "It all depends on how good a nose you've got and how strong a back."

Landry gave a short, sharp snort of a laugh. "I'm American, aren't I?"

Soon after his arrival Landry realized that his expectations of California were not entirely accurate. He had incorrectly assumed that he would need the friendship and support of his traveling companion Jonas Walker. Now that he had been in

San Francisco only a few hours, he understood that this strange place with its oddly energetic people was a place for loners. He did not need Jonas Walker, nor anyone else. He was sufficient unto himself—or would be as soon as he gathered a bit more knowledge. For the next three days he continued his friendship with Walker, gleaning from the man every scrap of information about gold that he might find useful. But when it came time for the engineer Walker to extend an invitation to Landry, Landry was prepared to refuse without fear for his own security.

Walker thought only in terms of a company, and he offered generously, "I'd like to have you as a member of my team, Morrison. We'll set up on the Yuba. I've got it on the best authority that the gold is pure there—of high quality. We can both benefit from the association."

Landry smiled, saying, "No thanks, Jonas. From what I've heard it sounds like the Middle Fork, or perhaps North Fork is more to my liking. I might even try the Feather River." He laughed at himself then, adding, "Actually it will depend on transportation. I am going to have to find a way to get anywhere —I'm no hand with mules."

"All the more reason to hire on with my crew," Walker pressed.

Landry shook his head. "Sorry, Jonas. I learned a long time ago that I am not much of a company man. You'd just get mad at me when I questioned your authority and eventually fire me. Sooner or later I'd be on my own anyway. That's the way life goes."

Walker began to protest, but changed his mind and put his hand out for Landry to shake. "I know you are making a joke of this to spare my feelings, but I want you to know that I'd really value you as part of my team. We need good men."

Landry looked at this man he had once cultivated thinking it would be to his advantage. Now he felt little friendship, and certainly recognized no use Walker could be to him, so he shook his hand and parted company, with Walker still believing in a friendship that had never really existed.

After leaving Jonas Walker, Landry returned to his hotel room, dressed in his finest New York suit, and set out to find Susannah. It took him several days. It seemed that few people in

San Francisco knew anything about a Susannah Morrison. He had met two Mormons, both of whom claimed that Susannah had come to a bad end. One said flatly that she was dead, the other wasn't as certain of her fate, but was sure she no longer lived there. Landry had believed neither of them, but still he found no information. Finally he began to haunt the saloons and gambling houses, asking every man he met at a faro table if he knew of a woman fitting Susannah's description. With only her description given, he met with greater success. By the time he heard the third reply that it sounded like he was talking about Cameron Gentry's wife, he was convinced Mrs. Gentry was his sister. Soon after that he learned that the attractive Mrs. Gentry ran a very exclusive, very expensive women's shop on Montgomery Street not too far distant from her home.

Five days after his arrival in San Francisco Landry visited the shop. For a moment he stood outside looking at the gold leaf script on the large showy glass window of the shop. "Gentry's Fine Apparel for Discriminating Ladies." Under that in small upright lettering it said, "Prop. S.M. Gentry." Certain now that this was his sister's shop, he stepped inside, and immediately felt like an alien. Heady French perfume permeated the air. For a town that complained of a very small female population, there was a large number of women examining the gowns, hats and jewelry. Susannah must draw every woman around to her shop. Landry's eyes flicked over each of the women in the room, but none of them was Susannah. He was about to conclude that he had been wrong, and this whole excursion into the female domain had been an error, when he heard her voice.

Breezily Susannah flipped aside a heavy, ornate brocade curtain that divided the front of the shop from her storage area and fitting rooms. On her arm she carried an elegant black silk gown. Behind her came Ann Eliza Brannan, talking in rapid staccato as she gave last-minute alteration instructions. Susannah's smile was bright and her voice cheerful as she answered Sam's wife, but she was annoyed, for Ann Eliza always insisted on telling Susannah what an expert seamstress she herself was, as if she didn't really expect Susannah would be able to come up to her standards. One of these days, Susannah vowed, she'd tell the haughty Mrs. Brannan to take her business elsewhere, or sew her own clothes!

Landry stood near the door, shielded from view by two dresses on display, watching the little scene unfold. His sister was just as sprightly and sure of herself as ever! A warm feeling of a nature he had not known for a long time crept over him. Of all his family, actually of all the people he knew, only Susannah did he trust or love. She looked happy and well—and pregnant! A smile of pleasure lit his face once again, and for a moment he regained that handsome, blameless look of sweetness that had marked him as a young man, before all the trouble came to rob him of innocence and vulnerability.

Shortly after this the women began to leave, for they knew that it was Susannah's practice to close her shop from one to three in the afternoon. Susannah moved toward the door with the last customer to leave. Only after she had shut the door and put the "closed" sign in place did Landry step out of his hiding place. Susannah cried out in startlement. Then her eyes grew big, and her face paled. She tried to smile and mouth his name, but her eyes rolled into her head, and she slumped into a swirling darkness.

Landry caught her and carried her back through the brocade curtain. In the back room he laid her on a chaise, and began to rummage in her desk and on the shelves against the wall, hunting for smelling salts. Finding them, he ran the pungent smelling bottle under her nose, and began to chafe her wrists.

Susannah recovered with a jolt and a quick memory of Landry's face. Laughing, crying, she sat up, assured herself it was really he, then threw her arms around her brother's neck, kissing his cheeks and eyes. "You came! Why didn't you tell me? When did you get here?"

The brother and sister talked for a long while, with Susannah scolding him royally for not telling her when he would arrive. "Cameron and I were at the wharf when the *California* dropped anchor! I even thought I saw you, and was forced to doubt my own eyes! I thought it was wishful thinking."

Landry laughed. "You couldn't possibly have been sitting in an elegant English-made carriage?"

"Yes! Yes, we were! You mean you saw us too, and didn't

recognize me? Oh, Landry, how many days have we wasted while you searched for me? Well, no sense in worrying about that now—you must leave the hotel and come stay with Cameron and me. Oh, and I'll have Papa and Mama over for dinner one evening, and—" She stopped, her hand over her mouth. She had been going to say "and Tollie"—Landry's wife, who was now her own father's unwanted wife.

Landry's eyes revealed that he had followed the path of her thoughts.

Embarrassed, she said, "I'm sorry, Landry—forgive me. That was cruel and thoughtless of me."

Landry shook his head. "It was bound to happen. We could hardly go on forever without Tollie coming into the conversation. But you must realize Susannah, that I have no intention of seeing Papa—at least not until it suits my purposes. And there will be no grand reconciliation. As long as I live I'll never forgive Papa. And if I'm able, I'll damn him from hell after I die."

"Landry!" Susannah cried, truly shocked at his vehemence. "You can't mean that! Papa did what he thought was God's will —now he knows that he was wrong. He finally understands that —and he'll take you back. I know he will. He pines for you!"

"But my dear little sister, I will not take *him* back. What is done cannot be undone."

"But Landry—"

"No, Susannah! This is a subject we dare not talk about any more. Please—if you persist, I will have to leave and not see you either, and I do not want that to happen. You're all I have left. I don't want to lose you too."

Tears came to Susannah's eyes. "Now it is you who are being cruel. You have no idea how much I risked—how much I lost— to bring you here so you and Papa could be reunited."

"You of all people should have known that that could never be."

"Well, I didn't—and I still don't. I won't accept that. What of Elisha—and Tolerance? Will you not see them either? Elisha is your son—"

His son. So he had a son. Landry's eyes had a faraway look, cold, hard, and angry. Only his words were mild. "I'll see them —in my own time." Then he smiled, and looked fully at Susannah. "I'd like to meet your husband. I've been told he's quite an important man hereabouts—and a good man."

Even though her brother disturbed her, Susannah couldn't help smiling at the mention of Cameron. "Yes, he is. I'm sure you'll like him—and you two will become friends." Suddenly, however, she was less sure of her words, and less sure of this brother to whom she had always been so close. "You will stay with us, won't you?"

He took her hands in his, and leaned forward to kiss her on the forehead as he said, "No. I will not stay with you, but I do want to meet Cameron, and spend what time I can with you. We have a great deal of catching up to do. But my plan is to take some of this gold I've been hearing about out of these California hills."

"You won't even be in San Francisco!" Susannah wailed.

"Ahh, Susannah, would you keep me here as though we were still children? It's time for us to be apart. Don't regret something that shouldn't be regretted. We will have our times together. We have this time."

Susannah put her head on his shoulder. "Nothing is the way I dreamed it would be, Landry. I feel as though I'm losing you all over again, and again this time I can do nothing about it."

For a moment Landry felt a choking sadness. "It is best, Susannah. Otherwise you might have discovered that you wouldn't want us to be together."

She looked up at him and took his face between her hands. "Never! No matter what, Landry, I could never wish to lose you."

Landry hid his face from her, but he was more grateful than she'd ever know. It was only Susannah who preserved a part of himself that was lost to him forever.

Cameron greeted his brother-in-law with mixed emotions. He had heard a great deal about Landry from Susannah, and was well aware how deeply she cared for her brother. Hadn't he had to rescue her from the consequences of her bold, dangerous plan to get the money to bring Landry to California? He could see in Landry the traces of the sweet and vulnerable young man whom Susannah had described, but he saw much more as well. There was a hardness over the old vulnerability, and a sly shrewdness Cameron didn't trust. He'd welcome Landry into his home for Susannah's sake, but he'd be glad when Landry left for the gold diggings.

One evening early in March, Landry and Brian Campbell were both dinner guests at the Gentrys' home. Brian had brought news to Cameron from Robin and Fiona, and another shipment of gold. Brian laughed, saying to Landry, "You can't beat this combination of the Gentry brothers. They make quite a team. One is systematically cleaning the hills of gold, and the other one waits in town to receive the gold and make more gold from it."

"You invest your brother's money?" Landry asked Cameron.

"Occasionally," Cameron answered cautiously. "Robin is and always has been his own man, but from time to time he asks me to handle certain of his investments. Mostly those he has here in San Francisco and the ones in Sacramento."

"I feel like the poor relation," Landry said. "I was feeling quite the well-to-do man when I left New York, but I'm nearly a pauper out here! I'd better get to the diggings quickly just so I can keep up!"

Brian listened quietly as Landry and Cameron continued to talk on a more serious level about Landry's plans. When the conversation petered out, he offered, "I'm heading up north day after tomorrow with supplies for the camps, Landry. You are welcome to ride with me if that suits you."

"Where are you heading?" Landry asked, then added, "And how much will it cost me?"

Brian chuckled, exchanging glances with Cameron. "Normally I'd rob a man of about sixty dollars to take him up to the camps, but seeing as how you're family, I'll settle for some pleasant company and a few wild stories about life in the East. As to where I'm going—that's a little more difficult to answer. I will be stopping at Spanish Bar, Big Bar, probably swing a ways up the Yuba, then on to Middle Fork and perhaps North Fork. Most likely, though, I won't get any farther than Fiona's and Robin's camp on the Middle Fork. I rarely do—those folks up there clean me out of supplies as fast as I can bring them. And what others don't take, Fiona does. She's a regular little money-making machine. The girl's got a nose for gold, and now she's decided she and Robin should keep extra supplies in their cabin and sell them to people passing through."

"You really miss them, don't you, Brian?" Susannah said.

He didn't say anything for a moment. It wasn't often that someone realized just how much he did miss the closeness he had shared with Robin and Fiona. He said quickly, "Yes, I do. I will be glad to spend a week or so with them. You know Fiona is expecting their first child."

Susannah smiled softly, thinking of her own child, thinking that the two babies, who would be so close in age, would be first cousins.

Before the conversation veered again, Landry brought the attention back to himself. "I'm eager to meet this brother of yours, Cameron. Unless I miss my guess, I won't find anyone better equipped to teach a greenhorn like me where to dig for gold in those first days."

Brian made arrangements to meet Landry early the next morning. Under Brian's direction, Landry learned the uses of various types of digging equipment and purchased the items he wanted for himself. By ten o'clock Landry had bought everything he would need and had parted with Brian, agreeing to be ready to leave from in front of the City Hotel at six o'clock the following morning to go to the gold camps.

With the rest of the day free, Landry set out to do the one remaining thing he wanted to do before he left the city. As he had tracked down Susannah's whereabouts, so had he done with Tollie. Many times after that he had followed her, taking note of her destinations. He had also understood quickly that she had changed as much as he had. There was about her a restive inquietude. Whatever his father had done, it was certain that he had not been able to satisfy Tolerance Morrison. She had the haunted, hungry look of a bored woman.

Twice in the five days he had followed her, however, she had entered a building and remained there a good portion of the afternoon. He had checked out all the stores and offices and the other exits, and assured himself that she had used none of these. All that was left was the apartment of one Samuel Brannan. Landry had made it his business to discover that Sam Brannan was a wealthy speculator, either loved or hated by his fellow citizens, and incidentally the First Elder of the Church of Latter-Day Saints of San Francisco. This last gave Landry a bitter amusement. At least in this the Mormon bishop's daughter had not changed. Tolerance had always sought to be close to the men of God.

The last convenient fact he had ascertained about Tollie's patterns was that she nearly always stopped at the newsstand right at the City Hotel to purchase a paper. On all the other occasions on which he had seen her, he had been content to remain out of sight and merely watch her, but today as she approached the newsstand, he stepped out of the hotel doorway and into her path.

Tollie halted her steps, and without looking up said, "Excuse me, sir, you're barring my way."

Landry said, with teasing laughter in his voice, "Is that any way to greet your long-lost husband, madam?"

Even before she looked at his face, Tollie knew, and her heart leapt. "Landry . . ." she whispered. "Oh, Landry . . ." Her eyes, her entire face softened with pent-up longing for him. Automatically her arms reached for him, but Landry turned away, looking around elaborately as though fearing detection.

He said, with the wistful little smile that he knew melted women's hearts, "I have missed you, Tollie."

"And I you. You can't imagine, Landry . . ."

"Well, I have some idea," he said briskly. "How have you fared as my father's wife?" He concealed the anger in his heart, and showed her only a tender concern.

Tears came to her eyes. "I—I made a dreadful mistake. When he asked me to marry him, I was in such turmoil—from your being excommunicated, you know, and Bishop Waterman divorcing us, and the baby coming—that I could not even plan. All I could do was pray—oh, Landry, I must talk with you, isn't there some place we can go and be private?"

He said softly, "Perhaps you know of some place, sweetheart. I've only just arrived here."

"I can't take you home, that much is certain. Could we go to your—have you found a place to stay yet?"

"Well . . ." he said hesitantly, "I have a room. It's not much, but—"

She said eagerly, "Let's go there. We can't stand here on the street, there's so much I need to tell you."

"Don't you think it might damage your reputation, if you were to go to a hotel room with a stranger?"

"Does it matter?" she asked dully.

"Of course it matters! I still care about what people say about you."

She smiled at him. "Well, this once I won't give it a thought."

"Then neither will I." He offered her his arm, which she took and squeezed, and they went to his hotel room. He had gotten the finest that the City had to offer, and she exclaimed over its appointments while Landry stood watching her with a little smile on his lips.

When she seemed to have run down, he took her hand in his and brought it to his lips. Then gently, finger by finger, he removed her glove, and kissed her hand again. His eyes never left hers. He saw with increased bitterness her love and longing for him. He sighed, and released her hand. "But I should not be thinking the thoughts I have," he said, and strolled to look out the window. Quite as he expected, he heard her footsteps follow him, felt her arms come around him.

"Oh, Landry, hold me," she begged. "Kiss me and tell me you forgive me. I have hardly been able to live with myself these past two and a half years—"

He did not turn around. "You are looking quite well, and prosperous," he pointed out. "So evidently Papa is providing for you sufficiently."

"There is more to life than clothing," she said. "I would rather be naked and be with you than—" She stopped, aware that she had said far too much.

He turned toward her at last. "You always did look good in the natural state." His smile was genuine, his eyes shining, the color in his face heightened. "I have thought of that often since I saw you last."

She leaned forward and nestled her head on his shoulder. She shuddered. "You cannot imagine how it is to be married to an old man!" Thus Tolerance at eighteen saw Ezra Morrison at age forty-four.

Landry felt his anger stiffen him, but he made his voice kind. "I'd rather not know, sweetheart. Please—let's not talk of him."

She went on, as though her mind were so full that she had to unleash some of her thoughts or burst, "He is so—so *soft!* His hands, his body—everything!" Landry felt a fierce surge of righteous gladness, for he knew that his own body . . . everything . . . was rock-hard and fit. "I am so glad he—he does not approach me anymore!"

"It must be very lonely for you without—companionship."

"Oh, I have friends—a few," she added hastily.

His voice was so tender, so persuasive. "A lover, perhaps?"

"Well, I—" Quickly she caught herself, thinking of Sam Brannan and their sweet afternoon trysts. She said, "I have no one. Oh Landry, my darling—are you ever going to kiss me? Ever forgive me?" Her eyes, filled with tears, sought his.

He touched her lips with his, and when she showed signs of responding, withdrew from her. He said, "There is nothing to forgive, Tollie."

"But you are holding back from me!" she said frantically. "You have not forgiven me! Landry, please! Please—say that you understand! Say that you love me still!"

"I do understand," he assured her. "And I have always loved you." With a sick lurch of his stomach, he knew that this, at least, had some truth in it. Which was one of his reasons for bringing her to this room.

"Thank you." She sighed. "Now kiss me as if you mean that."

He bent his head, and kissed her long, and ever more deeply. Her hands, which had been on his shoulders, moved slowly down his back, to his waist, and slowly around to the front of his trousers. He could feel his excitement growing, his heart pounding with anticipation. But he pulled back from her slightly, looking regretfully into her eyes. "We must not do this, you know."

"Do what?" she asked, smiling sensuously at him.

"You are my father's wife," he reminded her. "Sealed to him

for eternity. Think what punishment will be ours if we violate that promise."

She said tartly, "I didn't suppose you still held such reverence for the Church."

"I was thinking of you," he said, hurt.

"Let *me* think of me. Just kiss me, and hold me—and let us love each other."

He looked at her for a long moment, with that slow sweet smile on his face. "Don't you think you should remove your other glove?"

She laughed, and threw her arms around him. With her mouth on his, kissing him and teasing him, she said, "Landry, Landry, how I have missed your teasing!"

"And I yours," he replied with a different meaning. "You are still as beautiful as you were when we married."

"So are you," she whispered. Her hands sought the buttons on his vest, and undid them. Expertly she removed his coat and vest, and then she began on his trousers.

"Shouldn't you remove something?" he whispered lazily. "There are a lot of interferences . . ."

She jerked on the front of her dress, and he could hear snaps popping. He watched with wry amusement as she took off everything she wore, and stood naked before him. Just as she straightened up from the last garment, he grabbed his coat and headed for the door. "I must go now," he said. "I just remembered an appointment."

"Landry!" she cried, in panic, running after him. "You can't leave now!"

He allowed her to persuade him to return to the room. Her arms were warm around his neck, her lips left little buds of kisses on his face. He yielded at last, allowing her to take off his clothing. By this time they lay on the bed. He had never been so ready to take a woman in his life. Yet he prolonged the moment, for his own satisfaction, for his own revenge. To the very last minute he pretended cool indifference, even Christian reluctance. What they did was all Tollie's doing, all on Tollie's head. He was simply servicing her.

He had intended to heap the ultimate insult on her, to climax before her and then be unable to satisfy her. But in this he reckoned without Tollie's mad desires. He had barely entered her when he heard her little moans and felt the hard spasms of her satisfaction. Remembering well her capacity for long climaxes, he stopped his motion and said to her, "At least *you* are getting some pleasure from this."

"Don't stop," she said frantically, "go on, oh please go on."

In a desultory way he continued, out of rhythm with her, destroying her enjoyment while heightening his own. When he sensed that she no longer wanted him in her, then he thrust hard and cruelly until he found his own satisfaction. As soon as it was comfortable for him to do so, he let himself slip out of her, apologizing in such a way as to throw blame on her.

Tollie by this time was crying. "I'm sorry," she kept saying "I couldn't help it—Landry, please come back into me, let me make it right."

Pity he hadn't any clothes on, he'd have enjoyed checking his watch. He kissed her and whispered, "I have to go, Tollie—I've got an appointment with Samuel Brannan, and I'm late already."

He took pleasure in the expression on her face—astonishment, fear, disbelief—but most of all the fear. Then, recovering herself, she said, "You'll come back, won't you? I can meet you again, can't I?"

He was up off her, starting to put on his clothing. "Not tonight, sweetheart—Mr. Brannan said something about dinner and the gaming tables. I expect we'll make rather a long night of it."

She scrambled up from the bed and began to dress too. But her clothing was more elaborate than his, she needed more time. He was fully clad when she was still struggling with her petticoat strings. He reached over and cupped her breast in his hand, and kissed her gently. "I'll be here all day tomorrow, Tollie," he said softly, meaningfully. "If you'd come at eight in the morning, we could have more time together."

She stopped what she was doing and flung her arms around him. Something was still strange between them, but they could get it all ironed out tomorrow. She whispered, "And we'll make things right for each other. I promise."

He smiled lovingly at her. "Nothing was wrong this time—

nothing that a little practice won't fix. See you at eight tomorrow?"

"Oh, yes!" Then she panicked again. "You're not leaving without me?"

"I must," he assured her. "I can't keep an important man waiting."

Her eyes searched his face, but his bland expression told her nothing. "Tomorrow then, at eight."

He kissed her hand, gazing smiling at her. "Tomorrow." Then he was gone, quietly closing the door behind him.

Tollie looked around the room, remembering all they had done there, feeling again the thrill of satisfaction, living his kisses all over again. Yet something was wrong, something was missing.

She shrugged, stepping into her stylish brown silk dress. They had been apart for over two years. They could hardly be expected to get it right the first time. Well, they had tomorrow, and tomorrow—

She gasped. She had not even told him of Elisha. Landry didn't even know they had a son. Then she smiled with pleasure. Tomorrow. . . .

Fourteen

*L*andry and Brian were on their way soon after six the following morning. Landry, smiling a little to himself, wondered what Tollie would think when she discovered him gone. He would have liked to see her face.

The two men arrived at the winter cabin on March 11, 1849. Robin and Fiona had been able to hear for some time the laborious progress of the team and the wagon. The steep, crazy hills of Middle Fork were covered with a thick volcanic dust which during the rainy season and the thaw time became a thick, pasty black mud that sucked at the mules' hooves, pulling the animals down into the goo up to their fetlocks. The wagon became more and more difficult to move as the wheels mired heavily, growing to three times their normal size with the thick mud stuck to them. The two men struggled for footing as they walked alongside the animals, urging them upward and around the outcroppings of rock. Both Brian and Landry were covered with mud, wet through, and as tired as men could be when they finally managed to bring the wagon over the last ridge of rock and into the valley. Brian was too hard-pressed and tired even to smile when he saw Robin and Fiona come out of the cabin in greeting.

As they neared the cabin, Fiona put her arms out in welcome.

"Come inside," she said, immediately recognizing their exhaustion and choosing to ignore the usual amenities, and the fact that one of these men was a stranger. "Robin will see to the mules while you two dry off and get something warm to drink."

Her easy, hospitable practicality reminded Landry of other times and other days when his own family might have extended such a welcome to a stranger in distress. Then the Morrisons had been secure in their love for each other and in their faith. That was long ago, and since then Landry had learned how fleeting love and faith could be. He knew better now than to trust either, and pitied those poor fools who did so place their trust. He followed Fiona into her house. But there was no trust between him and this generous, no-nonsense woman, for he would not give it.

Both men took their travel bags from the wagon before Robin moved it to the lean-to behind his cabin. Fiona showed them to the small room that had been partitioned off from the main room and served as her and Robin's bedroom. She handed Brian a basin and a pitcher of water. "It won't do as well as a good soak, but at least you can get some of that mud off you."

When Brian, finishing first, came out of the room, Fiona was ready with a cup of hot herb tea. "Drink this, you'll begin to feel better in no time."

Brian smiled, patting her shoulder in great affection. Taking the cup from her, he drank deeply. With a sigh he said, "One thing these mountains teach you hard and fast is how pleasurable a dry shirt and a hot drink can be. This has been the worst journey I've made in a long time. The rivers—" He turned as Landry came forward. "Fiona, this is Landry Morrison. He's come to try his hand at the diggings."

"You're . . . Morrison . . . surely not Susannah's brother from New York?" Fiona asked, as she prepared a cup of tea for him.

"Surely I am," Landry said, with an engaging twinkle in his eye. He looked Fiona up and down in a cautious way that would not offend. He noted her pregnancy, and imagined what she had looked like before her figure had been distorted. Fiona Gentry was a beautiful woman, and Landry smiled, confident that she, like most beautiful women, would take to his particular kind of attention. Here, he was sure, he would have an ally.

He watched her move about her small house, and listened to the easy, pleasant chatter she kept up with Brian. He quickly concluded that in addition to being a beauty, she had no business being hidden out here in the mountains. She must hate living here with the mountains all around, the rivers hurtling past her door, and a sea of black muck that threatened everything.

His musings were just beginning to gain wing when Robin burst through the door. Finished with his task of seeing to the mules and putting the wagon under cover, he slammed the door shut behind him and headed straight for the fire, his hand extended. "It's raw out there!"

Fiona came to stand near her husband. "Robin, this is Landry Morrison, Susannah's brother."

Robin smiled broadly and stretched out his hand. "Well, then, Landry, that makes you a family member—a brother-in-law of sorts."

Landry's hand was swallowed up in Robin's. Cameron and Robin looked very much alike in features and general size, but that was where the similarity ended. This man was used to hard physical labor, and had the heavy, well-developed musculature that went with it. Robin's eyes were bolder, and there was an air of daring about him that Landry had not sensed in Cameron. Brian had been right, however—the Gentry brothers were forces to be reckoned with. Whatever qualities one brother had not developed, the other had. Landry graciously accepted the appellation "brother-in-law of sorts," knowing the man could give him invaluable information and direction if he chose. Landry always allowed the other man to name the terms of friendship; it always made it so much simpler to know how best to use him.

For the rest of that day the four of them sat around the cheery fire in Fiona's house talking, eating and drinking sparingly of the New England rum Brian had brought with him. The men were so engrossed in talk about new gold finds and the large number of new miners in the mountains that neither Brian nor Robin noticed that Fiona was very quiet. Landry, however, did notice. At first he took this as confirmation of his judgment that Fiona wasn't happy there, that she would prefer the city and the beautiful clothing and the entertainments and shopping the city could provide, as Susannah and Tolerance preferred. Fiona was most likely a naturally reserved woman, and a patient one, who was waiting for her husband to come to his senses and take her back where she belonged. He smiled at her, mildly flirtatious, but mostly to let her know he understood her plight.

Perplexed, because he hadn't been able to read her response, he paid more attention to what the men had been saying and less to Fiona. Soon after he had put her from his mind, he had the uncomfortable feeling of being watched, and too often he would look up to see Fiona's strange green eyes turned to him, probing him, examining him as though he were a piece of suspect meat.

With a sense of shock that ran deep in him, he realized that he had badly misread Fiona Gentry. She was not normally a quiet little mouse of a woman. It was his presence that was making her quiet, and that was due to an instinctive mistrust she had of him. He decided at that moment that he would not stay with the Gentrys a moment longer than was necessary or polite. He would gather the information he needed and then move on to a camp far away from here and from Fiona's too wise green eyes.

Then, as if she wanted him to be off-guard, later in the evening Fiona stopped watching him, and under the influence of the rum and the stories Brian and Robin told, she became her normal energetic self. She could tell a joke equal to the best offering any of the men had, and she even got up to dance a bit as the others sang and clapped a rhythm. For a time, Landry thought he had also been wrong in his second assessment of this enchanting, worrisome woman. She could not—any more than anyone else—look through his demeanor and see the hate and anger and turmoil that seethed beneath his calm exterior. He was far too practiced at deception for her to be able to do that.

But in the morning as she fixed breakfast and he was the only man awake to keep her company, she asked, "Have you and your father made peace?"

"No," he said, and knew he would have to leave as soon as possible. She knew his story from Susannah, perhaps, or—who knew, maybe the witch divined it. At this point he was willing to attribute all manner of powers to her. Then, because she seemed to expect him to say more, and because he wanted to try to splinter the single-minded purpose of her inquiries, he added, "It isn't that I don't want to make peace with my father . . . I just haven't had the courage to face him—yet. I'm hoping I can make something of myself before I go to him. You can understand that, can't you? I'm a grown man, I don't want to return a beggar to a home I lost as a result of my youthful folly."

Fiona said nothing. Her bright-green eyes bored into him, then when she finished kneading the dough for the morning biscuits, she looked away. When she spoke again, the subject was different. "Is Susannah well? Her baby is due soon, isn't it?"

"Susannah is always well—that is a knack my sister has. She can always find joy in life." Landry was on safe ground talking about Susannah, for he truly cared for and admired her. He smiled. "Her baby is due in July. I'll be an uncle."

Again Fiona fell silent, failing to pursue the subject, and again she surprised Landry. Babies should be one of those topics she couldn't bear to ignore, and he had tried to give her the impression that his was a friendly, receptive ear for such woman talk. Unable to restrain his curiosity, he prodded her. "When do you and Robin expect your child?"

"In June," she answered, and neither by look nor words did she indicate it meant anything to her or that she wanted to talk about it. What a strange woman she was, thought Landry. She was all pent-up vitality, and he didn't seem able to attract her in even the simplest ways. He was feeling distinctly uncomfortable. She was far too young to have the qualities he was attributing to her. She couldn't be more than seventeen or eighteen years old, he judged. Maybe it was the mountains, those spooky, menacing chunks of rock that scraped the clouds as they passed. They did strange things to a man, and probably to a woman too.

He got up, mumbling that he was going to see to the mules. Once outside he didn't know what to do. Aside from feeding the stubborn beasts and making sure they had water, Landry Morrison, spoiled child of his father, and city dweller all his life, didn't know what to do with them. He remained outside idle until he heard the comforting sounds of Robin's and Brian's voices.

Brian and Robin headed for their claim as soon as they had eaten, and Landry tagged after. Using as much of their time as the two friends would spare him, Landry asked questions, was shown, and watched what they did to find gold. He made a thorough pest of himself, constantly interrupting their work to be shown something that was by now obvious to them. Once when Landry was hacking at a piece of granite with his pick thinking it was slate, Robin stopped his work and came over to him, taking half an hour picking up different kinds of rock and explaining how one could tell the difference. At last he settled Landry out of the way with a piece of slate. He showed him how to separate the layers and take out the gold that was trapped between them.

Shaking his head, he returned to Brian. "He has a lot to learn. He may be a permanent guest."

Brian chuckled, but said, "I doubt it. Unless I'm wrong, that man is a loner. He won't stay here any longer than he has to. Anyway, Fiona doesn't trust him—did you notice?"

"She won't say a word about it," Robin commented. "I tried to talk to her last night and again this morning."

Talk petered out as they got back into the rhythm of working together. Then Fiona, Landry and all else was forgotten as they cracked open a cluster of rocks near a pool the thawing water had made, and found a pocket of gold. With great whooping and shouts, that were as sure a sign of spring as the birds returning, Robin and Brian announced their find.

"The spring flow brought it down—" Brian said when Fiona hurried to the dig site to see.

"—And left it right on our doorstep," Robin finished for him.

"We're rich again!" Fiona cried, and laughed with them over this latest bit of good fortune. How she wanted to jump down into the river with them and help, but instead she sat primly on a rock from which she could see their progress. She went back to the cabin only long enough to get her knitting and her sketchbook, then took her position on the rock again, and enviously watched Brian and Robin have all the fun of taking out the gold.

During the last season she had gotten so accustomed to a great amount of physical activity that she now found her inactivity chafing. She dared not do much, for she wanted this baby more than anything in the world, but still inactivity palled on her. It was only her love for Robin, and his child, and her dreams of their future that gave her the patience to wait out these last few months.

She was happier now, though, since Brian had returned. She and Robin had missed him far more than they had expected. They wished him well in his express business, and knew he was performing a much needed service, but it had been so grand to have the easy camaraderie that had sprung up among the three of them. She had asked him if Coleen might consider joining them, but as she had feared, Coleen would have no part of it. In her opinion her sister was a fool, always clinging to the past and wanting things handed to her. But that was Coleen's loss, she thought, quickly dismissing her. Fiona herself was happy now, and was once more useful cooking meals for Brian and Robin— and Landry—and keeping their clothes clean. It wasn't hunting for gold, but it was next best, and allowed her to feel a part of the whole operation. Thus reminded, Fiona got up and started back to the cabin to begin dinner.

Her departure brought an unpleasant thought to Brian's mind. He tugged on Robin's shirt. "Maybe we shouldn't let her go back alone to the cabin. In fact, I don't think she should be left there alone at all. I've wanted to talk to you since I got here, but not in front of Fiona, for I don't want to scare her. I've heard some disturbing reports in several of the gold camps about Indian raids. Have you heard them? Is it talk or truth, Robin, do you know?"

"I've heard the stories too, Brian, but I don't know. No one seems to have been attacked themselves, but everyone has heard about someone else who has. I don't know what to make of it. I've been thinking about taking Fiona home to her father's place, though."

"What does she say?"

"I haven't told her about it yet. I don't know what to do.

Maybe there is nothing to the talk, but on the other hand, all the reports have been about this region along the Middle Fork and some on the North Fork. I don't know what I'd do if anything happened to Fiona, but then if it is all talk, I hate to lose our claim for a foundationless scare."

Brian looked surprised. "Is it likely someone would move in on you?"

Robin gave a dry laugh. "I'm not sure of that either. The men coming in now are different from the first miners. There've been a few incidents, nothing too serious yet. But just a month and a half ago, five men were tried in Coloma for robbery."

"I heard there was a hanging in Coloma," Brian said softly.

"It makes a man think twice about any move he makes."

"Well, you know I'd be glad to take her to Coloma or to Sean's whenever you say the word. I think I'd feel better if you both left with me, until we find out the truth of these reports."

Landry packed his gear and equipment that evening. Brian and Robin both urged him to stay a bit longer, and become a little more adept at working the water, soil and rocks for gold, but Landry thanked them, and refused. He left with the first light the next morning.

Brian winked at Robin as they waved goodbye to their guest. "What did I tell you about him being a loner?"

Robin was thinking about Susannah and all that she had risked to bring this odd man who claimed to be her brother to California. He had never thought a great deal of the Mormons, had thought less of them after his experiences with Susannah, and now decided he had been right. They were a strange and rigid people he didn't understand or particularly like.

He and Brian went back to their digs, encouraging Fiona to accompany them and watch. They had not talked again of the Indian raids or the possibility of claim jumpers again. They still didn't know if the reports were rumor or stories concocted out of boring, cold winter nights around a camp fire, or if they were true.

Next evening they had just washed up from a fruitful day's labor and had sat down to eat the stew Fiona had cooked, when they heard a man screaming maniacally at his mules. The sound was disjointed and frantic. The mules hee-hawed in terror, and the wagon wheels made hideous grating and screeching noises against the rocks.

Thinking someone had misjudged the treacherous way down the rocks coming into the valley, both men jumped up from the table, grabbed their ropes that hung by the door, and ran into the yard, leaving Fiona to follow at her slower pace. As cautious and as prepared as her husband, Fiona took the time to gather the strips of clean cloth she always kept ready for bandages, and then took from her trunk the splints that Robin had made during the winter in case of a fall from the rocks.

But it was not a travel emergency. Zane Tyler's huge frame, standing in his wagon, dwarfed the mules he was attacking furiously with his whip. Fiona and the men halted in shock. Zane Tyler was usually a kind man to animals, and it was always to him others went when one of their animals was ailing. To see him wildly flailing at the poor beasts was dumbfounding. It took several seconds before Robin and Brian realized that there was a large red gash along Tyler's whip arm, and several other ugly wet red stains on his shirt and pants. Robin and Brian began to run across the valley.

Tyler got his frightened mules moving again, and the wagon shuddered forward, skittering and careering dangerously down the rocky path. The rear wheel skidded over the edge of the rock, then the wagon slid back and thumped hard against an outcropping. Then with a tremendous lunge, and splintering of wood, the mules pulled the wagon over the final rock ridge that brought them into the valley. The jolt sent Zane sprawling, and the wagon airborne. The wagon came to a wobbling landing. The mules, free of their master's mad hand, began to run, each pulling against the other.

Robin positioned himself on one side of the team's erratic path, and Brian on the other. Both men had their ropes coiled into lariats, awaiting the opportunity to halt the runaway team.

Fiona, seeing what was happening, ran back toward the cabin and safety. Brian and Robin threw the lariats, and threw them again and again before they finally had a secure rein on the mules. Out of the depths of the wagon Zane rose like a colossus. His face was streaked with mud and blood and tears, his mouth a gaping cavern through which he bellowed his anguish. The terrifying sound distracted Robin and Brian for a moment, and the mules once again began to run. Finally the two men brought the animals to a quivering halt and tied them securely to an oak tree.

Zane Tyler fell to the bed of the wagon. He gathered up a bloody bundle, then again fell atop it. Robin and Brian both heard the broken sobs that tore out of the big man as he wept like a child.

As they looked over the sides of the wagon, Tyler moved his arm to disclose his bloody treasure. Tyler's red eyes streamed tears, his mouth was a crumpled wound in his face. "They killed her," he wailed. "The God-damned bloody savages killed my Josie!"

Retching, Robin turned away from the sight of the dead woman with part of her scalp peeled back to expose her skull. Gaining control, he realized that Fiona might follow them, and he turned and ran back to her. He threw his arms around her, holding close as much for his own comfort as to prevent her from going on to see Zane's grisly cargo.

"Robin, what has happened?" Fiona asked with cold fear in her voice.

"It's Josie," Robin said brokenly. "She's dead."

"Oh, no!" Fiona cried, burying her head in Robin's shoulder. The two of them stood there clinging to each other. Finally, wiping the tears off her face, Fiona straightened up and moved out of the protective circle of her husband's arms. "Come, Robin, we'll have to see to her burial. That is why Zane brought her here, isn't it?" She began to walk in the ungainly fashion of pregnant women.

Robin grabbed her hand. "No! Don't go over there, Fiona. You don't understand, she—"

At that moment Zane shouted again. "The God-damned savages! I'll kill them all with my bare hands!" He was standing up in the wagon again, his face uplifted to the sky, flourishing his clenched fists. "As God is my witness, I'll have vengeance for her!"

Fiona's steps faltered. She paled, putting her hands to her mouth. "Indians," she breathed. "The stories were true."

Robin nodded. Keeping her hand securely in his, he pulled her nearer to him, saying, "I don't want you to see her. Brian and I can take care of what needs to be done."

Fiona's feet moved steadily toward the wagon. "You don't need to protect me, Robin. I'll be all right. Josie was my friend. I won't turn from her now—I will see that she is properly prepared for burial." She gave a tremulous smile. "I really will be all right, Robin—just stay close to me, please. I need you."

Together they approached the wagon where Brian was slowly helping Zane to calm down. The big man's whole body seemed to be shrinking in on itself now that he was no longer screaming his pain and rage. "Why'd they hurt Josie?" he asked pathetically. "She was always good to everyone."

Fiona fought fear and nausea as she saw what remained of the tall lanky Tennessee mountain girl who had so briefly been her friend. "Put that blanket over her, Robin, and bring the wagon up to the house. Zane, we must see to her now. The time for mourning will come after. Go fetch plenty of water," she ordered him, and by the force of her will brought him down from the wagon to go obediently to the stream.

Josie, the only name any of them ever knew for her, was buried that same night by the light of torches. As Fiona had prepared the corpse, Zane had dug a deep trench. However, he had refused to allow Robin or Brian to make a coffin for her, nor would he make one himself. For whatever reason, Zane Tyler wanted his Josie buried on a pallet, and covered only with a shroud. He did not answer their inquiries as to the reason for this. They concluded it must have been something Josie herself wanted, or some peculiarity of Zane's grief. Whatever the reason, no one argued with him.

The four of them gathered at the trench. Fiona offered the Bible to Zane, but he thrust it away. Robin and Brian lifted the pallet, then lowered it into the grave. Methodically, like a man in a trance, Zane began to shovel earth into the hole. With each mighty swing of the laden shovel he recited prayers that flooded into his mind from some previously forgotten catechism he had learned as a child.

Only after they had returned to the house, and Josie was reposing in her grave, would Zane allow Fiona to tend to his own wounds. He sat stoic and silent as she cleaned and tightly bound the deep gash on his arm, then worked on a small but deep cut on his scalp. His right shoulder was badly bruised, but overall his injuries weren't too bad. He said nothing about the way he had gotten them. The few things he did say were disjointed, so Fiona, Robin and Brian didn't try to put them together into some kind of sense until later.

Bandaged and as comfortable as Fiona could make him, Zane sat in a chair near the hearth and stared silently into the fire. He was inconsolable. He would take no part in the talk and healing reminiscences the Irish so loved to ease the pain. Zane Tyler chose to nurse his sorrow and his hate, drinking steadily from the bottle of rum he held tightly in his hand. He remained sitting like a stone in the chair by the fire, sodden with drink, refusing most food, and brooding alone for two days and nights.

The others talked among themselves and put together the fragmented bits and pieces that Zane had told them. "Apparently she was alone in the tent—I think he was still at the digs when they came out of the hills."

Robin asked Brian, "Did he say they just attacked, or were they looking for food—or guns?"

"I don't know. It sounds like they attacked. Maybe they were going to carry Josie off. He said he killed one of them, but the others ran."

"Well, he'll tell us later," Fiona said. "We'll just have to give him some time." She glanced over at him, a worried look on her face. "But how much time? He can't stay there like that."

"Zane isn't the only thing we need to worry about," Robin said. "His camp was only ten miles away, Fiona. You're not safe here either—I couldn't protect you any better than Zane could protect Josie." Robin looked away, hating the notion that he was helpless to keep Fiona safe. Then he said, "Brian and I have decided to take you to Coloma."

Fiona's emerald eyes flashed. "I have no objection to going to safety—provided all three of us go—but I will not have you and Brian deciding what will be done with me as though I am a piece of furniture to be gotten out of the way! You will include me in your thinking and planning, or I will take myself out of your decision!"

"You're a stubborn, willful woman," Robin muttered. "Hasn't what you've seen frightened you? This is for your own good!"

She said crisply, "Since it is my good, you could trust me to have the sense to preserve it as well as you and Brian."

Brian grinned. "She has a point, Robin."

Robin frowned at his treacherous friend. "This is nothing to make fun of," he growled, then said very humbly to Fiona, "What do you think we should do?"

"Is there any safe place closer than Coloma, or any destination that is an easier journey? These mountains are very rugged —I don't want to do anything that might bring on the baby before his time."

Granting her that they had overlooked the difficulty she would have traveling, they all racked their brains trying to think where else they might take her that presented fewer hazards. No one could think of an alternative to Coloma that wasn't as harsh a journey.

Fiona said, "All right, but we'll have to move slowly. One of you had better warn the other miners in the area that the stories are true, and they should take steps to protect themselves. I'll get ready to leave."

Fiona began to pack those things she thought would be necessary for them on a visit of undetermined duration, and Zane Tyler finally broke free of his morbid grief. In its place, however, was a hot, seething anger which he claimed could be quenched by the blood of every savage in the territory, and nothing else. That night he went to sleep and slept all that night, the next day and night, and then awakened on the morning Robin, Brian and Fiona were ready to leave for Coloma.

Zane was still refusing to eat, except for the smallest amount to keep him going. He seemed to be putting himself through some ritual that only he knew about. It gave Fiona a strange, eerie feeling. Zane Tyler had been one of the gentlest men she knew, and now he was a true primitive. She found both aspects fascinating and enticing, and had no doubt that once he had avenged Josie, he would return to behaving like the man he had been before this tragedy. She now knew him to be a man who felt deeply. She was sure he would love again as soon as he dared risk the depth of his own passion once more. It would be a fortunate woman who ended up with him.

The trail to Coloma was hazardous and arduous for the three of them. The Middle Fork was the roughest and rockiest of the rivers. Its banks were uncompromising granite. The trail, though frequently used, was difficult to follow, and required that Fiona do a great deal of walking and climbing on her own. This was difficult at the best of times, but now the rivers were running high with the spring thaw and the rush of water cascading down from the mountain peaks. The rocks were slippery and dangerous, so their progress was slow, and Fiona was exhausted long before they stopped each night. More and more frequently as they progressed, she had to stop and take rest periods. Though she didn't complain, she knew that Robin was frightened that she or the baby would come to harm and he would be unable to do anything about it. She had never seen him afraid before, and she didn't like it. Each day she mustered up her courage and her strength, and tried to show him that she was fine, and that he was guarding her well.

When they finally reached Coloma, the small town was in an uproar. Many reports of the Indian raids had come in, and the last was proved true. Five miners on the North Fork had been attacked and beaten to death. They had been robbed, tortured, and murdered. The town was a buzz of angry voices, with armed men preparing to hunt the Indians down. John Greenwood, son of the famous mountaineer Caleb Greenwood, had been summoned to lead a large group of men to track the Indians.

Robin found lodgings for Fiona in one of the wood and canvas buildings that boasted they were hotels. He left her with plenty of money to see to her board and lodgings, the cost of which was high in Coloma, and then went to join the other men.

"You must be very careful, Robin," Fiona said as she kissed him goodbye. "It will profit us nothing if I am safe and you are not. Neither of us will ever be whole without the other."

"I know, my love," he said, smiling tenderly at her. "No harm will come to me. I will be back for the birth of my son—in the mountains."

She smiled too. "I believe you," she said simply. She kissed him goodbye in the privacy of her canvas room, then came out on the street to watch the posse of men ride out of the town.

The men tracked the Indians to their *rancheria* on Weaver's Creek. Greenwood halted his men on a gentle rise that allowed them to take a good look at the Indian outpost. Giving brief, gruff directions, he aligned his men, then yelled for the attack to begin. Zane Tyler was surprisingly docile, and seemed willing to obey Greenwood's commands. All he was interested in was seeing the Indians punished—or dead.

The men rode out of the hills, their guns blazing. Indians poured out of the *rancheria* in disarray, streaking for cover. The posse spread out, each man selecting his human targets. Twenty Indians lay dead in the yard of the *rancheria* when Greenwood called for order once again. He and several of his more highly trained men had rounded up thirty more Indians. Surrounded by Greenwood's guard, the Indians were marched back to the mill at Coloma. Like ancient conquerors, the men rode back into town with their captives staggering in fright and fatigue in front of them.

Quickly a trial was held. That same afternoon the Indians were convicted of having been associated with the deaths of the five miners and of Josie. The Indians were taken out into the street and allowed to run. Twenty of Greenwood's mountaineers, and one Zane Tyler, stood waiting for a sporting shot, then fired their rifles, cutting down the fleeing Indians.

Robin and Brian returned to Fiona, joining her in the hotel. Greenwood and several other men formed expeditions determined to chase every Indian in the area out. Zane Tyler joined one of those groups, and left his friends in Coloma knowing he wouldn't return until no one would ever again suffer at the hand of an Indian as Josie had.

Fiona, Robin and Brian spent two days in Coloma. They talked a lot, ate food prepared by someone else's hands, and drank too much. It was a wonderful time of fun and relief for them. Then on March 20 the three started back toward their diggings on the Middle Fork. Soon Brian would leave with another wagonload of their gold, and life would go on. No one of them would look backward to their losses, only forward to the good things that were yet to come.

Fifteen

Asa Radburn was not especially tall, wide, or heavy; yet there was something upsetting about him, something that raised the hackles even before it became known what he did for a living. Perhaps it was the air of tension held tightly in check, the atmosphere of an angry man just ready to let his anger explode, that gave him overtones of menace. Until 1846, only three years before, he had been pudgy of body and ineffectual in most areas of his life. Then, while undergoing military training aboard the *Brooklyn* as a member of Sam Brannan's Latter-Day Saints, Asa had discovered the hard cold man under his soft and yielding exterior. Asa became that man. He turned his fat into muscles, his ineffectuality into deadly effective hate.

In August of 1846, after Brannan's Mormons had settled in California, Asa left, intending to join Brigham Young's party, which was then known to be traveling west overland. As he told his mother, he wanted to join the Sons of Dan, the close-knit secret society of Latter-Day Saints which had been formed originally in 1838 to protect the Mormons from the Gentiles in Missouri. Asa remembered his childhood in those bloody days in Missouri. It would suit him fine to be one of those hard-bitten men who protected their people no matter what it took.

Asa's dreams had more than come true. Early in 1847 he found Young's party at Winter Quarters on the Iowa-Nebraska border. He was welcomed into the Danites, discovering that their blood oath included the "utter destruction of apostates" and that they were instructed, among other things, to "take spoils of the goods of the ungodly Gentiles." He soon became close with Orrin Porter Rockwell, the devoted friend of the late Prophet Joseph Smith, founder of the Latter-Day Saints. Because Brigham Young trusted Rockwell, and Rockwell spoke favorably of Asa, Young came also to trust Asa. He frequently sent the two men on missions. Once they were to locate an Indian who had threatened to kill and scalp Young. When they found him, it was Asa who overpowered the Indian, garishly slit his throat, and removed his scalp as proof for Brother Brigham to see.

That was the first man Asa killed. He had found it remarkably simple and satisfying, and thereafter he devised new ways to take a life. But equally satisfying was the killing of a man while letting him live. It was the expressed purpose of the Church to have only large and strong men in Zion; so occasionally a Danite caught a small man and removed from him all signs of gender. One such victim had, the following night, hanged himself from a tree. Asa, grinning, had stripped off the man's clothes so that all who passed would see the power of the Sons of Dan.

Asa had thought never to marry until he could have the woman of his dreams. He had been obsessed with Susannah Morrison since he was fifteen. In 1836 his mother, Prudence, had married Susannah's father, Ezra. It was then that he first saw Susannah. She was merely seven years old; according to Mormon doctrine she would not be baptized for another year, for she was innocent before God. But already she was a woman-child, roguish if not devilish, favoring him with a level, knowing gaze from her deep-blue eyes, smiling at him and showing her dimples. Her exceptional beauty made his mouth fall open and his eyes grow wide. But the obsession was only his; Susannah had barely tolerated him even after they became adults. It was partly because of Susannah that he had left San Francisco.

Then, in the malarial swamp that was the Mormon Winter

Quarters, he met Fairy Meeks. Rockwell told him that Fairy's parents were recently dead of fever, and that the girl was without family. Asa made an excuse to stop at Fairy's tent. He saw a grief-worn black-haired girl with blue eyes and a complexion that bloomed like roses. She was Susannah all over again, but Susannah vulnerable, Susannah susceptible to him.

They stood and stared at each other for a moment. Then he said, "I've been told you're going to take a husband, and I'd like for it to be me."

Still she stared, her arms crossed under her shawl for warmth. She saw a stocky man of average height with long crinkly brown hair. She saw round hard eyes of a dark agate green, and a thin-lipped firm mouth accentuated by a heavy mustache and trimmed beard. "You're one o' them Danites," she said flatly; but in her voice was the hint of lost music.

Asa smiled. "They're not all bad men."

The corners of her tired mouth lifted a little. "P'raps not. Won't you come in an' set a spell?"

Unconsciously he answered in her terms. "Don't mind if I do." He waited until she sat on a small stool, then sat on a box near her. There were others in the tent, but for Asa and Fairy, it was Wonderland and they were alone. He learned that she was sixteen, born in Kentucky, and that her parents, like his, had been driven out of Missouri and Illinois by Gentiles. No husband had been named for her yet, but the Saints took care of their own; and a beautiful girl could not remain without protection for long. At the end of an hour, with Fairy seeming agreeable, Asa went to ask Brigham Young the favor of this girl as his wife.

So Asa married almost the girl of his dreams. For the first time in his twenty-six years he was happy. Fairy was a gentle girl, affectionate and pleasant, who cooked well, kept the buttons sewed to his shirts, and proved adaptable to his nighttime demands. She was Susannah as Asa would have molded her.

That she had a tough core he also found out. When they had been married some months, and she was large with their first child, Asa lost his temper over some trifle and slapped Fairy's face. He was appalled once he had done it, for Fairy's head snapped sideways, her hair flew, and a big red spot on her cheek quickly turned black and blue. She did not cry; Fairy never cried about anything. She gasped, and put her hand to her injured cheek. Then her eyes, brimming with hatred, met his. Even in fury, her voice was lilting. She said, "You'll pay. I swear it."

He fell to his knees before her. "Fairy, I'm sorry, so sorry, I never meant to do that—please, Fairy, say you forgive me. I'm so sorry—"

He did not see her face, as she had averted it again. But her hand patted him on the shoulder as she moved away toward the cook fire.

So he felt he had gotten off easily this time. All his years of gentle training at Prudence's hands came back to haunt him, and inwardly he took an oath never to hit Fairy again.

That evening at supper, Fairy got up to serve him another helping of mush. She seemed a long time in getting it, and he turned toward her just in time to see the heavy stick of firewood which she swung, hitting him hard on the skull. He felt intense pain, he saw whirling stars and then blackness.

He was days in bed recovering from his concussion. He felt helpless and afraid. But Fairy took care of him, feeding him, keeping him washed and his bed dry and comfortable. Sometimes she smiled at him and sang old mountain songs to him.

When his head was better, and he was able to stand, she said softly, "Just one thing I want to say, Asa Radburn. You kin hit me if you must, but next time you'd oughter kill me, for I'll kill you if you don't."

"It will never happen again, Fairy."

She said, looking into the fire, "No, it won't."

Their first child was a boy, born in November 1847. They named him Jarom. Asa was gone often on missions for the Church, and sometimes while he was away he had jealous fears that Fairy might be untrue to him. He always tried to return unexpectedly, so as to catch her in some transgression, but he would find her sleeping alone, or sewing, or cleaning, or rocking the baby and looking serene. And always she greeted him with a happy smile and arms that quickly laid down their son to give Asa her utmost attention.

He returned in 1848 in time to act as guide for the large

group led by Brigham Young, who had come back from Great Salt Lake City to take them to Zion. They were met midway by Porter Rockwell and three companions. Late in September they first got glimpses of the Great Salt Lake Valley, lying desert-parched and grey and unfriendly below them. The sun glittered on the Great Salt Lake, and lent substance to the Oquirrh Mountains that edged the valley. Asa, riding his horse some distance toward the rear, heard two women talking as they walked along. "It sure don't look like no glorious valley t' me," said one, "even if Apostle Woodruff did call it that."

"Men!" replied her companion eloquently. "You might know they'd pick *this*. Weary and footsore though I am, I'd walk another thousand miles rather than stay in this hellbitten place."

The first one sighed. "It ain't like we got any choice."

But as they drew nearer, the pioneers could see clumps of tough grass now and then, and cookfires, and a neatly arrayed city of tents with human figures working around them. Near the tents sparkled a stream of water that overflowed a newly made dam. Already the Saints were industriously transforming a hostile wilderness into a viable community. On September 20, 1848, Young's party of over 1,200 persons, 397 wagons and a huge herd of cattle arrived in Salt Lake City, to be greeted with cheers by the several hundred people living there.

Fairy, who had wanted their second child to be born in Zion, got her wish. Letha Belle Radburn was born the very night of their arrival. She was the image of her mother . . . but she reminded her father of Susannah.

Brigham Young was a busy man, what with personally overseeing many of the overseers of the activities of his new empire and his numerous wives; but he never lost track of his church members in California under the leadership of Sam Brannan. Over a year ago, he and Brannan had had a very unsatisfactory meeting at Green River, in which Young had demanded that Brannan turn over to him the tithes of the California Mormons, and Sam had replied that that money was needed for the work of the California church. They had exchanged even harsher words, and threats, but so far no money had come to Utah from

San Francisco. It was time, Young felt, to draw the fangs of that slimy apostate snake, and in so doing enrich the depleted coffers in Zion. So Young prepared a long letter to Brannan, detailing his instructions in this regard.

He arranged to send the letter with Apostle Amasa Lyman, who was taking a party on a mission to California. So on April 11, 1849, Young and the Council of Twelve Apostles gathered to bless Lyman's group and Porter Rockwell, who was to guide Lyman. Also being blessed was Asa Radburn, who, though he burned to accompany Lyman and confront Sam Brannan himself, had another mission to fulfill. Porter Rockwell's sixteen-year-old daughter Emily had run away with Hiram Gates to the gold fields of California. Evidently they had been helped by Levi Fifield, a former member of the Mormon Battalion. So Gates and Fifield had been charged with kidnapping.

Judge Heber C. Kimball issued a warrant for the arrest of the two men, and made his mark on the document on his knee before turning it over still wet to Asa. He said, grinning, "Now it might be you won't want to use them up, Brother Asa. It might be Hiram Gates wouldn't perform so good with his privates cut off."

Asa, nettled at being told how to handle a routine matter, said with gentle menace, "Leave it all to me, Brother Kimball."

Kimball glanced at him, pretending to shiver, then laughed.

Outside, Asa said to Rockwell, "Port, you never mentioned that about Emily."

Rockwell walked on with his limping stride. He said calmly, "Didn't bother me none. Gates is a decent man. It was Kimball got the blood up. He had hot britches for Emily hisself, only Gates beat him to her. Serves that son of a bitch Kimball right. Why, Prophet Joseph would sit up in his grave clothes if he knew the notions some o' them old elders get about young girls."

"You were close friends with Prophet Joseph, weren't you?"

Rockwell's light-blue eyes clouded. "Higher'n brothers. Met him when I was sixteen and he was twenty-four. I was one o' the first he baptized in the Church. Him 'n' me never had one cross word. We was both lame, see. Both had accidents when we was little, an' both had one short leg. We talked about it some, how we was friends with the same defect. But it never kep' us down. He went on t' be famous, an' I just followed him faithful-like. He'da never wanted the Church t' be what Brother Brigham's made of it.''

Asa had heard stories that Joseph Smith had approved a few shabby acts himself, but he was too shaky on Church history to refute Rockwell's devoted view of the martyred Prophet. He asked, "Do you have any ideas what you want done with Gates?" That was merely a courtesy; Asa had his own ideas.

Rockwell grinned. "Hell, Asa, Hiram Gates wasn't a good enough hypocrite to rise in the Church. He won't be missed one way or the other. Far as I'm concerned, you just do what suits you at the time. You got your orders.''

Although Asa rode west with Rockwell and the Lyman party until they reached Sutter's Fort in California, there was no further reference to Gates. Thinking over the conversation, Asa realized that even the feared and powerful Rockwell would not have dared to contravene Kimball's warrant. A Danite could be used up by another Danite. He might do well to remember that.

As they rode along getting nearer to the gold fields, Asa thought it strange that there were no Indians to be seen. Something must have happened to them. He shrugged. No Indians meant less trouble for him.

He had not been to Sutter's since the fall of 1846, on his way east to join Brigham Young. Then Sutter's Indian workers had been harvesting in the fields around the fort; the shocks of corn had stood neat row on row in the stubbled fields. Fat cattle and sheep and sleek horses and mules had grazed peacefully in the pastures. The fort itself had been a place of pleasant bustle and excitement, with several emigrant trains coming in every day. Now at the end of May three years later, everything had changed. There was an air of desertion, of abandonment, about the countryside. Mill wheels turned in the streams beside un-used mills. Farmhouses stood untenanted, little towns unpopu-lated. Crops had been planted, then left to grow untended while the farmer dug for gold in the red hills.

At Sutter's Fort, people who could not find room within the walls camped outside in a ragged temporary community of tents and brush arbors. There was a frantic twin stream of traffic going into and out of the fort. Teamsters and bullwhackers cracked their whips, whistling and yelling at their straining horses or oxen struggling to pull wagons precariously over-loaded with commodities. Men rode horses; they walked; every-body rushed. Goods and merchandise burst out of every avail-able storage facility. The many stores and shops that lined the streets were crowded with variously clad people, many mud-caked, who opened little bags and paid for their purchases with gold dust or nuggets, and hurried out again to load their vehi-cles or their saddlebags and return to the gold fields.

John Sutter, whose very name was synonymous with hospi-tality, was nowhere to be seen. It was said that his son Augustus had come over from Switzerland and found his father besieged by creditors, and that Sutter had monumental debts. Asa, view-ing the teeming activity, found it mystifying that Sutter could not have made enough there to pay even the largest debts.

Lyman and his party had gone to seek lodging at the hotel. Asa and Rockwell were lounging on the porch of a thriving general store. After an hour there talking with passersby, they had learned that Susannah Morrison ran a shop down in New Helvetia and among Sam Brannan's many enterprises was a huge store in a former granary here, as well as a hotel. A lot of Mormons were working around Mormon Island, and they had a tavern. Nobody knew of Gates or Fifield.

Rockwell said, looking at the milling activity around them, "Think mebbe I'll have a chop at them gold fields myself. A man don't get rich very fast bein' an angel of the Lord."

Asa considered this. He wasn't in any hurry to find his quarry. And he wasn't in any hurry to get back to Fairy and the children and the new baby which would be along this summer. He'd hang around the gold fields a while and pick up some of that magical wealth for himself. Meantime, he'd scout out Su-sannah and see how frightened she was when she finally recog-nized him under his growths of hair. His old notion of getting even with her for refusing him was still simmering under the surface. There were lots of entertaining ways of dealing with women. He'd see if it was worthwhile . . . yet.

As for Sam Brannan, who had tried to throw him out of the

Church, and whom Susannah preferred to himself, it would be a pleasure to waste that smug bastard. Pity he hadn't been assigned to escort Lyman. He'd give a pretty penny just to see the look on Brannan's face when he read Brigham's letter. And when Brannan got smart and refused—that would be like him—then would come the satisfying part. Asa smiled.

"You thinkin' about home?" asked Rockwell.

Asa replied swiftly, "Hell, no! Thinking about an apostate. You wouldn't want to trade, would you? Let me go with Brother Lyman to see Elder Brannan, and you track down your new son-in-law?"

Rockwell's lips curled sourly. "I don't take no personal interest in Gates. You do the job Kimball gave you, boy."

It was one of Apostle Lyman's duties to take the Gospel to the Mormons in the gold diggings, so the following morning the group set out for Sutter's mill up near Coloma. Asa knew that California was a big piece of land; yet he had blindly assumed that once he reached "the gold fields" he would be able to go through them much like a man searching for a street in, say, San Francisco. What he was not prepared for was the disorganized miles-apart layout of variously sized claims where any number of men from one to several hundred might be working. Tracking down Levi Fifield and Hiram Gates in these muddy tangles of tents and jakeleg equipment was the next thing to impossible. He had to have a base camp and somebody there in case information came in.

Asa spent that first week prowling around camps and asking questions, while Lyman and his party attempted to collect tithes from the Mormon miners. Everywhere they went it was the same story. "We already tithed to Brannan." "Sam Brannan's our First Elder, so we gave the church money to him." Amasa Lyman reflected that there should be a great deal of money waiting for the Church in San Francisco.

But meantime, Lyman himself had to get contributions to finance his own mission. Because of Brannan they had such dismal success that Lyman decided to work harder and longer, so as not to go back to Brother Brigham empty-handed from the rich gold fields. He could be seen every day standing in the back of a wagon, sermonizing to anybody who would listen, and attempting to collect money for his cause, which was to develop yet another Mormon settlement in California. From dawn to sunset Rockwell could be seen standing stripped to the waist in the cold streams off the mountains, swirling bottom mud and water around in a broad pan. Occasionally he picked some flakes of gold out of the mess and put them into a quinine bottle. At night the miners gambled and drank, sang and fought, and next morning might pick up stakes and head for a new camp.

Asa rode into camp one evening at dusk. His diligence so far had not unearthed Gates or Fifield, or even a woman in the diggings. He found Rockwell half-drunk and working to get drunker, sitting by himself staring into space. He looked up at Asa. "Gone," he said. "All gone. Every speck o' dust I drowned myself for a week to get."

"Somebody stole it?" asked Asa.

Rockwell belched loudly. "After a manner o' speakin', yep. One turn o' the cards, and my whole stash is gone."

Asa borrowed the whiskey bottle long enough to wash out his parched throat. "Port, that gives me an idea. Looks like we'll be hanging around the gold fields for a while, so we might as well make something at it. We haven't any reason to kill ourselves working in the fields, when there are easier ways. Now if we'd start up a tavern, or a hotel, it'd be us who'd be getting the gold."

"What in, a tent?" asked Rockwell sarcastically.

"Hell yes, in a tent. Sell whiskey by the drink. Have cots or pallets for men to sleep on. Have a new game for them to put their money on."

"Shootin' matches," said Rockwell, becoming interested. "I c'n make more on shootin' matches'n I could on booze."

"Is it a deal?"

Rockwell was not too drunk to be businesslike. "Soon's we get the dee-tails ironed out, it's a deal."

The next morning the two men left in search of the nearest distillery. They found it in Sacramento. As soon as they returned, they were in business. In a short time they were operating the Round Tent Saloon at Murderer's Bar, a locality populated with a hodgepodge of hastily erected buildings. When

Rockwell made his trips to Sacramento, returning with the whiskey by pack train, he would pause at the top of a hill nearby and sound a bugle call. Asa, tending the bar in Rockwell's absence, would then fire several shots as a signal to miners that there was fresh whiskey. Soon they had three establishments, including a hotel at Buckeye Flat and a "half-way house" near Mormon Island. When they had to go after supplies, they left a Latter-Day Saint in charge, knowing they would not be cheated.

During this time Rockwell developed some peculiar habits. Years before, while living in Missouri, he had tried to kill the deputy governor, Lilburn Boggs. Boggs was now living in California. Rockwell was sure that Boggs had men searching for him, so in the gold camps he asked the Saints not to call him Rockwell. He went by the name James B. Brown. He carried two revolvers and a dueling pistol loaded with buckshot. Always near him was an intelligent little white dog he had trained to protect him. The dog's name was Dog.

When he went out for whiskey, it was a fascinating sight to see him astride his big roan horse, with Dog perched on the horse's rump behind him. Sometimes Dog stood up with his paws on Rockwell's shoulder and looked ahead. At night if there was an alarm, the dog had been trained to lick Rockwell's face to wake him. The Danites were known and feared, but there was always someone willing to risk his own life to kill a killer.

"Brown's" reputation as a crack shot was always being tested. Boyd Stewart, a feisty ex-member of the Mormon Battalion, challenged Rockwell to a shooting contest. They set a prize of $1,000. Business boomed all morning at the Half-Way House, with hundreds of miners crowding around and laying bets on the winner. That afternoon the match was held. Rockwell's score was best. The men went wild, rushing to the bar and drinking round after round. At the height of the celebration Stewart climbed upon a rickety table and yelled for quiet. When the men had ceased to roar, Stewart said, "Got a 'nouncement. Got a fella I want y'all t' meet." He gestured theatrically toward James B. Brown. "Look close at him, boys. This here man's such a hot shot that he won his own contest—but he couldn't kill Gov'nor Boggs! Yep, like I say, this here's that famous an' fearful Son o' Dan—Porter Rockwell!"

Rockwell blanched. In the savagely drunken crowd were men from Missouri and Illinois, men who would give their right hands to be able to say they had killed him. Two or three started toward him, yelling, "Hang the son of a bitch!" Then, as Rockwell searched frantically for a way out, others surged after him. At his feet, Dog suddenly rose, his eyes glaring, growling and baring his teeth. Rockwell grabbed out his knife, slit the tent, and as he dodged out the back, pulled the bar over after him. He could hear bloodthirsty yells and roars, but found a horse and got on it. Dog leapt up after him. Together they galloped out of the camp.

Asa, thinking quickly when he grasped Stewart's announcement, grabbed the heavy box that held the day's takings in gold. While the men were still tangled up at the back of the tent, Asa forced his way out against the tide, ruthlessly using his knife against anyone who tried to stop him. He found his own horse and mounted. In a few minutes both Asa and Rockwell had left the teeming camp near Mormon Island far behind.

Sixteen

Fairy Meeks Radburn did a thing she never did during the day: She lay down on the bed and pulled a comforter over her. Both children, thank God, were asleep, and she was so tired she couldn't see straight. She was pregnant, and scared, and she'd been nearly talked to death. Elder Nephi Gunderson had been at the house again and spent the whole blessed morning. Poor little Jarom, Fairy thought—only eighteen months, he couldn't be expected to understand that his maw was busy and couldn't change his britches when he had filled them. And little Letha Belle at six months old still had to be nursed often, so she had screamed a lot, because Fairy's milk was drying up. But old Brother Nephi had instructed her to ignore the children; it strengthened their resolve to have to wait for comforts. As far as Fairy had noticed, it strengthened only the power of their screams. And when Brother Nephi shut Jarom in the bedroom all by himself, poor Jarom was petrified. He cries got hoarser and hoarser until they finally stopped altogether, and Fairy risked Brother Nephi's rage by going in to see about him.

She found her baby son cowering under the bed, hiccuping, his little face fiery red and streaked with tears. She hauled him out by his shirt and held him in a fiercely loving embrace, stinky pants and all. By this time Brother Nephi had followed her in, and was standing right behind her. The entire room reeked of Jarom's clothing. Brother Nephi said reproachfully, "Seems to me, Sister Fairy, that a good mother would not let such things occur."

"Not soil his britches, Brother Nephi? He can't help it. It's the thing babies do the best. But if you'll let me, I'll change him."

"*I* have not been preventing you," he said with high dignity.

Moving as quickly as she could with Jarom's frantic little fingers picking at her, she poured water out of the pitcher and wet a rag, and laid her son down on a changing quilt on the bed. Brother Nephi had backed out and was waiting impatiently by the door. Fairy deliberately took as long as she dared, talking soothingly to Jarom, cleaning up his plentiful mess and pinning on a dry clean diaper. In the living room she could hear neglected Letha Belle monotonously screaming, her voice diminishing but still strong. She'd tend to her too, she thought daringly. No old brother was going to stop her this time.

With Jarom sobbing and droning and clinging to her skirt, she somehow managed to pick up the baby and get a clean diaper on her too. Then, embarrassed but under a great necessity, she unbuttoned her dress and gave the baby her breast.

The sight evidently pleased old Brother Nephi a great deal, for he hitched up his chair and watched the process with complete absorption. Jarom watched too, and finally he made sounds that meant, "Me hungry too, Maw."

Fairy smiled pleadingly at Brother Gunderson. "They're only babies, both of 'em, Brother Nephi. I hope you don't mind if I fix somethin' for Jarom, so's he won't start up again."

Gunderson, staring glassy-eyed at her blue-veined white breast and the eager rosebud mouth on it, nodded absentmindedly. Fairy stood up with the baby in one arm, and prepared a bowl of bread and milk for Jarom and fed him with her free hand. She realized that Brother Nephi had followed her out to the kitchen and was still staring at her. The baby finished, and Fairy slipped her clothes shut.

"Go on, go on feeding her," he said eagerly. "I don't mind at all."

"She's done," said Fairy flatly.

"Can't you make her take more?"

Fairy's lips twitched a little, at Letha Belle sprawled in sleep, slack-mouthed and peaceful. "Not hardly," she said.

"When do you feed her again?" She hated the look in his eyes, as if he would like to be in Letha Belle's place himself.

She looked at him steadily. "Whenever she gets hungry."

He seemed to realize where he was, and the subject of conversation, and a speckled redness crept up over his old age-spotted features. "Well," he said. "Well, well."

Fairy let him stand for a moment longer, then said, "Have a seat, Brother Nephi? I'm nearly done with Jarom, though."

"I don't mind if I do," he said, and sat in Asa's chair at the table. Apparently emboldened by having seen Fairy's breast, he began, "There is something I have been wanting to tell you, um, Sister Fairy."

Hoping to discourage him from saying something unpleasant, she said briskly, "I don't keep secrets too well, Brother Nephi, if that's what's on your mind."

He smiled. His teeth were black next to the gums. She caught an appalling swampy whiff of his breath, and all but gagged. He said, simpering, "It concerns you, dear Sister Fairy."

She gave him another steady look. "I hope you're recallin', Brother Nephi, that my husband Brother Asa is one o' them Destroyin' Angels."

He seemed to falter momentarily; his eyes shifted as though he were thinking. But he went on, "Well now, we won't cross that bridge until we come to it."

She got very busy, wiping Jarom's chin before giving him another bite. "What bridge?"

"Why, your husband, Brother Asa. As you know, I am above him in the priesthood of Melchizedek."

"Yes, I recollect that. You're one o' the oldest elders." She smiled at him guilelessly, as though paying him a compliment.

His face tightened; he coughed slightly. "Nevertheless, I am still a man. A man of great vigor, and—long-lasting." He looked at her to see if she caught the significance of this statement.

She smiled blankly. "I'm sure that's a thing to be proud of at your age," she said. "Helps a lot when you got the kindlin' t' split, don't it?"

She had spread it on a little too thick, she saw, but there was no taking it back now. He said, "I am speaking—of—the—marriage bed."

"Oh." She kept her face stony. "That's a thing I never think of, Brother Nephi. It's a thing that never has pleasured me none." She was aware that she was repeating herself, but couldn't seem to help it.

"Perhaps you haven't had the right partner, dear Fairy," he suggested.

"Couldn't have a better than Brother Asa," she declared. "It's just me, I don't cotton to it noway."

"But you could learn to," he said insistently.

"Don't want to." She shrugged. "I get a baby every year as it is."

"Sister Fairy, I hope you are not forgetting woman's place in the Church, to produce children for the greater glory of God."

She said without inflection, "I remember."

He stared at her hard for an uncomfortable time, as though gathering courage to use the power his higher rank gave him to take Asa Radburn's wife. Finally he said, "It is my wish that you become my plural wife."

There. It had come out at last, the words she dreaded, the words she knew were coming from the first day Brother Nephi started visiting her. And now that they were said, there would be nothing in God's green earth that would save her from this rotting, slobbering old lecher. Fairy choked back a sob. It would go worse for her if she seemed to reject him.

She said tonelessly, "I thank you for the honor, Brother Gunderson."

Bearing down on his advantage, Gunderson said, "But you don't wish to be my wife?"

"It's a thing I never thought of. I just thought I'd go on bein' Sister Fairy Radburn. This is an awful s'prise to me." She looked around her small clean kitchen, seeking the everyday, the familiar, in the midst of shock. Bless the Lord, what would she do? What would happen to her babies? Jarom? Letha Belle? The little one still in her belly?

He said irritably, "You don't seem very grateful, Sister Fairy."

"But I am," she assured him. "It's just—here I was, sitting in my kitchen feeding my little boy, and a big priest in the Church pops the question to me—it ain't the kind o' talk I'm used to. That's all it amounts to, Brother Nephi."

He seemed satisfied, at least enough not to press any longer. He stood up, staggering a little before righting himself. "You think about it, dear Fairy," he advised her, boldly patting her on the shoulder. "I'll be back tomorrow, and we'll talk about it some more. But I don't want you to put me off, now that we've made up our minds. We deserve our share of earthly happiness, you and I."

"Yes, Brother Nephi," she said automatically. "I'll just walk you to the door."

After he had gone she bolted both front and back door, and put her children to bed as if in a dream. She returned to the kitchen and broke up the heavy brown everyday bread and poured milk over it. She dipped a spoon in it and began eating. No matter how upset Fairy might be, she knew she had to eat, had to try to make milk for Letha Belle, had to get her own strength from somewhere.

She ate two bowls, her eyes never once seeing what she did. She was living entirely in her own head now, figuring things out. Now that the old limberdick had spoken, she knew she had to act quickly. But she didn't know yet what to do, or where she could go.

For once in her orderly life she did not rinse the dishes she and Jarom had used. She left them sitting on the table, the little crumbs of bread drying in the milk. She lay down on top of the bed and pulled up a comforter. She was beginning to get an idea, and she'd need to be rested if she was to carry it out. In a few moments she was sound asleep.

She woke up alert an hour later, when Letha Belle cried. She nursed her again, and petted her, and put her on the floor to play. While she waited for Jarom to wake up, she put a few things in a bundle that she could hide under her skirt. There was a little money in the house—Asa was always so proud of having money around—and she sewed it all into the hem of her petticoat. Fortunately it was a cold day even for early spring, and she could just put plenty of outer wraps on the babies. She couldn't carry much food, which was what they'd need the worst, and only a few diapers, and those spread out evenly over her petticoat. What she'd do when they got wet or soiled—well, she'd have to figure that one out when it happened.

Fairy knew well what the penalty would be if she were caught. Women in the Church were like cattle—in fact, First Counselor Heber Kimball called his wives "my cows." The elders had just begun talking of The Laws of the Lord. These were rules in the process of being revealed to President Young and his Council of Twelve. So far all she had heard was that grave crimes would be punished by cutting off the head of the offender. President Young had said, "It is to save them, not destroy them." He meant the souls of those who apostatized, as she was about to do. The President didn't like for people to try to leave the Church.

She wasn't leaving the Church—not that it would help her any to explain that—but she was thinking of heading for Sutter's Fort, where Asa had said he was going. She didn't know if she would be safe there, if she would be safe anywhere if old Nephi wanted to have her, but she had to leave Salt Lake City, that was all there was to it.

Fairy Meeks Radburn was a simple woman. Her wants were few, but those few were strong. She believed in her God. She wanted to be a good wife to her man. And she loved her children. Brother Nephi was going to wipe out two of those three wants with one swipe of his lecherous hand.

Now that Fairy had made up her mind, she was left with the need to find a way to accomplish this feat of running away, and with a terrible fear. She was running to save herself and her children, but if she failed, and it was likely that she would, all of them were going to die anyway—so what would she be gaining? For the first time doubt entered her mind. Perhaps God wanted her to suffer the indignities Brother Nephi would heap upon her. Perhaps her children were meant to suffer under his uncaring. Being simple and direct, Fairy closed her eyes, calmed herself so that she could hear whatever voice might come into her head, and then she said softly, "Lord, am I supposed to stay here with old Nephi, or do You want me to hike out of here?"

She waited, eyes closed, hands clasped in her lap. No voice came into her mind. No magical thought appeared to show her the way. But still Fairy waited. The Saints were a people of miracles. Hers would come if she listened. Then little Jarom awakened. From his crib she could hear him happily chattering, "Da-da-da-da-da."

Fairy's eyes opened wide. For days she had been trying to get both Jarom and tiny Letha Belle to say Dada clearly and purposefully, so she could surprise Asa when he came home. Jarom said many things that were intelligible—at least to her—but he never said Dada. Now, she realized this was the voice she had been waiting for. This was her directioning, this was her answer. Her children must be taken to their father. With God's approval, she began to think practically of escape. Since there was no place for a pregnant woman with two children to go easily from Salt Lake City, Brigham Young would know she would have to have help or transportation. In these parts that would mean another Mormon—and that wouldn't happen—or a wagon train. Trains came through there almost every day now. It would be easy to catch up with one, but it would also be easy for President Young's Wolf Hunters—whose job it was to catch apostate "wolves" and keep them from leaving Salt Lake City— to search the wagon trains.

Wolf Hunters—Danites—Destroying Angels. Sometimes one man was all three. Sometimes he acted as spy, sometimes as killer. If Fairy had been customarily given to pondering, she might have pondered over the need for all those religious watchdogs just to keep people from leaving the realm of Young's authority. But once you became a Mormon, you were one for life. She heard sermons preached in which Young himself said, "The moment a person decides to leave this people, he is cut off from every object that is desirable for time and eternity. Every possession and object of affection will be taken from them who forsake the truth, and their identity and existence will eventually cease." She did not entirely understand that, but she knew what was meant by the statement that "hog-holes in the fences will be stopped up with apostates that try to leave." But she was accustomed to living with fear. It seemed to be President Young's way of keeping God's chosen people in line.

As she planned her getaway, she heard her guiding voice again. She could be with the wagon train and yet not. Pleased with that enigmatic notion, she set forth to do it. No one would miss her until the next day when Brother Nephi came to visit and she wouldn't be here. Even that certainty she might be able to delay a bit.

As soon as it was dark, Fairy set her table as though for lunch the next day. She put bread in her bowl and Jarom's, and added a great deal of milk. With luck, when the old man came, he would think she had been called away, rather than having run away. That would give her a few precious hours—minutes, she amended. Then with her sleeping children, one packed on her back in a sling she had improvised, and the other in her arms, she set out from her house for the last time.

The air on the desert was piercingly cold at night. She could feel little Jarom squirming, wrapping himself into a little ball against her back, trying to stay warm in his sling. She walked west in the direction she had seen a wagon train pass by earlier that day. Doggedly she walked across the hard cold sands until she was certain she was near to the train. She couldn't see it, but she could now hear the lowing of cattle, and every once in a while a woman's high-pitched laugh. She stood still, looking about her, her eyes searching for a dune, a rise in the ground, anything she could make use of. Finally about a hundred yards ahead she saw what she thought to be a hill, and headed toward it. Her burdens grew heavier with each step, and the dune that had seemed so near was a mile distant, rather than the hundred yards she had thought. Nothing was as it seemed on the desert. She should have known that, for it was what she was counting on to save her and her babies.

When finally she reached the rise in the ground, it was better than she could have hoped. The hillock turned out to be an old wagon, broken and dry, abandoned a long time ago, and now almost entirely covered with salt and sand. Close to exhaustion, Fairy slumped to the ground near her newfound haven, and began to think how she could make it secure. Always her restless eyes looked to the east. There was little time before dawn, and she still had a great deal to do. She had passed the point of returning. She either made herself and her children safe here at this wagon, or they would all die.

The one side of the wagon lay against the sand and seemed to be sitting on a depression, for little rivulets of sand kept sliding down under it. Putting the two babies as deep inside the hold of the wagon as she could, she began to dig. The sand moved swiftly to undo her progress, but Fairy was dogged, and driven by the lightening sky. On hands and knees, like an animal, she scooped out the sand. Testing it out, she found that she could get under the wagon. Just a bit more digging and she could manage to hide herself and her two babies under the sand and the wagon, and then it was up to God to keep the men who would come hunting for her away from their shelter.

Fairy waited until the sun was high and the desert was growing unbearably hot before she fed her children, then slid them down into the hole she had dug. The children were restive, especially Jarom. Fairy did her best to talk to them and play pat-a-cake in their cramped quarters, but she didn't do a great deal to keep them quiet. When the time came, she had but one means to quiet them, and she would use it then and only then.

She didn't know how long she and her children had been huddled in their hole when she first felt the tremors in the sand that told her horsemen were coming. The loose sand shifted down on them, and Fairy felt a moment of panic when she thought the hole would fill up again and smother them. Soon after, she heard voices. The horsemen were talking and laughing. Once she heard a comment about herself. "She can't be far. Where's a woman with two babies going to go out here?"

His mate responded, "We'll get her at the wagon train."

Whatever else they said was lost as they passed by, and other men on other horses came, shifting more of the loose sand into her hiding place and causing her great fright. At first the strange sounds and odd feeling of the earth shaking fascinated her children, then it frightened them, and both began to whimper. Quickly Fairy undid her blouse and hugged both children to her, placing a nipple in each of their mouths. Their interest in her milk overpowered their fear, and they suckled happily. Letha Belle was asleep in ten minutes, and Jarom's eyes were

beginning to lose focus in spite of his efforts to keep awake.
Fairy breathed a sigh of relief and a prayer of thanksgiving to
her Lord. All that was left was for the men to search the wagon
train, as she knew they would, find her not there, and return to
Salt Lake City to look for her in another sector.

If the men did not find her on their return, this might even
gain her a whole day. It might be assumed that old Nephi had
been rash in claiming that she had run away. Perhaps they
would wait near her home to see if she returned that night.
Perhaps they would think she had just been visiting, or seeing to
her mission of tending to sick children. Perhaps. . . . Fairy
closed her eyes and prayed. She fell asleep with her children,
and when she awakened stiff and uncomfortable, it was cold. It
was night. They had slept right through the men passing on
their return to Salt Lake City.

For a long time Fairy sat still, all cramped up in her hideaway
afraid to move, thinking that perhaps the men hadn't returned
yet, and she would come out just in time for them to catch her.
Perhaps they were standing in a huge circle outside waiting for
her, having known where she was. Jarom stirred, whimpering in
his sleep. Letha Belle's eyes opened, and her little head wiggled
back and forth as she sought Fairy's breast. She let the child
feed, then, taking all her courage in her hands, she began to
struggle out of the hole. Once she was outside, and had assured
herself that President Young's men were nowhere around, she
reached back inside and brought her children into the cold night
air.

Once more Fairy Radburn put Jarom on her back in the sling,
and wrapped Letha Belle in her blanket, and set off across the
desert. God had brought them through their first terrible test.
They had gotten out of Salt Lake City. They were free. But that
was only for now. Fairy knew that the men would come back,
once they found she truly had run away. And she knew the
desert itself was as much a killer as Brigham's Danites were.
Now she had to find a safe place for herself and her children,
and a means of travel; otherwise they would die of thirst and
exhaustion out here on these terrible pathless sands.

She knew that every moment she had was precious. If she
didn't catch the wagon train tonight, they would leave in the

morning, and with their animals and wagons they would far outdistance her the next day. Head down, her lips mouthing prayers, Fairy plodded through the clinging sands. She was tired and hungry, but she was afraid to eat, for if she consumed the little food she had, her children might die of starvation.

Dawn came, and again she could hear the sounds of the train, but could not see it. With a sinking heart she knew that those sounds she was hearing were made by a group of fifty or sixty people preparing for the day's travel. She was condemned to another blistering hot day alone on the desert, and another cold night's walking.

Tears slipped out of her eyes. Today she wouldn't rest. She daren't. She couldn't let that train get any farther ahead of her. It was her only hope, and she also knew that each day she had less time before the Danites came out of Salt Lake City after her. It was only God's protection that had kept her safe this long.

The sun climbed high in the sky, and beat without mercy on the hot sands. The heat scorched through Fairy's shoes and burned her feet. She no longer could trust her eyes, for the desert wavered and undulated, the horizon was unsteady and undistinguished by any landmark to guide her. The children were suffering, no longer really crying, but never did they stop their continuous whimpering. Fairy's heart was breaking. She wouldn't have brought them out of Salt Lake City to die like this. No one would even know they were dead. No one would pray for them, or mark their graves.

The last thing she remembered was the horror of thinking about the vultures and the scavenging animals that would most likely give her and her children the only burial they would have. Hysterical from hunger, thirst, and exhaustion, Fairy began to laugh in a crazy high-pitched wail that frightened her dying children. "If I turn to the east, the wolf-hunters will take us. If I turn to the west, the wolves will feast," she cried in her voice of awful high-pitched laughter. Trapped in the thought, she repeated the words over and over until there was nothing.

Titus Horner was always the odd man out. He missed appointments, he missed boats, and he had missed his wagon train when it left St. Joseph, Missouri. Titus wasn't worried. He was used to being alone. He never seemed to make friends. He wasn't a pleasant man, and few people had ever liked him, including his own parents and brothers. The kindest they had ever been to him was the day he told them he was leaving for the West and would never return. They had smiled at him that day, wished him luck, said goodbye, and went on with their lives. Titus had joined a wagon train, but had quickly gotten into disagreements with the wagon master and several other men in the group. Titus was too much the coward to get into a real fight, but he was a contentious man whose entire entertainment was argument. When they had stopped in St. Joseph, Titus had taken himself off to see the settlement, wondering if perhaps this was far enough west. But he found no one there who liked him either. When he returned to his train to continue his journey, he discovered they had left two days before. He was alone again.

He was a full three days behind the others when he entered Salt Lake City. He had intended to poke his nose around there too, but had quickly changed his mind. He hadn't liked those people. They were all het up over some woman who had run away. Titus could sympathize with her. He had been running to something or away from something all his life. He left Salt Lake City as soon as he had replenished his water supply and bought some more meat. He was in a hurry for another reason. If he was going to continue west, and it looked like he was, the one thing he didn't want to do was try to get over those mountains by himself. He was no fool. It was going to take a lot of strong backs to hop over those big hills, and he wasn't much for a whole lot of labor. He wanted company.

Titus was in a hurry coming out of Salt Lake City. His oxen, accustomed to Titus's usual lazy pace, found a whip on their backs and a loud voice shouting in their ears. Tracks didn't stay long in the sand, so on the morning of the third day when he could see vague traces of the other wagon ruts, he knew he was making good progress.

He had gone about four miles, and was just getting the oxen to move at a rapid but steady pace, when he saw something in his path up ahead. As he passed, he took a closer look. "Umm —umm," Titus muttered to himself. "Coulda took the time t' bury her. Don't seem right to jes' toss her outta the wagon an' go on."

He thought about stopping to bury the woman himself, then he thought how far ahead the others would get while he tended to his good deed, and decided against it. "She ain't mine," he said aloud, shrugging. He yelled at his oxen and they strained forward. Fortunately the animals had no real desire to move, for at that moment Jarom woke up and stood up near his mother's side. Seeing another human being, and wanting comfort, the little boy opened his mouth and let out an ear-piercing wail of misery.

"Crikey!" Titus exclaimed. "They done threw out the kids with the ol' cow!"

Jarom tottered to the man, hands outstretched.

"Crikey!" Titus said again. He didn't want to pick up smelly, wet and distraught Jarom. Letha Belle, hearing her brother, began to cry too. Her voice was small and pathetic compared to her brother's. Titus moved cautiously nearer to the body of the woman. He peered over and saw the infant. It was one thing to leave a corpse alongside the road, but what was he going to do now? Could he leave two infants to certain death? He looked all around. Nobody was near. Nobody was watching. Nobody would ever know. He glanced up at the sky. *He* probably wouldn't see either. Never before in Titus's life had God seemed to care what he did or what happened to him, so most likely that was the case again today.

The only problem was that, being a coward, Titus didn't want to go to Hell. Preacher said it was worse than this earth could ever be. As far as Titus was concerned it was hard to imagine anything worse, so Hell had to be some terrible place. He poked at the baby Letha Belle, causing the poor weak little thing to howl lustily. Titus wondered what would happen if he just put his big hand over that little head of hers for a minute—no more —just a minute. God wasn't likely to notice that, and it would quickly solve half his problem.

As he leaned forward to smother the baby, his knee pressed hard into Fairy's spine. She moaned, and Titus jumped back a full five feet. God had seen! Crikey! The dead bitch was gonna ha'nt him!

Something had hurt Fairy, and stirred her to consciousness. It took her several moments to get her bearings or think of anything but pain and thirst, then with swift fear she remembered her children. With a lunge that took all her strength, she pushed herself to a sitting position. Dizzily she sat, her body swaying and threatening to topple over again. She became aware of Titus hovering near, his whiskery face a mask of fear. Fairy thought only of Danites, and when she saw him, she burst into great racking sobs of despair. She would die and so would her children. God had not blanketed her with his protection after all. With what little strength she had left, Fairy cried and cried.

This very human action made Titus a bit braver. He sidled closer, "Be you alive? You ain't dead? You ain't a ha'nt?"

Fairy stopped her howling, and blinked her tear-shrouded eyes. Titus had an ingratiating look on his face, and he was bent almost double trying to get his face on a level with hers. She knew: this man was no Danite. She gulped hard to swallow her tears. She looked steadily at him. " 'Course I ain't dead."

"You that woman them Saint-folks is looking for?" he asked with an oily smile.

"Don't know what you're talkin' about," Fairy answered cautiously. "You got any water or food you could spare me an' my younguns?"

Titus handed her his flask. "Food's in the wagon," he said. As she drank, and gave some to her infants, he asked, "Any reward for you?"

Fairy laughed. "Not 'less you call gettin' your head cut off a reward."

Titus jumped back. "I ain't gettin' *my* head cut off!"

Fairy watched him shrewdly. If God had given her a fool for a savior, she'd accept that. "They find out you helped me, and them Danites an' Wolf Hunters'll cut your head right off."

"Mebbe they'll never find you," he suggested.

"They'll find me if you don't take me far from here. What's your name, man?"

"Titus," he said. "I could do you in—and then who'd know?"

"Jes' me, an' you, an' God," Fairy said simply, but she had said the right thing, because Titus still wasn't certain God wasn't hiding somewhere nearby, just waiting to chuck him into the hot place when he made a slip.

Trapped, Titus began to whine. "I ain't got much food—and not much money—an' it's a long hot journey an'—"

Instinctively Fairy knew she didn't dare mention she had money. She said, "Me an' the kids don't eat much, an' I kin work. I'm a strong woman. We won't be trouble. Most likely we'll be a big help to you." Then, taking a calculated risk of having him turn tail and run, Fairy ordered, "Give me a hand up. Let's get these younguns on the wagon. Time's a-wastin'."

Titus obeyed. With the children once again fed, their diapers clean and dry, and in the shade inside the wagon, they slept. Fairy catnapped, unable to trust Titus. He walked at the side of his oxen, making good time across the desert.

By nightfall, Titus and Fairy could see the wagon train ahead. Already they had made camp, and the wagons were loosely formed in a circle. Slightly out of line and off to itself, Titus pulled his wagon in too.

"Howdy, folks, I'm back! Sure did take me a while to catch up," he said jovially, as though these were his best friends.

"Well, well, aren't we the lucky ones," a wag said smartly. "We got ol' Titus back again."

"We sure did miss our mascot, Titus," another called, and several men laughed.

"Wait till you see what I found on the road," Titus yelled, sure everyone would be jealous when he displayed his prize. "Come out here," he snapped at Fairy.

Her face blistered from sunburn, and much the worse for wear, Fairy stepped out of the wagon. Proudly Titus announced, "I got me a woman. She was a throw-away, an' I found her."

The men sitting around the campfire didn't know what to say. Finally one lifted his hat, saying, "Howdy, ma'am." The others muttered unintelligible greetings, then fell silent. They waited for Titus to leave. They had never liked him, and they didn't like his story about finding a woman at the side of the road. They wondered what he had done. Then when they heard Jarom's cry, and they knew he had children in that wagon as well as the woman, they decided the less they know of Titus and his business the better. They looked at each other, stood up, abandoned their fire, and moved away from Titus and his woman.

Fairy watched with interest, but it suited her. The less anyone knew about her, the better. She got down from the wagon and took possession of the fire to make their evening meal.

The second day they had been with the wagon train, two things happened. Titus told Fairy that day after tomorrow, they would be out of this dad-blamed desert. The other event was that one of the men who rode guard with the train flashed past on his horse, announcing that riders were coming from the east. Fairy knew they were the Danites, and they wanted her and her children. She didn't need to see them, she simply knew it. She clutched at Titus's sleeve. "Titus, you can't let them find me— they'll kill all of us. You got to believe me. These are my people, and I know them."

Titus gave a nasty laugh, but she had frightened him. "Crikey, what'd they want with me? I'll jes' give 'em what they want. They won't take no 'count o' me then."

Fairy's eyes narrowed. "I'll tell them you defiled a Mormon woman, Titus. I'll tell them you forced me to go with you. They'll flay you, Titus, an' leave your mizzable carcass bleedin' on the desert. You know what'll happen then, don't you!"

"Crikey, you some bitch, ain't you," he breathed. But she knew he would hide her—unless he found some way of giving her up while saving his own skin. She had to trust, though, for Titus was the only chance she had. She couldn't run now.

The Danites were a powerful and rough-looking group of horsemen. They sent three men to the head of the train and stopped the lead wagons. Another man, the leader, sat on his horse midway down the train where most people could see and hear him. "We come for a woman and two children who are with you. Give them up, and you can be on your way."

"What'd this woman do?" a man shouted.

"She belongs to us," the leader said curtly. "You got two minutes to bring her forth." He sat astride his horse like a stone, not a muscle moving. His men slowly walked their horses up and down the line of halted wagons. The two minutes passed, and no one had moved or said anything.

Fairy was hidden under the floorboards of Titus Horner's

wagon, Jarom and Letha Belle wrapped tight against her body with a sheet. She had done something she had never before done in her life, and she prayed she would not live to regret it. She had given both her children diluted doses of laudanum. She had no idea if it would harm them, or merely put them to sleep as she hoped, but she had to keep the little ones silent, or there was no chance at all that they would live. Their little heads lolled to the side, their little mouths sagged. With tears streaming down her face, Fairy tried to hold them close, and through their unnatural sleep make them feel the depth of her mother-love.

The Danite leader gave a silent signal with his hand, and his men went to work. Roughly they jerked every man away from his yoke of oxen and yanked every woman from the wagons. Children were thrown cruelly sprawling to the desert floor from whatever height they happened to be. Then one man for each wagon was arbitrarily assigned, and with a Danite guard he was ordered to empty the wagon. The thirty-eight wagons that comprised the train of sixty-five people were emptied out. Chests, furniture, clothing, all were thrown out onto the desert. Barrels of flour and other precious food supplies were spilled and broken. Broken crockery lay about. Out of fear no one spoke. The Danites were so abusive and forceful that the emigrants realized if they revealed Fairy, the Danites would kill them all. The Danites did not find Fairy.

Satisfied that she was not in any of the wagons, the Danites lined the people up. The leader walked down the line of people asking questions. With the butt end of his whip, he poked men and women alike in the chest, threatening and menacing as he demanded they give him the woman and her children.

One man sneered at the Danite leader, saying, "Takes all o' you t' get one woman, huh? Some kind o' men!"

The Danite swept his hand back with lightning speed, bringing the whip butt hard across the man's face. He fell to the ground, blood spurting from his eyes and nose. The Danite walked on. Finally he came to the last man in the train. A skinny, frightened wretch of a man whose eyes shifted constantly. "Where's the woman?" the leader demanded.

Titus hunched his shoulder up in a way he had when he

thought he might have something to gain. "Is there a reward for her?"

"Just answer me!"

"But—but, if you want her so much, she must be worth somethi—" The whip butt smashed against Titus's jaw. He howled in pain, sprawled on his back. "What'd you do that for! I was gonna—" Another of the Danites kicked the fallen man in the back. Again Titus howled in agony, but he tried once more to tell the leader that he'd give Fairy to him. The leader, enraged and loathing the miserable being writhing at his feet, kicked Titus again, this time in his private parts. Titus could not tell him anything now. Doubled over, gasping for breath and retching, he would unwillingly keep Fairy's secret.

After one more march down the line of travelers, the lead Danite remounted his horse. He was satisfied that Fairy Radburn was not with this train. He signaled his men to ride off.

Fairy nearly fainted with relief when she heard the horses galloping away. As quickly as she could she freed herself from the platform under the wagon, and tended to her children. Jarom wakened after about an hour, but Letha Belle gave her the scare of her life by not moving or breaking her sleep until the middle of the night. Fairy left Titus where he had fallen. She had gathered up all she could of the food that the Danites had strewn all over, and she had tried to help others put their belongings back into their wagons. None of them would permit her near them. They wouldn't allow her to touch their belongings. They hadn't given her away—this time—but neither would they befriend her. Giving thanks to each of them, she walked back to Horner's wagon a small friendless figure.

Titus had managed to drag himself up into the bed of the wagon. Both babies cried on the floor where Horner had shoved them when he took the only tick for himself. He lay there moaning and calling for Fairy to tend him.

Fairy spit on the man. "You'da give me an' my babies to them if they'da listened to you. Greedy old man, you brought this on yourself." She picked up her children's belongings, wrapped them in their blankets again, and settled them down in a little nest on the floor. Together the three of them slept away what was left of the night.

Titus was a sore man in both body and spirit. With each day he became nastier and more cruel with Fairy. Even the end of the seemingly endless desert did not improve his temper. And if he had been unpopular before with the other members of the wagon train, he was a complete outcast now. None of them spoke to him or "his woman," and never did they offer him a helping hand.

Each slight Titus suffered from the others, he took out on Fairy or one of her children. On the day that Titus had asked another man to fetch water for him when he went to the stream and had received a scathing look for an answer, Jarom happened to be within reach of his hand. Titus smacked the little boy harder than he meant to and the child fell, gashing his head against a wagon wheel. Fairy ran around from the other side of the wagon where she had been starting dinner, and saw her small son with blood running down the side of his face, and Titus leaning over him. With the cooking spoon she had in her hand, she whacked Titus on the back.

Growling viciously, the man turned on her. He grabbed her by the hair and swung her around until she was on her knees in front of him. He slapped her hard across the face over and over, then drove his knee upward. Fairy, seeing it coming, twisted to the side to protect her unborn child, and Titus's leg crunched painfully into her shoulder. Fairy's whole arm felt as if it was going to fall off. She couldn't move it. Vaguely, for she was about to faint, she heard the shouted anger of another man.

She drifted into and out of consciousness, but Titus wasn't hitting her any more. She was cold when she fully regained her senses. She was on the ground, and it was the dead of night. Her first terrified thought was for her children. What had he done to them after he had finished with her? Staggering to her feet, she began her search. They were nowhere to be found. Titus was snoring, deep in sleep when Fairy slipped into the wagon. Jarom and Letha Belle were not there with him. Fear was choking her. What had he done with her children! Her lips drew back from her teeth, and she looked feral in her terrified rage. Her children! Her life!

Trembling, Fairy grabbed the bread knife from its holder, and drew it across Titus Horner's throat with all her strength. Her children! Oh, God, he had taken her children!

As Titus Horner lay on his pallet gurgling in his own blood, Fairy raced frantically around the wagon searching for her children, or at least for their bodies. If nothing else was left to her, she could at least bury the little ones. She looked under the wagon and in the piles of dirty clothes that Titus had left assuming she would wash them. She could find no sign of her babies. Now she looked at Titus, regretting only that she had not forced him to tell her where they were before she had slit his throat.

Then she straightened, her heart pounding painfully against her chest wall. The baby inside her tightened into a small hard knot, making her belly ache as well, but she *had heard a cry!* From somewhere outside she could hear Jarom's high piercing scream and Letha Belle's weaker but shrill cry. She nearly fell in her haste to get out of the wagon. Then again she stood still, determining from where the cries came. The cattle! In the cattle pen! Fairy ran across the expanse of grass and rock to the hastily built pen where the cattle were kept for the night. There among the thick, heavy legs of the cattle sat her two tykes, clinging to each other and screaming for their mother. Laughing with joy now, Fairy shooed the two cows that hovered near, and scooped her children into her arms. She hugged them and kissed them over and over.

Fairy had no cause to hurry now—except that in the morning someone would discover that Titus was dead. But she hardly cared. Her children were alive, and she was alive. That was all that mattered. Once more she cleaned her children, fed them, and sang them to sleep. Then Fairy got out of the wagon, hitched the oxen to it, and set out away from the train. If anyone saw her go, they did not stop her.

By the time first light dawned, Titus Horner had been thrown out of the wagon and left for the vultures and wolves. Fairy Meeks Radburn and her two children were miles ahead of the wagon train, and alone.

Seventeen

Jane Pardee quickly discovered that the express business she had entered into with her stepson Brian was both lucrative and wearisome. The lack of roads between the gold camps took its toll on a person's body, and Jane's most frequent companions on these trips were her mules. The mules were better company than none, but it did make a woman wonder if her powers of conversation would ever again extend beyond "Hippah mulah!" She tugged at the reins and got the ornery beasts back onto an old track left by the Hudson's Bay Company. She was grateful for that meandering track. Too often she traveled through territory where there was nothing, and she had to forge her own track. That took time, and it was dangerous.

Jane's usual route took her on a long loop north up the coast with a gradual movement east until she came to the mountains and traveled straight to Marysville on the Feather River. Then she headed farther east, and began the southern route zigzagging through the mountains to visit one small gold camp after another until she once again veered west, stopping at Sutter's Fort before she continued on the lower part of the loop on her way back to San Francisco and then home. It was a long, arduous trip, but Jane found a certain satisfaction in it. From the first trip she had made, it was apparent that this service was essential. Some of the men in the mining camps were suffering from a variety of aches and pains that Jane recognized and could immediately cure by putting vegetables into their diets. In her own brusque way, she had become the mama to these rough-edged men who could dig up the side of a mountain or build a city on the barren rocks and think nothing of it, but seemed unable to figure out that a potato would keep their legs from swelling and their gums from bleeding.

The miners' rough humor and their need of her good advice and express service pleased Jane. She liked being needed, but it also accentuated her loneliness, and her need for a more personal intimacy. She wanted to be needed all the time by one particular man. Despite her proximity to so many men, she had met no one who might become husband number five. "Maybe I already got all the husbands the good Lord allotted to me," Jane said to her mules. "What do you say about that, Lord? Think you could hunt around and find me just one more man to love?"

She moved her animals deftly through a narrow, meandering path that cut through the Sierras. Her wagon was only half loaded with supplies, and she hoped she'd have enough to bring needed sustenance to all the men in the camps she had to visit before she could get back to Sutter's and restock. The wagon rode well, however, for the supplies she had sold had been replaced by bags of gold and mail the miners she had already visited had given to her to take back to San Francisco. The trust the men placed in her with their gold and their mail—the only precious link many of them had to distant homes, wives and families—pleased Jane more than anything else.

It was good to know you were trusted and considered an honest, reliable person. The only problem with that trust which gave her some difficulty was that the miners did not stay in any one place for long. She always returned home with a few letters she had been unable to deliver, for the men had moved on and she hadn't been able to find them. Gold camps sprang up like mushrooms and then just as quickly met the end of their season and disappeared as though they had never been there. She never knew when she might round a bend in the road expecting to see a camp she had visited a month or two before, only to find a ghost town. Sometimes these transformations took place with such thoroughness that it gave her a sense of being in a dream, of imagining places that had never really been there at all.

Jane smiled as she thought of the many places that had vanished. It seemed that every man who ever stuck his shovel into the mountains thought the place needed to have a name to mark it, as though that would assure its success or place on a map. Like spinning snowflakes in a blizzard the names of new camps and ghost camps whirled through her memory. Dixie Valley, Rat Trap, Skunk Gulch, Coon Hollow, Foster's Bar, Shaw's Flat—come and gone, with others popping up and petering out with equal speed.

This leg of her journey she liked, for it was beautiful country, and at the end of the stretch came a few days of rest at Sutter's Fort. She would stop there and visit with old friends, exchange the latest gossip, and enjoy pleasant company while her wagon was being restocked with the supplies she'd need on the most southerly leg of her route. She'd also get to take a look at her town—Sacramento.

She smiled as she thought of Sacramento. On the advice of Sam Brannan she had bought ten lots there the last time she had come through. When Sam had first suggested the idea to her she had laughed and told him he was talking through the bottom of a whiskey bottle. Sutter's Fort was already a thriving community, and was no more than three miles from the low land that Sam Brannan was calling Sacramento. Sutter's land had much better drainage than the land Sam was talking about, and any fool could see that Sam's land would flood when the river was high. Jane knew all of that as well as she knew the contours of her own hands. But she also knew that Sam Brannan had a knack for knowing what people would do, and as he often said, good sense seldom had anything to do with final decisions. Sam said the low land would flood, but it would also become an important city—Sacramento. Jane believed him. It made no logical sense, but she had invested money in ten lots. Now she was anxious to see what had come of her investment in these months that had passed since her last visit.

Jane was shaken free of her thinking and her solitary chat with her mules by a persistent shrill cry. It sounded human.

Carrying as much gold as she was, she became instantly alert and wary. She daren't try to run—the ground was too rocky, and she could topple the wagon too easily. Instead she halted the mules and sat listening, watching, trying to identify the sound. Was it a single person in trouble? Was it a signal—one man to another or several others? Her hand moved easily and smoothly to the rifle on the seat beside her. She was a good shot, and she knew little fear. The dangers out here were far too great for flutterings of fear. Those she had left behind in Philadelphia nearly thirty years ago when she had headed west. Now she did the best she could. When she succeeded she was rewarded by the bounty of the land; if she failed she would bear the hardship of death. This was just another time when she would rise to the occasion and hope she could best it.

She sat still for a moment. The sound went on, and at least she knew it was not a signal, but neither did it quite sound like a man. She quickly made a mental inventory of all the sounds of animals she knew, and still she couldn't place what she was hearing. Cautiously she dismounted, secured the team of mules, and began to move toward the strange cries. She shook her head trying to rid herself of the irrational thought that kept coming back. No matter what this sounded like, there would be no baby up here—not here where there were no camps, no people, nothing but rocks.

Fifteen minutes later, however, she was proved wrong. A little boy, near to two years, she guessed, and another child considerably younger were huddled together in a shallow pit surrounded by piles of rock. The little boy, red in the face, was howling continuously, barely pausing to draw breath.

"Well, I'll be jiggered. The Lord sent me a man—a little young, but a man nonetheless," she said, chuckling. She reached down into the hollow, and scooped the little screamer into her arms. Nestling him securely against her hips, she leaned down and picked up the other child, who turned out to be a girl. She soothed the two frightened infants until they were reasonably quiet. But all the time her eyes roved restlessly over the rocky terrain, searching for sight of the adult who had left the children here, wondering where the man or woman was, and if he were friend or foe.

After waiting without results for half an hour, and realizing both children were hungry, Jane started back to the wagon. Beyond feeding them, she didn't know what to do. She didn't know if they had been abandoned, lost, stolen by Indians, or put in the hollow for safekeeping while their father dug for gold or searched for food. It was a shame both children were too young to tell her anything.

She smiled at the little boy, who was now quiet and sitting in the bed of her wagon munching happily on a biscuit and some grapes. His big eyes followed her every move. His sister had been fed and had already fallen asleep. "You two little tads are gonna make me late coming into the gold camps. Whaddaya think of that?"

The little boy waved his fists in the air, and attempted a crumb drenched smile as he jabbered unintelligibly.

"You know, feller, I have the feeling that if I could understand your language, you could tell me just what I want to know." She laughed at his antics, enjoying him. "Well, what does it matter? A day lost when you're in the company of a good friend doesn't mean much, does it?"

The sun began to dip toward the highest mountain peaks. "Shouldn't be long now before we find out if there is somebody coming back to fetch you two." Jane got up to gather wood to make a fire. The little boy watched her intently as she worked, setting the wood in place and making a circle of rocks, building them high enough to form a stove. She smiled at him. "Yes, sir, just a little while longer and your mama or your papa will be back—if there is such a critter to claim you." She looked away, and said more softly and to herself, "And if there isn't, then what am I gonna do? Lord, you wouldn't do that to me, would you? I know I prayed to you for children—but I haven't done that for a long, long time. I don't think I'm up to raising two kids now."

She made a thick broth with small pieces of shredded pork in it, and fed the children. Then she bundled them in a nest of blankets in the bed of the wagon, and settled herself to wait in front of the fire. The children were sound asleep when Jane heard the first frantic cries of their mother bouncing off the rocks.

"Jarom!" the voice called, shrill and panicky. "Jarom! Answer your maw!"

Jane got to her feet indecisively. She couldn't tell from where the original sound was coming. The woman was so panicky, she was shouting again before the reverberating sound of her first call stopped. Jane walked to the edge of the track where it began its descent. She stood on the ledge facing in the direction of the hollow in which she had found the children. Cupping her hands around her mouth she called "Whoo-eee! Whoo—eee!" She waited, and heard no break in the other's frantic calling. With a frown she shifted direction a bit. If the woman would just pause long enough to listen, it would be a simple matter to locate each other. Jane finally just stood silent on the top of the ridge waiting for the woman to quiet long enough for her to send a signal the other would hear. Finally the woman's voice broke and she began to sob. Jane took up her own call again.

An answer came. A high, quaking voice quavered, "Where are you?"

"Follow the sound—top of the ridge," Jane called loudly and clearly.

In the purpling dusk, Jane finally saw a small woman with a tangled mop of curly black hair scrambling up the rocks, not even aware that four feet to her left there was a path that would make her ascent easy.

Jane reached down for the woman's hand and hauled her up the last few feet of rock. Her sobs had turned to hiccoughing spasms. She could barely talk, and was completely unable to comprehend the message Jane had for her. "My . . . my chi . . . children . . . J-jaro—J-jjj . . ." she stammered, tearing at her hair, her eyes wild.

Jane put her hands on the smaller woman's shoulders, and held her firmly until she quieted. "Your children are safe! Listen! They're safe—right over there in the wagon. Shut your yap! C'mere and look at 'em—and don't you wake them up," she added gruffly.

The woman stumbled, nearly falling in her haste to get to the wagon. Jane took her arm and kept a hold on her. The woman began to cry again when she saw her two babies curled up in the blankets, their arms and legs intertwined as they slept puppy fashion.

"They've been fed and they're dry. You leave them to sleep, and let me get some warm food into you. You look in worse shape than the tykes."

As soon as she got her to the light of the fire and seated, Jane noticed the woman's near exhaustion, her painful thinness and her pregnancy. She shook her head, realizing it hadn't been two waifs she'd found today, but three. The woman was little more than a girl, not beyond eighteen or nineteen, Jane guessed. "What's your name, girl? How'd you come to be wandering out here with two tykes and another one on the way?"

The girl looked at her with fearful, wary blue eyes. "Are you a Saint?"

Jane guffawed. "Hardly! I like my little sins in big doses too much to warrant sainthood." To prove her point, she lifted her flask, took a long drink, then offered it to the girl. "Take some. It'll do you good. It's brandy."

The girl shook her head. "No—no, I mean are you—are you a M-mormon?"

"Lordy me, are you one o' them?" Jane sighed. "No, I'm not a Mormon, and it doesn't make any nevermind to me if you are either. What's your name?"

Fairy took a deep breath, unable to decide if it was safe to tell this big woman her name or not. The questions wouldn't stop there, she knew.

"Look here, girl," said Jane. "You can't stay in these hills alone—and I'm guessing you're alone or your man'd be here by now. I'll help you, but not without you telling me what it is I'm letting myself in for."

"Are you here alone? No man?"

"No man. I'm Jane Pardee. I run an express service to the gold camps. But if you've got it in your head that I can't defend myself, you're mistaken. I've been up and down these hills, and met and mastered the nastiest of them. Don't even think of tryin' to take from me what's mine."

"Oh! I wasn't! I'm—I'm just—"

"Scared simple," Jane finished for her. "Who are you running from? Your husband?"

"Oh, no," she said quickly, then paused again considering the possibility of trusting Jane Pardee and placing her safety and that of her children into this woman's hands. With a deep, trembling intake of air, she decided. She said, "I'm Fairy Radburn. It's my husband Asa I'm runnin' to, Miz Pardee. Guess I should tell you what you're lettin' yourself in for, for helpin' me and the babies."

"Radburn, huh," Jane mused to herself. Jane had never met Susannah's stepbrother, but she knew all about him. She made a mental note to warn Susannah next time she stopped in San Francisco.

Jane dished up a large portion of the thick soup, and handed Fairy a big chunk of bread and some cheese. "Here, eat this as you talk. You don't look like you've had anything decent to eat in weeks."

Fairy smiled faintly, saying, "I hain't, an' I thank you." After she had several satisfying mouthfuls of the soup, and some of the bread, she sat back and told Jane the whole story of her escape from Salt Lake City, starting with Brother Nephi's demands, and ending with the murder of Titus Horner and her time in the mountains. Ten days before, she had lost Titus Horner's wagon down a ravine. She had gone down after the wagon and brought up what little of the food she could gather, but it had been a long time since she or her children had eaten a nourishing meal. "I was afraid to let them eat much—I didn't know if I'd find anything else for 'em. I did save some of their garb." Fairy pointed down the path, vague as to where she had left the parcel now that it was dark.

"It's a miracle you survived at all," Jane breathed.

Fairy's face brightened, and in her eyes glowed a touching light of faith. "We are a people of miracles," she said.

Jane merely looked at the young woman. The biggest miracle of all was that after all Fairy Radburn had been through, she could still say that. Jane got to her feet and walked slowly to the wagon. She took from it another blanket, brought it back and wrapped it around her shivering charge. "You sleep now. You'll be safe. We'll decide what we want to do in the morning."

Gratefully Fairy curled up by the fire and slept with a confidence in her security she hadn't known since she'd left her home.

As Fairy and her children slept, Jane sat by the fire awake and alert, her rifle near her hand. She mulled over the problem these three presented to her. There was no question she was going to help them, but there were a few problems not easily solved. At any of the camps she entered to deliver mail, collect gold or sell supplies, she might be dealing with a Mormon—or worse yet, a Danite. She would have no way of knowing it until it was too late. Fairy and her children would have to be kept hidden while she conducted her business, and until Jane could deliver them to Asa Radburn in Sutter's Fort. It wasn't going to be easy. If it hadn't been for the mail Jane was carrying, and the fact that so many depended on her, she would have forgotten the rest of her route and headed straight for the fort.

And that made her think of the final problem. Asa Radburn had been at Sutter's Fort the last time he had written to his wife, but that was no guarantee that he would still be there when they arrived. Men just did not stay put these days. Jane had said nothing to Fairy about this. The woman didn't need any more trouble on a plate that was already full to overflowing. But thinking about it, Jane wondered again what she was going to do with the three of them if the husband couldn't be found.

Jane didn't really sleep that night, merely nodding off and awakening every half hour or so. She was wide awake and alert with the first light, another disastrous possibility coming to mind. Fairy had said her husband was himself a Danite on an assignment for Brigham Young. Fairy was going to present herself to him a fugitive from avenging Danites, thus making her husband choose between his family and his own place in the Church. Not only would her husband lose his status in his Church if he chose her and the children, but he would moreover bring the wrath of Brigham Young and his fellow Danites down on himself. Fairy was dead certain that Asa would choose his family—but Jane wondered, would he?

She got up, and tossed more wood on the low fire, bringing it back to a healthy blaze. While she waited for the flames to subside, and burn down to a satisfactory cooking fire, she put the coffee pot on, and went to feed and water her mules. She gave each of the animals an affectionate pat, and a little treat she carried in her pants pocket. "Well, Daisy," she said softly to the lead mule, "looks like I stepped into it up to my knees this time. I sure hope we all come out of this one all right." She moved down the line of animals, taking a moment with Hyacinth, Carnation, Bluebelle, Iris, and Lily.

She went back to the campfire to start breakfast. She glanced at Fairy, lying half on her back in innocent slumber. Funny, but she looked like somebody Jane already knew. She gave it a brief thought, and dismissed it. She'd never seen this girl before.

At the scent of food, Jarom awakened and began to jabber. His arms were stretched out toward Jane, an eloquent demand that she should come and get him. Letha Belle awakened moments later. Together the two children brought Fairy out of the nicest sleep she'd had in weeks. She got up, smiled happily at Jane, then went to hug her two babies, but she didn't take them from the wagon. She turned to Jane. "I'm goin' down the hill to get their garb—I left our passel down there on the rocks. All their clean napkins are in it," she explained.

After the two infants were washed and dressed in clean dry clothes, Fairy fed them. Jarom toddled after Jane as she broke up camp, and Fairy took Letha Belle with her to the stream as she washed their clothes.

When Jane set off again, the children's wet laundry flapped in the breeze from the side of her wagon. Jane yelled, "Hippah, mulah!" and they started along the ridge that would take them to the first camp along the North Fork. Jane left Fairy and her babies in a camp long before she entered the mining camps. She did her trading, then circled round to pick up her passengers before going on to the next camp. It was a tedious way of travel and added many hours to Jane's routine. When she crossed Bear Valley on her way to Sutter's Fort, she was already three days later than expected. About four miles north and east of the fort, Jane left Fairy again. Together the two women set up the camp, then the big woman hugged Fairy. "Don't you worry none. If Asa is here, I'll find him and send him out to you and the little'uns—if it's safe."

"Ought I go with you?" Fairy asked.

Jane shook her head adamantly. "Good Lord, child, no! We

don't know who we're likely to find with your husband. We've got enough problems for him without maybe causing him some more. Let me scout out the way of things with your man, then I'll send him to you if I can. If that doesn't work out, I'll come back for you myself and we'll figure out what to do with you."

Fairy looked down. "All I wanted was gettin' Jarom and Letha Belle safe away from Salt Lake City. But with Asa bein' a Danite and all, maybe he won't want us." She looked up at Jane's face, her eyes tearful. "Jane, I never went fer to git you in trouble too."

Jane gave her another quick hug. "You didn't get me in trouble. I did it all myself. I'm real good at that. Now, you take care of those two babies and yourself while I'm gone."

As always, Sutter's Fort was a beehive of activity. The streets and shops were crowded with wagons, men on horseback, and pack trains and freight trains like her own. And as had been usual during the last year, many of the faces she saw belonged to strangers, but even more belonged to friends and acquaintances, all glad to see her. She hollered greetings to several of them, promising to see them later in Brannan's Shirt Tail Store. She knew she would have a good supper tonight, and a few drinks, and be questioned until her throat was dry about the new gold camps and strikes, and about those places that were no longer good spots to hunt for gold. This was just another of her services, one she enjoyed a lot. Jane Pardee liked comradeship and a lot of gossip. As long as it was harmless, a little gossiping did the soul good. In her way, she was the miners' mobile newspaper.

Casually, she asked about new people in the fort, particularly Mormons. Often she would say, "When I was last in San Francisco I heard that Susannah Gentry's brother, Landry Morrison, has come to try his hand at finding the glittery stuff. I just thought if I could locate him, I'd give him a message from his sister and see if he might want to send a letter back with me."

One of the men at the bar chuckled. "You'd do anything to scare up a little more business, Jane."

"How do you expect me to get rich, Buddy, if I don't do a little scarin' up?"

"Well, I think you're out of luck. The only Morrison around

here is Dave. And the only new fellows that I know are Mormons are a tough lot runnin' a saloon a ways up the road. They get all their gold second hand."

Jane shrugged, and let the subject fade away. She had heard what she wanted to hear. Tomorrow would be soon enough to see if one of that tough lot was Fairy's husband Asa.

The next day Jane took some time to watch the saloon where she thought she might see Asa, waiting until she saw a man who fitted the description Fairy had given of her husband. When she was reasonably certain she could enter the saloon and find Asa Radburn, she walked inside. The man standing at the end of the long, dark wood bar glanced at her, but said nothing. For a moment she wondered if he was going to ask her to leave because she was a woman. He scowled, and turned his head away from her. Obviously he wasn't going to serve her, but that was all right. She squinted a bit as her eyes became accustomed to the dark interior, then she saw the man she thought to be Asa sitting at a table near the rear of the saloon. He had a half-eaten meal in front of him, and his attention was consumed by a tattered newspaper. She walked to his table, sat down, and rapped gently on its surface. The man looked up. Her first impression did not promise good things for Fairy. This was the man Susannah had so feared. A hard man, with hard dark pellets for eyes.

"Are you Asa Radburn?" she asked.

"What if I am? Who'd be wanting him, and why?"

Jane didn't like him, and she wasn't going to play the game by his rules. "If you want to tell me if you're the man I seek, then speak up. If you don't, I'll be on my way, with Radburn the loser." She sat upright, her hands on the arms of the chair ready to propel her to her feet and out the door.

He looked at her with his hard, peculiarly dull eyes for a long moment. He noted the gun on her hip, and she believed he knew she could use it well. Finally he said, "Sit down. I'm Radburn. What's your message?"

"No message," Jane replied softly. "I got a package for you, but you'll have to come with me to learn more about it. I won't talk to you here—it must be where certain ears won't hear."

"If you mean my partner, I've got no secrets from him."

"Not yet."

"Get out of here. Whatever you're selling I don't want it," Asa said, and buried his face back in his newspaper again.

Her voice very low but clear, Jane said, "I *thought* Fairy was countin' on the wrong man." She got up then, making the chair scrape loudly against the plank floor.

The paper dropped and Asa leapt up. "What did you say? Fairy? Did you say F—"

"Shut up!" she hissed. "Don't say her name again, do you hear? You want to know what I've got to say, follow me out—but shut up!" Jane stalked out of the saloon, and moved with swift steps down the street.

She was nearly at her hotel before Asa caught up with her. He reached out and grabbed her roughly by the shoulder. With a quick swing, Jane slammed the back of her fist across his face, and before he recovered she had her pistol out of its holster and aimed at him. "You don't touch Jane Pardee like that! Get up off the ground, you turd, and maybe I'll give you the information your wife asked me to give you."

"You old bitch," Asa muttered, wiping a trickle of blood from his cut lip as he got up.

"You're damned right I'm an old bitch, and next time don't forget it, 'cause with you it'll be my pleasure to shoot first."

It took a long time for Jane to lose her anger, and Asa had to resort to using all the good manners and courtesy that Prudence had so carefully inculcated in him in his youth before she would speak to him. Finally she told him what had happened to his wife.

"Where is she now?" he demanded.

"I'll tell you when I'm certain you mean her no harm."

"How could I mean her harm? She's my wife! My children—my son—"

"You're a Danite," Jane pointed out bluntly. "Brigham Young sent them after her. That means you choose between doin' your duty to the church for Young, or you protect your wife and kids—and put yourself in the same spot with Young that they are. Up to now you haven't shown me anything that says you've got the balls to stand by your family." Jane's eyes bored into him. She gave no sympathy, and no quarter. She didn't trust this man. Even if he swore to her that he would protect Fairy and the tykes, she'd hate leading him to them. "You'd better think it over. I'm staying here at the hotel tonight. I'll wait here until tomorrow noon. If you think you can face the world with Brigham Young's bunch of killers on your tail, you come talk to me, and I'll tell you how to find Fairy."

Asa began to argue, then thought better of it. He had been right. This woman *was* an old bitch, and he believed her when she said she'd shoot first if he bothered her. With a great number of disturbing thoughts on his mind, Asa Radburn sauntered back to the saloon. All the rest of that day he was moody and surly with his partner. Porter Rockwell accepted that, for on occasion that was how Asa was.

The thing that gave him the most grief was that if he protected Fairy he would be called an apostate, and that would make him no better than his good-for-nothing stepbrother Landry. It would lower him to the level of Sam Brannan—only Brannan had managed to plead his case before the Council and get reinstated, and Asa would never be allowed to do that.

All his life he had wanted to be something special, to find a place in life that singled him out as just a bit better than others, and he had finally found it. A Danite was a special breed of man. A Danite was a proud man. What was a man who had to hide, and constantly run? Fairy had brought this on him. Was she worth it?

He thought about his children. It was true, as Jane had said, that if they had been caught in the desert or the mountains, both children would have been killed right along with their mother. But they hadn't been caught. He wouldn't have to do away with his own children. He could keep them. It was only Fairy he'd lose—Fairy and his unborn child. The child might be another son. Asa liked the idea of fathering sons, men-to-be like himself, made in his image and likeness. They'd give him another wife. He could have several wives. All he'd lose would be Fairy—and the unborn child. He wanted the child. Maybe he could hide her until the child was born, and pretend he had found her only then.

He didn't sleep that night for a long time, and when he did his dreams were haunted by his pretty, raven-haired wife. Fairy was a loving woman. She suited him well, and though he seldom used the word to himself or aloud, he loved her as much as he was able. With an unexpected suddenness, his mind set itself to the task of figuring out a story acceptable to Porter Rockwell—er, James B. Brown—to cover a span of time during which he could be absent and get a good head start on anyone sent after himself or Fairy. Being an apostate was a tricky business for anyone, but especially for someone like him who carried out special missions for Brigham Young. Brother Brigham did not like losing one of his people from the fold, and firmly believed that death was preferable to defecting from the Lord's flock.

As Asa worried through this, an idea formed. The next morning he approached Rockwell/Brown. "I think I'm being tested," he said, and waited for a reaction from Brown. "I got a package from Brigham yesterday—secret orders to go waste a fellow in the digs south of here. I've never been sent on a mission alone before—what do you think it means?"

"Could be he wants to see if you can be trusted. Who are you s'posed to use up?"

"I'm not allowed to say—just inform him by messenger when the deed is done," Asa said. "Does he test men this way? Does he think I can't carry something like this off?"

Brown chewed heavily on a wad of tobacco, spat, and hit the brass spittoon with deadly accuracy, making it ring. "Snuff the guy out like a candle and send Brigham his head. Whatever he's thinkin', that'll settle it."

Asa smiled. "I worry too much."

"You do," Brown agreed. "How long you figure to be gone?"

Asa shrugged. "There's a lot of gold digs south of here—depends how lost he's got himself, and if he has an idea I'm on his heels. He could be hard to find if he knows someone's after him—a month?" The statement sounded more like a question, and Brown raised his eyebrows.

"Why're you askin' me? I'm not wastin' the guy, you are."

Asa cleared his throat. He had made a mistake, and he couldn't afford that with Brown. "I'll be back when the job's done," he said decisively. "I was just wondering if you could spare me for that long."

Brown shrugged. His own mission was not pressing, dependent on Sam Brannan making a mistake. He said, "Brannan will hold." Then, reminding Asa of his uncompleted mission to use up Hiram Gates and Levi Fifield, he added, "I heard tell Hiram Gates was over in Greenwood Valley."

Asa nodded, hitched his gun belt up and let it drop into place. "See you," he said jauntily, and walked away.

It was close to noon by the time he packed those things he wanted to take with him, and all the money he could lay his hands on. He was hurrying by the time he got to the hotel and asked for Jane.

"She left 'bout fifteen minutes since," the clerk said with sleepy indifference. "She might be still at the livery."

Asa ran the hundred yards or so to the livery stable where, breathless, he found Jane hitching her mules to a heavily laden freight wagon. He said accusingly, "You told me you'd wait until noon."

"You found me. What'd you decide?"

"Take me to Fairy—or tell me how to get there."

"I'll take you, but I'm going with you. Asa—don't think you're going to haul that poor little girl back here and turn her over to Brigham Young."

"That isn't the way it's done," Asa said with an oily smile.

"Hitch your horse to the back, and climb up on the wagon with me."

By a circuitous route, Jane headed away from Sutter's Fort. She let the mules move aimlessly about the countryside for several hours. Asa finally could stand it no more. "Where in the hell are you going? What are you doing?"

"Just making sure you don't have some of those rotten teeth you call Danites taggin' along behind us."

"I don't, damn it all! I told you I'm throwing my lot in with Fairy and the kids. Don't you understand every minute is precious? If we're to make it to a safe place, I have to get moving right now!"

"Then why the hell did you bring only one horse?" Jane snapped. "What're you gonna do, strap two babies, a grown man and a pregnant woman to one animal?"

Asa shook his head. "Is that what's bothering you? What did you think, I could take a cart or wagon out of Sutter's to go hunt a man down without making Porter suspicious? I told him Brigham had sent me on a mission. You don't go on out to kill a man in a donkey cart!"

Jane granted that, and set the mules on a course that would take them to Fairy and the children.

Asa was a different man with his family. His dark, pebble-dull eyes took on some life. He was enthusiastic and as gentle as he could be with Jarom. He seemed in awe of Letha Belle, almost afraid he would hurt her if he picked her up. Fairy showed no fear of him at all, but still Jane did not relax her watchfulness. At the first sign that he was not a man of his word, she had already decided she'd shoot him the same way she'd shoot and kill a poisonous snake.

Asa kissed Fairy gently on the cheek and then lovingly on the lips. His hand moved from around his wife to touch and rest gently on the small mound of her belly where his new child resided. Jane relaxed. Taking the children with her, she left the couple alone to talk. After the whole situation had been discussed, Asa came to her. "We're headed north—up along the Feather. Could you do one last thing for us?"

"Depends what it is," Jane said.

"Would you go into Coloma and get us a cart? I don't dare buy something like that right now."

Jane bought the cart. Again she was days late on her route, but it was with a good feeling she prepared to set out again. Fairy, smiling, hugged her mightily. "If my baby is a girl, I'll name her Jane. Thank you for everything. Thank you so much —we wouldn't be with Asa now if it hadn't been for you—we might not even be alive."

Jane grinned with pleasure and managed to blush. To cover the rush of emotion she said, "I'll be around bringing you supplies from time to time."

"But you won't know where we are," Asa said.

"You'll know where I am. When you need supplies you'll know where to get them without harm coming to you."

She sat on her wagon motionless, watching them move along in their cart. The mountains seemed larger than usual, and the donkey cart seemed very small.

Then Fairy turned to wave and smile at her, and Jane's heart jolted. She gasped. Now—now, when it was too late, she knew who Fairy reminded her of. Susannah. Susannah, who had known such fear of Asa. Oh Lord, Lord forgive her, she had led that lamb right to the slaughter!

Eighteen

Augustus Sutter was feeling panicky. Before him sat Colonel Stuart of the United States Army, who had come to foreclose at once on Captain Sutter's holdings of Fort Ross and Bodega, under the terms of his contract with the Russian-American Fur Company. Augustus eyed the colonel, cold and forbidding. His mind was whirling. What would his father do if he were here? What was the proper procedure, the legal thing to do? He said, "I shall consult our attorney, Peter Burnett."

Peter Burnett met them in his office. His welcoming look observed Augustus pale and tense, and Stuart, cold and composed. He made himself efficient with outer garments and drinks, and they sat down to talk. Augustus let Stuart state the reason for their presence. Burnett listened, then said to Augustus, "Didn't Captain Sutter expect to be back tonight?"

With his father one never knew; but Augustus nodded eagerly. "Yes, he did."

Afterwards Augustus could not have said how Burnett did it, but having obtained Colonel Stuart's word that Sutter's money was still good to pay off the debt, skillfully he persuaded Stuart to wait until Sutter returned before carrying out his foreclosure. Augustus took Stuart to Sacramento to Brannan's hotel with the promise to return for him at dinnertime. Then he hurried back to Burnett's office, where they spent some time combing the records in the dim hope of finding enough money.

At last Burnett slapped the account book shut. "This has me beaten. No matter how hard we try, we are short nearly ten thousand dollars. What a shame, what a pity and a shame." He wiped his forehead with his bandanna handkerchief.

"Is there any possibility Colonel Stuart will take part payment?"

"We have pushed that man as far as he will push, Augustus. Now we've either got to come up with the full amount or lose the entire property."

Tears stood in Augustus's blue eyes. "To think—I have stayed here with Papa, trying to protect him from just this, and now it's going to happen anyway."

Burnett put his hand briefly on Augustus's shoulder. "My young friend, you cannot save a drowning man who thinks he is picking water lilies. The seeds of this disaster were sown long before you had any power over the property."

"What will Papa say? I feel I have failed him."

"You have not failed him, nor have I. If we cannot produce a miracle, then we can comfort your father. Meantime, let us follow your suggestion of part payment. We shall create a proposition for the colonel, offering him as much money as we can, in case he is of a mind to be flexible."

That evening Burnett, Augustus and Colonel Stuart sat late in the parlor of Sutter's quarters, two of them waiting with mounting anxiety for Sutter to come home. They all knew that Sutter had probably camped and would not return for another twenty-four hours. Stuart showed no signs of impatience, but when the tall case clock chimed ten, he rose. "I can see our man isn't coming tonight," he said. "Will you have someone light me back to the hotel?"

Numb and miserable, Augustus found an Indian servant, gave him a torch and sent him with the colonel. He and Burnett waited a bit longer, avoiding each other's eyes. Then boots thumped on the porch, the door was flung open, and Captain John Sutter stood in the doorway. "Vell vell," he said heartily, his cheeks rosy and his eyes alight. "My friend Peter and my son Augustus. Such a velcoming party. 'Gustus, pour me a brandy and order my supper. Ve haff a downbreak on the road, othervise I had been home sooner." Neatly he hung up his outer coat and his hat. Then he turned around. "You are both so qviet. Vot iss?"

Augustus handed his father the brandy. "Drink this, Papa, you will need it."

"Aahh! Varm at last. Now tell me, for vot do you stand with long faces?"

"A man came today to foreclose on Fort Ross, Papa."

"Foreclose!? But he cannot! Ve vill pay him and send him off!"

"John," said Burnett gently, "there isn't enough money. He won't take a partial payment."

"How much do ve owe? Ve pay!"

"It's not only Fort Ross, Papa, it's Bodega too."

John Sutter flapped his hand as though shooing flies. "A little thing. How much?"

Burnett told him, and added, "We have a little gold, and several negotiable notes on the lots in Sacramento City. But we still need ten thousand dollars."

Sutter stared at him. "If dot don't beat the Dutch. I neffer see it fail. I get a dollar, a man needs my dollar. I get a thousand, a man needs my thousand."

Augustus felt hope rising, but clamped the lid on it. "What do you mean, Papa?"

"Today I say I will collect debts. You know it is my dearest vish to bring here your mother and our family. I say to myself, I vill collect a few thousand and I vill send for my Anna. Yes, yes, Peter, I know you say pay off efferything first. But I miss my Anna."

Unable to wait, Augustus asked, "How much did you collect today?"

"Vell . . . I do not know. I bring it in and veigh it, then I say."

Excited now, Augustus ran out to the wagon and brought in the heavy sacks of gold dust his father had collected. When weighed, their value totaled $10,500. Augustus's eyes met Peter

Burnett's. The youth let out a whoop that made his father jump. Then he grabbed his hat and ran out into the night.

"Vhere does he go, running like the vind?" Sutter asked.

Peter Burnett smiled in relief. "I suppose he has gone to Brannan's hotel to save Fort Ross and Bodega for you."

A few days later Sutter said, "Augustus, I vould like you to write for me several letters."

"Yes, Papa. To whom, and what do you wish to say?"

Sutter began pacing the floor of his office. As his son took notes, he began naming prominent men in Los Angeles, San Diego, Santa Barbara, Monterey. "And of course, Sam Brannan in San Francisco. Vot ve are going to say is that since the Congress does not see fit to grant California a government, then ve should create a government ourselves. Do you know vot I hear the other day? I hear a man propose that maybe murder is not a crime if there is no law against it! How do you like that, Augustus?"

"But Papa, even without law, surely there is some redress—"

"Redress!? A mob, a rope, and a tall tree! That is redress when there is no law! But ve vill fix that. Already in San Francisco the people haff meet in the little redwood schoolhouse to consider vays to protest the import duties ve are forced to pay on everything we use, to support this government we cannot haff. Ve must haff our own government soon. If not, then efferything I vork for ofer the years, efferything I own, is not mine. The American government comes in and poof! all is gone."

"If California had factories, instead of so many gold mines, then we could at least avoid this import tax," said Augustus.

"Then ve haff to pay some other tax instead. Vot gets my goat is that ve are paying for government, but we don't got one. So you tell these men that we should haff meetings, and elect officials, and begin to write a constitution for the state. Tell them that very soon Governor Mason will be replaced, and vhen the new man comes in, it vould be vell if ve had some order already established."

"You've already set a precedent here, Papa," said Augustus proudly. "We may be the first district to have elected a magistrate and recorder."

"Vell, vell, ve had to start somewhere," said Sutter modestly.

Augustus recapitulated the points his father wished to make in the letters and said, "I'll write a rough draft for you to look at first, Papa. Before you go, would you go over some of these accounts with me?"

Sutter hated accounts, especially those written down on paper, especially those which showed something unpleasant. "Pshaw, Augustus, you take care of that. Ask Peter."

"Now, Papa—" Augustus began, with a little smile.

His father sat down, evidencing every intention of springing right up again. "I take a minute, no more."

"First, I wanted you to look at the cost of supplies you are getting from George McDougall. He is cheating you. You pay him this much"—he pointed with his pen at a figure—"to run your ferry boat. In addition, he brings you supplies and charges you this much. Much too much."

"But he brings them in on my boat—he cannot be overcharging."

"Papa, he is. We could save several hundred dollars each week by getting someone else to supply us. And your stores at Coloma and Sutterville—"

"Fine stores, beautiful stores," Sutter said.

"Making a lot of money for someone else. Your agents there are cheating you too."

"They cannot be. I trust these men."

"They should not be trusted. They want your gold for themselves, and they don't care how they get it. Can you not find other agents, other men who are honest?"

"You say first my friend George McDougall is dishonest, then you say my two friends who are running my stores are dishonest. Are you saying that Captain John Sutter does not know how to pick his employees?"

"No, Papa. But I might say that Captain John Sutter has a kind generous heart and unscrupulous men take advantage of him."

Sutter shoved the account book from him and stood up. "No—no, I vill not belief this. These men haff honest faces. They vould not cheat me."

Augustus said patiently, "Whatever the cause, we are running short of money again. Your three thousand dollars in rents from the Fort are already overdrawn this month."

Sutter sat back down. "Augustus, vot is happening? You come ofer from home, you say you vant to help me, and you get your name on my property, and ve haff no money. I vant to know vhy."

"I told you why, and you refused to believe me. Possibly you have been too generous and openhanded with men who ask you for supplies."

"But I haff alvays done so," Sutter said. "I am a rich man, I share my riches. Are you trying to tell me how to run my business?"

"Yes, Papa. That is my job. I am telling you that you are no longer a rich man, that you cannot afford to give away so much."

"I am the richest man in New Helvetia!" Sutter exclaimed. "Or I vas, till you took ofer."

Augustus had frequently heard this complaint before and ignored it. Nevertheless, the undercurrent of distrust and competition between himself and his parent disturbed him. Now, weary of fighting his father to try to save his father's wealth, he said, "You are blaming me because the truth of your financial affairs has come to light. Is that it, Papa?"

"I do not think it is the truth!" Sutter exclaimed. "I haff plenty money!"

"So you trust George McDougall, and the two men who run your stores, and you pay the bills everyone presents to you true or false—but you do not trust your own son, who has collected money due you, and has paid many of your debts, and who speaks the truth to you."

Sutter shrugged. "You haff say it."

"I think we would be better off if I leave New Helvetia," said Augustus, standing up. "You are too stubborn for me."

"A Papa alvays knows best," Sutter said, his mouth set.

"Tell that to Peter Burnett, and see where it gets you. Good night, sir." Augustus left the room, heading for his bedroom.

" 'Gustus, vait!"

He turned around, asking respectfully, "Yes, Papa?"

Sutter said hesitantly, "Maybe a little mistake has been made, maybe these men who vork for me haff forget to pay me all they owe." His eyes pleaded with his son, Understand me, let me be right.

Augustus said, gently but firmly, "They are dishonest men, Papa."

Sutter said, angry again, "It is my money! You do not tell me vhat to do! I do vhat *I* vant!"

"Yes, Papa. Goodnight."

This time his father did not call to him. Augustus went to bed in a black mood, determined that as soon as he had written the letters for his father, he would pack his belongings and leave this place. He had had enough of wrangling and obstruction, of two steps forward and a step and a half back in his father's affairs.

He tried to avoid his father by eating breakfast late, but Sutter came knocking on his door. He came in shyly. " 'Gustus, I haff a confession for you."

"What is that?"

"I haff a little gold I don't tell you about. Might be you could use it to pay on my debt to Pierce over at the tannery."

This had happened before, usually after they had argued. "Where did it come from, Papa?"

"I collect it yesterday, a debt a man owed me. I safe it out so maybe I can sooner send for your mama. But I get more for that."

"Who was the man? I'll put his name and the amount down in the account book, so that we do not try to collect from him twice."

"No matter, no matter, it was neffer written down anyvay."

Augustus sighed, and put his hand on his father's shoulder. "Oh, Papa," he said and smiling, shook his head.

The time was nearing when Sutter felt he could send for his wife and other children. Accordingly, he was having a fine new house built on Hock Farm, his rancho on the Feather River. The house would face the river, with a white fence all along the front of the yard. It would be a story and a half, with high ceilings, many windows, and a long cool front porch with as many as twelve pillars. Conveniently nearby would be several outbuildings, plus a barn and farm outbuildings. There were tall trees to shade it, and the river was at hand for pleasure and transportation. This was expenditure Augustus did not protest, for he was as eager as his father to reunite the family again.

In March Sutter announced that he would be moving to Hock Farm to live. "I can oversee the building better from there," he explained. "I haff already rent out my quarters here in the Fort for two hundred dollars a month."

In April, as soon as the weather in the mountains had begun to clear, Sutter took a group of one hundred Indians and several Sandwich Islanders to dig for gold. They made camp on the South Fork of the American River, and found satisfactory diggings. Later Sutter moved his entourage onto Sutter Creek. By the end of April he had arrived back at Sacramento, where Augustus and Peter Burnett were still tending to his business affairs.

"Welcome home, Papa!" said Augustus, embracing his father. "We have missed you!"

Sutter smiled at his good-looking son. "I haff miss you too. But there is good news." He turned to a squat Indian who had come in with him. "Tondo, bring in the bags." After two or three trips, there were several leather pouches on the desk in front of Augustus. "Now veigh them," Sutter commanded. Their contents were poured out and weighed. "Ah, six thousand dollars. Enough," said Sutter with relief. "My boy, today I want you to go find my friend Heinrich Lienhard and bring him here. We are going to send him on a mission. He vill haff enough to pay back all my old debts in Switzerland. And by the end of this year—1849—he vill return vith your mama, and Emil, and Alphonse, and Anna Elisa!"

There was other news for Sutter. Brigadier General Bennett Riley had relieved General Mason as military governor of the province. Before Congress had adjourned on March 3, Mason and Riley had sent an inquiry as to whether or not Congress had provided California with a territorial government. For three months there was no answer. Then on May 28, word came to California on the *Edith*, a ship returning from Mazatlan. Con-

gress had not acted. So there was still taxation without represen-
tation in the Union.

Riley, whose language was spangled with oaths of many sylla-
bles, was as sensible as Mason had been. He was incensed—
colorfully—about this idiotic state of affairs. Riley immediately
issued a proclamation, setting August first as the date for the
election of municipal officers and convention representatives for
each district; further, on September first, the electorate would
assemble at Monterey and begin creating the State of California.

There were ten districts. Each had held meetings, as Sutter
had suggested. Peter Burnett had been elected Chief Justice of
the Sacramento District. Now they agreed to send properly
elected representatives to the constitutional convention. The
candidates for election toured the gold camps on horseback,
talking to the miners, taking with them little gifts of dried fruits
and tobacco that the miners missed so much.

The Sacramento representatives included Lansford W. Hastings, the daring, resourceful guide whose ill-considered "Hastings Cut-Off" had meant death for so many members of the
Donner Party; four other men; and as head of the delegation,
Captain John Sutter.

"Ve must become the thirty-first state in the Union," he said
to Augustus. "Ve vill!"

Nineteen

Spring and summer of 1849 was a busy time for the Gentry families, the Campbells and the Morrisons. With San Francisco changing daily—thirty new houses were being built every day—and streams of people flooding off the ships so crowded in the Bay that it looked like a huge forest, excitement and energy ran high. For those who thrived on this hectic kind of life, their personal lives ran apace with the city.

There seemed to be two distinctly different kinds of people in the territory: those who had early disappointments and failures in the gold fields and were crushed by them, and became disheartened and sickened by the rapid-paced vitality. Others simply grabbed like eager children for all the bounty that California offered, never looking backward or too far forward to times that might not be so blessed or rewarding. These were the true Californians, possessing a spirit and an optimism that were part and parcel of the makeup of the Gentrys, the McKays, and the Campbells. To any member of these families, even the slightest disappointment seemed an interference with the nature of life.

On a warm day in June, Sean McKay sat at his table in the kitchen eating his midday meal and grumbling fiercely to his wife. On the table beside his plate he had placed a letter they had just received from Fiona. His hard, blunt finger jabbed at the letter. "Why aren't she and Robin coming home? When am I going to get to see my grandson? That's what I'd like to know, Mary. Haven't you taught our daughters anything about respecting their father?"

Mary also wondered when Fiona was coming home. It was difficult to love someone as much as she loved Fiona, and want to see her so badly that the ache was with her daily, yet have that person show no sign the feeling was mutual. A part of her recognized that she should be grateful for Fiona's lack of need to come home, for it showed that she was happy with Robin, but it hurt nonetheless. She did so much want to see her newest grandson, Tyrone Gentry. Soon the child would be a month old, and she had never seen him for herself, did not know what he looked like except for Fiona's description in the letter.

Sean said querulously, "Mary! Mary, are you listening to anything I am saying? I want to see my daughter and my grandson!"

"I'm listening, Sean, and I want the same thing myself, but the letter makes it very clear that Robin and Fiona intend to remain at the gold camp and may not come home until the rainy season begins."

"What makes you think they'll come home then? Last year they stayed up in those mountains all winter. You'd think Fiona would have had enough of that after our experiences coming here from Illinois. Maybe Robin won't allow her to come home. Maybe—"

"Oh, hush, Sean McKay. You know perfectly well that's untrue. Every line of that letter indicates she is well and very happy."

"Well, I'm not!" he growled.

Mary laughed and came over to hug him. "I know, Sean, I can always tell."

"Coleen wouldn't do this," he asserted.

"No, but Coleen is quite different from her sister. Now that she and Brian have made up their differences, she's content enough on the ranch so long as she can see us often. But Fiona has always been independent and headstrong."

"I think you spoiled her."

"If anyone spoiled her it was you," Mary said placidly, taking a bite of applesauce.

Sean sat in brooding silence for a while toying with his food, then he said, "I'm not going to sit here and do nothing."

Mary laughed lightly again. "You know, Sean, you're the one who is spoiled. You have gotten accustomed to prosperity and having things your own way. You no longer tolerate being thwarted very well. Back home, you would not be talking this way."

"This *is* home, Mary," he reminded her. He said urgently, "Let's go to Fiona—Jim Herman can run the ranch for me. He's as able as I am." Sean was referring to the disappointed gold hunter whom Brian had brought to Sean, and who was now his foreman and right-hand man. "We could go at the beginning of August, and come home with Robin and Fiona and little Tyrone when they come back for the winter."

Mary said mildly, "Perhaps they won't want to come back."

Sean's blue eyes shone with determination. "They are not keeping my grandson in the snow! They will come home."

Mary smothered a smile. "Yes, Sean."

"Then you agree we should go?"

She did smile now. "I acknowledge that we are going, dear."

Mary McKay began to pack their wagon with the things she thought Fiona would want or need about the same time Susannah Morrison Gentry was giving birth to her first child. Prudence Morrison, feeling herself an old hand at births after her experience aboard ship with Tolerance, was in attendance. After Prudence had firmly ordered Ezra to take Cameron, a nervous father-to-be, to the closest saloon, she shut the door of Susannah's bedroom, and with relief turned to the business at hand.

Between pains, Susannah smiled at her. "It is a lot easier here than it was on the *Brooklyn,* isn't it, Mama?"

Prudence's eyes softened in sympathy for the tinge of fright and doubt Susannah expressed in that statement. "It is indeed, my darling, and it will be much easier. After all, you know what to expect and so do I. We are fortunate, Susannah. Some women go through their entire lives and know nothing about the birth process."

Susannah fought back weak tears, then she said softly, "Mama, if anything should happen—I mean, if everything doesn't go as it should—you'll see to the baby, won't you? I couldn't bear to lose him—I want him to live."

"Susannah Gentry! I won't hear talk like that!" Prudence said with some alarm. "You and your baby are going to be fine. We will have no difficulty." No more were the words out of her mouth than she was running to Susannah who was in the grip of a hard pain. She dabbed at her stepdaughter's forehead when the contraction subsided.

"I should have had more sympathy for what Tollie was going through." Susannah gasped, and clung to Prudence's hand.

"Don't think about that, dear. Keep in mind that each pain that has passed is one that will not have to be gone through again, and one of them will bring your child into the world. Keep looking for that pain."

Susannah, squeezing Prudence's hand, managed a giggle. "Mama, that is the worst piece of advice I've ever heard!"

Prudence gave her a sheepish grin. "I thought it sounded good."

Grimacing, Susannah tensed for the next pain.

"Try to relax, dear. I don't think it is good to fight against Nature."

Six and a half hours after her labor had begun, Susannah gave a last mighty heave and brought Simon Gentry into the world, a husky, lusty little boy.

By the time Ezra could no longer keep Cameron away from his home, his wife and his new child, Susannah was propped up in bed. Prudence had bathed her and the child. She had changed Susannah's nightdress, done her hair, and had her looking pretty, if tired. Cameron needed only to look at Prudence's homely beaming face to know all had gone well. Two at a time, he raced up the stairs to their bedroom. Bursting through the door, he got his first look at his son as the child rested peacefully in his mother's arms. Still very red and wrinkled, the baby was curled into a little ball snuggled as close as he could get to Susannah.

"Isn't he beautiful, Cameron?" Susannah asked, her eyes sparkling, her face a wreath of smiles.

Cameron's sight was blurred by tears. "You're both beautiful," he said in a low choked voice. He stood near the bed awkwardly.

Susannah patted the space beside her. "You won't hurt us—come join us. We're a real family now, Mr. Gentry. Come, I want you to see all of him." As Cameron moved nearer, Susannah peeled back the layers of soft cloth Prudence had wrapped Simon in. A tiny, perfectly formed little human being was exposed to his father's proud eyes. Simon had a thick covering of dark downy hair on his head, and even at that first sight Cameron could see his own bone structure in miniature. Simon Gentry would be built very much like his father. Cameron had never known before a feeling as deep or expansive in nature as what he felt in that moment he recognized himself in his son.

In the days that followed, Cameron bought cigars for dozens of friends and acquaintances, and drank more toasts than he had ever drunk in his life. Susannah was kept busy by a steady stream of visitors, and Simon had more baby clothes and silver spoons and cups than he could ever use. From Prudence and Ezra he received a set of gold tableware, and a bank account that would keep him in good stead all of his life.

"Oh, Papa, how can we ever thank you enough?"

With great pride, Ezra looked down at his grandson in his crib. How differently he felt about this grandchild from his older grandson Elisha. He said, "You have thanked me in the best of all possible ways, Susannah. You have presented me with my grandson—little Simon."

"But you have given him so much, Papa—"

Ezra smiled, and shrugged. "Over time, I would have done so anyway. This way, if something should happen to me, Simon will have what I intended for him in my lifetime."

"Papa! Nothing is wrong with you, is it?" Susannah asked with concern.

"No, no, Susannah, I am as fit as a man in his forties can be—but one never knows what the future will bring. I have spoiled too many opportunities in my life looking for the perfect time, the perfect person. I won't do that with Simon."

Susannah hugged her father. "Papa, you are the most wonderful father in the world."

Ezra patted her hand gratefully. It wasn't long ago that she would not have uttered those words, and certainly would not have believed them. Clearing his throat, he changed the subject, not wanting to revive sad memories better allowed to lie quiet. "Cameron tells me that Fiona and her child are well, and that Sean and Mary are going to their camp to see him."

Susannah's eyes were on Simon. "The Gentry men seem to have the knack of fathering boys, don't they? Two first born babies, and two boys. But Tyrone could not possibly be as beautiful as Simon is."

Ezra agreed, chuckling. "I wonder if Tyrone has his mother's flaming hair?"

"Do you know, that never occurred to me?" she marveled. "I just supposed he'd have had black hair like Robin's. Wouldn't it be nice if we could get the whole family together—a reunion? It has been over a year since I have seen Fiona and Robin."

"It sounds like a good idea to me. I'll put a bug in Sean's ear. He is determined to get Fiona to come home for a time anyway. This will give him added ammunition—not that he needs it. What a rare old Irishman he is," Ezra said, smiling affectionately.

Fiona and Robin Gentry were wealthy. They remained in the gold hills not to gain wealth, but because they liked the mountains, and so long as they had each other for company they liked the isolation. There was something invigorating about the strange straggling of men who came to the hills to seek their fortune in contrast with the long lonely months when they saw no one and heard nothing but the wild cries of the mountain animals.

Lately they had talked often of returning to San Francisco for a while when the rainy season began. Fiona, more than Robin, was loath to leave. Moodily she worked her pan in the stream. Tyrone, now two months old, lay on his blanket a few feet away from her on dry ground. The baby gurgled happily, content in the open air.

Robin, watching Fiona, got up and came over to her side. "What has hold of your mind, Fiona? Where is my usual little pepper pot of dreams and schemes?"

"If we go back to San Francisco this fall, maybe we'll never come back here," she said.

"But that isn't so. We've already decided we'll stay up here for at least one more season," Robin said with perfect truth. He pulled her to a seat beside him and put his arm around her.

What he had said didn't satisfy Fiona. She continued to stare glumly at the rocks. "That's what we say now, but what will happen when we get back to San Francisco? Maybe we'll think that it is wonderful there. Maybe we'll think it is as good there as it is here, and we'll decide to stay."

Robin shook his head. "If we feel that way, then perhaps that is what we ought to do. Why are you so worried about something that hasn't happened yet?"

"I don't want it to happen," she said. "I don't want to have other things that I like put before me so that I become confused. I know it is good for us up here in the mountains. We are thriving, and so is Tyrone. I don't want to lose that. I don't want to be fooled into thinking something else is better."

Robin just stared at her. "I don't know what to say. Do you not want to go home for a visit? I thought you wanted to see your mother and father and Coleen and Brian Og."

"See! You said go home," Fiona wailed. "This is home! We haven't even gone, and you are thinking about back there as home." She threw herself into his arms. "Oh, Robin, I don't want us to get stuck there. Hold me, and keep me right with you."

Robin didn't know what to do with his wife. He had known her to be this sentimentally emotional only one other time. He pushed her away from him a bit to better see her face. "Fiona . . . you are acting . . . very strange. You aren't . . . you couldn't be . . . could you?"

"I am," she said, and burst into tears.

"So soon after Tyrone," he murmured, more to himself in wonder than to her.

"Isn't it wonderful." She sobbed.

"I don't know . . ."

"I'm not exactly certain yet," she said, sitting up, taking his handkerchief, blowing her nose and dabbing at her eyes. "I'm only late—maybe—but I feel pregnant."

"But it's only been a little over two months since Tyrone—that's not very good for you, is it? Your mother told me—"

Fiona's eyes spurted more tears. "What difference does it make what my mother said if I am? See, that's just what I don't want to have happen. We'll go to San Francisco, and everybody will have sensible advice and we'll feel obligated to follow it. What if I want to have three dozen kids? Why shouldn't I? And that's not sensible—at least not to anyone else."

Robin began to laugh, his arms around Fiona. He rocked back and forth with her. "My God, Fiona, if three dozen kids don't kill you, they'll kill me." He kissed her tears away. "Come on, let's give it up for the day. I'll get Tyrone—let's go back to the cabin. Now that you're already pregnant I don't have to worry about getting you into that condition any more."

Fiona smiled and got to her feet immediately. She looked back at her handsome husband. "This is something else I don't want to give up, Robin. Up here, we do as we please. We work when we wish, we make love when we wish. There are no appointments to be kept, no obligations to be met. So long as we have food and shelter, we are completely free."

"I know, my love, but I promise you that wherever we go, we won't give that up. If life ever closes in on us, we'll leave. I won't ever let you be held captive by the unimportant things of life."

This time her smile beamed bright and true. "Thank you, Robin." Then, her mood completely changed, she said brightly, "Maybe this one will be a girl. Do you think that would be nice, or would it be better to have two boys, and then a girl?"

"I've always wanted a girl who looked just like you."

"But you do love Tyrone? You aren't disappointed?"

He took the baby from her, held him high, and kissed him on his rosy, chubby cheek. "I love him with all my heart—next to you. Always you will come first, and always he will be next to you."

Fiona was happy and content for a week, until she received a letter from her mother announcing that Sean was determined to see his new grandson, and that they would arrive at the camp sometime in mid-August. With that she dissolved into a mixture of highly volatile emotions. She was excited at the prospect of seeing her parents and having the chance to show off young Tyrone, and yet frightened that Sean and Mary would convince Robin they should go back to San Francisco for the winter.

Robin, usually very easygoing with Fiona, put his foot down. "I won't hear any more of this kind of speculating, Fiona. You are affecting Tyrone with all this worry, and you don't look well."

"But—"

He shook his head. "No buts—no more anything. It isn't a bad idea to go back this winter. Among the information you ignored in this letter is news of Sacramento City. Sam Brannan is going to be accompanying Sean and Mary that far, and according to this, Sean is thinking of investing. He says it is a thriving city. I think we ought to look into it ourselves. Another thing is that I have been thinking for some time we ought to head farther north—perhaps up along the Feather River or one of the streams that feed into it. If we leave this fall, we will be in a position of needing to build another winter cabin, and this time we'll have to do it without Brian's help, and you are pregnant."

"But—"

He raised his eyebrows, warning her not to carry the thought onward. Distractedly, she looked away, then back to him. "You would have to do all the work alone," she said.

"I would, but that doesn't bother me. What makes me uneasy is that I might not get it finished before the first snows. Then what would happen to Tyrone and you?"

"It does make sense to go down for the winter—but does it have to be San Francisco?"

"I didn't realize you didn't like San Francisco."

"I do like it—but all the letters we've had from Mama and Papa and Cameron indicate it is getting to be a very busy, crowded place."

Robin laughed. Her ideas of crowded had changed considerably since they had come to the mountains. Now she felt crowded if other people were living within five miles of them. There had been a time not long ago when she was comfortable only when she had been able to view her neighbor's house from her window. "We could stay in Sacramento—that is what I meant when I said we should take a look at it for ourselves. It wouldn't hurt for us to have a house there—even if we don't live there."

"That would make Mama and Papa happy. They would think that civilized."

"You might find it an advantage as well."

She laughed shortly. "I can't imagine how."

"You may find that two infants give you a desire for a little more stability and household organization than we have now."

"Never! I'll never choose to live in the city! Never, never, never!"

Sam Brannan's sentiments regarding the city were quite different from Fiona Gentry's. He had begun to look upon Sacramento City as a haven. His relationship with Ann Eliza was at best stormy, with thunderous passions both loving and hateful. Lately they had been worse to each other than usual, and she had taken up a new cry. He didn't know what to make of it. This time he wasn't certain that Ann Eliza's threats were merely threats. There was something different about her which made him uneasy. He would be more than happy to have a good excuse to be in Sacramento City with Sean. He could justify his absence to Ann Eliza, and that always made things easier.

With all good intentions, he brought home a large bouquet of golden roses for her. He found her in the parlor, her fancy work on her lap, a picture of placid hominess. For a moment he regretted the tension that always seemed between them. Ann Eliza Brannan was a beautiful woman—more than beautiful, she exuded an air of refinement that made her seem regal. Other times he saw this trait and accused her of putting on airs, but right now, without any heat or rancor to cloud his vision, he saw that she was a rare and desirable woman. He tiptoed the rest of the way into the room, and stood at her side.

"A penny for your thoughts," he said, and whisked the roses out from behind his back, presenting them to her with a flourish and a low bow.

"Oh, Sam! They are beautiful! What a lovely surprise." She took them and buried her face in them, inhaling of their delicate fragrance. With another grateful smile for her husband, she said not unkindly, "Are these to soothe me before I hear disagreeable news, Sam? Or might it be that this is a red-letter day, and I shall have flowers *and* a husband home for dinner?"

He kissed her cheek, and sat down near her. "You have both, my dear."

Without seeming to move a muscle, she rang a small bell that sat on the table beside her. When a primly dressed woman in starched black with a white apron appeared, she said quietly, "Tilda, please put these roses in water in the white Bristol vase and place them on the entry table. Mr. Brannan and I will have a glass of sherry before dinner. Set the table in my sitting room for two. The children may be served now."

Sam added, "But Tilda, send my little hell-raisers in here to their papa before you give them dinner."

"Yes sir." The woman curtseyed and left.

Ann Eliza barely managed to hold her tongue until the woman had closed the French doors to the parlor. "I do not want the children rough-housing in here, Sam. You are seldom here, and always you permit behavior that is not allowed at any other time. It is very difficult then for me to discipline them and regain order when you are once more off on one of your jaunts."

Sam ignored her. His children entered the parlor in orderly fashion. Almost shyly, as if they were confronting a stranger rather than their father, they greeted him in ragged unison.

Sam, laughing, got up, and one by one he lifted them high above his head, saying that he was gauging how much each had grown. He pretended to stagger under Sammy's weight, while the little boy giggled and squirmed. "Oh, my! You have become a giant, Sammy! You are as big as an oak! Look, 'Liza, my boy has grown up."

It was Ann Eliza's turn to ignore him, which she did, turning her attention to the little girls who were already squealing in delight. "Sit down, please. You are young ladies. Please reflect that in your behavior."

Sam looked fondly at his pretty daughters Addie and Fanny, ages two and three. "Nonsense! They are children! Come along, my little troops, if Mama does not want us to play in here, let us go outside. I want to see how fast you can run."

Ann Eliza started to protest, but with a sigh resigned herself to the fact that there were some unpleasant costs to be borne if Sam was at home. She heard him explaining as the children followed after him, "Sammy, we will give you a handicap because you are much bigger and your legs are longer than the girls'—but I'm betting you can make up the distance anyway."

Sammy's piping voice could be heard also. "I don't like to run fast, Papa."

The treacherous thought came to Sam that his wife was raising his only son to be a milksop. But he said lightly, "What foolishness! All boys like to run fast."

Ann Eliza heard no more as the front door closed. Sam, perhaps because he saw his family so infrequently, seemed not even aware that his children were far more like she was than they were like their father. For that Ann Eliza thanked the powers that be. Sam was overpowering, and though she loved him, and had a sinful lust for him, he disturbed her. She was both attracted and repelled by the furious animal power of him, and so very often she was hurt by him. She could not have borne it if her children had had that same power to devastate her. Somewhere in her life she needed the company and admiration of *civilized* people.

Listening to the faint sounds of her family at play outside the windows, Ann Eliza sat quietly thinking and trying to feel if this was giving her any real pleasure. How badly would she miss Sam if she left him? This was something that she had been thinking about more and more frequently. As she got accustomed to the thought, she was even becoming comfortable with it. At first it had seemed an impossibility, a terrible thing to allow into her thoughts. Now it just seemed like something possible but not probable.

Her reverie was interrupted by her children running back into the house at Tilda's call for dinner. Ann Eliza put out her hand to stop them from running to her. In only a few minutes their clothing had become covered with mud, and Sammy had grass stains on both knees. "Tilda!" she cried, forgetting the bell. "Tilda! Clean these children!"

"Their dinner is waiting, Ma'am," Tilda said meekly. "I'll see that their hands and faces are washed clean—and after dinner they can all have a good soak."

"That sounds like a marvelous idea, Tilda," said Sam.

"I said clean those children!" Ann Eliza insisted, her hand pressed to her temple. "I will not have them sitting at my table looking like urchins. Clean them now, and dress them properly for dinner."

"The dinner will get—"

"Clean them, or they will not eat! Not in my house!" she screamed, sounding far too much like the boarding house mistress's daughter she had been for her own liking. All her life she had striven to rise above her humble origins. Deliberately she lowered her voice and spoke in a controlled fashion. "That will be all, Tilda. See to the children now, please. I do not want them going to bed late."

Sam sat down. He leaned forward in his chair, his hands hanging limply between his legs, waiting for the children and Tilda to file out of the room. Before he could speak Ann Eliza said, "Please, Sam, don't talk to me about the children now. We have nothing to say that hasn't been said many times before."

"Do you realize that you are constantly complaining that I am never home in the evenings? That I do not spend enough time with you or the children? Do you realize that every time I am at home, or spend time with my children, we fight? The evening always ends like this. Tell me, Ann Eliza, if you were I, would you want to come home to this?"

She looked at him unblinkingly, a disturbing calmness in her demeanor. "No, I wouldn't, Sam. But let me ask you something. If I interfered with the organization of your business as badly as you interfere with my organization of this family, and on so erratic a basis, would you tolerate me?"

He felt uncomfortable. He could deal with her screaming. He knew how to handle his wife then, but this calm, accepting Ann Eliza was a terrible creature. He said in a low voice, "You know I wouldn't."

"So. There we are—nothing to talk about. Your behavior is abhorrent to me, and mine is abhorrent to you. Perhaps it would be best if each of us found a way to—to—" She ran out of words, still afraid to suggest that she leave, but for the first time while talking to him, she really wanted the words to fly from her mouth so fast that she would be unable to stop them. Tonight she couldn't quite manage it.

"To what, Ann Eliza?" Sam asked, curious yet fearful of what she might say.

She looked away from him, fighting back tears. "I don't know. I just don't know, Sam—I am just so terribly unhappy. When you are not here I am lonely, and I feel so—so mean, and I want you to be here. I need to know you are truly my husband —not just in our marriage bed, and when it comes time to pay the bills, but really my husband. And you see, it is so mad, and so awfully sad—I know you are not that man. I am tied to you for all my life, and I am the mother of your children—but you are not really my husband."

"What are you talking about?" he exclaimed, suddenly very angry. "That makes no sense at all. I am your husband. I will always be your husband."

She said nothing.

This was a time he should go to her, put his arms around her, comfort her, let it be known that he was there for her, and that he loved her—but he didn't. She was frightening tonight, and he much preferred to think of sweet Tollie, or of his trip to Sacramento City.

He stood up abruptly. "I am going to eat with the children. I'll tell Tilda to remove one of the settings from your sitting room. Good night, Ann Eliza. Oh, and I nearly forgot with all this talk, I will be leaving for Sacramento City in the morning. Sean McKay may buy some of those lots I have there. I'll be gone a week or two."

She didn't even look at him, but merely nodded her head.

By the time Sam met Sean and Mary, he had put Ann Eliza and her strange behavior out of his mind. He had decided what she needed was another child to keep her from growing morbid, and that ended his worry.

Mary had never been to Sacramento City, and its amazing growth meant little to her, but Sean was agog. All Sean remembered of Sacramento was the old ship store, and the flats that stretched out beyond it, peopled only by ancient oak trees. Now the tall masts of ships swayed at their moorings in the river, and on the plain, sheltered by the thick-trunked oaks, houses stood in orderly rows. Where recently there had been only scrubby grass, well-planned streets now crossed each other. From the landing to Sutter's Fort nearly two miles away, Sean could see houses. These were not tents, they were houses! Permanent dwellings that settled, stable people intended to live in for a long time.

"You're surprised, aren't you?" Sam said with relish.

"That doesn't even begin to express it," Sean replied. "Mary, you would not believe what a difference there is in this place—in just a few short months. There was nothing here! Nothing!"

"We're building a theater," Sam said. "And, of course, I have the finest hotel in town. You will be my guests—for as long as you stay."

"A hotel," Mary marveled. She had never spent the night in a hotel in her entire life.

"Yes," Sam said proudly. "It was John Sutter's grist mill until I took it over. Refitting it cost me fifty thousand dollars, but I think you'll agree it was worth every penny."

Mary's eyes lit up from her first sight of Brannan's hotel portico with its row of rocking chairs; and the chandeliers, the elegant flocked wallpaper, and the velvet draperies. And the bed!—the highest carved headboard she had ever seen, the softest feather ticks. To think she was going to sleep in such a contraption. Really, it made her feel giddy and girlish. She rolled her eyes at Sean, who was wonderstruck as she was, but hiding it better. They ate a grand dinner with Sam, who afterward went on to his own pleasures and left them to theirs. Hand in hand Mary and Sean strolled around, peering into every room left open, Mary anxious that none be finer than theirs, even though it was free.

"Here's the one you'll want, Mary," said Sean, chuckling. She poked her head around the door and saw a large dormitory room, with four tiers of bunks up to the ceiling. They were so high that they had to be reached by ladders. There were a few men in there already, seated at a table playing cards. There was a large mirror—with a hairbrush and a toothbrush chained to it. They backed out, stifling giggles.

All that evening Sean babbled on about the change in Sacramento City. "Now I expected houses here—Sam Brannan doesn't get excited over nothing—but Mary, Mary, this is beyond the imagination! I don't know how he has done it."

"Really, Sean, you make Mr. Brannan sound like a magician with a bag of tricks."

Sean shook his head. "I'm not sure that he isn't. I am going to invest here, Mary."

By the time Sean and Mary continued their trek to the mountains, Sean was the owner of six prime lots in Sacramento City. Sam was going to oversee them until Sean returned from the gold camps. Sean left the city confident that his investment was going to reap him great rewards. If Sam Brannan sold his properties, Sean was certain it would be at double or triple what he had paid for them.

With the days of delay at Sacramento City, and their miscalculation about the difficulty of travel in the mountains, it was late August before Sean and Mary finally pulled into the yard of Robin's and Fiona's cabin. It was late afternoon, and no one was at home. Mary looked around with concern. "Where could they be? Surely Fiona doesn't take that little baby to dig for gold! She wouldn't, would she, Sean?"

"Where else would she be?"

"I don't know. What should we do?"

"Make yourself at home, Mary my love. We'll wait, and soon enough you can give your daughter a piece of your mind."

When Mary finally spotted Fiona coming up the hill toward the cabin with Tyrone strapped to her back like an Indian child, she couldn't speak. Fiona was dressed like a man—a very untidy man. She was covered with mud, and her beautiful auburn hair was tucked up inside a weather-beaten, dirty slouch hat. Even the baby had smudges all over his face, and hands, and legs.

Fiona smiled as she saw her parents, and broke into a run. "Mama! Papa! We didn't know you'd be here today—I thought you'd changed your minds, because we were looking for you last week." Without thinking she reached to hug Mary, but stopped as she saw the stiffening in her mother's posture. "Oh," she said crestfallen. "You don't like me as I am now."

Sean said gruffly, "Let me see what you've done to my grandson."

"He's as healthy as a little animal," Robin said proudly, and took the child from the carrying pallet. Tyrone kicked exuberantly and squealed as Robin lifted him high in the air and then into Sean's hands.

"He seems to be in one piece," Sean said.

Fiona smiled at her father. "It is good for him up here, Papa. It is good for all of us."

Mary burst out, "I cannot believe you have allowed yourself to—do you always dress in this fashion, Fiona?"

"Mama, please—don't be critical. That is not like you. What would you have me wear when I am working in water most of the day? I can't very well wear a dress."

"I can't see why a decent woman would want to be working like a man in a stream in the first place. You have a home to see to—and a baby."

Fiona sighed. She had known a visit with her parents would be difficult. That was why she so badly wanted to stay in the mountains. She would never be like other women, she knew that now. "Come inside," she said. "Robin will get bath water for us, and I'll start dinner."

"If you don't mind, I'd prefer you bathe first, and I'll start the dinner," Mary said.

Fiona didn't argue with her.

The coolness between Fiona and Mary continued through the evening. Sean was content to get to know his grandson, and paid little attention to anyone else, except after the baby had been put in his crib for the night, and then he talked to Robin about the amazing growth of Sacramento City. Mary excused herself, having heard all this several times over. She got her shawl and walked outside.

Fiona sat listening to Robin and Sean for some time, then got up and put on her suede jacket that Robin had made for her and followed her mother outside. "Mama," she called into the darkness.

From a distance off, she heard Mary's voice. "I'm by the rocks, Fiona." That was a vague thing to say when one is in the mountains, and nearly everything is rock, but Fiona knew exactly where Mary meant. The rocks were Fiona's favorite spot to sit and think, or sketch and write, and she too called them "the rocks." Robin teased her about it often.

She joined Mary, sitting near to her mother. "I'm sorry you are so disappointed in me, Mama. I guess I knew you would be —but I am very happy. That counts for something, doesn't it?"

"I am more shocked than anything, Fiona. I wondered what would happen to our family in this vast place, but I never expected to see one of my daughters working like a field hand— and dressing like one. Haven't you any pride?"

"I have a lot of pride. Sometimes I think I have too much, and God will take all this away from me."

"Take it all away from you! Whatever can you mean? You and Robin are very wealthy, and you are living like the poorest of the poor. What is there to take away? A mud-floored cabin? Filthy clothing? What?"

Fiona began to cry. "If that is all you see when you look at Robin and Tyrone and me, Mama, I don't have anything to say."

"And what do you expect me to see?" Mary snapped. "What else have I been shown? My heart cries out for that poor baby. What can you be thinking of?"

"But he's healthy, Mama, and he's happy. He is a content baby, not afraid of strangers, strong and eager to learn. Does it really matter that he isn't dressed in lacy little garments?"

"Clean linen would be enough, Fiona."

"I've missed you, Mama, but I still miss you, because you are not the Mama I remember."

"Nor are you the daughter I remember," Mary said. "And I miss you too, Fiona. They say a mother has a special place in her heart for her firstborn, and that may be true, but you were always my shining star. Sean always said that I spoiled you—let you have your way too often. I'm afraid he was right." Mary picked up her daughter's hand. She did not need to see it in the dark in order to feel the calluses and the hardness of her skin. "The hand of a crone," she said.

Fiona cried.

Mary cried too, but she walked back into the house without saying anything else.

Sean had little to say to Fiona, knowing that to side with her would cause a donnybrook with Mary. He was courteous, but all of his attention went to Robin and Tyrone. The next morning, after breakfast, he said to Robin, "I'd like to try my hand at this gold panning. Think you could show me how?"

"I'd be more than glad to have a third hand down there."

"Third hand?" Sean asked.

"Fiona, Sean. She's very good—the best partner a man could have."

Sean wasn't going to be drawn into the argument so easily. He didn't like what Fiona was doing, but he wasn't going to join with Mary in discussing it. He looked at his wife. "Come sit in the sun on the rocks, Mary, and watch this old man wrest a fortune out of the river for you."

Mary smiled at him. She would do as he asked, for last night she had told him she wanted to go home as quickly as possible. Sean had asked her for a few days with his grandson, and then he would take her home. She would give him whatever he asked of her, for he would take her home as she wished.

Dressed neatly and carefully, she made her way down the hill, in an ill-tempered sort of way glad for the chance to serve as an example to her daughter. Fiona was again in her work clothes with Tyrone strapped to her back. Mary could barely stand the sight.

When they got to the diggings, Fiona laid out a blanket—a clean blanket—and placed her son on it. She spread out several toys that Robin had carved for Tyrone and gave him a cinnamon biscuit to gum. Within minutes, Tyrone had thrown all his toys off the blanket and had collected several rocks, which he seemed to prefer. Quietly Mary took the rocks away from him. Tyrone howled in anger.

Sean let out a yell for Mary. "Look! Mary, come down here. Look at this!"

Mary leaned over the rock trying to see what had so excited her husband.

"You can't see from up there, woman! Come down here—it's the biggest nugget I've ever laid eyes on, and it's stuck right here in this rock."

Robin sloshed through the stream to Sean, and Fiona followed. When she saw it, she threw her arms around Sean. "It's huge! Papa, you're a real miner now. That must be nearly a pound. Pick it up."

"Not until your mother takes a look," Sean said, his jaw set.

Mary made her way down to the edge of the stream, but still could not see into the crevice of the rocks. "Sean, you will have to lift it out. I just can't see it."

"Then come here!"

"I can't! I'll ruin my shoes."

"Damn it, Mary, my first big gold find and you won't even look."

"I'll take my shoes off," she said dutifully, and began to do so.

Fiona started to warn her parents that the rocks were slippery, and the current faster than they realized, but Robin took her arm and squeezed hard enough for her to keep her thoughts to herself.

Gingerly, clinging to Sean, Mary put her foot into the cold stream, drawing in her breath sharply. With her other hand she held her skirts out of the water. Carefully the two of them were moving toward the rocks when, with a scream, Mary lost her balance. She went down into the water, taking Sean with her. The stream was no more than three feet at the deepest part, but the current was swift, and both Sean and Mary were swept away from the bank and thoroughly soaked before Robin pulled them upright.

Mary's hair was hanging in wet clumps in her eyes and down her face. Sputtering water, she headed for dry land. Sean, blowing water from his mouth, grabbed her arm, almost knocking her over again. "You're not getting out till you see my bloody nugget, Mary!"

She glared at him, then both of them burst out laughing. "It had better be big enough to take me on a shopping spree," she said, laughing.

It was a full week before they could persuade Mary to go near the stream again. When she finally gave in, realizing that a "few days" in Sean's mind was a little longer than she had thought, she sheepishly asked Fiona if she had an extra pair of Hussar boots she could wear.

Slowly but surely, Mary began to take the shortcuts in living that her daughter had taken, and she was enjoying herself. She went to bed tired at night and woke up refreshed in the morning. The mountains had a magic of their own, and while they inspired awe with their size and beauty, they also gave one a feeling of peace.

By the time the weather began to hold a chill both morning and evening, and the trees were ablaze with September color, Mary understood what it was about her life that Fiona valued so much that she was willing to give up all else to preserve it.

Fiona greeted this transformation in her mother with relief and a deep gratitude, but Mary had not capitulated totally. "Despite my understanding, Fiona, there is something you must understand too. Manners and social courtesies came about for purpose. Those seemingly unimportant things teach us ways to talk to each other and reach agreements without rancor, and without the need to resort to more primitive methods of getting our own way. You need balance. What you have here is good, but what you are turning your back on is also good and has its place. Tyrone needs that in his upbringing as much as he needs this. I can see what you treasure here, but I can also see that it is not enough. I would like you to think about it. Unfortunately I don't have a convenient stream to dunk you in to make my point. I will have to trust you to examine on your own the validity of what I say."

Fiona agreed that she would, and later talked at length about it to Robin. Robin agreed completely with Mary, and added the weight of the coming baby, which Fiona had not yet mentioned to her parents. "I have already given you my word that I will not let you get trapped, as you put it, someplace you don't want to be. Now I would like you to be a little more flexible about combining the life we have back ho—back there and the one we have here. I haven't seen my family in over a year either, and I'd like to see my nephew Simon as well."

"That means you want to go back for the winter."

"Yes, I do. I'd like to stay there until this baby is born. Then, if you are up to it, we'll come back to the mountains and move to a more northerly camp."

Fiona took her time mulling it all over. She watched Tyrone, and thought how it would be for him once he began to walk and talk. Finally she announced at dinner on a cold September day, "Robin and I have decided to go to the coast for the winter. We'll be going back with you."

Sean took Mary's hand under the table. "We'd sure feel safer with someone to show us down the mountain. We had the Devil's own time getting up here." Then with a twinkle in his eye, he asked, "Have you got any other news for this old grandfather?"

Twenty

Sam Brannan walked from his home to his office
on Montgomery Street, taking a circuitous route. The long walk
allowed him two things. He could clear his mind of the wrangling he and Ann Eliza always seemed to be engaged in, and he
could look over "his city" with a tough and critical eye. San
Francisco was changing at such a rapid rate that even Sam had
a difficult time keeping up with its progress. However, in his
opinion, not all the changes were progress. He took this early
morning stroll to his office to sort out the new developments
from the old, the bad influences from the good. It was his time
for noting change and planning his own actions in accordance
with what he observed.

One of the changes that bothered Sam considerably was a
pretense of fervent patriotism that acted as a cover for a rowdy
group of men generally known as the Hounds, so that they
could commit mayhem on the Spanish-Americans who lived in
shanties on Clark's Point, Telegraph Hill and beyond, in the
tent and shanty district known as Little Chile. Sam, as a Mormon, had known too often and too well the hypocritical brand
of self-righteous patriotism the Hounds practiced, and he hated
that kind of bigotry and prejudice more than anything else he

could think of. He had had too many friends and acquaintances who had died or been injured or had lost everything in attacks made by the self-righteous. It made him think longingly of what might have happened if he and his group of 238 Mormons had been able to reach California before the Mexican War, and had declared it theirs before it had become a possession of the United States. With all his heart he believed that this kind of "patriotism" would never have existed in a country of Saints.

The Hounds had little right to claim anything decent, and certainly no justification for the claim that they were protecting American citizens against the Spanish-speaking foreigners. However, the Hounds did have a source of power and influence that was something to be reckoned with. They were not merely a gang of men easy to dispose of; they had political connections and protection that dated back to a time before they had arrived in San Francisco.

The Hounds' membership was composed of sixty men who had come to San Francisco as a regiment of volunteers from New York under the command of Colonel Jonathan D. Stevenson, organized to fight in the war with Mexico. When Stevenson had put out the call for men to join his volunteer regiment, he had asked for, and said he would accept, only those men of proven good character.

For the most part he got what he asked for. But some men were not so upstanding, and most of these ended up in Company E of the regiment. The sixty men who later made up the Hounds had originally been members of similar gangs in New York. There, as here in San Francisco, the gangs had existed under the guise of public protectors. They had come from the ranks of New York's Bowery Boys, the Plug Uglies, the Dead Rabbits, all volunteer fire brigades. With these "public servants" in their midst, the New York Volunteers had arrived in San Francisco too late to participate in the Mexican War. Stevenson broke up the regiment right after they arrived. By October of 1848, all the men had been discharged from the Army.

During the late fall of that year Sam Roberts, a member of Company E of the Volunteers, gathered all the former New York gang members and organized them into the Hounds. Thereafter Roberts became Lieutenant Roberts, keeping the military structure and flavor for the Hounds. All the Hounds strutted up and down the San Francisco streets in full military dress. They drilled regularly with swords and muskets. Then every Sunday afternoon, and occasionally on a weekday, they regaled the citizenry with a full parade through the streets with fife and drum playing, their members waving flags and banners. The Hounds loved their shows of patriotic strength, and used it to their best advantage, knowing that it confused the people as to what, if anything, their actual authority was. It almost guaranteed them a free hand in the raids they made on the Chileno quarters at the end of these parades.

For months now the Hounds had had a free hand to do whatever kind of mischief they chose, and Sam Brannan was heartily sick of it. They were nothing but hoodlums. So far, the civil authority—what precious little of it there was in San Francisco —had done nothing to stop the Hounds from plundering the Spanish-Americans' property at will.

A favorite hangout for the group was a saloon on Kearney Street known as the Shades, but their official headquarters was a large tent at Kearney and Commercial Streets, which they called Tammany Hall. It announced to all their origins and the source of their political protection. The Tammany organization had spewed politicians all over the country, and their influence and corruption was as much a part of politics in California as it was anywhere else.

Just thinking about the Hounds and those who used and encouraged them put Sam in a sour mood. More than anything he wanted a justification, an excuse, no matter how slim, that would enable him to move strongly against the brutish, arrogant gang. But for now, he dared not.

As Sam neared the waterfront, his mind released the problem of the Hounds for the moment. The Bay presented problems of its own, but these at least had a humorous side. Ships rocked at anchor in the heaving waters of the Bay so close to each other they nearly touched. It looked like a tub crowded with some child's whole collection of toy boats. Since news of the Gold Rush had spread wide, captains now took the unusual risk of losing their entire crews when they came through the Golden Gate and into San Francisco Bay. Often, as soon as a ship dropped anchor, the captain was the only able-bodied man left aboard. The crew would already have made away with the longboats and abandoned the ship, leaving the passengers, their luggage, and the freight stranded out in the Bay.

It wasn't unusual to see some hardy passenger lose patience and swim to shore, leaving his belongings behind. The more common sight was for an enterprising citizen who owned a lighter to take the small boat out to the ships and offer, for a price, to bring the passengers ashore. The lighter, however, would bring them only so far, so that they must wade the last few yards. Men could be seen almost any time with their prized possessions held high overhead to keep them from getting wet, while they in suits, hats and fine boots sloshed through the surf. Such antics had inspired one New York newspaperman to exclaim that "All San Franciscans are mad, stark mad!" Sam agreed, but that aspect of San Francisco he loved.

He took his time at the shore, enjoying the bustle and confusion that was always present there. The noises were comforting ones, ones that indicated that men were at work and making their own way. Lumber was piled in the open air, waiting for delivery; boxes of goods from all over the world crowded the wharfs and piers. And in his mind's eye Sam was envisioning the half-mile-long wharf he wanted to build for himself. There wasn't a nook or cranny of this city he loved that he did not wish to put his own stamp on. If a man wanted to read a newspaper, Sam Brannan wanted his name connected with it; if a stranger wanted a meal to eat or a hotel to sleep in, or a pier to dock at, or land to buy, Sam wanted his name associated with it all. If he had ever truly been in love, Sam knew that his paramour was San Francisco. What an enticing, captivating beauty she was!

However, by the time Sam turned away from the waterfront and had made his way to his office, he was once more brooding over the problem of the Hounds. They had become a constantly irritating thorn in his side, and he wouldn't rest until he found a means to rid his city of them. This summer they had been claiming the *alcalde* had told the group to rid San Francisco of the Spanish-Americans. Sam didn't believe for a minute that *Alcalde* Leavenworth had issued such an order to the Hounds. But he did believe that San Francisco was being afflicted by a Tammany-inspired blight of Know-Nothing doctrines, and men who already had their hands deep in the city treasury and were not above using the Hounds as henchmen.

About midsummer the Hounds changed their name, now wanting to be called the San Francisco Regulators. With the name change they also made the bold announcement that they expected the people of San Francisco to pay them well to protect the citizenry from the Spanish-Americans. The Hounds continued to terrorize, burn, steal, rape and pillage in the Chileno district, but they now also felt free to walk into any place of business and demand what they wanted without paying for it. On those rare occasions that a man was bold enough to dispute their right to steal, he might be beaten or stabbed, or his establishment burned down. As before, there seemed to be no way to stop the Hounds. They took what they wanted.

Throughout these spring and summer months while the Hounds were getting braver and more audacious in the crimes they perpetrated, Sam Brannan and other responsible residents seethed over the situation. Sam even considered using his own personal bodyguards against the Hounds, but thought better of that. He could not encourage the use of private armies.

In July of 1849, a storekeeper by the name of George Frank authorized the Hounds to collect a claim of $500 from a Chileno man, Pedro Cueta. Frank and Cueta had been wrangling over the debt for some time. Cueta claimed that he had never owed Frank the money. With no courts in California, the matter remained at a stalemate until Frank called in the Hounds.

On July 15, the Hounds, dressed in full military regalia, marched to their fife and drum from their tent Tammany Hall, showing off their prowess and might to all San Franciscans out and about. After this showy parade of power, the Hounds headed for the impoverished Chileno district. Spreading out, but keeping a kind of order that discouraged retaliation, the Hounds went through the Chilenos' houses, stripping them of everything of value, tossing other possessions into the streets, and roughly shoving people from their homes. Then they destroyed and burned the Chilenos' houses.

Frightened, but angry and impotently outraged, the Chilenos milled about, watching the destruction. Then the Hounds turned on the people. Injured people cried and moaned in pain as the Hounds, now in the boiling grip of blood lust, began to fire into the crowds of injured and frightened people. Men and women ran for safety where there was none. The Hounds kept up a sporadic fire. Children, crying and terrified, ran in panic searching for parents. No one tried to stop the slaughter.

But Sam Brannan had had enough, and this time the Hounds had committed a crime so heinous that he was certain he could force the politicians to action. Failing that, he would get the citizenry to act on its own. He wasn't called a firebrand for nothing.

On July 16 Sam and Captain Bezer Simmons paid a visit to the *alcalde,* Dr. T. M. Leavenworth.

"Some action must be taken now, Leavenworth," Sam demanded. "There is not a decent resident in this city who is safe so long as you continue to allow this gang of ruffians to thrive."

Leavenworth played the craven, wringing his hands, avoiding direct eye contact. "What can I do?" he asked pathetically. "The Hounds—I'm one man."

"You're the *alcalde,"* Simmons said heatedly. "Use the power you have for the benefit of this city."

"What power do I have?" Leavenworth asked, hands spread to show the emptiness.

"The power of the people," Sam answered curtly. "Call them together. One thing is certain: You will not find the people of San Francisco wanting."

With Sam and Captain Simmons at his side the whole time, Leavenworth issued a proclamation calling the residents of San Francisco to assemble in Portsmouth Square at three o'clock that same afternoon.

As Sam had promised, the people of San Francisco were not faint-hearted or wanting. They assembled en masse in the Square at the appointed time. However, it was not the *alcalde* who addressed the crowd and moved them to action, but Sam Brannan. The First Elder of the Church of Latter-Day Saints in his best, most carrying churchman's voice denounced the Hounds and all they stood for. He called for action against them, called again for relief for those Chilenos who had lost their property and all their possessions. Money was collected, and Sam moved on to stir the crowd further, to awaken their passion for justice and move them to take responsible action for their city. He asked that a committee be appointed to bring the gang members to justice.

Two hundred thirty men volunteered their services, and were made special deputies that afternoon. Each man was armed with pistols and a musket. With the sun still high in the afternoon sky, the special committee was ready to search until they had rounded up the Hounds and brought them back to the Square.

Lieutenant and leader Sam Roberts of the Hounds heard quickly that Sam Brannan was in the Square and at his hell-raising best. Roberts recognized that the wrong force had been loosed in the city and that the Hounds had little protection now. Inside Tammany Hall, the drum rolled furiously, summoning the Hounds together. Roberts told his membership of the dangerous turn of events. "There's not going to be any stopping him. Brannan's got the bit in his teeth and is running with it. I think we'd better do the same—run!" Roberts then led by example.

Most of the Hounds had left the city before the meeting in the Square ended. They scattered in all directions, some heading for the interior, others going by boat across the bay to make for the Sacramento River. About twenty clever gang members decided that the safest hiding place would be San Francisco itself. These men were caught immediately.

As the Hounds were captured, then arose the question of what to do with them. San Francisco had no jail. At last it was decided that the brig of the warship *Warren*, at anchor in the bay, would be used as a jail.

The trial was perfunctory. The case against the gang was so weighty that even the politicians on whom they normally counted for help dared not speak in their defense.

Sam Roberts and a sidekick named Saunders were sentenced to ten years at hard labor. Others of the gang were sentenced to lesser terms at hard labor. All of the men involved in the attack were fined heavily.

The true problem of the outlaw bands in California now came into the open to confound everyone. Aside from the *Warren,* San Francisco had no prison facility, no authorized agency by which to carry out these long-term sentences. The special deputies who had brought in the Hounds had already been disbanded. So, once public notice had been removed from the Hounds, things went back to the direction they had been going before the trial. The politicians on whom the Hounds counted came through for them again. One by one the Hounds were released, never having had to serve out their sentences. The only victory Sam Brannan and the residents of San Francisco had won was that the Hounds did not reassemble in the city.

Sam and A. L. Davis sat in a restaurant several days after the Hounds had been released. Over a magnum of the champagne Sam favored, they talked about the turn of events.

"We might as well not have brought the Hounds in at all," Davis said.

"It isn't all that bad," Sam said. "It is good to know that when we need to take action, our people are ready to do it."

"What is to stop another group just as bad as the Hounds from taking over where they left off?" Davis asked.

"Nothing," Sam said, and thought he knew exactly who that group would be. Ticket of leave men—criminals released from the British penal colonies in Australia—were arriving in San Francisco at a great rate. Everywhere a man looked he could see the British garb and hear the twang of the Australian speech. They already had a district where they congregated near North Beach, as well as favorite saloons they patronized or owned, their own gambling houses, and a name that made them a gang of sorts. They were almost always called the Sydney Ducks, and occasionally the Sydney Coves. By either name, they bore similarities to the Hounds, and boded no good for San Francisco. Something had to be done. Sam Brannan, as he sipped his champagne, set his mind to figuring out what that something might be.

Twenty-one

Not long afterward, Sam was gratified to learn that at least progress was being made. On August 1, 1849, at an election ordered by Governor--Brigadier General Bennett Riley, the ten districts in California elected municipal officers and delegates to the constitutional convention that would be held the following month. In San Francisco John W. Geary was chosen First *Alcalde*. Geary promptly appeared before the city council and laid the situation on the line. He said, "In San Francisco, every day, there are at least two murders. The murderers have gone free. What are you going to do about it? Those lawless thieves and assassins, the Hounds, were captured a month ago and properly tried, but it means nothing, for there is no place to incarcerate them for their sentences. What are you going to do about that?" He ended his somber speech by saying, "You are now without a single requisite for the promotion of prosperity or the maintenance of order. What are you going to do about it?" Then he sat down.

Stirred to action by Geary's harsh eloquence, and fearful that the people would again take matters into their own hands, the council appropriated money to purchase a ship for a prison. They chose the brig *Euphemia,* which had been abandoned in the bay. At the same time the committee appointed Colonel John E. Townes as Sheriff and Malachi Fallon as City Marshal. But to Sam's disgust, thievery and beatings, terrorism and murder continued the same in San Francisco.

By the middle of August all of Captain John Sutter's debts were paid. His son Augustus and Peter Burnett had put Sutter's property back in his own name, and Sutter was once more in control of his own affairs. Augustus, worn down to the bone with the constant frustration of dealing with his bullheaded father, and suffering frequent headaches and fevers as a result, was determined to leave. He said, "Papa, I need a holiday, a rest. I have heard that Mexico is very beautiful, especially Acapulco. I should like to see that. So next week I'll be leaving."

Tears sprang to Sutter's eyes, and he put his hands on Augustus's shoulders. "My boy, my boy, vhat a hard time I haff giff you. I hope that these frequent illnesses haff nothing to do vith me."

"I cannot say," his son replied diplomatically.

"Vell, I hope not," said Sutter dismissingly. "Now listen to me, my son. I know you haff vork too hard. You deserve some time to rest. But I am going avay in a veek myself, and vhile I am gone, then you rest."

"No, Papa. I must get completely away from Hock Farm and Sacramento."

Sutter's face took on the set look Augustus dreaded. "But I need you," he said persuasively. "At this convention I am going to, I might get elected to something, and then who vould do my accounts? Or Peter might get made something, and I vould lose his services. You are—"

"You can hire someone to take my place, and Peter's. Papa, I must go."

Sutter continued, as though no one else had spoken, "You are the only man I can trust. Yes, yes, I know ve qvarrel from time to time, but you alvays keep my interests at heart."

Augustus thought bitterly how he would have clutched those words to his heart during the past impossible months. He said, "But I have finished! Your property is your own now, and—"

"Vill you stay?" Sutter pleaded. "My boy, vill you stay, at

least until your mother and brothers and sister arrife? Then ve vill all be happy together!"

Augustus felt himself outmaneuvered, outargued, beaten. He sighed. "I will stay until Mama comes."

Sutter embraced him, and Augustus put his arms around his father. "Thank you! Thank you! Now go rest, my boy! Go lie down, do nothing today!"

"If you don't mind, I'd like to go horseback riding instead."

"Good! Good! In fact, I might come vith—" Sutter stopped. It had occurred to him that his presence might not be soothing to Augustus. He said quickly, "No, no, I cannot. You go. Haff a good time. But rest!"

Now it was late August. Sutter, Lansford Hastings, and the other delegates were sailing on Sutter's ship, the *Sacramento*, from Sacramento to San Francisco, thence to Monterey, the state capital. The men were quietly excited, for they would be making history at the same time they were creating a state. Of the forty-eight men chosen to draw up a constitution, six of them came from Sacramento. At San Francisco they left the *Sacramento* and promptly boarded the *Fremont*, a brig bound for Monterey.

Sutter's party was met by Thomas O. Larkin and Don Jose Abrego, who had been Treasurer of Mexico under Governor Pio Pico. "Welcome to Monterey, John, Lansford," said Larkin, clasping Sutter's and then Hastings's hand, and greeting the others. "You're the first to arrive."

Abrego said, in pleasantly accented English, "Monterey is a small place, senores, only twelve hundred inhabitants. We have no hotel and no decent restaurant. But we have arranged for rooms in homes for all of you."

Larkin said quietly to Sutter, "John, you'll be my guest."

On Tuesday, September 4, a quorum of delegates had arrived, and they were ready to begin creating a government for California. They assembled in Colton Hall, a porticoed building of white stone quarried from a nearby hillside. On the ground floor were school rooms; the large hall on the second floor was for public meetings.

Upstairs, a temporary railing divided the assembly room. Inside the railing the delegates were seated at four long tables. At one end was the dais for the presiding officer, decorated with two American flags over a picture of George Washington. A collection of candlesticks sat on a side table. From the hall a door opened on a small balcony with a view of the sea.

The delegates were scarcely seated when Guadalupe Vallejo said, "I move we appoint Captain John Sutter chairman of this body." Amid cheers and clapping, Sutter rose and bowed to his friend and then to the others. "I thank you all for your good opinion of me, but I respectfully decline," he said. "I move instead that we consider our noted ferryman, Robert Semple."

After a vote Semple, smiling, took his seat on the dais, where he looked good-humored and kingly. He slapped his long-fingered hand on the table and brought the convention to order. Thereafter events moved with amiable rapidity. Semple appointed committees and gave them a time at which they were to report. Copies of the constitutions of several existing states were made available for study.

William E. Shannon proposed the first amendment. "I propose," he said in a rich Irish brogue, "that neither slavery nor involuntary servitude, unless for punishment of crimes, shall ever be tolerated in this state."

That simply, California became a free commonwealth.

Sutter stood up. "Ve ought to haff a lottery," he declared. "It vould be a good vay to raise money for the state."

"No lottery!" cried out an opponent. "That's old hat!" He referred to the practice, back in the 1790's, of financing public enterprises through lotteries. "We want something new!"

"It's qvick, it's cheap and sure," Sutter argued. There was a loud, hot debate but in the end the lottery amendment was defeated.

Over the next days the delegates settled several issues, some of them—such as suffrage—taking up days of discussion. They chose San Jose for the new state capital. A special committee prepared and submitted a design for a state seal, which was accepted. During a land discussion, General Vallejo brought a laugh when he misunderstood the word freeholders for the Spanish *frijole,* and he rose up out of his seat to say, "Why have we started talking about food? This body has serious work to do!"

During the six-weeks course of the convention, Monterey enjoyed an economic upsurge. Four hotels were built, and several houses, and a few stores opened. A Chinaman owned one hotel; an Italian tinsmith who had gotten rich from his trade built the Washington House and rented his rooms for $200 a month. Some of the hardier outdoorsmen delegates slept at the "Point Pinos Hotel," which was to say wrapped in a blanket under the stars and the pine trees, to escape the bedbugs, lice and fleas to be found in the less pretentious homes.

John Sutter was appointed chairman of the special boundary committee, whose members all had a broad general knowledge of the territory. Throughout the convention they studied the boundary question. Sutter presented the committee's findings and recommendations to the assembly. There was a bitter debate, but in the end Sutter's boundary suggestions were chosen. The delegates had no way of knowing that their boundaries would stand for 135 years just as they had accepted them.

The convention was nearly over. A schedule was prepared to enable the assembly to submit the constitution to the people and to install the new government. The document was then taken to an engrosser, a person who would write it all in large clear letters.

At one-thirty in the afternoon of October 13, the engrosser completed his work. At two, the delegates met for their final act. The entire assembly demanded that John Sutter sit as chairman of the convention for that last session. Outside, vessels of all nations in the harbor displayed their colors, with the Stars and Stripes above them. The commander of the fort, Captain Burton, prepared to fire a national salute.

There was a hush, and tears stood in many eyes as John Sutter rose and set his hand to the fine new document. As he did so, the flag was run up to the peak of the flagstaff of Colton Hall, signaling to the fort that the signing had begun. The first salute was fired, and a great roar echoed in Colton Hall, over the land and out to sea. As the delegates came forward one by one to sign their names, the guns continued to boom at regular intervals. The cheering was constant, from every spectator, every delegate, everyone within earshot of the marvelous cacophony, welcoming the new state.

Sutter, to whom the sound of cannon was music, had tears of joy laving his face. He stood upon the rostrum waving his arms. "Gentlemen!" he shouted. "This is the happiest moment of my life! It thrills my heart to hear these cannon salute our new state! The State of California has just been born! God grant her honor and eternity!"

Twenty-two

*L*andry Morrison had left the Gentrys' camp on the Middle Fork heading north. He stopped at several camps on the North Fork, and had good luck. It had taken very little time for him to conclude that he had a knack for finding gold—a nose for it, as Robin Gentry would say. The North Fork was nearly as rich as the highly productive Middle Fork. With good fortune, and a habit of listening carefully to the advice of more experienced prospectors, Landry had done very well. He had sent several shipments of his own gold back to San Francisco with Brian Campbell, and could now consider himself a wealthy man.

Landry was far richer than he had ever dreamed while he was in New York. The kind of wealth he now had tucked away in the Miner's Bank was well beyond his previous wildest hopes. He knew that he could, if he wished, leave the gold diggings to others and set himself up in business, or simply be a gentleman of leisure, but he wouldn't do that. He had been infected by the incurable disease of the Sierras: gold fever. Now it was a game, a constant restless urge to go on, to find one more strike, to find the richest pocket of all. It wasn't long before he left his new friends on the North Fork and began a meandering exploration of the secrets of the Feather River. Gold fever victim that he was, he wanted to find as much along the Feather as he was able before the winter set in. He had filled up his leather pouch again before the weather turned nippy, and he began to search for a permanent camp to winter in.

Soon he found a place that gave promise of being rich diggings in the spring, and seemed to have a congenial group of five other men who had already built a snug cabin. That looked very good to Landry, for except for the work involved in finding gold, he still was not one to enjoy physical labor. Pleased with his new place, he settled in for the long snowbound siege of winter in the Sierras, as content as he could be in complete idleness. He listened to gossip, and to the other men talking of their luck in one area or another, and their preference for one kind of mining over another. He slept a good deal, drank too much, played cards, and waited for spring to come, or something, anything to break the winter monotony.

One blustery cold day fit for nothing but sleeping and drinking, Landry lay half asleep and half in a drunken stupor trying to stay warm. He was roused by cries of men outside the cabin. He could hear the excitement and perhaps alarm in their voices, but it didn't cause much response in him. Even the most minor break in routine was considered cause for jubilation. He rubbed the window by his bunk momentarily free of frost and saw several men dragging another man toward the comparative warmth of the cabin. Staggering a bit as he got up, Landry opened the door, hunching his shoulders against the cold blast of air that pushed into the room.

He peered out into the blowing white, the men obscured to his sight. All of them looked alike, long-haired, heavily bearded and garbed, and covered with snow and frost. Landry was no different. His slick sophistication of the city had been left behind at the base of the mountain. He spat a warm brown stream of tobacco into the snow, then yelled, "He dead?"

"Naw—got an arrow in him," came the call back.

They brought the half-starved man into the cabin and propped him up in a chair by the fire. Jacob Durer, the only man in the camp who knew much of anything about healing, saw to the wound in the man's heel. Durer seemed as concerned about the way he had come by the wound as he was about the wound itself. After non-stop questions, the injured man told the group that he and his partner had been prospecting in the hills. On their way back to camp one night they had been set upon by redskins, and he had been wounded in the skirmish. He didn't know what had happened to his partner.

"You got a name?" Durer asked curtly, binding up the heel in clean linen.

"Stoddard," the man said. "I sure could use a good meal. Been a long time since I had anything in my belly."

Durer nodded to one of his cabin-mates, and Nate Fairgate dished out an ugly-looking but nourishing pottage that passed for stew. Stoddard ate with relish, great globs of the grayish mixture hanging in his long, straggly beard. Once Stoddard was fed and had begun to warm up, he became more talkative, but that in no way satisfied Jacob Durer.

"How far from here was it that you came across the savages?" Durer persisted. No one had forgotten the Indian attacks of the previous winter, and the Indian's whereabouts was a matter of great concern.

Stoddard shook his head, then waved vaguely to the north. "We were way up in the hills. I been wanderin' around out there for days. Me an' my pard . . ." He paused, his voice trailing off as though he had lost the train of thought. But his eyes glowed with a peculiar fanatical brightness, then again he seemed to lose the thought that had animated him. He said, "I don't know what happened to my pardner. We were gonna be real rich— yeah, live like kings . . ." His voice trailed off to little more than a murmur.

"How far in the hills?" Durer asked, then thinking that the man's mind had been affected, Durer turned his attention to his cabinmates. "We'd better post a guard."

Gerald Forbes, a big, heavy-set, bluff man, laughed. "Those damn redskins aren't crazy enough to attack a camp with six healthy armed men in it."

"A band of them wiped out a camp of five healthy, well-armed men just last year with no trouble at all," Nate Fairgate reminded them.

"Yeah, and they paid for it. I don't know where this old

geezer came from, but it had to be a ways. There aren't any Indians left around here."

"There's redskins—there's plenty of them," Stoddard muttered, gingerly lifting his bandaged foot.

Forbes shrugged. "Post a guard. We got nothing else to do with our time, and nothing to lose but a little sleep, and we get too much of that anyway."

No one was paying attention to Stoddard now. They were talking among themselves, and as so often happens in ennui, their attention strayed from one subject to another. But Stoddard went on mumbling, "We were gonna live like kings—"

Four-foot-ten inch Pete Allen, whom all the men called Eenie, was listening. "How'd you figger that, Stoddard? You find yourself a bar?"

Stoddard's eyes crinkled up and he made a disparaging face. "A bar? Hell, no, we found ourselves somethin' a whole lot better'n a bar. We found a whole lake. A whole goddam lake. A gold lake. There was nuggets big as my fist lyin' all over the banks. Everyplace there was gold. And it had the sweetest, purest water a man ever touched to his lips."

Eenie laughed, and asked in his piping voice, "You wouldn't be pullin' the leg of a little man, now would you, Stoddard?"

Stoddard looked aggrieved. "If I say I found a gold lake, I found a gold lake, and there's no mistake about it. You can stake your life on this man's word, young fella. Me an' my pardner found it. We had nuggets fallin' outta our pockets, and we'da brought back a fortune if them damned savages hadn't jumped us."

Landry's attention had been caught by this exchange between Eenie and Stoddard, and now he moved closer to the man. "Could you find that lake again? In the spring—you going back up there?"

"Sure I'm goin' back up there—soon's I get another grub-stake."

"You need another partner," Landry suggested in a low, confidential voice. "I've got the stake. Do you know the way?"

"Mebbe I do, an' mebbe I don't," Stoddard said with a look in his eyes that promised that he did know.

"Where were you when the Indians attacked?" Durer said,

once more on his favorite topic. He had been voted the peace-keeper, the only law of the camp, and he took his responsibilities seriously. Now he was showing proper concern for the safety of his camp and people.

"Way up in the hills—way up there," Stoddard insisted. "We got lost after we left Goldlake. Took us a hell of a long time tryin' to find our camp, and then those damned savages came a-screechin' out of the hills, and we run for all we was worth till we had to stand up an' fight. I never did get back to camp. Don't know what come o' my pardner."

"Goldlake?" Jacob said in confusion, this being the first time that anything Stoddard had said on any subject other than the Indians had registered on his hearing. Durer pulled up a stool and began questioning Stoddard all over again, this time about the gold lake.

Liking the attention, Stoddard patiently repeated his story. By the time he had repeated himself several times over for one man or another, he had acquired the nickname Goldlake Stoddard.

Goldlake considered himself as lucky and as well set up as Landry did. He had congenial company, a cabin that was tight and warm, plenty of food, and there was always conversation. More often than not he was at the center of it. His gold lake was keeping this winter alive with talk, speculation, and anticipation. With greater frequency, Stoddard hinted that he could find that lake again with little or no trouble. He also hinted that maybe it was farther up in the hills than he had first suggested. All six men listened raptly. A lake of gold was something worth dreaming about.

Landry Morrison listened to every word Goldlake Stoddard mouthed, and soon realized that he was beginning to make up a more elaborate tale with each telling. There was no question in Landry's mind that the old man liked the attention he was getting, and that alone was egging him on, but Landry's concern was in being able to tell if there was a nugget of truth in the gold talk. Often he had thought the old man was crazy and hadn't any idea of what he was talking about. Sometimes he thought the old man was crazy but actually had seen a lake of gold. And sometimes he thought Stoddard was just shrewd and that as soon as the weather broke he'd sneak off and go back to the gold lake alone, cutting Landry and the other men out of the chance to have some of the gold that the lake offered. As a means of entertaining himself Landry debated the question with great frequency, but he had already decided that when spring came, he was going to follow Stoddard and find that gold lake.

One afternoon, when the snow seemed that it would never stop and the wind howled around the doors and seeped into the windows causing the rudimentary chimney to smoke, Landry wrapped himself in blankets on his bunk and wrote to Susannah telling her about Goldlake Stoddard and his bizarre tale. For a while after Stoddard's arrival, he had said nothing to anyone, but slowly the news had spread from this camp to others in the area, and the number of men dreaming about the gold lake had increased to the point where Landry saw no reason not to tell his sister. There was little danger anyway, for Susannah wasn't likely to get the gold bug and come hunting for the lake, and neither was Cameron. To them it would be an amusing story and nothing more. It was nice to have something of interest to write about for a change.

The day Susannah received the letter from Landry happened to be the day that Robin and Fiona had come to town to visit and meet their young nephew, Simon. The two brothers greeted each other with hearty rib-crushing embraces. Susannah and Fiona were more reserved, but equally happy to see each other. Susannah's hands plucked eagerly at the coverlet over Tyrone's face. When she finally found the sleeping child in his nest of blankets, she drew in her breath. "He is beautiful!" she cried. "Oh, Fiona, we are both so lucky! Such beautiful boys, and they are so close in age—I hope they will be the best of friends growing up."

Fiona smiled proudly, then said, "Well, you must be fair now —where is Simon? When do we get to see him?"

Susannah started for the bell that would bring the maid, then she whirled to face Fiona. "Why don't we go upstairs to his playroom? I'd rather you see him in his own surroundings, and Tyrone can be made comfortable there as well. Come on—Cameron and Robin won't even know we are gone."

"Oh, yes, they will," the twins said in unison, laughing.

Robin said, "I want to see my nephew too." When both babies were together in Simon's crib, he said, "I'll be damned, Cameron. Another pair of twins!"

After the two infants were comfortably settled in, with Simon's nurse Livie Jenkins in charge, the adults gathered in the parlor, with Cameron showing off his prowess as bartender, and Susannah happily chatting about her brother's successes in the gold diggings, and the strange story he had told in his last letter about the lake of gold. Susannah shrugged after she had told the story. "I don't know if he is fooling us with an elaborate tale, or if he really is on the trail of a lake of gold. Is that possible, Robin? Cameron doesn't think so."

Robin laughed, but his interest was roused. "I am beginning to believe anything is possible up in those hills, Susannah. Half the things I have seen since Fiona and I have been there I would have called improbable a year ago. I suppose there could be a lake of gold. Where is Landry? Did he say where the camp is?"

"I think somewhere on the Feather River, but he said the lake is north of that—somewhere way up in the mountains."

Fiona said with a giggle, "All of these places we're talking about are way up in the mountains."

Susannah made a face. "All of it sounds like imaginary tales of derring-do to me. I don't see how you stand it, Fiona. How do you manage with an infant? And soon there will be two! You have none of the conveniences we have in town. You don't even have servants."

"We live a much simpler life, though. We haven't nearly as much to take care of as you have. And anyway, you're a fine one to talk. You have an infant, a house to take care of, and a shop of your own!"

Fiona and Robin spent three pleasant days with Cameron and Susannah, then bade them goodbye. "I promised Sean we'd meet him in Sacramento City," Robin said. "He has some property there, and has just had houses built on two of his lots."

"Sacramento City is a good place for making money." Cameron grinned. "You own five lots there, you know."

"I do?" Robin exclaimed.

"Certainly—your brother is your business agent, isn't he? Well, I purchased ten lots when Sam first started talking about Sacramento—five for you, five for Susannah and me. And a fine old time I had getting Peter Burnett to sell me more than four altogether. The man is so conservative that he has tried to discourage speculation. They cost you two hundred fifty dollars each for two by Sutter's Fort, and five hundred each for three near the river. I'd guess they are now worth fifteen thousand. They'll be worth more if you hold onto them."

Robin shook his head. "What else do I own that you haven't told me about?"

"Some property here in San Francisco, and a few lots in Benecia. Part interest in a general store in Stockton—uh, let's see—part of a race track—" Cameron looked at his brother uncertainly.

Robin looked at Fiona. When their eyes met, both began to laugh. "This is fun, isn't it?" she said. "When did we acquire a race track, Cameron?"

"Well, actually, there isn't a track yet, but we are in the final stages of completing financial arrangements. We have the land, but I'd like to find a third partner before we actually start constructing it. I haven't found the right man for it yet."

"If you'd like a suggestion," Robin said, "I know a man—honest as they come, has the money, and is a good sort to work with."

"Are you talking about Zane?" asked Fiona.

"Yes. Zane Tyler is a good man, Cameron. I'd like you to meet him, and keep him in mind for our partner. I've heard he is going to be in Sacramento this winter. Perhaps you and Susannah could come for a visit with us then."

"Are you going to be living in a house?" Susannah asked quickly, then covered her face in embarrassment as everyone chuckled.

"Of course they are going to be living in a house," Cameron said, then looked over at his brother. "She has the strangest ideas about how the gold miners live—none of it is real to her since we left New Helvetia." He put his arm around Susannah's shoulders. "It's a good thing we don't have need to live outside of the city at anything less elaborate than Agua Clara. Susannah wouldn't know what to do." He smiled tenderly at her. "But about December. We'd like very much to visit then, and to meet Zane Tyler. You are not the first person to mention his name to me. James King of William thinks very highly of him. I'd consider that a dubious compliment, except that his opinion still stands after your Mr. Tyler refused to do business with him."

"I wonder what Jim wanted with Zane?" Robin mused.

The next day Fiona and Robin left for Sacramento. Sean and Mary were comfortable in one of the two houses Sean had built on his lots, and Mary had already begun to see to the furnishing of the other, where Robin and Fiona would live.

"It's going to be such a treat living right next door to you, even for a little while," Mary said, and gave her daughter another hug. "It makes me feel like a mama again, and I can spoil Tyrone like grandmothers are expected to do."

Fiona rolled her eyes up and made a face at her mother, but she was pleased. She had missed her mother too, and hadn't realized how much until she'd been with her again. So as daughters often will, when their mothers need to do a bit of mothering, Fiona sat back while Mary bustled around the house getting it into order.

"I'd like to go out to the ranch for a while and visit with Coleen," Fiona said, enjoying her idleness. Tyrone played happily on the rug at her feet, working ceaselessly as he tried to pull himself to a stable sitting position. She laughed gently as he rolled over. "He wants to walk. He will start young."

"Brian Og runs Coleen's whole household now," Mary said. "You should be grateful for every day Tyrone does not walk. He'll be difficult to keep up with. Have you thought about that? How will you watch him in the mountains?"

"I'll just keep him with me," Fiona said complacently.

"It won't be as easy as it was last year. There will be two children to keep your eye on, and this new one will need a great deal of care."

This was not a subject Fiona liked to think about, and certainly she did not want to talk about it. This problem was one of those she tucked aside hoping it would disappear, or would present a solution on its own, though she knew neither was possible. "We'll work it out, Mama," she said weakly, hoping that Mary would drop the subject.

"What is it, Fiona? You never were one to hide from the truth. You are going to work it out by ignoring it. And it isn't something that is going to go away. I know you know that, so why do you pretend there is nothing to be discussed?"

Fiona began to breathe very rapidly, holding back tears. Mary came over to her and scooped her into her arms as she had when Fiona was a child. "I am still your mama, Fiona. Tell me what is making you so unhappy, perhaps I can help. Is it Robin?"

"Oh, no, I love Robin very much—I don't want anything to change with Robin and me, not ever, Mama."

Mary rocked back on her heels, her mouth open in sudden understanding. "Is that what this is all about?"

Fiona nodded her head, her eyes leaking tears that dropped down onto her round little belly.

"But my darling, what do you call having two children—one right after the other? You said you were delighted to discover you were going to have another so soon."

"I am," Fiona wailed.

"But children cause change, Fiona. You and Robin have lived quite an unusual life for married folk—you surely didn't think it could go on so forever, did you?"

"It will! I won't—I can't let anything happen to our way of life." She looked at Mary beseechingly. "We have such fun together, Mama. Robin and I do everything together—I don't want to be like Coleen. I don't want to be stuck in a house all day while Robin is out in the world. I want to be with him doing whatever he does."

Mary knelt quietly at the foot of her daughter's chair for a moment, silent, thinking. Finally she asked, "Is this what Robin wants?"

"I don't know. I'm afraid to ask, because he might say what he thinks he should say. He knows everyone thinks my going to the diggings with him is peculiar. And he's always worrying about what is good for me and the babies. I don't know if he'd tell me what he really wants."

"But you think you know what that is?"

"I don't know, Mama. All I know is what I want."

Mary bit her lip. "I'm not sure that you didn't marry too young."

"See! That is just what I mean. Just because I don't want to be like everyone else—like Coleen, or Susannah, it's because I'm too young, or I'm too headstrong. Well, maybe I'm right, Mama! I love Robin. I don't want to settle for just being his wife —some—some attachment to his household like an old bedstead or something useful, but very replaceable. I want to be part of his life. I want to live with him, really live—"

"I understand, Fiona. I do. There is no need to go on. I know what you want, but I can tell you that what you want is not going to work out in a gold camp in the mountains. Perhaps you do have the right idea, dear, but you are choosing the wrong place. Surely you can see two little children and a woman in a gold camp will quickly become more burden than joy to either you or Robin."

"I don't want to live in San Francisco—or here."

"Tich, Fiona, don't be so narrow in your thinking. After all, these are not your only choices. What about a ranch?"

"Robin doesn't want to raise cattle—and he hates farming wheat."

"Well, then another alternative must be thought of. But, Fiona, hiding from it is not going to make it better. You must give it some thought, and find a place and an occupation that will preserve what you have together that you so treasure, and at the same time make the order of your lives reasonable."

"I've tried, Mama, but I get afraid. I always feel like I have to hold onto the gold camp as tightly as I can, because if I don't there won't be anything to take its place, and then Robin will leave me behind and go on alone."

"Sometimes if you fear something too much, you bring it upon yourself. Perhaps what you're forgetting is the power of that love you are claiming to protect. You know, my dear, if you have no trust in it, you have nothing to treasure anyway. If you do love Robin, then believe in him. Trust him to join with you in finding the right place for your family. You say both of you like doing your life's work together? Then why are you not seeking it together? What your papa's life and mine is to me is not so very different from what you are telling me you want with Robin."

Fiona just stared at her mother. She so seldom thought of Mary young like herself and burning up inside with dreams.

Mary's cheeks reddened a bit, then she smiled. "Your papa and I started over many times. Who do you think was in the fields beside him before we had the money to hire a man?"

"You?"

"Of course—me. I was a good helpmate, and I know the joy of walking beside my man. But I also know that it demands patience, and the man must find his own way. He'll not thank you for trapping him into a way of living, any more than you would thank him for leaving you behind to become a bedstead in his household—useful, but replaceable."

Fiona put her arms around her mother and cried. "Thank you, Mama . . . thank you."

The young Gentrys and the McKays settled in to a pleasant but uneventful winter in Sacramento. It was a good time for all of them, providing plenty of time for Coleen and Fiona to visit back and forth between ranch and town, and talk endlessly of what had happened to the two very young, very inexperienced McKay sisters in the three years they had been in California. "Do you remember not wanting to leave your boyfriends behind when we first started out?" Fiona asked Coleen.

"Yes, but it is just awful, Fiona. It seems like it was another person. I don't even remember who it was I thought I was going to pine away over. I've often wondered why I remember so little. Maybe something is wrong with me."

"I doubt that. More likely it just isn't very important to you. Life moves so quickly out here. I can't speak for you, but I have barely enough time to keep up with Robin and Tyrone and myself, let alone sit around remembering what happened to me when I was fifteen." Then she gave her sister a wicked little smile. "And Brian being with you might have a little to do with it. I bet those stolen little kisses back in Illinois are nothing compared to now."

Coleen blushed to the roots of her hair. "Some things never

change! You still have no control over your thoughts or your tongue! You shouldn't say things like that!"

"Why ever not? We're alone, and we're sisters. Why can't I say it? It's true, isn't it?"

Coleen said, with righteous smugness, "That's private—not something to be talked about." She asked, "When is your baby due?"

Fiona giggled. "That's private—not something to be talked about."

"Oh, Fiona! That's not the same at all, and you know it!"

"Well, it does point up what an old prude you are, Coleen. It's a good thing Brian married you. I can just imagine what a prissy old stick you'd be if you were an old maid."

That was too much for Coleen. With a shudder of indignation, she got up from her chair, gave Fiona a withering gaze, and left the room.

Fiona made a face at her sister's back. Coleen had no capacity for accepting happiness, even when it was handed to her. When Brian came home from his express route, instead of enjoying him, she seemed to go out of her way to pick fault with minor things, and to keep him constantly off balance during his brief visits.

Fiona remained sitting complacently. Pregnancy under the watchful eyes of her mother and father was a tedious process, and she felt restless and ornery. If nothing else, shaking up her sister's rigid notions gave her something to do, and it really did little harm. She expected Coleen would have forgotten all about it by the time the family was ready to go to the theater that evening.

The opening of the Eagle Theater that winter had been another event that had broken the tedium for Fiona. The canvas theater building, fronting on the levee, held performances three times a week. Many of the miners attended every performance given. Often she and Robin had met Zane Tyler at the Eagle, and each time he had shown up with a different woman, always pretty, but never again had Fiona seen the easy camaraderie between Zane and any of his new partners that had existed between him and Josie. Robin had commented that for a territory that boasted few women in comparison to the number of men, Zane seemed to have no difficulty in finding the prettiest. Fiona still felt sorry for him, and was certain he was in need of close and continued friendship from herself and Robin.

As she went to her room to dress for the evening, her mind was still on Zane and on the play that night. She especially hoped he would be there this evening, for Mrs. Ray of the Royal Theatre of New Zealand was scheduled to appear in *The Spectre of the Forest.* The coming appearance of Mrs. Ray had been a topic of conversation for quite some time, and there was no one in Sacramento City who was not eager to see the celebrated actress performing.

Fiona sorted through all the gowns in her closet, searching for one which did not accentuate her pregnancy. She finally settled on a warm and becoming dark-green velvet gown with a matching cape. Robin came into the bedroom just as she was struggling to latch a pearl and emerald necklace he had given her. He came up behind her, their eyes meeting in the mirror of her vanity table. He kissed the top of her head, then took the necklace from her hands. His pride in her beauty was evident as he stood back and admired her.

He sighed happily as she got up and stepped into his arms. "Mrs. Ray is going to look faded and plain compared to you," he breathed. "Sometimes I think I'd be smart if I didn't take you to the theater. I can name at least ten men I know of who hate dramatic productions, but hold a box just so they can watch you."

"Then I must always make certain to look as beautiful as possible—one should never disappoint one's admirers." Fiona's green eyes twinkled, and she rubbed her nose against his. "You'd better get dressed, darling, or we'll be late. Did Papa finally give in and agree to escort Mama and Coleen to the theater?"

"You know perfectly well your mother never loses that kind of discussion. I abandoned Sean as he was struggling with a very unruly collar that did not want to stay put." As Robin talked and pulled clothes from his drawer, Fiona put them back and replaced each item with something new she had bought him, or something she considered more fashionable. Finally he stood in the middle of the bedroom, his arms folded across his chest looking at her, exasperation clouding his face. "I think I liked you better in the mountains. You never interefered with my clothing there."

She raised her eyebrows in impish reminder. Then she said cheerfully, "But here, you must look like the dashingly handsome, important man you are. And anyway, I warned you that allowing me, or rather making me, live in a city was a bad idea."

It was pleasant to be able to banter once again with Robin on subjects such as these without having that edge-of-a-problem tinge to it. After her tearful talk with Mary about her love of working with Robin, and of living away from others, Fiona and Robin had talked at length and come to an understanding. Her baby was due in May, and Robin had agreed he would remain in Sacramento until the baby was born and Fiona could travel safely. They would then return to the mountains for one more season of gold digging, returning to the city next winter. On their way to and from the mountains, they would take their time and investigate every possibility and location for their life's work. Fiona conceded that though it would not be in the city, they should be close enough that they could visit the other members of the family readily. Though their plans were necessarily vague, the mere reaching of agreement had restored Fiona's natural sense of well-being. Once again she was happy, and optimistic about their future.

Robin, Sean, Fiona, Mary and Coleen entered the theater smiling and nodding to acquaintances. Even in a canvas makeshift theater there was a certain magical excitement. Fiona kept searching through the crowd hoping to see Zane.

"Don't worry about him," Robin said. "If he is in town, he'll be here. He knows where our box is."

"I hope he doesn't miss this show," Fiona said, her eyes sparkling with excitement.

Robin smiled, shaking his head. "I hope you're not disappointed. You're putting a lot of faith in Mrs. Ray."

"But Robin, she must be superb—the Royal Theatre of New Zealand! Now how could she be anything but excellent?"

"Do you know anything about New Zealand?" he teased. "Or about the Royal Theatre?"

"Well, no, but—wouldn't it have to be good if it is royal?"

Fiona asked, then began laughing. "Oh, dear, you don't suppose she is going to be awful?"

They sat in the rough gallery at one end with about one hundred other "box" holders, and stared for several minutes at the dropcurtain. The scene was of a dazzling yellow sky, vividly purple mountains, and dark-brown trees in the foreground. It was designed to keep the drowsy awake.

At the sound of a bell, the dropcurtain was rolled up, and the audience looked upon a darkly bloody-red forest. They knew at once that this was going to be a play dotted with derring-do and bloody scenes. Hildebrand, the robber, stood in the midst of the red forest, his sky-blue mantle brilliant and startling. The scene was set for a noble knight in royal purple and his trusty servant in scarlet to lay siege to the robber's den to rescue the damsel held captive and in distress. In the midst of the terrible fighting and speechifying, the specters of the forest made their appearance, looking eerie and strange in their tent costumes and carrying lighted tapers.

"Where is the famous Mrs. Ray?" Fiona whispered, already bored with the wait.

Almost as soon as she said it, Mrs. Ray glided gracefully across the stage and struck a posture front and center. Fiona covered her mouth to keep in an irreverent giggle. "What does that mean?" she asked, for Mrs. Ray's action seemed to have nothing whatever to do with the play. When the action was repeated several times during the three acts, Fiona determined never again to be impressed with anything or anyone simply because they were called royal.

As they rode home later in the carriage, Fiona was dramatically emoting to Robin, parroting Mrs. Ray's final words to Hildebrand, "I'd rather take a basilisk and wrap its cold fangs around me, than to be clasped in the embraces of a 'eartless robber."

Robin grinned at Sean. "Do you get the impression I'm going to hear this line frequently, Sean?"

"Fiona, me love, you're all ham," Sean said with a chuckle. "Given a bit more practice, you can be as bad as the famous Mrs. Ray."

"I think the only reason they had Mrs. Ray perform was so

that the miners could see a woman was actually in the play," Mary said sourly, for she too had expected an outstanding performance that night. "The next time we go, I think it should be for one of the musicians. I like the little Swiss organ girl. I think she is quite good."

The discussion about what was the best kind of performance to see at the Eagle Theater continued for several days, but when it came time for the next performance, no one cared what it was, they all simply wanted to go and be a part of the crowd.

The McKays, Campbells and Robin Gentrys celebrated the New Year together. Mary prepared a goose and all the trimmings, and Robin and Brian managed to find a good vintage champagne and red table wine, along with a bottle of the finest French brandy for Sean. Sean had his own surprise. He had haunted the *Embarcadero* and accosted every newcomer to Sacramento City until he found a man who had a bottle of Irish whiskey he was willing to sell.

The Sacramento River, however, had its own way of heralding the first month of the new year, and began to rise. Everyone knew that the land on which Sacramento sat was low, so little was thought about it. Water in the streets and thick oozing mud was an inconvenience, but nothing that was not expected from time to time. But the river kept on rising, and soon shop-keepers were piling full barrels of goods on top of empty barrels to keep them dry. Those who were fortunate enough to have two-story dwellings or businesses moved furniture and goods to the second floor. Still no one was unduly dismayed. Life went on as usual with the minor inconvenience of a flood.

The Sacramento continued to rise, and the McKays, the Gentrys, and the Campbells were living only in the second floor of the two houses. A great deal of laughter passed between the upper-story windows. Neighbors would row by in the boats, and stop to talk at the window. Robin and Sean rigged a line between the two houses, so a boat could be drawn back and forth to be used as a ferry, and also for the families' only means of transportation. Often the boat was drawn by pulleys from Mary's house to Fiona's with a cup of sugar to borrow sitting in the bottom.

Robin spent part of each day taking people from the roofs of the one-story buildings and finding places for them to stay until the water went down. A one-story adobe bakery could not withstand the onslaught of the water and crashed in. But the spirits of the people in Sacramento remained high. They all seemed to be having a merry time, and thoroughly enjoyed themselves.

One evening when Mary and Sean, Coleen and Brian and Brian Og had rowed over to Fiona's house, and they had had dinner together, a man rapped at the window, and handed in to them a water-soaked letter. Apologetically he smiled. "I hope you can read it. I tried my darnedest to keep this pouch dry, but we ain't got anything but water 'round here. Sorry, folks."

"It's from Susannah," Fiona said, as soon as she had thanked the man and shut the window.

"Can you read it?" Sean asked.

"It's pretty smeared, but fortunately Susannah has a large round hand, and I think I can make out what—oh, no! There was a terrible fire in San Francisco!" Fiona concentrated harder, quickly making out the smeared ink to see if Susannah's and Cameron's house was damaged. She put her hand to her heart. "Thank God, their house wasn't damaged. All three of them are all right. But there was a lot of damage done on Montgomery Street, and Susannah's shop was burned." They all looked at each other, thinking that this had happened to Susannah before.

"Was it a complete loss?" Sean asked.

Fiona frowned hard, trying to make out the smeared writing. "I'm not sure what this says, Papa, but I think it was only the front—yes, here she says she should be back in business before the end of the month. It must not have been too bad." Fiona studied the writing for a bit longer, then said, "Oh, what a time for a fire—this happened on Christmas Eve. Gosh, it took a long time for this to get to us."

"It floated here," Robin said.

Though the group huddled on the damp second floor of Fiona's Sacramento house didn't know it, Susannah's shop and the other fifty structures that had been ruined in the San Francisco fire had already been rebuilt, and the hardy, optimistic San Franciscans had put that unpleasantness out of their way.

In mid-February Susannah, Cameron and Simon arrived for their winter visit. After hugs and greetings were given all around, and Simon was admired and put to bed, Robin introduced Zane Tyler.

Susannah reached for Cameron's arm and intertwined hers with his. She kept staring at Zane as the men talked. Then suddenly she remembered where she had seen him before. With a cry she released Cameron's arm and pointed at Zane. "My pie pan!" she exclaimed.

All talk stopped, and several pairs of eyes stared in amazement at Susannah's outburst. She could feel her cheeks turning rosy.

Only to Zane did her remark make any sense, and he threw back his head and laughed heartily. "What a joy it is to be remembered," he gasped, and if Cameron had not been standing right there, and virtually a stranger, he would have grabbed Susannah around the waist and whirled her about the room.

"What is this about a pie pan?" Cameron asked, confused but laughing too, without knowing why.

"He—Mr. Tyler—is the man I told you about who burst into my store in New Helvetia wanting digging equipment, and when I told him I didn't have any such thing, he said 'this will do' and stole my pie pan to use."

"Now wait a minute," Zane protested jovially. "I didn't exactly steal it. I offered you three dollars for it, but you wouldn't take it. So in a way, you gave it to me. You can take credit for my new-found wealth, Mrs. Gentry."

"I never gave it to you!" Susannah breathed. "You took it!"

"Well, they say borrowed money is the luckiest," Zane said.

The following day he presented Susannah with a small, gaily-wrapped package. As she sat in the parlor, with everyone watching, she opened it to find a royal blue porcelain pie pan. Her eyes lit up with pleasure, and she giggled ruefully. "Mr. Tyler, it's beautiful. I take back everything I said."

"But is it enough to repay you for the theft of your other one?" he asked, an impish sparkle in his eyes.

"More than enough," Susannah said, blushing.

The silliness of the pie pan incident set the tone for the entire visit. The families went to the theater together as often as they could, ate at the finest restaurants Sacramento City could offer, and spent pleasant evenings playing parlor games and talking in

Fiona's parlor, or in Mary's. No one was happy to see Cameron and Susannah return to San Francisco at the end of a week, nor did they want to let Zane go two days later. It seemed as if much of the winter fun left with the three of them.

By April the weather and life in general was returning to normal in Sacramento City as well. A new theater opened, but the Gentrys did not get a box this time. Fiona was merely waiting out the last few weeks before her second child was to arrive, and she and Robin spent much of their time preparing to leave for the Feather River as soon as she was able. Tyrone was nearly a year old, and had mastered his legs sufficiently to get into every cupboard and drawer his mother wanted him to stay out of. Quickly she was learning that Mary had been correct; two infants were a far cry from having one. Tyrone was no longer her sweet, amiable child who was grateful for her attention and obedient to her wishes.

Fiona gratefully accepted Mary's help, and also Robin's. It was going to be a long difficult time until she gave birth to this new baby. But despite the difficulties a toddler was giving her, Fiona was looking forward to the new child and the new gold camp with much of her old zest.

Twenty-three

*F*iona McKay Gentry had been impatient for the birth of her second child almost since its conception. Perhaps Fiona had imparted this sense of haste to the child, or perhaps it was a part of a natural inheritance from her mother. Whatever the cause, Maeve Gentry was nearly as impatient as her mother, and made her appearance on the family scene in the middle of the night May 2, 1850, nearly three weeks earlier than expected. Maeve was a tiny baby full of fight, and sporting a full head of brilliant, carroty-red hair that stood on end, giving her a look of bristling, excited energy.

Robin watched his kicking, fist-waggling, screaming daughter dumbfounded. All he could think was that she certainly wasn't like Tyrone had been just after birth. He had been prepared for Maeve to be weak, coming early as she had, or even sickly, but she seemed only determined to announce to all within hearing that she was here to stay, and her presence would be felt.

Mary was in thrall. Maeve had captured her heart and would never relinquish the hold.

Fiona was weakly trying to control her laughter, because it hurt to laugh. But Robin was funny with his bafflement. Mary was funny with the love-struck expression on her face, and Fiona's ranting minutes-old daughter was even funnier.

Sean peered cautiously over Mary's shoulder at the squirming child Fiona held loosely on the bed beside her. He whispered to his wife, "Do you think her hair . . ." he began, then started again. "Will it always be like that, do you think, Mary?"

"It'll darken as she gets older, Papa," Fiona said, still giggling and wincing with the effort.

"She'll be a true beauty," Mary declared, her blue eyes shining with love and the vision only she could see of Maeve Gentry in years to come.

"She's so angry," Robin said softly, still in awe of the tiny creature.

"Wake Tyrone up, Robin," Fiona said to him. "He should meet his little sister."

Robin hesitated. "It's the middle of the night."

"It is no more, and it doesn't matter," Fiona said. "I would like him to see his little sister. Tyrone will go right back to sleep. Please, Robin, bring him to me. I'd like to have both my babies here for a moment."

Robin brought sleepy Tyrone into the room and sat him on the bed next to his mother and sister. Tyrone's eyes widened. He had none of the hesitation of his father, and Maeve's persistent yelling meant nothing to him. He grabbed her hand in one of his chubby fists and promptly rolled over on her, pushing his face into hers. The two babies were tangled like puppies, their noses all but touching.

Maeve stopped squalling, blinked in an unfocused, confused way at her brother, then shortly after went to sleep.

Mary watched with tears in her eyes as she saw what she believed was the sealing of a bond between the two children.

Robin still stared and had said almost nothing about his daughter. Fiona now looked at him, a touch of concern clouding her green eyes. "Don't you like her, Robin? Are you disappointed in your daughter?"

Mary saw Robin's hesitation, and knew as Fiona knew that it had happened too often this night. She picked Tyrone up from the bed, cradling him in her arms, then signaled to Sean they should leave Fiona, Robin and Maeve alone.

"What is it, Robin?" Fiona asked.

Robin tore his gaze away from his sleeping child. "She's so tiny . . . but did you hear her? Tyrone never screamed like that. Is something wrong with her?"

Fiona smiled, touching her new daughter. "She is very small, of course, but she seems fine. She is a healthy baby. We are fortunate, Robin."

Robin gave Fiona a sheepish grin. "I think I'm afraid of her."

Fiona giggled again.

"Well, she isn't what I expected—Tyrone was so quiet," Robin explained hastily, now more than a little embarrassed at such a confession to his wife.

Fiona answered in prophetic words, "She may be a more demanding child than Tyrone." As Robin moved closer, she kissed his cheek. "Maybe there's a bit of wildness in Maeve that we didn't give to Tyrone. Each child we have will be different from all the others, you know. We have only one Tyrone, and that is how it will be. And now we have Maeve. Yes, Maeve, our little wild one."

Robin listened to what Fiona said, and was lulled by the sound of her voice, and slowly he too came under the spell of Maeve Gentry. When he spoke again, his voice was softer, and a new warmth had come into it. "She's not a full hour old, and she's already taking on the battles of her small world . . . and yet she seems so . . . fragile . . . so small . . . so in need of protection." His voice faded into silence, but he continued to watch the baby. She stirred in her sleep. As she turned her head, he realized that despite her frantic red hair and her pinkish, purplish skin, still discolored from the birth process, she looked very much like her beautiful mother. Maeve then entered the warm embrace of Robin's heart, and he found that she was a very comfortable little presence there.

The news of Maeve's birth traveled quickly to the Campbells' house, to Jane Pardee, and to the Carl Gentrys at Agua Clara and the Cameron Gentrys in San Francisco. Jane managed a quick visit on one of her trips into the mountains. Coleen and Brian came for several days, and Carl and Rowena came bearing a cartload of gifts for the new grandchild and for her mother. Susannah and Cameron, however, had to rebuild from the fire, and just managed to send off a note congratulating the new parents and promising to visit when they could.

Their full attention was taken by the city in which they lived. San Francisco was burning again. Once more their house on Montgomery Street was spared, but this was a terrifying fire, and Cameron had insisted his family leave their house and move to safer ground.

For seven hours the leaping, licking flames of the fire danced from one building to another along three blocks of the city. It crept up the slope of Clay Street hill, consuming all in its path. The fire area was bordered by Montgomery Street and Dupont Street. From their vantage point north of the city, up in the hills, the Gentrys watched as nearly three hundred homes and businesses were turned ember and ash by the passing of the raging fire.

The acrid odor of charred wood, burnt canvas, and soured water on ash hung over the city after the fire had lost its heat. Millions of dollars of damage had been done in those seven frightening hours. But as it had in the past, the spirit that seemed to come automatically with residence in the town sprang up. Even as Cameron cautiously returned his family to their home, already a few eager, hardy people were clearing away the smouldering remains of their houses and businesses in preparation for the rebuilding that would begin immediately.

Susannah and Cameron, as soon as they reached home, began their own preparations to help in the rebuilding process, as they had in the past. Susannah ransacked their house searching for items that could be spared and used by those who had lost everything in the fire. As she gathered goods, Cameron loaded the carriage, then placed in it last food that would be needed immediately. He took the supplies down to the burned district, offering them and his own strong arms and back in the rebuilding. Susannah would see little of him in the next few days.

But few days it was, for in ten days nearly half of the burnt buildings were rebuilt. The fire had done nearly four million dollars' worth of property damage, but just over a week later, no stranger entering the city would ever have realized the devastation. All he would have seen was a frantically active town. San

Francisco was a beehive of rapping hammers, ripping saws, the clatter of new lumber, and the bustle of busy men.

One of the busy residents of San Francisco who was more than pleased to see all the activity was easy-going, well-dressed, back-slapping Honest Harry Meiggs, owner of a lumber yard. Harry Meiggs had come to San Francisco with the Forty-Niners, but had resisted the temptation to head for the gold hills. He had brought with him a load of lumber, and elected to remain in San Francisco and sell the wood. It had been a wise choice and had made him a wealthy man, as well as a noted and respected leading citizen of the growing city.

Along with the industrious sounds of lumber being hammered into place was the loud, exuberant sound of Harry's voice as he encouraged each and every one of his customers. Most often Honest Harry was on his way for a visit to his banker, for Harry's original load of lumber had netted him fifty thousand dollars even before he could legitimately call himself a resident of San Francisco. Now he had five hundred men working for him cutting wood, and he even had his own pier to unload the lumber from. It gave him a good and benevolent feeling toward one and all, and left him secure and therefore free to attend to his second passion.

Harry's other obsessive love, which he fully expected would make his second fortune, was the North Beach section of San Francisco. He was certain the city would grow in that direction, and to ensure his second fortune, Harry had invested every penny he could in property in North Beach. His bankers agreed with his judgment and had lent him, and were still lending him, considerable sums of money so that he could continue to gobble up huge tracts. So today, although he felt sorry for some of the people who had lost so much, on the whole was a good day. Honest Harry Meiggs felt good that he had his first gold mine in lumber, and was well on his way to securing his second in land. With a pleased smile, and a few more encouraging words to his neighbors, he knew he was set for life.

Landry Morrison was not in circumstances dissimilar from Harry Meiggs. Landry had certainly done well in California, and by any man's standard he was well off. Landry had found gold, but he wasn't satisfied yet, and did not consider what he had found his "gold mine." He thought of himself as one of those still searching, still waiting to cross the next ravine, the next mountain pass—or to sit on the shores of the gold lake.

News of Goldlake Stoddard had spread quickly through the gold camps along the Feather River, and north of there. Only that spring did Landry come to the conclusion that he had picked the wrong group of men to winter over with. Nate Fairgate, Eenie, Jack and the others were congenial men, but they were not especially quick of wit or action. Other men in other camps listened to Goldlake's tales and pumped him for enough information that they made plans to set out and find the lake of gold, while Landry and his companions merely talked among themselves, did a little daydreaming and speculation, but brought forth no plan of action. It came as a shock to Landry when he found out that others were about to do what he had thought of.

In May of 1850 twenty-five men of the other camps gathered equipment and, with Goldlake Stoddard as their guide through the mountains, set out to find the wonderous lake of gold. The expedition was all ready to leave by the time Landry found out that the search for the lake was a fact. Hastily he left his claim, threw his gear into packs, and hurried after the group of adventurers. Some hours later he caught up with them, only to get his second shock. There were nearly a thousand men who, like himself, had heard about the expedition into the mountains and decided to pack up all they owned and follow. It was a strange straggling mob who struggled up the mountain passes that spring.

During the first few days and nights of the group's travels, the camps were lively, and the talk was merry, and the companionship rich and comradely. However, as the distance grew, and they were all high up in the mountains where the air was thinner, Stoddard still said nothing about their coming nearer to the lake. Some of the men dropped out of the search, and either panned for gold where they were or headed back toward the Feather and the claims they had left behind. There were still several hundred men following after Stoddard. However, their mood was shifting. More and more frequently complaints could be heard, and from some mouths came serious grumblings.

"He had us headin' straight north for five days, an' now he's sayin' maybe it's south," said one of the thousand Landry traveled with. "Ask me, the guy don't know which way it is—if there ever was a lake of gold."

"He said he picked up chunks of gold big as your fist," another said. "A man ain't gonna lie about that—not when he's got better'n a thousand men followin' him. He'd have to be loco with all of us here."

"That's just what I'm thinking," the first man replied. "Maybe old Stoddard ain't wrapped too tight. Maybe he is just plain cuckoo."

"Well, we'll never know unless we follow him to the end, will we?" Landry said acidly. "I don't see anyone behind you fellows pushing you over these hills. You think Stoddard is loco or a liar, turn back."

"You'd like that, wouldn't you?" the first man said belligerently. "We come all this way, then get sent back while you line your pockets with gold."

Landry gave a dry bark of a laugh. "You are nothing but a complainer. Either the gold is there or it is not. You want to find out, then follow along. You want to go back—no one is stopping you. But for God's sake shut that mouth, or I'll stop you." Landry touched his hand to his pistol.

Ellis and his friend veered off from Landry, but remained on the trail of the gold lake and kept on grumbling, now out of Landry's earshot.

Stoddard still seemed confused and uncertain of the whereabouts of the lake. He indicated that it should lie just over the next ridge, so men, animals and equipment made the difficult descent and climb, only to hear Stoddard claim the lake was farther to the west. Over yet another ridge, and Stoddard was certain they had to bear east.

Tired now, and losing faith, the huge group of miners were all grumbling, and the comments were getting nastier and nastier. Several times Landry had heard the sentiment that Stoddard ought to be hanged. "There's no gold lake. The man's done us dirt."

The original party of twenty-five who had organized also realized that something had to be done. They had no more time to waste trotting over the mountaintops if the lake wasn't there, and the crowds of uninvited who straggled along after them were getting in a surlier mood with each passing hour. They called a meeting to determine what should be done. Many of the followers came to the meeting to offer suggestions and information.

The meeting started in chaotic fashion with people shouting at no one and everyone that something had to be done. Then came the other remarks that Landry had been hearing privately for days.

"The old man is crazy!"

"He never did see a lake of gold!"

"Yes, he did—it's just that the winter covered it over with a landslide," a true believer cried out. "It ain't so easy findin' a place when the land changes. We'll find it."

"Yeah! Give Stoddard time. He'll come across it again."

"How many chances will we get to find a whole lake of gold?"

Several of the original twenty-five had come to their own conclusion. One of the men, a tall burly fellow with a commanding, rich baritone voice said, "Stoddard, you've got twenty-four hours more. We've walked these hills from one end to the other, so you lead us to the lake by camp tomorrow night, or by God, man, we're going to hang you to the nearest tree. That's our final word on it. You've had your chance, now either you show us the gold lake or we've got to think you've pulled a funny one on us."

Stoddard nodded his head vigorously. "I'll get you there. Goldlake Stoddard is no liar—I'll get you there."

The man smiled, and shook Stoddard's hand. "I hope you do, old man, for your sake, for my sake, and for all of their sakes."

Smaller campfires and tents and sleeping rolls sprang up around the periphery of the main camp. Everyone went to bed early and slept well in anticipation of the long haul on the morrow. At first light men began to stir and prepare food, for this promised to be a long day. The general mood of the camp, however, was much better than it had been in the previous days.

The spirit of hope had revived. Today would tell the tale. By the end of it they would all be rich, or it would be ended.

Landry had just gulped down a cup of steaming hot coffee when he heard a stir and shouting in the main camp. Two men rode off on mules, and others scurried about madly. Landry held his breath. Somehow he knew without knowing what had happened. He got up from his camp, and strolled almost casually to the main camp to verify what he suspected. He walked up to a group of three German men conferring with each other. "Did Stoddard leave last night?"

All three men looked at him. All three sets of eyes were the peculiarly cold blue that so many Germans seem to have. "He did," one said, then spat on the ground at his feet.

"Are you going after him? Is anyone, besides those two I saw ride out a while ago?"

Another of the Germans shook his head. "Why waste our time chasing a crazy man?"

The other two remained silent, looking at Landry. Landry had spoken to these men on other occasions, and while they were not particularly talkative, they had always been friendly and willing to be drawn out—not at all like they were today. He smelled something afoot. These men had something in mind, and Landry wanted to know what it was. "You must be pretty miffed to have him lead you up here to nothing, aren't you? Are you going to do something about it?"

The three men exchanged glances. "He is gone, let him be gone."

The shortest of the three added, "He has sealed his own fate. He would not dare come back down from the mountains with so many angry with him."

"Then you are not going after him?" Landry persisted.

The three men shook their head, all murmuring that they would not be so foolish.

"I agree, it would be foolish," Landry said in a friendly fashion, then walked away. He believed them. They were not going after Stoddard, but they were up to something. He wondered if they had talked to Stoddard and had gotten information that made them think they could find the lake on their own, or if they knew of something else of equal value up in this section of the Sierras. Whatever it was, Landry decided that where the Germans went he would follow, at least until he had satisfied himself that there was nothing of value to be gained from them. He had little to lose. His choice to follow Stoddard had already caused him to lose his claim on the Feather River, and much time. He could afford to give another week or ten days to pursuit of the Germans and whatever they thought they might find. It was a good bet, he thought, for the one thing he knew about these men was that they were serious and did not waste their time or energy.

The hundreds of men who had toiled up the mountains with Stoddard, after hearing the news of his disappearance, broke camp and dispiritedly began making their way back down the mountain, most of them hoping to return to the claims they had left behind. The Germans, however, moved farther to the east on their way back to the Feather River. Their route took them much farther inland than prospectors had been going, and they stayed farther north than where most of the good claims were located. Landry followed at a respectable distance.

The first day they camped near the mouth of a small stream that fed into the Feather farther south. Landry followed suit, and was rewarded, as were the Germans, by color dotting the rock. It was nice to see gold worth picking up and putting into a pouch again, but it still was nothing worth shouting about. Landry sat alone in his camp wondering whether he should move the few yards or so to try to join with the Germans, or stay where he was. For now, he decided, he'd keep to himself. He wasn't certain how long he would follow after them. He could always be friendly when and if it suited him.

All of the men needed water for camp, and walked the short distance to the junction of the Feather and this stream. The footing on the rocks was precarious, and it was in taking the greatest caution, and watching carefully, that both Landry and the German who was getting water for his group stopped dead in their tracks, their breath caught in their throats. In every crevice and every crack of every rock was gold! Neither of them could move without stepping on gold. Gold to be picked up by the fistful. Landry had never seen so much yellow rock in his life. It was everywhere!

All of the men staked claims immediately and began to gather in the rock as fast as they could. In less than a week Landry estimated that he had gathered nearly $30,000 worth of gold, and he hadn't washed a single pan of gravel yet. He had merely picked up the rock.

He talked to the Germans in their camp, and all agreed that they should keep this fabulously rich find a secret. But secrets such as that are not meant to be kept. Somehow, almost as if the news was carried on the wind, men in Nelson Creek, and Poorman's Creek, and all along the Feather River heard about the rich bar the Germans had found, and came with their picks and shovels.

The diggings were so rich, and so many came, that it was quickly agreed that the claims would be limited on the bar itself to ten square feet and to forty square feet on the hillside. That small amount of ground was enough to make a man wealthy for life.

In the first few days the men had only picks and shovels and pans to mine with, but within a week there were two Long Toms in operation, and the strike was already well known, and named Rich Bar.

Men, eternally hopeful, thought that if there was one rich bar in this area, why shouldn't there be two or three or even more just like it? So half a mile to the east of Rich Bar some other treasure hunters located and found Smith's Bar, and half a mile to the west, Indian Bar. The men and camps in this area were in high spirits, and everyone there knew he had at last found his El Dorado. This included men like Brian Campbell, who immediately put the new camps on his route and hauled tons of gold to San Francisco.

Zane Tyler heard about the strike on Rich Bar almost as fast as it happened, and moved his operation there. Asa Radburn heard about it, and weighed the risks of taking Fairy and the children to a place where they might be recognized. He decided it was worth the risk. Anyway, it wasn't as if he couldn't take care of himself. So they, too, packed up the few belongings they had accumulated in the months they had been hiding, and started for Rich Bar.

Robin and Fiona heard about Rich Bar when they went to San Francisco to talk with Cameron before leaving for the mountains. Robin wanted to discuss several investments with his brother before he and Fiona were to leave again for an undetermined length of time. There were always letters written between the brothers, but those were never so satisfactory as one visit.

While the men talked business, Susannah and Fiona showed off children, comparing notes and cute stories. And they shopped. Fiona went on a buying spree that nearly cleared out Susannah's small shop.

"I don't know where I'll ever go to wear these gowns, but this is fun," Fiona said, and whirled before the pier glass in the shop. She was wearing a lime silk gown that hugged her figure, and gave her a look of height she didn't ordinarily have. She touched the lace bodice that Susannah, with her eye for color, had dyed just two shades lighter than the body of the gown. "This is just beautiful, Susannah."

Susannah stood back, pleased with her design and handiwork, and finding that she liked this beautiful sister-in-law. "And it doesn't hurt the dress to have you in it—it's almost as if I designed that with you in mind."

"Perhaps you did," Fiona said with a smile. The smile vanished instantly, to be replaced with a look of alarm. Outside in the street came a bloodcurdling Chickasaw war whoop.

Susannah made a face, then began to giggle. "Don't worry. All that means is Pegleg Smith is back in town."

Fiona pressed her hand to her chest to still her pounding heart. "Who—or what—is Pegleg Smith?" She hurried to the shop window to get a look at the man who had brought forth such an ungodly outcry.

"Pegleg is a real character—he is rapidly becoming one of the landmarks of San Francisco. He was supposed to have stumbled upon a tremendously wealthy mine up in the mountains, then lost it. People are always hunting for it—the lost Pegleg Mine. No one knows if it really exists or not, but then Pegleg certainly has his share of gold, so maybe it does." Susannah watched out the window with Fiona, then said, "He's an interesting man. The Indians call him Wa-na-to-ko, the man with one foot. I guess he lived with the Chickasaw and the Choctaw for some time, did a lot of trapping with them and had several Indian wives." She laughed. "He should have been a Mormon."

"How did he lose his leg?"

"He was shot by an Indian in the ankle. The bone was shattered. He is said to have severed the muscles with his knife, and then his friends cut the rest of his leg off. How he survived, I don't know. But then with Pegleg nothing makes a whole lot of sense, you just have to take him as he is and believe him, because there isn't anything else to do. I kind of like having him around. He makes the rest of us seem so sane."

Fiona laughed. "He is colorful," she agreed, and thought that San Francisco seemed to be drawing a lot of colorful characters. Since she and Robin had come, she had met Honest Harry Meiggs, who was an upstanding citizen, but a character nonetheless; today she had seen and heard Pegleg Smith; and the other day when she and Robin were out walking they had run into three street preachers. One had called himself Hallelujah Cox, another was Crisis Hopkins, and the third man went by the descriptive appellation of Old Orthodox.

She had heard of, but not met, Joshuah Abraham Norton, who though he had gotten rich was still a bit weird. Then there was Madame Ah Toy, who was involved in a court dispute with some miners who had paid her, she said, "for the privilege of gazing upon her countenance" not with gold, but with mere brass filings. San Francisco was becoming a strange but exciting place to be—but Fiona still didn't want to make it her home. Now more than ever she wanted to find the right place for her and Robin and the children to settle.

As Fiona was learning about the characters of San Francisco, Cameron was regaling Robin with the tales of Goldlake Stoddard and the resulting strike at Rich Bar. By the first of June Robin was too restless to stay in the city one more day. He wanted to go to Rich Bar himself. If this was to be his family's last foray into the gold fields, why not make it the best of all? Rich Bar sounded to him as though it was the place to go.

Cameron had wanted Robin to take a look at Benecia as a possible place to speculate on land, so Robin and Fiona stayed nearer the coast than usual on their way north. As they moved north of San Francisco and began gradually moving eastward, they entered the Napa Valley. Fiona was entranced. This was the most beautiful place she had ever seen. "Robin, can we camp here for a few days—please?" She was thinking, but not yet certain, that this was the place for them to live. She wanted time. She turned pleading eyes to him, for she knew he was impatient and would want to hurry on.

"Fiona . . ." he began, in a voice that told her he was going to urge her to keep traveling.

Quickly she said, "Robin, please—forget about Rich Bar for just a moment—long enough for you to take a good look at this valley. Look at it, Robin. Doesn't it seem like perhaps it is home?"

Robin tried, but Rich Bar wouldn't leave his mind. All he could think of were the stories of great wealth that Cameron had told him. One man had brought out $2,900 worth of gold in *one* pan. That had been the biggest single pan haul that Robin had heard about, even where pans worth $1,000 or $1,500 had become ordinary. How could he look at a lush green valley when his blood was racing with thoughts of thousands of dollars' worth of gold waiting in the stream and on the ground for him?

Fiona, seeing where his thoughts were flying, tugged at his sleeve. "Robin, this is as important—no, more important to us than Rich Bar."

"Two days," Robin said, giving in because she was as afire about the valley as he was about the gold.

"Two days," Fiona agreed, and hopped down from the rig without help. Robin set up the camp for them. That night when the children were asleep Robin and Fiona walked together in the valley. The air was fresh and clean, and carried on its back the scents of rich soil and wild flowers. Overhead the stars seemed to sail down to earth so close Fiona reached up laughing, trying to catch them. She was in love. This would be her home.

That night as they made love, she told Robin, and he agreed. He had fallen under the spell of the valley too. They stayed there for four days and then, anxious that someone would buy the land before they had the chance, hurried on. Robin stopped at Sutter's Fort and sent a letter back to Cameron asking him to buy a thousand acres of land in the Napa Valley.

They arrived at Rich Bar by the end of June, and discovered several people whom they knew already living in a thriving community. Zane and Robin greeted each other with a bear hug, as well as several war whoops that put Fiona in mind of Pegleg Smith. Maybe the characters weren't making San Francisco; perhaps San Francisco had that effect on people. The other person they felt they knew, if only slightly, was Landry Morrison. Robin was surprised to discover that not only was Landry there, but he had been among the first, and was now an extraordinarily wealthy man in anybody's book.

Rich Bar was a different place from other claims Robin and Fiona had made. It was well on its way to being a town, with more people coming in all the time. Robin built a house in the town for Fiona and the children, and instantly made life easier all around for them.

Right from the start Robin's claim paid heavy dividends. Not a day passed that he didn't return home in the evening with a story of great success to report to Fiona. She accepted the news with a new sense of warmth and well-being. For her the search for gold had changed character. She no longer worked the claim with Robin on a regular basis. She tended her new home and kept a hardy garden in the back, which she watched over lovingly, and imagined that she was in the Napa Valley. While Robin still dug in the earth and washed tons of rock, Fiona was looking to the future, and learning those things she would need when she and Robin began to cultivate that rich valley.

Twenty-four

Ezra, Prudence and Tolerance Morrison stepped outside of the one-room redwood schoolhouse on Portsmouth Square where Sam Brannan held the Mormon services. Little Elisha Morrison clung to his mother's skirts, shy and slightly overawed by this congregation of big people milling about. This was the first year his mother and father had insisted he attend services with them regularly, and he wasn't certain he liked it. All these people who seemed to know him much better than he knew them gave him an uncomfortable feeling. Nearly four years old, Elisha already had many things in his young life that were confusing, and often occupied his quiet moments when he tried to sort it all out. Ezra was his father, or at least he was the man Elisha called father, but many, many times he had heard Prudence and his mother and Ezra talking about another man they said was his father. Elisha finally decided that he must have several fathers, just as it seemed that Mormons thought of everyone else as brothers.

Now, almost to his horror, the tall handsome man who had been standing in front of all of them and talking in a deep thunderous voice about their Father in Heaven joined his family, and Elisha sought the safety of his mother's skirts. Sam Brannan scared him.

Sam looked down at the big-eyed little boy who peered out from behind his mother, and felt a twinge of unaccustomed guilt. He liked Ezra Morrison very much, and if there was ever a man he respected, it was Ezra, but somehow Sam always seemed to be clandestinely involved with the women of Ezra's family, and that made him uncomfortable. It gave him the feeling that Fate had her twisted sense of humor leveled right at him. First there had been Susannah, and now there was Tollie. He had to concentrate to understand what Ezra was saying as he complimented Sam on his sermon this day.

He thanked Ezra, then he met Tollie's eyes. He knew she had been looking at him the whole time, communicating to him that she was looking forward to seeing him later that night. Unable to stand the mixture of feelings that Elisha stirred up in him, Sam bade the Morrisons good day, and hurried off to talk with some other people.

An hour later he was alone, and grateful for it. He wanted time to shake himself free of the brooding gloom that had come on him. It was either solitude, or go to the saloon and drown himself and his feelings in the best champagne San Francisco had to offer. Women were his nemesis. In all other things Sam Brannan was a forceful, successful, farsighted man, but when it came to women, he might as well have been a callow pimple-faced boy for all the expertise he had in handling the situations that arose. His marriage to Ann Eliza was a constant battlefield —or less. They no longer had the fire and passion that a battlefield brings, it was more like a siege for the duration, with both parties to the war huddled in their camps waiting—waiting— waiting for something to happen, only days went by and nothing happened.

And there was Tollie, as well as several other young women he saw from time to time. To him these women were diversions, but these "diversions" developed feelings, and memories, and expectations in which he figured prominently, and once more he was in trouble, unable to satisfy that side of their needs. If only everything were as simple as sex, if only the release it brought was enough for women as it was for him, his life would be complete.

Sam was unable to shake the mood. As he did so often in his dealings with the women in his life, he compromised, trying to satisfy everyone and ending up satisfying no one. He decided he would go home to Ann Eliza and his children. Before he headed for his Bush Street house, he stopped to have a few glasses of champagne with friends. It was a mistake, and he knew it was a mistake, for Ann Eliza hated his drinking, but it was so difficult to face her without some fortification, some of the mellowing wine to make him feel calmer. He didn't know how to behave with Ann Eliza. He had the slickest manners around, and could small talk any woman into his bed, but one did not small talk one's wife—at least not all the time. He could put together any business deal a man could want, yet he could not put together one whole evening of pleasant company that his wife wanted. He just didn't know how. It hurt him deeply to fail her time after time. That constant personal failure was something he just couldn't face, so he went home anaesthetized against that failure.

Ann Eliza had just helped Tilda put the children down for their naps, and was sitting in her parlor. Already she was knitting new small things for the baby she had told Sam about just a week ago. He had thought that having another child would please her and act as a new challenge for her, as one of his business deals did for him. However, she seemed more depressed and sour of temper than ever. As he entered the room, she glanced up at him, then away, but that flashing look had been sufficient to let him know that she knew he had been drinking, and that she didn't want his company.

Sam stood in the doorway of his own parlor in his own home and didn't know what to do. Ann Eliza was barring him from the comfort of his home as effectively as she might have done by erecting a fence across the doorway. Walking stiffly and unnaturally, he came over to her and kissed her cheek. Trying to be affectionate, Sam caressed her shoulder. "Have you had a good day, my dear?" he asked, his voice sounding loud and stilted in the quiet room.

Her face averted, Ann Eliza bit her lower lip and squeezed

her eyes shut before speaking to him. There was nothing so painful as a falsely affectionate touch when one had once known true affection. She didn't know what had happened to her and Sam, but their marriage had not worked almost from the start, and yet she had loved him so much. She tried to smile, but knew it was just another form of expressing her disappointment. "It has been fine, Sam. What has brought you home this afternoon? I expected you'd spend the day with your Mormon friends— you usually do after services."

"Yes, I know," Sam said hesitantly. There was so much he could say, so many questions he would like to have her answer for him, but how did one ask one's wife of many years to teach him how to be her husband, in such a way that he could still feel like a man in his own right? Even if he had the temerity to ask, he knew it wasn't something she could possibly answer. He smiled. "Today, however, I wanted to be at home—with you."

Ann Eliza heard the sincerity in his voice, and once more a slender frond of hope for them weakly struggled to life. She put her knitting down and smiled genuinely at him. For now, at least, she would ignore the scent of liquor on his breath. "Would you care to play cards, Sam? The children will not awaken for at least another hour."

Sam got up, and placed Ann Eliza's favorite chair near the table, and then got out the cards. Ann Eliza, with a glance at him to affirm, told Tilda he would be home for dinner. Then she sat down to play cards with her husband.

Sam put forth a Herculean effort to make the afternoon and evening a pleasant one. He avoided all dangerous subjects, which was nearly everything he was interested in, and allowed Ann Eliza to dictate their activities and conversation. By the time the children awakened from their naps, Sam was as tense as a taut wire. He had been sitting still all afternoon, his eyes focused hard on the cards, his mind chained to the fairly restricted rules of the game. He felt caged, and he no longer had the mellowing effect of the wine to keep his restless impatience or his temper in check.

At eight o'clock, after dinner, and after he had played quietly with his children, he said, "I must go out for a while, dear. I have promised Ezra Morrison I would meet with him this evening about a business matter he is considering. I won't be late."

Ann Eliza's suspicions leapt immediately, but with as great an effort as Sam had put forth earlier, she now quelled them, smiled at him, and offered her cheek to be kissed.

As soon as Sam stepped out into the street, he felt at home again—alive! The city was his home, far more than the four walls that comprised the shell of his house. He took a deep breath and straightened his back; his eyes sparkled, and he ran down the front steps and out onto the street, a jaunty swagger to his walk. He had no appointment with Ezra Morrison or anyone else. The small, believable lie was merely the cost of his freedom.

With the whole city at his fingertips, he considered where to go first. As he often did these days, he headed for the waterfront. Long Wharf, the wharf he had envisioned so often, was in the process of becoming a reality this summer of 1850. He stood on Liedesdorff Street and looked out at his wharf stretching, unfinished, out into the Bay. In his mind's eye sometimes the wharf would stretch out two miles, other times it seemed to him it would reach all the way out into the ocean itself. However he envisioned it, it was a magnificent piece of work, and he loved it, and was proud of his part in it as he was of everything he did in this city.

Long Wharf was going to become the main wharf of San Francisco, he felt certain. He looked around him. To his left was the two-story Pacific Mail Steamship office. A lot of business could pass from Long Wharf to that building. Beyond the Pacific Mail building there were innumerable smaller buildings belonging to a variety of merchants, all of them in the midst of a boom. They were so confident of continued or accelerated profits, in fact, that when it was determined that a sidewalk to Montgomery Street was needed, they had sunk hundred-pound cases of the best Virginia tobacco, at 75 cents a pound, into the tide-flat mud until a solid sidewalk had been built up. Sam smiled at the memory of watching that take place. Stark mad San Franciscans—how he loved them!

He looked out at the Bay in the direction of Clay Street. He could see the clipper ship *Niantic,* which had sunk in shallow water and was now embedded in the mud. She was going to become the foundation for the Hotel Niantic. Again he smiled, a rush of warmth flowing through him. Who but a San Franciscan would build a real hotel on the hulk of a sunken ship?

Sam now felt restored, rid of the stultifying afternoon he had spent at home. He was full of himself, and wanted entertainment, a little excitement, and some loving—loving that had no strings attached, loving that could be engaged in and then forgotten until it was wanted again. And he was hungry. In spite of having eaten with his family, he felt as though he had had nothing.

With a twinkle in his eye Sam spun around on his heel and headed for Dupont and Washington Streets. He knew just where he could satisfy both his hungers. With a quick step, and whistling merrily, Sam began to think of Mammie Pleasant's boarding house long before he got there. Mammie was an understanding woman. She knew what a man wanted and needed, and she knew how to deal in his own coin. It fascinated Sam just how adept Mammie was at making deals that would benefit her later and benefit her clients right now.

Mammie Pleasant had arrived in San Francisco about the beginning of the year, but her reputation as a wonderful cook had preceded her. She had barely set foot on San Francisco soil when several prominent men, and a few mine owners, bid for her services, offering her as much as five hundred dollars a month. Mammie had turned them all down and had opened her own place.

She hadn't needed to take a position, nor did she need financing. Mammie had married well, and had been left a considerable amount of money from her first husband, James W. Smith. After Smith died, Mammie had married again, this time John J. Pleasant, an overseer of her late husband's. John Pleasant and his wife had set sail together on the voyage to San Francisco, but somehow when the ship docked, only Mammie was aboard. No one seemed to know or care what had happened to Mr. Pleasant. It was enough that Mammie was there, and ready to cook for and make the most important men of San Francisco happy.

Sam was smiling broadly as he opened the door to the heavenly odors that permeated Mammie's place. He was seated at a table that always seemed to be ready for him whenever he came in. It was almost as though Mammie knew he was coming before he knew it himself. And it was said that Mammie had learned the black arts from her Louisiana mother. She was a mysteriously powerful woman, there was no doubt about that.

Sam ordered Louisiana shrimp, one of Mammie's specialties, and some corn pone, which he had developed an especial liking for ever since Mammie had convinced him he should try it.

As Sam ate with relish, Mammie appeared as if from out of nowhere and sat in the seat opposite him. "Is my magic chasing the blue fingers from off you?" she asked.

Sam sat back. "Ahh, Mammie, you always know just what I need. How do you do it?"

Mammie laughed.

She was a strangely attractive woman. Her skin was as dark as the finest ebony. Her mother had been a black woman from the bayous. Some said her father had been a Kanaka man, others said he was a Cherokee Indian. Mammie said nothing. Mammie's face looked as if it had been carved from that fine ebony. Her expression was stern, and her features were distinctly refined, patrician. Sam liked to sit back and look at her almost as much as he liked eating the food she prepared with such flair.

"I already told Myra that you'd be coming over to the boarding house for a visit," she said confidently.

For the first time Sam noticed that she had with her a brilliant scarlet shawl. It was almost a trademark with her. He thought how often he had seen Mammie sitting poker straight in her carriage, the red shawl prominent on her shoulders, and a brightly colored bonnet. "You're going out tonight, Mammie," he commented.

"You are not the only one who may have need of an assignation to rid you of the blue fingers of the heart." Mammie's small smile made her face even more classically intriguing.

Sam sat back in his chair, his eyes narrowed as he looked at her speculatively. "But that still is not to say that you are the one to have the blue fingers, is it, Mammie?"

She smiled at him enigmatically.

Sam finished his meal. "Sometimes, Mammie, I think there isn't going to be one influential man in all of San Francisco who will not owe you a debt, and who will not entrust to you some secret that you will call due one day."

"You are a wise man, Sam Brannan, but you must also remember Mammie does not do anything that is not to the benefit of all. That is as it should be. Even between conspirators there must be trust. Now, come, allow me to make you comfortable with Myra, and then I can be on my way in peace, knowing you are well taken care of."

She led the way, through a large public room then down a tastefully decorated hall, into the boarding house section of the building. Mammie Pleasant actually did run a boarding house— a select one which attracted the famous, wealthy and influential men who visited the city—and those who lived there. They came to dine on Mammie's delicious meals, to sleep in the comfortable beds in beautifully furnished rooms, and to find that pleasures of their own devising could be brought to them there.

Sam followed her up the stairs that led to the back. He really didn't know why he should trust her, but he did. There were few people in San Francisco whom Mammie didn't know, and that included Ann Eliza. If she chose, she could make plenty of trouble for Sam, but he didn't think she would—at least not now, not until she asked him for some favor he could not grant. In that event he had no idea of what she could, or would, do. In the meantime he would enjoy the lush blondness of Myra and allow her to soothe him in her own special way.

Despite his diversions, Sam did not forget that he had made a step forward that afternoon with Ann Eliza, and he had high hopes that this coming child would improve their relationship still further. He had not felt this way about his other children, but for this little one his heart was open and ready. He left Mammie Pleasant's place early, much to Myra's surprise and consternation, and returned to his home and Ann Eliza.

As he had expected, Ann Eliza had retired for the night, and was lying in the darkness of her own bedroom. She would most likely behave as though she was asleep whether she was or not, but he would stick his head in her room and say goodnight to her anyway. He wanted her to know how early he had come home.

He opened the door quickly, noting the gentle, flowery odor of her perfume that permeated the room. It was so like Ann Eliza, light, dignified, understated. For some reason tonight that amused him. "Are you awake, my dear?" he asked softly, not at all in accordance with what he had planned.

"Yes," came her reply, equally a surprise. "You are home early, aren't you? Did your meeting with Brother Morrison go well?"

"Very well indeed," Sam said, and entered the room. He walked to her bed, bent down and kissed her on the forehead. "Sleep well, my dear," he said, and left the room before she made a greater effort to please him, and both of them would end the night dissatisfied, thus negating all the small progress toward each other they had made today.

In the following days, Sam was pleased with the relative peace in his home. He and Ann Eliza were at least able to carry on conversations, a little stilted perhaps, but they were talking in civilized fashion with each other. He considered this a reasonable way to live. He had Myra to satisfy his baser needs, and if he could fill in the hollow of himself that needed stimulating female conversation and companionship, he and Ann Eliza might be able to tolerate each other in their marriage.

When he thought of this, his mind went immediately to Tolerance Morrison. Tollie was attractive, she was companionable, she was sweet, she was not abrasive to his nerves, and she was married. With her a workable arrangement could be made. He and Tollie already met at his apartment on occasional afternoons, and he had taken her to dinner a few times. Now that he was looking upon his whole domestic situation in the same fashion he did a business problem, things seemed as though they might fall into place. Keeping his businesslike approach in mind, he spoke to Tollie that very afternoon, telling her what he had in mind and concluding with "But you must understand, my dear, that I am devoted to my wife and family, and that is as it should be and will remain. In no way should our seeing each other socially interfere with the lives of our spouses, for you too have a devotion to Ezra, I understand that."

Tollie looked at him with sad eyes. "I don't know if I have a devotion to Ezra. I don't know if I have a devotion to anyone. Once I thought I did, but now . . . I just don't know."

Sam thought of Mammie's expression "the blue fingers on the heart." He put his arm around Tollie and drew her over to the settee. "I believe I know what you are feeling," he said. "Ann Eliza and I also have not an easy marriage, but that does not end the devotion."

Tollie gave a small, sad laugh. "Is that what I mean, Sam?"

"Isn't it?"

She laughed again, took a deep breath and let it out. "I don't think so."

"Then what do you mean, my dear?" Sam asked.

Tollie turned her eyes on him. "You are my religious leader, aren't you? It is strange to be confessing my innermost problems to the First Elder of my Church, who also happens to be my lover. That is peculiar, don't you think?"

She was making him uncomfortable. Sam cleared his throat. "Yes, I suppose it is. But I am prepared to listen to you, and to guide you in whatever way I may be able."

Tollie made a little motion of demur with her hands. "It is really quite simple. I love Landry. I was married to him. I had his child. I betrayed him, and now he has betrayed me, but I still long for him. So—am I in any way devoted to my husband Ezra? Am I in any way better than Landry who was dis-churched when he questioned? He denounced a precept—a belief of our church. He did not even do that fully, he only questioned, and yet he was sent away from his family, his wife, denied his child—everything—and here I am . . ." She stopped talking, her face blank with the hopelessness of true depression. "You can't help me or guide me. No one can."

"My dear!" Sam said with true alarm. He had really thought very little about Tollie herself. He had always thought her a rather superficial young woman, whose life could be made happy and complete with possessions, fine clothes, and exciting places to go. He'd had no idea she harbored such dire thoughts and feelings within her. "You were but a child when all of that happened with Landry. You must understand that Bishop Waterman and Ezra—all concerned did what they thought was best at the time. What were you to do?"

"I don't know. That's just it, I don't know. I pray, but I never get an answer. Everything might have been all right—except that Landry came here." Dispiritedly she told him of her meeting with Landry and how she had gone to the City Hotel the next morning expecting to spend the day with him. "But he had gone to the mountains long before the time he told me to meet him. He did that on purpose. He drew me out, made me confess my love, my longing for him, my lust for him—and then he left." She stared at the wall, eyes brimming with tears of humiliation and hurt.

Sam didn't know what to say. He wondered if there was any way at all for a man and a woman to love each other and be together. When he thought of Ann Eliza and heard tales such as the one Tollie was telling him, he thought not. He waited for her to regain her composure, then he said, "I hardly know where to begin, Tollie. You have been terribly wronged—"

She said calmly, "No. It was an eye for an eye."

Sam didn't argue; instead he said, "Well, be that as it may, the real question is what are you going to do now? I take it you do not want to be Ezra's wife."

"I don't know what I feel, but I know that he doesn't want me to be his wife. I caused as much pain for Ezra as I did for Landry. Prudence is the only woman he wants—but I find I resent Prudence terribly." She looked up at him for guidance. "Does that mean I am jealous?"

Sam closed his eyes for a moment. How could she not know? How could he ever think of forming such a liaison with her as he was contemplating?

"I shouldn't ask you these things, Sam," she said contritely. "It isn't fair."

Sam laughed harshly. "Who but me should you ask? As you pointed out, I am your spiritual leader. If you can't come to me with these problems, who can you go to?"

"I've made you angry."

"No, my dear, you haven't made me angry. You have merely thrust me full length into the desperate muck of the human condition—a place I do not like to be, for I am not sure there are any answers. We are pathetic creatures, and we do not seem to have any rules that are completely faithful to us. All we can do is keep trying to find the best place for ourselves, to learn to serve others and thereby make ourselves reasonably comfortable in this life. That is not much in the way of advice, and certainly not what a spiritual leader is supposed to say, but it is all I have to offer."

Tollie's eyes widened. "Surely you do not feel that way! You always are so busy, and so . . . so vital. Everyone looks to you, Sam. We all know how capable you are. You are involved in everything of importance."

"Yes, I am. I keep very busy. That is my way of avoiding what I think of as the pit of human existence. I run past anything that might drag me into it . . . ."

Tollie sat quietly, looking at him, thinking of him and of herself. It was a long time before she spoke again, and when she did, she felt better and had made some decisions for herself. She was no longer the pampered only daughter of a Mormon bishop. She was no longer the adored young wife of a Mormon elder. All the bright dreams of her world going right, with someone always there to keep her safe and happy, were not going to happen. There never was going to be a magic wand to make things right, nor a fairy godmother to guard against tragedy. If she was to find happiness, she would have to do it on her own; and it would not be the high-minded pure joy she had always dreamed about. Her happiness would be a series of compromises and settling for what was available. Sam Brannan was available. And he could enable her to see things and go places she wouldn't be able to do otherwise.

"I'd like to . . . I'd like to have that arrangement . . . liaison with you, Sam."

"Oh, but Tollie, after all you've told me, I don't think—"

"Have you changed your mind, Sam? Do you no longer want me?"

"No, no, my dear, it isn't that. I don't think it would be very good for you. When I first suggested it, I had no idea you carry such a burden of sorrow."

"But I have concluded that this arrangement between us would be helpful to me. Perhaps it was meant that I should talk to you as I have today. We are a people of miracles, and in a small way this was a miracle—at least for me. I suddenly feel strong enough, capable enough to find some happiness and pleasure in this life for myself and on my own. I don't need Ezra, and I can't have Landry, so that leaves . . . me. Just me. I couldn't face that before. I'd like to try now, and I'd like to be with you."

Sam considered for a moment, then smiled. He hugged her to him. "There is far more to you, little Sister Morrison, than I ever dreamed." He held her at arm's length, looked into her eyes. "Though it does not help you, I must tell you that Landry Morrison is a fool. If he were half the man you think he is, no man other than him would ever touch you."

Tollie smiled brilliantly, her face coloring prettily.

With Sam Brannan as escort, a whole new world opened up for Tollie. Once she had decided to be on her own, she grew very bold, and urged Sam to take her places that before she would never have considered, let alone entered. She gave full vent to her baser side.

Tollie was fascinated by Portsmouth Square. On the western, or quiet, side of the Square stood the redwood schoolhouse, where public meetings were covened, the Saints held services, and the Odd Fellows lodge met. There also were a few hotels and small stores, and the Old Adobe house from Mexican days, from the steps of which the Reverend William Taylor could usually be heard, fulminating against gambling. He had something to fulminate against, for gambling houses filled the eastern side of the Square and much of the other three sides. In the saloons and in the barrooms of the hotels were also tables for play. Outside, in fine weather, were often set up arrangements for monte, faro, and chuck-a-luck games. The gaming operated ceaselessly; most of the houses had pianos or orchestras which were usually playing a variety of songs; crowds of people came and went; shouts, oaths, cheers and screams issued from the gambling houses which bore names like The Empire, The Mazourka, Tontine House, Aquila de Oro, La Soucidad, The Verandah.

One of the places that had always attracted Tollie the most, and that she had studiously avoided, was the El Dorado, the famous and infamous gambling palace, the first to open after the discovery of gold. When it had first been in business the El Dorado had been a canvas tent, but by the time Tollie had decided she wanted to know about gambling, the place was a large square room built of wood. Rather than being just another gambling spot, the El Dorado was already looking to the varying whims and wants of its customers. It was going beyond the mere practice of throwing the dice, or watching the wheel spin. It had a few private rooms where a man could entertain his inamorata, and this suited Tollie just fine. She could see what took place in the El Dorado, have Sam place bets for her, and still maintain a bit of decorum and some privacy.

The first time Sam took her into the private booth, Tollie studiously avoided looking at the walls, which were decorated with extremely expensive and extremely lascivious paintings. Instead she showered all her comments and attention on the rococo furniture that was crammed to superabundance in the small room. But as soon as Sam left to place her bet on the Rouge et Noir, she looked carefully at the paintings. Even when she was by herself they brought a blush to her cheeks, but she liked them.

By the time they had gone to the El Dorado for the fifth time, Tollie did not feel so strange entering the gambling hall, although it was definitely frowned upon by "decent" folk. But she liked the music that was played constantly, and she liked to see the musicians as well as hear them. That she couldn't do from the booth. So she stood for a moment near the long bar at one end of the room, and watched the musicians who played from a raised platform gaily decorated with bunting and flags and brightly colored streamers.

Sam stood behind her, enjoying this colorful view of the El Dorado through her enchanted eyes as he had never enjoyed it through his own. Along the walls were fine mirrors of plate glass, which reflected the gaming tables positioned all over the large room, surrounded by eager men with bags of gold dust and clinking gold coins just waiting to be placed on the spin of a wheel. The lively music of the band rose above the constant hum of men's voices, the thud of the gold dust pouches, and the dealer's call, "Place your bets, gentlemen!" Croupiers and bankers all talked in aloud clear voices, and occasionally a whoop of triumph would drown out all other sound.

Tonight there was a group of Negro singers, who were performing the songs currently popular in California: "The Bullwhacker's Song"; "The Ballad of the Happy Miner"; "There's a Good Pile Coming, Boys!"; and one which Sam always liked, and joined in on:

> *"Oh, what was your name in the States?*
> *Was it Thompson or Johnson or Bates?*
> *Did you murder your wife and fly for your life?*
> *Say, what was your name in the States?"*

Tollie's eyes glistened with the enchantment. Sam could feel the waves of excitement flowing off her. She clung to his hand like a child released to wander the roads of a fairy tale. Shivering with emotion, she tore her eyes away from the sight of the gaming tables and looked at Sam. "Oh, why must this be just for men?"

Sam laughed and shrugged. "I guess men just assume women wouldn't like this—or approve of it. I really don't know why."

"We are always left out of all that is fun, and then we must pretend that we don't approve, and nobody ever knows why. I like this. I wish!—I wish I could walk up to one of those tables and slap my own gold coin down and say, I want number thirteen, sir!"

"Thirteen is unlucky," Sam said.

"Not for me!" Tollie said stoutly. "Everything about me is backward. Thirteen is a lucky number for me."

Sam took several pieces of gold from his vest pocket and placed them in her hand. "Why don't you just walk right up there and do what you want?"

Tollie looked at him open-mouthed. "You'd let me?"

"I'll escort you," Sam said with a smile, and with his hand on her back gave her a gentle nudge in the direction of the table.

Tolerance Morrison made the first bet of her life. In the El Dorado a man could place any bet he wished; the sky was the limit. She put all thirty dollars' worth of coins Sam had given her on number thirteen, and won. With a squeal of laughter, she and Sam gathered up her winnings and retired to their private booth.

"How does it feel to be a gambling lady?" Sam asked, as he poured champagne into the glasses for them. He held up his glass to toast her.

Tollie didn't give a thought to the fact that she never drank alcoholic beverages. Until recently she hadn't even had tea or coffee or any hot drink, adhering faithfully to the Mormon Word of Wisdom. She took too big a sip of the champagne, and the bubbles got in her nose and she choked, laughing and sputtering champagne on both of them. When she could speak, she threw her arms around his neck and said, "Oh, Sam, this is the most wonderful night of my life. I love it! I love you for bringing me here! I love everything! Everyone!"

Sam didn't go home that night, and neither did Tollie. They had a wonderful time, and ended up back at his apartment making love and drinking champagne until the sun had risen to start a new day.

Tollie was worried when she finally realized what she had done. "Prudence is going to know I've been out all night, and I can't cover this with a simple-minded story about visiting friends. What will I do?"

"Do you mind if Prudence makes a fuss? What can she do to you that you would care about?"

Trying to imagine the worst, Tollie said, "She couldn't take Elisha from me, could she?"

"I don't really think Prudence would do that. Do you?"

"No . . . I don't think so, but she would be angry and she might tell Ezra. She'd probably love telling Ezra."

"And how would that affect you?"

Tollie thought for a moment. "I don't think I care. All I care about is my son."

"Then take your son and move out of Ezra's house."

"Live alone? I couldn't! How would I? I have no money—I couldn't."

Sam didn't argue. She was right, of course, but he also knew that she was moving in that direction whether she realized it or not. Now that Tollie had taken the first steps in breaking away from a very strict upbringing, she was discovering she was a free spirit. He doubted very much that she was going to calm down with time. More likely there would be many more nights when she would not return home, and her dress and speech and behavior would become more extreme. If she didn't leave Ezra's house, Sam was willing to bet that one day Ezra was going to put her out. He had planted the idea in her mind, but she wasn't ready yet to act upon it. That was all he could do for now.

He called a carriage for her and had her taken home.

The next time they went out, on a whim he took her to the Bella Union. There the roulette wheel, Tollie's favorite game, was run by someone who had caused a great stir in the city, and had caused the editor of the *Alta California* to write indignantly about gambling houses not being suitable places for women. Sam didn't think Tollie would have read the editorial, so he said nothing to her until they entered the Bella Union.

An old hand going to the gaming houses with Sam now, Tollie entered the place with some confidence. Sam led her straight to the most crowded wheel in the house and said, "How do you feel about number thirteen tonight?"

Tollie looked up and stared into the face of a strikingly beautiful Frenchwoman. Mademoiselle Simone Jules had enormous dark-brown eyes, so dark they appeared black. She wore her hair stylishly, and was the center of attention. Tollie didn't take her eyes off the woman as she placed her bet on number thirteen. Mademoiselle Jules, with a slight nod and smile, acknowledged Tollie's presence, then spun the wheel. Tollie did not win that time on the table, but she had won something else. She turned to Sam and asked him if they could leave right away. Once outside, he apologized. "I'm sorry, Tollie, I thought you'd enjoy seeing another woman at one of the houses. Mademoiselle is highly regarded. I didn't realize it would upset you."

"It hasn't," she said tensely. "I want to do that too. Then I could leave Ezra's house. I could make my own way in the world. I could live my own life as I want to. Can you teach me, Sam?"

"Teach you?" he asked, again taken aback by Tollie's vehemence and force when her mind was made up.

"How to deal—how to work the wheels. I don't know anything. All I've done is put a few coins down and watched the wheel spin. How do you play faro, and chuck-a-luck, and vingt-et-un? I don't know the simplest things. Can you—will you teach me?"

Sam threw his head back and laughed until his sides hurt. "Yes, my dear, I, Samuel Brannan, First Elder of the Church of Jesus Christ of Latter-Day Saints, your spiritual leader, will teach you how to gamble, and do it damned well."

Twenty-five

San Francisco of 1850 was a town feeling its oats. Hardly a man in town didn't have gold coin or gold dust in his pockets, more of it than he knew what to do with. Even those who had no luck in the diggings had only to get a spoon and a pan, and take the gold right out of the dust on the streets. With a little diligence he could be assured of extracting about an ounce a day, which made him a worthy man at the gaming tables. A spirit of *joie de vivre* permeated everything. The dealers at the El Dorado liked to call out that the sky was the limit. That was San Francisco. Her slogan might have been the sky's the limit.

With all the proper fixtures in place now here and at the state level, California had only to wait for Congress to vote and allow them their proper spot in the Union. All of California and particularly San Francisco was keeping an eye on Congress as closely as any man ever watched a Faro table. For California, 1850 was an all-or-nothing year. The final die had been cast on November 13, 1849, a rainy day in one of the rainiest rainy seasons in history, when the people of California had voted on the constitution and elected state officers. It had rained steadily for five weeks, and on election day the mud was knee-deep. The turnout was small but decisive. The constitution passed. Peter Burnett, Sutter's attorney, was elected governor. Edward Gilbert, a former lieutenant in the New York Volunteers, was elected as congressman along with George Washington Wright. On December 17 Governor Burnett and Lieutenant Governor John McDougall were formally installed in office. Burnett, in his acceptance speech, said that California should assume "all the functions of sovereignty now." He added that if the state were refused admission to the Union, they would go for broke. If the United States didn't want her, California would become sovereign unto herself. That afternoon the legislature elected as United States senators William Gwin and John Charles Fremont.

On New Year's Day 1850, Gwin, Fremont, Gilbert, and Wright sailed for Washington via Panama. They arrived in the national capital in February, and soon applied to Congress for admission to the Union, under a state constitution that prohibited slavery. Congress debated the issue some more. Ordinarily in these circumstances the territory in question had developed laws, and order, and had written a state constitution. As a Congressionally recognized territory, California could have sent a delegate as envoy to Congress to keep them informed of progress regarding the area. But California had not even been granted territorial status yet. It was still under the military government left over from the Mexican War.

There were in Congress two groups of men, violently opposed, the one wanting slavery and the other wanting abolition of slavery. The newspapers called both these groups the Ultras. The Ultras would not yield to any suggestion from the opposing group. Between these two screaming extremes were the Soberheads, men of reason and good judgment who argued that it was the duty of Congress now to give California the safeguard of an organized government.

Henry Clay, "The Great Pacificator," proposed the Compromise of 1850, under which California could be admitted as a free state and New Mexico and Utah could be formed into territories with their people deciding the slavery question for themselves. Daniel Webster, the great orator, spoke for California. President Zachary Taylor died; and in his place Millard Fillmore became President. Fillmore instructed Congress to vote. Not until September 7, 1850, did Congress cast the final vote to make California a state.

On October 7, San Franciscans got word that the issue of their statehood had passed the Senate on August 13, but it still had to pass the House. That vote had already been taken, but no one in California had received word of the outcome.

Jane Pardee had come into San Francisco from her freight route, supplying the gold camps and bringing back bank deposits. As soon as her business was taken care of she stopped in to see her friend, Sam Brannan. Without waiting to be asked, Jane sat down in the most comfortable chair in Sam's office.

He grinned at her. "Make yourself at home, Jane."

"Thanks, Sam, I have. Well?"

"Well what?"

"Is Fillmore going to get a chance to sign the papers for statehood or not?"

Sam laughed. "How should I know? Congress is as fickle as a pretty girl with two proposals of marriage."

Jane cocked her head to one side. "True enough, but you know. You always know these things. What plans are afoot? Any truth to the rumor that a grand ball can be put together on a day's notice, and Mr. and Mrs. Samuel Brannan would act as grand marshals?"

"I wouldn't deny it," said Sam, enjoying Jane as he always did.

"Then it is just a matter of time—maybe days," Jane said, her eyes beginning to sparkle.

Chuckling, Sam repeated, "I wouldn't deny it."

"That settles it! I'm staying in San Francisco. If California is going to become a state, that's one event I'm not going to miss out on."

"I didn't know there was any event you missed out on, Jane," Sam said. Then with a wickedly mischievous gleam in his eye, he turned to her favorite subject. "Have you found number five yet, Jane?"

"Nope. I swear, Sam, there just doesn't seem to be a man I can take to my heart. Maybe there'll never be a number five."

"Live in hope, Jane. I don't like to hear you, of all people, giving up. Anyway, if you get desperate, I've got a lame old elder up in Sacramento who'd like a young wife. He's toothless, and wouldn't cause you any trouble."

Jane laughed with pleasure. "Don't offer what you're not prepared to give, Sammy. I might take you up on it. You just never know." She got up, came around the side of his desk to cup his face in both her hands, and gave him a resounding kiss. "Maybe I'll set my cap for you. Got to be going now. Give those kids of yours a kiss for me." She left his office as much a whirlwind as when she had entered.

Sam grinned. She made him feel good. Jane was always a slightly cockeyed oasis of sanity in a crazy world. By the time the day was out she would have visited the Gentrys, and the Morrisons, and two or three dozen other people she knew from here or Sutter's or one of the gold camps. There was no one, it seemed, whom Jane didn't know.

Jane did exactly what Sam thought she would do, and her visiting didn't stop then. If she was going to wait around in San Francisco for word of statehood, she had to keep busy. The one thing Jane Pardee could not abide was idleness. She could tolerate just about fifteen minutes' worth, and then she had to be up and doing.

She tried her hand at gambling, and lost fifty dollars in Bill Briggs's place. That was enough for her. Gambling, even chuck-a-luck, wasn't her cup of tea. But she did enjoy Bill Briggs's company, and spent the rest of the night talking with him, and accompanied him to the market to toss coins to the gamins gathering refuse for their goats.

Fortunately Jane—and San Francisco—didn't have long to wait for news of statehood. On October 18, 1850, the *Oregon* fired her cannons while still at sea. By the time she sailed through the Golden Gate into the Bay, hordes of people had gathered at the waterfront. As soon as the big ship neared, a cheer went up from the crowd. Stretched from mast to mast was an enormous canvas sheet, reading CALIFORNIA ADMITTED! on one side and CALIFORNIA IS A STATE! on the other.

Shouts of victory could be heard all around the wharf. Men drew pistols and shot into the air. Ships in the harbor fired their guns. Jane Pardee flung her arms around the man standing next to her and danced him down the pier. With the same suddenness that she had grabbed him, she let the man go, and he staggered backward. She hurried back to her hotel to pack. She'd be on her way now to carry the news to Sean and Mary, Brian and Coleen and others in the gold fields, especially Robin and Fiona.

In a lather to be on her way, Jane almost didn't hear Sam Brannan call her name. "Are you going to join in the race to San Jose to bring the news of statehood?"

"I'm headin' north," Jane said. "Who's driving?"

"Jared Crandall. Governor Burnett says there's no better. He's the prince of drivers. Ackley and Maurison won't stand still for that, you know. They say they'll beat the governor and Crandall to San Jose and give the news themselves. I wouldn't think you'd want to miss that."

"I don't guess I do," Jane admitted with a grin. "What do you say you and me go down to the Square and watch the start of this race?"

"We'll get a better view up around the Mission," Sam said, and helped him into his carriage.

The stagecoach for the Hall and Crandall Stage Line that ran every day between San Francisco and the state capital at San Jose was a Concord, a Yankee creation, built in a New Hampshire plant, and it had not yet been surpassed. The builders, Abbott, Downing and Company, had constructed a 2,500-pound, smooth-riding vehicle. The body of the coach was suspended by two heavy thorobraces that allowed the coach to rock back and forth, absorbing the road shock. And perhaps most important of all, the Concord wheels were the most durable to be had. The regal Concord was durable, reliable, and attractive. She could carry nine passengers in her upholstered interior, and another ten on top, plus luggage in the boot. She was a fine vehicle, and Jared Crandall the best of drivers.

Governor Peter Burnett mounted the steps of the coach and waved to the crowd gathered in Portsmouth Square to watch his leavetaking. Across the Square the driver for Ackley and Maurison, arch rival of the Hall and Crandall line, waited for the start. He might not have been chosen to carry the governor to the state capital with the news of statehood, but he could sure give his competition a run for their money, and perhaps beat Crandall to San Jose. In their advertisements, Hall and Crandall emphasized safety, while Ackley and Maurison stressed speed. Today they'd see who was the best for both.

Crandall, on the box, gave a quick wave to his rival, then yelled at the horses, and the two Concords tore out of the Square heading for the sandy road to the Mission.

All along the road people stood three and four deep, waving scarves and flags, and calling cheers to the governor flying past, with Crandall looking like a man possessed as he cracked his whip and shouted encouragement to the horses.

Behind the Crandall coach came the Ackley and Maurison Concord, its driver straining himself and his horses to the utmost as he strove to come even with Crandall. The two coaches were side by side, the two teams of horses almost neck and neck. Jauntily both the governor and Crandall, the prince of drivers, took off their hats and waved them to the crowd, shouting, "California is admitted to the Union!" Both Crandall and Burnett were in their element. Pegasus himself could not have touched the flying hoofs of Crandall's team.

Jane pounded on Sam's shoulder. "Look at that bloody son of a bitch drive, Sam! Look at him!"

Sam was hanging out the window of his carriage, waving a flag madly.

With only dust in the air left to mark the passing of the two Concords, Jane fell back against the seat. "Whew! I feel like I'm in that race with 'em." She sat up, and nudged Sam. "I am, by jiminy! Tell your driver to lash these beasts and get me back to the hotel. I'll be damned if anyone is going to get to my family and tell them the news before I do. Hurry, Sam, I got a race of my own!"

Jane dressed in her driver's outfit. With her pants, loose-fitting shirt, and slouch hat, one would not have known she was a woman, and that was how she wanted it. Men didn't trust a woman driver to get them where they were going, or to be able to protect them on the road. Well, what they didn't know wouldn't hurt them. She wasn't any Jared Crandall, but she could out-drive most men, and there were damned few she couldn't outdraw and outshoot. With that thought, she strapped on her gunbelt, and slipped her pistol into the holster. She grabbed her carpetbag, paid her bill, and was on her way out of San Francisco within the hour.

Inspired by the example Jared Crandall had set earlier, and with her big spurs jingling, Jane got upon the seat of her freight wagon and imagined what it would be like to sit on the box of a Concord stagecoach. She took the reins and shouted at Daisy, "Hippah mulah! Hippah mulah!" With a bone-rattling jolt, Daisy inspired the other mules to move, and Jane was off on her own race to tell Carl and Rowena Gentry at Agua Clara the good news. Then it would be on to Sean and Mary's, and to Brian and Coleen's house, and finally to Rich Bar and Fiona and Robin. She wasn't sure what pleased her more, the idea of bringing them the news of statehood, or seeing the children. With Brian Og and Tyrone and Maeve to love and call a part of her family, Jane Pardee felt blessed as she had never felt before in her life.

She was about four miles out of San Francisco when she heard a great commotion in a thick stand of trees just off the rutted trail that passed for a road. She came close to ignoring it; but just then a worn-out nag, bedecked with three carpetbags inexpertly tied to the saddle, ploughed in knock-kneed fashion out of the trees. Moments after, she heard a man yelling for mercy.

"All right, Daisy—Carnation—Iris—get mean, girls!" She turned the mules in the direction of the noises. With all the speed the mules could muster she headed them right into the trees, her head tucked down into her shoulders, her pistol already out of its holster. With a blood-curdling imitation of an Indian war cry, Jane charged into the midst of four men. Daisy was a biter, and Iris loved to butt. Carnation would kick if she could get a good shot at her target, but it was difficult for her in harness. Iris sent one man headlong into a tree, then threw her head back, baring her big teeth and bellowing in triumph.

"Don't shoot me!" a small man cried out, his hands high in the air.

This creature was obviously the subject of the attack. He had a bruise on his chin, and one of his eyes was very red and already swelling shut. He wore a heavy black woolen suit that must have been death in this heat. But Jane wasn't interested in him. Daisy had a healthy mouthful of the pants bottom of one of the rascals, and Iris was pulling the whole wagon sideways in her effort to give her target another thumping with her hard head. The third man was running like a sprinter and had already put a quarter-mile's distance between himself and his partners in crime. "Get out of my way, you little squirt!" she shouted. "He's getting away!"

The man moved directly in front of the wagon. "Sorry!" He looked up at her, his arms still high over his head. "I'm trying! Don't shoot!"

Daisy's victim was screeching his head off, and Iris's was now comatose. "Daisy! Let the bugger go!" Jane ordered, giving up any hope of a truly heroic citizen's arrest. As soon as he was free, this ruffian, too, headed for the hills. She climbed down from the driver's seat, gave the prone man a kick in the rear to be certain he was really out cold. He was. She turned her attention to the little man. "They attack you on the road?"

"May I put my hands down now?" he asked meekly.

"Who in the hell told you to put 'em up?"

"Oh, sorry—I just thought that was the proper procedure—I wanted to do things correctly for you . . . uh, sir? Are you a sir?"

"No, my name's Jane Pardee."

"Oh, my," he breathed.

"And that's just why I wear men's duds. Soon's a man knows I'm a woman, it's 'oh, my!' " Feeling unaccustomedly bashful, Jane kicked at the dirt, causing clouds of dust to fly up onto the black pants the man had just brushed off so painstakingly. "Who are you?"

"I'm Zeke Rumbard, gentleman farmer."

"Gentleman farmer?" Jane repeated loudly, in puzzlement. "What is a gentleman farmer? That mean you don't work?"

Zeke's pleasant face lit up when he smiled the most angelic smile she had ever seen on a man. "It means I farm gently. Tulips are my specialty," he said proudly.

Zeke stood no more than five feet two inches, and Jane was a husky, healthy, self-dependent six feet in her stockings, but somehow that smile he had bestowed on her made her feel like the most pampered, cosseted, protected woman ever born. With a suddenness that shocked her, she wished she was wearing her pretty blue dress and not the baggy driver's outfit she had on. "Tulips, huh? That's a nice occupation for a man, Zeke."

Zeke puffed out his narrow chest as far as it would go. This was a lot of woman, he decided, and he was the man to handle her. All he had to do was hear her respect his tulips, and he knew he would be able to find his way into her heart. There was something very special and tender about people who loved flowers. "I'd like to thank you, Miss Pardee, for coming to my rescue."

"Oh, I near forgot. Was that your horse that tore out of here?"

"Yes, poor Penelope was terrified with all the shouting and wrestling about. Those ruffians knocked me right off her back. I don't suppose I'll ever find her now."

"Hop on up," Jane said, pointing to her wagon. "We'll find her. She'll probably be grazing not too far off. Unless she knows her way home, she won't have gone far."

"Well, she certainly doesn't know her way home. We don't have a home yet. We've just arrived in California, and I was about to find the right spot for my garden."

Jane got up on her seat beside Zeke. Before she could pick up the reins and call to her mules, Zeke grabbed her hand and brought it to his lips. "What lovely, capable hands you have, Miss Pardee."

Jane blushed to her hair roots. "Do you think so, Mr. Rumbard?"

"I do indeed. You are a magnificent woman."

Jane didn't know what to do. She was completely flabbergasted. She hadn't run across a man who affected her like this since Mr. Pardee, and here he was scarcely bigger than a mouse. Life sure was strange. "Hippah, mulah!" she cried, and let Daisy get the mules back onto the rutted track. "I'm on my way to visit some friends and bring them news of California's admission to the Union. Would you care to look at the land in that direction, and give a lookout for poor Penelope?"

Coyly Zeke smiled and looked at her from the corner of his eye. "Whither thou goest . . ."

"Oh, Mr. Rumbard . . ." she fluted.

"Zeke. Please, if you don't think me too forward on such short acquaintance, I'd like it if you'd call me Zeke. That's what my mother called me."

"I will, if you call me Jane."

"Oh! What a beautiful name! It suits you so. I will develop a new tulip and name it the Jane. I think—mm, red—no, a deep royal violet tulip named Jane."

It was a good thing Daisy was as much a mule as she was, for from then on Jane was almost worthless as a driver.

They stopped at Agua Clara, the Gentry ranch, and visited for a short time, then went on, intending to go to the Campbells'. Instead they stopped and were married by an itinerant preacher. Jane Pardee Rumbard had found her fifth husband.

It was the end of October, and snow had already fallen in the mountains when Jane and Zeke arrived at Rich Bar and Robin and Fiona's house.

"Wait 'til you meet these two," Jane said proudly to Zeke. "Robin's not mine, and neither is Fiona, but by heaven, Zeke, I feel like they are. You're going to fall in love with Maeve. She's the wildest little imp you'll ever meet."

Jane pounded on the door. As soon as Fiona answered it, Jane said, "I took so long in getting here I suppose you already know California's a state, but I got some other news you don't know about."

Fiona laughed and put her arms out for a hug. "Oh, it's good to see you! We've missed you, and we need cheering up. It's been too cold for Tyrone to play outside, and he has the sniffles." Only then did Fiona see the small man who had been hidden behind Jane. "Oh. I'm sorry, I didn't realize you had someone with you, Jane. Please, come in—and sit down."

Robin, one of the few men who was taller and broader in the shoulder than Jane, gave her a crushing hug and kissed her on the cheek. "What brings you up here in the snow?"

Jane's smile illuminated her face. "I've got news. You are

looking at Mrs. Zeke Rumbard, and this is the man responsible. Meet my new husband—Zeke."

"I'll be damned!" Robin exclaimed, and put out his hand to Zeke. "Congratulations! You've got yourself the best of women."

Zeke looked at Jane and nodded calmly. "I am well aware of that, Mr. Gentry."

"Call me Robin—and this is my wife, Fiona. We don't stand much on ceremony here."

Jane had stood back, glowing with pride as she watched Robin and Fiona and Zeke getting to know each other. Then she noticed Fiona. "Well, I'll be jiggered—you're with child again!"

Fiona blushed. "Jane! I haven't even told Robin yet."

Robin said, "But Fiona, you've just had one!"

"Well, I wasn't completely sure, honey."

He protested, "But Maeve isn't even walking yet," as if that was a criterion.

"Don't worry, Robin. She will be before this one is born," Fiona said, and then changed the subject. "Come on, Jane, let's you and me head for the kitchen and have a little girl talk while we fix dinner for these men."

During the next few days Jane and Zeke settled in. They all talked and caught up with the events in one another's lives, played a lot of cards in the evening, and generally enjoyed one another.

"How long will you stay up here, Robin?" Jane asked.

"Fiona and I have agreed that this will be the last year. We had thought about going to Sacramento again this winter—but it's hard to say goodbye when you've enjoyed a place. Rich Bar has been good to us."

"Your dad said you've bought land in the Napa Valley. Are you going to settle there, or is that for speculation?"

"Oh, we're going to live there," said Fiona eagerly. "That's where I want to raise our family. Robin and I decided that last year."

"The Napa Valley is said to have some of the best crop land around here," Zeke said dreamily. "I was on my way there when I was set upon by bandits, and Jane saved me. Isn't it strange how we are taken off our intended track only to find later that the detour leads to the same place? I mean, look at me. I was on my way to the valley. And it seems that I went in a completely different direction—Rich Bar, and now here we are talking about the Napa Valley where you own land and plan to settle. Don't you find that strange?"

"Perhaps it was just that you were not supposed to go to the Napa without Jane," Fiona said with a smile. Jane and Zeke were so well suited to each other. "Do you realize that if you also settle there, we might be neighbors?"

They talked on for quite a while until the obvious became clear, and Robin said, "If you are looking for a small plot, Zeke, why don't you let me sell you fifty acres? I don't think Fiona would object, and then we'd be sure to be near each other."

"That would be wonderful!" Fiona cried, her eyes sparkling green. "It would solve everything! Robin and I have been trying to think of a way we could build our big house so that it would be ready for the whole family when we are ready to live there. But I couldn't do it alone, and Robin can't be spared here, and it is so difficult to find someone to do the work for you that we had just given it up as impossible. But if Jane and Zeke were there, Zeke could supervise the building, and that would leave Robin free to work our claim—and the house would be built!"

"That's a mouthful, girl. Cripple that and walk it by me slow," said Jane.

Zeke said mildly, "She wants her house built. They will sell us land for my tulip garden, and we will, in turn, see to the construction of their home. It so happens," he added, "that before I retired, I was a master carpenter and house builder."

Jane said in delight, "Why, that's amazing! Why didn't you ever tell me that?"

He said modestly, "I wasn't sure you'd be interested in my former life."

"I'm interested in everything about you, sweet man," Jane assured him enthusiastically.

From that evening on, the cards were put away, and the pleasant wintry nights were spent with the four of them planning and designing the two homes. Fiona kept making hers larger, adding another wing and several more bedrooms.

"What are we building? It looks like a barracks," Robin objected.

"Let her alone," Jane ordered. "The way you two are going, you'll be needing a barracks."

Fiona and Robin looked at each other and chuckled.

"As soon as the first good break in the weather comes, we'll go to the valley," Jane said, then looked at Robin. "And you'll follow as soon as you wind matters up here. Is that right?"

"That's right," he said, putting his arms around Fiona. "You two keep her safe."

"Oh, we wouldn't think of doing anything else," said Zeke sincerely.

Fiona shivered with joy. "I am so excited! This is a dream for me. Our own home—a place for our family. I love you all!"

Twenty-six

*A*sa Radburn was not a happy man. Nothing was sitting right with him these days. Jane Pardee had brought him the unpleasant problem with his wife Fairy, and he had done the only thing he could think of at the time to make certain his children were safe. But he hadn't liked it, and he still didn't. He had lied outright to Porter Rockwell about having an assignment from Brigham Young, and sooner or later that lie was going to be made known. He didn't want to lose his standing in the Church. For the first time in his life he had become a man of note when he became one of Brigham's Destroying Angels. That esteem, and the fear in which other men held him, meant the world to him, and now Fairy was jeopardizing all of it.

When he married her, he had thought he had the best of all possible women. She looked like Susannah, and even had a rougher version of some of Susannah's finer qualities. Fairy also, or so Asa had thought, was a good loyal woman, totally unlike Susannah, who would betray anyone and anything to get what she wanted. Now, it seemed, Fairy wasn't better than Susannah. They were two peas in a pod, and he was the fool who had chosen to love them both. Just as Susannah had ruined his reputation in San Francisco and had him driven out of the church

there under Sam Brannan, Fairy, just by living, was threatening
to have him drummed out of Brigham's church in Salt Lake. He
couldn't stand that, yet he hadn't been able to bring himself to
do anything about it. Fairy was the mother of his children, and
no matter how hard he tried to close himself off from her love,
he couldn't bring himself to kill her. He was in a real bind. No
matter how he turned, he was going to lose something or someone very important to him.

When Fairy and the children first arrived in Rich Bar, she
had been so relieved to reach safety that she hadn't noticed that
Asa was not entirely pleased. Her entire attention had been
focused on feeding her children properly for the first time in
months, and to taking care of herself and the baby she carried.
She hadn't noticed that Asa had been cool toward her, or that
he had not been insistent in bed. After all, she was far gone in
this pregnancy, and she accepted his coolness as consideration
for her and the child. Fairy actually accepted everything Asa
did as a kindness. He had found a place for them right away. It
had been a tent, but that was much more than what she had had
on her escape from Salt Lake City. And he had wasted no time
in building a real house for her and the kids. He had even
seemed to enjoy building a separate kitchen for her, so Fairy
went through her days happily making a home for her small
family, completely oblivious to the undercurrents that ran so
strongly in her husband's mind and heart.

The first indication that all might not be well came to Fairy's
attention when Asa decided he would not pan for gold in Rich
Bar itself, but would dig over at Indian Bar. Fairy had questions, but she didn't ask them, for she was too grateful to him to
think of imposing her will or wants on him right now. She
merely smiled, packed his belongings for him, made a good
meal, and kissed him goodbye. "The children and I will be fine,
Asa. There are good people living here. We won't want for anything."

Asa took a lot of time hugging Jarom and talking to him as
though he were a grown man and could understand what the
responsibilities of a man were. He took an equal amount of time
bidding Letha Belle, his pretty little daughter, goodbye. He gave

Fairy a quick kiss on the cheek, ran his hand across her swollen belly. "Now you take good care of that baby," he said, again turning his attention to the children. "Your daddy's going to make you rich little children, you hear? What do you want me to buy you with all that gold, Jarom? A pony?"

Jarom hesitated, but Letha Belle cooed at him. He laughed. "So it's you, Letha Belle, who wants to be a cowboy, eh?"

Fairy laughed too at the words Asa was putting into Letha Belle's garbled language. But she was pleased, and glowed with pride. No one could mistake the pleasure Asa took in his children, and that made Fairy feel good. She knew they were really a family then.

Asa went off to Indian Bar, promising that he would return in a few days. "As soon as I stake my claim and get the digging started, I'll be home," he said with a final wave goodbye.

Fairy set up her house, always with Asa in mind. She sewed and mended other people's castoffs, and soon had her house looking homey and colorful. Many of the things she got for the house came from the woman who had become her best friend in Rich Bar. She had met the woman through Jarom, of all people. Jarom was a husky, outgoing little boy who knew no fear and had never met a stranger. If Fairy turned her back for one minute, Jarom was gone. She'd hate to have to count the number of times she had run out of her house, her hair wild, and her eyes just as wild with fear she had lost him this time. On one of the days she was running through Rich Bar like a chicken with its head off, she had raced into the yard of the Gentrys' house, and there was Jarom just as happy as could be. A beautiful auburn-haired woman was feeding a baby, and Jarom and another little boy about Letha Belle's age were munching on cookies sitting on the ground by the woman's chair.

"Jarom!" she had cried. "Mercy, child, I've been all over this place looking for you. I'm truly sorry, Missis. Jarom just loves to get out an' go visiting. Without tyin' him down, I just can't seem to keep him in the house."

"My name is Fiona—Fiona Gentry. I enjoy having Jarom, and so does Tyrone. Please sit down. You look hot and harried. Let me get you something cool to drink."

Fairy plunked down onto the three-legged stool near the children. "I thank you. I'm Fairy Radburn." She put her hand on her large stomach. "With this little one nearly ready to come, runnin' ain't the thing I do best. I'd sure like a cold glass of water."

Fiona put Maeve into her basket, and went into the house. She came out with a tray and glasses, one pitcher of lemonade and another of water. "I thought you might like a little lemonade after you've quenched your thirst. I just made it this morning, so it is fresh and tart."

Fairy made a quick trip back to her house and brought Letha Belle to the Gentry house, and the two women and four children spent the whole day together. Fiona was glad to have another woman to talk with, and Fairy had never been much for friends, so it was nice to meet someone she'd really like to have for a friend.

"Does your husband have a claim here?" Fiona asked, wondering if he was a prospector, or if he was one of the new people who seemed to be flocking to Rich Bar to set up businesses, saloons, doctors' offices, and general stores.

Fairy shook her head. "I thought he might, but he decided he'd go to Indian Bar. He built us a house here—guess he thought we'd do better where there were more people living near us."

Fiona nodded agreement. "He's probably right. From the look of it, Rich Bar won't take long to become a city. News of this strike spread faster than any other I can think of. It seems like one day no one was here, and then the next people were flooding in."

"I kinda like that," Fairy said. "It's nice to have neighbors, especially people as fine as these. I knew Asa picked us a good place when I heard how them American miners settled their claim jump with the Frenchies. Other places I've heard about, that would have meant a shootin', but those men settled it in real fine fashion."

"I guess so," Fiona said, thinking that it could have been solved even more simply. Men won and lost fortunes on the flip of a coin, why not a gold claim? In this instance the group of Americans and the Frenchmen elected one man from each side to do battle for his whole group. It was to be a fight to the end, with no gloves and no rules. When the Frenchman could no longer get to his feet after the last battering from the American, the American group was declared the winner of the claim. But it was questionable if they'd won in the end. Fiona said, "Isn't it strange how things work out? I'm not so sure they couldn't have solved the question some better way. The Frenchmen ended up with the best claim after all. Robin says that Frenchman's Gulch may be the richest strike in these parts."

Fairy smiled. "Oh, I don't know. I'm kinda glad they fought. I like to see a man want something so much he'll risk himself for it."

Fiona was quiet for a time, thinking that of all the men, only one from each group had risked himself. Then she asked, "Has Asa ever done that for you? Risked everything, I mean."

"He's never fought somebody for me. But Asa has risked everything for me." As she said it Fairy got a strange feeling, and not a comfortable one. For the first time she questioned Asa. She was grateful to him, and he hadn't done anything to her to make her think he was unhappy, but all of a sudden she wasn't so sure of him as she had been. She just couldn't shake this odd feeling of danger that had come over her. She shivered, then laughed. "Goose runnin' over my grave," she said, unable to get her mind off that, now that she had set the fear loose. "I guess a man would always have to keep lookin' at what he fought over and wonderin' if it was really worth it."

She wanted to go home. The afternoon had lost its sunshine for her. She gathered up her children, thanking Fiona for her hospitality. "Maybe you and the little 'uns could come over to my house this week. Mine is a humble home, but I'd be pleasured to have you."

It was then that Fiona first suggested that Fairy was welcome to some of the things she had in abundance. "My brother-in-law runs a freight service, and he is always hauling things up here thinking I'd like them." Fiona laughed. "I do like them, but Brian is always so certain that we do without everything in the gold fields, that he is a little excessive. I have far more furnishings than I need. You are welcome to whatever we aren't using."

Tears came in Fairy's eyes. "Why, thank you, Fiona, you sure are good people. We could use just about anything. Truth to tell, that house of mine is close to barren, and I'd like to surprise Asa with a nice homecoming on his first visit back. I'd sure like that."

Fiona quickly discovered that while Fairy was in great need of many things, she was also a proud woman, and placed a certain value on herself that would not be violated. Fairy was determined that she should give something back to Fiona that was of equal value, if not of the same ilk. After innumerable days in the sun with the children, and cups of coffee, and tea and lemonade, Fiona found out that Fairy could bake bread that tasted as if it had just been delivered from heaven by the hands of an angel. Fiona was certainly a competent baker, but her loaves couldn't hold a candle to Fairy's. On this, they made a basis of exchange. Fiona spent so many afternoons in Fairy's kitchen watching her knead and mix and bake that she had to laugh just to think of it. Fiona tried and tried, but she never did seem to acquire the touch with dough that Fairy had so naturally.

As Fiona was trying to learn the secrets of heavenly bread, Robin was the daily guinea pig. Fiona always handed him two slices of bread and asked him to tell which was best. Without exception he always chose Fairy's bread, and brought a great howl of frustration from his wife. Even when he tried to cheat, he was always wrong.

"I'll never get it right!" Fiona would wail, and pretend to tear at her luxurious hair.

As soon as they were alone, Robin would kiss her and say, "I chose the worse piece of bread, because I thought it would be yours."

"It was!" Fiona cried in despair.

"No! Don't you see, because the one I chose was Fairy's. That means yours was really the best."

"No, it wasn't! Oh, Robin, I'll go through life poisoning you and all our children with terrible food. How can you stand me? I cannot stand myself."

Robin put his arms around her and held her close, never once thinking that she was teasing, and had gotten just what she wanted from him, until she would start to tickle him and laugh. "Take me to bed, wretched man, the only thing I can do well is bear you children! Oh! Oh! Robin! Take me to bed, man, before I've burnt another loaf of bread. Let me not near the cookstove, but lay me on silken sheets and make me into a wanton woman."

By the time he caught onto what she was doing, Robin was in no condition but to comply with her desires, and would take Fiona squealing and roaring with laughter to their bed.

Asa's visits to his home in Rich Bar were infrequent, and of short duration. If it hadn't been for Jarom and Letha Belle, he probably wouldn't have come any oftener than was necessary to give Fairy money with which to run the house. She was very large with child now, and Asa didn't like making love to her in that condition. Though he knew it was ridiculous, it seemed to him that she was in that physical condition just to thwart him. To Asa's mind, she could do nothing right. "Where'd you get all this stuff?" he asked this time, making a large sweep of the room with his large hand. "I didn't give you leave to buy all this."

"It's a surprise for you, Asa. I wanted you to come to a real home. Isn't it cheery?"

"Where'd you get it?"

"Mostly I got it from our neighbor woman. Her brother-in-law carts all sorts o' truck up here for her. She didn't need it all."

"You've been begging!"

"Asa! You know better. In my whole life, no matter how bad things was, I never begged for so much as a scrap of bread," she said indignantly.

"How much did you pay?"

"We traded," she said proudly. "I bake bread for her family and I been learnin' her how. That's what she wanted to trade."

Asa made a derogatory snort of laughter, but said nothing. He walked around the room, touching the chair, the small round table, a footstool, and a low table with a lamp on it. "Give it back."

Fairy didn't know what to do. She had never seen Asa like this. He had his moods, but this was worse than a mood. He had been getting more and more bad-tempered ever since Jane had brought him to her and the children back at Sutter's Fort. It was like something was eating him and making him mean. She stammered, "I can't do that, Asa. These people been good to us. They're my friends. I can't throw these things back at them like they was worth nothing. 'Sides, it wouldn't be true. We need this stuff. We ain't got anything else."

Asa rounded on her. "Are you saying I don't provide for my family? Is that it, Fairy—you've got yourself a nice little place and now things aren't good enough for you? You want more? Maybe some pretty clothes? A handsomer husband?"

"Oh, Asa!" she cried, and ran to him. "That ain't so! You know it! Why are you doin' this? You're my man—I ran all the way crost the mountains t' come to you."

Asa pushed her away and picked up his saddlebags. He dumped the contents out on the seat of his chair, then threw the empty bags over his shoulder. At the door, he looked back. "Get that into a bank. Use some of it to pay fair for this stuff."

"Asa, don't go!" Fairy cried, and ran awkwardly to the door. "Asa! Please, I didn't mean no harm. I'll take it back. Asa—" She began to cry, not understanding. "Oh, and I haven't even packed food for you." She was talking to herself now, for he had ridden away.

Fairy did as Asa had bidden her. That day she made arrangements for the gold to be taken to the Miner's Bank in San Francisco, but she couldn't shake the heavy sadness and fear that bore down on her. She walked slowly, carefully back toward her house. It wouldn't be long now before the baby came. She could tell, for her back was hurting fit to double her over, and every now and then she'd get a stitch and have to stop walking. She stood catching her breath, holding onto a hitching post.

She realized a man had come up to her. "Are you all right, ma'am?" he asked.

Fairy was a pretty woman with dark curly hair and large blue eyes, but she had little idea of her beauty or the effect it had on those who saw her. She looked now at the man, and saw a slender, medium-sized fellow with kindly brown eyes. "I just had a little stitch," she admitted, smiling at him.

The man stared at her, a mixture of amusement and surprise

on his face. He shook his head a little and smiled as though mystified.

"What's the matter?" Fairy asked, uncomfortable under his stare. "Is my petticoat hangin' or what?"

The man laughed pleasantly. "No, it's just that I can hardly believe my eyes. You look so much like my sister, I thought there for a moment that you were Susannah. It—the resemblance is really uncanny." He laughed again, then took her arm. "Here, let me help you to your home. You look a little washed out."

Fairy pulled her arm back. "It's right nice for you to want t' help a stranger, but I don't know you. I'll be just fine after I rest a bit."

"I'm Landry Morrison. Now we are not strangers—or I am no stranger to you. Now. Come along. Let me help you inside before you are fainting away out here on the road."

Fairy did feel light-headed. The argument with Asa and her other worries were more than she could deal with today. She let the man take her arm, and they began to walk in a leisurely way toward her home. "My husband has some family by the name of Morrison."

"It's a common enough name."

"I 'spect it is. Asa's maw married a Mister Morrison after Asa's daddy died."

"Asa?" Landry said, a tight, cold feeling coming into his belly. "Your man's name isn't Asa Radburn?"

Fairy looked at him, her own eyes now filled with questions. "Why yes, it is. Do you know Asa?"

Landry's face was taut, and his eyes no longer held the sweet concerned look that had been what made her decide to trust him and let him guide her home. He said, "You might say I know him. He's my stepbrother."

Fairy smiled. "If that don't fell the trees. What a little world we live in. Imagine that! I'm helped on the street by a stranger who turns out to be kin."

"No! Asa and I are not kin," Landry said with a curt vehemence that brought Fairy up short. "In fact, you would be wise to keep our meeting to yourself. Asa will *not* like your having talked to me. He and I aren't kin, and we aren't friends."

"You don't like him?"

"No, I don't like him. I never did."

Fairy pulled her arm free from Landry's loose grasp and began to walk faster and on her own. "I thank you kindly, Mr. Morrison. I am feelin' better now. I can get home alone."

He doffed his hat. "Good day, Mrs. Radburn." He started to walk off, but stopped. He had liked Asa's wife. He really didn't want to be the cause of trouble for her. If Asa were anything like he had been as a younger man, she had trouble enough without adding the name Landry Morrison to it. He turned and said, "I meant what I said, Mrs. Radburn. You shouldn't tell Asa you know me—or have talked to me."

Fairy hurried home as fast as she could. This was a terrible day, and she felt uncomfortable in every way in her body and mind. She was sitting listlessly in the chair Fiona had given her when Fiona knocked on the door. Taking one look at her friend, Fiona immediately hurried home, got tea, and returned to brew it hot and strong on Fairy's stove. "I know you Mormons don't hold with stimulating drinks, but you need something right now." She put in half a spoonful of sugar. "You look like a ghost."

Fairy was too weak and strained to argue. She gratefully took the hot tea and sipped. As she relaxed, all of her problems overwhelmed her. Jarom and Letha Belle and Tyrone ran and played in the room around the two women, and Maeve in her basket cooed, but neither mother seemed to notice or be disturbed by their noises. Fairy's eyes filled with tears. "I don't know what is happening to me an' Asa."

"You had a quarrel?" Fiona asked shyly, not certain if Fairy would welcome her prying. Fairy was a very private woman.

"I don't even know—I was so pleased to have him home— then it all went wrong. Fiona, I don't know. He said it was all this stuff you an' me traded for, but that ain't it. It's something else—something inside he's been chewin' on for a long time." She stopped talking, her lips pursed shut as though afraid that some awful thing would tumble out if she didn't hold it back.

"You know I'll help you, if I can," said Fiona, for lack of something better. "Has Asa left again?"

Fairy nodded, her lips still locked shut so hard they were white.

Fiona looked around, waiting for something else to be said. When the silence continued she suggested, "Perhaps it's time for the baby—maybe that is making you blue and too sensitive. When Maeve came earlier than I expected, I was just awful the last week. I don't know how poor Robin put up with me. This may be the same kind of thing for you."

Fairy said, as if confessing, "Asa is a Danite."

Fiona looked at her. The term Danite meant nothing to her. She said, puzzled, "Does that have something to do with the baby coming?"

Fairy began to laugh and cry at the same time.

Later, as she and Robin, Landry and Zane were having dinner, Fiona asked, "Have any of you ever heard of Danites?"

"It's a Mormon sect," Landry said curtly.

"Are they midwives?"

Robin looked at her. "Is it her time?"

"I'm not sure." She told him of the strange afternoon she had spent with Fairy. "I suggested that she was probably feeling blue because the baby is coming soon, and then she became so distraught that I didn't know what I should do. So I gave her tea and finally got her to sleep. I sent the Ames girl over to watch after the children. I hope Fairy is all right."

Robin made no comment, but he was very disturbed to find out that Asa Radburn was their neighbor.

Landry said nothing as the others discussed Fairy and what they might do to comfort her. Up until this moment he had no idea that Fiona and Fairy were friends, nor had he known that Asa had become a Danite. He finished his dinner in quick order and excused himself.

"There's a strange man," Zane said after Landry had gone. "One minute he's as friendly as can be, and the next he runs off with that tight look on his face like the devil is right on his heels."

"Did you know that he is Susannah's brother?" Fiona asked.

Zane glanced at Robin. "Cameron's wife?"

"The same. Cameron asked if we'd try to befriend him, and we have, but as you say, he is a strange man, a peculiar combination of a fellow you think you'd like to know and a man you wouldn't trust for anything."

"I think he keeps secrets," Fiona said.

"Secrets?" both Robin and Zane parroted.

"Yes. I think there are all kinds of things he thinks and does that nobody knows anything about. He's like a shadow—but I think maybe—I'm not sure, but maybe I'm beginning to like him."

Both men laughed at her romanticism. Robin got up and produced a bottle of brandy. "A Frenchman over in the Napa Valley made this. Told me to try it and see what I think. This seems like a good time."

Zane was in hearty agreement, and the two men sampled Pierre LeBeau's brandy as Fiona tidied up the kitchen.

Landry left the Gentrys' house and walked directly across the way to the Radburns'. He gave a perfunctory knock at the door, tried it, and, finding it unlocked, walked into the house. Betty Ames looked up alarmed.

"I want to see Mrs. Radburn," Landry said, before the young girl could set up a howl, which she seemed inclined to do. "Go tell her she has a visitor."

Betty scurried up the open stairs to the loft as quickly as she could. Landry could hear low voices, then Fairy appeared on the steep stairs, ungainly and precariously balanced.

Without a trace of welcome in her voice she asked, "What do you want, Mr. Morrison?"

"I want to talk to you—privately. Please, Mrs. Radburn, it is important. Will you ask the girl to go home—it is *very* important that we talk about—about something important to you."

Fairy hesitated, then said, "It's all right, Betty. Mr. Morrison is kin. You can go. I thank you kindly for seeing to the children."

"I'll finish putting Jarom to bed for you," said Betty, giving Landry a scathing look.

Using the rest of the tea Fiona had brought that afternoon, Fairy brewed a pot while they waited for Betty to complete her task.

After the girl had gone home Fairy got right to the point,

showing little sign that she wanted Landry in her house. "What is so important for you to say to me, Mr. Morrison?"

"I'd appreciate it if you'd call me Landry. Although you do not seem to think it, I am your friend, and have your best interests at heart. 'Mr. Morrison' makes me feel as though I'm a tax collector here to plague you."

"Are you goin' to talk to me or not, 'cause if you don't have nothing to say, I'm tuckered and want to go back to bed."

Landry took a deep breath. "This isn't easy for me to start with, Mrs. Radburn, and you are making it more difficult." His brown eyes were soft on her, asking her for consideration.

Fairy was tired of strife. If she could have brought herself to be rude, she would have told him that to the depths of her soul all she wanted was to be left alone to sleep for a long, long time, but she didn't. "All right, Landry, what is it? I'll listen."

"Fiona told me that when she saw you this afternoon, you said Asa is a Danite. Is that true? Is Asa one of them?"

"It's true." Instantly Landry picked up the current of discomfort that ran through her. Lines of strain appeared white around her mouth, and she held herself more tightly.

Landry felt he was a fool to talk to her at all, except that he knew what it was like to have those hounds of hell on your heels and to live in fear of them. But if he told her of his own situation, he would be putting himself in danger from his vindictive stepbrother Asa and his henchmen. "I know a little about the Danites—and I sense you do too."

"Why wouldn't I? I just told you my husband's one."

"I didn't mean that kind of knowing," he said, still unable to bring himself from plunging right into it.

"Look, Mr.—uh, Landry, I don't know what you're tryin' t' say, but truth to tell, I don't feel too good tonight. Can't we talk some other time?" She got up from the table, waiting for him to rise.

"Are the Danites hunting you?" he asked quickly and bluntly.

Fairy's knees buckled, and she sat down heavily on the chair. Her face was sheet white, and both her hands clutched her stomach. "Are you one o' them? Were you sent?"

"No! Dear God, no! Rest easy, dear lady, I'm no Danite—I'm

not even a Mormon any longer. It's just that today I thought you were in trouble, and then tonight when Fiona said what she did, I—I thought I'd better talk to you and offer my help, for what it's worth."

Fairy looked at Landry in some surprise, more inclined to trust him now that it appeared he was a friend of Fiona's. Encouraged, Landry asked, "Does Asa know you're being hunted?"

Fairy nodded, then looked up at him. "That's what I'm so afraid of—maybe he thinks he's made a mistake protecting me. Maybe he—I oughtn't to be talkin' to you like this—it's disloyal to my husband."

"You are merely talking to kin," said Landry with a wry grin. "There is nothing you could tell me about Asa that I don't know. I grew up with him, remember?" Fairy's eyes were still wide with fear and distrust. "And we didn't get along. Are you afraid that when Asa loses his position with the Danites because of you, he may think the price too high and turn on you?"

Her face buried in her hands, Fairy nodded. "I don't know what to do. He ain't given me cause to be so disloyal. He saved us, and brought us here, and built this house for us, and give us all he could, but every day I keep feelin' more and more afeared and . . . and it's him I'm afeared of."

Landry came around to her side of the table and put his arm on her shoulder, then he hunkered down so she was looking into his face. "You are not being disloyal. What you fear is real. I understand that Asa is your husband, and you feel beholden to him, and I'll grant him more backbone than I thought he had for sticking by you this far, but other people's respect is important to Asa. It is possible that he would turn on you."

"What can I do?"

"You can count on me. You can count on the Gentrys to help you, and there is a man by the name of Tyler who would help." Landry paused. "If Asa ever touches you in a threatening way, you scream your head off."

"Oh, my God." Fairy moaned at the horror of the thought of having her friends and neighbors bursting into her house to save her from her own husband. "What will come of my babies?"

"You will take care of your babies," Landry said, trying to

soothe her, his hand moving easily and gently across her back. "Right now you have to think about the new baby. I just wanted to tell you that you are not alone. I thought perhaps knowing there were others who understood would ease your mind a bit."

Fairy struggled to gain control of herself. Nearly exhausted, she sat back and took pleasure in Landry's caressing touch. "It does. I don't know what happened. It's like one day I woke up and everything changed. All the things I counted on were gone, and only ugliness and hardship were left."

Landry said, "I know that feeling well. And I can remember how hard it was wishing that somehow you could live that one day over again and rid yourself of all the horror that followed."

"Are the Danites after you too?"

"I don't really know. They were for a time. I think they gave it up, though, and until now, talking to you, no one knew I was here—the Danites, I mean."

Fairy looked more closely at him then. She realized he had taken quite a risk talking to her. If he had been wrong about her, she could have sent Asa after him. "Why did you risk your own safety just t' talk to me?"

"Because of what I told you. I remember too well what it feels like to have your life torn apart, and then be hunted."

"I'm sorry," Fairy murmured.

"Sorry? For what? You've done nothing to me."

"I'm sorry for what happened to you. You can call me Fairy —if you'd like."

Landry smiled, and it lit up his face, restoring to him the fresh look of open innocence that had marked him years ago. "Does that mean we are truly friends?"

Fairy smiled too, and Landry had a peculiar feeling of *déjà vu,* a sense of being back in their big house in New York with Susannah, talking over some childish prank they had joined in. The warmth and love of those old days seemed to be here as well, and thriving between him and this woman named Fairy.

Landry became a frequent visitor to Fairy's house. Using the techniques of stealth he had learned so well in New York, he always arrived without being seen, and knew whether Asa was at home or not before Fairy ever realized Landry was in the

house. It amused her, it made her uneasy, and at the same time
gave her confidence that Landry would always look out for her
interests when it came to Asa. After she got used to his strange
ways of entrance, it became a game for both of them. With
Landry a little lightness once more entered Fairy's house, and
she could laugh again, and for hours at a time not worry about a
stranger coming up to her and ending her life without so much
as a qualm. Even the pains in her back had diminished, and she
entered the month of July without having the baby come too
soon.

Asa Radburn was being consumed from the inside out. More
and more he was thinking about Porter Rockwell waiting north
of Sacramento for him to return from having performed the
secret mission for Brigham Young. Too much time was passing,
but Asa could not think of a way to return to Rockwell and still
keep Fairy and the children a secret. He couldn't keep going
back and forth. He'd have no reason, and Rockwell wouldn't be
fooled for long. As he did every time he thought his way around
his particular circle of discomfort, he concluded that he would
remain in Rich Bar and dig the lucrative claim he had found on
Indian Bar. The only real difficulty was that every time he returned home to Fairy, shades of Brigham Young and Porter
Rockwell came to haunt him, and he was in a foul temper all
the time. He was a man who had peace of mind nowhere.

Asa returned home from Indian Bar at the beginning of July,
and again left several pouches of gold for Fairy to arrange to
send to the bank in San Francisco with the next freight carrier
who came through Rich Bar. He spent little time with his wife,
instead going nightly to the Bluebird Saloon in the town. He
and Landry came close to meeting there the first night Asa was
home. Landry had agreed to meet Robin and Zane for drinks
that evening after dinner, and he had entered the Bluebird and
was looking around just as Asa, sitting at the bar, turned to look
toward the door. Landry's breath caught, and with a quick motion he slid inside the door and along the wall into the shadows.
Asa gave no indication that he had seen anything, but it was
enough to give Landry a sour stomach. As soon as Asa had

gone back to nursing his drink, Landry slipped out of the bar and went home.

Asa stayed in Rich Bar longer than was his custom. He seemed in no hurry at all to return to the diggings, but it gave Landry enough time to observe his stepbrother and see what Fairy had tried to describe. Asa Radburn was, without doubt, a man with a heavy problem on his mind. Seeing that for himself made Landry as uneasy as Fairy was. There were few things a man could count on in life, but one was certain: A Danite could upon occasion turn off all his human feelings and kill anyone, even a loved one, under the order of his leader.

That was something outside of Landry's ken. He could seek revenge, but it was a hot feeling. The idea of killing on order was something that made his blood run cold. He couldn't imagine being able to do it himself. He felt more protective of Fairy now than he had before. Landry and Fairy had truly become friends, and what happened to her would affect him. He wished Asa would leave again. It was so much easier to think everything would be all right when he wasn't around.

Asa left Rich Bar on July 11, just two days before Fairy gave birth to Lemuel John Radburn. Landry was with her, as he was most days when Asa wasn't in town. He had all but given up digging at his claim to spend most of his time with Fairy and her children. He wasn't too certain why he was doing that, but he had no inclination to stop. Sometimes he thought being with her was just an excuse to keep him from working, something to give him the feeling of being needed and important to someone. Other times he wondered, then pushed the thought away that he might be coveting Asa's wife. That didn't sit well with him. As far as he was concerned, he had married Tolerance Weber five years ago, and she was his wife. He didn't feel kindly toward her, but nonetheless she was his wife and she owed him something. Until the score was settled one way or another he wanted no other entanglements. Yet he kept right on seeing Fairy, and becoming more and more involved with her. There was seldom a day—or a night—that passed without her entering his mind and residing there comfortably a part of himself.

So, on the day her pains began, Landry was there. Fairy had

been listless all morning, and he had been taking care of the children just as if they were his own. He had just fed them and put them into bed for their nap, and was coming back to fix something for Fairy and himself to eat, when Fairy stiffened in her chair.

With a gasp she said, "Landry, I think you best get me to the bed."

"Is it time?" he asked with a certain amount of panic. He had thought often of this moment, but now that it was here, his heart was beating like a drum, and his hands were clammy.

"We better hurry," she said, her face white with effort. "I don't think it's gonna take much time."

"Oh, God!" Landry breathed, and walked around in a complete circle, before he could get himself going in her direction. He got her to her feet, and she groaned. "I'll carry you," he said, then couldn't think how to pick her up without hurting something. "Oh, God!" he said again.

"Hurry, Landry." Fairy panted. "The baby's comin'."

He let go of her as though she had suddenly become terribly hot. She teetered and almost fell. "Oh, shit!" he cried, and grabbed hold of her again, this time swinging her into his arms and heading toward the steep, impossible staircase. He was sweating and trembling almost as much as she when he finally got her into bed. "I'm going for Fiona—you'll be all right while I'm gone?"

"Hurry!" She moaned.

"I'll be right back—don't move," he said, stopping once more at the head of the stairs. Then he lurched down three steps, craned his neck to look at her again. "I'll be right back," he said, and raced down the final steps, tripping at the bottom, righting himself and flying for the door yelling, "Fiona! Fiona! It's time!"

By the time he pounded on Fiona's kitchen door and stuck his head inside, Fiona already had a basket full of clean cloths, and tea and other things she expected to need. She laughed when she saw him all wild-eyed and disheveled. "My goodness, Landry, you'd think this was your baby. Here, take the basket. Don't drop it."

Glad for something useful to do that was easy, Landry

clutched the basket with both hands, and followed after Fiona. "I feel like it's mine," he said. "She'll be all right, won't she?"

"I imagine so. Landry, you really shouldn't be feeling this way, you know. No good can come of it. Fairy is married."

"I know, Fiona, but it isn't what you think. I'm not sure what it is. I care a lot for Fairy. Sometimes I think it's just because she reminds me so much of Susannah—I feel very young and carefree again when I'm with her. It reminds me of home a long time ago."

"It still isn't any good, Landry. It will cause both of you heartache." They came to Fairy's door. She stood for a moment, hand on the doorknob, and looked at him. "Be careful."

He nodded, and followed her inside. While Fiona worked with Fairy in the effort of bringing the child into the world, Landry remained downstairs and out in the yard. He cleaned the house, tended Fiona's children, cut wood for the stove, and fixed everything he could find to mend.

His heart beat faster when finally, three hours later, he heard the lusty cry of the infant. Fiona came downstairs with the child, preparing to wash the baby before giving him back to his mother. Landry watched in fascination as Fiona gently bathed the newborn in warm water, then wrapped him in swaddling. Landry had such a look of longing on his face that Fiona handed the baby to him. "Give me a few minutes to make Fairy presentable, then if it is agreeable with her, why don't you give her her son?"

Landry's eyes shone, and he held the child with great gentleness. Once again Fiona thought what a strange man of secrets he was. But she still liked him. Peculiar and close-mouthed as he was, every now and again that flash of deep capacity for love sprang forth, and she liked that in him. It meant a great deal to her.

As Landry sat gingerly on the side of Fairy's bed, watching her as she examined the baby, he trembled with his emotion. He had missed all this with Tollie and his own son. Somehow it seemed as though God were giving him that special time back to him.

Fairy smiled at him. "His name is Lemuel John Radburn. Do you like it?"

Landry nodded. "I have a son named Elisha. But I didn't help name him. I didn't even know what his name was until a few months ago."

"Oh, Landry, how awful for you. I know how you love children—I've seen you with mine. What happened?"

"That is a long, unpleasant story. Not anything to be told now. This is a time for celebration."

In the days that followed Lem's birth, Landry was extremely solicitous of Fairy, not allowing her to do anything strenuous. She was merely to enjoy herself, and care for Lemuel and play with the other two children. He did everything else there was to be done in the house, and saw that Jarom and Letha Belle were cleaned, fed, and put to bed on time. Fairy had never been so pampered in all her life, and she blossomed under his care.

Fiona looked on with concern. "Robin, hadn't you better say something to Landry? Asa is liable to come back any time, and he is all but living there. There's going to be a lot of trouble over this."

"He's a grown man, Fiona. What can I say to him that you haven't already? And there's Fairy to consider. I think she wants him there."

"But what about Asa?"

"What about him?"

"He's not a nice man, Robin."

"Landry knows what he's doing. If anyone knows Asa Radburn, he does."

Fiona had to agree. She had no cause whatever to say anything bad about Asa Radburn, but it didn't stop her from feeling it. She was afraid for both Fairy and Landry. She wished Landry would go back to digging his claim.

It was nearly a month before she got her wish. Asa finally made an appearance at his home in the middle of August. This had been the longest period of time he had stayed away, and Fiona thought it most peculiar that it had been at the time when he knew his child would be born. It wasn't as if he wasn't a father already, and didn't know the time a baby would come. He had to have realized the child would be born while he was away. Robin might say that he had never done any cruelty to his wife or children, but in Fiona's view, deliberately leaving

Fairy to contend with the birth and the two other children alone was an unforgivable cruelty.

Landry, by some means, knew when Asa was returning. He kissed Fairy goodbye, assuring her he would return as soon as it was safe. "In the meantime, don't you worry. I'll be near enough to know what is happening. If you need me, I'll be here."

The one thing neither Fairy nor Landry had paid much attention to was Jarom's development. His continued growing and his baby speech had not been given special consideration. But soon after Asa returned home, and admired his new son, Jarom came to Fairy asking her about "Landy." At first Asa paid no attention to the garbled word, but Jarom was an insistent little boy, and had finally repeated it enough that Asa asked, "Who is Landy?"

Fairy had fought down her panic by now, and had control over her voice and her shaking hands. "Landy . . . he's kin of yours."

"Mine?" Asa asked in surprise, then his face darkened. "Landy . . . Landry Morrison hasn't been here, has he?"

"Yes, he was looking for you, and he seemed right pleased to meet your family. Jarom took a liking to him."

"God *damn* it! He's here? In Rich Bar?"

"Well, yes, I imagine he is," Fairy said, relieved that his strong reaction would make her nervousness seem natural. "What's wrong with that? He's your stepbrother—isn't he? He said he was."

"He's a damned apostate!" Asa growled. "Don't you ever let him through that door again. By God, you shoot him if he ever shows his face here when I'm gone."

"Asa! You're frightin' me."

"You damned well ought to be frightened! You don't have the brains of a pea. You should have known not to let him in here."

"How? How was I to know? You never spoke his name, and he came here as kinfolk. How could I know?"

"Because I *didn't* mention his name!" Asa shouted. "Where does he live?"

"I don't know," Fairy said, in a small, fearful, truthful voice.

"I'll find him. Rich Bar's not big enough to keep a secret."

Asa stalked out of the house. Fairy cowered, not knowing what to do. She didn't dare warn Landry, and she didn't know but that Asa was going to kill him. She clung to Lemuel, and prayed.

Asa found Landry in the Bluebird Saloon, and this time Landry didn't have the advantage. He had to sit there at the bar and pretend pleased surprise at Asa. It wasn't easy, for Asa was in a rage, and it showed plainly on his face. The only saving grace was that Landry was with Zane Tyler and Robin Gentry, two men not to be taken lightly. Asa wasn't going to do anything with these two in Landry's company, but from now on, Landry was going to have to be careful of his back. That would be more Asa's style.

"Asa!" Landry said in greeting, and extended his hand.

Asa was too angry even to make a show of courtesy. "You went to my home," he snarled.

"Yes, and I met your wife and children. That's a fine little family you have."

"Keep the hell out of there if you value your hide, Landry."

"That's no way to talk to your step-brother, Asa. We haven't seen each other in years. The least you could do is say hello like a civilized fellow."

Asa reached for Landry's shirt, his thick, hairy hand pulling, then pressing into Landry's throat. "You know I'd be rewarded for bringing back proof of your death, don't you?"

Asa moved quickly as he felt the nose of a pistol pressed hard into his side. Robin Gentry, his light-brown eyes looking like fire-hardened metal, said, "Take your hand away from him easy, and sit down. If you've got words, make sure they are just words. Quietly now, Radburn."

Asa sat on the stool next to Landry. "You'll be alone one of these days," he said under his breath.

Landry smiled. "So will you." He let that sink in. "You travel a lot, don't you, Asa? Lonely roads between here and Indian Bar."

Asa gave a short bark of a laugh, but Landry could hear fear in it. Goaded by the knowledge that Asa could still be intimidated even slightly, he said, "Couldn't get the real Susannah, I noticed, so you picked second best."

With a lightning motion Asa brought his fist around, connecting with Landry's jaw. Landry fell off the stool onto the floor, and Asa stalked toward the exit. He stood there, and looked directly at Robin. "Keep him away from my house, or I'll kill him next time."

Zane and Robin helped Landry to his feet. Robin looked grim, and Zane was puzzled. There was more to this than he had thought. Zane had known from the moment Asa walked in that the man hadn't known about Landry and Fairy, or Asa wouldn't have been talking at all. Holding that kind of anger, he would have shot first. So whatever precipitated this went beyond the current situation.

Zane asked Landry point blank what there was between them. "This man is out for blood. I think you'd better let us know what it's all about."

"Asa's my stepbrother—there's always been bad feelings between us."

Zane shook his head. "You sure do like to tempt fate, don't you, Morrison? No sensible man would have gone near his wife."

Landry was looking at the door through which Asa had passed minutes before. "Yeah, maybe I do like to tempt fate where he's concerned."

Asa returned home to find Fairy peering out the window. "What happened?" she asked as soon as he came in. "You didn't kill him?"

"No, God damn it, I didn't kill him, but I sure laid him out. I let him know the feeling of Asa Radburn's fist."

Fairy gasped, then covered by grabbing her husband's hand. "Are you all right?"

He pulled away from her. "I'm fine."

It was a week before Fairy was able to find out that Landry was all right too. Asa stayed as close to Fairy as a mustard plaster, refusing to allow her to visit with Fiona, her only source of information. Asa hadn't forgotten that it was Robin Gentry who had pressed that pistol into his side in the Bluebird. He wasn't likely ever to forget it, just like he had never forgotten the score he had to settle with Cameron Gentry.

Things were not going well in Rich Bar. This was not the place for him and his family. He began to think where they might move to. Always he came back to the problem of the Danites. He couldn't go on like this. He was afraid to move his family for fear of walking right into a community where a Danite was in residence, but he couldn't stand the thought of staying here either. And he was so sick of not being able to make up his mind, he was in a constant state of frustrated anger. He had walloped Jarom the other day before he even realized what he was doing. The kid deserved it, he reasoned, but still Asa didn't like doing things—anything—without being in control.

At the beginning of September he finally told Fairy what was on his mind. He said at the dinner table, "I want to move on."

"Move where? I thought you were satisfied with your claim. I thought this place was safe."

"Not with Landry here—and I don't like those Gentrys either. We're going to move on."

"When?"

"I've got to go back to Sacramento first," he said through a mouthful of food. "I'm sick to death having to hide you all the time, so I'm going to get this settled for once and all." He watched her reaction. It pleased him to see the fear leap into her eyes, but she said nothing. "I'm going to see if I can make a deal with Rockwell. Maybe if I can find Hiram Gates, Rockwell will do what he can about getting you straight with Brigham."

Fairy held herself tense. "And if he can't—or doesn't want to?"

"What do you think?" Asa asked with a grin.

She felt sick. "I think they'll know where I am."

"Uh-huh," Asa said, the grin broadening. "And all that'll stand between you and them is me. Just like now. You haven't forgotten that, have you, Fairy?"

She looked down at her plate. She swallowed. "No, Asa. I haven't forgotten it. You hold my life right in the palm of your hand. I know that. I don't ever forget that."

"Good. That's the way it should be."

She took a breath. "When will you leave?"

"End of the week, I expect. It's already getting damned cold up here. I want to be able to get down there and back before we get snowed in. If Rockwell isn't of a mind to deal with me for your life, the best time for us to go on the sly is winter. Rockwell's a lazy son of a bitch. He won't follow in the snow."

On September 20, 1850, Asa packed his gear and headed down the mountain under leaden skies for Sacramento.

On September 21, Landry Morrison and Fairy were sitting comfortably in front of the fire in Asa Radburn's house, playing with Lemuel and Jarom and Letha Belle. Late that night as they were still by the fire after the children had been put to bed, snowflakes fell softly outside the window.

Twenty-seven

With relief, Asa saw the cheap outline of the tavern he owned, halfway between Sacramento and Dry Diggings, with Porter Rockwell. Er, he meant James B. Brown. He'd never gotten used to Rockwell's alias. So the building was still there, anyway. He shivered, partly with apprehension, but mostly with the penetrating cold of the day. God damn Fairy anyway. If he hadn't hooked up with her, he wouldn't be out in this snow and rain, running back to Rockwell to try to set things straight. He'd have been in the warm all day instead, standing around chewing the fat with his friends.

He left his horse at the livery stable and walked into his tavern, looking around like a man does who has left his business for somebody else to run, and is checking to see that everything is all right. The saloon was pretty full, and should be this late in the afternoon, but funny, he didn't see anybody much whom he knew. A couple of men looked up when he entered, but nobody paid him special attention. He shook the snow off his clothes elaborately, saying, "Brr-rr! That damn wind's like an auger!" He was gratified when some of them laughed and made answering comments.

Rockwell/Brown was standing behind the bar, watchful as

always. Asa didn't see Dog, but now there was a new dog in the old one's place. Rockwell's gaze caught Asa's, and Rockwell's was sour and mean. Asa smiled. "Hey, Jim, how's things going?"

Brown shrugged. "Well enough, no thanks t' you."

Asa stood in front of the bar, aware of the other men standing near and listening. "Give me a whiskey, Jim. I'll get my guts warmed up, and then I'll be back at work."

"High time, Radburn." Brown poured him a short whiskey and turned his back as he put the bottle away.

Asa made no move toward his glass. "Brown." He said it with extra emphasis, to remind Rockwell he knew his real name. "Fill it up," he commanded.

Brown said to the wall, "I did." Then leisurely he turned around to see the glass still untouched. He laughed. "Must be losin' my ex-pertise," he said. He sloshed in some more whiskey, overflowing the glass and making a mess on the bar. Again he seemed not to notice, but looked directly into Asa's eyes. "Had a good time while you were gone, Asa?"

"Chrissake, Jim, you going to leave that slop there?"

"Here's a rag. See if you can still run one."

Asa debated for a second. Then he picked up the rag, carefully wiped his glass and carefully wiped the bar. He said, making a motion like one of the queers Brown hated so much, "There. I think that looks very sweet." He batted his eyes rapidly at his partner. Several men standing near him guffawed.

Brown laughed in spite of himself. "Son of a bitch, Asa, you're always a jump ahead, ain't you?"

Asa shrugged, but drank quickly. He'd been thinking all the time he was gone that Brown ought to be piling up money for him. But that would have to wait. There were other matters more important. He said confidentially to Brown, "Got the job done, Port."

"It's *Brown*, asshole—James B. Brown." Louder, but still quietly, Brown said, "Sure as Old Ned took you long enough. You chase him clear to hell, or only partway?"

Asa forced a grin. "He took the long way around, and I had to follow."

"D'you sent Brigham his head?"

"Hell no, there wasn't any head left, time I got done with him."

Brown said nothing further, merely glanced at Asa again. Asa had the quelling feeling that Jim had been playing with him, and had known the truth all along. Asa said casually, "Business been pretty good while I was gone?"

Brown's face got that snake-mean look that Asa knew well and dreaded from times when they'd done jobs together. He said, "Maybe so. I was gone some myself."

Asa looked around. There were too many men listening to suit him. He said, "C'mon, Jim, bring the bottle and let's sit a while and talk." There was a table in the corner with men just sitting there drinking, and Asa walked hard-ass over to them. "Sorry, gents, we need this table for somebody else." He expected a fight, and would have been glad of one to relieve his pent-up anger and bewilderment and downright fear, but with some muttering the men got up and stood by the bar.

Brown seized the advantage. He hadn't even sat down before he demanded, "Where in the hell was you for a year and a half? I give you up for dead, you stupid eejit."

"I told you, I was chasin' after that fellow."

"You ain't only stupid, you're a sumbitchin' liar." Rockwell watched the tiny lines of tightness leap into Asa's face. "There never was no man you was s'posed to use up. Least, Brigham don't know 'bout him."

"I never said Brigham. I said Kimball."

"Stupid—sumbitchin'—eejit—liar," said Brown contemptuously. "Well, it ain't up t' me to take care of you. Brother Shit, you're out."

"Out of what!?" Asa said, too loudly. He remembered to drop his voice. "I had a confidential mission for Brigham Young himself. Do you think he'd break his own confidence and tell somebody else about it? Don't be silly!"

Brown grew red. "If there's anybody silly here, it ain't me, boy. It's Asa Radburn they're out to burn. You get sent on a mission, and a year later you ain't back from it, and there ain't no word neither. Your wife run off and they never found no trace of her. What d'you know about that?"

Asa felt a stab of fear for himself so genuine that he let it all show. "My wife—ran off? From where? Salt Lake City? What the hell happened?"

"Sure you don't know?" Rockwell asked cynically.

"Look, I've been gone a long time, Jim. I'll tell you all about it later. But listen, man, Fairy's my *wife!*"

"Wifes don't mean a damn thing," said Brown, whose hadn't. His first wife had left him and taken the children, and he had remarried—with her at gunpoint—the wife of another Mormon. She had never seemed content since.

"Tell me what happened," Asa begged, just as if it were all news to him.

Rockwell/Brown seemed convinced that Asa knew nothing, and he told him all that he had heard. "That old codpiece Gunderson was mad as hell, as you'd expect. Brother Brigham sent his Wolf Hunters out, an' they combed the desert, an' shook out a tu-three wagon trains, but there never was a track of her."

Asa looked down, pouring more whiskey. "I expect she got lost in the desert. What happened to the kids? Little Jarom, and —what's 'ername, the baby, Letha Belle? Who's got them now?"

"Never found them neither. They prob'ly got snake bit an' died. I even hunted for 'em some myself, but it's like they all walked into a hole."

Asa shook his head and let Brown see some tears in his eyes before he ground them away with his fists. He said tremulously, "Nothing in this life is assured, Brown. Nothing."

"Well, I can tell you she's better off dead than she would be if Young's Wolf Hunters woulda caught 'er. I heard 'em talkin' about what they was gonna do 'fore they let 'er die." Brown grinned, showing greenish teeth. Then, remembering it was Asa's wife, he added, "Yep—better off dead."

"You told me I was out. What do you mean, out?"

"Why, out o' the Danites, acourse. Christ a'mighty, Asa, you didn't even get Hiram Gates."

Asa said eagerly, "Yeah, Port—er, Jim, I was going to talk with you about him. I have a deal you might be interested in."

"Yeah? Say on."

"Look, Gates ran off with your daughter Emily."

"Tell me somethin' I ain't heard."

"Well, suppose I do get Gates for you? What would that be worth to you?"

Brown shook his head. "Radburn, your brain ain't any bigger'n my thumbnail. I told you when we left Salt Lake, I don't give a personal damn about Gates. I said then I thought Gates was a decent man and it wasn't in my interests t' kill him. I ain't changed my mind." He waited, watching Asa's face fall. "'Sides, Gates is dead anyways."

"Now what the hell! Did you do that? What for? Tell me that!"

"Gates fell over dead less'n a month ago. But Brigham don't forget. Gates left two boys by his first wife, fourteen an' sixteen year old."

"Well, why don't I get them?"

"Indians got 'em last week."

"Real Indians?"

Brown said slyly, "I don't know zackly if they was converted Mormons or not. Radburn, you been out o' the business too long. You ain't careful any more. And them Danites on the lookout for you's gonna find you."

Asa felt his heart leap jaggedly. He blustered, "I've remembered more than you've forgotten . . . Brown. No Danite's going to get Asa Radburn. Besides, what are they after me for?"

"Usin' you up for an apostate. You was gone on your little expedition too long. Brother Brigham don't take kindly to apostates."

"I never apostatized! It was Church business I was gone on! Look, Jim, are you willing to listen to my story?"

"Hell, sure, why not? I got nothin' aginst you 'cept stupidness."

So Asa told him a long and rather involved tale, the details of which he had been working out the entire way here from Rich Bar, about a man who had done him wrong, and in so doing had denigrated the Church, and Asa had taken on wasting him as a personal mission. He concluded with a fascinating account of his confrontation with the enemy and the despatching of him. At the end he was still not totally sure that Brown believed him, but he was able to answer all Brown's questions in a convincing manner.

Then Brown changed the subject, maybe too soon. He said, "You'da done good to been here the first part o' January, boy."

So it was back to that, stupid Asa, the boy.

Asa said savagely, "What for?"

"Me an' Amasa Lyman went t' San Francisco t' collect from Sam Brannan. I remembered how you hate Brannan, and I'da took you along."

Asa knew that Brannan was still alive when he left Rich Bar. He said, feeling malicious, "Did you waste him?"

"Waste the goose that lays the golden eggs? I ain't no numbskull. 'Sides, all me an' Lyman was s'posed t' do was hand him Brigham's letter, and pick up Brigham's money an' deliver it."

They couldn't have been successful, or Asa knew he would have heard it. He said, "How did that go?"

"Wait'n I tell you. We get to his office first thing in the morning, and it's bristlin' with bodyguards. Man, they came out o' the *walls!* Worse'n Brigham any day. So we're standin' outside in the hall, an' they've all got piss-olivers pointed at us, an' we got to give up our guns. So then we go in, and Brannan's laughin'. God damn, Asa, I was so mad I could chew crowbars an' spit nails. Lyman's got the letter. If I'da had it, I'da rammed it up Brannan's—but Lyman ain't like that. He's got t' be a gentleman an' *talk* his way through. Talked the whole friggin' time."

Asa said sympathetically, "He's a gold field preacher, isn't he? Probably thinks he's got a silver tongue." Asa liked that analogy—a silver-tongued preacher in the gold fields.

"Ahh, who gives a rip. Finally Lyman give him this letter, so Brannan reads it an' hands it back. He's sittin' there so Goddamn prosperous an' handsome it hurts your eyes, and laughin' fit to kill."

"What did the letter say? Did you find out?"

"Got it right here." Brown reached inside his greasy vest and took out a stained and smelly letter. "Read it yourself." He watched Asa like a man who cannot read, trying to find out if the other man can.

For Brown's benefit, Asa read parts of it aloud. "Hmm . . . he asks for 'at least ten thousand dollars' in tithe money. Then he goes on to say, 'And when you have settled with the treasury,

I want you to remember, that, Bro. Brigham has long been destitute of a home and suffered heavy losses and incurred great expense in searching out a location and planting the church in this place, and he wants you to send him a present of twenty thousand dollars in gold dust' "—Asa looked up at Brown and whistled.—" 'to help him in his labors. This is but a trifle when gold is so plenty, but it will do me much good at this time.' "

"Doesn't want much, does he?" said Asa. "Then he says, 'I hope that Bro. Brannan will remember that, when he has complied with my request, my council will not be equal with me unless you send twenty thousand dollars more to be divided between Bros. Kimball and Richards, who like myself are straitened; a hint to the wise is sufficient, so when this is accomplished, you will have our united blessing, and our hearts will exclaim 'God bless Bro. Brannan and give him four fold, for all he has given us.' " Asa read on in silence then concluded, " 'But should you withhold when the Lord says give; your hopes and pleasing prospects will be blasted in an hour you think not of—and no arm can save.' " He looked at Brown again. "Brother Brigham sounds like business, eh, Jim?"

"Brannan didn't think so," said Brown sourly. "Want t' hear what he said?"

"What did he say?"

"He said, 'I'll give you the Lord's money when I get a receipt —signed by the Lord.' "

"That took moxie."

"He had it, 'specially with all them bodyguards around."

"So what did you do?"

"Wasn't nothin' we could do. I watched him for a few nights, but he didn't go noplace without them bruisers, and I couldn't find out nothin' useful about him in town 'cept he owes everybody, so I come back. Sure, I coulda used him up, you know I'm a fine shot with a rifle, but Brigham'da nailed my skin to the barn door for killin' him afore he paid."

Asa sat saying nothing for a long time, so that even Brown knew he was thinking. He said finally, "Brown, I know a lot about Sam Brannan. He was First Elder on that boat we came over on, you know."

"So?"

434

"And I talked to him a lot of times while I still lived in San Francisco. I know some of his habits, and where he might bank, and who his old girlfriend was. And," he added on a hunch, "I'm right at home in big cities."

Brown said, probably before he thought, "Well, they mix me all up. I don't hardly know what I'm doin' in a city."

"And I was just thinking, maybe I could do you a favor . . . Jim."

"Like what?" Brown asked suspiciously.

Asa hesitated a moment, a man who is about to reveal one of his life's close-kept secrets. "I never told you this, never told it to anybody before, but Sam Brannan and I wanted the same girl. She loved me the best, but he was way above me in the hierarchy, and she didn't have any choice, she had to go with him. I told him some day I'd get even with him. He's forgotten all about me by now, but that girl hasn't. No way she could."

"So you want to kill Brannan?"

Asa looked pained. "Nothing so crude. All I want to do is ruin the bastard. Take his money for the Church and make him into a virgin queen."

Brown laughed. "You think you could do it, do you?"

"I know it. I know Brannan. I know San Francisco like the end of my dong. But you'd get the credit. I can keep my mouth shut."

"And then what would I owe you?"

"You could talk Brigham into reinstating me. You'd be sitting in the catbird seat, he'd listen to you because you'd done Brannan. You could get me another mission, and I'd do it, and Brigham'd know I was trustworthy like I've been all along."

"You want me to lay my neck on the choppin' block for a stupid bastard like you?"

Asa measured him coldly, long enough that Brown felt uneasy. Asa said, "I don't think you've got anything to lose, Rockwell."

Brown looked right and left quickly, to see if anybody had heard his name. "There ain't nobody after me, Radburn. I'm the one still in good with the higher-ups."

"Want to bet fifty cents on it?"

Brown's small eyes narrowed. "That all you figure my life's worth?"

Asa grinned. "I didn't say that, did I? I was only thinking of friends of ex-governor of Missouri Lilburn Boggs."

"SShhh!!"

"I can go to San Francisco, see, before snow time. The Sacramento's still open, will be for weeks. I can get Brannan, and bring the money back to you. You can take it to Brigham and get me a new mission. We can both look damn good to him."

"Yeah. *If* you come back with it."

"Look, Jim, I know you think I'm stupid, just because I can read and you can't, but if I didn't mean to play this one straight, would I tell you? Now would I?"

"I reckon not."

"Well, is it a deal?"

"You bring the money and Brannan's balls back to me, and we got a deal."

Asa laughed, going hot shivers all over at the idea. Nothing would suit him better than the exact thing he'd said by accident, take Brannan's money and relieve him of his manly parts. Excitedly he shook Brown's hand. They drank a toast to the job, and sat chatting like friends. Then Asa brought up the other thing he had to mention. "Uh, Jim."

"Not thinkin' about backin' down already, old buddy?"

"Hell no, it's the finest idea I've had since I found out about Mother Hand." He waited for Brown's chuckle, then said, "No, it's just—I hate to ask you this, but I'm close to dead broke. And you and I are partners, you remember I put in half on this tavern—so I'd be obliged if you could give me my half what we made this last year."

Brown's good humor vanished. "Boy, you are lyin' to yourself if you think I got any gold dust to give you."

"Why not? What's wrong?"

"Nothin's wrong. But I worked for that all by myself, and I ain't about to give it up to you."

"But it's mine!" Asa couldn't help saying, feeling childish. "We made a bargain—a deal!"

"One little thing you forgot," said Brown. "When I had to be gone, you got all the profit. That was part of the bargain too. So while you were gone, I earned it all. I had all the expenses, I keep the profit."

Asa was stricken. How could he have forgotten that? Had he ever agreed to that? He couldn't remember now, he'd been away so long. What had he done when Rockwell left on that mission to use up Abraham Holt? He couldn't remember. Or at least he couldn't remember being able to keep it all for himself. Rock— Brown was foxing him, he was sure, but he simply could not remember. He said, but it sounded weak, "I don't remember that!"

"Well, you will," Brown assured him, getting up. "That deal still on?"

"Sure," said Asa. "I'll be leaving in a few days, soon's I get rested up." One thing he had to remember was to get that letter from Young to Brannan. He'd better mention that tonight.

"No hurry," Brown said, and went back to work behind the bar. Asa drank up and joined him. After all, he had put up half the partnership.

Asa watched the weather anxiously for the next day or two, while he put in time behind the bar and buttered up Brown without seeming to. He didn't even let himself think of the plan he had in mind, for fear he'd say something accidentally and put his own neck in the noose. He might be doing that anyway, but it was a bold enough plan to throw everybody off guard, and if it worked, he'd be back in good with Brigham again.

On the third evening Asa and Brown divided up profits, Asa got the letter to present to Brannan again, and had a drink and a last laugh about Brannan. Early in the morning, before Brown was out of bed, Asa would set off for San Francisco.

Except he wasn't going to go to San Francisco first. First—he was heading straight for Salt Lake City and Brigham Young himself.

Once on his way into a freezing cold rainy dawn, Asa had to laugh. Who would think that Asa Radburn—target of the Danites, sumbitchin' liar, stupid, boy eejit—had balls enough to brace the President of the Church of Jesus Christ of Latter-Day Saints? Nobody, that's who. But it was worth the chance. If Asa pulled off his scheme, Rockwell would be on the waste list and he'd be tall in the saddle again. If he didn't—but Asa refused to think of that now. He had lost control of his life, and he had to regain it. It was daring that got men places, and this sure as hell was daring.

The first chance he had, he shaved off his whiskers and cut his hair. One of his trademarks had been his whiskers, wide and wiry and bushy. That, and his broad-brimmed hat. He stuffed the hat into his saddlebag and got out one he'd bought a while back. Damn, but his face was cold without that protective covering. But nobody knew him without his whiskers, so it was worth the loss. Now he'd have to remember to shave most every day, like a regular greenhorn. He'd wear a scarf over his ears till he got used to the cold. And he'd better put a little grease on his cheeks too.

Asa looked at himself in the hand mirror he'd brought along. Not bad as a disguise. Did his face really look like that—tough, with those lines bracketing his mouth? And those eyes as hard and wary as a grizzly's? He smiled at his reflection. One hell of a mean smile too. He'd forgotten what his face looked like naked. Men would think twice before they messed with him.

Now what would he say his name was? Rockwell wasn't the only one who could assume a new identity. He'd be . . . Joe Jackson. That sounded hard. Joe Jackson. He practiced saying it. "Name's Joe Jackson. From San Francisco." He talked to himself constantly as he rode, working out his story for Brigham, working out his ploy to get in to see him in the first place.

Everything was going his way, going like clockwork—until the snow began. There had been rain, and sleet, and rain mixed with snow, but this snow that was falling now was going to be a long hard one. He'd been real lucky, actually, to have avoided it before. Usually by this late in October he'd have been snowed in till late spring wherever he was. And now that was just what was happening. Joe Jackson's heart quailed a little bit, wondering if he had gone to all this trouble to make himself over and start a new life, only to die out here all alone in a snowdrift. He forced the horse to move as fast as possible, praying that he'd come on a house or something.

The snow had gotten nearly a foot deep, and he was walking, leading the exhausted animal, before his prayers were answered with the smell of smoke. He stumbled around some more before he found the snug little winter cabin of some gold miners. He opened the door and stuck his head in. "Name's Joe Jackson. From San Francisco. I've got some supplies. Got any extra room?"

It was a long winter, one during which Asa cursed the fate that held him here when he wished to be elsewhere. But it gave him a lot of time to tell Joe Jackson's stories, to practice being Joe Jackson. By springtime, Joe Jackson had taken over Asa Radburn's days and nights, his thoughts and his hopes. Jackson's voice was lower, steadier. Asa even learned how to walk differently, with a longer stride and his hands out ready at his sides, like a gunfighter. Joe Jackson was a man to reckon with.

The weather was still cold as Asa rode into Salt Lake City. Asa's heart beat painfully fast as he went past his old house, and a man peered out the window at him curiously. For a second he thought maybe Fairy had gotten another man, but then Fairy was in Rich Bar. He rode on, sitting up straight like Joe Jackson, not letting himself think of Asa Radburn at all.

It wasn't easy, getting Brigham Young's bodyguards to let him in, but his powers of persuasion were goaded by underlying terror. He had to succeed before the wrong man recognized him. Finally he got into a waiting room—of course escorted and constantly under guard—and sat waiting for Brigham Young to see him. At length he was taken into an inner chamber where the great man himself stood before the fireplace.

Brigham Young wasted no time in amenities this day. Asa stood because President Young stood. "So you're Brother Jackson. Now what's all this nonsense about Sister Fairy Radburn? Who told you about her?"

The heart of Asa Radburn shook within Joe Jackson's boots. He answered in his new voice, "Brother James B. Brown, sir."

Young's eyes lost focus, as though he were going through some long file in his mind. "Never heard the name."

"Also known as Orrin Porter Rockwell, President Young."

Young was all attention. "Rockwell!" he said with something like gladness in his stern voice. "Where did you find him, Brother Jackson?"

"He's running a tavern about halfway between Sacramento and Dry Diggings, sometimes called Placerville."

"Tell me about him. How did you get to know him?"

This was one of Brother Brigham's tests, Asa knew. He could not fail it. In his Joe Jackson voice he described Rockwell, being sure to mention his expertise as a marksman, telling little stories that were typical Rockwell occurrences, until he was certain that Young was satisfied. He took a deep breath. "And he's got a partner, a skunk named Asa Radburn who stole my wife."

"Asa Radburn? He ought to be—" Young stopped himself from saying "dead by now." He said instead, "How did you find out about Sister Radburn?"

"Brother Rockwell and I were drunk together one night, President Young, and he told me about killing her himself."

Young frowned. A Danite who drank and talked was dispensable. "Funny he never sent back word," he said dubiously. "Tell me more about that."

"Oh, but this was after I confided in him that I wished to become a Danite. When he heard I had hoped to have audience with you, he sent the message to you that Fairy Meeks Radburn is dead as a doornail." Asa went on to supply details, including Rockwell's supposed description of Fairy and her children, and a grisly account of her demise. By the time he had finished, his shivers were totally realistic, though manly. "And then," he concluded, "his partner Asa Radburn coveted my wife, and took her away from me, and married her."

Brigham looked angry. "That God damned apostate," he said, and the real Asa stiffened momentarily.

He used the gesture to advantage as he said, "I became a Saint in San Francisco under First Elder Sam Brannan—and now I wish to become a Son of Dan."

Asa could tell by Brigham's expression that he was doing well. He knew enough about everything he was telling that he could be quite convincing. This Joe Jackson was a wonderful person.

"And tell me, Brother Jackson, what was your opinion of Elder Brannan?"

"Well . . ." Asa frowned. "At first I thought he was a truly dedicated and inspired leader in the Church, a man who knew the religion inside and out. At least he inspired me, he gave me the faith I have been waiting for all my life." Asa smiled as though uplifted to think of it. "But as time passed, I entertained some doubts of him. I do not believe he is totally sincere—though he is a firebrand as a speaker, and he somehow gets his people to do the work of the Church."

"How was he about collecting tithes?"

"Determined, or so it seemed to me. However, it is hard to see what good they are put to in the Church there—although I wasn't in a position to judge."

Young spat generously into the fire. "Sit down, Brother Jackson," he invited. "Take that chair over there."

"Oh, but, sir, you're still standing, and—"

Young laughed. "Then I'll sit too. There. Better?"

"Thank you," said Asa.

"Now. What in hell gave you the idea you want to become a Son of Dan? And what do you think they do?"

"Danites," said Joe Jackson, drawing on Asa's recollection of the Danite oath, "enforce the commands that the Lord saith. They assist in the utter destruction of apostates. And I would like to become one because it fits in with my former occupation."

"Which was?"

"A bounty hunter."

Brigham Young laughed. "What kind of bounty, and for what?"

"I lived in the East for a while. There the states offered bounties of one or two dollars for the heads of wolves and panthers. I earned a good living, for I was the best marksman around."

"And now you want to hunt men for the bounty?"

"Yes, sir. If you want to test me, give me the mission to waste Brother Asa Radburn. I'd like to even the score—and be of service to you at the same time."

Young looked at him for a long time, possibly wondering if he had seen or talked to this man before. Joe Jackson sat perfectly straight and alert, not meeting Young's eyes but focusing on a mark on the wall until the Mormon leader had concluded his scrutiny. Asa remembered how tough and hard his fresh-shaven face had looked in the mirror. Then, although Young had not seemed to signal him, a bodyguard opened the door. "Come in, Brother Bennett," he said. "We have a prospective Son of Dan here. Put him through the routine and bring him back tomorrow."

Joe Jackson came through the harsh testing of a Son of Dan. By the time Bennett delivered him back to Young, he had sworn the Danite oath to regard the First President of the Church of Jesus Christ of Latter-Day Saints as the supreme head of the Church on earth, and to obey him as the Supreme God in all written revelations given under the solemnities of a "Thus saith the Lord," and always to uphold the Presidency, right or wrong. He had learned the Danite password, to be spoken at the moment of giving the hand of fellowship. Who be you? Answer: Anama, meaning friend. He managed to perform the rather obvious Danite signal of distress, clapping the right hand to the right thigh, then raising it quickly to the right temple, the thumb extending behind the ear. Bennett assured Young that the new man had done well.

Brigham Young was smiling, which gave his stern countenance a warm and friendly look. He extended his hand to Asa. "Who be you?"

"Anama," answered Joe Jackson.

"So you want a mission, Brother Jackson."

"Yes, sir. Anything you say." Mentally he crossed his fingers.

"And you have a good reason to use up Brother Radburn."

"Damn good, sir."

"Very well. That is your mission. But first you must serve a trial period here in Salt Lake City, getting used to our ways, and we getting used to your ways. Sometimes this trial period is three months, sometimes a year. Much depends on the man and how quickly he learns."

Joe Jackson concealed his dismay. He said, eagerly, "I promise to do my best at all times, President Young."

Young's smile was not totally benign. He said, "Yes, of course."

Joe Jackson's spine crawled. He had forgotten his trial period with Porter Rockwell. Now he would have to undergo it all again, and conceal his true identity all that time. Well, he knew the ropes. He'd make the trial period just as short as they'd let him.

It was midsummer before he was summoned to Brother Brigham's chambers again. By the grace of God, he had committed no errors that anyone caught. His personality had become completely Joe Jackson, a man he liked very well by now.

"So you are ready to undertake your mission, Brother Jackson?" said Young.

"Yes indeed, President Young. More than ready," said Jackson.

"You may leave tomorrow morning. Use your own methods to rid the church of Brother Asa. Brother Bennett will go with you."

"Thank you, President Young. I am honored to be a Son of Dan."

"Well, we'll just see how you do. Good day, Jackson."

"Good day, President Young."

Bennett and Jackson rode out of Salt Lake City, heading for Sacramento, into bad weather. The clouds were low and baggy with rain; the air felt wet. As surely as Asa knew anything, he knew Brother Bennett was suspicious of him. That was natural; it was Bennett's duty to be suspicious, and to watch Asa's actions at all times, and to ask him penetrating questions sometimes and then lapse into pregnant silences which were supposed to make the new man nervous. It was a little difficult to be as alert as an old Danite would be but to make it seem as if he really was a Danite only three months in the making. Even harder was faking sleep, when he needed the sleep desperately. But somehow Joe Jackson managed. As the days passed, and Jackson responded well to emergencies, Bennett came to trust him a little.

One night, after Bennett had been snoring heavily for some minutes, Joe Jackson killed him. With his knife he cut his throat and mutilated his bearded face. Then he dug a hole in the desert sand and buried Bennett. On the man's chest, he put Asa Radburn's hat. Before long, nobody would be able to distinguish Bennett from the man whose name would be on his grave marker. With the same knife, Joe Jackson crudely carved ASA RADBURN on a piece of board from some luckless wagon train, and stuck it into the sand.

The next day Jackson wrote a brief letter to Brigham Young. Couched in cautious Danite terms, he said that he had recognized Asa Radburn a few days out of Salt Lake City, and wasted him and buried him at such and such a place, with a marker. And Bennett, Joe Jackson wrote, had deserted the mission. He signed the letter simply "Jackson." Later on the trail, he met a party heading for Salt Lake and entrusted them with the letter to Brigham Young.

It was over. Asa Radburn was dead. His last act as a Danite had been one of great courage, resourcefulness, bravery, boldness, daring—and it had been eminently successful. Now Joe Jackson—or whatever name he took next—could live wherever he wished with Radburn's wife Fairy. Hell, he could do anything, now that Asa Radburn was dead. In Asa's twisted mind, his plans were perfectly clear. It was time now to carry out his boast to Rockwell about Sam Brannan.

Jackson touched his horse with his boot heels. He was headed for Rich Bar, where he'd pick up his wife and kids and take them somewhere safe. Once they were settled, he'd make for San Francisco and Sam Brannan just as fast as hoofs could carry him.

Twenty-eight

The year 1851 was going to prove as exciting and chaotic as any year Sam Brannan had ever experienced in San Francisco. As he had predicted after the Hounds had been gotten rid of, the city was going to be afflicted with other groups just as brutal and criminal as the Hounds.

The presence of the Sydney Ducks, however, was not the lone cause for crime. Perhaps far worse than any single gang was the ineffectiveness of the law enforcement agencies in the city. San Francisco had grown too fast. The problems its neophyte government had to handle were monumental, and included wharfs and roads and water and construction and taxes. Law enforcement wasn't high on the list of priorities. San Francisco was ripe for trouble.

Trouble came on a cool evening in February. On the nineteenth, at eight P.M., the dry goods store of C.J. Jansen and Company on Montgomery Street was still open.

Several men walked slowly along the street, keeping in groups of two and three, their eyes on Jansen's store. One of the men had discovered that Jansen kept a stock of gold sovereigns. The eight men had also concluded from rumors that Jansen's store might have as much as ten to fifteen thousand dollars in cash.

The shop was a long narrow room. It was dim inside, lit by a single candle near the back. Several of the men went up to the store and looked in the window. One of the Sydney Ducks, Old Jack, slipped into the store hoping to pull a sneak-thief maneuver that would allow him to lift the money unseen and get out without Jansen ever knowing. He was too slow, and a compatriot, English Jim Stuart, took matters into his own hands. English Jim had been in and out of trouble many times, and would avoid killing if possible simply because it aroused the citizenry and caused him trouble he didn't want. His weapon was the slungshot. English Jim used a piece of lead about the size of an egg affixed to a stick.

Jansen was relaxing in the rear of his store awaiting the time he would close up. Jansen's friend Theodore Payne had a shop right across the street, and the two men had plans to go out to dinner after they closed for the night. Jansen hoped that Payne's store was busier than his. He got up, thinking it was hardly worth the bother staying open, when he noticed a man in the shadows. Squinting to see better in the murky room, Jansen saw a small man with a dark hat pulled low over his forehead.

Jansen, a good-natured man, asked courteously, "Can I help you, sir?"

"Blankets," Old Jack said. "I want some blankets."

"If you'll follow me, please, the blankets are at the rear of the store," Jansen said, leading the way. He reached for the topmost of a pile of dark blankets.

"No. Not those. I want white," said Old Jack.

Jansen frowned. This grubby man wouldn't be buying anything white. Then he noticed another man in the store. The man walked back to them. He wanted blankets too, he said. As soon as he was positioned near Jansen, English Jim yelled, "Now!"

Jansen felt a terrible pain as Jim brought the lead shot down on his head. He fell to the floor, slipping in and out of consciousness. He could hear the men ransacking his store, but he didn't move. He knew that if he could get to his feet they would kill him. He lay still until he was sure the men had left. He tried to rise, but couldn't. He crawled to his back door and once in the cold air he yelled for help.

His calls attracted people almost immediately. From across

the street his friend Ted Payne came, and took Jansen home to bed, then brought the doctor to see him. Jansen lapsed into a coma.

Returning to Jansen's store, Payne discovered that a shot bag of cash had been stolen, and Jansen's watch. He also found the weapon English Jim had used on Jansen. There was little more that Theodore Payne could do for his friend that night, but he went home worried. The terrible thing was that although San Francisco had a marshal and seventy-five policemen, no one was certain to what degree these supposed enforcers of law and order were in the pockets of the criminals.

News of the robbery and beating spread quickly. By next morning it was one of the main topics of conversation in the city. Newspaper editorials and men in the street spoke scathingly of the police. After Jansen regained consciousness he was questioned. He described the two men, one tall with a mustache and wearing a round topped hat with a wide brim; the other small and wearing a cap pulled low.

The first men the police interviewed were Jansen's clerks. Both men were able to prove their innocence immediately. By the end of that day the police had done nothing. No one was in custody. The *Alta California* let the people know about the inaction. Some letters to the newspapers were suggesting the real solution was to use the Lynch Law.

Sam Brannan was incensed when he heard about the attack on Jansen and the delay in arresting the culprits. If other San Franciscans had little faith in the police and the legal system of the city, Sam had none. He was far more in favor of the quick, decisive kind of justice that was practiced in the gold camps than the delaying tactics favored in the city. He wanted the people of San Francisco to realize that if they did not wish to continue to be victimized, they would have to do something forceful, and by themselves.

The next day the police arrested William Windred. That same day English Jim was arrested in Sacramento. He denied everything, saying his name was Tom Berdue. He was a man of substance. The police found on him a gold watch, a certificate of deposit on a bank for $1,700, and a considerable amount of gold dust.

The two men were taken to Jansen's house. Jansen's face was barely recognizable. His eyes were swollen, his face misshapen and black. He was dazed and hardly sensible, but he said that the tall man was his attacker and the short one might be the other. With the arrests, everyone settled down and assumed life would go on as usual.

The following day was Washington's birthday. There would be parades and street shows, and the Washington Guards in uniform and full armament would march through the streets. San Francisco was a city that liked to celebrate, and a good portion of the population was out for the occasion.

In City Hall, however, there was a businesslike atmosphere that had nothing to do with the celebration. About noon the police took their prisoners back over to Jansen's house, and asked Jansen under oath to identify them again as his attackers. Jansen said he believed these were the two men, but he refused to swear to it. The man could still barely keep his eyes open or his head up.

While the authorities were attending to business, word spread, and a crowd gathered around City Hall. When the prisoners were brought back for examination at about two o'clock, the crowd was already calling, "Lynch 'em!" "Hang them!" With amazing speed and force, the mob surged forward as the police ushered the two men back into City Hall. Several men reached out, grabbing for the taller prisoner. The police split up, some taking the prisoners inside the courtroom, the others beating back the more forward of the mob.

Mayor John Geary asked for and got a volunteer force to form a guard line all around City Hall to protect the building and the court. All the volunteers were armed, but then so were the people who were now milling about the building. No one was comfortable with the situation, and every man in the court was afraid there would be a bloody confrontation between the cordon and the citizenry before the hour was out. The recorder adjourned the court until Monday morning. He hadn't completed his statement before someone cried, "Now is the time!"

The courtroom was flooded with flailing, angry men. Pushed by the force of the mob behind them, the first men into the court leapt to the benches and crashed through the railings. The police were being quickly overpowered.

Into the fracas marched the Washington Guard, still in uniform from the Washington Birthday parade earlier, their bayonets fixed. The room was packed with fighting bodies. In confusion and disorder, some of the Guard mounted the desks and benches, and with their bayonets began to jab at the men in front of them. Slowly the crowd gave way and they managed to clear a space. Voices from everywhere were shouting, "Hang 'em! Bring 'em out!" Finally the guard managed to clear the room, and the police hurried the prisoners out and into the station house.

Sam Brannan was pleased when he read the flyer that was being distributed in the crowd as they were jeering the Washington Guard. The flyer was addressed to the CITIZENS OF SAN FRANCISCO. It declared that the legal processes had failed and the city was in a state of anarchy. At the end was an invitation: "All those who would rid our city of its robbers and murderers, will assemble on Sunday at 2 o'clock, on the Plaza." The only unfortunate aspect about the flyer was that it was anonymous.

From City Hall, men of prominence came out to talk to the crowd and try to get them to disperse.

Slowly the crowd dwindled, and most of the men wandered off to the restaurants and taverns to eat and drink. Some went to their homes, others just continued to mill about in small groups and talk, but the heat of the afternoon was gone.

Something was in the air, however. As darkness was falling, the crowd reassembled in front of the City Hall. The crowd was bigger and surlier than it had been that afternoon, and many of its members had been well fortified in the saloons. These men meant business and were going about it in far more organized fashion. They elected leaders.

The city officials were once more back in City Hall. Many of them were on the balcony of the building. The mayor, several judges, and a number of residents were called upon to help. D. M. Howard, a wealthy, respected man talked, urging moderation. Several others followed, and gave the same message. Above all, the idea was to keep the men in the street listening and thinking, and not acting on what they had come here to suggest—instant and immediate justice.

The crowd didn't disperse, and the city officials had said over and over the only message they had to deliver. Something had to be done, or the mob was going to act. To allow Sam Brannan to speak was taking a chance. Sam was thoroughly out of patience with a legal process that didn't protect its citizenry. No one knew for sure what he would say; he might move this crowd to riot here and now. But the city officials moved aside anyway, and Sam stepped to the front of the balcony outside the second-floor rooms of City Hall.

The people began to shout and cheer. He was their man. The noisy racketing in the plaza was deafening. Sam didn't even try to gain control. Not only was he glad they were finally cheering about something, but he liked it. It was good for a man to hear this kind of adulation every now and again. It also gave him time. He knew what he wanted—he wanted the law in the hands of the people—but timing was all. He raised his hands, and the crowd quieted.

"I am not going to tell you what you should or should not do to protect your homes, your families, your city. But I will make a suggestion. I move that we appoint a committee of twelve good men to cooperate with the city officials. I further move that we guard these prisoners . . ." He paused and grinned down at the crowd, knowing that many of them would realize what he meant. "Protect them overnight."

There was some laughter, but mostly the sound that rose to the balcony was one of approval. Twelve men were appointed, among them Sam Brannan, D. M. Howard, and Theodore Payne, Jansen's friend and rescuer.

That night, as soon as the men had been appointed, the committee met. After they had wasted some time in trying to be official and give proper speeches, and make motions, someone said bluntly, "Why don't we appoint a jury ourselves and try the prisoners?"

"You can't bypass the courts," said another. "That really would bring us to anarchy. We have a legal system, we must use it."

Sam Brannan was now ready to test his idea. He stood up and

said, "I am very surprised to hear people talk of a legal system. I am tired of such talk. These men are murderers as well as thieves. I know it, and I will die or see them hanged by the neck. I am opposed to any farce in this business."

"The use of the courts is not a farce!" a man said hotly. "We have lawyers, judges, recorders, and mayors just to avoid what you would thrust us into!"

"No!" Sam said with passion. "No, you forget something very important." He looked at the eleven other men in the room. "*We* are the mayor and the recorder, the hangman and the laws. The law and the courts have never hanged a man in California. Yet every morning we are reading fresh accounts of murders and robberies. I want no technicalities. Such things are devised to shield the guilty."

There. He had put it on the table. A first test. He sat down and waited to see what would happen. Were they ready for this kind of action yet?

The men of that committee were not. They voted his proposal down. But they passed a motion to form a patrol to guard the prisoners. They wanted no escapes.

D. M. Howard moved the meeting adjourn. Sam got to his feet again. "I move that the committee recommend to the people that the prisoners be hanged at ten o'clock on Monday morning."

No objection was registered, and a vote was taken. Sam received three other votes in agreement with his own. Eight refused the motion, but he had a full third of the committee agreeing with him. It wasn't full victory, but he could go home that night knowing that a positive step had been taken.

The committee made its report, and did not satisfy the crowd. All night long the streets were noisy and crowded, with patrols moving about, groups of men talking and spreading rumors that the Sydney Ducks were out committing crimes, while others said that there were plans to burn the city down in retaliation for the arrest of English Jim. It was a tense and terrible night.

By nine the next morning, Sunday, February 23, a crowd had already gathered in Portsmouth Square by the courthouse. The two major topics of conversation were about how the Washington Guards just happened to appear armed and prepared at the right time to make an appearance in the courthouse; and argument about who had been the author of the anonymous handbill. A few people thought it was Sam Brannan.

On Sunday morning, Sam took special care with his toilet and dressing. He was in a good humor, which meant he was determined.

Ann Eliza came into his room and sat down on the settee near his bed. "This situation is quite dangerous, isn't it, Sam?"

He turned to give her a faint smile. "It couldn't be much worse. I don't want you or the children to venture out at all today."

"And you are going to place yourself right at the heart of the controversy. Why must you do it? Why must you always be in the midst of turmoil? No one will ever thank you for your efforts."

Sam, determined to maintain his good humor and his purpose, took her chin lightly in his fingers, and kissed the end of her nose. "It is nothing for you to worry about, my dear. It is a complicated matter at best. Trust that I know what I am doing."

Ann Eliza pulled away from him. She hated being patronized. "I *do* know what is being said, Sam. I understand perfectly well what you are doing, and it is very dangerous. You are placing yourself between the lawless and those who call themselves patrons of law and order. You will stand between two powerful sides. The Sydney people hate you, and now many of the prominent residents of the city will be opposed to you as well."

She still had the capacity to surprise him, occasionally, with her perceptions. He said, "But if I win my point—"

"What will you have won?"

"We'll rid the city of the Sydney Ducks, and make these streets fit for decent folk again. We can't play act with these men. They are brutal ruffians, miscreants, convicted felons. We need strong action. So far none of our city officials seem inclined to take it."

"And if you do not win your point? What then, Sam?"

"Then they are fools. But I am a patient man, and I'll wait, because if something forceful is not done immediately, this wave of crime will grow worse. If they do not listen now, I will speak out again at the next opportunity. This situation will go on, until the people approach me, begging for assistance."

"Oh, Sam," she said softly, "can't you ever think of your safety, or ours?"

He came to sit beside her, his arm around her shoulders. "But I am, my dear. I know you do not understand, but I do think of my family." He gave her a little squeeze. "I must go now. The meeting is going to start soon."

She nodded, received his goodbye kiss and watched him walk to the door. Just as he was about to pass through it she said, "Sam, be careful—please."

In the square nearly a quarter of the population of the city, six thousand strong, stood in an orderly manner, waiting to hear what had happened. As Sam's committee listened to a variety of suggestions, such as the one made by Mayor Geary that the committee appoint twelve men to sit with the examining judge the next day, and that their verdict be final, the people in the streets were being bombarded with long speeches. The idea was to wear the people down and allow boredom to set in, and soon the crowd would disperse, ending a volatile situation.

The committee liked Geary's suggestion, for while it was unusual in court procedure, having been suggested by the mayor of the city, it had some legality by virtue of his office. The motion was approved.

Outside, a young man, twenty-seven, good-looking, slender and intelligent, stood among the crowd. He realized that the tactics the city officials were using to calm the crowd were not working. Though the people were orderly, there was an undercurrent that he sensed, and it was growing. Soon it would burst forth, and then there would be trouble. William Tell Coleman did not like trouble, particularly the ugly kind of trouble that could come out of a disorganized, angry mob on the move. He began to push his way through the dense throng of people, making his way to the City Hall. Once inside he had no doubt that he would be allowed to speak. After all, he was a merchant of some note in the city.

As Coleman edged his way toward the building, Sheriff Jack Hays came out on the balcony, and the crowd began to cheer. Hays was enormously popular with the people, and for the moment anyway, the mood in the streets shifted. That gave Coleman some time. He was granted leave to speak. Many of the men, Sam Brannan included, wondered what this man would have to say. Coleman wasn't a practiced speaker, and the great numbers were intimidating, but he spoke clearly, in a voice that could be heard across the Square.

"With just cause we have gathered here in agitation. We all want to see to the safety of our city, and we have that right. I'd like to put forth a proposal to you that I think may solve our dilemma. I would suggest that we who are gathered here today in peaceful meeting form ourselves into a court. We can do so right here in this building. Each of the prisoners can be appointed counsel. The testimony may be taken and the trial proceed fairly. If these men, or one of them, be found innocent, then he should be allowed to pass out of this court this very afternoon and be free, without recrimination from any of us. Should one or both of the men be found guilty, then they should be despatched before the sun sets this evening." He paused, nodded at the crowd, then said, "I thank you for listening."

Shouts of approval resounded in the Square. Finally someone had stepped forward and said something definitive, placing himself before them as a leader. Shouts went up for a new committee to write up Coleman's suggestion into a proper motion. Men moved to do so immediately.

Sam Brannan let nothing show on his face, but inside he seethed. He had missed his chance. With the lightning speed that marked him when he elected to move, Sam had a handbill printed and distributed while the committee worked: TO THE PEOPLE OF SAN FRANCISCO. Four names were on the sheet, Sam's own and the three others who had voted with him when he had proposed citizen action in the meeting the night before. It was a minority report. "The undersigned, the minority of the committee appointed by you, report as follows: That the prisoners, Stuart and Windred, are both deserving of immediate punishment, as there is no question of their guiltiness of crime. The safety of life and property, as well as the name and credit of the city, demand prompt action on the part of the people."

By now there had been so many committees appointed for various reasons that the men in the Square assumed that this was the word of the most recent one, and rushed to the station house to get the prisoners. They were stopped at the door. It was pointed out that this was a minority report and not something to be acted upon. The throng rushed back to City Hall, now worried that they would miss a word of the committee in session.

The current committee reported, recommending that thirteen men be appointed by the citizenry as judge and jury. The trial was set for two o'clock that same afternoon.

Amid the confusion the trial moved forward. Most arguments that revolved around legal points were shouted down with cries of "Go on with the evidence! Never mind the speeches!" Around seven P.M. the jury went to Jansen's house, and for the third time, the injured man told authorities what he remembered of his attackers.

It wasn't until midnight that the jury had finally weighed all the evidence and had come back to the courtroom with a decision. The court was hushed with expectation. The surprise of the day came when it was announced that the jury was not unanimous. Three men had not agreed on the guilt of the prisoners.

The courtroom burst into a cacophony of shouting. "Hang them anyway!"

"Majority rules!"

"Order! Order!"

"Hang the sonsabitches!"

Despite the heated emotions that were running rampant, the crowd finally went home. For almost three days few people in the city had had any rest or sleep.

On Monday Windred and Berdue were brought to trial before Justice Shepheard. Shepheard held them over for trial, and placed each man on $10,000 bail. Neither man wanted to try to make the bail. They had spent all Sunday hiding under beds, and had no wish to be loose on the city streets. That was sure death.

Shaken by the vehemence of the population, the city council instituted a chain gang that same day.

But the city didn't lose its anger. A man was found with stolen goods, and as quickly as he was caught, two men came forward with a rope. Someone in the crowd that had gathered begged for reason, and not a lynch mob. Strangely, the crowd agreed, then set upon the robber and beat his face to unrecognizable pulp. Then freight-truckers came, and with their whips lashed the man as he screamed, "Murder! Murder!" When he was a bloody mess, he was tossed in the Bay, whence the police fished him out and took him into custody. The mood of the people hadn't noticeably improved.

Sam Brannan didn't like this any better than he liked the lackadaisical, do-nothing courts. What he wanted was a vigilance committee, which would have a semblance of firmness and organization.

During the next weeks, San Francisco went about its business with the tensions still boiling beneath the surface of everyday life. In March the Pioneer Race Track at the Mission Dolores opened the racing season. There was a huge free-for-all fight among the spectators. No one was injured, but the demonstration showed the temper of the people. Roxana Coxin in the heat of the excitement stripped herself naked and danced in the streets. She was sentenced to ten days' hard labor.

On March 26, Captain E. M. Jarvis was walking in the evening with his wife near the Mission. Out of the darkness came a man who plunged a long knife into Jarvis's back. Jarvis died. A man named Slater, a Sydney Duck, was charged with the murder.

The election of city officials was scheduled for April 28. The Whigs were in good position to sweep the incumbent Democrats out. They came forward with the slogan "Throw the rascals out!" There was hardly a person in the city who disagreed with that idea, but it wasn't always easy to identify the rascals.

The streets had another attraction, and another noise these days. A steam paddy, a twenty horsepower excavator, was tearing down the sand hills south of Market Street, and filling in Yerba Buena Cove. The steam paddy, which was changing the face of the city, was a curiosity that drew crowds daily.

All in all, the city was a hive of activity, sitting atop a problem that was not going away: crime. No one knew what to do. Every man in San Francisco realized that something was going to happen—something bad. The city was poised, waiting for it.

April brought with it dry weather and chaotic fear. At three o'clock in the morning of April 13, the fire alarms rang throughout the city. No one in this city of tents and wooden buildings took a fire bell lightly, especially one that clanged in the middle of the night.

Cameron Gentry grabbed Simon, wresting him from a sound sleep, and with Susannah ran outside prepared to hie for safety. People tumbled out of houses all up and down the street, blinking in the night, and searching for the ominous smell of smoke and the column of flame. It was a false alarm.

On April 14 at eleven o'clock at night, the fire alarms sounded again. Again Cameron and Susannah took Simon from his bed and hurried outside. At his house Sam Brannan did the same with his family, marshalling his young children cranky and sleepy into the street. There was no fire. But the lack of flames did not help anyone to rest easier. The Sydney Ducks were known incendiaries, and San Francisco was terrifyingly vulnerable to fire. False alarms brought everyone to the high peak of fear.

On April 23, eight prisoners escaped from the jail, among them Windred, one of the men accused of attacking Jansen. The consensus was that the police had known about the break, and had perhaps helped the criminals.

On April 24, the *Alta* editorialized: "Truly the branches of government, judicial, aldermanic and police, are all of a piece—just good for nothing."

Another false fire alarm sounded on the April 25. This one most people regarded as less threatening than the preceding ones. The Democrats had been holding a meeting, and since it was so close to the elections, it was thought that likely the alarm had been sounded to break that meeting up.

By the 28th, the city had a new and Whig government. R. H. Waller was the recorder; Robert Crozier was the new marshal; Frank Pixley, who had defended English Jim Stuart in the past, was city attorney. The Whigs were due to take over the offices and exercise the power of the city government on May 4, 1851.

On May 3, there were a lot of happy men in San Francisco, and a few who were experiencing butterflies in the stomach at the prospect of making good on campaign promises. Questions of whom to appoint to the various positions in city government were paramount that night for the Whigs. But for the rest of the city, it was a night similar to any other. The weather was nice, and as usual a northwesterly breeze whipped through the tunnel formed between Telegraph Hill and Russian Hill. For a change, it was a quiet night. No new tragedy had been reported in the newspapers, and no patrols or milling mob of concerned inhabitants roamed the streets.

About eleven o'clock most of the houses were dark. On the west side of Portsmouth Square in a paint shop, smoke curled upward, to be caught in the swift breeze coming in through the gap in the two hills. With a suddenness that caused the walls to shake before the building caught fire, a single column of flame leaped up. The fire alarm began to peal almost immediately. Faces appeared at the windows of the nearby Union Hotel on Clay Street. The wind whipping down through the hills made the blaze dance and leap, spreading out from the bottom of the building like a huge, lethal orange flower, its petals of flame touching, then touching again the wooden planking of the road.

In minutes people were spilling out of the Union, and on the heels of their departure, the hotel burst into flame. From second to second terrified people saw one frame house after another smoke, then crumple in engulfing flame. Almost as if it had a mind of its own, the fire ran down the blocks of the city like a crazed horse. It swept along Kearney Street, down Washington, eating all in its path. Montgomery Street became an oven in which nothing would survive.

Susannah knew without looking that her shop was gone. Now she and Cameron and Simon would be lucky to outrace the fire as it lunged up the street toward their house. Grabbing anything useful she could lay hands on, she helped Cameron put their belongings in the carriage. Hurrying out of the house, she dropped the last load of clothing and blankets to the ground, for the fire had taken another giant leap and was consuming the house two doors from theirs.

Cameron was holding the reins tight as the horse whinnied, stamping its feet and walling its eyes. "Hurry!" he shouted. "I can't manage this horse!"

Susannah jumped into the carriage beside Cameron and a

screaming, terrified Simon. Lashing the animal furiously, Cameron jolted and bounced them with all the speed the horse could give for high ground and safety.

Volunteer firemen pulled the engines to the fire, which meant they could stop almost anywhere. With the hoses in the cisterns, the volunteers began to pump water manually on the unbearably hot flames. But it was useless. The cisterns had dried up when no rain fell.

Brick houses reached such heat that the brick disintegrated. Others who had built houses of cast iron, thinking them to be fireproof, found themselves inside ovens that went red hot, then white hot. Hinges melted on doors, effectively welding the occupants inside. The walls glowed white, hot beyond touching.

Desperate, the firefighters brought out gunpowder in an effort to blow the fire out. With one tremendous blast, competing with the raging scream of the fire, the flames leaped skyward, then lunged along the streets. California Street was engulfed in flame, then Sansome. The business district sizzled and burst, throwing sparks and huge chunks of fiery lumber into the air.

Running ahead of the blaze, those who had escaped the fire searched frantically for safety. The streets of San Francisco, made of wood planking over the rutted bumpy mud flats, formed an air tunnel through which the wind howled and the fire followed. The streets blazed, carrying the path of the fire up one route and across yet another to meet the flaming fury on the crossroads.

Every newspaper in the city was burned out except the *Alta California*. At five o'clock in the morning, with the fire still raging and consuming fresh houses in the city, the *Alta*'s editor sat at his desk and wrote, "San Francisco is again in ashes. The smoke and flames are ascending from several squares of our city, as if the God of Destruction had seated himself in our midst."

The fire kept up its terrible unrelenting path until finally it turned toward the less densely built-up section around Battery Street, Bush Street, and Hillside, and to the waterfront. Cornered there, the fire burned itself out by seven o'clock that Sunday morning of May 4. Eighteen blocks of the city had been burnt out. The streets were gone. What little planking was left was charred and brittle. Five other blocks were destroyed for the most part, only a random few places left untouched. The main business district was gone, and most of Sydneytown had burned. Almost three-quarters of the city of San Francisco had vanished in one night, to be replaced by a pile of stinking, smouldering ash.

For several hours—a long time by San Francisco standards—the sentiment in the streets was that they should move to another location, because San Francisco was gone. Others noted that one year ago on that date, San Francisco had burned. Could that be coincidence? Soon it was discovered that while people ran for their lives, others had been looting homes and businesses, systematically taking advantage of this tragedy.

But soon most San Franciscans recovered from their depression, and throughout the city could be heard the sounds of a populace cleaning up and rebuilding. Among these was William Tell Coleman, who had lost four-fifths of his stock, and his building. Coleman already had new lumber in the street on Sunday afternoon, and had made arrangements for a load of goods to be brought from a ship in harbor. He would be open for business on Monday.

Cameron took Susannah to see her shop, or what had been her shop. It was not even a shell, just a pile of charred lumber in the ashes. She closed her eyes and turned away from the sight.

"We can rebuild it," Cameron said, pressing her head against his shoulder.

"I don't know. This is the third time my shop has burned down. Let me think about it for a few days. I may not be as resilient as Mr. Coleman. I don't even know if I want the shop." She looked up at him, her eyes bleak, yet filled with love. "Perhaps it is time for me to stay at home. Simon might enjoy some company in the family."

Cameron's eyes kindled. "It isn't fair to say things like that to me when we are standing on a public street." He smiled at her.

"Where else can we stand?" Susannah asked, smiling back at him. "We have nowhere to hide now—I have no shop, you have no office, we have no home."

He put his arm around her, helping her back into the carriage. "Maybe that's not true. Come on, let's go see."

But Susannah had been right. The house that Cameron had built for her, where they had made love first in the washhouse, and later in every room, was gone. Susannah, holding Simon, stood in front of the cold ashes of her home and sobbed. "I feel we've lost a part of ourselves. It isn't fair, Cameron! Why doesn't somebody do something! Everybody knows this was arson. What good will it do us to rebuild? Someone will burn us out again."

"I don't think either of us would want to live here now," Cameron said sadly. "The city has changed too much these few years. I haven't felt easy living on Montgomery Street for a long time now. We have land on Hillside where we can build a new house. We'll be better off there."

"Take me away from here now, please, Cameron," Susannah said, no longer able to view the wreckage of her house, any more than she had been able to continue looking at her shop. "I don't ever want to come back here again. I can't look at it without thinking what would have happened if we hadn't gotten out in time."

"But we did, Susannah, we did. We are all safe and unharmed. We're together. Be thankful, my darling, not frightened."

Susannah's blue eyes swam with tears. "But I am frightened, Cameron. I don't think I'll ever go to sleep at night again without being afraid."

She was not alone in her fear, and the person or persons unknown seemed determined to keep it that way. During the last two weeks of May, two more fires were started, but discovered and put out before they could do harm. The city officials posted a reward of $2,500 for the capture of incendiaries.

With June came a vicious outbreak of robberies, and more fires, all put out safely. On June 2 there was another jail break. Among the fugitives were Sydney Ducks. A celebrated burglar named George Adams escaped, and another who had already escaped on three previous occasions, and James Burns, a notorious ex-convict who went by the name of Jemmy-From-Town.

On June 2, the night of a set fire in a lodging house, a Sydney Duck named Benjamin Lewis was arrested for the crime. He was taken to jail to be brought to the recorder court on June 3.

San Francisco again waited to see if anything would be done to stop the crime and violence.

Sam Brannan waited to see if finally the city would act on its own.

Twenty-nine

On Sunday morning, June 8, 1851, the *Alta,* the only paper that published on Sunday, printed a letter written to the editor regarding the crime situation in the city. The writer, who called himself "Justice," suggested that it was time the people formed themselves into a committee of vigilance. He said that it did no good for the police to arrest criminals, robbers, and arsonists if the courts did nothing to them or let them go again. He concluded, "We must be a law unto ourselves, and there are enough good men and true who are ready to take hold."

"I say we should go talk to Brannan," volunteered George Oakes. His neighbor and fellow merchant, James Neall, agreed with enthusiasm.

"I've had enough! It's time we did something, just as this letter says."

Oakes and Neall set off at once to see Sam Brannan in his office at the northeast corner of Bush and Sansome Streets. The fire had stopped just one block away from Sam's office. Oakes commented, laughing, "It probably didn't dare come any closer. Sam would have put the fear of the Lord into it."

Sam and his clerk Wardwell were at the office working as they did every day of the week when Sam was in town. Sam looked up, greeted the two men, and asked how he could help them.

Oakes put the *Alta* on Sam's desk. "I don't know if you're the man who wrote this or not, Brannan, but I've heard you say often enough that we'd better do something about this situation or rue the day we sat idle. Neall and I agree. That's why we're here—to join you." Neall and Oakes smiled brightly.

"What are we waiting for?" Sam said. "Wardwell, are you ready with pen and paper? Let's get started."

For several minutes the four men questioned each other about possible names to put on their list. By the end of half an hour they were satisfied they had enough people for the first meeting, and they began to discuss time and place.

George Oakes, a member of the California Engine Company, said, "I have access to the room at the fire house. It'll do for the first meeting, and it will be easy to keep others out."

"Tomorrow?" asked Neall, his eyes seeking a sign of agreement from the others.

"Tomorrow," Sam said, and Oakes nodded.

"All right, Wardwell," Sam said, smiling at his clerk. "Do you think you can get them all written and delivered this afternoon?"

"I certainly can, sir." He gave the others a jaunty little bow. "If you gentlemen will excuse me, I have some writing to do. Invitations to a little party, you know."

The timing of the four men could not have been better. San Francisco had had about as much tragedy inflicted on it as its inhabitants could stand. When the men on Sam's list received their invitations, many were already convinced of the necessity of such a meeting or such action as Sam was noted to favor. Those who teetered on indecision were pushed toward Sam's view by the Monday morning *Alta*.

"Another Attempt To Fire The City," the article began. "This could not possibly have been an accident, and it is now rendered positive and beyond a doubt, that there is in this city an organized band of villains who are determined to destroy the city. We are standing as it were upon a mine that any moment may explode, scattering death and destruction."

The editor also had a few choice words of his own. After

using a quote from Cicero about how much can the patience be tried, he asked of San Franciscans, "Have they no spirit, no indignation, no life, energy, character? . . . If we are willing to let the felons burn us up, let us say so, and the sooner it is done the better. Men that have no resentment ought to be abused and kicked by villains and cripples and everybody else."

On that same day, Judge Parsons declared the Grand Jury no longer legally constituted, which meant that nothing would go on in the court until after the first of July, when another Grand Jury would be in session. This came at a time when all the locations San Francisco had to detain criminals were filled to bursting, and the city was riddled with crime and fear as well as annoyed, harassed, and irritated inhabitants.

Sam, George Oakes, and James Neall looked upon the day's events with raised eyebrows. "Somebody up there wants us to succeed, I think," Sam said.

Neall laughed. "Maybe we ought to send an invitation to Judge Parsons. He's helped as much as anyone."

The three men were joined by Wardwell, and started off for the meeting feeling certain of their success. They were not disappointed. Every man who attended that first meeting by invitation was indignant, and ready to act. After a general discussion of the situation and all its ramifications, the men agreed they wanted to continue with the committee as it had begun, but that it should be larger. Sam and a few other men were designated to draw up a constitution for the group that afternoon, and they agreed to hold another meeting later that same day.

"I can see we are going to need considerably more space for tonight's meeting," said Sam with a pleased smile. "I offer one of my storerooms for the meeting. It isn't pretty, but we'll have plenty of space."

Filled with determination, and a feeling that finally steps that were good and proper were being taken, the men adjourned to go seek other men of like mind to bring to the later meeting.

Sam and the others spent the afternoon working on the constitution. All had the sense that there was not a moment to spare. Too much time had already passed.

That evening the men, nearly a hundred of them this time, met in a long narrow storeroom. It was poorly lighted, and built of rough wood, but no one cared what the surroundings were when decisions of such magnitude were to be considered. The proposed constitution was read, the question of a name for the group was discussed, and a miscellaneous conglomeration of matters were brought up and disposed of by the group.

As the fledgling vigilantes were hard at work in Sam Brannan's storeroom, one of the Sydney Ducks, a man called Simpton or Jenkins, was also busy. It was about eight o'clock in the evening. As was his custom George Virgin, a shipping agent, came ashore from a steamboat. He headed for his second-story office in a building on Long Wharf, not too far from the room where the Vigilantes were forming themselves into a cohesive group. This was the last task of George Virgin's day, and when he had placed the money he had collected for his firm in the strong-box safe he kept in the office, he could go home. The Sydney Duck, who had his own plans for the night and for the money Virgin was about to lock up, watched Virgin's actions from the shadows of the wharf.

Jenkins was patient. He did not want to confront George Virgin. All he wanted was the money, and he had planned well how to get it without causing any trouble for himself or others. He had watched Virgin go through his routine many times. Jenkins had a boat at the ready; tied with a single, quickly released knot, so that as soon as he got the money he could be off across the water, and no one would ever know he had been there.

Virgin completed the paperwork necessary, put the money into the safe, which was simply a heavy box, checked over the office, and prepared to leave. He hesitated for a moment at the door, having the nagging feeling he had forgotten to do something. Finally he gave it up and went out the door, locking it securely after himself.

Jenkins watched with satisfaction as Virgin came down the outside steps of the office at long last. Having waited this long, the Sydney Duck didn't mind waiting a few more minutes for Virgin to be well on his way home. Then Jenkins came out from the shadows and headed for the office door. With a chisel, he worked quietly and patiently to break the lock free. He had to be cautious, for next door was the bookseller's shop, and any unusual noise might be noted. Jenkins was good at his business, however, having been reared in London and having experience of this sort going a long way back. In short order he had entered the building. Being a strong man, he picked up the entire strong box and put it in a bag that had once been used for coffee beans. He could open the box later and extract the money safely at his leisure.

Then George Virgin remembered what it was he had forgotten earlier. He turned around and headed back to his office.

In Sam Brannan's storeroom, the first official vigilante meeting was drawing to a close. One hundred three men had signed the pact that made them vigilantes, and had selected the name Committee of Vigilance for themselves. Sam was elected their first president, and Isaac Bluxome was the first secretary. Their password would be "Lewis." As the final event of the meeting, Colonel Jonathan D. Stevenson, the man who had organized the New York Volunteers and brought them to California, made a speech. At fifty-one the oldest man in the group, Stevenson felt called upon to remind these young men that the move they had taken was of a most serious nature, and that every one of them would have to face up to the responsibility they had taken upon themselves. After that, the meeting broke up. Some men stood around in groups still going over that evening's decisions.

George Virgin hurried along the wharf, and started up the stairs to his office. He met a man coming down the stairs carrying a bulky burlap bag. The big, encumbered man stepped to the side to let Virgin pass and continued on his way. Virgin smiled at the man, thinking his burden was a load of books just purchased from the next door bookseller.

As soon as Virgin tried his key, however, he knew that the man had not purchased books, but had robbed *him*. To be certain, Virgin opened the ruined door, and saw the office in disarray. He turned, chasing after the big man, who was now heading down the wharf at a clumsy run. "Stop, thief! Stop that man!"

Jenkins stood out in the bright moonlight. His gait was awkward, but he didn't stop. He had planned well, and if he could just make it to his boat, he would be off and away, leaving Virgin to scream "thief" all he wanted on the side of the wharf.

Hearing the cry, a number of men on the wharf, and several boatmen who made their living rowing people back and forth to the ships and wharves, joined Virgin in the chase.

Jenkins threw the heavy booty into the boat and, with a quick flick, released his boat from its mooring. His powerful shoulders now put to the oars carried him away from the pier quickly. Behind him he could hear the hallooing and calling of the boatmen as they ran for their own crafts to give chase.

Jenkins would have had no difficulty outrowing the pursuing men had it not been for John Sullivan. Sullivan had just taken a fare out to a ship in the harbor and was returning to the wharf. Hearing the excited cries, Sullivan maneuvered his boat so that he would intercept Jenkins and leap on board.

The Sydney Duck was trapped. With one oar unshipped and Sullivan in his boat, prepared to knock him silly, Jenkins could do little. Thinking ahead to his probable trial and the leniency of the courts, he heaved the strong-box, the evidence of his guilt, into the water. By then the other boatmen had arrived and towed Jenkins back to the wharf. There they beat on him for a time, then took him in tow to turn over to the police.

The chase and capture of Jenkins had caused a stir, so the constantly curious San Franciscans who were out and about at nine o'clock in the evening gathered and formed a crowd escorting Jenkins to the authorities. One of the men joining the group was a volunteer policeman, David Arrowsmith. He took charge of Jenkins. Arrowsmith also happened to have been the twenty-fifth man to sign the constitution of the Committee of Vigilance just under an hour ago.

The idea of a Committee of Vigilance had not completely settled in Arrowsmith's mind, so for the time being he was content to take Jenkins by one arm while John Sullivan, the hero of the evening, took the other, and the two men marched him to the station house. That might have been the end of it, with Jenkins out on the street within a few days, but for George Schenck, the seventy-second man to sign the vigilante pact. Schenck was on his way home when he ran into the stream of men escorting Jenkins. After hearing the night's tale from Arrowsmith, Schenck said, "Why, you're a member of the Committee of Vigilance. We formed it to handle just this sort of thing. Take him back to the committee headquarters. The men will still be there—and those who aren't can be summoned."

Arrowsmith suddenly felt the enormity of the committee's actions that night. He said, "If you say I should, I will."

"I do say so," said Schenck decisively. "This is why we organized, and here we have the first man caught. Let me take hold of him, and we'll go right to the committee."

Sullivan gave up his place to Schenck, and the men changed directions and started for the warehouse.

At the committee room Oakes, Ryckman, McDuffee and some others were still there. Oakes hurried to the fire house and just before ten o'clock struck the coded bell alarm to call the Committee of Vigilance to a general meeting.

The members began to make their way to the meeting room from all parts of the city. Others, knowing that something big was afoot, followed. At the door the committee had posted a guard. Those who could not give the secret password were refused admittance. Soon 80 of the 103 Vigilantes were there.

Now, with all assembled and faced with their first opportunity for action against a Sydney Duck captured in the commission of a crime, no one knew what to do. They had just concluded their first official meeting, and had established a good many of their procedural rules, but the one thing no one had thought to do was establish how they would proceed with a trial. They put the prisoner in another room and discussed the matter. Some of them wanted to turn him over to the authorities until they were better prepared to handle matters like this. Others agreed they weren't prepared, but merely wanted to delay the trial until they could determine the committee's method. Sam wanted an immediate trial and to hell with procedure.

In the middle of the room a large man got up, took off his sailor's cap, and strode to the front table, where he slammed the cap down. Captain Howard said, "Gentlemen, as I understand it, we came here to hang somebody."

With his words Captain Howard mobilized the others. Cries from all over the room concurred. "Let's do it!"

"We've taken charge—or we haven't. Now's the time to decide."

"Hang him!"

Quickly the court was organized. Sam was brought forth to act as the presiding officer. Other members served as jury. George Schenck was the prosecuting attorney, and while they appointed no one to act on behalf of Jenkins, he was allowed to speak for himself.

Outside, rumors were flying, and a crowd of huge proportions was growing. The police had gotten word that this new group calling themselves the Committee of Vigilance had taken a prisoner and were in the act of trying him. Others had heard that the Sydney Ducks were going to rescue their mate and retaliate on the citizenry. Jenkins seemed to think that was true, for he was cocky in his defense and felt no qualm in calling the members of the committee a variety of profane names. Between the police and the Ducks, the vigilantes wondered if Jenkins didn't have good cause to be cocky. If anyone was in a precarious position it was the fledgling committee. Then the police knocked at the door, demanding the committee turn over their prisoner to the proper authority. The committee did not want an all-out confrontation with the police, so they put off Captain Ben Ray, telling him to wait just a while and all would be straightened out.

David Broderick, a local politician, seized upon this night as a good vehicle to promote his own views. Under the cry of law and order, Broderick called out all his henchmen. The mayor had called the military companies to assemble. This last caused no consternation, for many of the members of the military companies were members of the committee, but the other assemblages could cause trouble.

It was midnight before the committee jury voted. Unanimously they stood for conviction, and unanimously they stood for the punishment of death. One of the committee members slipped out and went to the fire house. A few minutes after midnight, the bell of the California Engine House tolled mournfully, signaling that the vote had been for death for the prisoner.

Jenkins finally realized how serious his position really was and began to shout loudly, begging, "Shoot me like a man! Don't hang me like a dog! Shoot me!"

Outside the crowd was rampant with speculation, and disorder was only minutes away. Everyone had an idea of what was going on, but fact was mixed with rumor, and the crowd was restive. Someone was going to have to speak to them, but no one, including Sam, wanted to do it. Ryckman punched Sam's shoulder, giving him a look that said, you got us into this. Ryckman said, "You'd better go out there and talk to them, Brannan. You'd better get that mob rallied behind us."

Sam gave him a look of pure acid. That was a tall order, and Ryckman didn't seem to be fighting his way to the door for the honor of accomplishing it. Sam remained standing in the room for a while, trying to think of some way to approach the crowd. The onlookers might support the Vigilantes, but they also might turn into a mob that would sweep away the whole committee this very night. With a surge of noise coming from outside, Sam squared his shoulders, opened the door and stepped out into their midst.

He found a mound of sand, and stood on it to address the mob. He calmed himself, trying to convince himself that this was no different from many times when he had spoken to a hostile and resentful group of Saints. Things had not always been peaceful within the bounds of the Church either. He had come through tougher times than this.

He started out slowly, letting his magnificent voice work on the crowd. He reassured them, telling them of the circumstances of Jenkins's capture and trial. He assured the people that all would be carried out to their satisfaction. "This is no mob. These men who have committed themselves to serving you are not acting hastily, or in the heat of passion. Your Committee of Vigilance is your insurance that you will be safe in this city." He stopped talking for a moment, letting his mere presence hold the crowd. Then with a smile he raised his arms and asked, "Have we done well for you?"

The crowd roared their approval. The noise was deafening, but in spite of that a few nays could be heard here and there.

Someone shouted, "Who's the speaker?"

Another, who had recognized Sam, gave his name.

"Who are the committee?"

Suddenly the crowd closed ranks, and cries from all over went up. "No names! No names!"

Inside the meeting room the committee were arguing about whether to hang Jenkins at night or to wait for daylight. William Coleman argued that it would not be manly to hang him at night. "It will make the committee appear cowardly."

Others less bold just wanted it done while they had the chance, and before someone stopped them.

Outside, the crowd had split up. Some of the people had hurried over to the Square so that they could get a good position from which to view the hanging. Others milled about outside the meeting room, waiting to see the prisoner brought out.

Jenkins had realized by now that no one was coming to his aid and that this committee was deadly serious in their intent to hang him right now. He asked that Reverend Flavel Mines, the Episcopalian minister, be brought to him, as he needed spiritual guidance. Reverend Mines was summoned, but Jenkins couldn't quite rid himself of his arrogance or his profanity. Reverend Mines made a valiant effort to reach Jenkins, knowing he was in a mortal battle with Satan, but eventually even Mines gave up. He pleaded with Jenkins and prayed with him and for him until nearly two o'clock in the morning.

Ryckman brought the agonizing to an end. "Reverend, I mean no disrespect, but you've been with this man for a long time." He hesitated for a moment, then in the harsh direct manner that was natural to him, he said, "I am going to hang this man in half an hour."

The committee had agreed to hang Jenkins in the Square, choosing the Old Adobe, a government building that still stood from Mexican days and which conveniently had a cross beam running its width that would make an excellent hanging place. Wakeman, Schenck and Coleman had chosen the site, and Wakeman had appointed himself hangman.

A little before two, the committee chamber door opened. The members, each armed with pistols, came outside, forming a solid column. The men directly in charge of Jenkins had a rope around his neck, and each man had ahold of the rope so that they would stay together should there be a rush to rescue or capture their prisoner. Thus four abreast and twenty deep, the Committee of Vigilance marched with its prisoner up Sansome Street toward the Square. Jenkins's arms were tied. Behind him came a small man named George Ward. Ward said loudly and boldly, "If the police should try to take you, sir, I am telling you that I will blow your head off."

Wakeman laughed, and muttered to his partner, "Take that pistol away from the boy before he hurts somebody."

At California Street the procession turned, going to Montgomery, then on Montgomery to Clay and then to the Square. It gave them the feeling of doing the right thing, for they were passing through an area that had been devastated by the fire that everyone agreed had been set by the Sydney Ducks. As the committee moved up the slope of Clay Street, everyone got a little more tense. If the Ducks were going to make a move to free Jenkins, it would be at the corner of Clay and Kearney just before the group came to the Square. As anticipated, the Sydney men rushed, but the Committee was prepared, and closed tight around Jenkins. The Square was crowded with men who had come to aid Jenkins. The Ducks rushed again, then gave it up, leaving Jenkins to his fate—or rather to the action of the police or of Broderick's men. Police were milling through the crowd rallying the many who were opposed to a vigilance committee. Broderick was speechifying to the crowd, trying to make them rush the committee and take the prisoner away.

The committee, wanting only to get the prisoner despatched, kept a steady, single-minded path through the crowd, but now they became confused. Some helpful souls had placed a rope from the one-hundred-foot Oregon pine that served as a flagpole in the Square, and had erected a platform on which Jenkins could be placed. Thinking someone had changed the plans, the committee began to move Jenkins to the flagpole.

Two policemen now broke through the committee lines and grabbed hold of Jenkins. Immediately committee members had shoved their pistols roughly into the chests of the officers. "I'll blow your heart out!"

Officer North cried out, "For God's sake, stop! Are you a Christian?"

"Let go of the prisoner."

The officers backed away.

Someone else saw where the committee were taking Jenkins to be hanged and yelled, "The Adobe! It's desecration to hang him from the flagpole! The Adobe!"

The Old Adobe was about 125 feet from the flagpole, and the men were fighting in closer and closer quarters. Police Chief Ben Ray grabbed the rope around Jenkins's neck and tried to take command. One man pressed a pistol into the back of Ray's head, and another threatened to club him. Ray let go.

The committee, pulling Jenkins along by the rope, began again to move toward the Adobe. Ray's men, deciding they would have the prisoner, grabbed Jenkins's legs, and put the man in the awful position of having one group pulling on his neck and another on his legs. He was very nearly hanged with the effort to rescue him. Men shoved and hit one another and struggled for control of Jenkins. Breaking free for a moment, some of the committee, now near to the Adobe, ran with the rope and slung it over the beam. Just as quickly they began to move outward, making the rope taut and dragging Jenkins with it. Jenkins was hauled up. Captain Ray ran forward with a knife to cut the felon down. Men fell upon him, beating him down to the ground and taking his knife away from him.

The men holding Jenkins in the air were unsteady, and Jenkins bobbed about like a crazy doll. Captain Wakeman, used to being aboard ship, yelled mightily for a belaying pin. Lacking that, the men tied the rope to the porch railing. Jenkins dangled, jerking spasmodically.

The crowd began to struggle out of the Square and toward their homes. The Committee stayed, guarding the body so that the Sydney Ducks would not steal it before it could be handed over to the coroner in the morning. A reporter for the San Francisco *Herald* hurried off so that he could have tonight's doings in the early edition. At two-thirty in the morning he said, "He is probably dead at the time of this writing." He concluded sometime later, "Four o'clock—he is still hanging—dead."

Sam Brannan did not get home before the morning light. This moonlit summer night the Committee of Vigilance had been born, and Simpton, or John Jenkins, or whatever his real name had been, was dead. Sam wasn't clear on what he felt other than tired. Action was needed to protect the city, but then, as if in keeping with the nature of San Francisco and the men who were drawn to her, the Committee of Vigilance had had its first trial in chaos and black comedy and the heat of passion. On that thought, Sam fell sound asleep still in his clothes.

Because of the speech he had given, Sam was the only Vigilante identified that night. Later that year, when Mormon Elder Parley P. Pratt brought his mission to San Francisco, he was to use Sam's involvement in murder against him before the Church.

Thirty

*L*andry Morrison and Fairy Radburn were as happy as they had ever been in their lives. Rich Bar was snowed in. Nobody could get in, nobody wanted to go out. They had supplies to last until spring. As good neighbors they had the Gentrys, who could help them out, or whom they could help out, in case of any need. They had Jarom, and Letha Belle, and Lemuel. There was no fear that Asa would come back unexpectedly and interrupt their idyll. They had all the time in the world, till spring.

In October Fairy had gotten a letter from Asa, saying that he was going on a mission and would be back before snow. But he didn't get back, and the snow piled up. When it was plainly safe, Landry moved in with her. He had been spending all his time there anyway, so why not? he asked.

"Why not?" Fairy said, laughing, ignoring the good sense that Fiona had tried and tried to instill in her. Landry was good company. Until this time, Fairy had never had a lover while Asa was gone; now she was learning what intense happiness a man could give her. Before Landry, the nighttime before sleeping was something to be gotten through, a performance she had to put on for her man's benefit. Lord knew *she* thought little of it.

The first time Landry persuaded her into bed, she looked on it as another time to play-act, but for his sake she didn't mind doing it so much. He was so kind, and his mouth tasted so sweet and fresh against hers, that she even felt a low-key desire of some kind. She started out by doing for him some of the things Asa had taught her, but he stopped her gently. "This is for you, Fairy," he whispered against her lips.

"What d'you mean?" she whispered back.

"Don't you know?"

Not only did Fairy not know, she did not know what it was she didn't know. But when Landry kissed her in places she didn't know people could be kissed, and caressed her over and over until she was crazy-hot for him, she began to understand. Then he entered her, leisurely, though his own wild passion demanded hurry, and Fairy felt the first throb of anticipation. He said, "Wait. Just lie still, and feel me in you."

Fairy did, her mind rushing to the point of their joining, and she blushed at her own heat growing. It was thrilling, but it was frightening. What if something happened? And if it did, what would it be? As he began slowly to move deeper into her, and out, and in deeper, she grew anxious. She kept wanting to take more breath, felt that something "down there" was nearly bursting. Suddenly she was overwhelmed by passion, by an event so tremendous that she moaned his name, over and over. At that moment she experienced the familiar spasms of the man in her, and her body went on responding, carrying her high and yet leaving her too weak to do anything more but pant, and laugh, and at last say, "Landry, what did you do? That was— uncommon fine."

He chuckled, smoothing back her hair and kissing the end of her nose. "Yes, it was—wasn't it?"

"Nothing like that ever happened to me before."

He said gallantly, "Nor to me. It must be something special, just for Us." He always said it like that, Us with a capital U. It was being snowed in with plenty of wood piled out back, and sunshine, and giggles, and kisses on her neck, and hands touching, and babies held in two pairs of arms, and youthful joy that Fairy had only with him.

"Can we ever do that again, d'you reckon?"

"We might." He was still in her, resting his weight on his elbows, and her pelvis, and his knees, so that unlike Asa who always flopped his full weight on her, he felt warm but light between her legs. Until now she had never thought there might be a difference from one man to another. Usually by this time Asa would have turned over to sleep, but Landry hadn't, and she discovered she liked still feeling him down there. Especially when he was going on kissing her, nibbling at her lips and her earlobes, and his fingers were playing with her nipples. Tentatively, she rubbed the muscles of his back, and felt him growing hard within her again. They went on, and this time she expected it, but it was still wonderful.

After that she began thinking of it all the time, hardly able to wait between times before they did it again. They spent the winter months touching and hugging, talking and laughing, their spirits unquenchable because of the amazing thing they could do together.

Landry enjoyed it as much as he had enjoyed Tolerance in that way, but there were times when he wished Fairy *were* Tolerance. Sure, he and Fairy had a lot to talk about at the first of the year, and they still did have—yet he was starting to feel restless. Anybody would, he argued to himself, cooped up in a little town all winter. He loved Fairy's kids, taking almost as much pride in their growth and development as if they were his own. And Fairy never got boresome. She was like Susannah in that respect, with a saving good humor toward nearly everything. She was sensitive to his moods, having stepped lightly around Asa for years, and when Landry showed signs of withdrawal, she never tried to jolly him out of it, but occupied herself contentedly with stitching on a quilt or the children's clothing. When Landry felt like coming back to her—even though he'd only been upstairs—she welcomed him with a smile and an affectionate hug. It was the same the two or three times he went down to the Bluebird and came home staggering drunk. Fairy was afraid of drunkenness, for Asa in that condition was unbelievably cruel. But she had courage, and she helped Landry to bed, and was grateful that he didn't beat her or try to take her.

She never mentioned Asa's name. Jarom, three and a half, had seen so little of Asa that he never mentioned Daddy; his hero was "Landy." Letha Belle was a year younger, and Lemuel not even a year yet. It felt sometimes as if Asa was dead, and she and Landry were the maw and the daddy. But they had to prepare for Asa's return. When winter let up and the thaws began, Landry moved all his belongings out of the house and back into his own cabin. As soon as the weather permitted, he began spending the whole day at the diggings again. He revived his natural caution, always checking for signs of Asa's presence before he entered Fairy's house. Finally he devised a particular arrangement of a window blind as a signal.

Through the winter Fiona had remained Fairy's best friend, even though she disapproved of her household arrangements, not from a moralistic viewpoint, but out of concern for Fairy's safety. Like Fairy, Fiona feared Asa. She tried her best to persuade both Landry and Fairy that living together was a mistake, that one of the children would talk, or that it would all come to light somehow. To this Fairy only glowed with contentment and said, "It'll be all right, Fiona." Fiona told of her own stubbornness in not thinking out her future with Robin; but her persuasive words lit on fallow ground.

Fiona and Robin seldom quarreled, but over Fairy they did. Robin had made his own disquieting assessment of Asa, and he did not want his wife and children associated in Asa's mind with Fairy and her children. He feared that when the man came home, something terrible might happen that would involve Fiona. But therein lay Fiona's blind spot. She might be able to help Fairy, she argued; which gave Robin a coldness down his spine.

That aspect of the situation solved itself when the weather broke early in February 1851. Fiona and the children left Rich Bar to go live in Napa Valley with Jane and Zeke, and supervise the building of the Gentry mansion. So Fairy was left without a woman friend. She had her children, and Landry.

The summer wore on, and still Asa had not come or sent word. Landry had begun quietly asking new arrivals in Rich Bar if they knew of Asa Radburn. There was no concealing his relationship with Fairy; everyone who had wintered over in the community knew where Landry had lived. He and Fairy might easily have grown careless, naturally thinking Asa dead after the long silence. But Landry had a feeling—a gut feeling that had never lied to him before. And its message was that Asa would come back.

Funny, along with that was the feeling that he and Tollie would get back together. He clung to that idea, torn between the delicate harmony of his winter love for Fairy and his longer, more anguished love for Tollie. He and his wife would have a lot of things to settle if they decided to try to make a go of it again. But in the time since they'd met and made love in San Francisco, he'd ironed out most of the old hurts in his mind. After Asa came back, and he was sure Fairy was all right with him, he might go to San Francisco.

Meantime, he was forcing himself to see less and less of Fairy, concealing his presence at the house from neighbors. She understood why, for they had talked about it. They were back on the early cautious footing—though once he got in the house, nothing had changed between them. It was just that now, when Asa had been away for nearly a year, and everything seemed safe, it paid to be extra careful.

It was late in September. The grasses had gone dry, and the dead stalks of goldenrod littered the slopes. Already there had been heavy lasting snow in places, but Joe Jackson was almost home. He had made pretty good time from Salt Lake City to Sacramento to Rich Bar.

Nightfall had caught him still a distance out from Rich Bar. But he went on. Dark never stopped Asa Radburn, or Joe Jackson either. He grinned, thinking how he always managed it so he got in at night, just in case Fairy had a little something going on. But she'd never dare. He had left that woman so scared of him—

He wondered how Fairy would like his new look, the leather outfit, his hair kept neat and short, his face shaved every single day. He knew his mother would like it. He felt better about himself, that was sure.

He had his new life all figured out. While it was still dark— maybe not until tomorrow now, the night was starting to feel over—he'd bundle up Fairy and the kids and the stuff they'd want to take with them, and get them out of Rich Bar. He'd moved them down to Monterey. It was a nice place, big enough so that new people wouldn't make any splash. There they could live the pleasant life of Joe Jackson and Family, and he'd go out sometimes and dig for gold, and sometimes use up some sucker. Yes sir, he had his life all planned.

He was at the edge of Rich Bar now. The community was bigger, but he could still find his own house.

They had made tempestuous love and had fallen asleep where they lay, tangled in the blankets, her legs slackly wrapped around him, his head tight beside hers on the pillow. "Landry, don't fall asleep," she had said. But next thing she knew, she was waking. There was a noise in the house, and it wasn't Jarom out of bed and running around. It was footsteps on the stairs . . . a man's footsteps. Coming up. Slow but sure, like a man who owned the stairs. Like Asa.

In a flash, Fairy was wide awake, terrified, on the point of screaming. She punched Landry in the ribs, hard. "Go out the window," she hissed.

He woke up seconds too slowly. "Whaffor?" he asked, bewildered. He had been deep asleep and dreaming. Now somebody was telling him—

"Go out the window. Drop to the ground. I'll follow. You catch me." She said it all clearly, and in his muzzy state, he trusted her. Naked, he perched on the sill, looking back at her. She motioned him on, and he jumped to the ground. Recovering himself, he realized where he was and what must be happening. Yet he stood naked in the darkness, waiting to catch her.

Fairy didn't come. The window was slammed shut.

Landry's mind raced. He had no weapon, no clothes—they were in Fairy's bedroom. Asa had returned, and Landry had nothing with which he could defend Fairy's life. He had to get a gun.

His legs thought for themselves, and he found himself tearing down the empty streets to his cabin, a few blocks away. Pray God he wouldn't be too late. Asa would find his clothes, and he'd be angry, but how angry? Furious? Raging? Murderous? God, please, God, please, Landry kept saying. He could hear his breath, feel it searing in his chest, but spurred by thought of Fairy, he ran. God, please. . . .

The most terrifying quiet sound Fairy had ever heard was the closing and latching of her bedroom door. She turned from the window, unable at the last moment to leave her children to face Asa's wrath unprotected. She was aware of the telltale smell of their lovemaking, on her and on the bedding. In the dark room, she could see a man's shape. "Who is it?" she asked. "Asa? Is it Asa?"

Asa's voice answered, dryly amused. "Name's Joe Jackson. From San Francisco."

"Wha—what d'you want?" She was groping for the little chair she laid her clothes on, trying to get it between her and him.

Asa laughed. As Fairy shrank against the wall, he passed her, peered out a corner of the window for a moment, and slammed the window shut. He looked different in the faint light, Asa and yet not Asa. He said, "So. You and Landry."

She did not answer, hoping to be able to cross the room, unlatch the door, and run to safety. But with a slight creaking noise of his leather jacket, he had reached out and grabbed her arm. His hand whipped across her face, right and left, again and again until Fairy saw stars and her head rang. She grunted with the force of his blows, but would not let herself cry out. She wouldn't give him that pleasure.

He shook her, and her head bobbed on her neck. "You—were —in bed—with Landry— Weren't you!"

Automatically she said, "No! Never!" and was rewarded with his knee in her belly. She gasped, grabbing herself against the bursting pain, and slid to the floor in a heap. Her hair fell over her face. She was aware of her nakedness, and aware of thinking that if she only had her things on, the way he was kicking her wouldn't hurt so bad. She felt his hard boots, swiftly propelled, on her thighs, in her ribs, on her tailbone. Each blow was more agonizing than the last, but she had to stay and take it. She couldn't pass out, for who would protect Jarom, and Letha Belle, and baby Lemuel?

Then he jerked her to her feet, crouched over still holding

herself together, and his fist rammed into her jaw, and some of her teeth broke and flew across the room. She cried out at that, and felt herself falling again. Just before she fell, something hit her in the pit of the stomach. Something hard as iron. Something that tore her apart inside. Something that killed her.

Joe Jackson went on kicking the woman who lay on his bedroom floor, laying bruises on every inch of her head, and her face and body, marking her so that nobody who saw her would ever forget the man who did it to her. He would knock everything out of her, and she'd never want some other man again. None would ever look at her, she'd be so ugly.

Then he realized that she wasn't moving. Her arms had fallen limp, and her body lay twisted and grotesque as if Susannah had abandoned it there and gone on somewhere better. "Susannah, damn you—get up!" he said, giving her another vicious kick. Just like her to play possum, damn her. He'd teach her.

He bent over to grab her and stand her up again, and as he did so he felt a paralyzing fear, as though Fairy stood over him with a stick of stovewood, the way she had once, and would hit him with it. "What's that?!" he grunted. He raised up suddenly, whirling around to peer into the darkness. Nothing was there. Only his wild imagination.

Or was it? Something had entered this room that wasn't there before. Some unearthly force that threatened him. Some evil presence . . . Quickly, like the coward he was, Joe Jackson ran out of the bedroom and down the stairs.

Landry Morrison, panting, whimpering in his fear for Fairy, jammed his legs into his trousers, buttoning them at the top only, then found his other boots and got them on. He grabbed a shirt and slung his arms into it while he was pawing around in the chest trying to find extra ammunition for his revolvers. His motions were frantic as he strapped on his gun belts and filled his pockets with bullets. Barely five minutes had passed since he had dropped out the window. Grabbing his boot knife off a little stand, he left his cabin on the run.

The stars were fading; the faraway night skies had gone slightly gray and had come nearer. Landry ran in a zigzag pattern, from this bush to that building, hiding behind trees momentarily, going across back yards and through ditches, until he came to Fairy's house. His pounding heart strained for air. Crouching at the back corner, he muffled his hoarse panting with the tail of his shirt. As soon as he could, he held his breath and listened. Nothing, except the swish-thud of his heartbeat. There was no sound at all.

Oh, God! God, please! Tears came into Landry's eyes and he rubbed them away impatiently. Carefully he worked his way around to the front door. It stood open. The house felt empty, yet the children had to be still in there. With both guns drawn, and terribly aware that if he shot anyone, it must be Asa Radburn and no one else, he entered. He listened, with his ears and with his consciousness. The children were there, but no one else was.

Positive of this, he took the stairs two at a time and rushed into Fairy's bedroom. He smelled blood. Blood and lovemaking. In the dim light he saw her body, lying crumpled and broken like trash thrown on the floor. He did not have to touch her to know that she was beyond his help. He took a brief, sobbing breath, and another. There was not enough air in the world to fill his lungs now.

He rubbed both hands on his trousers legs, trying to put aside his grief. Then he bent over and got his hat and his gun off the chair where he had left them. He looked at her one last time. He whispered, "Fairy, I'll take care of him. He'll never hurt anyone again. I swear this to you."

Quietly, so he wouldn't wake the children, he slipped downstairs.

For a while he stood at the windows, away from the edge, looking out all around the house. Asa would be hunting for him. Was he hiding in the bushes, expecting him to come out now? With great care, Landry went out the back door. When nothing happened, he retraced his erratic course to his cabin, more cautious than before because it was getting lighter. He reached it at last, but his gut feeling told him Asa was not there. He had been, though—several things had been smashed. So Asa was after him.

Landry didn't want to stay in his cabin. He felt trapped here. He went outside, searching in his mind for Asa. Where would he likely go next? Where would Asa expect Landry to go? Of course. His claim on the river. Asa would go there, and simply wait up on the cliff for him to come and try to kill him there.

Landry started running again, this time not so careful. He was staking his life on a hunch anyway, why not play it to the hilt? Not that Landry wanted to get killed—in fact, he realized all that he had to live for now. But he'd promised Fairy, and he'd carry out that promise.

There were a few miners on the streets already, headed toward their claims. Every day was precious at this time of year, toward the end of the mining season. He knew them, but paid no attention to their called comments. He had to get to the diggings before Asa got there first and found a good place to hide.

He was too late. He saw no one around, but as, panting hard, he climbed the rocks above the river, a shot sounded, and a bullet bored through the air past his ear. Then another, and another. With the speed of desperation he found a crack in the rocks and crouched there while Asa emptied two guns all around him. Landry had never been under fire before, but he knew how many bullets were in a revolver, and Asa had used his up. Landry cautiously held up his hat, but nothing happened. During the respite while Asa reloaded, he crawled to another position, where he would be hidden but he might be able to see his enemy.

He scanned the entire countryside within his view. Nothing. It would have helped to know what color Asa was wearing, but he saw only rocks. He waited, listening for the rattle of stones falling, any little sound that would reveal the other man's location. He might have been alone, except for the eerie feeling of his enemy's presence. He peered out a little farther, looking down, sickened by the sheerness of the drop down to the river.

A shot rang out, then another. Landry knew where they were coming from now, and he peppered the spot with his own bullets. He saw earth fly, and bits of rock, but there was no sound. Quickly he reloaded, though he had two more guns. Now that he knew where Asa was, he might be able to sneak up on him.

Asa had the same idea, for as Landry negotiated an especially tricky passage through the rocks, the shooting began, this time in earnest. A big piece of rock broke off above Landry and hit him hard in the shoulder, knocking him off his feet. He slipped down the face of the cliff into the river. He smacked in the water with the inertness of a corpse and was swiftly borne downstream, around a bend and out of sight.

Above him, Joe Jackson took off his hat and wiped his forehead. Got the son of a bitch, he thought. If he'd ever seen a dead man, that was Landry Morrison. Served the bastard right for ever getting born.

So now he might as well make a clean sweep of it. Wipe out the whole Morrison clan. First Susannah, and then Ezra. And after he'd tended to that little business, he'd go after Sam Brannan.

They'd find out it didn't pay to mess with Joe Jackson.

Robin went outside and picked up the child. Jarom clutched Robin's neck, sobbing heartbrokenly, his chubby little hands patting Robin for his own comfort. "Can't find Maw," he said over and over.

Robin held the little boy tight. "It's all right," he said soothingly, brushing back Jarom's hair. "We'll take you to your maw," he said.

"No!" said Jarom, squirming, burying his nose in Robin's shirt. "No—scary. Scary!"

Robin began walking toward Fairy's house with Jarom in his arms. "Did you have a bad dream, Jarom? Is this what's scary?"

"No," said Jarom, still sobbing.

"Come along, then, we'll find what's scary, and we'll just fix it."

"No," Jarom insisted. He was squirming, but would not let Robin put him down. Robin went in the open door, calling softly, "Fairy! It's Robin Gentry! Are you awake? I've got Jarom with me." When there was no answer, Robin tried again to put the boy down, then started up the stairs carrying him, talking in a loud voice but hoping he wouldn't awaken the other children this early. There *was* something scary here—and odd, too, for Fairy was the best of mothers, always alert to the wants of her babies. Robin hardly knew what to do. He shifted Jarom to his other shoulder, and got out his gun. Then he took the child back downstairs and seated him in a chair. But Jarom would not let go; he screamed hysterically, clinging to Robin. In the end Robin took him along on his back, hoping that if someone was upstairs who meant trouble, he would not harm Jarom.

No point in trying to be quiet, with Jarom shrieking bloody murder. He could hear the other two awake now. He knocked on Fairy's open door, then poked his head in. What the hell!? He saw the bruised and bloody mess on the floor, knew it was Fairy, and knew Jarom had found her. His stomach lurched. At his back, the child was pinching him with his hands and screaming, "Maw! Maw! Maw!" until Robin could hardly bear it.

He turned, and shut the door behind him, and got the other two children out of their beds, and took them out of the house. Led by Jarom, they were all screaming by now.

Landry Morrison heard them, and knew the sounds. He

could not run any longer—he was in such pain and exhaustion he could barely walk—but he hurried the best he could toward Fairy's children. Jarom saw him and scrambled down from Robin and flew to his "Landy," who picked him up and held him against his wet clothes and began to sob like the boy.

Robin Gentry didn't know what to do next. He was holding two small, wet-diapered children, and there in front of him was the third child and the man Fairy had probably died for.

Landry collected himself, and looked up. "You saw her?" When Robin nodded, he went on, "He thought he'd killed me too—but he knocked me into the river and the cold shocked me back to consciousness."

"Who?"

"Asa," Landry answered. "I just happened to see him heading down the trail, lickety-split for Susannah."

Momentarily, Robin had forgotten Asa's early obsession, even though he had played a part in rescuing her from it. *"Susannah?!* Why Susannah?" he exclaimed, but even as he said the words he knew the answer.

"He married Fairy as a substitute for her," said Landry, standing up now. "Now that he's killed Fairy—and me—guess who's next."

"My *God*. And Cameron—" Robin looked from one baby to the other, trying to decide which one to put down first. "Landry, will you take care of these kids? I've got to try to get to San Francisco before—"

Landry's warm brown eyes were cold as stone. "He killed somebody I loved, Robin. It's up to me to keep him from it again."

"But—"

But Landry had gone, once more able to run. In a few moments Robin heard the clatter of hoofbeats fading into the distance.

He stood there paralyzed, then was galvanized into action. If ever he needed Fiona's expert hands with children, it was now. He had to get to San Francisco too. Meantime, he had three babies, wet and hungry and without a mother. How . . . ? A devilish grin broke over his face. Robin stood in front of a nearby house, and in his most stentorian bellow he cried, "Zane! Zane Tyler!"

"Never let it be said that I failed a friend in need," said Zane Tyler, as they bounced along the uneven road toward the Napa Valley and Fiona, "but this is the sonofabitchin' livin' end, damn my eyes if it's not."

Robin laughed, looking around at his friend who was doing a poor job of holding Lemuel's rag tit for him. "You've got to pick the little booger up and hold him, Zane," he directed. "Don't be afraid of him."

"Christ, what if he wets on me?"

The two men's eyes met, and they started laughing, and eased off, then one of them made a silly remark and they started up again, and went on that way for some miles. Their hilarity was a needed release, but they did not slow their pace for even a moment.

"Hoo—hoo, boy oh boy," said Zane as they wound down. "At least it's better than crying, or shoving your fist down somebody's neck."

"I'll do that too, if I get the chance," Robin assured him. "Here, you take the reins a while, and I'll hold Lem." He checked on the other children, who were tied onto the seat with long strips of rag. Jarom looked solemn, but he was a solemn child; and Letha Belle, a smiler, was smiling. So far they were enjoying the ride.

It had been a wearing morning. Robin had roused other friends in Rich Bar, one who helped Zane dig Fairy's grave in her backyard, two more who sought out diapers and blankets and little clothing, and packed the wagon with supplies while Robin cleaned up the children, changed their diapers, and fed them breakfast. Word spread, and others built a coffin, and took care of the children while Robin and Zane struggled to clothe Fairy decently for burial. That was almost impossible, so Zane slit her dress down the back, and then arranged it nicely after she was in the coffin. They could hardly bear to look on the face of that sweet and pleasant woman. They held a brief service, with quite a number of miners in Rich Bar attending. Afterwards they all had a stiff drink, and Robin and Zane loaded the children into the wagon and they began their journey.

Fiona was astonished to see them, capering with gladness until she saw the children. Then her face fell. "Oh, Robin," she said in a hushed voice. "What's wrong?"

He told her, but not everything. Then Fiona cried, and held all of Fairy's children, and thanked God for the safety of her own. They got them into the house, where Jane and Fiona tended to them while Robin and Zane filled their stomachs with cold food left over from the previous meal.

"You're not going on?" Fiona cried. "Oh, Robin, it's nearly dark! Stay here tonight! Sleep a little bit and I'll get you up before dawn."

"I'm afraid to," he said. "We've lost so much time already."

"Oh, Robin . . ." She left the rest unsaid; but her eyes said it all.

He smiled at her. "I'll be all right," he promised her.

She caught his hand and pressed it to her lips. "You promised, now."

"Brave Fiona," he said. "I'm glad we have each other to love."

"So am I."

He kissed and held his children, giving special notice to Mark, who was four months old and whom he had seen only once before. Mark had his father's handsome face and coloring. Robin looked at Fiona. "Is this the pattern, all the boys look like me, and all the girls like you?"

"Well, for now," she said, grinning.

Zeke had saddled two horses and had packed two blanket rolls. As the men left, Robin's eyes lighted at the sight of their mansion, looming large in the evening sun. "When I get back," he told Fiona, "I'll be coming here to live. I'm done with Rich Bar forever."

They took off at full gallop, two big men on fine horses, desperately hoping to make up time in their pursuit of a madman. Fiona smiled and waved until they were out of sight. Then slowly, she walked back to the house.

Susannah, Cameron and Simon had settled into their new house on Hillside. The house was far from finished, and nearly every day was noisy with the sounds of hammer and saw; but they had to live somewhere. Susannah was as content as a setting-hen. For the first time in years she did not feel the insistence of business ambition butting at her. She knew she would want another shop sometime, in a few years—but for now her ambitions were encompassed entirely by her husband, her home and her family.

At the breakfast table she took two-year-old Simon onto her lap, kissing him fondly. He was an attractive child, already much like Cameron in his humorous but steady approach to life. She said, "Simon, how are you going to feel when you have a baby brother?"

Simon giggled. "Baby butha," he mimicked.

She hugged him luxuriously, saying, "Oh, Simon, you fit so good."

"Are you feeling all right this morning?" Cameron asked.

She smiled at him happily. "I've never felt better. I don't think I'm going to be sick in the mornings any more. Cameron, don't go to work today. Stay at home, and let's just go on a picnic, or do something to declare independence of the marketplace."

He said wickedly, "I knew it was a mistake not to get you another shop. You're going to be a constant temptation to me, Susannah."

She pouted prettily. "Well, is that so bad?"

"It's wonderful—except when I yield to it and have to work twice as hard to make up."

"What would happen if you didn't make it up?"

"Then I'd remain a day behind all the rest of my life. I'd always have Wednesdays Tuesdays."

"Unless you took another day, and then had Wednesdays Mondays."

"Wendy Mondy," said Simon, and they laughed.

"But if you took a *half*-day," Susannah persisted, "you'd only be behind from midnight to morning, and you wouldn't even notice it!"

He got up to put his arms around her. "I'm gradually getting the notion, darling. But this is a day full of appointments. Why don't I come home for lunch?"

"But you do that *every* day!"

"So I do," he said, feigning surprise. "Well, that's what I'll do today!"

She dissolved into giggles. "Oh, Cameron!"

"Oh . . . Susannah," he said, kissing her and smiling deep into her eyes.

After he had gone she contentedly washed the dishes and straightened the house, happily played with Simon, and serenely contemplated the next child they would have. She thought of their new house, and her pleasure in it, and the guests who would people it over the years. She smiled, rejoicing in the wonderful prospects that she and Cameron had.

She outdid herself on the lunch, serving fish poached in wine, a colorful fruit salad, hot biscuits, tea and crisp vanilla cookies. Together they put Simon to bed for his nap. As she closed the door, her eyes met Cameron's, and they smiled like conspirators. The workmen had not come today. They were all alone. She said impishly, "Could you come to the wash house with me, Cameron? I might need a little help . . ." He reached out to embrace her.

The knocker on the front door sounded, and Cameron uttered a sharp sibilant word. Susannah said, giggling, "I'll get rid of him, darling, don't go away."

They went down the stairs together, Susannah a little bit first, so that she was the one who opened the door.

It was like having ice water suddenly turned on in her veins. It was not so much who stood there—though that was shock enough—but the expression on his face. "Asa!" she gasped, her eyes wide. She was terribly frightened. Her hand went to her throat and she could feel the caged bird of her heart beating its wings to get out of there.

While she stood there unable to move, he stepped inside. She had never seen a smile so terrible. He said, "Name's Joe Jackson. From San Francisco."

"What do you want, Radburn?" Cameron asked. Almost roughly, he shoved Susannah behind him.

"Came to get Susannah," he said.

"Well, you can't have Susannah," said Cameron patiently. "And if you know what's good for you, you'll get out of my house."

"Cameron, don't," Susannah pleaded. She had never seen this expression on Asa's face before. The fear it gave her was ghastly.

There was a gun in Asa's hand, and he waved it at them carelessly. "Just sit down, right over there on that couch where I can watch you, and we'll have a little talk."

"Asa, please leave," said Susannah. "We have nothing to talk about now, after—"

"After all these years?" The terrible smile flashed again. "But it's all these years I came to talk about with you, dear Susannah."

Cameron seated himself carefully, trying to remain in a position to pull out the revolver he wore at his waist. He knew Radburn must see it, yet he seemed not to care about the threat it might pose to him. The man must be insane.

Cameron was aware of Susannah, shaking as she sat next to him. He did not dare take her hand, for that might hinder him in getting off a shot at Radburn. He was immensely proud of her calm as she said, "Very well, Asa. What do you wish to say?"

"You always were the lady, weren't you? Perfectly poised, even when you're staring death in the face." He seemed amused at her quick intake of breath. "Yes, dear Susannah, I came to kill you. It was you who ruined my whole life, and now I'm going to make you pay with yours."

Cameron pressed his leg against hers in warning not to speak. He said, with reasonable curiosity, "Why do you say that? How could one person have ruined your life?"

Asa's eyes never left Susannah. "You turned me down. You spurned me. I loved you from the time I was fifteen, and you never had anything but contempt for me. Then you took to lying about me—lied to Sam Brannan, lied to Gentry here, trying to make people believe I attempted to rape you." Susannah took a breath, but said nothing. "I had to leave here, a hunted man, ruined in the eyes of everybody who counted."

She said courageously, "Asa, you did that to yourself. You *did* try to rape me. I—"

"You tempted me," he said; and the accusation was the ultimate indictment of woman ever since Eve. "You foully tempted me. You put in my mind the lusts of the flesh! And you gave your body to other men! Now I will repay you for the hell you put me through." He raised his gun casually. The barrel was pointed right at Susannah's breast.

Cameron moved quickly, in front of Susannah, jerking out his gun and firing at the same time Asa fired. Cameron's aim was deflected, and his bullet hit the wall opposite. Asa's bullet struck Cameron in the throat, and a little fountain of blood began gushing out. In the next second, before Susannah could move, there was another gunshot. Asa Radburn fell dead, with a hole through his temple.

Susannah sat paralyzed, in shock, unable to take it all in. Cameron fell to the floor—and it was Landry who rushed across the room to him. But it was too late. Cameron Gentry was dead. Susannah turned white, then green, and lost consciousness, her body falling across Cameron's.

Landry Morrison, covered with sweat, and mud, grieving for one death already, exhausted from his long futile ride, covered his face with his hands and cried.

Fifteen minutes later there were booted footsteps on the porch, and Robin and Zane burst in through the open door.

Thirty-two

*E*zra Morrison was as close to collapse as a man can be and still function. Zane Tyler had come ashen faced to his door to tell him what had happened at Susannah's house earlier that day. Such an overwhelming rush of anger, grief and horror had poured through him in the hours since then that Ezra could not separate one feeling from another. He had been so stunned at the news, he had not even thought to prevent Prudence from accompanying him to Susannah's house. Vaguely he remembered, or thought he remembered, Zane telling him not to permit her to go, but he hadn't, or perhaps it was that he couldn't stop her. Asa was his son. He didn't know what had happened exactly. Maybe he'd never know.

He did know that Prudence was at the edge of insanity now. When she saw what had taken place she had seemed to fold in on herself. He had brought her back home and put her into their bed, but after that small consideration there had been nothing else he could do. He could hear her upstairs now. She still cried, even though her poor, racked body could produce no more tears. He wished he could share this with her, but she didn't want him, and for good cause.

Ezra understood that, but he hated it nonetheless. He could

not pretend grief for Asa without being a liar, and Prudence couldn't bear that. Only she had loved her son, and only she would mourn his passing. It was a cruel fate that had brought them to this place of sorrow, and Ezra had a deep fear. Landry, his son, had killed Prudence's son, and Asa had killed his daughter's husband. What would that do to him and Prudence —to all of them? He and Prudence had withstood other devastating times in their life together, but there was nothing to compare with this. He didn't know what to do. His heart, his mind, his soul was encased in icy dread.

Moving like a mechanical man, Ezra did the only service for those he loved that he was capable of doing. He put on his coat and hat and returned to Susannah's house. Someone had to see to the dead, and it was not going to be Susannah or Prudence. That much he could do for his daughter and his wife. There seemed to be precious little else. This tragedy—he still couldn't bring himself to look upon it as murder—had started a whirlwind of regret and guilt in Ezra that went all the way back to when he had lived in New York in 1846. Somehow today, he could not get it out of his mind that the horrible events of this day had taken place as a direct result of what had happened to Landry back then, and he, Ezra Morrison, was to blame. In his own conscience he was the murderer today. It was his fault that his son now sat in confinement at the station house accused of killing his stepbrother. Ezra fought the urge to allow tears to stream down his face.

He made arrangements with the undertaker, then turned toward Bush Street to Sam Brannan's office.

Sam jumped up from behind his desk as soon as he heard Ezra's voice talking to Wardwell. Something was terribly wrong.

"Ezra," he said, and went out to his friend. "My God, Ezra, what has happened?" He helped him to a chair, saying to Wardwell, "Bring brandy, and be quick!"

"No, no, I want nothing," Ezra protested.

"Want it or not, man, you'll have it. You look on the verge of passing out. Now here. Slowly . . ."

Ezra sipped at the brandy as if it were his cup of life. "Sit down, Sam, I need to talk to you, and then I need your help. My whole family needs your help."

In a voice as devoid of life as Sam Brannan had ever heard, Ezra told him of the events that day at Susannah's house. A sharp pain shot across Sam's chest, and his throat was dry. "Susannah—" he croaked.

"Robin and Zane Tyler have taken Susannah and Simon to the Parker House. She couldn't stay in that house . . . she . . . she just couldn't remain there . . ."

"Oh, dear God, and Robin—I wasn't thinking. Cameron was his twin. How is he?"

"I don't know. I can't tell what is happening inside Robin. He is . . . quiet."

"How can I help, Ezra? What can I do?"

"We need your guidance, Sam. We cannot hate our enemy, for he is our brother, and we cannot properly grieve for our dead, for his slayer was his brother. We need help."

Sam's brown eyes lost their luster. "The one time I wish with all my heart and soul that I could be the Lord's man for you and your family, Ezra, I cannot. I am barred from the services of the Lord. Parley P. Pratt and his mission have voted me out of the Church. I am no longer your First Elder . . . I—I cannot do as you ask."

Ezra's eyes snapped, life lighting them again. "I did not ask for the First Elder, Sam. I am asking you as a man of God. No one can take that from you, except yourself. Have you relinquished it?"

"No, no, of course not. You know I could never do that—but I have been judged unchristian, neglectful, lawless . . . unfit. . . ."

"I have not so judged you, and I ask you now, in the name of God, come to us when we need you so grievously. Help us. Please . . . help us." Ezra buried his face in his hands, and the tears that he had held back all day flowed from him with great racking sobs.

Sam Brannan's eyes stung, and tears rolled down his cheeks. "I am with you. God guides us all, Ezra, but I am with you, and will remain so until the end of this awful time."

Tolerance Morrison had heard of the shooting while she was in a shop buying a hoop for Elisha. The women she overheard had no idea who she was, nor what a terrible effect their words were having on her. She grabbed the edge of the counter, steadying herself until the threatening blackness at the back of her eyes receded. They hadn't actually said Landry's name, but they had mentioned Asa and a stepbrother. Who else could it be? As quickly as she could trust herself to walk steadily, she put the hoop down and left the shop. Once inside her carriage, she couldn't think where to tell the driver to take her. She didn't want to return home. Ezra and Prudence would be there, and she didn't want to be. She wanted to be with Landry. Above all else she wanted to be with Landry. Tollie knocked on the top of her carriage for her driver.

"Where do they take people who commit mur—who—what happens to a man who shoots another?"

"To the station house, Ma'am—there or to the Committee of Vigilance."

"Take me to the station house," she said, her voice shaking. Dear God, she hoped he was there and not with the vigilantes. Everyone knew that enough money would buy a man out of the hands of the police or the courts, but she didn't think that was true of the committee men. But Sam was a leader—no, Sam believed in what he was doing. He wouldn't help her. What had happened? Had Landry just shot Asa in cold blood? Terror choked her, and she had to concentrate on her breathing, or she would faint.

After she had talked, pleaded and cried, Police Captain Ben Ray allowed Tollie to see Landry, with the warning, "He's already killed at least one man, Mrs. Morrison."

"He's my husband!" Tollie shrilled hysterically. "You can't accuse him of anything!"

Ben Ray didn't argue with her, but shook his head. He knew as well as anybody that Tolerance was Ezra Morrison's second wife. But if Ezra was going to let a handsome woman like her run on the loose, he wasn't going to stop her. He decided he might send a message over to Ezra's house to let him know where his wife was. He took Tollie back to where Landry sat in a cell, his head down.

"Landry!" Tollie cried, and ran to the barred door. She turned to Captain Ray. "Oh, open the door!"

"No, Ma'am. I can let you see him, but only from out here."

Landry looked up and saw her standing at the door, her hands white as she pulled herself up on tiptoe to see through the opening. He felt sick at his stomach. The sight of Fairy swam in his mind. "Go home, Tollie. You shouldn't be here. Captain Ray, take her out of here—send her home."

"Come on, Mrs. Morrison. You heard the man."

"No! I won't go! Landry, please! Landry, you've got to tell me what happened! Oh, please!"

"Take her out of here!" Landry cried in a breaking voice.

Ray took Tollie by the arm, and applied pressure. "Come with me now. You can come like a lady or I'm going to have you hauled out of here like I would anyone else who caused trouble."

Tollie whirled on him. "Take your hands off me, sir! You may find yourself treated like anyone else who lays hands on a woman against her will!"

Ben Ray had all he could manage to hold his temper. If it hadn't been for bits and pieces of this story coming in from all quarters, he would have had her in a cell of her own. "Look, Mrs. Morrison, I don't want this to get ugly. You asked me to let you see him, and I have. The man doesn't want to talk to you. So go home. Come back tomorrow if you want, but please go home now."

Tollie had no choice. Quiet and defeated, she turned and walked out of the station house. She told her driver to drive—anywhere, just to drive. They had gone only a block when another carriage passed. Tollie, staring out the window, sat up straight. Robin Gentry, Senator Gwin, and Governor Burnett were in that carriage.

"Stop!" she shouted to the driver. "Turn around, I want to see where that carriage is going." She no more than had the words out of her mouth when another carriage carrying Sam Brannan and Ezra raced past. "Quickly! Turn!" she cried frantically, rapping on the top of the carriage.

Her carriage stopped outside the station house once more. Both carriages were there. Tollie didn't know what to do. She didn't know what this meant—if it were good for Landry or bad. She waited. The driver asked her several times if she wanted assistance in dismounting. She just shook her head, her eyes fixed on the door to the station house. Soon Ezra and Sam and Landry walked out together. Tollie grabbed her skirts and jumped down from the carriage. She ran to the three men. "Landry . . . Landry, are you all right?"

He was pale and haggard. She had never seen him as anything but the essence of youth, but today she was seeing far into the future, and knew how he would look as an old man. "I am fine," he said.

"You have heard?" Ezra said dully, then gathered his wits. "We have just witnessed the act of a noble man. Robin Gentry came down here to secure my son's release." His eyes wandered away from Tollie to stare indiscriminately at the tops of the buildings. "I wonder if I could have been so aware of another's need as he was. I could not. I was not."

Tollie barely heard him. "Landry, please, I beg you, let me talk to you. Please, come with me in my carriage."

Robin walked out of the station house and down the steps past the Morrisons without so much as a glance. He and his friends climbed back into his carriage and drove off.

Landry watched the receding carriage. "Mr. Brannan has offered me the use of his apartment until . . . until this is over. I am going there now."

Tollie's heart pounded for a minute with sickening slowness. Sam's apartment. Did Landry know about her and Sam? Was he being cruel? Now? No, he couldn't be, not now. Even she didn't deserve treatment like that. "I would like to talk to you, Landry. It is very important to me."

Landry nodded, then looked at his father. "This won't take long. I'll see that she comes home soon."

Ezra had already begun to walk slowly toward the carriage. "It doesn't matter," he said vaguely.

Landry looked from him to Tollie. "You should see to him. He is your husband. He needs someone."

"He is not my husband," she said under her breath.

She and Landry didn't say a word on the way to the apartment, and even once they were inside Sam's attractively furnished, comfortable suite of rooms the awkward silence remained between them.

Infinitely tired, Landry sat down on the couch, his hands limply in his lap. "I was living with Asa's wife up in Rich Bar," he said bluntly. "I cared about her, Tollie. There was a . . . a goodness between us. She was sweet, and she deserved better than to be beaten to death by Asa." Tears began to roll down his face. "Do you know why he killed her? Because of me . . . and because she looked like Susannah."

Tollie swallowed hard. Her throat pained. "Did you—did you love her, Landry?"

"Oh, yes, I loved her. She brought me back to life. I loved her." He stopped talking and made a helpless gesture with his hands, then let them fall limp again.

Tollie began to speak.

"No, don't say anything, Tolerance. You don't understand, no matter what you think—you don't understand about Fairy and me. You see, she reminded me of Susannah, too. We laughed like children . . . like Susannah and I did as children, and we played together. She brought me back out of that death I had gone into . . . after you left me. But in doing it she revived in me all that meant. She . . . made me realize that the only woman I've ever loved as a woman is you. Fairy was my friend, she was my lover, my sister, my salvation, and because of me she is dead."

Tollie was crying as hard as Landry. "No, it is because of me she is dead . . . and Asa and Cameron too." Miserably she looked up at him. "Don't you see, Landry, if I had just believed in you and stayed by you when the Church turned you out, this would never have happened. It was I, the faithless wife, who caused all this. I loved you. I love you still, but I took myself, our child, everything away from you because I was selfish and frightened and—and sinful."

Landry got up and crossed the room to her. She stood up and threw herself into his arms. "I never knew what sin was until now. Oh, Landry, forgive me!"

They clung to each other, the sobs of one shaking the body of the other.

Susannah Gentry, sedated, rested on the hotel bed tossing and moaning. She kept seeing Asa's gun, pointed first at herself and then exploding in fire and din as it was turned on Cameron.

Zane Tyler sat at the side of the bed, a cold, wet cloth in his hand. Gently he washed her face. Every turn of her head, every agonized sound that was torn from her, tore at him as well. He, far better than the others, knew the enduring, unendurable pain of not being able to get the vision of a murdered loved one out of one's mind. Even now, on occasion, the horror of Josie's death would come back to haunt him. He knew what Susannah was suffering, and neither he nor anyone else could soothe the wound she bore.

He got up when he heard Robin coming back into the suite. "You got him freed, Robin?"

"He's staying at Sam's apartment. I didn't do a good job of it, Zane. The man saved Susannah's life, and did the best he could to save Cameron's, and I couldn't bring myself to say a word to him."

Zane gripped his friend's shoulder. "You're asking too much of yourself. Give it time. Landry was probably grateful he didn't have to talk to you either."

Robin nodded, then put his hands up over his eyes. "God damn it! Why Cameron? Why in the hell did it have to be Cameron?"

Zane said nothing, but he understood now why Robin had been unable to speak to Landry. After considerable time had passed he said, "I sent someone to tell Zeke and Jane and Fiona. Your mother and father should arrive tomorrow morning, and I'd guess Sean and Mary will be in tomorrow."

"Did you send someone for Brian?" Robin asked.

"Yes. I didn't forget anyone."

"I wish Fiona were going to be here."

"It would take her too long, Robin, you know that. Everything will work out better if you let her prepare for Susannah and Simon to live at your house after the funeral."

"If Susannah will go," said Robin.

"She'll go, because you will take her there. You're going to have to do what is best for her. It will be some time before she is thinking for herself."

Robin cried, "But Zane, I look like him! It must be hell for her to see me with his face, and have it not be Cameron. Good God, I hate looking in the mirror at myself. I can't . . . without seeing him."

"Damn Asa! Who in the hell is Asa Radburn anyway?"

Robin didn't answer for a long time. He was remembering that night escape from San Francisco they had arranged for Susannah. Who was Asa Radburn? He was the man Cameron had rescued Susannah from. And that night on the trail, on the way to Agua Clara, Cameron had told Robin that he loved Susannah. How long ago that all seemed. He sighed. "Asa . . . was a nothing . . . he was a stepbrother who wanted to be more than that to my brother's wife."

Zane shook his head. "Somehow it always comes back to the Ten Commandments, doesn't it. You listen to the preachers, and kind of laugh out of the side of your mouth at them, but by God, then something like this happens and you're sitting right on top of those ten stone tablets again, and you don't feel like laughing."

The two men fell silent. Around five the doctor came to the hotel and looked in on Susannah. He gave Robin a small bottle of laudanum. "I think she will be all right without it, but I am going to leave it with you. If she is too restless give her one dose —but no more. We have the baby to think of."

At seven o'clock Sam Brannan knocked on the door. He spoke with Robin for a time, then asked to see Susannah. Once again Zane gave up his seat of vigilance beside her to someone else. Susannah was asleep. Sam sat in the chair Zane had vacated, but he didn't awaken her. He had been the first man Susannah had ever loved, and he had failed her then. Perhaps this time he could do something for both of them. He could not give her back the man she loved, but perhaps he could help her gain the courage to go on. Whatever happened, he couldn't bear for Susannah to lose the joyous vitality that was her hallmark. How often the Lord gave us a second chance! Perhaps this was his. How often men were given that chance, but because the form was different and the end result would be different, they did not even recognize it for what it was.

The other members of the family began to come into San Francisco early the next morning. Carl and Rowena Gentry took a suite of rooms in the Parker House next to the suite Robin had gotten for Susannah and Simon. Sean and Mary, Brian and Coleen arrived at noon. Half the Parker House was now filled with members of the family, or friends who had come for the funeral. With the McKay women there, all the rituals of death began. Zane Tyler, strangely quiet, watched Mary gather the families together, getting them to talk and reminisce about Cameron, encouraging joking or even a bit of roughhousing. By the time they went to dinner that night, Zane could see that Mary's effort had brought about an easing of tense grief.

Carl and Rowena Gentry took Susannah and Simon in hand, and escorted her. Zane felt a quick jab of loss. He had come to think of himself as the only one who understood Susannah's pain, and had nominated himself her protector. Now unable to be with her, he found Mary McKay. Just to look at her made him smile. She was a woman from whom warmth flowed. He introduced himself, then said, "But I already know who you are. You are Fiona's mother. You are the only woman here beautiful enough to have such a daughter."

Mary smiled brightly as she plucked at Sean's coat sleeve. "Did you hear the man, Sean! His tongue has been touched by the little people."

Sean grinned and shook Zane's hand. "More likely the golden liquid from a bottle, Mary. It's good to see you again, Zane, even if it be in such awful circumstances."

"They are," Zane agreed, then said with deep seriousness, "But not so awful as they were before your family came, Sean. Your Mary works wonders."

Sean thought for a moment. "It is good to grieve hard and fast, for it helps to clear the heart of soreness, but when that time is past, it is wise to move with life as quickly as you can, leaving the grief behind. There is a bad place in between grief and life that a person can get trapped in, and that is no good. Mary's way is a good one. It's the way of the living."

Sean smiled. "Don't you worry, my Mary won't let anyone get caught there, not even Susannah. Susannah is a strong woman, and when we all go to Robin's house, my Fiona will help. All my girls were created for life. You'll see."

"I hope I will," Zane said.

"You think highly of her, don't you, Zane?"

"I thought a great deal of Cameron. I suppose in a way I envied him—but I also loved him as a brother. Robin and Cameron and I have become very close over the years since I met them. But Susannah . . . Susannah . . ." His voice broke. "Susannah . . . is my pie-pan lady. She is someone very special. I don't want anything bad to ever happen to her again."

Sean blinked and looked away. "The time will come, lad, never fear. God watches out after those who love. The time will come."

Both men were to be buried in the cemetery at Mission Dolores. To the Morrisons and the Gentrys this cemetery symbolized what California meant more than any other place. The whole history of the territory could be seen there, written in short epitaphs on old, old gravestones.

As Susannah came out of the services that Sam had performed for the families, she drew in her breath, blinking in fascination, surprise and weary gratification at the number of brightly polished black carriages that awaited the journey to the Mission Dolores. Eighty or ninety of them crowded the street. Susannah squeezed Rowena's hand. "Oh, Rowena, look how many have come." Her voice failed, and she whispered, "He was so loved."

The cemetery was a rich green tangle of myrtle and ivy. The Mission cast a spell of contentment and haven over the ground. It was a rich, fertile place. Susannah managed to stand straight and brave until Cameron's casket was lowered into the ground, then with a cry she stretched her arms out to bring him back to her. She swayed, and before anyone could think what was happening, Zane Tyler moved through the people to her, and caught her as her knees gave out. He carried her back to the carriage.

Once more the family gathered after the funeral. The doors to the Gentry suite were all opened, and Mammie Pleasant had catered a repast for the mourners. Susannah had retired to her room and refused all invitations to join the others. Sam Brannan stood in the large group of men and women talking in the effort to put this behind them, thinking and wondering if this was the time of his second chance. Was this the moment that Susannah needed someone to guide her? He gulped down a glass of champagne, then purposefully walked toward Susannah's room.

Tollie and Landry stood off to the side by themselves. The elder Gentrys had been quietly polite to Landry, and Ezra had been ridiculously courteous to him. Prudence, thin, her homely face further ravaged by crying, had not been able to look at him. No one knew how to treat or approach Landry. No one had yet come to grips with the way to deal with such a tangled family tragedy. So Landry had stayed as much to himself and in the background as was possible.

Tollie felt that her mind was clear for the first time in her life. She finally knew what she wanted and had the courage to stand up for it. She wanted to be Landry's wife and the mother of his children. She stood beside him even when he had discouraged her from it at first. Nothing was going to dislodge her from the place she now recognized as her own.

Finally Landry said tentatively, "Tollie, are you sure?"

Her eyes, though grief-worn, were calm and serene. "I am sure."

"And what of my father?"

"We must talk with your father, Landry." She bit her lower lip. "I know this is not the usual time or place for such a thing, but this isn't the ordinary circumstance, and when you leave this place later, I am leaving with you. If I must sleep on the stoop of your house outside in the cold, I'll never leave you again."

Landry looked across the room where Ezra stood brooding, his eyes fixed on the glass he held in his hand. He took a deep breath, then took Tollie's hand in his. As they came to Ezra, the name Papa nearly spilled from Landry's lips. Flustered by the old term of affection coming so easily for a man he had thought he hated, Landry could think of no name to call Ezra. He said, a little curtly, "Tolerance and I would speak to you, if we may, sir."

Ezra nodded. The icy lump in his chest shifted, prepared for more pain.

Landry had never felt more like a disowned child in his life. All the fine words that had seemed possible only moments before were gone. He was awkward and tongue-tied. He blurted, "Tollie and I love each other."

A dam of pent-up emotion broke free in Ezra. His blue eyes warmed, and swam with tears. Impulsively, he grabbed Landry to him. "Oh, my son, forgive me! How I have wronged you."

"Papa . . ." Landry murmured.

With another broad sweep of one arm, Ezra grabbed Tolerance and crushed her to both of them. "And you, Tolerance—forgive me. Please, both of you forgive the arrogant pride of a fool."

"Oh, Ezra, you aren't angry with us?" Tollie asked, once more standing free of Ezra's embrace.

"Angry, no. Contrite, my dear. I was never a husband to you, not as I should have been, nor was I father to my son as I should have been. I praise the Lord that He should bless me with the opportunity to take part in reuniting you and Landry." Ezra looked as though he were in ecstasy, then the worry lines returned, and he looked hard at his son. "But can you forgive me, Landry? I never wanted to be your enemy, yet I was. I, more than anyone else, made myself an enemy for you."

Landry couldn't speak. He shook his head. "I was my enemy," he managed to whisper. "And I forgive . . . and ask forgiveness, Papa."

Ezra hugged them both again. He took several deep breaths, and smiled with a warmth that touched them all. He was a free man once more, and right here in the midst of all the grieving, he wanted to sing, and share his joy.

Sam Brannan had no song of joy to bring Susannah, but he did have a sincere heart and a pure wish that she should be healed. At first Susannah refused to permit him entrance. Sam persisted, knocking on the door each time she refused until the entire situation had become ridiculous. Finally she opened the door. "Sam, I have told you I don't want to see anyone. Leave me alone. I want to rest, can't you understand that? I just can't face anyone right now."

Sam pushed the door open and stepped inside, shutting it behind him. "I understand better, perhaps, than you would like," he said. "I won't permit you to do this to yourself, Susannah. You and I go back too far, and there is too much affection between us for me to stand idly by while you bury yourself with Cameron."

Susannah turned away from him, and walked across the room. When she had sufficient distance between them she turned and said harshly, "I don't know what you're talking about, but if you have had your say, I'd appreciate it if you would leave now." She glared at him, bitterness and anger marring her beauty. She wanted to hurt someone as she had been hurt. "I'm sure we have an adequate supply of champagne—even for your appetite."

Sam lowered his eyes. Ann Eliza said similar things to him regularly, but somehow her remarks didn't hurt as deeply as this did coming from Susannah. He looked at her without defense. "Susannah, I love you, and so do many of those people in the other rooms. We can scarcely bear the loss of Cameron—we could not bear at all the loss of you to us."

"Oh, stop that nonsense!" she snapped. "I am alive, and I'll be alive for many years, too many. Leave me alone!"

"No, my dear, I'll never leave you alone. Whatever it takes, however long it takes, I'll keep talking to you, keep reminding you that none of us will allow you to close yourself off from us. I will continue to speak for Cameron until you listen."

"Cameron?!"

"Yes, Cameron. We were friends, you know. Under the circumstances, I'm not certain how that happened, but it did, and I've always been grateful for his friendship. Cameron and I shared a love for you—his was the greater, but mine was sincere, and he knew that. He came to respect it, and he talked to me about you from time to time."

Susannah sat down. "What did he say?"

"That you were his courage, because you knew how to take a joy from life that he didn't know how to do without you."

The grief in Susannah's eyes went beyond reach of tears. She said softly, "Ohh . . . Cameron . . ."

"You're not listening, Susannah. The message isn't about Cameron, it is about you. Your gift is a delight in living—it is passed to those around you. The one thing I can be sure of is that Cameron would die by his own hand if he thought or believed that because of him you extinguished that gift."

"Cameron is dead—how dare you suggest that he would have killed himself with his own hand! He was murdered! He was happy and we had the whole world before us and it was taken away from us in the cruelest fashion. I did die with him! I did. Asa didn't shoot me, but he might as well have."

"He didn't because your husband wanted you to live!" Sam shouted back at her. "For God's sake, Susannah, the man gave his life rather than see you dead. Are you going to throw that away? Is that all he meant to you?"

Susannah leapt up from the chair and began to pound on Sam's chest in rage. "How dare you! I hate you! I hate you!"

Taken aback by her vehemence, Sam fended her off, then merely tried to contain her blows. As she tired, he put his arms around her and held her still while she cried. "Sam . . . Sam, what am I going to do? I'll never see him again . . . he'll never tease me about anything again . . . never look at me again when I've done something that pleases him and say 'Oh . . . Susannah' . . . What am I going to do?"

Sam crooned, "My little love, listen in your heart. You haven't lost Cameron, he is here with you. Listen to the whispers in your heart, Susannah."

She sobbed into his chest. "Do you really believe that, Sam?"

"Oh, yes. I can't say I *know* too many things in which I have utter faith, but I do believe that. Cameron will remain with you —always."

"It will be easier than living alone, but—"

"I am not suggesting that you live with a ghost." Sam paused, knowing that what he was going to say next would not sit well with her. "I mean that Cameron would want you to go on with your life—even if that means with another man."

Surprisingly, Susannah said nothing and did not react at all. She looked terribly sad, as if he had made her accept something she had been warding off with all her might. After a time she said, "It is really over, isn't it, Sam? There is nothing I can do. Cameron is never . . . coming back."

Sam took her in his arms again and held her. Dry-eyed and calmer, Susannah rested her head on his shoulder, content to remain safe there until she could think what to do next.

It was growing dark outside when she stirred, saying, "I . . . I will join the others now." She gave him a weak, grateful smile. "Thank you, Sam. Come, I want to find Simon. He must be missing his mama. I haven't been very good to him the past few days."

The Gentrys and the McKays and the Campbells set out for Fiona and Robin's home two days later. Carl and Rowena and the McKays were going to stay just long enough to meet their new grandson Mark Gentry, then go on back to their own homes. Susannah and Simon were to have a home there in the great mansion for as long as they wanted or needed.

Zane Tyler, with proprietary authority, took the task of driving Susannah and Simon to the Napa Valley. As he sat in the driver's seat, his mind was racing ahead to the day that Susannah would be prepared to take on new challenges, and look not toward the past, but to the events—and the man—of her future.